MEXICA

By Norman Spinrad

THE DRUID KING

MEXICA

MEXICA

Norman Spinrad

ABACUS

First published in Great Britain in November 2005 by Little, Brown
This paperback edition published in September 2006 by Abacus

A CIP catalogue record for this book
is available from the British Library.

ISBN-13: 978-0-34911-904-5
ISBN-10: 0-349-11904-X

Typeset in Plantin Light by M Rules
Printed and bound in Great Britain by
Clays Ltd, St Ives plc

Abacus
An imprint of
Time Warner Book Group UK
Brettenham House
Lancaster Place
London WC2E 7EN

www.twbg.co.uk

For Dona Sadock
with whom this novel's long strange trip began

and

Bruno Delaye
'El Embajador'
without whom it never would have arrived

and in memory of Mouse
who never got to wear his sombrero

1

WHY, DEAR READER, assuming that you may one day exist, am I writing yet another account of Hernando Cortes' heroic conquest of 'New Spain' for King and Cross?

I ask it of myself as I embark on this wine-dark sea of narrative up here in the chilly mists, for down below, the minions of the Church burn every Mexican codex they lay their hands on in the name of the suppression of blasphemy, so it is hardly likely that they would allow this account to reach you or its author to survive should it come to light.

Still less should they finally learn who Alvaro de Sevilla really is.

Perhaps they know already. I am not about to descend from my refuge to find out, for if they have learned that Alvaro de Sevilla was once Alvaro Escribiente de Granada, the price for satisfying my curiosity would surely be paid at the stake. Worse still, should they see who was hiding behind *that* mask.

Who am I? Where am I as I write this? And when?

It is the Year of Their Lord 1531 by their calendar, 5291 by that of my people, and matlactli omei acatl as the Mexica not the span of a man's life ago would have counted it in their own language, Nahuatl.

I am writing this true story in a hut in a small village of similar dwellings high enough on the slopes of the great volcano Popocatepetl to remain untouched by the rise and fall of the great empire far below, small and poor enough to remain beneath the interest of the conquistadores, now that they have caused the Indians to be baptized and erected a tiny stone church.

Having left this singular mark of the conquest in the care of the local teopixqui, a sort of lay priest of the rain god Tlaloc turned lay priest of the tripartite God of the Church for the sake of his people's tranquility, the friars and their armed escort left, hopefully never to return. In the service of which this village shall herein remain nameless, and likewise this priest of two gods who has succored me, to shield it and him from their wrath.

I was born Avram ibn Ezra, though even that is not quite the full truth of it, since 'ibn Ezra' is an Arabization of the Hebrew 'ben Ezra', for I come from a Jewish family distinguished by a long line of scholars and poets and a shorter line of less famed advisers to the sultans of Granada, of which I was the last.

I was baptized Alvaro Escribiente de Granada shortly after the surrender of my patron Muhammad Abu 'Abd Allah (known as Boabdil to the victors who wrote the history) made him the last of these Islamic rulers of Spain in the Year of Their Lord 1492 and before the Inquisition was to reach its full baleful flowering. I had seen the handwriting inscribing itself on the fallen walls soon enough to become one of the earlier conversos, converting at a time when openly forswearing Judaism in favor of Christianity was enough to save me from my minor notoriety as a member of the last Islamic court.

Later on, when the times changed, and the Inquisition began its fanatically diligent rooting out of marranos – conversos secretly still observing the rites of the sons of Abraham – being known as a convert who had been baptized in a manner which in hindsight appeared just as opportunistic as it actually was lost its protective magic.

And so, like second and third sons of noble families, backers of the wrong sides in the struggles afflicting the former petty principalities attempting to become a nation called Spain, starry-eyed dreamers and bullion-eyed schemers, I set off in 1518 for those lands discovered by Columbus in 1492 and then beginning to be styled 'the New World' by freebooters unaware of how true that would prove to be.

Thus I became Alvaro de Sevilla somewhere in the ocean between Spain and the isle of Cuba, my baggage consisting of my skills as a scribe and secretary, and laudatory letters of recommendation to its governor, Diego Velazquez, forged by myself, which enabled me to secure service in his employ.

Thus, on a tropical isle thousands of leagues across an ocean from the memory of Europe, then but thinly settled by Spaniards of the sort mainly concerned with securing plantations and the Carib slaves to wrest wealth from them, as the most learned man in the employ of Velazquez, I soon enough also became the most valued whisperer in his ear.

Thus did Avram ibn Ezra thoroughly disappear.

But not from the heart of he who now sets pen to Mexica paper. For however great a weight of paper may have been burned in the bonfires in Mexico, however great a weight of flesh may have been burned at the stake in Europe, memory cannot be burned from the hearts of those who survive, even if they may wish it so.

And now I find it is Avram ibn Ezra who is compelled to relate the true story of Hernando Cortes' conquest of the Empire of the Mexica and the part Alvaro de Sevilla played therein.

Why, dear reader, you may well ask, *am* I compelled to inflict upon the unknown future one more version of a great tale of which there is sure to be a surfeit?

Because what has already been written and what is likely to be written is at best half the truth and at worst farragos of self-serving lies.

Why should the reader swallow *this* version as the truth when its author has spent the bulk of his life lying about his own identity?

The answer is that I secretly transcribed Montezuma's own account of many of these events, and, having saved the manuscript from destruction, I have it with me now, and moreover I presume to believe that I was the closest intimate among us that he had. For I fancy that only one born into a Jewish family bred for generations to survive in a mighty civilization not their own, only to see it fall, could hope to even begin to achieve such communion with a soul as alien to the European mind as his hideous gods were to the Christian clerics who sought and still seek to supplant them here with the singular one on the Cross.

The fathers of the Spaniards who arrived on the jungled coast of what they first believed to be a mere island inhabited by savages little different from the Caribs of Cuba and the Antilles had lived the heroic history of the Reconquest of Spain from the Muslims, leaving them with the firm belief that they had triumphed in the service of the one true God.

Their sons, lacking the opportunity to be the heroes of such a noble cause, inverted this sense of moral certainty into the conveniently sincere belief that they too served God as they conquered and stole, as long as they did so marching behind the True Cross; that as long as they converted the Indians they enslaved to the True Faith, God served their cause as much as they served His.

Montezuma, Emperor of all he surveyed, nevertheless enjoyed no such hubristic moral fantasy. He not only sincerely believed he was the servant of his gods, but agonized endlessly and sacrificed profusely, sparing not his own blood either, in a lifelong attempt to discern what they wanted him to do.

To a one-time Jewish scholar there was something familiar about this priest-king's obsessive quest for knowledge of the will of his gods. For while the Christian faith expediently adopted by Alvaro Escribiente de Granada is founded on the certainty that the nature of God is set out in the Bible and His will clearly enunciated in the words of Jesus Christ, the sophisticated cosmopolitan Judaism of Avram ibn Ezra consisted of a philosophic and moral argument between God and Man that neither wished to see concluded.

And while I found Montezuma's metaphysical system horrifyingly repugnant in many of its aspects, its complexity and sophistication appealed to my mind, and therefore, I have reason to believe, did my mind appeal to his.

As for my insight into the mind, if not the heart, of the great Cortes, all I can claim is that I was with him from the beginning, all too often his secret vizier, to my present sorrow, but not that I even now can fully comprehend a man who combined such virtue with such evil, whom I came to both love and hate, often at the same time.

Hernando Cortes was not an uneducated man. He was reasonably versed in the classics, he could write a decent enough poem, he was a great orator, and a more than competent general, if not the Caesar he thought himself to be. He was also a masterful plotter, liar, and double and triple betrayer, who could charm the carrion birds out of the trees, blessed with the sincere Christian belief that whatever he did served God and hence absolved him from any necessary sin committed in the process.

For this master sophist was the product of a civilization able to convince itself not only to believe that it was anointed of God to rule over lesser breeds, but that he and the Church were doing these people a special favor by conquering them and converting them to the True Religion. For if they didn't, would not their souls burn in hell for ever?

But when you reach a state of sophism so exalted that you can apply it perfectly to yourself, how to comprehend the mind of a ruler who sprung from a civilization whose capital made anything in Europe seem like a backwater provincial seat, whose philosophical theology rivaled the Egyptians' in its complexity and its concept of time, and whose cuisine put that of Spain to shame?

Still less when the said cuisine included the meat of its prisoners of war, and the civilization believed *we* were insane because we sought to kill as many of our enemies in battle as we could instead of capturing them, sacrificing them to our gods, and savoring them in our banquets as a civilized people should.

And therein lies the tale.

Where to begin? With the landing of a few hundred conquistadores on the coast of a mysterious and unknown land under the command of the hero of the tale, Hernando Cortes? No doubt that is how a mediocre dramatist would have it, but for your narrator it began earlier, in Cuba, for this was where I met him.

What did I expect to encounter upon landing in the harbor town and seat of government, such as it was, of Santiago de Cuba? A path to easy riches via a grant of land and Carib slaves?

The island being large, sparsely inhabited, and much of it unexploited jungle, this would have been easy enough to obtain from its conqueror and governor, Diego Velazquez, who, being dependent for his continuance in that position upon remitting ever more tribute back to King Charles of Spain, was ever in need of more tribute himself, which could only be obtained by opening up more land to cultivation and husbandry, which is to say by bestowing plantations and slaves on reasonably competent arrivals, and given the mediocrity of those washing ashore from the other side of the ocean, I would have been eminently qualified.

Indeed, as Velazquez was to whine to me often enough when I had gained his confidence, the situation had grown dire in that regard. The natives of Cuba being quite primitive and innocent of the higher military arts, he and his kinsman and general, the irascible and not particularly competent Panfilo de Narvaez, had had an easy time conquering the island, but once installed as overlord of Cuba, Velazquez, being a shortsighted and slovenly administrator, had made rather a mess of things.

True there had been a certain amount of gold to be panned and Carib slaves to do the work, but not enough to satisfy the needs of the Spanish King, who was engaged in endless military ventures in the Old World and growing ever more dependent on tribute from the New to finance them. And, moreover, at the time I arrived in Cuba, the veins were running thin.

So the plantations were fast becoming the main source of Velazquez's income and hence of the tribute with which he must maintain his position. But the Caribs had turned out to be slaves of a quality the Romans would have relegated to the lead mines, and the supply thereof was drying up fast, as disease, despair and harsh treatment caused their numbers to dwindle towards the vanishing point. Then too, the Spaniards in their wisdom had introduced cattle and swine, enough of which had escaped and bred wild to ravage the man-made farmland hard won from an isle that was mostly wooded.

And even had Cuba been an agricultural paradise, becoming the landlord of a plantation would hardly have been the ambition of the son of a people who had forcibly been banned from agricultural pursuits for something like a thousand years.

Did I imagine living the rest of my life on the funds I had brought with me in a balmy tropical paradise where fruit fell from the trees into my arms and fish leapt up from the sea into my lap in the company of a harem of beauteous dusky maids?

Perhaps in the dreams of my sea voyage, but Santiago de Cuba proved to be no such paradise. The climate was clement enough, but the town itself was a pathetic colonial mimicry of provincial Spain. Inland from the fine harbor which was the reason for its location, it was built around a central plaza with a market, some shops, two taverns, Velazquez's administrative seat and a church to be sure, but everything was built of either adobe or roughly-hewn wood, including the governor's 'palace' and even the church, and most of the houses were roofed for the most part with rapidly drying palm fronds which need be changed as soon as they browned to avoid the risk of fire. Nothing was paved, and when the weather was dry the streets and the plaza were plains of dust, and the infrequent but occasionally torrential rains turned them into a slough of mud and soaked through the roofs.

As for the dusky maids, what was available were grimly sullen Carib women, some of whom might be found comely to a certain taste for the exotic, but most of whom would have been hard put to find employ in a Spanish seamen's brothel.

This is not to say that the Spaniards did not avail themselves of their services in their desperation and even take them to wife, for, aside from securing more land and slaves, extracting what wealth they could from what they had, carousing in the taverns, and exchanging florid fantasies of the mountains of gold hovering somewhere in the vast unknown lands elsewhere in this New World, there was little else to entertain their idle hours.

In short, Santiago de Cuba was a dismal and boring provincial backwater and most of its denizens dismal and provincial bores. In this atmosphere, Diego Velazquez, a large boisterous figure of a man, his blond hair going grey, his robust body aging to fat, was at least amusing company.

He might be a greedy rogue, but his lust for wealth was not that of a miser piling it up for its own sake like an Egyptian beetle hoarding its balls of dung, but rather a means of preserving his position and perhaps enlarging it so as to enhance his already exhalted opinion of himself and holding forth as a lavish and loquacious host, which he forthrightly enjoyed like a small boy.

True too that he was prone to sudden fits of temper, and even more prone to playing everyone off against everyone else, granting and with-drawing his favor on whim and suspicion like the only beautiful coquette in a townful of crones.

'Why do you keep them so stirred up like a man poking around with a stick in an anthill?' I asked him when I had gained his confidence and perhaps a measure of his friendship, over perhaps a bit too much wine.

'Why *does* a man poke around in an anthill?' Velazquez replied with a bleary impish wink. 'For entertainment! I'm an old man who has probably already reached the highest station I am likely to attain and I must do *something* to keep myself amused.'

And when I replied with a skeptical stare: 'Mark me, Alvaro, I am surrounded by ambitious schemers, such is inevitable in this place and my position. Far better to keep them scheming to gain or hold my favor than having them turn to scheming against me!'

Such a man might be impossible to trust but difficult not to enjoy.

My other main source of enjoyable company in those days was Cortes himself, the closest thing I had in Santiago to an equal intellec-tual companion, though his own high opinion of his learning and erudition was not exactly matched by mine.

At the time, Cortes was high in Velazquez's favor, having not only been granted a large plantation and a good supply of slaves, but also appointed alcalde of Santiago, mayor of the town, and therefore Velazquez's chief lieutenant. Indeed it was my impression, though Velazquez would never admit such a thing to himself, that Velazquez, having no son, had in his heart adopted Hernando as a kind of substi-tute, though Diego being Diego, he trusted him no more than he would trust anyone else, a true child of his flesh included, had he had one.

Hernando, it seemed, represented the sort of son such powerful, aging, rough-hewn men so often wish to have and seek to raise up when the raw material is actually at hand – a kind of fantasy of himself as he could have been, were it possible to be magically transported back to his youth with his mature wealth, position, memories and cunning intact.

For Hernando, then in his middle thirties, was a fine martial figure of a man, well-built, handsome save for a certain thinness of hair, a scion of minor nobility and appropriately aristocratically fair skinned, given to finely tailored if not foppish clothing, an accomplished swordsman, horseman and seducer, in which capacity he had compromised the honor of a lady, been jailed for the manly offense by an unconvincingly outraged Velazquez, then released by him with an avuncular wink and nod when he agreed to restore it retroactively by marrying her.

In short, just the sort of dashing grandee Velazquez might have wished himself to have been as a young bravo back in Spain, or, failing that, to have raised up as a son to become in his stead.

But there was more to Hernando Cortes than that. I sensed it immediately when Velazquez introduced us at an impromptu luncheon in the small salon adjoining his offices when Cortes had chanced to arrive unannounced at the appropriate hour.

'This is my alcalde, Hernando Cortes,' Velazquez declared once we were seated, 'and this is Alvaro de Sevilla, my new scribe and secretary, recently arrived from Spain. I do believe the two of you have certain things in common.'

'Do we?' said Cortes, and as was natural under the circumstances our gazes met.

Or perhaps confronted each other, for in those dark eyes I saw someone guarding hidden depths measuring my own, and suspicious that mine were likewise regarding his from behind a mask. I had too often been forced to endure such scrutiny, for there were far too many men in Spain who fancied they could immediately smell out a hidden Jew, and, so my fears whispered in my ear, perhaps some truly possessed this power. Yet there seemed to be both something more here and something less, as if we were both acknowledging something mysteriously covert in each other's natures.

Velazquez seemed unaware of any such thing passing between us. 'Indeed!' he said. 'You are two men of erudition and learning, the two most educated men on this entire island, I warrant.'

'Oh?' said I.

'Hernando is a graduate of the great university of Salamanca,' Velazquez told me, and at this Cortes' mien softened, and I took this at the time to be a becoming intellectual modesty in the face of his patron's flaunting of his protégé's academic credentials. Only later, when he confessed the truth, did I learn that he had been sent there as a callow lad of fourteen and left after only two years under something of a cloud.

'And you?' he asked.

'Oh, I am a self-educated man of modest family background, book-ish even as a boy, but unable to attend such a formal seat of learning, however much I might have wished to enjoy the privilege,' I answered quickly, which was the lie I had palmed off on Velazquez. 'But it is gratifying how much one may learn from diligent and passionate read-ing and discourse with those who have been blessed with such an advantage.'

'Oh yes!' Cortes declared, with more sincerity than I realized at the time. 'How much more pleasurable it is to read all that one will and share the company of like minds who truly love literature, poetry and philosophy, than to be tutored by dry pedants!'

He smiled at me, and when Hernando Cortes smiled upon you like that, you could not but love him. 'Perhaps we might meet sometimes to share such conversation?' he suggested eagerly. 'No insult intended to present company, but Cuba is not exactly brimming with those who enjoy such discourse as much as food, drink, and simple feminine companionship.'

And so it came to pass.

Cortes and I would meet in the larger of the town's two taverns, where the interior walls were well finished and adorned with a few third-rate paintings brought over from Spain, which boasted a fire-place, however pragmatically useless in these tropics, where more or less acceptable meals were available and the wine was of a somewhat finer coarseness than in the other one and the prices somewhat higher; and which therefore was frequented by what passed for the higher society of Santiago de Cuba rather than sailors off ships in the harbor, tradesmen and craftsmen, overseers and the like.

Here we did discuss literary matters, of which Cortes proved rea-sonably knowledgeable in a conventional sort of way, and his interest in the life of the mind proved sincere, if hardly informed by thoughts or insights that one who had enjoyed the discourse of the court of the Alhambra could find particularly profound.

Like a carefully courting Spanish swain, he gingerly proceeded to the next level, and with downcast eyes and a shy nervousness ventured to show me some poems he had written. These were more or less what one would have expected of a man earnestly modeling himself as a proper Spanish aristocrat worthy of reception at the royal court – technically proficient but conventional in form, rhyme and meter, celebrating chaste courtly love with bloodless allusions to the Virgin, painting word-pictures of landscapes, professing adoration of the True Faith and the martial virtues.

What they revealed was a man who wished to be a grandee of the mother country, far from the metropoles of such possibility, a would-be warrior who yearned to emulate El Cid and the heroes who had so recently rescued Spain from the evil heretics for King and Cross, but bereft of a proper war and noble cause.

A man who seemed to me, and to himself, born too late for those heroic times, fitfully whiling away the days in a dusty colonial back-water. A man confined by circumstance to a life too petty for his ambitions, a spirit too large for the part he found himself playing, like an actor who would be the heroic man of destiny playing out instead a minor role miswritten for his talents by the fumbling pen of fate.

I surmised that he simply harbored grandiose political ambitions, that in the secret dreams of his heart he was a Caesar or a Cid, for such is common with men trapped by birth and a hierarchical system where birth so constrains destiny. But one evening over a barely passable paella concocted of the fruits of the local sea but entirely lacking in costly saf-fron, he revealed to me that there was more to it and to him than such huge but conventional dreamtime ambition.

'Do you never ask yourself why we are here, Alvaro?'

I was immediately put on my guard, for Cortes I knew to be as loyal a Catholic as any, and of course theological matters were something I must avoid discussing as I would avoid the stake.

'To serve God and the Cross, of course, and seek to attain His Grace,' I replied quickly.

Cortes waved his hand dismissively. 'I mean why we are here in Cuba, in the savage Indies, thousands of leagues of ocean away from true civilization, from Spain, from the center of the world.'

My shrug was as much from relaxation as anything else. 'Does the driftwood on the beach wonder why it was cast up on this particular shore?' I answered idly but truthfully.

Cortes chastised me with a frown. 'We are not salt-grayed scraps of wood from some distant land!' he told me with no little passion.

'Are we not?' I replied, still lightly. For that was indeed how I more or less saw myself, a piece of human debris from the wreckage of Al Alhambra, adrift on the sea of flight, who had managed to find refuge on this shore.

But not Hernando Cortes.

'Not I, Alvaro! I believe I am here for a purpose, and I do not mean only here on Earth by the Will of God, but here in this New World, driven across the ocean by a will of my own, though of course such an impulse could not have been placed in my breast save by the Holy Spirit Itself which moves all things, be it a piece of wood adrift on the sea, or the hearts of men.'

'And what might be that purpose which God has entrusted to you?'

Cortes shrugged, but his intensity did not waver. 'This I do not yet know,' he admitted, 'for God has not yet seen fit to reveal it, which is to say I have not yet found it, nor has it sought me out. But it is here.'

'In *Cuba*?' I scoffed.

'In this New World, Alvaro, in this *New World*!'

'Such as it is,' I said dryly, for in truth this seemed to me rather ridiculous hyperbole.

Columbus, in his attempt to reach China, or the Spice Islands, or India, the long way around had stumbled instead upon an archipelago of islands inhabited by easily conquered and enslaved savages whose highest civilized attainments were rude pottery, crude agriculture and the use of fire. A much larger landmass, be it a larger island or some sort of continent, might have later been found to the north, and more islands or conceivably also something more massive had been encountered by tentative explorations to the south, but it was all thinly settled by much the same illiterate primitives whom the ignorant had taken to grandly styling 'Indians' as if they had discovered the outskirts of the mighty civilization encountered by Alexander east of Persia.

To style this wilderness a 'World', new or otherwise, was then, by my lights, the equivalent of granting the same grandiose honorific to the icy wastes north of Russia or the jungle south of the Sahara, or indeed to that vast desert wasteland itself.

But Hernando Cortes had a vision.

'Consider all that has happened within the lives of living men,' he admonished me. 'Our homeland has been liberated from the heathen for Christ and the Cross. Where we so recently believed the world ended across a trackless ocean in a great fall of water over its edge, we now know that there lie vast lands unknown since Adam and Eve were driven from Eden by fire and the sword.'

'Surely you do not believe that we only need cut our way through thousands of leagues of jungle to reach the gates of Eden!'

Cortes laughed, but briefly, nor did the moment lessen his passionate intensity. 'Who am I to say?' he declared. 'Who knows how far these lands stretch in what directions, when all we have thus far done is to settle a few islands and touch upon their shores? Who therefore is to say what does or does not lie beyond, and how far? China? India? Greater civilizations unknown? Lost Atlantis? And why not Eden itself, if God so wills it? And if not, if only more of the same, then surely He has brought us here not only to save the souls of benighted savage tribes but to bring the light of civilization to their ignorant darkness that they might serve His cause the better and our own as well. I tell you Alvaro, the one thing certain is that we *have* landed on the shores of a New World, whether it be inhabited by some true civilization that need only be brought to Christ to become our equals, or whether God has given it to us as a gift to make it our own.'

I was taken aback by this vision, but who could but be seduced by it? And who could but be seduced by him who so passionately revealed not only it, but depths to his soul previously quite unknown?

'Consider also, my friend,' he went on, 'that our fathers were granted by God the boon of living at a time when it was possible to be the heroes of the great Reconquest of the last bastion of the heathen heretics of Mohammed for His Son and the Cross. Is it not to denigrate His Great Good Mercy to suppose that He has not granted our generation this New World which He withheld from our knowledge since before Adam bit into the apple in recompense for our birth too late to take part in *that* holy cause?'

And I found myself shamed, for while all the talk of God and the Triumph of His Holy Cause might raise my gorge, the grandeur of

Cortes' vision shamed the shrunken state of my own, indeed showed me the depths to which my spirit had fallen.

For had I not once been an intellect of insatiable curiosity, no seeker after empires, or glory, or the saving of savage souls, to be sure, but just as lustful after what lay beyond the ever-expanding frontiers of my knowledge as Cortes was for whatever lay beyond the frontiers of what little we knew of these new lands?

And had I not so recently proclaimed myself but a shard of driftwood washed up on the shores of this unknown vastness shorn of the ambition to know anything more?

2

C ORTES HAD AWAKENED something in my soul, if nothing more than the memory that I had one. I had come here with flight to safety foremost in my mind, and, having achieved refuge, my dreams and fancies had been occupied with melancholy ruminations on all that I had lost, my vision directed backwards towards a lost golden age rather than towards what might lie ahead.

I realized that my curiosity had died, or rather, I realized upon its awakening that I had allowed myself to regard the rest of my life as a storm-racked remnant of what had been, like that scrap of grayed and skeletal driftwood indifferently adrift on the tides that I had proclaimed myself to be.

I might be too long in the tooth and enfeebled in limb to dream of a second life as a robust romantic adventurer like Cortes, but there are other modes of adventure, those of the mind and the spirit, and I had not so long ago counted myself quite the swashbuckler thereof.

From time to time, I had stood on the docks to watch the tropical sun set behind the silhouettes of what ships might be in harbor into the mirror of a boundless sea stretching back beyond the horizon and sending the lengthening shadows of their sail-bare yards back toward the old world that I had lost, a gloriously golden but melancholy crepuscular beauty all too emblematic of my mood.

Now, at the end of a fitfully sleepless night, I was moved to go there to watch it rise. The docks and the strand were abandoned. I was the only soul abroad in the darkness and a bleary one too, and once more the vista mirrored and mocked my mood.

But the fiery globe arose from the black and endless sea in a penumbra of flame, and when it had banished the last star and risen, burning white, into a brilliant and cloudless sky, I beheld that same sea transformed into a scintillating mirror of the cerulean heavens, a blank tablet upon which anything might be written, and beyond it to the south, to the west, in any direction but the east, lay lands unknown, Cortes' New World.

Columbus had been right in his faith that the world was round: one need only stand on a strand like this one and watch a ship disappear beyond the curve of the horizon to know that. The Greeks had understood that two thousand years before he set sail. But he had been ignorantly wrong about its size when he set forth to reach China or India by sailing west from Spain. For the calculations of the Greek mathematician Eratosthenes had shown that the Earth was twice the size of what had then been the 'Known World' and was now called the 'Old', and for that to be possible, this vast ocean would have to cover half of it.

I had long known this from my readings, but in that moment, I knew it in my heart, and contemplated what it truly meant, which was that either the God of Abraham, Jesus and Mohammed had played a grim pointless joke, or there was as much unknown out there in this New World whose outskirts we had merely touched as in an Old World which contained all Europe, Araby, Persia, India, China, and whatever lay south of the Sahara besides.

And so I took new and far keener interest in everything, in matters which had previously flitted through my attention like the butterflies and more noxious insects with which the isle abounded. An apt analogy, for Santiago de Cuba being the seat both of Velazquez's government and of the intrigues with which it was infested and the port from which explorations went and to which they returned, there was an abundance of both hungry and contentious flies forever hovering about the dung-pile and extravagantly colored tales flitting in and out on the sea breezes that came and went.

Many of the former revolved around Hernando Cortes, though of course Velazquez himself was the main object thereof. My literary friend was not only one of the richest men in Cuba, but perhaps the most charismatic, as I now had reason to know myself, nor was there anything shy in his nature. He was also one of the most ambitious, though cloudy as to purpose; the sort of man who loved intrigue for its own sake, who drew allies to him and created enemies, both of whom would exchange places with the airy ease of the political breezes. Whether he loved power at the time or not is hard to say, but power, albeit at the time unused to any end, was an attribute generated by his nature as surely as Velazquez's appetite for food and drink generated amusing loquaciousness at one end and odoriferous wind at the other.

Velazquez, like the governors of other of these island outposts of Spain, from time to time commissioned and at least partially financed exploratory expeditions with the aim of finding new sources of wealth, particularly gold, and founding new subsidiary colonies which, with the concurrence of the authorities back in Spain, might be added to their dominions.

A few years back, one of these, under the command of Francisco Hernandez, had been blown off course by a storm and chanced upon a previously unknown island, where they encountered an Indian town with buildings of stone rather than thatch and wood, and a temple of some sort where horrid rites were practiced, human blood sacrifice chief among them, if the lurid tavern tales were to be credited. These Indians had worn well-woven and decorated cloaks and loincloths, feathered headdresses of no little splendor, and some of them, more to the pecuniary point, jewelry and trinkets of gold.

They were also much better armed than the Caribs, equipped not only with bows and lances, but something vaguely described as either a sword or an ax sharper than any barber's razor, and some of them were protected by quilted body armor. They proved to possess an unwelcomingly warlike disposition, and after some bloody skirmishes, the Spaniards were driven off, though not without a modest amount of booty and two captives, bizarrely christened by them as 'Melchior' and 'Julian'. They continued to another island, or perhaps a mainland coast, where they spied some more such towns and even larger numbers of hostiles, and decided that the prudent course was to return to Cuba.

This had occurred before I reached the island, and I knew it only as one of the many garbled third-hand tales of greater wealth to be seized in shadowy elsewheres in circulation at the time and paid it little heed, but in 1518 it had proven enough for Velazquez to send out a follow-up expedition under the command of his kinsman Juan de Grijalva.

Nothing was heard or expected to be heard from Grijalva's expedition until some months after my fateful conversation with Cortes, but then a single of its ships, under the command of Pedro de Alvarado, sailed into the harbor, and the island erupted into a pandemonium of excited avarice.

Alvarado – tall, eagle-eyed with a predatory beak and mien to match, and golden of hair and beard – was an even more dramatic figure than Cortes, higher-born than Hernando, and with an even higher opinion of himself, known as a fearless bravo by those who aspired to emulate him, a great warrior, as it were, in need of a great war.

Alvarado's florid tales of martial feats, in which his own part tended to be the most heroic, might be discounted heavily to braggartly nature, but the gold jewelry he had brought back with him was quite real, if its weight as bullion swiftly became highly exaggerated in the tavern tales, as I was to learn in the process of rewriting Velazquez's accounting of it to the royal court, though he had probably minimized its amount in the report so as to shave off a bit of what was the King's rightful share in favor of his own coffers.

What captured *my* avid attention was not the gold as such, but the craftsmanship of the objects which had been made from it, or more justly the art, for there was nothing primitive about it. Parrots, ducks, unknown animals, flowers and the like, rendered in fine realistic detail. Impossible creatures limned with equal perfection. Abstract arabesques as meticulously drawn in metal as the finest calligraphy done with ink on paper.

Surely no race of unsophisticated savages could have created such jewelry, nor did the style thereof at all resemble what little I had seen or heard described of what Marco Polo had brought back from China or the trinkets from India which had wended their way back to Europe.

My pulse quickened at the sight and my excitement soared, for whoever these artists were, they had to be members of a race worthy of being deemed a *civilization*, and wherever it was out there in the vast unknown, it had to be a civilization never before encountered by our own or even by any other that we knew of. We – or at that moment in my fancy *I* – were presented with an opportunity for intellectual and spiritual adventure no man had known since Polo reached China, since Alexander marched through Persia into India.

Unknown oceans were mere water, unknown continents mere land, but an unknown civilization with its arts, its sciences, its literature, its knowledge, as Marco Polo had demonstrated, might indeed be justly deemed a New World for the mind and the spirit, and one lay out there somewhere waiting for us.

I took to haunting the taverns in a largely futile quest for more detailed and reliable knowledge, but there was not much to be had from the mouths of sailors and soldiers off Alvarado's ship, for since all and sundry were forever plying them with drink in hopes of learning the location of the by now mythical gold mines, they were therefore more or less continually drunk, and took to inventing all manner of fantasies in the successful attempt to stay that way at no expense to themselves.

Alvarado's battle tales held no interest for me, especially since, had they been true, Hannibal would have been hard-pressed to hold his own against these Indian hordes with all the elephants in Africa. His vague and imprecise descriptions of the land and its 'cities' seemed more of the braggartly same, a fantastic and inextricable mixture of fact and fiction.

And so my quest was largely frustrated until at length the other three ships of the expedition returned to port laden with more treasure and eyewitnesses.

For several days, it was much of the same only more so, but then I succeeded in winkling out a young man in his twenties who seemed sharper-eyed and less inebriated than most of the reveling horde of returnees, whom I encountered in an early morning hour wandering the beach and gazing out to sea with a keenly thoughtful expression.

I introduced myself, not entirely untruthfully, as a scribe in the employ of Diego Velazquez, commissioned to produce a report on the discoveries to send back to Spain more scholarly and coherent than the confusion of tales presently circulating, and intimated that he who served as my reliable informant would be fairly credited as such therein, and that his name might very well be read by the eyes of the King himself.

Whether seduced by this promise or simply more thoughtful than most of his comrades and eager to share knowledge for its own sake in the manner of a budding scholar, he readily enough agreed, and introduced himself as Bernal Diaz del Castillo, taking care to spell it out letter by letter so that it would reach King Charles in its proper form.

Over a long breakfast in the larger of the taverns, empty at this bleary hour save for ourselves, he marshaled his thoughts, and proved to be an excellent observer.

According to Diaz, the Grijalva expedition first made landfall on an island the locals called Cozumel at a small village whose inhabitants fled at the sight of their ships, leaving behind only two old men hiding in a maize field. Through the interpretation of 'Melchior' and 'Julian', they learned the name of the island, and then sent them to fetch the chieftains of the village, known as caciques. They never returned, nor did the inhabitants.

Grijalva gave up, crossed the narrow channel to a large island or mainland, and thence to the town of Champoton, even though its inhabitants had given the previous Hernandez expedition a hostile reception. Grijalva took half his troops ashore, armed with small cannon, crossbows and arquebuses.

This proved wise, for they were greeted by a large war party – if not the mighty force of the tavern tales – and a battle ensued in which the Spaniards suffered significant casualties from Indian arrows but succeeded in driving the natives off into the nearby swamps with their firearms and crossbows.

'After three days in the empty town, we sailed on to the mouth of a broad river—'

'A *broad river*?' I interrupted sharply, for a broad river mouth meant a large river, and a large river needed mountains of some size to feed it or else a system of tributaries, and that was a sure sign of a continental landmass, not another island.

'Well, it turned out to be a lagoon, and onward we sailed until we did arrive at the mouth of a wide river, with what seemed to be a good harbor. But there was a bar at the river mouth over which our larger ships could not pass, and so we left them there and proceeded upriver in boats of shallower draft with most of our forces, for the banks were lined with armed Indians in canoes and also those fishing with nets, so there must be a large town nearby.'

Better and better, for only a folk of some sophistication would site a town upriver from a coast where it would be safer from storms sweeping in from the sea rather than on the more obvious natural harbor.

And easier to defend too, for as Diaz related, the natives had set up barriers and fortifications on the banks about a mile or so downstream from the town, called Potonchan, behind which they lurked in force, prepared to repel the invaders. Seeing this, Grijalva put his forces ashore on a marshy headland deemed a safe distance away, but as it turned out there were Indian 'marines' lurking in their canoes in the nearby system of rivulets.

Ordinarily, I would have paid indifferently polite heed to his soldier's detailed descriptions of these military tactics and maneuvers, but the sophistication of the Indian deployments seemed quite telling.

The Spaniards were about to fire on them with their cannon and crossbows when someone found the wit to try to treat with them through Julian and Melchior before commencing a slaughter, and this proved successful when their 'peaceful' intentions were announced and backed up by gifts of worthless trade beads and mirrors, which the Indians took for precious jewels and perhaps magical objects.

'Grijalva told them that they must provide us with provisions in exchange for these goods, for we were vassals of a distant and mighty King, and that they must accept him as their lord too—'

'He said *what*?' I exclaimed, manfully resisting the impulse to smack my brow with the palm of my hand at this amazing piece of imbecility.

These Indians, who called themselves 'Tabascans', were likewise dumbfounded, for two of their leaders, one apparently a cacique and the other a priest or 'papa', informed the Spaniards in no uncertain and to my mind quite reasonable terms that they already had an overlord, thank you very much, and were in no pressing need of another. They warned Grijalva against attacking them, boasting that they had already marshaled some twenty thousand warriors from the surrounding provinces, and, moreover, further reinforcements would be speedily available to repel them should this parley end in war rather than peaceful commerce.

Grijalva was prudent enough to opt for the latter, and the Tabascans reciprocated with the required provisions and promised to provide gold later as a gesture of their good will, as they did the next day, along with cloaks of cloth and feathers, their own version of cheap trade beads, and the like, all presented with the burning of fragrant incense and high ceremony.

The gold, however, served only to whet the avid Spanish appetite, for there was little enough of it by their lights, and it was of mediocre purity. When more was demanded, the Tabascans whined, truthfully or not, that they were a minor province who had no more, but that there was a great mother lode conveniently far to the west in some place called 'Anahuac' or 'Mexico'.

Grijalva opted for sailing on in search of the said mother lode, for he had verified the presence of gold in these new lands, for all he knew these people might just be telling the truth, and there was no point in pressing the issue with their army.

Roughly southwestward along the coast they sailed, passing a seacoast town, another river debouching into a bay, and then yet another where they sheltered from bad weather, where in the far distance they spied snowcapped mountains.

'You are sure?' I demanded. 'In the *tropics*?'

'Quite sure. They gleamed whitely at their peaks, and at times the sunlight flashed as brilliantly off them as off mirrors.'

This fairly took my breath away. For there to be snow atop mountains in the tropics and at this season, they must be higher than the Pyrenees, mightier than the Alps even, and I could see no way such a cordillera could exist on a continent much smaller than Europe.

A New World indeed!

Before noon or not, I ordered up wine with which to digest all that I had thus far heard, calm my excitement, and gather my wits to frame questions which would elicit information more pertinent to the nature of my curiosity than Diaz's soldierly account.

Clearly what Grijalva, and Hernandez before him, had visited was a continent, and one inhabited by far more than scattered primitive tribes, for the Tabascans had styled themselves provincials, and had spoken of their fealty to some mighty overlord. Moreover, minor provincials or not, they had not only received the news of the Spaniards' advent at Champoton rapidly enough to greet them with a large force in good array and secured behind fortifications apparently thrown up for the occasion, but, unless they were dissembling, had already alerted the surrounding provinces of what must therefore be a well-organized empire by some means of communication whose speed those of Europe would be hard-put to match.

'Did you not visit any of these towns you passed?' I asked Diaz.

He shrugged wistfully, or so it seemed. 'We would have had to fight our way inside, I believe, and cannon and firearms or not, we were heavily outnumbered. And furthermore Grijalva's commission was exploration and trade, which the Indians seemed to insist upon conducting well outside their towns, and so we sailed on and on seeking the main source of the gold, which we never found, though we managed to accumulate more by trade. At one point, Alvarado sailed ahead up another river, trading with the Indians along its banks and seeking to reach a town called Tacotalpa, which he never did. This he did against orders, to the great consternation of Grijalva, and I do believe that that is why Grijalva dispatched him back to Cuba in advance, to be rid of him before his adventurous spirit should cause him to bring the wrath of forces much greater than our own down upon us.'

Young Diaz paused, and took a draught of wine as if to fortify himself. 'And aside from their greater numbers, we did visit two of the Indian temples, and what we beheld went a long way to dissuade us from provoking their ire.' He shuddered. 'First we were drawn to an island by pillars of smoke. When we arrived, it was deserted, but there were two stone buildings of triangular shape, with well-hewn stairways leading to altars atop them. And presiding over these altars were idols of a hideousness too terrible to describe, and . . . and what lay upon them was far worse. There were five corpses, their breasts rent open and their hearts ripped out, their legs and arms nowhere to be seen, and the altars, the steps, awash with blood still congealing, beginning to stink, and the whole a feast for foul insects and carrion birds.'

Now it was I who shuddered, not only at the description of this horror, but what further horrors must lie in the hearts of those who had perpetrated it.

'You grimace, as well you might,' Diaz told me. 'But there was worse to come.'

'What could be worse?' I whispered.

'The ceremony itself, whose immediate aftermath we were proudly shown as if this were a special favor. This was on another ceremonial island, where there was a larger such pyramid, presided over by four of the priests they called papas, a grim jest on our Holy Father in Rome, for though they wore black-hooded robes like Dominicans, these were filthy, ragged, and stinking, like their hair, and the stink was that of a crusted accumulation of ancient dried blood. They escorted us up to the altar, perfuming us with sweet incense from censers much like priests of the True Faith, but what we beheld there . . .'

He poured himself more wine from the jug and bolted it down. 'There was another monstrous stone idol, likewise befouled with a decade's worth of dried blood. On the altar upon which this demon leered down were two small boys, their chests sliced open and still oozing blood. On the top of the altar was a depression, horribly reminiscent of a baptismal font, filled with blood as a chalice might be with sacramental wine, and a channel from it over the edge through which that blood still flowed. And swimming in the pool of blood were two hearts. The papas were quite proud, hospitable in their awful manner. Had we so wished, they made it clear that they would favor us by anointing us with the incarnadine results of their ceremony as if it were so much holy water. As indeed it must have been, though that of Satan.'

And he crossed himself.

3

WHILE I COULD HARDLY share in Diaz's righteous horror at what he perceived to be a perverse and Satanic parody of the rites of his One Truth Faith, a Black Mass as it were, it certainly filled my heart with dread. For never had I heard of such a foul ceremony practiced by any people anywhere, and were it not for his calm and honestly straightforward account of the rest of the tale, so unlike the extravagant fantasies put about by Alvarado and the other returnees, I would have discounted it as all too reminiscent of the evil slanders of Israel – the kidnapping of Christian children, their sacrifice by Jews and the drinking of their blood in just such a Black Mass – put forward by the Inquisition to justify their equally cruel and vile burning of such heretics, myself potentially included, at the stake.

After our conversation, I walked the beach, staring out to sea in an effort to clear my mind, not only of too much wine at too early an hour, but of the confusion of conflicting impulses which so roiled it. The sea was calm and smooth as glass and the sky above it an untrammeled blue, but at the limit of my vision, a thin line of dark clouds seemed to hover, whether real or painted there by my mind's eye, it was impossible to tell.

Either way, it seemed an omen, for I now knew that out there beyond that horizon was an unknown civilization capable of the finest of art, marshaling and deploying large armies with a speed that seemed impossible by means unknown, erecting towns of stone, yet also given to evil horrors previously unknown even to the worst imaginings of the dark spirit of the Inquisition itself and entirely beyond my moral comprehension.

Now, up here on my misty mountain so many years and events later, dwelling among remnants of a people to whom such omens were, and still are, taken as messages from capricious and contentious gods, I have come to believe that such omens, such visions – whether thrown up by artifices of the mind or truly passed down to the world of knowledge by higher entities – are real.

I have the evidence here before me, in the opening pages of the journal of Montezuma, for there, rendered in the cunningly succinct pictures and symbols which served the Mexica as both writing and chronological annotations, and put down before any Spaniard set foot on his shores, is the record of such omens, which, if they did not predict their future advent in detail, all too accurately foreshadowed the eventual baleful result thereof.

A red sun in a black night sky dripping blood. A temple burning. Another temple being struck by a bolt of lightning. A fire streaming across a night sky, possibly a comet or a great meteor. An enormous wave of water swamping tiny houses. A monstrous fish, gray and scaled, with the fanged head of a vicious snake, ensnared in a fisherman's net.

All these glyphs depict omens seen before the advent of the Spaniards, and one need not be a Mexica monarch to immediately discern that they predicted that a great disaster was to befall Montezuma and the empire he ruled.

But this, like the omens themselves, is getting ahead of the tale, for as I stood there on the beach contemplating that omen of my own, soiling the pristine horizon and the seductive marvels with which my imagination filled what lay beyond it, none of this was known to me or to any Spaniard.

Writing so now, I glance at the next pages of Montezuma's pictorial journal, and wonder how daunted I or Cortes would have been had any Spaniard's eye been privy to them before the minions of King Charles set out in their ridiculously meager numbers to conquer this empire of 'primitives'.

For there, meticulously dated, are skillfully rendered paintings in natural color, and what they depict, discounting understandable mistakes owing to the utterly alien nature of the subjects to the artists' eyes, are reasonably accurate portraits of sailing ships and armored and bearded Spaniards, and most chilling of all, had those Spaniards seen them, scenes of both the trading and battles related to me by Bernal Diaz and the comings and goings of the previous expedition of Hernandez.

Would we have set out with our little fleet and tiny army had we seen *these* omens? Would Cortes have presumed to so confront the armies of an Emperor of whose very existence we were innocent were it then known that *he* knew so much more of us than we of him from before the very beginning?

The gold brought back by Alvarado and Grijalva excited the greed to go back for the much more promised, truthfully or not, by the Tabascans to be found in the land called 'Mexico', and in no one more so than Diego Velazquez.

There must be another expedition, someone would have to lead it, and there was no lack of volunteers eager to assume the position and campaigning for the potentially lucrative honor. No one was more avid than Hernando Cortes, no one more popular than Cortes, and no one his match at the persuasive arts. But Grijalva, being not only the leader of the previous expedition but a kinsman of the ever-suspicious Velazquez, would seem to have had the advantage.

Such an outcome, however, would not have been at all to *my* advantage, for I was determined to be among the company setting forth, and, being advanced in years and lacking all military skills and experience, would not have been likely to be chosen to go by the likes of Grijalva. My hopes lay with Cortes, and my advantage, and therefore his, lay with my access to the ear of Velazquez.

'Whom may I trust?' Diego moaned to me when the importunities of the many had left him severely vexed.

'Why not the one man on all Cuba that you *know* you can trust?' I suggested sardonically.

'You don't mean—'

'Yourself!'

Velazquez regarded me as if I had gone mad before realizing I spoke in jest. He was, after all, more advanced in years than myself, excessively corpulent for such martial adventures, and of course, Velazquez being Velazquez, he would hardly venture to put himself incommunicado across the sea for an unknown time, turning his exposed backside thereby to a writhing nest of conspirators against him, real or imagined.

'Well, Hernando Cortes would seem to be the natural leader, close to you, and the popular choice as well,' I ventured.

'Cortes! I am supposed to entrust such a venture to a man more popular than I am? I'd be better off with Grijalva, a man of both less ambition and fewer powers of persuasion, and at least my kinsman, for however little that may be worth in these dishonorable times.'

Velazquez frowned deeply. 'But there is a weightier matter causing me to delay my decision,' he said unhappily.

'How so?'

Velazquez rubbed the thumb and forefinger of his right hand together. 'To have any hope of being a financial success the next expedition is going to have to be larger than the last, and therefore—'

'Far more expensive,' I said, seeing where he was going, and realizing the advantage of arriving before him.

'Just so,' moaned Velazquez. 'Twice the number will have to be sent—'

'Or more. A fleet. An armada.'

'You exaggerate, Alvaro,' he protested, 'but in truth it will require a dangerously large investment, a large risk for potentially even larger gain to be sure, but on the basis of what? Some samples of gold barely enough for Grijalva's expedition to turn a profit and a tall story told to him by the Indians perhaps simply to see him gone.'

'Why then take the risk yourself?'

'Where then is the money supposed to come from?'

'Cortes!' I told him.

'Cortes . . . ?'

'He is rich, is he not, thanks to the lands and slaves you have granted him.'

'But mostly in land, not bullion . . .'

'Against which he could secure loans at interest . . . perhaps even from you, or to be more discreet about it, from you through intermediaries . . .'

'And being the governor, I would be entitled to a share of what he brought back on that basis alone . . .' Velazquez began to muse. 'And if he did not bring back enough to cover his expenses, the loans could be called, his lands would become mine—'

'And if he were successful, you would not only collect a handsome share of the results, but the interest on the loans into the bargain.'

Velazquez laughed. But then he frowned once more. 'All well and good, Alvaro,' he said, 'but why would you imagine Hernando Cortes would agree to such a compact? He would surely realize that while my wager would be well covered either way, if he failed to bring back plenty he would be quite ruined.'

'I believe I know his heart well enough to persuade him,' I told Velazquez quite truthfully. 'For Hernando Cortes, wealth is but a means to glory, to writing his name in the annals of history, to becoming the great man he believes is his rightful destiny. The man is no miser but a soldier of fortune and an adventurer.'

'Just so,' grunted Velazquez. 'What you have described is a man of overweening ambition. How is such a man to be trusted?'

'*Trusted?* Who said you need trust him? You will hold all he owns hostage, will you not?'

'Are you sure there is no Jew somewhere back in your bloodlines, Alvaro?' Velazquez exclaimed with a laugh.

'Are you sure there is none in yours, Diego?' I rejoined to cover my discomfort.

'I like it not, Alvaro,' said Cortes.

'Oh yes you do, Hernando,' I told him. 'Or is *this* how you would spend the rest of your days?'

We lounged on the porch of his large but roughly built plantation house gazing out at the vast expanse of his holding, where teams of half-naked Carib slaves stooped toiling under the parching tropical sun.

'Is this the destiny for which God has chosen you?' I purred in his ear. 'I tell you, Hernando, whether or not there really are vast amounts of gold waiting to be seized on the other side of the southern sea, there is for a certainty your New World to be conquered, and I speak not of an endless jungle infested with primitive tribes.'

'Well the gold had better be there too, for I will be gambling my all on it and there will be no great destiny for a hero who returns with his tail between his legs as a pauper,' Cortes grumbled, and I knew I had him, or at any rate almost.

'If you return at all,' I told him.

'I fear the risk of my life less than the risk of my standing.'

'That's not what I meant. Consider: how did Velazquez himself become governor of Cuba?'

'By conquering the island for Cross and King and being rewarded with the royal mandate of course,' said Cortes. 'Oh . . .'

'And we are not talking about adding merely another little tropical island to his domains, now are we?'

The gleam that came to Cortes' eyes belied his dismissive frown. 'We should not speak of such things, Alvaro,' he told me unconvincingly. 'We should not even think them. Such is exactly the sort of ambition that arouses Velazquez's mistrust. Also, the pursuit thereof while under his aegis would not be honorable.'

'But there would be nothing dishonorable about sending dispatches on our exploits directly back to the King, now would there? For surely His Majesty is a just and generous man with a mind of his own, and no one would dare to deem any unsought boon that he might choose to grant dishonorable.'

'*Our* exploits, Alvaro?' Cortes said with a sly grin.

'*Yours* of course, Hernando. I myself am entirely content to remain invisible to history. But while my respect for your literary skills knows no bounds, such dispatches are not poetry, but documents of a political nature and intent that need be most carefully rephrased from your drafts by a hand well versed in the politesse thereof, a skill I have learned in doing the same for Diego's rude and contentious ramblings. Moreover, he trusts me, at least to the extent that he trusts anyone, and I can see to it that he believes me an eye sent by him to watch over you.'

Cortes laughed. 'Should I rise to high position at court, I would do well to appoint you my secretary,' he told me. 'Indeed, were I a sultan of Araby, I would straightaway appoint you vizier.'

'Inshallah,' I muttered.

In the end, as history well knows, Cortes' expedition did set forth, but Cortes being Cortes and Velazquez being Velazquez, it was something of a hair's-breadth escape.

Before the ships – eleven of them, though only four were major vessels – had been purchased, several hundred gold-hungry men had already flocked to Cortes' banner, among them such known cronies or admirers of Hernando as Hernandez de Puertocarrero, Gonzalo de Sandoval, Bernal Diaz himself, Cristobal de Olid, Alonso de Avila, and first and foremost Pedro de Alvarado, with four of his own brothers in train.

Alarmed at this, Velazquez inflicted upon Hernando his own cronies to serve as a counterweight – among the more obvious Diego de Ordaz, Francisco de Montejo, Francisco de Morla, and his kinsman Juan Velazquez de Leon, as well as an unknown number of other men more or less loyal to him hidden within a larger list of 'suggestions'.

Constrained to appoint Cortes Captain-General, Velazquez loaded him down with a set of instructions and restrictions that had Hernando rolling his eyes towards the heavens when he read them.

His primary task was supposedly to convert the Indians to the True Faith, for which purpose he was supplied with two friars, the dourly righteous Juan Diaz and the rather more sophisticated Bartolome de Olmedo. Supposedly secondary, he was to impress upon them the greatness and magnanimity of His Majesty and the advantages of becoming his vassals, as token of which they were to 'manifest it by regaling him with such comfortable presents of gold, pearls and precious stones as, by showing their own good will, would secure his favor and protection'.

Given the lack of enthusiasm with which Grijalva's suggestion of same had been greeted, Cortes was allowed to fit out his 'peaceful' expedition with cannon, arquebuses, crossbows, cavalry horses, and fierce mastiffs and greyhounds for 'purely defensive purposes'. These he was enjoined not to employ unless directly threatened, and above all, he was *not* to implant a colony.

When Cortes protested that this last made no sense whatever, conflicting as it did with the order to persuade the Indians to swear fealty to the Spanish Crown, Velazquez shrugged ingenuously and told him that he at present had no authority to invest his agents with the power to colonize, for this could only come down to him from the Crown, and authority to grant it had not yet arrived.

This I knew to be true in the usual Velazquez manner, which is to say that he had requested no such authority for the purpose of conveying it to Cortes.

I agonized for a time as to whether I should tell this to Cortes, for I could thus far convince myself that I had committed no betrayal of Diego in the service of my own desire. Call it sophistry if you like, dear reader, but in the end I opted for betraying no such secret, instead pointing out to Cortes that if fortune truly smiled upon him, the King might just decide to bypass Velazquez and confer the same power directly. Especially if we sent letters for his personal attention crafted to imply that such a colony would become the seat of territories and riches that would make a sleepy little island like Cuba pale into utter insignificance.

Thus the period of preparation was a serpent's nest of intrigues and changes of mind by the ever-suspicious Velazquez which turned the departure itself into low farce.

Velazquez had in his entourage a madman who served him as a kind of court jester, and one day this fool advised him to 'have a care, or we shall some day have to go hunting after this Captain-General of yours'.

This ignited Velazquez's suspicion, tinder-dry under the best of circumstances, and the jealous bootlickers around him had little trouble fanning it into flame, to the point where he mused to two supposed 'loyal advisers' that it might be prudent to replace Cortes as leader of the expedition.

These worthies straightaway reported his remark to Cortes. Though his fleet was not yet fully provisioned, Hernando immediately boarded his men, myself included, and set sail that very midnight under cover of darkness, and while I was still in my hammock, the town of Santiago awoke at dawn to the sight of empty docks and the fleet laboring slowly out of harbor on a meager wind.

Someone roused Velazquez, and he galloped up to the quay, 'in a greater lather than his horse, and still wearing his bedclothes', or so Cortes told me upon my awakening.

'I just could not resist it, Alvaro. I had a boat lowered, and had myself rowed back within shouting distance. "This is how you take your leave of me, like a thief in the night, Hernando?" he roared like a corpulent purple-faced lion.

'"Time presses, Diego, and I must fly," I replied sweetly. "Have you any final commands?" And before he could marshal fitting words of invective, I ordered the oarsman to row me back to the ship, so that I was conveniently out of earshot and waving a fond farewell and so was spared whatever he shouted back waving his fists in the air.'

Cortes found this hilarious. Knowing Diego as I did, I could only moan in dismay. Only half provisioned, we could hardly put out to sea, and Cortes sailed around the coast seeking more.

First he docked at the little town of Macaca, where he presumed to requisition what little was to be had from the royal farms, 'as a loan to the King to be paid back with rich interest'. Thence we proceeded to the larger town of Trinidad, where he erected his standard, invited the locals to rally to it, seized the cargo of a supply vessel and 'paid' in personal script.

While this was in process, a letter arrived from Velazquez informing Verdugo, the governor of Trinidad, that Cortes had been relieved of command, and ordering his arrest. But the terrified Verdugo wisely decided to go no further than informing Cortes of this order, since to carry it out would be quite beyond his powers.

I was appalled at how Hernando was conducting himself, but Cortes was blithely confident.

'Having seen that his orders to remove me cannot be carried out, Diego will now have to pretend they were never issued or have his impotence revealed to the detriment of his authority in Cuba,' he assured me. 'By now, his fondest wish must be to see me gone.'

But there was more to come. Cortes sent Alvarado to Havana in search of more provisions, and upon arriving there with the fleet, he proceeded to invest the town with a large landing force armed with cannon, crossbows and arquebuses.

Once more the commander of the town, one Don Pedro Barba, received a letter from Velazquez ordering him to arrest Cortes and this time also to prevent the fleet from leaving. Once more the recipient of the order knew full well he was powerless to obey it.

This time, though, to enhance the farce, Velazquez also sent a letter to Cortes himself by a different courier politely requesting him to postpone his departure until he himself could arrive to see him off personally.

Even knowing Velazquez's sudden changes of mind, I was powerless to fathom these two seemingly contradictory messages. But not Hernando.

'It is Diego being Diego,' he told me. 'In the unlikely event that Barba was able to carry out his order to arrest me and detain the fleet, he would have achieved his aim, so he might as well give it a try. But Velazquez is surely not fool enough to suppose that this was likely, hence the letter to me.'

'He surely doesn't expect you to await his arrival?'

Cortes shrugged. 'I doubt he intends to come at all, for if he did, he would be unable to carry out his own order himself! This way, he can pretend that the order to Barba was never issued, Barba that his letter to me arrived too late, and Barba will have no interest in contradicting him. Thus will Diego's authority be preserved in the face of disobedience to his orders which never happened, and his ample backside adequately covered. With the aid of his friends.'

'*His friends?*'

'You and I, Alvaro. You will compose a letter to be left behind for Velazquez praising his virtues in a suitably flowery manner, and thanking him most profusely for the confidence he has placed in me, and his invaluable aid in lending me the money to finance this expedition, reminding him in a delicate manner that if it succeeds it will be repaid with abundant profit, whereas a change in leadership would rob me of the opportunity to confer such a boon upon him. And I will sign it with my own loyal hand.'

And so it was done, and so we departed on the nineteenth of February 1519, under fleecy skies, with what I was told was a good following wind. Five hundred and fifty-three soldiers, including thirty-two cross-bowmen and thirteen arquebusiers. Melchior, our interpreter, Julian having expired, perhaps of homesickness. Two hundred Carib slaves. Sixteen horses and a pack of war dogs. Two priests. Ten heavy cannon and four lighter ones. And a crew of some hundred and ten sailors to convey it all.

As I stood on the forecastle of the flagship gazing forward across the blue tropical sea at the future of our adventure, it finally came to me how ridiculously tiny an armada this was to presume to confront the forces of an unknown empire whose outlying province alone had already demonstrated the ability to marshal forty times our forces.

On the other hand, I told myself sardonically as I looked back and watched the Cuban shore and the unseemly manner of our departure disappear behind the curve of the Earth, were we not in truth the largest fleet of pirates ever to set sail?

4

THE WIND HOWLED, the sail flapped and snapped, the yards
creaked and groaned, the greater of the waves broke over the
deck at unpredictable intervals, the ship tossed and heaved, and so did
my entrails as I leaned, soaked and miserable, over the forecastle rail in
the savage teeth of the storm, gagging endlessly and from time to time
spewing bitter bile over the side.

I had never been a believer in Divine Justice or heavenly retribution,
but my lack of faith therein was now severely tested, for it seemed to me
that this storm might be an answer to Diego Velazquez's prayers for
vengeance, or worse still, a warning of what might be to come.

Below decks the few not afflicted by nausea huddled relatively warm
and dry, if not tranquilly, for the horses neighed piteously, kicking at
their stalls, dunging and pissing copiously in their terror, filling the
close air with the sickening stench, and sending all but the strongest of
stomach up into the roiling air.

I was advised by a sailor to fix my gaze upon the horizon to relieve
my seasickness, but such advice, perhaps sage under other circumstances, was useless under these, for the heavy driving rain rendered the
horizon as invisible as the rest of the fleet.

Cortes, emerging from the captain's cabin from time to time to scan the seas for it, seemed immune to the seasickness, but at least I was spared any of his hilarity at my own, for his mood was as foul as the weather. He had ordered the fleet to stay close together and affixed a lantern to the stern of his leading flagship to maintain formation during the night, but now the other ships could not be seen, not the most experienced of mariners could surmise where they were, and even our pilot was not sure where we ourselves might be.

The fleet's first destination was the offshore island of Cozumel, where the previous expedition had been more or less well received by the locals, and whose language was known to Melchior, our interpreter, and which therefore seemed to Cortes the prudent place to begin whatever was in his mind to begin.

'It is important that we all arrive there together so as to present an imposing spectacle,' he fretted during one of his forays on deck. 'But how am I to achieve that when all our ships are being blown hither and yon by this storm, and there is no way to even arrange a rendezvous after it has passed?'

I gagged again, but came up dry, much to the agony of my ribs and stomach, before I was able to express my befuddlement. 'Why should that concern you so? All know the destination, and we will easily enough rendezvous there when we make safe harbor.' I gagged once more. 'If we ever do,' I groaned.

'There is more to it than that,' he told me. 'Should some of our fleet arrive piecemeal before I arrive, I fear that some of my captains may take it upon themselves to put their men ashore after such a gut-wrenching voyage, and what then might happen, without even anyone who knows the local language . . .'

'But the denizens of Cozumel are by all accounts too few to pose a threat to even a partial force of ours.'

'That's not what I'm afraid of,' Cortes growled, and renewed his anxious seeking.

The storm finally broke, and at length we found ourselves alone on a choppy but tolerable sea, though the lightening of the skies did little to lighten Cortes' humor until a few seabirds appeared, a sign, so the sailors told us, that we were nearing land.

Then the lookout high up on the mainmast shouted out its distant sighting, everyone came up on deck, and soon the horizon became tinged with a misty line of greenish brown. A while later, this became a distant island, then a rocky coast crowned with lush green foliage above a narrow sandy strand.

Even Cortes' mien brightened when the subtle but unmistakeable odors of land – distant vegetation, the sun's heat upon sand, the tang of seaweed rotting and drying on a beach – reached our nostrils on the breeze, a perfume otherwise too faint to discern rendered blissfully tangible in contrast to the previously all too prevalent stormy sea stench of salt, tar, dung, urine and vomit.

We sailed anxiously around the coast of the island, until, rounding a headland that guarded a decent enough natural harbor, we spied masts and spars, then a ship, then another and another and another, and a cheer of relief went up, and this was greatly enhanced as we approached anchorage, for ten were counted. The entire fleet had survived.

Our joy was somewhat tempered when we saw in what condition. Spars were splintered, cracked and missing, rigging hung in tatters, some masts had even been reduced to jagged stumps.

'Fear not,' the captain of our flagship reassured Cortes, 'I've seen such tempests in these seas do much worse. This is nothing that ship's carpenters can't set straight, what with all that timber ashore.'

This mollified Cortes, and as we dropped anchor, close enough to the beach now to see them, our spirits were further raised by the sight of several score men awaiting us on the beach, who, by the gleam off their armor, and by the standards planted in the sand, were easily enough recognized as our comrades waving to us in welcome. Indeed, I could make out not only the standard of Pedro Alvarado, but the golden hair and beard of the bareheaded figure standing beside it.

I say our spirits were raised by this sight, but this was not true of Cortes. 'They landed against my orders,' he grumbled.

'How can you charge them with disobedience to orders that were never given?'

'I would have given them were I there!'

'How were they to know that?'

To this Cortes made no direct reply. Instead he issued the highly unpopular order that everyone was to remain aboard for the moment, myself included, while he went ashore in a boat to discern the situation.

As one might well imagine, the mood aboard the flagship grew more and more sour, then iresome, as the 'moment' stretched on towards an hour, while we watched Cortes being rowed ashore, being greeted by the party there, then engaging in some kind of long gesticulating conversation with Alvarado before being rowed back to the ship.

Our petty ire, however, was nothing to what burned on the face of Cortes when he climbed back aboard. His normal sallow skin was reddened with rage, and his scowl darker than the departed stormclouds, to the point where no one dare approach or speak to him, myself included.

But as he stormed into his cabin, he wordlessly beckoned me to follow, and once inside slammed the door behind us and poured out his fury.

'That arrogant halfwit Alvarado! I would chop off that golden head of his if I did not know that it is as empty of malice as it is of wisdom or even cunning!'

'What did he do?' I inquired mildly as Cortes paced the little cabin seeming fit to attack the furnishings with his sword at any moment.

'What did he do! Not content with landing his troops without orders, he whiled away the time awaiting my ire not merely by barging into the town armed to the teeth like a pirate raider but behaving like one too, looting the temple of its few worthless trinkets and so terrifying the natives that they have disappeared into the jungle. And do you know what he told me?'

'I surmise that you are about to tell me,' I all but whispered.

'"You are not pleased, my Captain?" he said with an air of wounded innocence. "True, we found no great treasure, but I assure you on my honor we secured all there was to be had." "You call unprovoked looting and desecration *honorable*?" I roared at him. And then . . . and then . . .'

'And then?'

'And then the man had the effrontery to display righteous outrage rather than contrition!' Cortes shouted, slamming his fist down on the tabletop, no doubt as if it were the head of Pedro Alvarado. '"You were not there to see it," he told me. "A hideous idol caked with the blood of

I dare not imagine who or what and these loathsome creatures done up in vile parody of priests of the Cross conducting some sort of evil ceremony while the benighted savages paid it obeisance! An outrage to the honor of Christ Himself! What true Christian's honor would not demand that he put an end to it and teach them a lesson?"'

Cortes shook his head and took a deep breath. He sighed and sank down into a chair, and when he spoke again, his rage had been tempered, though with nothing better than a certain despair.

"'A fine lesson you have taught these heathens with whom we would trade and win to the True Faith," I told him. "To fear and hate us before our mission is even begun." To which he replied: "I thought we were here to conquer these lands for the King and the Cross."'

'Well he *did* have a point,' I ventured cautiously, 'didn't he?'

'One way or another,' Cortes said with a sigh, 'but surely not like this! Save for the tales brought back by Hernandez and Grijalva, we know nothing of this savage empire we confront, not even if that is truly what it is, and the first Indians we encounter who might supply useful intelligence are frightened off into the jungle to spread tales of our forthright thievery.'

His anger now spent, Cortes motioned for me to be seated beside him. 'What am I to do now, Alvaro?' he asked plaintively.

'Well, I can tell you what you are not going to do,' I told him. 'In the dispatches to be sent back to the King, this fiasco must never have happened.'

'To be sure, but how am I to retrieve the situation so as to make it disappear?'

'Are there any of the natives left in the vicinity?'

'I believe Alvarado mentioned something about taking captives, but I was paying little heed at the time . . .'

'And unless I am mistaken, our Melchior speaks the local tongue.'

'So?'

'So we had best redress the natives' grievance against us with largesse and the promise of more,' I told him.

'*We* must redress their grievance against us?' said Cortes, getting my drift. 'Not quite, Alvaro. I have a better idea. And one that I shall find both just and amusing.'

*

And so our first congress with the subjects, however few, of the great Montezuma, took the form of a most bizarre formal ceremony.

Cortes unloaded his grateful forces from the ships – though leaving the poor horses and dogs behind for fear of giving further fright – lined them up behind his standard on the beach, sweating in their full gleaming metal armor under the tropical sun in the steaming humidity, and took his place before them, a fine martial display meant to impress rather than intimidate.

To his left stood Pedro de Alvarado, his handsome face an impassive mask, only his darting eyes betraying his discomfort. To his right was poor Melchior, a pathetic spectacle dressed as a parody of a Spanish grandee in a threadbare blue velvet tunic and green pantaloons a size or two too large, but with his hair long and unkempt in the Indian fashion, and the downcast, furtive and uncomprehending eyes of a forest creature plunked down at mass in a cathedral. Before them was a cloth sack and a small wooden chest.

Dragged forth by four soldiers to confront this august company were two aged and cowering Indians, wearing white loincloths and cloaklike affairs, beardless but sporting long graying black manes, and wearing copper earrings embedded with blue stones. Copper tablets likewise embellished depended from their lower lips, their modest weight serving to draw them down to display purpling lower gums and unsmiling yellowish teeth.

'Tell them that we are vassals of the great King across the sea and followers of the True Faith come to this shore in peace and friendship to convey to them the gifts and advantages lavished upon those whom he would in his gracious magnanimity befriend and liberate them from their darkness,' Cortes declared, turning to Melchior.

The poor man, whose Spanish both Cortes and I knew to be minimal, must have comprehended little more of this than we did of whatever he then proceeded to babble to the captives in their own language, and to judge from their expressions, it was insufficient to convey to them the honor being bestowed upon them and their people.

'Tell them that this man, overwhelmed by their beauty, sought only to examine their treasures, not to steal them,' said Cortes, pointing to the hapless Alvarado, 'and when their people, misreading his intent, fled, rather than leave them unguarded prey to thieves, he thought it prudent to take them into his care for safekeeping against their return.'

Had this been delivered by a great orator in their own tongue, it no doubt would have been difficult enough to swallow, and many of those comprehending it in Spanish were hard put to repress their sniggers, so there was no surprise when Melchior's rude translation was met with utter incomprehension by the two captives.

These ridiculous niceties being concluded to the expected no avail, Cortes nodded to Alvarado, who, grimacing, picked up the sack and gently poured its contents out upon the sand – copper implements of unknown use, several blades of a shiny black substance, handfuls of jewelry, some of it gold but most of it copper set with stones that were neither diamonds, rubies nor sapphires, though there were some with pearls.

The captives were then shoved forward to observe with incomprehension becoming amazement as one by one, displaying each item first with the utmost politesse, Alvarado replaced them in the sack.

'Tell them that we now return their safeguarded treasures to them, and they will find that nothing is missing,' Cortes said, giving Alvarado a sidelong glance that clearly said there had better not be.

Melchior's translation may or may not have been understood, but it did not need to be, as Cortes himself handed the sack to one of them.

He then opened the little chest, and one by one displayed its contents: a glass mirror in an iron frame, a steel knife with a leather-wrapped handle, a handful of rosaries, several base metal crosses on chains, a pair of scissors, a cheap miniature portrait of the Virgin and Child, a Bible, and handfuls of colored glass beads.

Closing the chest, he handed it over to the other Indian. 'These are precious gifts from His Majesty King Charles to your people as token of his friendship,' he proclaimed. 'Take them back to your people, and tell them to return to their homes without fear. Tell them also that there is much for them to have, in return for what presents they may wish to give to us as tokens of theirs.'

This time Melchior's translation seemed better understood, greatly aided no doubt by the obviousness of the gestures which needed none, and the Indians' eyes lit up with no little relief and pleasure, albeit of a somewhat tentative and disbelieving kind.

When their guards released them and stepped aside, they stood there numbly for a moment, then, at a farewell wave from Cortes, began slowly backing away towards the forest fringing the beach with their shoulders forward, their backs bent, and their heads lowered, like obsequious courtiers departing the royal presence. Only when they neared the treeline did they deem it meet and prudent to turn their backs and disappear therein at a dead run.

A word must be said, however reluctantly, in defense of the character, if not the sagacity, of Pedro de Alvarado, a man whose conviction that all those who did not adhere to Christ and the Cross were certain future inhabitants of Hell did not endear him to me, and whose cavalier indifference to military discipline was not only to vex Cortes but was to prove quite disastrous.

Nevertheless, he was a man whose unswerving courage made him a fine leader of men on a tactical level, nor did he believe himself insubordinate while committing insubordination, nor was he any more of a thief than the rest of them. He was like a fierce mastiff well trained to battle and loyal to his master, but best kept on a short leash when not released to attack, unwise to trust with anything more complex than well-supervised combat leadership.

There, dear reader, I have said it, and displayed one of the Christian virtues in which he was lacking, to wit forgiveness, which I doubt he would grant me should he read the foregoing – fortunately unlikely, since he was of little disposition to read anything.

Be that as it may, in Cortes' first letter to the King, rewritten several times by me, Alvarado was not even mentioned. The locals had fled into the woods at the very sight of our ships, and, through Melchior, Cortes had sent a message via two who had chanced to remain behind that 'he was there to do them no harm, but to bring them to the knowledge of our Holy Catholic Faith, that they might become loyal vassals of Your Majesty, like ourselves, and all that we desired was that the chiefs and the Indians of the island should likewise obey Your Majesty.'

And if that was not enough to grease the royal goose, I went on to declare that when he 'reassured them in this manner, they lost much of their fear, and the chief replied that he was content to do so, and sent for all the other chieftains of the island, who rejoiced greatly at all that Captain Hernando Cortes had spoken.'

Cortes rolled his eyes when I showed him this draft. 'You surely do not believe that the King is fool enough to swallow such a farrago, Alvaro,' he said incredulously.

'Rest assured, Hernando,' I told him, 'monarchs, being lords of all they survey, are well accustomed to believing whatever tale enhances their absolute belief in their own absolute grandeur, and think it only natural that anyone informed thereof will immediately wish to bow down to it.'

What actually happened after the events on the beach, you will readily enough surmise, dear reader, unless you too are a monarch, was quite different from what was vouchsafed to King Charles.

We set up a tent camp on the beach and lounged about getting our land legs back as Indians began to arrive in dribs and drabs. First came a few tentative scouts, then, when these were received peacefully with trade beads, larger parties, including women, offering examples of their cuisine in return. These consisted mainly of round, flat, dryish unleavened breads not unlike sacramental matzoh, served with a brown mash of what we learned to our relief were beans when we worked up the courage to bite into it, for it looked like sickly feces, though actually quite tasty. There were also roasted fowl called turkeys, larger than chickens though tasting quite similar. There were also sauces too fiery for most of us to tolerate, fruits to cool our palates from the effects thereof, and clay jugs of an oily drink they called pulque, somewhat more powerful than wine, with an aroma and taste reminiscent of lamp oil.

While this may not seem like much of a feast to the educated palate, it was quite an improvement over the shipboard staples of cassava bread and salted pork, and our honest gratitude was displayed by sending these parties back laden with beads, rosaries, and metal kitchen implements which might aid them in the more facile preparation of more of the same.

Within a few days, the natives had returned to their nearby town, and our camp became quite a little trading market, albeit not in the bargaining manner of an Arabic bazaar, but rather a continual exchange of 'gifts'. We gave them beads, rosaries, crucifixes, shears and scissors, knives, mirrors, and the like. In return, we received food, pulque, cloaks of rough cloth – a few of them inlaid with the brilliantly colored feathers of birds in patterned effects strangely like Arabic tapestry and quite beautiful – razor-sharp black knives, opaque green and blue stones, and bits and pieces of jewelry, all too few of which were crafted of gold.

Even so, since what we gave them was of little value by our own measure, our general feeling was that we were getting the better of the non-bargaining, though the Indians, from their expressions as they hauled it off, seemed of a similar belief: the ideal atmosphere for a successful bazaar.

There was no attempt at proselytizing in this bazaar, much to the chagrin of the friars, Father Diaz in particular righteously chafing to get down to Holy Business, for Cortes prudently forbade it for the moment in favor of leaving the said atmosphere untrammeled by theological disputation, since even though communication through Melchior was problematical, as in any good bazaar, this one mixed tales with commerce, whereby we might acquire useful information before acting further.

The language problem resulted in a paucity thereof, but we did manage to get the gist of one story that might aid in its resolution, to wit that one or two men with fair skin and beards had years ago washed up on the shores of the land across the strait and might still be counted among the living.

'If this is so, and they are Spaniards, they might prove extremely useful,' I told Cortes, 'for if they have indeed survived for years, surely they would have acquired more of the local language than Melchior has of Spanish, and would surely prove much better interpreters.'

So Cortes sent Diego Ordaz with two brigantines to the coast – called Yucatan – to seek them out, sending with him two Indian traders from Cozumel with what he hoped was ransom enough to buy them out of bondage should that be their condition. Ordaz was to dispatch these emissaries, wait eight days for results, then return.

This might be laid to my wisdom, but the further wisdom of Cortes lay in the fact that Ordaz was known by him to be excessively loyal to Velazquez, and sending such captains with questionable loyalty to himself off on separate missions would prove to be a favorite ploy of Hernando's. It removed them from the main force for a time, and hence from taking part in any unwanted intrigues, and who knows, with adequate ill luck, they might fail to return.

While awaiting the results, Cortes decided to mount an overland expedition to explore Cozumel, to better learn the lie of the land and relieve the boredom of a good portion of the idle troops, who were beginning to grow restive. Despite my softly and carefully worded advice to the contrary, he decided to mollify Father Diaz and Father Olmedo by taking them with him, along with the Holy Armaments of their priestly mission.

Cozumel proved to be an island of no great size, and no great fertility of soil, where a meager population of Indians, clustered mainly in scattered villages, eked out a modest living from the surrounding fields of what they called 'maize' and the beans from which they made their brown mash.

The maize was not a grain crop like wheat, but a stalk-like plant nearly as tall as a man when ready for harvest, from each of which depended several large oval pods containing thick stems coated with grain-like fruits. These must be scraped off, dried, processed with some sort of white solution, then dried again to be ground into the flour from which their flat bread was made. The beans grew on bushes, as did several species of peppers, some red, some green, of different sizes and degrees of fiery power.

The land being somewhat sandy and parched, these crops were often irrigated by systems of ditches bringing water from streams and springs, so that the croplands might justly be styled true farms.

They also made much use of a large thick-boled cactus-like plant called the maguey, which needed no irrigation or cultivation and grew wild. From the interior sap, they fermented their pulque, the fibers of the leaves and bole provided the thread from which they wove rough cloth, and, as I was to learn later, pulp from which the higher civilization of the Mexica made the very sort of paper upon which this account is being written. The strong sharp spines became needles useful in sewing, and, as it turned out, for darker purposes.

Save for the village temples, stepped pyramids of stone which might rise for several stories, their houses were modest single-story windowless and doorless affairs, but these too were of dressed stone, and often whitened with something like paint.

Though they possessed implements of copper and the black glass called obsidian, brittle stuff which nevertheless took an edge keener than that of steel, no smithing activity was in evidence, nor did we discover a local source of obsidian. The village chieftains and some of the notables sported modest amounts of golden jewelry, but we found neither goldsmiths nor gold mines, and you may be sure not for lack of avid searching and inquiry.

Taken all together – the relatively sophisticated system of agriculture, the craftsmanlike working of stone, the systematic utilization of the maguey, the modest presence of jewelry and implements which would have had to come from elsewhere – it seemed to me that Cozumel had to be a primitive backwater in sporadic contact with a distant and higher civilization.

The village temples themselves, though clearly not beyond the architectural powers of the people who had built the houses, seemed also somehow something of an importation. The veneration with which the locals regarded them might seem natural to their own venues of worship, but it seemed tinged with a dread that did not.

The 'papas' who presided over them were as Bernal Diaz had described to me – the long filthy hair, matted and felted rather than woven into braids, the ragged black robes reminiscent of the habits of Dominicans long since gone to seed, the foul stench – but he had not been able to render into words or perhaps even to perceive what I saw in their eyes.

It was as if some other being were staring out at you balefully from behind the holes in their skulls, or even the same being regarding you from all of them; if they were not truly possessed by their gods, if those gods might not even truly exist as we understood existence, I was certain that these papas were no cynical mountebanks but creatures whose spirits were no longer their own, like Hebrew prophets in permanent merger with the Ain-Soph, like Mohammed in the act of receiving the

Koran from Allah, like the most adept Sufi dervishes living forever in the climax of their trance.

Father Diaz, being an unsophisticated cleric lacking interest in such speculatively mystical matters, deemed them to be simple charlatans. Father Olmedo, a much more thoughtful man, seemed to be of a similar opinion to my own, but he, of course, was certain that what possessed them could only be Satan – not that I was entirely convinced that it was not. Nor did Bernal Diaz's account of the rite he had seen them conduct on the mainland exactly serve as an aid to my disbelief.

In every village we stopped at, Olmedo sought to enlighten the benighted darkness of the inhabitants. Our troops would be drawn up as close to the temple as the papas would allow, for Cortes at this point was not about to provoke a violent confrontation. A wooden Cross whose upright had been sharpened to a point for the purpose would be driven into the earth and a portrait of the Virgin and Child set up on an easel.

Olmedo would then preach a fiery sermon declaring that these were the emblems of the One and Only God Who had created and ruled the universe, that all other so-called gods were false and non-existent, or worse, aspects of Satan, the evil worship of which would condemn them all to an eternity of torture in Hell, which, when he was truly inspired, he would describe at length in gory detail, and that they therefore must be baptized with Holy Water if they knew what was good for them. When he was of a somewhat more positive mood, he would attempt an explication of the Trinity, of how the One True God had gotten a Son on the Virgin, and how Jesus was also somehow the One True God, which was to say (though he certainly didn't!) that God was both His Own Father and His Own Son, and, moreover, also a third entity known as the Holy Spirit.

Even with my studies of several theologies and any number of philosophical systems, this has never been quite possible for me to parse, so what these poor Indians might make of it I could not fathom, all the more so since it all need be conveyed by Melchior's halting translation, which for all we might know, could just as well have been a description of his nauseous ocean crossing or a recitation of his own lineage.

Despite this, the Indians usually seemed to enjoy the entertainment, and often several of their number would come forward to be baptized with Holy Water, probably amused at being invited to play a part in the incomprehensible but amusing spectacle.

Olmedo would end the proceedings with a magnanimous offer to replace whatever evil idols lurked atop their pyramid with a Cross and a portrait of the Virgin and Child, with which we came liberally supplied. Whether Melchior ever dared properly translate this is doubtful, given the fear and awe with which he regarded the papas, but it was certainly never accepted.

Nor would Cortes accept Father Diaz's impatient entreaties to accomplish this mass conversion by force, though he certainly had the means to do so easily enough.

'However my heart demands that I do so,' he told the priests, 'my intelligence tells me that it would be futile. Worse than futile, for there are many of these little villages, I cannot garrison them, and no sooner would we be gone, than these heathens would tear down Cross and Virgin, trample them in the dust, or worse, pervert them into objects in some Satanic ritual too ghastly to contemplate, and out of the most noble and virtuous Christian passion, we would blacken our souls as accessories to blasphemy and desecration.'

The practical disadvantages of creating such a conflict as such action would provoke in every village we passed as we toured the island – to wit hostility both fore and aft – were no doubt apparent to him, and as I have said, Cortes was the most accomplished of liars, no more so than when bending the truth served his own tactical purposes, but, having witnessed him speaking thusly on more than one occasion, the earnestness in his voice and the passion on his face convinced me that in this he was quite sincere.

And when he was finally pushed too far, baleful events proved me all too correct.

Cortes had received word that Ordaz had returned from the mainland without any shipwrecked Spaniards, which put him in something of a foul humor, and did little to improve the mood of the friars either, for the continued failure of the Indians to show any real interest in cleaving to the One True Faith despite the most eloquent and passionate preaching at length made plain Melchior's utter inadequacy as a translator when it came to such theocratic complexities.

We were on our way back to our main encampment, when, of a late afternoon, we encountered a village larger than most, and so too its pyramidal temple, though it was hardly a grand edifice.

What must have been most of the village was gathered silently around the foot of the temple gazing up at the stone hut which crowned its flattened summit, and at a respectful or perhaps fearful distance, though no papas were in evidence to enforce it. Though nothing seemed to be happening, it was an eerie unsettling sight, with the blue of the sky deepening, and the shadows of the surrounding trees lengthening, and the ominous shadow of the temple itself enfolding that silent congregation of what to my eyes now seemed savages, with their half-naked bodies, long black hair, and lips, ears and noses pierced with metal embellishments.

Cortes marched his troops into the village and brought them to a halt a discreet distance behind this somber gathering, whether out of curiosity, unease, or the tentative aspect of respect one tends to assume as a witness to the ceremonies of a faith other than one's own, I could not tell, and perhaps he could not either. There was such a pregnancy in the heavy tropical air that even Fathers Diaz and Olmedo fell silent, nor did our advent serve to distract the Indians from the object of their worshipful attention save but passingly.

How long we all stood there so still and silent, I cannot tell you, dear reader, for time itself seemed to have stopped until—

A hideous scream rang out from the summit of the temple, a sharp cry of sudden pain that rose into an even worse ululating, blubbering howl of terrible agony, that had Cortes himself and many of our company drawing their swords and rushing forward.

Before the Indian congregation could do more than turn in reaction to the commotion behind it, they were through their midst, and Cortes had mounted the lower steps of the temple with a cordon of steel swords and armor behind him as the horrible screaming guttered into a silence somehow even worse.

Then, as all seemed to freeze into mutual uncertainty, something large came tumbling and bouncing down from the summit of the temple, obscured by shadow and motion, until it all but collided with Cortes as it came to its final rest close by his feet.

Only then did he and the rest of us realize that what we had seen thrown down from on high like so much refuse was the corpse of a man, his chest a gory gaping hole, the path his body had taken down the stone steps drawn in gouts and rivulets of fresh and still dripping blood like a red stream burbling across the rocks of a rapids.

Cortes shouted in wordless outrage and dashed up the steps two at a time, sword in hand, several men behind him, while the others menaced the outraged Indians with their own swords. Someone in our party behind them gave the order, and four of our arquebusiers fired off their weapons, the unprecedented loudness of the reports and the alien tang of gunpowder dispersing the crowd in terror as Cortes gained the summit.

'The hut atop the temple was redolent with a sweet incense blasphemously reminiscent of that in a cathedral, filling the enclosed space with dense smoke, which, nevertheless, could not draw a merciful veil over the Satanic ritual my poor eyes were forced to behold, and I must cross myself immediately against it,' he told me later.

'Four black-robed papas stood before an idol half as tall as a man which seemed to be carved of stone, though it was hard to be sure, for it was caked with some brownish stuff that might have been dried mud or just as well shit, which softened its monstrous features; great bulging eyes over a leering mouth, and the top of the head a kind of bowl as if its skull had been opened.

'Before this demon was a rude altar of stone with a depression in it filled with blood. Blood ran down onto the floor from a channel cut in the stone and likewise dripped off the edges of the altar. One of the papas held a dagger of black stone coated with more blood. Another was in the act of anointing the head of the idol with blood from a clay bowl, and I realized to my horror that the brownish substance caking the idol, the walls, the floor, was neither mud nor feces, but a thick accumulation of old dried blood, indicating that herein this obscene black mass had been conducted many, many times.

'Try as you may, Alvaro, you will never be able to imagine the force of my outrage. I was upon the idol at once, and such was my fury that God granted me the power to budge it even before the soldiers mounting behind me rushed to aid, and while two of them held off the shouting papas with their swords – and it must have taken great restraint not to simply run them through – the rest of us rolled the Satanic thing out of the entranceway and threw it down the stairs.'

And indeed, a statue of stone came crashing and smashing down the temple façade to crack in two smaller pieces, a number of shards, and one large one, to land at our feet.

I was not entirely surprised, having heard Bernal Diaz's tale of a similar ritual, but the true horror of it was that now I was confronted with the sudden unavoidable realization that his tale was true and I was living in it, that the souls who inhabited this New World were far more foreign to my own than I could have ever believed or imagined, that it might truly be that Satan or something even worse possessed them.

The smashing of their cherished idol caused many of the Indians to screw up their courage to return, some armed with stone-tipped lances and arrows, all clearly outraged, but none daring to be the first to launch an attack.

Seizing the moment, Cortes ordered all present to draw swords, save the priests, and the arquebusiers whose fusillade had frightened them off in the first place; these he had take aim at the Indians at point-blank range as a precaution. He then had a sack of our usual trade goods brought forth, and its contents spread upon the ground before them like the disgorged plenty of a cornucopia, and, through Melchior, managed to convey that these presents were theirs for the taking.

There was a great confusion among the Indians. Their temple had been desecrated and their god destroyed by mysterious strangers possessed of magical weapons with which they were now menaced. But these invaders were now offering them wondrous and perhaps equally magical gifts. I cannot imagine what they must have made of this contradiction, and it would seem that they didn't either, as they milled about, some helping themselves, some standing back, some still brandishing their weapons in frustrated outrage.

Father Olmedo took it upon himself to plant his Cross in the soil close by the fallen idol, a mysterious gesture, which if nothing else served to draw the Indians' attention.

Rather than make another futile attempt to preach a sermon against Satanic and blasphemous idolatry, he summoned Father Diaz, who anointed the largest piece of the idol with holy water, then spread a sacramental cloth across it, converting it to a communion table.

The wine and wafers were then produced, the appropriate prayers were said, and all present were offered communion.

'The body and the blood of Christ . . .'

One by one, led by Cortes, all knelt and partook of the transubstantiated wine and wafer.

'The body and the blood of Christ . . .'

Bizarre as it might be to me as an unbeliever, I could understand why it comforted the Faithful after such grim and blasphemous events.

'The body and the blood of Christ . . .'

I not only thought it prudent to eat and drink of it myself, as I always did under such circumstances, but though I could not quite bring myself to believe that I was taking the godhead into my flesh as I did so, even I drew a measure of comfort from the familiar ritual.

I was among the last to do so, and, wonder of wonders, when I arose, I saw that a score and more Indians were lining up behind me to do likewise, as Melchior moved among them.

'What did you say to them?' I asked him, drawing him aside, as, one by one, formerly benighted savages knelt before the blissfully beaming Father Olmedo to partake of the Christian sacrament.

'Ask what is ceremony,' Melchior replied in his broken Spanish. 'Tell them is Christian magic. Tell them Christian magic turn bread and wine into meat and blood of their god.'

'*And?*' I demanded.

'Tlaloc must be fed blood and meat of men so rain comes,' said Melchior. 'But Jesus Christ God of Heavens give Christians *his* blood to drink and meat to eat.'

He shrugged. 'Is strange, men eat god instead of god eat men,' he said without a trace of humor. 'They not understand, I think, but they like it.'

5

'IT WAS A MIRACLE,' Father Olmedo declared every time he mentioned that bizarre and mysterious partaking of Holy Communion by savages so recently celebrating a human sacrifice.

And who was I to gainsay him the augmentation to his faith that it brought at the expense of exposing Melchior's part in it and provoking his ire, and perhaps Cortes' as well, against the poor man? Especially since the arrival of Geronimo de Aguilar in our midst, which he also hailed as a miracle, put Melchior in a fragile enough position.

Ordaz had returned without any shipwrecked Spaniards, nor had the Indian traders dispatched with their ransom returned with it to his two ships before he set sail, leaving Cortes quite vexed. In such a mood, he decided to quit Cozumel for the mainland, but no sooner had we set sail than one of the ships sprang a leak and we were constrained to return to repair it, and this was Father Olmedo's second miracle.

For had God not inflicted the crack below a ship's waterline that detained us, the fleet would have been long gone when the traders returned in their canoe with Aguilar, who, as it turned out, had delayed their return by insisting on first making a detour to bring his fellow castaway, one Gonzalo Guerrero, with him.

And while I myself am not about to declare such a transformation of bad luck into good divine intervention, it was no small thing. Language problems are usually glossed over lightly in traveler's tales, but had a previous expedition not captured Melchior and had he not learned some rudimentary Spanish, we would have been at an even greater loss at Cozumel. And had we departed for Yucatan without Aguilar, it would have been much the same thing, for while Melchior probably spoke his native Mayan better than Aguilar, his Spanish had proven minimal. And, as we were to learn later, neither of them spoke the Nahuatl of the Mexica and their vassals, something which would determine the fate of an empire when Marina entered the tale.

Geronimo de Aguilar and Gonzalo Guerrero had been shipwrecked on these shores eight long years ago. Guerrero, the more practical of the two, had made his peace with fate, married an Indian woman, fathered three children, adopted native ways, had himself pierced and tattooed, and despite Aguilar's entreaties, was not about to give up his relative domestic bliss and favorable status among the Indians.

Aguilar had eschewed such marital arrangements, had been enslaved by a cacique of some standing, but, by his firm adherence to his alien god and his superior knowledge of matters of which his master was ignorant, had risen to the status of a sort of pet sorcerer.

'But . . . I count . . . I still counted myself the Spaniard, the civilized man, and a servant of Christ,' he told me in the halting Spanish with which he arrived. 'I go down on my knees to thank Him for the miracle of my rescue.'

And so he had when he climbed out of that canoe, and fervently kissed the first crucifix offered to him. At that time he was a pathetic reverse image of the equally pathetic Melchior. Whereas the latter appeared as a confused and naive child of nature stuffed dazedly into the vestments, language and customs of a world he would never become equipped to truly comprehend, Aguilar stepped out of the canoe looking like a European who had costumed himself as an Indian for a masquerade ball.

Admittedly, it was an excellent costume, not merely the maguey-fiber loincloth and cloak, but the long wild hair, the sun-bronzed skin, even large copper bands depending from pierced earlobes, and beard roughly shaved, no doubt frequently and with an obsidian knife at no little discomfort, in order to emulate the general beardlessness of the natives.

Like Melchior, he appeared as a creature out of place and time, but unlike Melchior, he was returning to his own element. And yet, not quite, for while he was to remove his earrings, become properly barbered, and dress himself as a hidalgo if anything more punctiliously than most, recover his Spanish, and wear a conspicuous silver crucifix, there was always about him a certain lost air; like Melchior, but much more subtly, that of a man caught between two worlds and unable to quite find comfort in either.

And so, reinforced by a single man, who by his good knowledge of Spanish and the language of Yucatan was worth more than another shipful of soldiers, we set sail once more, not venturing out to sea but hugging the coast, first northward, then, rounding a cape, we followed what proved to be a peninsula as it curved west, then south past the town of Champoton.

Although this was the largest and most impressive town we had seen thus far, we kept our admiration and our curiosity at a good distance, since the inhabitants had given the expeditions of both Hernandez and Grijalva hostile and unpleasant welcomes, and continued along the coast as it bent westward once more until we reached the broad mouth of the river the Indians of the country called 'the Tabasco', which Grijalva had in all modesty renamed after himself.

Which is as good a place as any, dear reader, to make my apologies for the confusion of names with which this account, like all the others, cannot help but be rife, for the natives of these lands had several languages and no means of putting their place and tribal names into writing, the tonal palettes of their tongues differed from ours, besides which the Spaniards were forever renaming things in Spanish.

Thus the large city upriver has variously been called 'Potonchan' and 'Tabasco', where, by either name, Grijalva had been confronted by a very large force of Tabascans willing and very able to defend it, and upon attempting to persuade its caciques to swear fealty to King Charles, had been informed in no uncertain terms that they already

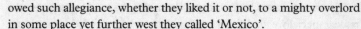

owed such allegiance, whether they liked it or not, to a mighty overlord in some place yet further west they called 'Mexico'.

More to Cortes' current point, when Grijalva, rather than pressing the issue with his much inferior force, had opted for trade, he had secured a modest amount of gold, and upon inquiring after more, had once again been told 'Mexico, Mexico', so he determined to proceed up the 'Rio de Grijalva' to their city.

From Grijalva's account, he also knew that the mouth of the river had an underwater sandbar which would prevent the entry of his larger ships, and so we were constrained to proceed toward Potonchan with something like half our forces in the brigantines and some small boats.

From the beginning it was an ominous passage, for the river soon narrowed, and both banks were overgrown with thickets of mangrove trees whose interlocking trunks slithered down the muddy embankments and into the water like the tentacles of enormous squids, forming overarching and deeply shadowed wild arbors from which cover lurking parties of Indians could be dimly perceived tracking our passage, scowling, waving their fists, and brandishing spears, arrows and curious wooden paddles studded with sharp black obsidian blades like the upright scales on the lethal tails of crocodiles.

Several hours upriver, the land on the banks became somewhat drier, the mangrove jungle along the banks thinned out, and our little flotilla reached a wider space where a large number of Indians, several hundred, had gathered, and, by the look of them not exactly to welcome us, for not one was unarmed.

Still, though there were many archers among them, no arrows were launched as Cortes brought our boats gingerly within shouting distance, crossbows cocked, the small cannon called falconets and arquebuses loaded, primed, and ready just in case.

Through Melchior, Cortes expressed his peaceful intentions to trade and nothing more, and requested permission to land in a most civil manner. The Tabascans, however, refused to grant such permission in a most uncivil manner, jabbing spears in our direction, slashing the air with their paddle swords, shouting fiercely, no doubt swearing obscenely in their own tongue and making equally rudely threatening gestures.

Firearms or not, Cortes did not deem this the moment to press the issue, especially with the sun beginning to set over jungled territory our potential adversaries knew a lot better than we did, and so we repaired to an island in the stream, where he set up a strong guard, and we passed a fitful and largely sleepless night.

At dawn, the beauteously golden tropical sunrise revealed a most unwelcome sight. The bank of the river on the side leading to the city was crowded up and down for a league and more with Tabascan warriors, thousands of them now, rather than hundreds. Canoes by the hundred, or at least by the score, laden with more warriors, lined the shore below with their prows pointed towards us like the pickets of a fence.

They confronted us silently now as we likewise confronted them, as if each side were waiting for the other to attack, or perhaps daring it to do so.

We all armed ourselves, myself included, donning metal armor and helm for the first time in my life, and buckling on an unfamiliar sword.

'Well we all knew it would come to this sooner or later, did we not?' Cortes said in a fine good martial humor as he held council on the beach.

For my part, I certainly did not. The cuirass chafed, the helmet was unnaturally heavy, I was already beginning to sweat, and the thought that I might soon draw a sword with lethal intent or at least necessity was as unreal to me as being soon confronted with a howling savage intent on my slaughter.

'There is, as I remember, a grove of palm trees about a league down-river from here and therefore out of sight,' Alonso de Avila, a veteran of the Grijalva expedition, told Cortes, 'and a road nearby it leading to the city, which from the look of things here must be left but lightly defended . . .'

Cortes studied Avila but briefly, for while the man was no particular intimate of his, neither was he any partisan of Diego Velazquez, and his suggestion therefore to be more or less trusted.

'Take a hundred men and march on it,' he ordered, glancing in the direction of the Tabascan force, greatly outnumbering us, which awaited across that all-too-narrow stretch of water. 'The rest of us will fight our way through the main force here, and thus we will catch the city itself between us,' he said blithely, and my stomach dropped towards my knees and my bowels began to loosen.

Avila loaded one of the brigantines and several small boats with soldiers, sailed to the far bank, and then turned downstream as if fleeing in terror, much to the gleeful derision of the Tabascans on the other bank, while the rest of us boarded the other boats.

Cortes waited a good hour after Avila's boats had disappeared from sight around a bend in the river, then brought our flotilla across the water to within earshot of the Tabascans, but hopefully out of effective arrow range. He then proceeded, at the top of his lungs, to issue, through Melchior, likewise constrained to shout, one of those proclamations, utterly pointless to the Indians even had they understood it, meant primarily to be duly recorded by our notary and therefore to cover whatever came next with a cloak of royal legality, however threadbare.

'We come in peace at the command of His Most Royal Majesty King Charles of Spain who commands you to grant us safe passage to your capital for the purpose of establishing the most friendly of relations, and if you do not obey, and if blood be shed, it shall be upon your heads, and in any case resistance is useless, since one way or another we shall camp tonight in your city.'

It is doubtful that the Tabascans comprehended any of these words, Melchior's attempt at translation or not, and if they had, the result would have only been to further enrage them, but the arrogant pomposity with which they were delivered would have sufficed to inflame a tribe of Barbary apes, and the Tabascans replied with a spontaneous and ragged fusillade of arrows.

Half of these fell short, some clattered against the hulls, a few whizzed overhead, several struck armor, but at this range none were able to do real damage. But Cortes ordered our boats forward to close with the canoes, which came out to meet the challenge, and then it was another matter.

Though we might be outnumbered even by the warriors in the canoes alone, their tactics were less than effective against armored men defending against them from behind gunwales with swords and lances. Which is not to say that I did not find the short fierce struggle quite terrifying.

While oarsmen rowed towards us at the highest possible speed, archers in the canoes launched arrows, drawing their bows, firing, reloading, firing again, in rapid succession, three or four of their arrows to one of our crossbow bolts. But the canoes were pitching and rolling, their aim was therefore quite random, they were firing upward, and the chief effect was to keep our heads down, none lower than mine, as I found myself kissing the planking as arrows hummed overhead.

When they closed, it was obsidian-tipped lances, rude wooden clubs, and those paddle swords, which we later learned were called 'maquahuitls' in Nahuatl, whose fringes of obsidian blades were extremely sharp but also quite brittle, none of which were very effective against steel swords, steel-tipped pikes, shields and armor. The Tabascans, moreover, were seeking to clamber up aboard larger boats from small canoes.

Although they outnumbered us, their obsidian blades shattered upon contact with our metal, and even the quilted knee-length jerkins which served many of them as armor were of little use against our swords striking downwards, and soon we broke their assault.

I say 'we', but in all honest truth, that is hyperbole, for being long in years for such matters and untrained in the martial arts to begin with, and with saving my own skin taking precedence over any impulse to prove the mettle of my manhood in battle, I hung as far back from the fray as I could.

When the canoe assault was broken, though, and Cortes, leading from the front with sword in hand, shouted for us to take the offensive and fight our way ashore, without thought, I found myself leaping over the side into the waist-deep water with the best of them, though not as ardent to gain the forefront of a short and terrifying hand-to-hand combat.

In memory, it all passes in a blurry tempest of churning water, overturning canoes, screams and shouts of pain and fury and triumph, the crack of obsidian and wood against metal, heavy wading through sucking mud, thumps against my helmet, my breastplate, the horror of feeling my sword slice thickly across an arm, blood, intestines, bodies floating face-down in incarnadine water.

Strangely enough, or perhaps not so strangely since I have heard its like reported often afterwards by soldiers, I do not remember feeling anything much like fear; not because I count myself as having been courageous, but because it was all happening too rapidly and disjointedly for such a rational emotion to cohere, for in such a situation one loses thought in favor of spontaneous action like an animal of the wild or one does not survive.

At any rate, the Tabascans battling us in the water were driven back towards the riverbank, or perhaps made an intelligent retreat by their own lights, for there they were reinforced by much greater numbers, and we must fight our way climbing up slippery mudbanks against long odds to gain the shore.

Our first attempt proved bloody and futile, and so too our second. Cortes, who had lost a sandal to the mud and thrown off the other to fight barefootedly balanced, shouted to us to fall back to the boats.

But this was only the briefest of tactical retreats. Once we were standing a score or so paces back, he had the arquebusiers and crossbowmen take aim at the front ranks of the Tabascans on the nearby bank and fire a fusillade.

At this close range, the damage done was terrible. Crossbow bolts passed through bodies like so many melons, quilted cotton armor or not. Metal shot shredded faces, necks, cracked open skulls like coconuts. But the tremendous and to them unprecedented roar of exploding gunpowder and the clouds of acrid smoke probably terrified the Indians as much as the sudden carnage within their midst inflicted by magical means beyond their comprehension.

The front rank – or what was left of the front rank – broke and sought to flee, pressing back against their comrades behind, and that only gave our arquebusiers and crossbowmen time to reload and fire again before they were all fleeing from the river bank.

We scrambled and slithered up the muddy but now abandoned bank, fired another fusillade, and then, shouting and screaming in triumph, we were chasing a far larger force across a marshy flatland towards a rude barricade of freshly cut mangrove logs.

Here they took more heart, at least for the moment, loosing volleys of arrows and javelins that wounded several of our number, and caused us to retreat back out of range. But once again, the arquebuses proved an overwhelming advantage. While they were hardly even as accurate as the Tabascan arrows at any given distance, and an archer could loose three or four missiles by the time an arquebusier could fire, reload and fire again, their range was greater and so was the force of their impact, and the thunder and smoke was terrifying to the uncomprehending Indians.

Cortes kept his force back out of harm from arrows while the arquebusiers fired volley after volley at the log barricade, cracking the wood, sending large jagged splinters flying back into the faces of the defenders huddling behind it, until the magical destruction of their fortification from a distance sent the Tabascans fleeing once more.

We pursued them at a measured distance – measured by how far one of their arrows might fly effectively – as they retreated in ragged order back towards the outskirts of the town of Potonchan itself, which was surrounded by a more formidable barricade, low wooden walls of long standing, to judge by the weathered conditions of the logs from which it was constructed.

Here they made another stand, and here we first encountered the weapon we later learned was called the 'atlatl' by the Mexica, though fortunately not in any great numbers, for this device hurled a kind of outsized obsidian-tipped arrow the size of a spear or javelin with great force and range. The butt of the feather-fletched javelin was placed up against a round depression in the rear of an arm-long pole or narrow plank, and the warrior then whipped the atlatl overhand, so that the missile was released with the leveraged force of an arm twice as long as was natural. While this had little effect when it struck metal armor, at medium range, if well aimed, it could go right through the quilted cotton armor used by the Indians, and which the Spaniards were later to adopt in sweltering tropical heat or when on the march.

Realizing that the arquebusiers would soon run out of shot and powder, Cortes had them reload together one last time, but ordered them to fire in sequence, under cover of which we charged the wall.

I indeed did join in the brave sword-waving dash forward, though due to my age, or perhaps my prudence, I was fortunately unable to gain the front of the pack. Confounded by the arquebus volleys and the speed of our charge, the Tabascans were able to inflict no serious damage before we closed with them, and then it was swords of steel against bare limbs and necks and quilted cotton armor, wooden maquahuitls fringed with obsidian razors against steel armor.

Though the Tabascans fought bravely and did not break and run again at the gates of their city, even outnumbering us as they did, they could not hold their own at such close-quarters fighting. For as many of them as there were, only two or three at a time could confront any Spaniard, their obsidian blades, though capable of inflicting agonizing wounds on exposed flesh, shattered against our shields and armor, their cotton armor was no defense against steel swords, and even I, I must confess, to both my pride and shame, seriously wounded, or perhaps even killed, several.

Soon enough we were fighting them in the streets of Potonchan, and streets these were, well-laid-out avenues of earth between well-crafted single-story houses of adobe or dressed stone, crossing each other at intervals, the whole centered on a large central square, with its inevitable temple, this one by far the largest and most elaborate we had yet seen.

As the Tabascans were constrained to fall back on this city center, their efforts to protect it grew even more valiant, or perhaps desperate, if little more effective. But as we forced them into it, we heard a great cry or moan of woe and disbelieving outrage issue from their rear ranks.

This was followed by the reports and smoke of arquebus fire, and then the Tabascan force rapidly disintegrated, the Indians fleeing every which way, down streets, around the square, dispersing into the city, and then, to our relief and joy, we beheld the reason for the collapse of their defense and their courage.

Avila and his men had circled round the city, entered it from the other side, and surprised and quite dismayed them with a sudden attack on their rear from the other side of the square they were seeking to defend, and our two victorious forces now faced each other unhindered across it. We cheered and ran to embrace each other.

Thus did the tiny army of Hernando Cortes win its first battle on the soil of what was to become 'New Spain', thus did it capture its first city, and thus did a great war begin, though no one realized at the time how enormous its magnitude would be.

It was an unsettling victory. We encamped in the central square in the shadow of the temple, the venue made ominous by the silence and emptiness which had descended upon it. There were simple adobe kiosks in the square, for apparently it served as a market as well as devotional center, but these were not only empty of goods, but seemed carefully so, for there was no debris in evidence. There was a stone house of the sort occupied by the papas, but there were no priests in it, and its rooms had been stripped to the walls.

So too the rest of Potonchan. The warriors we had scattered had exfiltrated through the streets into the countryside. The dwellings were empty of women and children and most possessions that could be carried, and again there was no sign of hasty disorder. Potonchan had not been abandoned in panic, it had been methodically evacuated before the battle had begun.

We victors huddled uneasily in the central square of the silent empty city as the afternoon sun began to wane. Cortes surely sensed the disquieted mood, for we all shared it. Perhaps that is why he did what he did, simply to calm our skittish disposition with some sort of victory ceremony, though I suspect he had planned to do the thing all along. A seemingly small and vain little thing that, knowingly or not, put his feet on the road to great consequences.

There was a large tree near the center of the square and Cortes gathered us all before it, ordering our notary to take down his words, and fateful words they would be, the first pronouncement of the so-called 'Requerimiento' on the soil of New Spain, and far from being the last.

For those of you, dear readers, unfamiliar with this legal formula, the 'Requerimiento' is the declaration with which territory was claimed as a possession of the Spanish Crown, previously uttered over each of the Caribbean islands thus far so favored and blessed, and now so presumptuously applied to what we would soon enough learn was territory owing fealty to the empire of the great Montezuma. For those of you who cannot credit such hubristic presumption, I swear it is true. I was there as witness to this first occasion, and at so many others.

'In the name of Charles, King of Spain, I, Hernando Cortes, his most loyal vassal and servant, do take possession of this city and any and all of its dependencies for the Crown of Castile,' Cortes declared.

And he slashed the trunk of the tree three times with his sword, though this was not a legal requirement. Perhaps, I remember musing at the time, not sure whether Hernando entirely understood what he was doing, he was cutting the three rules that bound him.

First, by disobeying the order of Velazquez *not* to found a colony or seize territory, he was severing his subservience to the governor of Cuba.

Second, he was declaring himself the direct agent of the King of Spain, a sovereign who had no idea that he was thus commissioning him.

Third, and I am sure he did not at all comprehend this at the time, by so doing he had declared a war of conquest on the Empire of the Mexica, a war that he would fail to win only at his great peril, for only by delivering the same to the Spanish Crown could he hope to validate his amazingly insubordinate actions retroactively and thus escape the otherwise formidably heavy consequences.

With those few words and those three sword strokes, Cortes cut his ties to the past and irrevocably committed himself to a future that I am equally sure was quite beyond even his most extravagant imaginings.

6

THE ONLY SOUND THAT greeted the sunrise the next morning was birdsong, as we rubbed the sleep from our eyes in the empty square of the deserted city. Cortes had posted guards around the square, and at the entrances to Potonchan, but they had not sighted a single human being. The only thing they did find was something that Cortes took as an ill omen, pantaloons and a jerkin found hanging in the branches of a tree, the discarded European vestments of Melchior, who had fled during the night.

'Why does it so trouble you, Hernando?' I asked him soothingly. 'We now have Aguilar as a translator, whose command of the native tongue here is little less than Melchior's and whose Spanish is far superior.'

'Why does it trouble me!' Cortes responded peevishly. 'The traitor will now inform the Tabascans of our small numbers, and who knows what else!'

'But we have sent thousands of them fleeing who *already* know how few we are,' I pointed out gently, 'and as for what else of military value Melchior might tell them, I doubt that he really understood half of what he saw.'

And as for being a traitor, I thought, but dared not add, that it was while ludicrously garbed as a Spaniard that the poor man had been a traitor to his own kind, and he had probably simply seized the opportunity to try to find his way home. I found myself wishing him well, imagining him as a man of advanced years in a little Indian village somewhere, telling tall tales of his brief sojourn among the Spaniards to enthralled but disbelieving grandchildren.

Cortes, though, was in no mood to be mollified, fearing that the disappearance of so many Tabascan warriors could only mean that they were marshaling somewhere to mount an attack to retake their city. And so he sent out two separate parties to reconnoiter, one under Pedro de Alvarado, the other led by Francisco de Lugo.

While we waited for them to report back, breakfast was eaten, wounds were dressed, mass was said before the glowering pagan temple, and then Cortes gave leave for his troops to gather what loot they might in the deserted city, but to return to the square before lunchtime.

As it turned out, most of the soldiers returned long before then and mostly empty-handed, for there was little booty to be had in the evacuated dwellings of Potonchan: some obsidian blades and arrowheads, odd bits of clothing, a few small sacks of maize, three or four golden trinkets of little value.

This did little to relieve the gloom, nor did the glum repast of cassava bread and salt pork from the ships and stale maize flatbread and bean-mash taken aboard at Cozumel, still less since the skittish Cortes forbade the drinking of wine or pulque while we waited.

The meal was not quite finished when one of the sentries that Cortes had posted came running into the square. 'They've returned!' he shouted breathlessly. 'We're under attack!'

Cortes hardly had to issue any order to have us all up, armed and running, but when we reached the vantage of the wall, we saw that it was the scouting parties of Lugo and Alvarado who were returning, and *they* who were under attack, not our main force in the city.

Four score or so Spaniards were retreating towards the city across a grassy coastal plain, all but surrounded by ten times their number of Tabascan warriors. In such close quarters, neither bows nor atlatls, nor for that matter arquebuses or crossbows, could be brought into play, and it was wooden and obsidian maquahuitls and lances against metal armor, steel swords against quilted cotton armor and wood and leather

shields, and our comrades, despite the unfavorable numbers, were holding off the Tabascans before them, while cutting their way through
those seeking to block their retreat, retiring towards us in more or less
good order.

Cortes nevertheless led his forces out onto the plain to their relief,
once more shattering the valor of the Tabascans with our magical
weapons, to the point where the scouting parties were able to gain the
walls of Potonchan with several prisoners, and it was the Tabascans'
turn to retreat, back across the plain.

But the encouragement engendered by this victorious skirmish was
short-lived, for when the prisoners were interrogated through Aguilar,
they were quite forthcoming and rather gleeful in apprising us of our
precarious position.

The Tabascans had been scorned as cowards by the surrounding
tribes for failing to attack Grijalva's previous expedition, which was
why they had fought us at the river, nor were they exactly congratulating themselves for being forced out of their own city. They had
therefore now marshaled not only the forces of Tabasco, but of several other neighboring tribes, to wit those who had called *them*
cowards, by challenging their manhood in return, and on the morrow,
or soon thereafter, an enormous army would storm our position in
the city.

The captives probably took this for the whole truth, but much later
Montezuma was to tell me of his own hand in the matter.

At the time, we were ignorant of his very existence, but the Tabascans
certainly were not, for while Mayan-speaking Tabasco was no ally or
even quite a vassal state of the Mexica, it was constrained to pay tribute
to Mexico by a well-developed fear of the mighty and invincible armies
of the great Montezuma.

And though *we* were ignorant of *him*, the great Montezuma had been
well informed of the Spanish advent on these shores since the expedition of Grijalva, and, moreover, his spirit had been disquieted and vexed
by omens predicting some dire disaster for quite a while before that.

'Was the fifth world about to come to an end as the omens seemed to
say? Was the great disaster they predicted about to fall upon us in the
form of these creatures who wore metal and arrived in boats the size and

whiteness of the highest mountain peaks? Perhaps not if they were men, but if they were Teules . . .'

'Teules', I should explain, was a Nahuatl word that might be translated as 'demons' or 'minor gods'. I would say simply 'supernatural beings', but the Mexica had no such distinction between the 'natural' and 'supernatural' and I am no longer so sure they were wrong.

'If they were men, they could be slain in battle,' went Montezuma's logic, 'but if not, must they not be Teules? Therefore the Tabascans should have tested them, and I showed my displeasure by requiring a thousand more hearts for Huitzilopochtli because they had not. And I let it be known to them that should they appear in their lands once more and should the Tabascans fail to test them in battle again, I would offer them the honor of testing their valor against the armies of Mexico instead.'

Cortes did not want to defend a captured city against a horde of its rightful inhabitants with only a portion of his own meager forces. Prudence, in my opinion, would have had us retreat back to the ships, but I was no general, prudence was certainly not Hernando's cardinal virtue, and he chose instead to pass to the attack.

Those too badly wounded to fight were sent back to the ships and reinforcements were brought up to Potonchan; more soldiers, more shot and powder, but also six heavy cannon on their wheeled carriages, and all sixteen horses.

Speaking of prudence, my first taste of battle had proven to me that I had neither the taste nor the aptitude for such close hand-to-hand combat, and as for enlisting in the minuscule cavalry, I had passed from youth deep into mature manhood without ever being constrained to plant my buttocks on the back of a horse and I saw no advantage, either to our army or myself, in doing so now.

The cannon, however, by their very nature, must remain well behind the front line of any battle, must be hauled gruntingly about, must have their barrels cleaned of sooty and odorous residue, and thus the grandees and would-be grandees who comprised Cortes' little army, almost as avid for glory as for gold, were not exactly competing for coveted positions crewing them.

Cortes found it amusing when I volunteered, and readily enough granted my wish, and so it was as a lowly assistant cannoneer – which is to say a human dray animal, a cleaner of bores and a stuffer of charges – that I witnessed the subsequent battle and as many of those that were to follow as I could manage.

Diego de Ordaz, being closer to Velazquez than to Hernando and therefore expendable, was given command of the infantry in the most dangerous vanguard, some four hundred men, while Cortes appointed himself commander of the cavalry, sixteen knights in all, if he was included.

We passed a fitful and sleepless night, and when the sun rose on the morrow, we set off. According to Aguilar's interrogation of the captives, the Tabascans and their allies were encamped close by the city in a field or meadow known as the plain of Ceutla. Cortes commanded the glum Ordaz to march his infantry and supporting cannon directly there and launch a frontal assault as soon as he contacted the enemy, while he rode off at the head of the cavalry, circled round, and fell upon their rear.

However, our unwilling local informants had left out a detail or two of the intervening terrain. In the direction of the plain of Ceutla, Potonchan was surrounded by a wide expanse of fields of chest-high maize interspersed with lower crops planted even more densely, and, the land being dry and sandy but the river conveniently nearby, this farmland was irrigated via an extensive system of canals, reservoirs and ditches. What was so salutary for the local agriculture made for very slow and rough going for foot soldiers, and getting the cannon to the other side seemed impossible, until Francisco de Mesa, our chief gunner, discovered that there was a narrow path which crossed the whole area in one continuous line, barely wide enough for us to haul the carriages single file.

Then it became merely an arduous and unpleasant task, made all the more tedious by the need to take care that no wheel slipped off the edge of the precarious causeway into a ditch, for getting the carriage back up on it again was something none of us cared to contemplate.

I was beginning to regret my enlistment in the cannon crews as I tugged, back bent, sweating and grunting, on a rope that had begun to fray my palms, towing a cannon with my comrades like a team of yoked oxen well behind the infantry, who, while having a difficult time of it too, had no such heavy burden to drag with them.

That is until at long last we sighted the end of the quagmire of plantations and the enemy which awaited us on the broad expanse of the apparently firmer ground of the plain of Ceutla. It was a daunting and terrifying sight and yet also beautiful.

The plain was quite flat and the formations of Indians upon it seemed to stretch all the way back to the line of the horizon. It is customary in accounts such as this to estimate the number of the enemy as grandiosely as possible, but I will simply say there were far far too many of them and leave it at that.

All of them were wearing long vests of quilted cotton armor and most of them headdresses of brilliantly colored feathers, so that as we approached from the distance they appeared as a vast field of whitish-barked bushes topped with blue, red, green, yellow and purple flowers waving in the breeze. Buckled to their left arms were round shields painted in bright designs, and in their right hands javelins, bows, maquahuitls, atlatls.

Standards were set up at regular intervals, tall poles festooned with more feathers, embellished with wooden and metal ornaments. When we were close enough to make out individual figures, we saw that there were men who must have been their captains standing beside these standards, extravagantly dressed in long cloaks done in a multitude of iridescent feathers or wearing the spotted pelts of some unknown animal, some with the head of this lionlike creature adorning their own, others crowned with immense and elaborate feather headdresses.

By the time we were close enough to pick out these captains, the enemy, thousands upon thousands of them to our paltry hundreds, had certainly spied us, and they were beating on drums, screaming out taunts and battle cries, waving and brandishing a huge maizefield of javelins, wooden swords, axes, lances.

How can I convey my perception of that moment to you, dear reader? You would have to have been there, wishing fervently in your terror that you weren't, for it was obviously utter madness to attack such a vast army with what we had at hand, and yet feeling privileged to be granted such an awesomely beautiful sight even at the cost of your life.

Well perhaps not quite, for any regrets I might have had for my decision to enlist in the cannon crews were wiped away by appreciation of the wisdom thereof, since the cannon could only be brought into play positioned well behind the front line.

Whether by happenstance or cunning, and probably both, the Tabascans had positioned themselves on the plain well back from the treacherous footing of the irrigated farmland, but not so far back that we would be out of range of the front line of their bowmen and atlatl-augmented spear-throwers as we crossed it to close with them. That was the cunning of it.

The happenstance was that our cannon, constrained to approach via the narrow causeway single file, could not take effective aim from safety there, and would have to be brought forward to the plain behind the advance of our infantry, indeed well behind, since we would then be firing over the heads of our own men or through a gap left in the formation for the purpose.

Like it or not, and Ordaz certainly didn't, he was not only going to have to cross the rest of the canals and ditches under fire, and once across charge a much larger force, but he was also going to have to push at least a section of the Tabascans far enough back to make room for the cannon to deploy and fire from firm ground.

And so it began. Our gallant foot soldiers formed a shoulder-to-shoulder skirmish line and made their way to the plain as rapidly as possible with their shields held up before their faces against a furious bombardment of arrows, stones and lances. The shields and helmets were good protection against the arrows and stones at this range, but, although they were not so many, the larger missiles launched by atlatls arrived with sufficient force to knock aside shields, making way for the arrows, and many wounds were taken, though none fatal, before the plain was reached. We, meanwhile, were still painstakingly wheeling the cannon in slow single file up the narrow causeway, not yet in effective range of the Tabascan missiles.

When Ordaz had his men assembled on the edge of the plain, he paused to look back at us, then waved us on, seemingly decided not to charge forward until we were close behind. But this would have forced us to lug the cannon slowly further forward under a hail of Tabascan arrows and spears without significant protection. So Mesa halted us where we were, and waved Ordaz forward in his turn.

While the Tabascans continued to bombard Ordaz's position, this contrary signaling continued, swiftly escalating into angry arm-waving and cursing, while the enemy, viewing this unseemly spectacle, hooted and jeered.

This finally proved too much for Ordaz, who formed his few hundred men into a tight wedge with the arquebusiers at the point, raised his sword high above his head, and ordered the charge. As soon as the arquebusiers were in range, they fired a volley, then dropped back behind the line of shields to reload on the run.

The noise, the smoke, the sight of a dozen or so of their comrades smashed to the ground from afar screaming and bleeding, caused great pandemonium among the Tabascans in the section of their front line confronting the wedge of charging Spaniards, though to their credit, they did not break and run.

Reloading an arquebus on the run being no mean task and one for which the arquebusiers were not well-practiced, they managed only one more volley before Ordaz's infantry closed with the Tabascans.

From our vantage hauling the cannon towards the plain, what we saw was a wedge of armored Spaniards pressing forward into a sea of howling savages behind a wall of shields, a well-ordered formation from this distance, though no doubt in the heat of the hand-to-hand battle, a bloody sword-against-sword chaos.

To our advantage as we finally gained the firm ground at the lip of the plain, the Tabascans, no doubt entirely unaware of the nature of our tiny and seemingly insignificant party, had little attention to spare for us, occupied as they were with attempting to engulf the wedge of Spanish swordsmen pushing a section of their formation back, and we were little harried by javelins or arrows.

Mesa positioned his six cannon in a line about ten feet apart, we loaded the first charges, tamped them down with the ramrods, and put the heavy balls down the bores. Mesa ordered the gunners to cant the barrels at about a thirty-degree angle to maximize the range, so as to fire well over the heads of our own men, and burning ropes were touched to the breaches.

The roar of six cannon going off together so close to one's ears was all too literally deafening. I had never experienced such a sound in my life, nor breathed in such a cloud of smoke both noxiously acrid and somehow intoxicating.

The effect on the Tabascans was devastating and terrifying even to behold from our distance. Six heavy cannonballs tore into their tight formation well back of the front, and in a moment scores of them were torn to pieces as limbs, heads, feathers went flying, along with two of the elaborate standards. Screams and shouts of fear and pain rose up but also howls of outrage and fury. Ordaz's men pressed forward but did not get very far.

We reloaded and fired another volley, but not before I had ripped two strips of cloth from the sleeve of my tunic and stuffed them in my ears, affording some small relief from the noise of the cannon. Once more scores of Tabascans were blown to bloody pieces, but well behind the front line, so that Ordaz's infantry could not really take much advantage to advance against the overwhelming numbers.

We fired a third volley to much the same effect, and then a fourth, while Mesa, fuming and cursing, made spreading gestures with his arms. Whether Ordaz spied these signals I know not, or whether he understood their import if he did, but at last he seemed to do what Mesa demanded.

The Spanish infantry seemed to break, or allowed itself to be broken, in two by the Tabascans, two defensive wedges being forced further and further apart as the Tabascans widened the gap between them.

Mesa, grinning, lowered the angles of the cannon barrels and had us advance a score of yards forward. When the gap between the two wedges of Spanish infantry was four times the width of our line of cannon and packed with Tabascans seeking to come up behind them, we fired.

This time, with the balls tearing into the Tabascans at closer range, flatter trajectory and therefore with greater speed and force, the carnage was horrendously greater. In a moment too rapid for the eye to even follow a hundred and more living Indians had been reduced to a bloody mash.

We reloaded and fired between the formations of Spanish infantry again to the same terrible effect. Ordaz brought his formations together

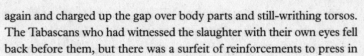

again and charged up the gap over body parts and still-writhing torsos. The Tabascans who had witnessed the slaughter with their own eyes fell back before them, but there was a surfeit of reinforcements to press in from the sides, seeking to surround them.

The barrels of the cannon were raised again, and we fired a volley into the Tabascan rear, in a not too successful attempt to ignite general panic, for it seemed that these Indians were valorous well beyond the point of madness.

Ordaz repeated the maneuver of dividing his forces in two, and this time the Tabascans hung back, sensibly not too eager to pour into the gap, but since Mesa lowered the trajectory again, this was to no avail, for there was no room for them to retreat to escape our next fusillade.

And so it went, for something like an hour. Ordaz opened up a gap. We fired into it. Tabascans sought to surround his divided forces. He brought them together and advanced, then opened a gap again for the cannon to fire into.

Screams and howls rent the air, now filled with the pungent grayish smoke of gunpowder. Arrows flew. Cannon roared. Arms and legs received bloody wounds by the score. Men were blown to pieces by the hundreds, the thousands. All around that terrible battlefield, weapons were clashing, men were wounded, men were slain, the Tabascans rushed forward, were blown to bits, the Spaniards pressed forward slashing and thrusting, were all but engulfed by Tabascans doing likewise. The battlefield boiled with furious and lethal action like ground contested by two rival nests of ants.

And yet, in a certain sense, it seemed that nothing was really happening, for no useful purpose was being achieved, nothing seemed to change despite the endless frantic and desperate motion. The far greater number of Tabascans could not overwhelm the metal-armored Spaniards backed up by the massive destructive power of the cannon, but they could not push the Indians back very far, nor could our cannon panic them into fleeing no matter how many we slew with each volley.

Or so it seemed to me at the time, entirely occupied as I was with the rhythm of loading and tamping my crew's cannon, like a miller servicing his grind stone. But as I was to learn later, in reality it had been a close thing.

'We had powder and ball for perhaps three more volleys,' Mesa told me after the fact. And as Ordaz would chide Cortes later for his cavalry's almost fatally tardy arrival, the sheer overwhelming numbers of the Tabascans and their relentless assault were at the point of wearing his men into exhaustion.

But before our cannon could run out of shot and powder or our infantry drop from exhaustion, there was a commotion far in the rear of the Tabascan army. At first, from my distant vantage, it was like the expanding ripples caused by tossing a stone into a pond, albeit of men rather than water, as the tiny figures were suddenly fleeing in all directions from some invisible center.

I must confess that it seemed magical to me as this unseen force moved towards us, perceivable only by the wake it drew through the Tabascan army, as whole sections of their formations disintegrated on either side of its trajectory. Zigging and zagging ever closer it came, ripping the Tabascan force apart with its passage like a knife tearing a jagged rent through cloth.

Then it was revealed as a phalanx of horsemen riding through the enemy army, steel helmets and whirling sword blades flashing in the sun, scattering the Tabascans before them. Closer still, and I could make out Hernando Cortes at the head of his cavalry, leaning down from his horse to cut down Indians with his sword as a reaper cuts grain with his scythe, shouting something impossible to hear at this distance over the din of the desperate screams of the fleeing Tabascans.

Ordaz's infantry broke into cheers, and I cheered too at the sight of our little cavalry contingent, hoofs pounding, horses' nostrils flaring, swords cutting the enemy down from the side, from behind, as the huge Tabascan army fell apart before them, warriors tossing aside lances, maquahuitls, bows, standards knocked to the ground and trampled, as what had been an army became thousands upon thousands of terrified individuals fleeing the plain of Ceutla in all directions.

Screaming 'Saint James! Santiago!' Ordaz's infantry charged forward into a battle that had suddenly been won, that was already effectively over.

Many were those present on the plain of Ceutla who afterward claimed to have witnessed the miracle; to wit Santiago, James the Patron Saint of

Spain himself, rather than Cortes, leading the cavalry charge which decimated and scattered the hosts of the heathen.

Cortes claimed to believe it himself, and perhaps he did, for it was certainly to his practical advantage, and Hernando had little trouble coming to sincerely believe in whatever served his purpose, even if it meant ceding to Saint James the credit for leading the charge which won the battle in which Tabasco was conquered for King and Cross.

And Santiago or not, it was hard to deny his fervent conviction that this great victory had been something miraculous. 'Explain to me if you can, Alvaro,' he told me when I expressed a certain skepticism, 'how a few hundred followers of the True Faith could slay thousands of heathen and put scores of thousands to flight without Divine Intervention. And with the deaths of only two good Christians!'

This I could not do, for such a seemingly impossible military feat did indeed seem supernatural even to me, nor would it have been politic to try, all the more so since Cortes speedily put the miraculous victory to good use.

Some Tabascan chiefs had been taken prisoner. These he released with a message for their caciques. 'Come at once to Potonchan to submit to our great sovereign and bearing tribute sufficient to slake his present ire, or I shall be constrained to slay every man, woman and child in your lands with the same ease with which your army was decimated and put to flight.'

And then he blithely marched his forces back to our previous encampment in the main square of the city to await their obsequious arrival.

I had winced fearfully when I heard him deliver this outrageous ultimatum through Aguilar, for it seemed certain to infuriate the Tabascans, who still had scores of thousands of warriors out there to our mere hundreds, and whatever had happened on the plain of Ceutla, miracle or not, it seemed sheer lunacy to wager our survival on it happening again.

But I was proven quite wrong two days later, when the Tabascan caciques *did* arrive, and, moreover, with a long train of porters bearing tribute of maize, turkeys, cotton, pulque, some reeds stuffed with brown cacao seeds, cloth of maguey fiber, cloaks embellished with bright feathers and the like, and a few golden torques, necklaces and lip tablets.

These items Cortes received with good grace but little enthusiasm, for the precious metal was the main object of his greed for tribute, and there was little of it here, nor was he particularly enthused by the twenty female slaves laid on as well, even though most of them were comely enough, and one of them was to prove to be worth a hundred times her weight in gold.

When he demanded from whence what little gold they offered had come, the caciques pointed in a generally western direction and, with expressions that might have been awe, or fear, or possibly both, uttered the word 'Mexico'. The same reply with which the natives had answered the same question on Cozumel.

As he had done on Cozumel, Cortes dipped into our bountiful supply of trade beads, mirrors and other such trinkets and gifted the Tabascans with them, who seemed more genuinely pleased with the bargain than he was, and within two days, most of the population of Potonchan had trickled back.

While the Tabascans kept a wary distance from the Spaniards, there seemed to be no hostility in evidence, and life in the city seemed to have returned to normal. Cortes, and most of the others, blithely took this as the natural order of things, for they were knights of the One True Faith, were they not, and Santiago himself had made an appearance to lead them to a miraculous victory, thus proving that God was on their side.

To me, though, being neither graced with nor blinded by such certainty of belief, there was nothing normal about such normalcy. These people, after all, had resisted our arrival with force, had been driven from their own city, had suffered a terrible defeat at the hands of a few hundred of us, still had the potential to raise a vast army outside the walls, and yet seemed willing if not content to let us lord it over them.

It seemed to me, if there was any miracle, that was it; I did not understand it and therefore could not trust it. Far from being tranquilified by this unnatural civic calm, the longer it continued, the more it disquieted me, and it was with no little relief that I finally heard that Cortes, having had the city scoured for more gold with but pathetic success, had decided to depart while the Tabascans still remained pacific and sail on westward along the coast to seek out golden fortune in this fabled 'Mexico'.

But not without fitting ceremonies, both secular and ecclesiastical.

Cortes had already recited the Requerimiento claiming Tabasco for the Crown of Spain, and since this had been duly recorded by a notary, the legal requirements had been fulfilled, the presence of Tabascan witnesses to the ceremony not being one of them. Nevertheless, the punctilious Cortes deemed it meet to repeat the ceremony for the benefit of their caciques and notables.

These he caused to assemble before the same tree close by their temple where he had previously recited the Requerimiento to Spaniards alone, delivering much the same little oration, but then adding for their benefit that since they had been so roundly defeated, and since they were now vassals of the Spanish King, any rebellion, resistance, or failure to provide required tribute would therefore be perfidious treason and dealt with accordingly without the least hint of mercy.

Since it was Aguilar, fluent in both tongues, translating this, I expected an outburst of anger when he had finished, or at least expressions of consternation. But the Tabascan caciques and notables stood there with expressions as animated and readable as those of their stone idols.

The next day was Palm Sunday, and Hernando and Father Olmedo chose to use this coincidence to good advantage.

Our entire army was marched out onto the savanna bordering the city on the side opposite the irrigated farmland, followed by a crowd of curious Tabascans. Here grew palmettos, only about half the height of a man, but sufficient to provide acceptable palm fronds for the ceremony.

Each of us cut himself a palm frond, and a number of the Tabascans, though they could have had no concept of why, found it amusing or prudent to do likewise. When this was accomplished, a procession was formed up with the friars at the head, followed by Cortes, his captains, the rest of us, and then the Tabascans, and back to Potonchan we solemnly paraded, through the streets thereof to the square with its temple, drawing quite a crowd with us to the spectacle.

Father Olmedo, accompanied by four soldiers, ascended the stairs to the pinnacle platform of the temple. Two of the soldiers entered the hut where the idol was kept, and, grunting and puffing, dragged it out into the daylight, and threw it down the steps to the ground, where it cracked in four pieces.

The assembled Tabascans let loose a collective groan but otherwise said or did nothing.

Three more soldiers then ascended, bearing a large wooden Cross, a small portable wooden altar, and a portrait of Mary and the Baby Jesus, followed by Geronimo de Aguilar. The soldier carrying the cross held it up triumphantly while Olmedo delivered his usual sermon. Since Aguilar was far more conversant with Christian theology than the hapless Melchior, his translation took as much time as the sermon itself and he must have been rendering it to the Tabascans in considerable detail, but their response was a still and stony silence.

The portrait of the Virgin and Child was then placed in the sanctuary previously graced by the stone idol with the stern command that it be kept clean and intact and never under pain of mortal sin be removed.

Father Olmedo then celebrated mass. When he had finished, hymns were sung in Latin by the Spaniards. Though they did not know the words, many were the Indians in their hundreds or even thousands who joined in wordlessly chanting out the solemn rhythm.

If you, dear reader, should happen to be a fervid and unquestioning believer in the One True Faith, paradoxically enough, these events will not seem as miraculous to you as they did to me at the time. But for a man of a more inquisitive and skeptical mind such as myself, they were utterly mysterious.

How had fewer than five hundred Christians defeated a heathen army the more extravagant chroniclers claim numbered as many as forty thousand warriors? Why did the Tabascans, who had put up such fierce resistance at the river bank and the gates of their city, meekly accept vassalage to an unknown monarch after a single defeat on the plain of Ceutla? What persuaded them to allow the overthrow of their stone god and its replacement with the Cross, the Christ and the Virgin without demur when they could hardly have even understood the third part of what Olmedo had told them, Aguilar's translation or not?

These seemed to me miracles far more mysterious, far more

powerful, than any apparition of Santiago on a battlefield. For the latter could be laid to fervor or wishful illusion or even if you prefer to Divine Intervention Itself, and therefore miracles of the world of appearances, but the former were deeper mysteries and miracles of the human heart.

As I write of these events up here on my mountaintop, they retain a certain miraculous mystery still, for if I have learned one thing in the years since, it is that the forces which move the souls of men can never be fully understood by them. For if they could, would we not ourselves be gods, or God if you prefer, omniscient and perfect captains of our own destiny, the Ain-Soph Ourselves?

The Kabbalah teaches that all reality, the world, its people, those entities which we rightly or wrongly deem gods, derive from that same Unknowable which is not merely the One True God but the One Source of truth and falsehood alike.

What truly happened on the plain of Ceutla to work these miracles?

I saw Hernando Cortes leading a charge of Spanish cavalry.

Many were those who saw the Divine Intervention of Saint James.

And I have before me a painting reporting the event to Montezuma, perhaps done by an eyewitness, perhaps crafted by an artist working from tales told by those who were there.

On this sheet of maguey-pulp paper Tabascan warriors, clearly identified by their dress and standards, can be seen fleeing in abject terror from what just as clearly are monsters in the eye of the artist.

Before the fleeing warriors huge grayish serpents belch smoke and flame from gaping fanged mouths. Behind and among them gallop creatures that the Greeks might recognize as centaurs, for torsos that are almost human arise out of the bodies of quadrupeds that might almost be horses. But second heads arise from the bellies of the torsos, their eyes whirling comets, smoke pouring out of their nostrils and flame from their maws, and the heads above are hardly what we would recognize as human, rather crested and beaked like hideous birds. The arms of these beasts end not in hands but in clusters of black obsidian blades.

Leading this demonic charge and rendered by the artist thrice the size of any other figure is neither Saint James nor Hernando Cortes.

It is shaped like a man. It has two arms and two legs. The legs end in claws that might be those of an eagle. The body is a confusion of tints and daubs, angled scales in a profusion of colors, feathers, things my eye still cannot identify. One hand grasps some strange bird around its long serpentine neck. Its head is crowned by a corona of jagged multi-colored feathers that might be reminiscent of a Spanish helmet if you wished to be so persuaded.

The face is vaguely that of a man with the blunt snout and grinning fanged mouth of a snake. The eyes are round and blue. This visage is ruffed around by golden and black and purple spikes that might be hair and beard or might be plumage or just as well flames.

This is what the Tabascans told Montezuma they saw.

This is Quetzalcoatl.

The Feathered Serpent.

Who saw truly?

None?

Or perhaps somehow all?

7

WERE THIS A ROMANCE, rather than a true account, I would no doubt now be describing some fateful moment of instant attraction between the hero of the tale and she who would become his inamorata, Doña Marina. But nothing of the sort happened when the slave women were loaded on to our ships along with the paltry rest of the booty from Tabasco, and while Cortes, Marina and myself were aboard the same ship as our fleet made its way westward along the coast, neither I nor Cortes was particularly aware of her existence until we reached the isle of San Juan de Ulua.

This was a small island of no consequence, but it lay close by the continental shore, and as our little fleet sailed between it and the mainland on a balmy afternoon, with our white sails billowing in the breeze and our bright ensigns trailing from the masts, we were quite visible from the mainland beaches, and must have presented a fine and wondrous spectacle to the crowd of Indians who gathered there to watch our stately passage.

The island *was* large enough to shelter our ships in its lee from the sudden storms which had an unfortunate habit of sweeping in off the sea, so Cortes decided to anchor there at least for the night, parley with the locals in the morning, and depending on the outcome, perhaps tarry longer.

But the locals took matters into their own hands. We had not been at anchor long enough for the sun to begin to set when a large canoe, paddled by half a dozen men, was launched from the beach and made directly for the flagship, which they no doubt recognized as such by its size and by the large red and yellow Spanish ensign, the largest flag flown by the fleet.

The rowers wore loincloths and nothing more, but there were two men standing upright in the canoe in a lordly manner, with their arms crossed and their aquiline noses in the air, wearing long cloaks of red, green, blue and yellow featherwork and headdresses in a similar style; clearly men who deemed themselves personages of importance and wished others, ourselves included, to be well aware of their station.

Cortes therefore dashed into his cabin to don a black velvet cloak trimmed with some white fur and a dashing hat sporting a large pheasant tailfeather. He also turned out Aguilar, myself, what officers were aboard, and six of the women we had been given at Potonchan as beauteous embellishment to our greeting party and sigils of our pacific intent. Among them was Marina.

That, of course, was not her name at the time. As she was to make clear to me later during her amazingly rapid assimilation of Spanish, her real name, that is the one she was born with in her own language, was 'Malinal'.

'I was born . . . *princess*, you say, Alvaro? In the province of Coatzacualo, I grew up speaking the Nahuatl of the *Mexica*, not you would say *barbarian*? Mayan. My father was a great cacique! But he died when I was small, my stupid mother married a greedy man, they had a son together, rob my . . . heriting from my father. They say I die, kill other poor child to show . . . *body*? *corpus*? Sell me to ugly traders from Xicallanco, who sell me to the Tabascans, this is how I learn Mayan. Tabascans give me to your Cortes and his Teules, so now it is Spanish I learn. Third language not so difficult after first two, you understand, Alvaro?'

But I see I am getting ahead of my tale.

A rope ladder was dropped over the side and the two lordly Indians understood its use well enough to clamber aboard, followed by three of their retainers, who had a more difficult time of it, since each bore a reed basket. One was filled with an inviting assortment of succulent and varicolored fruits, the second fairly overflowed with a gorgeous arrangement of red, orange, blue and brilliantly iridescent purple flowers, and the third, much smaller, was half-filled with some gold ornaments, jewelry and little statuettes.

Cortes stepped forward to greet them with Aguilar a step behind at his side, obviously not quite knowing the local custom. Did one hold out one's hand? Both of them? Bow? Offer an embraso?

The taller of the visitors, though, straightaway delivered an oration of some length in his own language in what seemed like a welcoming tone of voice, though for all any of us knew of their tonal modes, it could just as well have been a frosty ultimatum.

When he was through, Cortes turned to Aguilar for a translation. Poor Aguilar had exchanged his barbarian finery for civilized European dress and cut his hair to a proper length, but he had never ceased to appear, at least to me, like a fish who had somehow survived a long sojourn in the air, but, having found his way back to the sea, was no longer quite comfortable breathing water. His only source of status among his newfound compatriots was his standing as the only one among us who could speak the local language. But now he shrugged miserably.

'This is not Mayan,' he was forced to admit. 'I understand none of it.'

Apparently sensing the nature of the difficulty, the Indian lord picked up the basket of flowers and handed it to Cortes, with a graceful gesture and a little smile. Cortes likewise accepted it, and then the fruit. When he was handed the small basket of gold, I could see his eyes light up even from my position about six feet away, and likewise his frustration at his inability to demand how he might obtain much more.

'Nahuatl!' a female voice cried out from behind, and turning, I saw one of the slaves make so bold as to take three steps forward.

Marina was then in her mid-twenties, shoulder-high to your average European, with the long straight lustrous black hair and bronze skin common to Indian women, and she was wearing an ordinary cotton shift which obscured her form rather than served to well display it. There was nothing particularly beautiful about her slightly beaked nose, but her large dark brown eyes fairly glowed with intelligence and interior power, and she stood and moved with the carriage of a confident princess, no cowed slave girl she.

One of the nearby soldiers moved to gently constrain her, but she shrugged off his hand, strode forward, and before anyone could do anything else, was standing before Cortes and Aguilar babbling in what I had begun to understand was Mayan.

For a moment, Cortes frowned angrily at this interruption, but then he met those eyes, and was at least provisionally captured. 'Well?' he demanded of Aguilar. 'Do you understand what *she* is saying at least?'

'She says they are speaking Nahuatl, which is the language of the Mexica, and one which she understands even better than Mayan, it being her native tongue,' Aguilar told him rather glumly.

'Ask her what this chief was saying,' Cortes ordered.

A short conversation followed between Aguilar and Marina.

'In brief,' Aguilar told Cortes, 'he welcomes you to the land of the Totonacs, the rest being a series of formalities expressing much the same thing.'

'Tell her to thank him for his kindness in the same manner, and ask him who rules here,' Cortes told Aguilar, who relayed it to Marina in Mayan, who then spoke for Cortes in Nahuatl.

Hearing his own language spoken, the Totonac lord replied in it to Marina, who translated to Aguilar. For some reason, her speech was noticeably longer than the original.

'He says this part of the lands of the Totonacs is ruled by Teuhtlile, who resides in the city of Cuetlaxtlan, not far from here,' said Aguilar. '*She* says he dissembles, omitting to mention that well within living memory Totonaca has become a vassal state of Mexico, and therefore this local overlord is probably Mexica, though he would not like to admit it.'

'Have her ask him then whether this Teuhtlile is Totonac or Mexica.'

When this question was put to the Totonac lord, his displeasure was apparent and no translation was necessary when he spat out the word 'Mexica'.

'Tell her to tell him to tell us more about this Mexico we are beginning to hear so much about,' Cortes ordered Aguilar. 'In particular whether the gold comes from there.'

Through the same process this question was put and the Totonac lord replied that it did. He was then asked to what extent gold was abundant in Mexico, and replied at some length in a tone that seemed to combine awe, envy, and a bit of anger.

'She says that he says the lands paying tribute to the Mexica are vast, many of them are rich in gold as well as cacao, the beans for making chocolatl, making Mexico very rich indeed, and its Emperor the great Montezuma the most powerful ruler in all the world, though far from the most merciful or generous.'

Cortes then sent for presents to be conveyed to this Mexica overlord Teuhtlile of a somewhat finer quality than the usual beads, mirrors and ordinary knives and scissors, including a sword and a set of blue pantaloons with matching tunic.

'Tell him to inform the noble Teuhtlile I wish to meet with him, and will await him on this shore,' Cortes told Marina through Aguilar when these were gracefully accepted.

'Who is it who would meet with him and from whence have you come and what sort of beings are you?' the Totonac lord inquired, through what by now had become the accustomed tedious process.

'Tell him that I am Captain-General Hernando Cortes, vassal and representative of King Charles of Spain, and we come from *his* vast empire far across the great ocean, and as for what manner of souls we are, assure him that we are devout Christians and followers of the One Truth Faith and the One True God, the nature of Which and Whom we shall be most pleased to illuminate to both Teuhtlile and Montezuma when we meet them.'

As Aguilar put this into Mayan for Marina, her deep powerful eyes rolled, her lips creased in a frown which might have been one of hard concentration, likewise her brow furrowed, for after all, no doubt these were concepts Mayan was ill-equipped to convey very clearly, concepts she herself must find difficult to comprehend, and indeed, when he had finished, she paused for a long reflective moment before attempting to put whatever she might have understood of it into Nahuatl.

Whatever she said in Nahuatl, though, had a powerful effect on the Totonacs, and it would seem the desired one, for they then came to regard Cortes with no little awe, and a like amount of fear, as the formerly haughty chieftains took their leave in an almost grovellingly obsequious manner.

'Ask her what she told him!' Cortes demanded excitedly of Aguilar as soon as the Totonacs were over the side.

But before Aguilar could put the question to Marina, Cortes stayed him. 'No, better alone in my cabin.'

And he led Aguilar and Marina inside.

After well over an hour, Aguilar emerged shaking his head, frowning, and in no mood to communicate further with anyone in either of his languages.

Neither Cortes nor Marina emerged until well after sundown.

The next morning, to everyone's pleasure, except for mariners necessary to keep the ships crewed, our entire party put ashore, horses and dogs included. The immediate environ was a sandy plain dotted with unhealthy-looking palm trees and pocked with dunes upon which sparse salt grass struggled to grow. The climate was hot and made steamy by the nearby marshes, but while it was no one's idea of a tropical paradise, the Totonacs seemed friendly enough, it was terra firma, and Cortes set about organizing an encampment of some permanence.

Friendly Totonacs or not, the first order of bivouacking was to unload the cannon from the ships and drag them up to the summits of appropriate sand dunes so as to position them to defend the camp should this prove an illusion. Lugging cannon up sandy hillocks in broiling sun is not a pleasure I would recommend to you, dear reader, and it was several hours before the task was finished.

By this time trees had been felled and bushes stripped of foliage, and many Totonacs had proven their friendship by aiding in turning these materials into crude huts, even supplying mats to cover the sandy ground within, which otherwise would have made exceedingly uncomfortable flooring.

My work having been mercifully concluded, after slaking my thirst I sought out Cortes to slake my curiosity as to what had transpired in the privacy of his cabin, not, I assure you, any salacious details of what amorous adventures he might have had within with the Mexica woman, but what she had told the Totonac lord that had had him fawning before

Cortes as if he were some sultan or djinn, for it hardly seemed likely that
a literal translation of Hernando's talk of King Charles and the One
True God could have produced such an effect.

Nevertheless, Cortes did not spare me the said salacious details when
I caught up with him supervising the construction of the huts. 'It had
been quite a while, Alvaro, my wife being so far away and not the most
passionate creature I have ever encountered anyway, and this girl, who
gave me to understand that her name was Malinal, was, shall we say,
entirely forthcoming once we disposed of Aguilar, and no interpretation
was necessary to make her intent plain, for she straightaway threw off
her shift, revealing a trim and somewhat muscular nubility, and proceeded to perform such a series of amorous figures as convinced me
that I was hardly despoiling an innocent virgin.'

'No doubt your manly charms immediately overwhelmed her,' I said
dryly, 'and the fact that you are Captain-General of this expedition was
entirely irrelevant.'

Cortes laughed. 'Perhaps not *entirely* irrelevant, for this Malinal is
plainly a woman of wiles and quick perception, as witness how speedily she sized up the situation and the outrageous fable she palmed off on
that Totonac chieftain.'

'Oh?'

Cortes shook his head in rueful amusement. 'According to her artful
translation, behind the false name of Hernando Cortes is hidden my
true identity, to wit a creature or mythic hero or even god – Aguilar
could not make it clear – known as "Quetzalcoatl". Or perhaps I am
supposed to be his chief vassal and it is King Charles who is
Quetzalcoatl, this is also not very clear. But either way it seems that
Quetzalcoatl, historical personage or mythical creature, disappeared to
the east lifetimes ago, promising to return to bring back a lost golden
age or to destroy this one by tearing his enemies to pieces, or some such
thing, I'm afraid that Aguilar couldn't make much sense of that either,
and by that time, shall we say, my attention was drawn to more immediate pursuits in which his presence would have not only been
superfluous but bothersome.'

'Why on earth would she tell him that you or King Charles is . . .
is . . .'

'Some sort of second coming . . . ?' Cortes suggested with a laugh of modesty that seemed the slightest bit false.

I nodded.

'Obviously to increase my status in the eyes of the Totonacs.'

'Obviously. But why would she want to do that?'

Cortes laughed again, this time rather haughtily dismissive. '*Obviously*, Alvaro,' he said, 'you are not much of a student of women, a study to which I have applied myself with some diligence. Malinal had no trouble in recognizing me as the cock of this flock, as it were, and no trouble either in discerning that it would therefore be greatly in her interest to gain my favor, in which she has certainly succeeded.'

'Even a dry pedant such as myself could figure that much out, Hernando,' I replied. 'But why—'

'I am no woman's fool except to the extent that I want to be, Alvaro—'

'I doubt that you are the only man to claim that—'

'—and I know full well that a woman such as Malinal would seek to gain my side and cling there were I as fat as Velazquez, ten years older than you and with the breath of one of the mastiffs. I will allow her to do so knowing that because it will please me.'

'But why—'

'Since it is her ambition to become my consort, it is to her advantage to enhance my status and power, and therefore hopefully her own,' Cortes told me confidently. 'It is as simple as that. Which upon reflection is not so simple at all, but rather the means whereby, in the absence of martial or political possibilities, women seek to rise in the world, and after all, for a slave girl, even to become the harlot of a chieftain is quite a promotion.'

'Better still if you can promote him to mythical hero . . .'

'There you have it!' cried Cortes.

Having commissioned Aguilar to teach Malinal Spanish, Cortes commissioned me to oversee the process, realizing upon reflection that while Aguilar was the only of our number with whom she shared a common language, it was not in his self-interest to rapidly render himself superfluous.

I eagerly agreed, for I realized, as Cortes seemed not to, that we really knew next to nothing about what we were confronting on these shores, and Malinal was presently our best hope of alleviating our ignorance.

We knew that the inhabitants worshipped hideous idols and performed obscene human sacrifices. We knew that our armaments were superior to theirs. We knew that we were vastly outnumbered. And we knew there was a source of gold somewhere in 'Mexico'. And Mexico was a vast and powerful empire ruled by a mighty and all-powerful potentate called Montezuma. And now we also knew that there was or had been a hero or mythical figure or deity called 'Quetzalcoatl' whom at least the Totonacs held in awe or feared or worshipped or some such thing.

And that was all we knew. It was as if an expedition of black Africans had made their way up the Nile and across the Mediterranean to Italy and were trying to make enough sense of the Roman Empire of the Caesars to attempt to conquer it.

Montezuma, on the other hand, as I have told you, dear reader, knew much more about us than we knew about Mexico, thanks to the pictorial reports of his agents, something we only began to learn and whose means we first became aware of only when Teuhtlile arrived in our encampment with these painterly imperial informants among his considerable retinue.

If the Totonac nobles had seemed haughty, Teuhtlile was doubly so, as no doubt befitted a Mexica governor. He was tall for an Indian, of regal posture and grim of lip, with dark deep-set eyes squinting from under a heavy brow. He wore a golden earring in each ear, and one of those horrid labrets which pulled his lower lip downward to reveal his gums, this also of gold and inlaid with a pattern of greenish-blue stones. His long black hair was topped by a tall and elaborate headdress of green and red feathers, he wore the inevitable loincloth and sandals, and a flowing cloak of elaborate and brilliantly colored featherwork so long it all but dragged behind him on the ground.

His retinue included several score warriors armed with maquahuitls and shields, and at least as many porters, known as 'tamanes', Marina told me, carrying baskets of gifts, as well as a number of well-dressed men, though not as splendidly turned out as Teuhtlile, who seemed to be notables of some sort.

Cortes came out to greet him, and this being Easter, Teuhtlile was constrained to stand through a mass and communion, which strange rite he viewed with a lofty interest, before being invited out of the sun and into Cortes' tent, where he had gathered his principal lieutenants, Aguilar, Marina and myself.

After the usual amenities, Cortes personally and most ceremoniously served the Mexica governor his first goblet of wine. Teuhtlile seemed to recognize the red fluid at sight, but then seemed to be at a loss at what to do with it, and when Cortes took a sip of his own to enlighten him, Teuhtlile gave him a look of astonishment.

Through Aguilar and Marina, he asked what the red liquid was. 'Wine,' Cortes said. Marina, as she explained to me through Aguilar afterward, knowing no word in Nahuatl for this but having learned something of Christian sacraments and seeking to impress Teuhtlile in Cortes' service, told him that it was 'the blood of the Teules' god'.

'The god of these Teules favors them with his own blood?' Teuhtlile exclaimed in awed amazement.

Marina decided to press things further. 'Only to those he holds in the highest esteem as almost fellow gods themselves,' she told him. 'You are offered a great honor and it would be a terrible offense to refuse.'

At this Teuhtlile took a sip of wine and seemed greatly confused and indeed somehow disappointed at the taste, but never took enough to test its effect, inquiring immediately instead as to who these strange visitors were and from whence they came.

Cortes ordered his interpreters to tell him the usual tale of the great King Charles and the enormous empire across the sea which he held, where uncounted princes and even kings were joyfully content to bow down to him as vassals.

But when it came out the other side through Marina, she modified it for the local taste, as she told me later. 'I told him for now this great Teule calls himself Hernando Cortes because true name might cause terror if revealed to other but Montezuma, but I do tell him Teules with hair-feathers on the chins come from across waters in direction of the sunrise, and he understands what I say.'

At the time, Teuhtlile did respond with a knowing nod which seemed to mask a certain disquiet.

'Understood *what?*' I demanded of her through Aguilar in our post-seance interrogation.

'You say . . . *foretelling?*'

'Prophecy?'

'Prophecy!' she squealed in pleasure and in Spanish upon learning this new word. 'Prophecy that men from across the sea in the direction of sunrise will come to end this age and bring next one. Men with hair-feathers on faces!'

'Beards,' I corrected.

'Men with *beards*. Some say Toltecs coming back. Some say come with their god Quetzalcoatl, head of snake . . . *beard* of feathers.'

'And you led him to believe that Cortes just might be . . .'

Marina shrugged. Had it been the custom of her people, no doubt she would have winked.

When Teuhtlile then asked the purpose of the Spaniards or 'Teules' in coming to the lands of the Mexica, Marina put the question straight, and so too Cortes' reply, more or less, for this time it was he engaging in hyperbole, or not to put too fine a point on it, lying, and telling one which did not fit too badly with the implications of her little story.

'Tell him that the great Emperor across the eastern sea is not only all-powerful but all-knowing, and has heard tales of his brother Emperor Montezuma, and so has sent myself to establish communications with gifts and presents to delight and honor him and a message which I am ordered to deliver to him alone and in person. And ask him when this meeting can be arranged, impressing upon him that the sooner the better.'

At this, Teuhtlile at first took umbrage. 'You have just arrived and you presume to demand an audience with the Emperor Montezuma!' he exclaimed with frosty hauteur.

But then, taking advantage of the delays in translation to calm himself and more practically assess the situation: 'It is interesting to know that there is another Emperor almost as powerful as Montezuma, and if this is true, no doubt Montezuma will wish to make his fellow Emperor's acquaintance. But of course only Montezuma can decide, so if you wish, you may entrust your gifts to my care, my tamanes will convey them to him, and couriers will then return with the Emperor's reply.'

Cortes had a quick conversation with Ordaz, who he then dispatched to the ships to assemble the most suitable presents for an Emperor we had available, and while considerable scrambling was done to put these together, Teuhtlile, who had arrived more properly prepared, laid out his own gifts for King Charles or Hernando Cortes or Quetzalcoatl or whoever Marina had led him to believe he might be treating with.

Into the tent marched his tamanes, one by one, displaying the contents of their baskets. An abundance of cotton cloth, much of it quite beautifully embroidered. A dozen of the stunning featherwork cloaks, like tapestries done with plumage rather than thread. And one large basket filled with jewelry, pendants and cunning little statues of animals, humans and monsters, some of them mounted on little wheels, some unrecognizable as anything from nature, but others rendered with such lifelike precision that it was obvious that this was not the result of a failure in craftsmanship.

And all of them made of gold.

This was more gold than all we had yet seen, and it took those present a manful effort to refrain from salivating, no one more so than Cortes, who had mortgaged his entire fortune to mount this expedition and must at the least return with enough gold of his own to redeem it or else return as a pauper.

While Cortes and his captains were still in the process of stuffing their eyes back into their heads and their tongues into their mouths, Cortes' gifts for Montezuma arrived, looking quite niggardly in comparison, though hopefully not in the eyes of the Mexica governor who would be ignorant of such European goods.

To wit, the carved and somewhat garishly painted oaken armchair from Cortes' cabin, someone's red velvet cap, a gilded medal of Saint George and the dragon, and two whole water barrels filled with worthless glass beads masquerading as exotic precious stones.

These Teuhtlile accepted with good grace if not with visible enthusiasm. But then, seemingly like a Spaniard, his eye was caught by the golden helmet of one of the captains, Alvarado, I think but I am not now certain. I say 'golden' when of course the helmet was of gilded base metal. But how was the Mexica to know that?

Teuhtlile pointed to it and said something in excited Nahuatl. 'He says Montezuma would certainly wish to see that,' Aguilar told Cortes when Marina had translated. 'He says it resembles the . . . crown of . . . of . . .'

'*Quetzalcoatl!*' said Marina, addressing Cortes directly.

'He may have it then,' Cortes said, visibly suppressing a laugh, while plucking it from its owner's head and handing it to Teuhtlile. 'And tell him that it would be interesting if Montezuma would return it filled with the gold of his own country so that we may see if ours is of equal quality.'

Aguilar all but groaned at being forced to deliver this to Marina. Marina flashed a little smile at Cortes, then said something to Teuhtlile, who grinned, nodded, and the meeting in the tent ended amicably.

'What did you say to him?' both Aguilar and I demanded of her as soon as we could, for neither of us could imagine it had been a literal translation of Cortes' words.

'Teules . . . *Spaniards* have disease of . . . you say *heart*?' Marina said, in her then quite limited Spanish, thumping her bosom. 'And gold is you say *cure*?'

Cortes, accompanied by Aguilar and Marina, then conducted Teuhtlile on a tour of the camp.

'I was simply trying to show him our hospitality,' Cortes told me later, by way of explaining why he had laid on the extravagant military display I was then witnessing. 'But then, as we walked the beach within sight of our anchored ships, I noticed one of the men in his entourage gazing out at them and sketching their likeness in quite a cunning manner on a kind of paper tablet with plume and colored ink. And once my attention had been drawn to this, I saw that several other of these Indian artists were moving about the camp doing likewise.

'When I inquired, Teuhtlile told me that they were depicting we Teules, our animals, arms, clothing and so forth, for the eyes of Montezuma, who would therefore gain a more full and accurate understanding of us than would be possible with mere words.'

This Cortes told me as we stood on the beach some distance from Teuhtlile and his painterly scribes, who were busy putting to paper the splendid sight of a dozen Spanish grandees, in well-polished helmets and sweating in the wet heat within impressive metal cuirasses, astride a dozen horses in full parade display trotting by in formation, rearing them, wheeling them around, and returning at a full gallop with lances outthrust.

'I decided that if these painters were recording matters here for the eyes of Montezuma, I had best take advantage to impress him with our might by giving them a proper martial display, especially since these Totonacs and Tabascans and Mexica seem to have no horses or other riding animals to serve in their stead, and to judge from events at Ceutla seem quite terrified of the beasts. And as for cannon . . .'

Cortes raised his arm high in the air, then brought it down as a signal to a trumpeter, who blew a long loud fanfare. This in turn was a signal to the gunners some distance away on their sand-dune positions fringing the camp, who fired off their ten cannon in unison.

Even at this distance the report was deafening, the clouds of smoke quite considerable, as was the damage done to several copses of palm trees, reduced in a moment to flinders and flying fronds. All this was quite terrifying to Indians who had never witnessed even a single cannon being fired, and even the lofty Teuhtlile jumped into the air with his hands over his ears.

Cortes stood there grinning like a small boy having just pulled off a particularly impish prank, no doubt exclaiming in the privacy of his own mind: 'Have a look at *that*, great Montezuma.'

Which indeed the great Montezuma did, for the sketchers might have been dazed momentarily, but they recovered immediately and went on with their duties.

Montezuma showed their drawings to me during one of our seances and I have many of them with me now up here on my mountaintop.

They may not match the work of great European masters working with canvas and oils, but then they were never intended as works of fine art, but rather as reportage to a monarch such as those of Europe have never enjoyed. Considering how previously unknown these things were to the artists, their colored drawings of armored men, sailing ships, fiery steeds on parade, fire-and-smoke-breathing cannon, as well as details of swords, lances, shields and implements are quite astonishing. They may have gotten a few things wrong, they may have utterly neglected perspective, they may have simplified figures for the sake of clarity and swiftness of drawing, they may have embellished their images with a few superfluous swirls and curlicues, but for the purpose for which they were intended, these pictures are exemplary.

They were also, as I was to learn, conveyed to Montezuma with exemplary speed by a system of runners, who proceeded with them as fast as they could run for as long as they could, then passed them on to the next runner waiting at a system of stations, and thus were they conveyed from the coast, up through the passes between mighty mountains, a hundred miles or so to his capital in a matter of a day or two.

'I was alarmed by this advent, Alvaro,' Montezuma told me in the days of his captivity, 'for first there had been a series of terrible omens, then reports of Teules visiting our coasts and then departing, then the terrible defeat of the Tabascans at the plain of Ceutla, where it had been told to me by those who had not seen it themselves that Quetzalcoatl had appeared leading an army of monsters. And now these unknown beasts and men with beards arriving from the east in magical ships as huge as mountains! And their leader claiming he was Quetzalcoatl! That was all I then knew, and I ask you even now, Alvaro, as I asked myself then, what was I to do, how could I have done better?'

At this point, dear reader, you are probably telling yourself that were you Montezuma, you would have dispatched a hundred thousand or so of the warriors at your command and dispensed with the problem. But for poor Montezuma, nothing was so simple, and at this stage in my narrative, you know little more of his personality, the nature of his empire, and the spirits that moved him than Cortes did when he staged his military display for the Emperor's edification.

So in order that what Montezuma then did shall make sense to you, it would seem that I must now move somewhat ahead of my knowledge at the time to inform you.

Montezuma was the second in his line to bear the name, and the first had been the great Montezuma who had consolidated their empire, so that the name was both a burden and a challenge. Nor was his empire ancient. The Mexica had only ruled their present lands for two centuries or so, having migrated down from the north as latecomers, and both they and the tribes they now ruled venerated the memory of the Toltecs, the previous overlords, the fount of their civilization. Even the Mexica acknowledged the Toltecs as greater than themselves in every art save the martial, much as the conquered Greeks were regarded by the Romans, save that these proprietors of a lost Golden Age had vanished, to the east, it was said.

And the chief god of the Toltecs, who had likewise vanished, but who had promised to return one day to bring back the said Golden Age, was the 'Feathered Serpent', Quetzalcoatl.

'So what else could I have done?' the captive Emperor demanded of me plaintively, and more than once. 'If these Teules were mere invaders surely Huitzilopochtli would have me destroy them, but if this was the prophesied return of the Toltecs and they were led by Quetzalcoatl, how could I presume to do such a thing, and even if I did, surely all the signs of catastrophe had already told me that such an attempt could only end in failure and disaster.'

I should mention that Montezuma had been a priest before being elected Emperor, and that absolute temporal ruler or not, he truly believed that his mission was to discern, follow and express the will of the gods.

Cortes and the conquistadores might share such a conviction, but in their case there was only one God whose will must be fathomed and they were convinced that His Divine Will and their pragmatic self-interest happily coincided. Montezuma had a much more consternating theocratic pantheon to cope with.

He had the wills of many gods to discern and contend with. The paramount god of the Mexica was Huitzilopochtli, their Mars, natural for a martial people who had followed him down from the north to dominance over Anahuac, as what the Mexica were now pleased to call the 'Valley of Mexico' was otherwise called by its diverse tribes, each of which might be most favored by (or most favor) a different paramount god, and the Mexica in general and Montezuma in particular believed in and gave relative credence to the word of them all.

Thus the supersession of the Toltecs by the Mexica could be read as the ousting of Quetzalcoatl by Huitzilopochtli. So if Quetzalcoatl had indeed returned at the head of an army of Toltecs, the result would be as much a war of gods as of men.

Thus the dilemma facing poor Montezuma. If these Teules were mere barbarian invaders, Huitzilopochtli would wax wrathful if he failed to dispose of them. But if they were not, he could find himself on the wrong side of a war among the gods, and even an Emperor might well quail at that. To my mind, a better argument for the merits of monotheism over polytheism would be hard to make.

'I had to know the will of Huitzilopochtli, or failing that, at least discern whether Quetzalcoatl had truly returned from across the eastern sea,' Montezuma told me, 'and so I designed a test.'

8

W E WAITED FOR WORD TO come down from the distant Montezuma in luxurious if anxious repose, for there was little to do, and the Totonacs arrived in great numbers as a welcoming army of servants; setting up huts, cookfires, and all supplies necessary to feed us in fine style, and all of it free of the slightest hint of demand for recompense.

And excellent fare it was too, almost as good as what I had enjoyed at the court of Boabdil, far better than anything available on Cuba, and veritable ambrosia compared with what we had been constrained to nourish ourselves on since we set sail.

There were several sorts of fish from the sea and more delicate fresh-water fish too, as well as pork, turkey, and other viands unknown, almost all of which were either stewed in appropriate sauces or, if roasted, accompanied by such on the side. These sauces were all savory, many of them quite fiery, combining herbs, spices, red or green peppers, a small red fruit called the 'tomatl', and even the hard brown seeds called cacao, a local luxury, ground fine and mixed in. There were maize flat breads in abundance, all sorts of sweet or tangy local fruits, and strange vegetables also sauced in several styles.

This was washed down with plentiful pulque and more limited

quantities of a thick and frothy brown drink called 'chocolatl', made from powdered cacao beans, a longer brown bean likewise powdered, water and honey, which immediately became a favorite, for not only was it quite delicious, but, unlike the pulque, had a stimulative rather than soporific effect.

I indeed did have more than sufficient idle time for feasting, but Marina and I, along with a necessary but reluctant Aguilar, took the opportunity to improve our linguistic skills. I picked up a certain amount of rudimentary Nahuatl, but Marina's progress in Spanish, whether a matter of greater inherent talent or of stronger motivation, put me to shame and greatly disquieted poor Aguilar, for it was obvious that his services as an intermediary between her and Cortes would soon be rendered superfluous.

And all the more so since she was spending her nights in his tent engaged in exercises which needed no interpretation, and this was when she acquired the name 'Marina', with which she was baptized later, Cortes bending the unfamiliar mouthful of 'Malinal' to something with which he could feel more intimately familiar.

As for her baptism itself, I do not remember exactly when the ceremony was conducted, for it was no great thing, and certainly not to 'Doña Marina'. Indeed, as she told me after the fact when we had become intimate co-conspirators, once she had understood the Spanish system of honorifics, having the 'Doña' appended to the 'Marina' was, as far as she was concerned, the main point of the exercise.

'Easier for me to change favorite god than for you, Alvaro,' she told me. 'Your God of Abraham, and your Allah, and the Spanish Three-in-One are all so jealous of each other that each foolishly claims to be the *only* god. So to choose a new one, you must risk anger of the previous. But we have many gods, different ones for different purposes. Tlaloc for rain, Mixcoatl for hunting, Tezcatlipoca for the things of the night, Huitzilopochtli for war. True, they are jealous too and hungrily demanding, but they do acknowledge each other's existence. A much more reasonable arrangement.'

But I see that once again I seem to have raced ahead of my tale, at least linguistically, for it is hard for me to remember the 'Malinal' of that week of feasting and learning as less fluent in Spanish than the 'Doña

Marina' she would later become. No doubt had I attempted to communicate with her at the time in my few words of Nahuatl, she would have deemed me an utter oaf.

If we were waiting in avid impatience for Montezuma's reply to Cortes' request for an audience, we were in no particular hurry for the idyll to end. Indeed we lazily assumed it would go on longer than it did, for we were given to understand that the Emperor's seat was some hundred miles distant over rough mountain country, and surely it would take at least two weeks and probably more for Teuhtlile's messengers and tamanes to reach him and for Montezuma's reply to wend its way back, innocent as we were of the superior rapidity of the Mexica system of communication and transport.

You may imagine our surprise then when Montezuma's embassy arrived long before even our most optimistic estimates could have expected, a surprise quickly overwhelmed by awe and soon thereafter by joy at what arrived with his representatives.

Teuhtlile led the procession into the camp, but only in the sense that a king might be preceded by his lowly herald, for the previously haughty local governor was quite eclipsed by the Mexica grandee proceeding immediately behind him.

He wore a feathered cloak of the utmost splendor, his head was crowned with green and red plumes arising from a golden torque, heavy golden earrings studded with emeralds depended from his earlobes and a grotesque pendant from his lower lip, likewise of gold and jeweled, and his chest was draped with a vast necklace of gold and precious stones. He was flanked by more modestly accoutered servants perfuming the air he deigned to breathe with a floral incense burning in silver censers, and were that not sufficient, he held up a fragrant bouquet of red flowers to his nose.

Immediately behind him came two warriors – one wearing the pelt of some feline creature replete with the fierce head as a hooded cloak, the other extravagantly costumed as a fanciful raptor – bearing tall standards made of feather tapestries hung between poles and both depicting an eagle in the process of seizing a serpent. Behind them came several score warriors in formation, and behind the warriors, at least a hundred tamanes dutifully bearing up under heavy loads.

By this time Cortes' tent had been enhanced by a fenced courtyard, the tentside area of which was roofed by palm fronds against the sun, large enough for his officers, Marina, Aguilar, myself, and indeed most of our company, to gather therein to greet the Mexica parade, even Cortes remaining standing as a gesture of respect.

Teuhtlile stood aside as the ambassador of Montezuma approached, still within his perambulating cloud of incense. Up close, he bore such an amazing likeness to Cortes – give him a beard, lighten his skin, dress him as a Spaniard and he could almost pass for Hernando's twin brother – that it was impossible to believe that this was other than some arcane imperial jest.

Cortes, with some difficulty, masked his astonishment as his double touched his hands to the ground and thence to his face, which we later learned was the Mexica gesture of respectful greeting, akin to a Spanish bow, and introduced himself, via Marina and Aguilar, as Prince Quintalbor.

He then summoned forward the first of the train of tamanes, who unfolded enough maguey-fiber mats, known as 'petatls', to cover at least a hundred square feet of the courtyard before us, the better for the others to display the presents and treasures laid on by Montezuma.

First came weaponry, albeit it would seem of a ceremonial kind: shields, a few maquahuitls, an abundance of a sort of helmet, quilted cotton armor, all embellished with gold and silver ornaments and adorned with feathers. Then gold and silver collars, necklaces, bracelets and labrets. Many, many of the beautiful and extravagantly colored featherwork cloaks, as well as much larger items which appeared to be wall hangings similarly crafted. Incense. Reeds filled with cacao seeds.

And then came statues, as small as the tiny birds they portrayed and as large as a cat, of animals, birds, fabulous creatures, all done with amazingly accurate and finely graven precision, some in silver, but most of solid gold.

You may imagine, dear reader, the joyous effect this display had upon Cortes and his minions, not unalloyed with visible – at least to my eyes – greed for more. And there *was* more, much more.

A single tamane brought forth the gilded Spanish helmet that Teuhtlile had requested for the inspection of Montezuma, and gave it to

Quintalbor, who, with a sly little grin, handed it over to Cortes, seeming intent on studying his reaction.

And no wonder, for though Cortes' request had been made half in jest, the helmet had indeed been returned filled with nuggets and granules of gold.

But this was mere prelude to what came next.

Puffing and grunting, two teams of tamanes emerged from the rear of the train lugging two round disks the size of wagon wheels and laid them on the petatls directly before the astonished Cortes. One was engraved to represent the Moon and carved with a profusion of tiny figures. The other, crafted likewise, was an enormous portrait of the Sun.

The Moon was entirely of silver.

The Sun was solid gold.

This treasure was more than enough to redeem the debts Cortes had incurred in mounting the expedition, with profit above that amount besides, so the ill-concealed glee of his reaction and those of his lieutenants need not be described. But the keen measuring regard with which Quintalbor seemed to be recording it in his memory for future description, no doubt to Montezuma, must be mentioned.

Cortes, believing that Quintalbor's gift-giving had now been concluded, then inquired as to what the envoy bore as a message from Montezuma.

Quintalbor then delivered a short speech in Nahuatl with a visage made void of all expression and a voice as empty of emotional import as that of one of those talking parrots from Africa. Marina frowned as she delivered it to Aguilar, who was not at all happy to translate it into Spanish for Cortes, fearing his reaction, and not without reason.

'He says that Montezuma is pleased to have opened communications with, uh, King Charles, of whom he has long known, and for whom he has the highest respect, as witness these admittedly modest gifts, which he hopes you will convey to him as a token thereof. And he regrets that he will be unable to meet with you in person, since the distance to his capital is too great, and the journey too difficult and dangerous, as it passes through formidable mountains, and the road, such as it is, passes through the territories of dangerous enemies. He therefore enjoins you, for your own comfort and safety, to return to your own land with these presents for your esteemed Emperor as proof of the friendship of his brother Emperor, Montezuma.'

Aguilar ended this with a cringe, but Cortes, though he must certainly have been angered at this smarmy dismissal, to his credit betrayed no such emotion, but – after summoning forth a few paltry presents for Montezuma – replied in diplomatic kind.

'I am sure my sovereign would be pleased at Montezuma's munificence should I now return to his presence with it, but having been ordered to speak directly with Montezuma by King Charles, and having been dispatched on such a long and perilous voyage at no little expense by my King to do so, he would, with good reason, count my mission a failure, myself both disobedient and a coward, should I allow a short overland journey to dissuade me from its completion. As for the dangerous enemies we might encounter, you may thank Montezuma for his solicitude, but you may also assure him that any danger associated with such an encounter will be to those who would presume to impede us.'

This was quite a mouthful for Aguilar to translate into Mayan, though I would imagine that Marina was more successful in conveying the subtleties of it to Quintalbor in Nahuatl. The Mexica envoy accepted the presents – some fine ruffled shirts, a gilded goblet, a silver-handled dagger, nothing of much value – with good grace and without turning up his nose, as I would have done were I him.

'I will convey your message to Montezuma,' he replied, 'but I doubt it will be of any avail.'

The meeting then appeared to have been concluded on this unsatisfactory note, but it was not. At a gesture from Quintalbor, three final tamanes came forward, each bearing a large basket, and withdrew from each a panoply of items of adornment, laying them out before Cortes as a servant might lay out alternate court vestments for a king.

To his left was a conical golden helmet engraved with what looked like stars, golden earrings from which depended bells of gold, a tunic embellished with bright yellow and black feathers, and a long dark blue featherwork cloak.

To his right was a cap of some black and tawny brown mottled fur, earrings of blueish-green stone, a painted wooden mask more or less in the likeness of a serpent's face, a green and yellow featherwork vest, a shield of gold fringed with iridescent green feathers, and a matching cloak to be fastened with a kind of gold diadem inlaid with a large emerald.

Between them was a headdress of the glowing green feathers with a centerpiece of mother-of-pearl, earrings of blue stone in the form of serpents, a red featherwork cloak, and an elaborate vest with a collar in the form of a necklace of the blue stones and a large golden breastplate.

Quintalbor spoke briefly to Marina, then crossed his arms across his chest and gazed most directly at Cortes as his words were relayed by her and Aguilar.

'These are not gifts for your Emperor, but *personal* gifts from Montezuma to you, a great honor. But of the three, you must choose only one.'

You may be sure that Cortes' face showed consternation when he was told this, and you may also be sure that he had to have been quite aware that this was no simple offering of a present, for even had Hernando been innocent enough not to understand that this was some sort of puzzle or test, Quintalbor's rapt scrutiny would certainly have given it away. And since the man had conducted himself as a diplomat throughout, this was no doubt his deliberate intent.

Cortes hesitated for a long uncomfortable moment. Then Marina sidled up to him and spoke three words I was close enough to overhear. They were in Spanish so that Quintalbor could not comprehend.

'Right. Feather. Serpent.'

Hernando Cortes smiled. He touched his hands to the ground and then to his cheeks in emulation of Quintalbor's formal greeting.

Then he picked up the fur cap and placed it on his head.

And donned the mask of the serpent.

And with a flourish, draped his shoulders in the mantle of Quetzalcoatl.

9

No sooner had Quintalbor and his entourage departed our camp than Cortes summoned Marina, Aguilar and myself to his tent and demanded explanation from her as to just what she was doing and why.

I shall gloss over the linguistic complexities of this conversation so as to avoid inflicting upon you, dear reader, the confusion we inflicted upon each other, for Marina had gained enough Spanish to wish to speak to Cortes directly, but was unable to do so without Aguilar's intervention, and I was anxious to practice my smattering of Nahuatl, and so it was conducted in an intermediate patois.

Quetzalcoatl, Marina told him, was either the paramount god of the Toltecs, or their paramount hero, or somehow both. How this could be possible, she was at a loss to explain. 'I am woman of some . . . you say *education*?, but I am not papa who learns such . . . *mysteries*? *secrets*? *magics*?'

'Well at least then, who are these Toltecs?' Cortes asked.

'Master . . . you say *builders*? Great tribe ruled before Mexica. As Mexica are people of Huitzilopochtli, god of war, Toltecs were people of Quetzalcoatl, god of . . . of creating.'

'So the Toltecs were conquered by the Mexica?' I interjected.

Marina shook her head in what she had learned was our gesture for 'no'. 'The Toltecs . . . went away before coming the Mexica. Two worlds before.'

'Went where?' demanded Cortes, his brow beginning to beetle in frustration.

Marina shrugged. 'Direction of rising sun. Direction you . . . Teules come from.'

Comprehension began to enlighten Cortes' visage. 'So what you've had me doing is pretend to be this Toltec god or hero, or whatever he is, returning from the east to . . . to do what?'

'Make people think maybe Teules you . . . lead . . . are Toltecs returning from rising sun direction as in . . . *prophecy*? *story*?'

'Legend?' I said. 'A tale from the past which may or may not be true . . . a prediction from the past which may or may not *come* true?'

When Aguilar managed to put this into Mayan for her, Marina nodded her assent. 'Is legend men with beards come from across waters in direction of rising sun to . . . rule again? conquer? Different . . . stories. Some say Toltecs, some not. Some say leader is . . . you say . . . *will be*? Quetzalcoatl. Some say he is god, some say old emperor, some say Teule.'

'You've had me playing a god or hero whom the Mexica in general and Montezuma in particular will regard as a usurper!' Cortes shouted at her angrily.

From the look on her face, Marina understood neither his words nor his consternation. But when Aguilar had translated for her, she fixed Cortes with a knowing, unwavering stare.

'You come here to become the . . . *usurper* of Montezuma, do you not, Hernando Cortes?' she said in quite clear Spanish.

Cortes locked eyes with her for a very long moment of silence, during which, I am reasonably certain, he was confronting this proposition in all its blunt clarity for the first time.

'You tell caciques to become you say . . . *vassals*? to Emperor across ocean, not Montezuma,' Marina purred insinuatingly. 'Pay tribute to your Charles . . . through you. If *is* Emperor Charles, not just *you*, my Quetzalcoatl?'

'Surely you don't believe that I'm really Quetzalcoatl!'

'You throw down other gods,' Marina said teasingly, 'you give blood of new god to drink . . .'

I was amused, but Cortes was not. 'You're speaking blasphemy, woman!' he shouted in righteous Christian outrage.

'You *do* blasphemy, man,' Marina said with a fey little smile when Aguilar had explained the word to her in Mayan. 'Blasphemy Tlaloc. Blasphemy Tezcatlipoca. Blasphemy *Huitzilopochtli* himself, god of Montezuma. God of Mexica. God of *war*! Only other god not be afraid to do that!'

'Don't be ridiculous!' Cortes told them. 'None of them even exist!'

'Montezuma does not exist?' Marina said slyly.

'I'm not afraid of him either!' Cortes blurted.

'So then you *must* be a god, my Quetzalcoatl!' Marina told him in Spanish, and burst into laughter. And, finally, so did Cortes, and, sweeping her up into his arms, dismissed Aguilar and myself.

I did not have the opportunity to speak with Cortes for two days afterward, for Hernando was preoccupied with the factional politics beginning to evolve among his troops.

Idleness, it is often said, breeds the Devil's work; here in our encampment it consisted of excess consumption of pulque, an argumentative mood, and a desire among a growing number to return to Cuba with gold in their pouches and tales to tell. This faction was championed by Francisco de Montejo and Velazquez de Leon, loyal to Diego Velazquez, or at least as loyal to Velazquez as any of the gold-hungry freebooters in this company were by now loyal to anyone save themselves.

Cortes finally dealt with the problem by dispatching Velazquez de Leon and a score or so of this faction on a meaningless exploratory excursion into the nearby interior, and Montejo, with two brigantines and close to a hundred more men he wanted to see the back of, up the coast in search of a better anchorage for the fleet.

By the time we caught up to each other, the environment of our encampment had turned as foul as the mood of its denizens. The weather had turned oppressively hot and humid, and malodorous vapors from the nearby swamps drifted in on sluggish breezes, along with clouds of much more energetic stinging mosquitoes and flies. Latrines were well outside the encampment, but within there was much debris and food remains scattered about, for these warrior grandees were not about to bend their backs to keep the area free therefrom, especially since this detritus attracted the mosquitoes and flies. Nor were they much moved to pass the time cooking their meals, fishing, hunting, or gathering fruit and vegetables, for the encampment was enclosed in a half-circle of Totonac huts where all this could be had for handfuls of trade beads.

'What *is* the woman doing with this Quetzalcoatl ploy?' were the first words Cortes spoke to me by way of greeting. 'Why pit me against Montezuma? Or more to the unfortunate point, him against me?'

'Since it seems she does not truly believe you are a god or a mythic hero, perhaps because being consort of the ruler of his former empire is the next best thing?' I suggested.

'I am to throw my five hundred men against Montezuma's hundreds of thousands to please the selfish whim of a woman?'

'It wouldn't be the first time such a thing has happened,' I told him dryly. 'And you came here to be the usurper of Montezuma, did you not, Hernando Cortes?' I said in an admittedly lame imitation of the lady in question.

'Did I?' said Cortes. 'How could I, when before we left Cuba, I had no idea he or his empire even existed?'

'You embarked on this adventure to seize your destiny, you told me so yourself. To found an empire if there was none, to seize one if it was here.'

'Did I?' Cortes mused in a more thoughtful tone.

I shrugged. 'If it were only a matter of gold, there is now more than enough to return to Cuba with wealth aplenty, as Velazquez would surely have you do, as Montezuma recommends . . .'

'As Ordaz, de Leon, and Montejo, among others, would convince the men to have me do . . .' Cortes muttered. 'And yet, it would be madness to march on Mexico with the force at my command.'

He sighed, he threw up his hands. 'But if I obey my commission from Velazquez and simply return now with what we have gained, surely the next expedition will be mounted by him under some lackey's command,

and with a much greater force, and I will have missed my chance for ever. And so . . .'

'And so . . . ?'

Suddenly Hernando's face lit up with one of those abrupt lightenings of mood to which his relentlessly cocksure spirit was prone, and which went a long way towards making him the charismatic leader of men that he was.

'And so I must win Montezuma to the One True Faith,' he said, as if he had discovered the obvious solution to a minor problem.

'In the service of what . . . save of course the salvation of his immortal soul?' I demanded, quite befuddled.

'King Charles's partisans have been scheming to elect him Holy Roman Emperor even before the ailing Maximillian has expired, and for all we now know here, the latter may already have died and the former succeeded, so why not assume for present purposes that this is so?' Cortes said quite blithely.

'I'm afraid you've quite lost me, Hernando.'

'It's simple, Alvaro. It's one thing to persuade a heathen Emperor to swear fealty to a mere King, but a Christian sovereign should be easily enough persuaded to become a vassal of the Holy Roman Emperor consecrated by the Pope, since many such have already done so. And therefore to the King of Spain, since they are, or will be, one and the same. And who, being a just and honorable sovereign, will surely reward me with the stewardship of his empire.'

'And if Charles should never become Holy Roman Emperor, will you not have told a most dangerous lie of literally imperial proportions?' I said, overwhelmed by the hubristic audacity of such a scheme.

Cortes shrugged. 'His Majesty can hardly fault me for wishing it were so, now can he? Especially if I succeed.'

'And how do you imagine you will accomplish the minor task of converting Montezuma to the One True Faith, upon which all this depends?'

'Surely I will be aided by Divine Intervention, for by so doing, will I not save countless thousands of souls from eternal torment in the pits and fires of Hell, Alvaro?' Cortes said without the slightest hint of sarcasm in his voice.

'You will do well by doing good?' I replied, hoping I had succeeded in keeping it out of mine.

'Indeed! I will be doing the work of Our Lord Jesus Christ, and therefore He will surely stand by my side.'

'As simple as that, is it?'

'I must conquer Mexico for the King and myself by conquering the heart of one man for the Cross.'

After which, you will do what, walk on water? I managed to refrain from saying.

'Now that *is* a task for the likes of Quetzalcoatl!' I said instead.

The mood in our encampment continued to darken, soured not only by the idle waiting for the return of Montejo's ships and some reply from Montezuma to Cortes' latest request for an audience, but by the stepwise deterioration of the relationship with the adjacent Totonac market.

I now call it a market, for that is what it had become. First handfuls of trade beads were required to purchase the foodstuffs that had been provided as gifts of friendship, then the prices were put up, then what was available at these inflated prices was reduced from bounteous and varied plenty to maize flat bread, bean mash, pulque, scrawny turkeys, and blueish meat that had seen better days quite a while ago. It was not only a practical displeasure, but a continuous omen of ill fortune and ill will.

Marina passed the nights alone with Cortes in his tent, and the better part of the days with me in the absence of Aguilar, for she was determined to master Spanish well enough to dispense with the intermediary language of Mayan as quickly as possible.

I had never before pondered how I had learned Arabic as my daily language and Hebrew as the language of liturgy and Kabbalah, and then Spanish as a matter of practical survival, and finally the Nahuatl I began acquiring in the process of teaching Marina Spanish. Although I had mastered three tongues by the time I met Marina, I had never considered myself a linguist, having no particular talent for it, and having never evolved a method of study.

But Marina was not only a linguistic prodigy, she did have a method, albeit one that I could not apply.

'Better to spend days talking with you in my bad Spanish and your very very bad Nahuatl, than speak Mayan through Aguilar,' she told me. 'And much more Spanish to be learned from nights alone with Hernando. No man makes sex for as long as it takes to eat a meal, rest of the time there is talk, and Hernando likes better to talk than to listen. So I listen, he talks, when I not understand, I ask him to explain, and because is his only language, he must explain in Spanish. And so, at night, I must *think* in Spanish. This makes me more stupid than I think in Nahuatl or Mayan but makes me get smarter in Spanish faster.'

Needless to say, there was nothing stupid about this woman in any language! She was almost frighteningly intelligent, charmingly cynical, and yet intensely passionate in a curious manner.

Although I was too cautious to be anyone but Alvaro de Sevilla in her presence at this stage, she was entirely forthcoming about her history and how it had shaped both her cynicism and her passion. Indeed not only was she the first passionate cynic I had ever met, only in meeting Marina did I discover that the squaring of that circle was even possible.

'Mother sells me to traders, traders sell me to Tabascans as slave, Tabascans give me as present to Spaniards along with beans and turkeys,' she told me when I asked her how it was that, by all appearances, she had become so loyal to Cortes so quickly. 'To who am I loyal? You are looking at to who I am loyal, Alvaro de Sevilla! Only person who has ever been loyal to me!'

'And this is why you are willing to worship . . . uh the One True God?'

'One True God? *What* true god? Tlaloc brings rain, need rain, give him hearts of children. Time to plant, sacrifice to Xipe Totec. Win war, give hearts to Huitzilopochtli. Become . . . you say . . . *mistress? consort?* to Quetzalcoatl, drink blood of Jesus Christ, eat his meat. Same thing, Alvaro. As long as Tlaloc brings rain, be loyal to him. Corn grows, be loyal to Xipe Totec. But if lose war, no more hearts for Huitzilopochtli!'

I was sorely tempted to reveal both my appreciation for this theological pragmatism and some of my own story which so made me favor it, for this was the moment, I do believe, when the seed of some sort of bond between us was sown. But I had not survived to that moment by being less than cautious about such matters, and the time was not quite ripe.

'You really believe that Cortes is Quetzalcoatl?' I ventured instead.

Marina shrugged. 'Who is Quetzalcoatl? What is Quetzalcoatl? Man? God? Spanish Teule? Toltec hero? *Legend*, Alvaro. Good story. Many different good stories. But where important, all the same.'

'All the same?'

'I am woman sold as slave when a girl. I am not stupid, but I do not go to calmecac, you say *school*? *university*? so I do not know long story . . . you say *his*-story? of Toltecs, Mexica, Texcocans, Tacubans, Totonacs, all very . . . complicated. But three things I know. Quetzalcoatl is god, or hero, or dead king, of *Toltecs*, not *Mexica*. And Toltecs were strong when Mexica were nothing. And all . . . you say *subject*? tribes hate Mexica. Mexica strong, others weak. Weak fear strong, men hate what they fear. And much to hate beside. Mexica take taxes. Mexica feed thousands of hearts to Huitzilopochtli.'

'So?' I said, still not quite understanding.

'So many follow Quetzalcoatl if Quetzalcoatl fight Mexica. So many follow Hernando Cortes if believe he is Quetzalcoatl. Simple.'

'But what *do* you believe?'

And she grinned at me slyly, and those big dark eyes seemed to look straight into my hidden heart.

'I believe like you, Alvaro de Sevilla,' she said. 'I believe what is good for me to believe at the time.'

Ten days after Quintalbor's grand embassy had departed, a deputation from Montezuma finally did arrive, but its approach seemed an ill omen, for it was not led by Cortes' lordly double but by Teuhtlile and one Pitalpitoque, who, by Teuhtlile's far less deferential bearing towards him, was clearly a lesser personage, and while they were accompanied by gift-bearing tamanes, the train of them was less than half as long as before.

Cortes awaited him with his entourage beneath the palm-frond-shaded courtyard before his tent, and formal greetings were exchanged. But the atmosphere was tinged with tension as soon as the meeting began.

The tamanes bore no petatl mats upon which to display the ceremonial gifts, rather they were all but dumped on the bare earth as if to give deliberate affront. There was a goodly amount of cloth, but less than half of it was cotton, the rest being of the coarser and more common maguey-fiber variety, and little of it was embroidered. There were half a dozen featherwork cloaks, but they looked a bit the worse for wear. There were a dozen or so wooden shields which had been brightly painted, but they were adorned with neither feathers nor gold. There was some golden jewelry and statuettes, but precious little by previous standards.

And the climactic offerings, far from being enormous wheels of gold and silver, were four large opaque stones, which, though roughly the color of emeralds, were deemed of little value by those of our number with a knowledge of gems.

'The great Montezuma sends you his greetings,' Pitalpitoque told Cortes through Marina and Aguilar, 'and sends his greetings through you to his brother King Charles across the sea, and bids you bear these precious chalchuites to him as tokens of his respect.'

From Pitalpitoque's frosty attitude and Cortes' glowering reception of these items, it was clear that they were meant as a form of insult, and both of them knew it.

'Having obtained the gold to cool the fevers of your hearts, and having been given these gifts to take with you,' Pitalpitoque went on in the same vein, 'the Emperor Montezuma is confident that you will now return across the sea to the land from whence you came.'

Had Cortes been a dragon, smoke would have come pouring out of his nostrils when these words were translated to him. It was difficult to tell whether he was more vexed with the Emperor's envoy or Marina.

'Tell this . . . personage that we accept these . . . *tokens* in the name of our sovereign,' he commanded her directly in Spanish. 'And tell him that by command of that sovereign I am forbidden to do as Montezuma suggests until I have spoken to him face to face.'

Pitalpitoque's visage likewise darkened with diplomatically suppressed ire when this was put to him. 'Perhaps the translation has not made my meaning clear,' he replied, glowering at Marina as she rendered this. 'The great Montezuma does not *suggest*. The great Montezuma *commands*. The great Montezuma commands you to advance no further into his lands and to return to yours while you may still do so unharmed.'

What might have happened if the exchange had proceeded much further in this direction mercifully remained a mystery, for at this point there occurred a divine intervention of sorts. The bell for vespers rang, and Cortes prudently took this as an opportunity to cool the atmosphere and his own evident ire by interrupting the meeting for the required prayer, rather than let it continue to what just might have turned into blows.

Everyone filed out into the center of the encampment where a large wooden Cross had been set up, the evidently curious Pitalpitoque and his entourage as well as Teuhtlile, who observed the proceedings as Englishmen who were entirely ignorant of Islam might observe the bowing to Mecca in massed unison at one of the five appointed hours in an Arabian souk.

After it was over, Cortes said something to Father Olmedo, then drew Marina and Aguilar close to the Cross where the three of them stood.

'Father Olmedo has an important message for the great Montezuma!' he bellowed loudly. 'The most important message he will ever hear! For this is the most important message ever given to any man! This is the Word of God Himself!'

Marina, without waiting for Aguilar, at once shouted this out in Nahuatl, stopping everyone in their tracks.

And while I stood there groaning to myself, Olmedo, under orders from Cortes, via Aguilar and thence through Marina to Pitalpitoque for delivery to Montezuma, proceeded to preach the more or less standard sermon to potential converts.

You probably have some familiarity with this material, dear reader, so I need not burden you with the tedious details. He began with a short version of Genesis, proceeded rapidly through Moses and the Burning Bush, the handing down of the Ten Commandments, the evil of idolatry via the story of the Golden Calf, the punishment of the Flood, the birth, passion and resurrection of Christ, ending with the usual vague description of the eternal bliss to be enjoyed by the faithful in Heaven and a far more detailed portrait of the horrible tortures awaiting all heathen in Hell.

He concluded with a fiery injunction directed at Montezuma personally to repent of his heathenish idolatry, accept baptism in the

One Truth Faith, and thereby lead his benighted people into the joys of the former and away from the path leading to the eternal damnation of the latter, amen.

Cortes, it would seem, had been *serious* when he told me that he intended to conquer the empire of Mexico by conquering the heart of Montezuma for the Cross!

How Marina had translated Aguilar's Mayan version of all this, I had no way of knowing, and what Montezuma would make of whatever eventually reached his ears was hard to imagine. All that I could observe was the glazed look in Pitalpitoque's eyes and the grim set of his lips, no doubt at the thought of having to convey *any* version of this message to his sovereign's ears.

When it was over, Father Olmedo handed him a little statue of the Virgin and Child, with the instruction to give it to Montezuma with the injunction that he place it over the altar of his principal temple in place of whatever hideous idol presently defiled it.

Pitalpitoque regarded it as if he had been handed a very dead fish.

'You have made Montezuma believe I am his enemy with this Quetzalcoatl masquerade!' Cortes shouted at Marina.

'And you are not?' Marina answered calmly. 'You did not tell him, or you say *order* him, to replace Huitzilopochtli with Jesus?'

'An act of friendship to save his immortal soul!'

Marina rolled her eyes upward. 'If your friend Montezuma tells you to replace Jesus with Huitzilopochtli for good of your soul, this you will do, Hernando?'

'Of course not!'

'You will not obey him, but he must obey you!'

Aguilar cringed in the back of the tent, no doubt wishing he could disappear.

It was left to me to attempt to calm the stormy waters.

Cortes had summoned the three of us to dine with him, but there had been nothing cordial about the invitation. Hernando blamed Marina for Montezuma's blunt refusal to meet with him and even blunter command to advance no further towards his capital and be gone. Marina believed, quite rightly by my lights, that demanding that the Emperor of the Mexica accept Christ and the One True Faith and order his subjects to do likewise was utter madness that could only inflame his outrage.

'It seems to me both of you have perhaps forgotten that Montezuma is a sovereign . . .' I ventured.

'I hardly think either of us have overlooked that, Alvaro,' Cortes said dryly, but still peevishly.

'Marina is right about one thing, Hernando,' I told him. 'This is a man used to being obeyed by everyone, and you can have only offended him by demanding that *he* obey *you*.'

'Not me, but the Word of God!' Cortes exclaimed. But there was a certain defensiveness in his tone now, and when I fixed him with a squint-eyed stare, he shrugged, and some of the heat drained out of the atmosphere.

'And *you* must be right, Hernando,' I told him, 'in believing that Montezuma could hardly be expected to welcome back the long-lost god-king of the Toltecs to challenge his legitimacy.'

My last seemed a bit too much Spanish for Marina to completely understand directly, and so she was constrained to resort to Aguilar for an exegesis in Mayan, toward the end of which she began to nod slowly in comprehension.

'You are right, Alvaro,' she said. 'Montezuma obeys no man. Only his . . . *favorite*? god if he speaks to him, and this is Huitzilopochtli. He will not listen to your Three-In-One, Hernando, or only if Huitzilopochtli tells him to, and I think not this Huitzilopochtli will do.'

'But then—'

'*You* are right, Hernando, if Quetzalcoatl returns, Montezuma fears him, because Quetzalcoatl is . . . greater than him, and Toltecs were greater than Mexica, even Mexica believe this—'

'Then why in the name of the Virgin and the Twelve Apostles have you had me pretending to be him?' Cortes demanded.

'Tribes who hate Mexica maybe follow Quetzalcoatl, who Montezuma fears,' Marina suggested softly. 'Enemy of enemy is maybe . . . you say *ally*?'

There was a long silence as Cortes digested this.

'You're talking war,' he finally said just as softly.

'And you are are not, my Quetzalcoatl? If not to conquer, you came to do what?'

'With five hundred men against . . .'

Cortes caught himself short.

'Oh,' he said.

'Oh,' said Marina with a sly little smile.

10

WHEN THE SUN ROSE on the morrow, the Totonac market which surrounded our encampment was entirely deserted. During the night, every last one of its proprietors had fled, taking every last scrap of food with them.

Ill omen though it was, the practical disheartenment it raised in our encampment was equally dismaying and much more immediate, for we were abruptly forced back onto reliance on the stale ships' stores we had brought with us and what our own foraging parties could secure from the surrounding environs. Worse still, since while we were being so liberally supplied with meals well cooked for us by the locals, no one had really studied just what could be found where and how it might be properly prepared.

Then too, as the season waxed even hotter and more humid, clouds of voracious mosquitoes emerged from the marshes to feast far more lavishly on our blood than we were able to do on the local fauna and flora, bringing pestilence that slew over a dozen of our number and sickened many more.

The general mood was improved when Montejo's ships returned with news that he had discovered a cove suitable for a permanent anchorage, and relatively nearby westward down the coast close to a

Totonac town called Quiahuitzlan. But the factionalism that had died down to sullenly smoldering embers was rekindled when Cortes announced his intent to move there as soon as feasible.

Diego de Ordaz, Velazquez de Leon, Montejo, all known to be loyal to the governor of Cuba, and one Juan Escudero, who had not been, stormed into Cortes' tent as a 'deputation' from the like-minded demanding instead that we return forthwith to Cuba.

'How many supporters they really had, I did not know, nor did I deem it prudent to ask, for Escudero's presence among them seemed to indicate that the sentiment might be all too general,' Cortes told me later. 'And the longer we lay idle on this mosquito-infested coast, the more there would be, and as I slapped at the foul creatures, I began to wonder how long it would be before I myself became one of them.

'But I assured them that while the Totonacs here had disappeared, those at Quiahuitzlan had been friendly enough, and we could therefore no doubt resume profitable commerce there. Since it was Montejo himself who had reported their pacific disposition, there was much grumbling and muttering, but it quelled the rebellion, if that was what it was about to turn into, for the moment.'

While we were in the early stages of preparing for our departure, five Totonacs appeared out of the jungle of an early morning, made directly for Cortes' tent, and, to hear him tell it, interrupted himself and Marina in the midst of an amorous embrace.

They hastily dressed, I was sent for, and Aguilar as well, though by this time Marina's command of Spanish had progressed to the point where he was swiftly becoming a supernumerary.

The five Totonacs were unescorted by warriors and unaccompanied by gift-bearing tamanes. They were dressed quite alike in cotton loin-cloths and capes, and all wore the same gold rings, blue-green jewels in their ears and nostrils, and light leaves of gold affixed to their lower lips; indicating, at least to me, that they must be of equal rank. As it turned out, it was not a particular lofty one.

'We are messengers from the caciques of Cempoala,' the one who appeared to be the leader informed Cortes through Marina, 'the capital and greatest city of the Totonacs, to which all Totonaca owes fealty.'

Another of them, this one older and somewhat corpulent, then favored us with a brief lesson in Totonac history and the current relationship between that tribe and the Mexica, which, since it was the first such briefing we had, was a welcome favor indeed.

The Totonacs had originated on the high plateau beyond the great mountains separating it from this coast. Several centuries or so ago, they had crossed the mountains and descended their slopes towards their present territories, for the most part fairer and more fertile than either their ancestral lands or the steamy beaches and marshlands of this coastal area.

There they had long prospered until their conquest by the warlike and rapacious Mexica and their quite literally bloodthirsty god Huitzilopochtli within the memory of living men.

'The Mexica require of us very heavy tribute,' moaned a third. 'The fruits of our fields and orchards. Turquoise and cotton and feathers. Turkeys and pigs and cacao. The better part of what little gold is to be found on our lands.'

'But worse still,' said the fourth, 'is the tribute they require for Huitzilopochtli himself.'

'The hearts and the blood and the flesh of our best young warriors.'

'Which feeds Huitzilopochtli and thus makes him grow ever stronger.'

'And so more demanding.'

'And the Mexica more impossible to resist.'

By then we were all too well aware that the natives of this continent from time to time practiced odious rites of human sacrifice, so while we were hardly inured to such tidings, we were less than surprised.

'And . . . how many warriors does this Satanic demon consume as tribute annually?' Cortes inquired through Marina.

'In an ordinary year, no more than several hundred,' came the reply.

'If there are special ceremonies or circumstances, perhaps a thousand.'

'But when Montezuma became Emperor, of the twenty thousand hearts offered up on his altar to Huitzilopochtli, two thousand were slashed from the breasts of Totonacs.'

'*Twenty thousand human hearts . . . ?*' Cortes whispered hoarsely in genuine horror, as any civilized human being would. But any civilized human being was not Hernando Cortes. Most men would have quailed in fear at the thought of confronting such monstrosity with a force not the tenth part of the mere *victims* its machineries of slaughter were capable of consuming in a single unspeakable ceremony, but that was not what I saw in the eyes of Cortes.

'Why have you come here to tell me this?' he demanded in a tone of cold anger.

'Our caciques very much wish to invite you to Cempoala.'

'And why do they wish to do that?' demanded Cortes, but in a rhetorical tone that told me, and Marina as well, who broke into a little self-satisfied smile, that he had already caught the drift.

'Tales have been heard about . . . the bearded strangers from the east who arrived in canoes as big as snow-covered mountains . . .'

'What sort of tales?' asked Cortes, casting a lidded sidelong glance at Marina.

'Of their magical weapons . . .'

'And fierce beasts.'

'And the terrible victory they won against the Tabascans . . .'

'And . . .'

'*And?*' demanded Cortes.

The five Totonac messengers regarded each other furtively.

'It has been said that they are . . . Teules . . .'

'Or perhaps even the Toltecs returning . . .'

Marina's smile became a smug grin.

'And that you might be—'

Cortes abruptly held up his hand for silence. 'Tell them they must not speak of such things!' he ordered Marina. Marina scowled. Cortes shrugged. 'Well then, tell them now is not the time to speak of such things. Tell them . . . perhaps they might be discussed with their caciques when I accept their invitation.'

Marina spoke in Nahuatl to the Totonacs. When she was finished, they regarded Cortes with expressions verging on awe, though he seemed not to notice as he ushered them outside to welcoming hospitality.

'What did you really say to them?' I demanded of Marina when they had departed.

'What Hernando told me to tell them,' she said.

'Nothing more?'

Marina laughed. 'Only,' she said, 'that it was the wish of Quetzalcoatl.'

The troubled waters in our encampment were further roiled when Cortes decided to march the bulk of the troops overland through Cempoala, while the ships sailed down the coast to the harbor below the town of Quiahuitzlan. For while no one was unwilling to quit these dismal environs, those Velazquez partisans demanding a return to Cuba knew that moving the ships to a more favorable harbor was a sigil of Cortes' intent to delay that homecoming an indefinite time longer.

And while they had all been told that we had a friendly invitation to the Totonac capital, not even Cortes' closest allies had been told that his intent in going to Cempoala was to explore the possibility of more than peaceful and profitable commerce.

These supportive comrades he told that following Velazquez's mission to the letter and returning now with the seemingly impressive amount of gold already acquired would, after all, hardly enrich all and sundry, himself included, in the manner to which they wished to be accustomed, for a fifth would be due to the King, and much of the rest to Velazquez, and they would be left to share but a minority of the current spoils.

'Any nation who would gift us with those enormous wheels of gold and silver just to see us gone must have done so to protect a store of a far greater amount,' was the argument with which he armed the likes of Alvarado, Olid, Sandoval and Puertocarrero, and that was the verbal armament that they carried into verbal battle with the proponents of Velazquez, who, after all, would find themselves in more or less the same financial position if they prevailed.

But even this was dissembling, as Cortes confessed to me when I was finally enlisted in the plotting I had sedulously attempted to avoid. Instead of summoning me to his tent, he arrived at my hut, appropriately enough in the dark of night, long enough after midnight so that he was constrained to awaken me.

'I need your assistance, Alvaro,' he told me when I had rubbed the sleep from my eyes. 'For I intend to announce our departure to Cuba, and I must be prevented.'

'Would you mind repeating that?' I muttered blearily. 'Either I am still asleep or I must have misheard.'

Cortes' laugh was brief and dry. 'You are awake, and you have heard correctly. When the time is made ripe, I will relent to Velazquez's lackeys and agree to return to Cuba.'

'When the time is *made* ripe?'

'I have no intention of really returning to Cuba. I must be prevented from doing so by an outcry from my own supporters, which, of course, must not be seen to emanate from me, so that their wrath against me will be sincere enough to be convincing. Which is why I need you to help me arrange this spontaneous demand.'

'*What* spontaneous demand?' I grunted dazedly. 'It's the middle of the night, you've just awakened me, and I do not seem to be in full command of my senses, so you'll have to move a bit more slowly, Hernando.'

'The demand that, rather than return to Cuba, I agree to the founding of a colony here under direct royal auspices rather than under the meager commission from Velazquez, which grants me no such power.'

'Thereby reducing Velazquez's share of whatever gold we secure,' I said, now coming fully awake.

Cortes favored me with a smile, that, were he a wolf, would have had him licking his chops. 'Or eliminating it entirely,' he said.

Or was I fully awake?

'You seem to have forgotten that you have no such commission from the King!'

'Not yet. But if this plan succeeds, I will have the means to obtain it.'

'You will? How?'

'I will buy it.'

'*Buy* it! Defy Velazquez's authority and found your own colony, and buy a commission to do so from the King after you have already done it!'

'There you have it, Alvaro,' said Hernando Cortes.

'Have what? How do you expect to bribe a King?' I demanded.

'With gold, what else?' Cortes said blithely. 'And new lands, of course. And bribe is such an unjust term, Alvaro. I will simply do what

Velazquez himself and his general Narvaez did when they conquered Cuba and presented it to His Majesty as a gift. Only my gift of the royal fifth will be much more generous, since there is little gold in Cuba, and certainly a great deal of it here.'

I laughed. 'Ingenious, Hernando,' I had to admit. 'But wait! It seems to me you have forgotten one minor detail.'

'How so?'

'The small matter of conquering the Empire of the Mexica with fewer than five hundred men. Surely, after what we have now learned, you still don't imagine that this can be accomplished by winning the heart of Montezuma to Christ and the Cross?'

Cortes frowned. 'And why not, if God so wills it?' he said with what seemed like sincerity.

'An Emperor who sacrificed twenty thousand people to this Huitzilopochtli for one ceremony? Who won't even let you get close enough to him to even try?'

Cortes' frown grew somewhat choleric. 'We'll see about that later, one way or another,' he grumbled.

'After Quetzalcoatl has raised an army of Totonac auxiliaries?'

'I'll have none of that talk now!' Cortes growled quite angrily.

'What angers you so much about making good use of—'

'I'll not endanger my immortal soul by telling the blasphemous lie that I am a heathen demon who never existed in the first place!'

'Well it certainly would be a princely lie,' I said banteringly, knowing when to back off by giving him room to make the inevitable ecclesiastical jest.

'And we know who the most Princely of Liars is,' Cortes replied, following my lead.

'Speaking of which,' I said dryly, 'just what is my part in this . . . princely plot supposed to be?'

'Let us call it a . . . stratagem, if you please,' Cortes said with a sly little smile, and I saw that his momentary anger had dissipated as quickly as I had maladroitly called it forth. 'And your part in it will be to aid me in composing the letter to the King that will be sent with the gold after the deed is done, and shall we say . . . instigating its inception beforehand.'

'And how am I supposed to do that? I certainly have no standing to broach it to your friends myself.'

'Put it into the ear of someone who can. Someone whose innocent purity will be beyond their suspicion. Sandoval . . . or young Bernal Diaz. Was it not Diaz in his fervor who brought you and I together to begin this adventure in the first place?'

And so, like it or not, and I certainly didn't, I found myself involved in Cortes' plot, a plot that would have done the most Byzantine Emperor of Byzantium proud, at least to the point of covertly setting it in motion and watching it unfold. As such things go, it was a work of genius; indeed as it unfolded it seemed that Cortes had conceived a new *form* of plotting, one which might delight future connoisseurs and historians of this black art.

I sought out Diaz, tracking his movements from afar until I saw him strolling at the water's edge for a breath of air at the height of the next afternoon, when the heat was at its worst but the fewest mosquitoes were abroad, and contrived to have him encounter me doing likewise.

'A far cry from our meeting on that other beach in Santiago,' I ventured after we had exchanged perfunctory greetings. 'I deemed Cuba far from congenial at the time, but it begins to seem more and more like Paradise as our days here wear on.'

'Surely you are not among those wishing to return to Cuba, Alvaro?' Diaz exclaimed with rhetorical righteousness. 'I thought you an intimate of Cortes.'

'Hernando keeps his own counsel these days,' I told him. 'He seems less his own self, vexed by this growing demand to return to Cuba, his own inclination to press on here, and his fear that if it comes down to a confrontation, those who want to return can win the day by forcing the notary to produce the text of his commission from Velazquez.'

'Why should that so vex him?' Diaz asked with an ingenuous innocence upon which it was easy enough to pounce.

'Because, I believe, it does not grant him the authority to do what is really in his heart.'

'How so?'

I pulled Diaz closer and all but whispered in his ear as a theatrical gesture of secret confidence even though there was no one in sight to overhear. 'I was present at his meeting with the messengers from Cempoala . . .' I hesitated. 'This, you understand, you'd best not repeat, for if it became known, it would only inflame matters further,' I told him, knowing full well that was exactly what would happen.

'We were given to understand that the Totonacs, and not just the Totonacs, chafe grievously under the yoke of the Mexica,' I went on when he had dutifully nodded.

'So . . . ?'

'Cortes believes that it might be possible to enlist their allegiance against Montezuma, and by so doing to acquire sufficient forces to—'

'March against Mexico and conquer an empire!' Diaz exclaimed with all the gleeful fervor of glory-hungry martial youth.

'I said no such thing!' I replied in a tone confirming that I had indeed let this confidence slip. 'And you must not put this abroad either, for he has no authority to do so, and those demanding a return to Cuba could use it to force his hand by accusing him of planning insubordination, which Hernando has far too much honor to do.'

'But if it be possible, such an opportunity to add such a great territory to the Crown and to our own enrichment must be seized!'

I sighed unhappily. 'But Cortes has no authority from Velazquez to found a colony as you suggest and—'

'I said no such—'

'Still, your idea is a clever one, Bernal.'

'It is . . . ?'

'A legally constituted colony could indeed petition the King for his direct commission after the fact . . .'

'As Velazquez himself did in the process of conquering Cuba . . .' Diaz muttered thoughtfully, beginning to be as impressed with his own cleverness as I had pretended to be.

'It would be risky of course, for Velazquez would certainly become wrathful, and if we failed to present the King with a richer prize than Cuba—'

'Let us not speak of failure!' Diaz proclaimed excitedly. 'Let us not even think of it! Instead let us seize the moment and fill our hearts with the determination to succeed!'

'Please, Bernal, this must go no further!' I told him, putting on a display of fearfulness. 'We have both said too much, and it will be Cortes who will become wrathful if it gets bruited about promiscuously, and at us!'

'We must be discreet about it then . . .'

'Please, I beg you, Bernal, in my heart, I am all for this clever stratagem of yours, but in my mind and my stomach, I know all too well that I have neither the courage nor the talent to pursue such inclinations.'

'A bit too long in the tooth, eh . . . ?' the young bravo replied sympathetically. 'Fear not, I shall be careful, and I shall leave your name out of it.'

Well, dear reader, it was hardly possible for a junior officer whose heart had been filled with dreams of glory, and in whose mind I had sown a clever strategy whereby they might become fulfilled that he was now convinced was his own, not to play the part I had written for him.

Within a day our encampment was alive with a buzzing that put even that of our horde of camp-following mosquitoes to shame.

A buzzing which became akin to that of a tribe of hornets whose nest had been disturbed when, as was equally inevitable, Velazquez's partisans became aware of the perfidy that Cortes' partisans were plotting and, not being totally naive, sensed his hand behind it.

Matters came to a head immediately after mass on the following morning, when our entire company was gathered before the small portable altar and the large rude wooden Cross that Father Olmedo and Father Diaz had set up in the encampment.

Francisco de Montejo stepped forward to confront Cortes; of less than average height, stocky, swarthy, and a man whom Hernando could have trusted as a good leader of men had he not emerged as one of those leading the Velazquez faction.

'Is it true that you are planning to found a colony here?' he demanded.

'Wherever did you get such an idea, Francisco?' Cortes answered ingenuously.

'The encampment is full of such rumors, spread, it would seem, by your supporters, that that is exactly what you are planning to do.'

Cortes laughed good-humoredly. 'The encampment is also full of buzzing mosquitoes,' he said. 'Next will you accuse me of plotting with *them*?'

'You deny it then?' called out Diego de Ordaz.

'Of course I deny it!' Cortes answered more sternly.

'Then prove it!' demanded Juan Escudero.

Cortes let his hand move towards the hilt of his sword. 'Prove it, Juan?' he said not quite threateningly. 'You impugn my honor?'

There was a long moment of tense silence as Cortes and Escudero glared at each other. 'I cast no aspersion on your honor, Hernando,' Escudero finally said. 'I only meant——'

'He only meant that it is time we returned to Cuba and your agreement to doing just that would be a deed to back up your word, which we all trust,' declared Montejo, in an oratory tone of voice meant to be heard loud and clear by the hundreds of men gathered round. 'I speak for many who intend to do just that, one way or the other.'

'Do you, Francisco?' Cortes said evenly, then, at the top of his voice: 'Does he?'

Scores of those present raised their fists, waved their arms, shouted out their general agreement.

'You see, Hernando?' said Montejo.

'What I see is insubordination!' Cortes shouted out.

'You're a fine one to talk of insubordination!' Escudero said in like manner.

'So it is *what* that you accuse me of, Escudero. *Treason?*' Cortes shouted, and now his hand did come to rest on the hilt of his sword.

'He only meant that you have fulfilled all that the governor of Cuba has commissioned you to fulfill,' Montejo said hastily. 'You have explored the coast, done what it is presently possible to do toward converting its inhabitants to the True Faith, demonstrated the force of Spanish arms, and secured a far greater amount of gold and silver than the previous expeditions, which is all you have been authorized to do. It is therefore time for us to return to Cuba with what we have won to receive the praise of the governor who sent us for a mission completed so successfully and a job so well done.'

This time Cortes let the silence go on much longer before withdrawing his hand from his sword and declaiming to the gathering:

'Francisco de Montejo is entirely correct in his description of what we have thus far achieved, and indeed it is a job well done. But it is no mission completed, for the riches we have thus far won, however great by the pitiful standards of previous expeditions, are as nothing to what remains to be won. And there are untold souls here whom we abandon to their eternal damnation by failing to even attempt to bring them to Christ and the Cross, and therefore put at risk our own salvation. And while my commission from Diego Velazquez goes no further than to grant this expedition the right and the mandate to explore, trade and convert, there is no limit upon the territory in which we may perform these duties or the time we may take to do so.'

'Well spoken!' called out Pedro de Alvarado.

'Well spoken indeed!' cried Puertocarrero.

And there were general shouts of approval and support from the majority of those present.

Cortes waited patiently for it to die away. 'I have spoken for myself and for a number of those present,' he finally said, then shrugged. 'But not for all, or so it seems. I would prefer to remain and build upon our successes, but I see that there are many who would not, and among you no few who might believe I would be exceeding the powers granted me by the governor of Cuba in so doing. Nor do I believe I could successfully lead a force divided in its heart . . .'

He paused, he sighed, he shrugged again. 'Therefore, I see nothing for it but to return to Cuba, and my orders are to make ready to do so, and board the ships and set sail for Cuba tomorrow,' he declared, then turned on his heel and stalked off to his tent leaving pandemonium behind him.

He scarcely had time to duck inside before it was surrounded by an outraged crowd of those who had counted themselves his friends and supporters, among them Olid, Puertocarrero, Sandoval, Alvarado, and of course Bernal Diaz, demanding he emerge to face their wrath.

'You have betrayed us!'

'You have listened to cowards rather than men who would serve the Cross and their King!'

'What would you have me do?' Cortes demanded. 'Remain here with half of my already modest forces? Order those who demand departure for Cuba to remain and risk an insurrection? Do you suppose this is to my liking, I, who have mortgaged my all to mount this expedition, and who, by the time the King, Velazquez and our company have taken their shares, shall have barely enough to redeem my debts? What else am I supposed to do? Speak out and tell me, or leave me in peace to nurse the wounds to my spirit and my finances which I have just been forced to inflict upon myself!'

The furtive manner in which the most forward of them exchanged uneasy and reluctant glances was choice to behold, no more so than for Cortes, who nevertheless managed to await what he knew was the inevitable with a sorrowful look painted on his face.

It was Cristobal de Olid who finally screwed up the courage to deliver his own stratagem to Hernando Cortes. 'Diego Velazquez is governor of Cuba and nothing more,' he said. 'He does not rule here, and has no mandate from the King to do so.'

'This is obviously so,' said Cortes, furrowing his brow in incomprehension, 'since it is Montezuma who rules here, and no other . . .'

'Who *presently* rules here,' said Alvarado. 'But if the King of Spain should replace him as sovereign of the lands of Mexico due to our . . . *persuasion,* what would that have to do with Diego Velazquez?'

'I still do not quite comprehend . . .' said Cortes.

Now Bernal Diaz spoke, delivering the words Cortes had put in his mouth through me. 'Since the Crown has given Diego Velazquez no more authority to establish a colony here than the governor of Cuba has granted you,' he said, 'only the King himself may grant such authority . . .'

'Well I suppose this is true,' said Cortes. 'But he is not here to do it, and it would take weeks or months for a letter to reach him and for him to send back such a legal grant, and we can hardly wait—'

'Then why do so?' said Puertocarrero. 'Establish a colony now *in the name of the King,* not Velazquez, and send a report back to Spain telling him what we have done, which is to say won him new lands and riches, and begging his authority to win him much more—'

'—accompanied by enough gold to whet the royal appetite for the much more!' said Alvarado.

'You see?' Diaz said earnestly. 'Surely His Majesty cannot be but greatly pleased, and surely he will hardly listen to any complaints from Velazquez, when by so doing you have done him such great good . . .'

Cortes actually scratched the whiskers of his chin thoughtfully at this, a gesture which I found a shade overdone, but which seemed to arouse the suspicion of no one else present.

'It sounds feasible as far as it goes,' he mused, 'but it seems impractical unless there is some way of changing the hearts of those who would return to Cuba . . .'

His eyes brightened with sudden inspiration, though at least he refrained from snapping his fingers.

'There may be a way,' he said. 'I cannot appoint myself governor and Captain-General of such a new colony, since Velazquez has granted me no such authority nor has the King given him the authority to do so, but a new *municipality* might not be stretching things too far . . .'

The recondite niceties of Spanish law distinguishing the foundation of a 'town' from that of a 'colony' were beyond my ken, but not that of Hernando Cortes, and apparently they allowed the Captain-General of an exploratory expedition to do so on his own authority, or at any rate that was the position that Cortes assumed when he called an unexpected general meeting before the Cross to announce a fait accompli.

'I have been prevailed upon by a delegation of our comrades to found a municipality on these shores, which shall be called—'

'You have no right to do any such thing!' shouted Francisco de Montejo, setting off an angry display of verbal outrage by the Velazquez partisans.

'Hear me out—'

Curses and shouts continued, but they emanated from no more than a quarter of those present, and when Pedro Alvarado roared 'Let him speak!', drawing his sword and brandishing it above his head, enough of Cortes' loyalists did likewise to produce the desired effect.

'The new town shall be called Villa Rica de Vera Cruz,' Cortes declared, 'for the town shall surely become a rich one, and its citizens dedicated to bringing the heathens of this land to the True Cross.'

'You still have no legal authority to do this!' insisted Diego de Ordaz, but his tone was more subdued than Montejo's had been, since it was apparent which side would emerge victorious if the vote should degenerate into one of arms.

'Vera Cruz shall be founded in the name of the Spanish Crown, which certainly has the authority to do so,' Cortes replied mildly.

'But the King has not conveyed this authority to you,' Montejo pointed out, as much in confusion as in outrage now.

'True,' said Cortes, 'and if His Majesty wishes to dissolve the municipality of Vera Cruz, abjuring the benefits of the royal fifth of all wealth obtained and the expansion of his territories, he certainly has the right and the power to do so, though it is difficult for me to imagine why he would want to.'

This brought a long silence produced more by befuddlement than anything else, including my own, for Hernando had now passed beyond the elements of this complex ploy vouchsafed to me, and I was as much at a loss to know what would come next as anyone else, including all of his partisans, to judge from the looks on their faces.

Cortes produced a piece of paper from which he read out the names of the men he was nominating as members of the town council, or regidores, the lowest and most numerous officers required of a municipality, these being chosen mostly but not entirely from among his own supporters, and easily enough approved by a majority vote.

By the time Cortes proceeded to higher offices, nominating Alvarado 'commander of expeditions', whatever that might mean, Olid quartermaster, Gonzalo Mejia treasurer, Juan de Escalante constable, and so forth, the Velazquez faction had long since come to realize that it would be outvoted every time, and chose to abstain with sullen silence.

Working from the bottom up, Cortes finally came to the alcalde, or alcaldes, which, dear reader, if you are no more familiar with these legalities than I was at the time, is the highest office of a Spanish municipality, the chief administrator or administrators, for there may be one, or more than one.

'In the interest of restoring harmony, I have decided to nominate two alcaldes, and I ask you to vote for or against both of them at once,' said Cortes. 'Alonso de Puertocarrero . . . and Francisco de Montejo!'

There was a stunned silence and then a great cheer, in which even some of the Velazquez partisans joined. Montejo himself looked as if he had been hit on the head with a club. I nearly burst out laughing in delight at this capstone to Cortes' magnificent edifice of intrigue.

'In favor?'

The cries of approval were of course the loudest yet heard.

'Against?'

Who could raise a voice in opposition now?

Surely, I thought, appointing one of the opposition's main ringleaders to the highest position was the ultimate disarming masterstroke.

But I was wrong.

Summoning the newly elected alcaldes forward, Cortes produced another document and handed it to Montejo.

'This is the document whereby Diego Velazquez, governor of Cuba, appointed me Captain-General of this expedition, and since its authority has now been superseded by that of the magistracy of Vera Cruz, I now must respectfully resign that position,' he said with the ghost of a little respectful bow, and he turned his back and walked away.

'I must confess I do not at all understand what you have just done, Hernando,' I told Cortes when I joined him in his tent, to find the former Captain-General enjoying a goblet of wine in high good humor.

Cortes laughed heartily, bade me be seated, and poured me some wine himself. 'I have quelled a rebellion, established a city which in effect will become a colony, and removed Diego Velazquez as the source of my authority.'

'What authority? You've just resigned as Captain-General.'

Cortes laughed. 'Oh, the municipal council I have arranged to have elected will re-appoint me Captain-General soon enough, since it is dominated by my own supporters, and I shall require the appointment to the office of Chief Justice as well before I so gracefully accept the onerous responsibility. And since the responsibility *will* be onerous, I think it only just that my share of all the gold and silver obtained be increased to, oh, let us say, the equivalent of the royal fifth.'

'But they'll never agree to increase your share at the expense of their . . .'

I caught myself short.

Cortes nodded. 'There will be plenty to go around out of his former share now that we are under the authority of the municipality of Vera Cruz rather than that of Diego Velazquez,' he said.

And so the city of Vera Cruz was founded before Cortes and most of its officers and citizens had even seen its eventual site by the harbor below Quiahuitzlan.

And so did Hernando Cortes seize sovereign power, or rather power under the direct authority of the sovereign himself, which, since the King would know nothing of what had happened for a good long while, in pragmatic terms amounted to the same thing.

And as fortune or God's Grace would have it, though we would not learn of it for the same good long while, on that very day, the previous holder of the title having expired, King Charles of Spain was elected Holy Roman Emperor.

Thus did Hernando Cortes accomplish this masterly coup based forthrightly on deceit without having to tell a single lie or deny a single truth himself.

11

CORTES' BRILLIANT COUP HAD infuriated the Velazquez faction once they realized what had come out the other side, while rendering his own partisans even more enthused about his leadership than before, and this angry contention had to be pacified before we could march or sail anywhere.

So while our preparations were under way, Cortes arrested a few of the most vociferous troublemakers, Diego de Ordaz and Velazquez de Leon among them, confining them to the ships to contemplate matters in calmer circumstances, and a goodly portion of the rest of the objectors were dispatched as an extended foraging and scouting expedition under Alvarado.

Cortes used the time awaiting the return of Alvarado to render the temporary tranquility more permanent. In this he was greatly aided by the cupidity for gold, for once those confined in the ships had the enforced leisure to reconsider things, they realized that the altered situation would result in greater shares of the proceeds for themselves than if Velazquez were still taking his overlarge share for doing nothing.

By the time Alvarado's expedition returned with a good supply of turkeys, vegetables, fruits, and even a few deer, even the most stalwart Velazquez supporters had been won over by their own greed, and the reconciliation was celebrated with a feast, such as had not been enjoyed for far too long.

Having no role to play in these events, I was free to attempt to extract the general lesson from the specifics of Cortes' most original coup. The whole thing had been based on deceit, but Cortes had avoided telling a single lie himself, and therefore the danger of ever being caught in one. But he had gone inventively beyond that by doing something that ached my mind when I attempted to encompass it.

He had caused others to 'force him' into doing what he wanted to do in the first place by denying that he had any intention of doing so. It wasn't quite lying, but rather refusing to acknowledge the truth, or at least a good enough Sophist, as Hernando certainly was, could so argue. More difficult to grasp, however, was his method of proceeding through the whole thing backwards, as it were.

I mention my wrestling with this concept because during this period I was spending many of my daylight hours with Marina, perfecting her Spanish and acquiring a bit more Nahuatl and listening to her complaints against Cortes' foolish and stubborn refusal to take advantage of what she and fortune had so artfully arranged and play the part of Quetzalcoatl.

'You have his . . . *ear*? you say?' she said as I was packing up my few belongings on the morning of our departure. 'You must talk to him, Alvaro.'

'I may have his ear,' I told her archly, 'but you are the mistress of his more . . . sensitive parts.'

'Pah! Mexica, or Totonac, or Tabascan, or Spaniard, men will not listen to . . . you say *strategic*? advice from a woman!'

'What would you have me tell him, exactly?'

'These Totonac caciques convince themselves to await Quetzalcoatl already, and Montezuma gives Hernando the . . . you say *vestments*? *finery*? *costume*? of Quetzalcoatl as a gift—'

'You're not seriously suggesting he march into Cempoala wearing the cloak and the serpent mask!' I exclaimed, all but bursting into laughter at the image her words inflicted upon my mind's eye.

'Of course he must wear the finery of Quetzalcoatl when he appears in Cempoala,' Marina told me in no little exasperation. 'You are as stupid about this as Hernando is, Alvaro!'

'It's ludicrous!' I told her. 'He'd make a fool of himself.'

'I know not what means *ludicrous*—'

'Silly. Ridiculous.'

'—but he'd make not a fool but a . . . not god . . . not hero . . . both . . . neither . . . ah!' She threw up her hands in linguistic frustration. 'You must help me with this word, Alvaro. Means maybe god, maybe Teule, maybe hero, maybe all, who comes to make things better, like . . . like Jesus Christ on the Cross!'

'*Savior?*'

'Yes, yes, one who comes to save people from . . . from *evil*. Jesus saves people from their own evil, and Christian papas promise he comes back when this world ends to bring new one that is better, yes?'

'More or less . . .'

'So Jesus is *savior*. Story, promise, legend that people believe, maybe because they want to believe, yes, says that Quetzalcoatl of the Toltecs comes back from where they have gone to save people from evil of Mexica and Montezuma, he is . . . *savior!*'

'More like . . . *messiah,* I'd say.'

Marina frowned at me. 'What is the difference?'

This question gave me pause, for while Marina had become my closest intellectual companion, she was not yet my lover, nor, given her history and forthright professions of self-serving pragmatism, was I yet about to trust her with the secrets of my identity. So this was a dangerous question, for who knew what might come up in the pillow talk between her and Cortes, and it cut to the heart of what distinguished the Jew from the Christian.

For while Jews still awaited the coming of the Messiah who would set both their spiritual well-being and their fallen worldly state right, Christians believed that the Messiah had already come in the form of Jesus Christ the Savior from Sin alone, which was perhaps why He had failed to convince the Jews that He was the Messiah, but which was enough for them, since their worldly state was doing quite well, thank you very much.

'Jesus is our Savior because He saves our souls from sin,' I told her as a good Christian. 'And some say He was therefore the Messiah,' the secret son of Abraham could not quite keep from adding.

'There can only be one?'

'Christians believe this, and so do another people called the Jews, but the Jews believe the Messiah who will . . . set things right has not come yet, since things are not yet set right. And then there are the Muslims whose Mohammed was a man and not a god or a Teule but nevertheless was their Messiah who founded both their religion and their empire . . .'

'Ah,' said Marina. 'Messiah can be man, god, Teule, depending on whose Messiah he is, but he must be . . . general leading warriors, not dead man on the Cross.'

'Uh . . . so at least the Muslims believe, though the Jews are not quite sure, and most Christians consider Christ the Prince of Peace even as they do battle in His name,' I muttered, anxious to get off this topic.

'Is simple. Jesus Christ is One and Only Savior and Christian Messiah. But Muslims have their own Messiah who already arrives and sets their world right, Jews wait for theirs, and Totonacs and the other . . . vassals of the Mexica wait for the Toltec Messiah, Quetzalcoatl.'

'I couldn't have explained it better myself,' I answered quite truthfully.

'So why can't you understand that Hernando must wear the finery of Quetzalcoatl to Cempoala?' Marina demanded.

'Because while it might impress the Totonacs, it would make him look a fool in the eyes of his own men.'

'Why such finery would make a man look foolish in *anyone's* eyes, I do not understand. The vestments of Quetzalcoatl are very rich and very beautiful, much more rich and beautiful than metal suits and cloth hats and . . . silly . . . you call the stupid things *pantaloons*?'

'And a mask making his face look hideously ugly?'

'Ugly!' Marina cried in indignant outrage. 'The serpent is . . . you say, what, *sign, picture, symbol*? of wisdom, and feathers . . . *signify*? power and beauty! So to put on the mask of Quetzalcoatl means to wear the face of beautiful and powerful wisdom! How can you call this ugly?'

Christian art, and that of the Romans and Greeks out of which it grew, sought to capture men and the world as they appeared to the eye. That much of the art of the civilizations of these Indians, and particularly their depictions of their gods, which struck our eyes as both ridiculous and loathsome, sought to depict not their physical forms but their *attributes*, as the Sephiroths of the Kabbalah are not 'gods' but represent aspects of the Ain-Soph, was a concept I would not even begin to understand until much later.

'I assure you that it would make him look both ugly and foolish in the eyes of the men he leads,' was the best that I in my ignorance could then manage.

'And I assure *you*, Alvaro, that wearing the vestments and the face of Quetzalcoatl would make him look beautiful and wise and powerful in the eyes of the men he *must* lead if those few he leads now are not to be crushed by the armies of the Mexica any time Montezuma decides to do it,' Marina insisted. 'If he will not wear the finery, cannot you at least . . . you say *persuade*? Hernando to *speak* as Quetzalcoatl?'

'But you have him doing that already in your translations.'

Marina laughed. '*You* know this, Alvaro, but not . . . *exactly* Hernando,' she said. 'Would be better if he could be allowed to know everything he was saying, no?'

I smiled at her. 'I'll try,' I told her. 'At least he hasn't denied it yet.'

The fleet finally sailed for Quiahuitzlan, and the rest of us began our march to the Totonac capital Cempoala, moving inland from the dunes and marshes of the beach onto a sere and sandy plain little less dismal, save for the welcome lack of mosquitoes. As I trudged across this grim and boring landscape enlivened only by a distant view of the ocean and the occasional glimpse of mighty snowcapped mountains, I had a surfeit of time in which to struggle with Marina's explanation of how the hideous head of a serpent with feathers sticking out of it could appear beautiful in the eyes of her people.

But *my* last words were what came to obsess me during that first day of the journey. For in truth, Cortes *had* not yet denied he was Quetzalcoatl. He might not have claimed it, but he hadn't denied it. And Cortes had so recently opened up to me the arcane possibility that one might *affirm* something by one's artful denial thereof, or better yet, by having others affirm it for you while you denied it with a wink and a nod.

Eager as I was to broach these matters to Cortes, he rode at the head of the column, and I trudged afoot in the train, and there was no opportunity to do so until we had encamped for the night.

The road we were following had bent inland, and there the country rose up and became less oppressively hot and dry, becoming cooler and humid enough to support a verdant green savanna, across whose expanse we could see the edge of a forest. We came to a river, forded it, and the sun beginning to set by the time we had, encamped on its far bank.

When supper had been prepared and eaten and all began to retire, I told Marina to make herself scarce for a time so that I might converse alone with Cortes.

I found him preparing their bedding before the entrance to his tent, for it was a clear and brilliantly starry night, the temperature balmy to the point of perfection, and there were sufficient trees growing along the riverbank to provide sturdy trellises for a species of vine whose abundance of small reddish flowers incensed the air with a sultry sweet perfume, so that even the most unromantic of lovers would not have wished to pass the night anywhere but outdoors.

Nor with me.

'What is it, Alvaro?' Cortes asked brusquely. 'As you can see, I am preparing for . . . other company.'

'A brief moment of your time on a matter of importance, since we are now on our way to Cempoala—'

'Marina sent you, did she not?' Cortes interrupted crossly. 'And I need not guess what this is about! She has been using her feminine wiles to try to convince me to collaborate in this blasphemous charade of hers, and now, failing that, has enlisted you in her campaign—'

'—as she would enlist Quetzalcoatl in yours. Why can you not see that it is a strategy which—'

'You really think I don't understand the strategic advantages?' Cortes said more calmly. He ceased his puttering with the bedclothes and favored me with his full attention. 'Of course I do. And you will notice that I have taken pains to avoid quite contradicting what I know full well she is broadcasting in her own language behind my back. But . . .'

'But what?'

Cortes sighed. 'But unfortunately there is my immortal soul to consider,' he told me. 'Surely we are both aware that to worship false gods or idols is a mortal sin.'

'You are serious?' I exclaimed.

'Can you imagine anything more serious than burning in Hell for eternity for committing a peculiarly Satanic form of blasphemous idolatry?'

This gave me pause. Not because I could take such Talmudic theological nitpicking seriously, but because I realized that this master dissembler actually did.

'But pretending to be Quetzalcoatl, who you do not believe is a god, is hardly to *worship* him,' I said carefully.

'Is it not? Or is it the invention of a new sin that is worse, worshipping *oneself* as a god?'

'You can hardly be taxed for that if you don't believe that Quetzalcoatl *is* a god!' I replied.

Cortes seemed to chew that one over thoughtfully. 'Perhaps . . .' he muttered. 'But by so doing, do I not lead others into idolatry and thus to Hell, and is that not even a worse sin?'

'But the natives here are committing that sin already,' I pointed out. 'And by telling a small lie, a venal sin at worst, in order to enlist them in a crusade that in the end would bring thousands of their souls to the True Faith, would you not be performing a mighty . . .'

I caught myself short, for the word I had been about to utter was 'mitzvah', and this was a Jewish term and concept for a selfless good deed whose performance, paradoxically, conferred great virtue upon the doer's soul, and this of course I could not say.

'. . . service to them and Christ?' I said instead.

Fortunately, Cortes did not seem to notice the pause. 'You tempt me, Alvaro,' he said slowly, regarding me as if I displayed the visage of a serpent, not the one with feathers, but he who, coiled in the branches of the Tree of Knowledge, had held out its forbidden fruit to Eve.

It was an uncomfortable moment, bordering on the dangerous, for I sensed that I had perhaps gone too far, or at any rate should go no further. Fortunately, at that moment, Cortes spied Marina approaching in the distance.

'But I see a much more pleasurable temptation about to arrive, and this one I certainly do intend to succumb to,' he said in quite a lighter mood, and the moment passed. 'Time for you to be gone, Alvaro.'

'Before I go, might I suggest a page from your own book, Hernando?' I said quickly, in a tone seeking to emulate his own. 'In your recent dealings with the schism between your supporters and those of Velazquez, you have shown me a new art . . .'

'How so?'

'You've demonstrated how it is possible to use others to promulgate something you wish to be believed and affirm it by the very exaggeration of your denial. Could you not see your way to doing likewise in this matter?'

'Perhaps it is you who should don the mask of the serpent, Alvaro, or perhaps you are wearing it already,' he said, but with a knowing grin and a little laugh that stifled my pang of fear. 'I'll tell you what, I'll set you a little task in the same spirit. As Captain-General, I dare not bring such a matter to one of our priests lest the very question cast my piety into doubt. But should *you* so dare, I would certainly be willing to take advantage of any favorable ecclesiastical dispensation.'

'Spoken like a well-feathered serpent already, Hernando,' I replied with a grin myself.

'We'll see about that later,' said Cortes, rising to greet Marina. 'But right now, I have better sins to attend to. So be gone!'

As our paths crossed, Marina cocked an interrogatory eyebrow, and I replied with the slightest shrug of my shoulders and the ghost of an ironic smile. No more than that. But then it was, I do believe, that something new began between us.

The next morning we followed the river inland and upland toward its source in the great mountains which we could vaguely discern peering over the horizon like a misty front of thunderheads. Here the savanna stepwise gave way to an idyllic tropical landscape luxuriating under a bright sun, but cooled and freshened by the presence of the river and the air tumbling down the slopes of the far mountains onto the gentle slope of the plateau rising to meet them. Palms and cacao trees grew in wild profusion along the riverbanks, and more widely separated copses across the plain, surrounded by a sea of cacti and flowering bushes, and overgrown by vines of wild grape, red roses and abundant honeysuckle, the atmosphere redolent of the sweet perfumes of the Islamic paradise or lost Eden. Brilliantly colored parrots, singly and in flocks, swooped and squawked, mockingbirds sang melodiously, clouds of butterflies drifted on the breeze like multicolored snowflakes or handfuls of celebratory confetti.

Balm for the soul it indeed was, but the pleasure of mine was clouded by the thought of the task that Cortes had set me, or more honestly that Marina had cozened me into setting for myself, namely that of playing an earnest game of theological wits with a Franciscan priest.

I had gone so far as to fix my sights on Father Olmedo, for broaching such subtleties to the likes of Father Diaz was out of the question, besides which Olmedo was the senior cleric, and so his dispensation, if I could secure it, would be definitive.

As you may well imagine, dear reader, I had kept a measured distance from our priests, attending mass, taking the sacraments, favoring them with boring confessions, but otherwise avoiding anything but the most trivial congress. But now, and soon, I must inveigle Olmedo into the deepest of discourses, and moreover, without either appearing to be speaking on behalf of Cortes or betraying my considerable knowledge of religions other than that of the Cross.

And so I temporized as I strolled through paradise towards Cempoala, working up both my courage and my arguments, until, at length, my opportunity arose in the midst of an unwelcome Satanic intrusion.

We had passed through several little villages situated by the source of fresh running water that the river provided, apparently abandoned in haste by their inhabitants as the word of our approach preceded us, for freshly dressed deer and fowl, clean and well laid-out items of clothing, cooking utensils and instruments, had been left behind, as well as censers, obsidian knives and the like in the huts adjacent to their modest stone temples.

But then we entered a village where a horror had been left behind. At the foot of its temple lay three corpses whose hearts had been ripped out. Worse, these bodies had been expertly butchered, their arms and legs hacked off at the pubis and shoulders, and should we harbor any doubt as to the use to which they had been put, there were the embers of a large cookfire, around which were strewn bones whose identity could not have been mistaken, even had there not been meat remaining on the fingers of two of the hands.

Our company made its way past this obscene midden in haste, most glancing at it quickly, then just as quickly looking away and moving on, but Father Olmedo stood before it for long moments muttering something under his breath, then producing a vial of oil, anointing the brows of the mutilated bodies with it, and offering up his prayer.

Seeing my opportunity, and also touched by this gesture, I came up beside him as he made the sign of the Cross, and did likewise myself.

'You give these poor heathen the benefit of Supreme Unction and Absolution after the fact of their deaths?' I said softly. 'This the Church allows?'

Olmedo sighed. 'Supreme Unction the Church does not exactly forbid under such circumstances, but as for Absolution, this no priest can grant to idolaters who died in utter ignorance of the grace of Our Lord, and I fear the only soul I have comforted is my own, for surely I have not saved theirs from the fires of Hell.'

He was a hard-faced man, but this display of a softness of heart softened my own heart towards him, and so, call it a kind of grace if you will, gave me the courage I thus far had lacked.

'But we must try to do whatever we can . . .' I ventured.

Olmedo nodded. 'I see you made the sign of the Cross on their behalf yourself,' he said, as, side by side, we turned our back on the awful sight and began to walk away.

'God, it would seem, has set you an arduous task, Father,' I said sympathetically, and in that moment not insincerely, 'and indeed perhaps an impossible one.'

'Nothing is impossible if God so wills it,' he told me. 'But still . . .'

'And poor Cortes perhaps a more difficult one still . . .'

'How so?' Olmedo demanded, fixing me with a sharp eye.

'As you know, I am something of a confidant of his, and while as Captain-General he must betray no doubt or qualm, I believe that as a Christian, his soul is uncertain and troubled.'

'This he confides to *you* rather than his confessor?'

'This he truly confides to no one, Father, for how can he? But I have been commissioned to help our translator learn our language better, in which capacity I have conversed with her extensively, and she has . . . had extensive converse with him, and so I have inferred, as it were, that he fears the consequences of the sin she would have him commit . . .'

'But he has confessed to his adultery, of course, since he has scarcely kept it hidden!' Olmedo exclaimed in confusion. 'And if he truly fears it will cost him his salvation, he need only cease committing it.'

'That is not the sin I am talking about, Father,' I told him, 'and if that were to condemn all men who commit it, repent, and commit it again, to Hell, I fear that Our Lord would suffer for lack of a Heavenly Chorus.'

Olmedo did well in stifling a laugh, and covered it by adopting a stern mien and a gruff tone of exasperation. 'Then what sin *are* you talking about?' he demanded.

'Perhaps something akin to the sin of Mohammed,' I told him, 'pretending to be more than a man, and leading others into the sins of blasphemy and idolatry.' This I knew to not be the truth, for Mohammed had never pretended to be more than a man, and the word 'Muslim' means 'slave of Allah', which is what all who profess that faith must be, his worldly Prophet included. But this, whether versed in the Koran or not, was a comparison a Christian priest would find meet.

'You speak of this pretense abroad that he is the return of this . . . this . . .'

'Quetzalcoatl.'

'Quetz-al-coatl,' Olmedo repeated, with difficulty in wrapping his tongue around it. 'As serpentine a sound as that which it names, a demon with the visage of a snake, indeed perhaps that of the Prince of Darkness himself, for as we have just so appallingly seen, these people are flagrantly in thrall to Satan!'

We had now put that Satanic sight well behind us and once more were strolling through a blissful tropical paradise enlivened by butterflies riding the zephyrs like the pure souls of the saved and gaily colored parrots that presented nothing but a pleasant sight if hardly a Heavenly Chorus as we descended into this theological pit.

'I think not,' I ventured.

'*You think* not? After what we have just seen!'

'Satan may indeed be abroad in these lands,' I told him, 'but he most certainly is not Quetzalcoatl. I have learned that the Mexica worship a monster they call Huitzilopochtli, who indeed may be the Devil, and while I know not who or what the Totonacs worship, they regard Quetzalcoatl as his *adversary,* as we regard Jesus!'

'*What?*' roared Olmedo. 'You dare compare this . . . this . . . Quetzalcoatl to the Christ!'

'No, no, no,' I assured him hastily. 'But *they* do, I think. To them, Quetzalcoatl was either a hero who, like Frederick Barbarossa, left behind the legend of a promise to return at his people's hour of need, or a deity like Jesus, who departed from their world with the promise to return as their . . . savior. Or somehow both.'

'Blasphemy!'

'That is the sin I believe Cortes fears committing by donning, as it were, the mantle of Quetzalcoatl.'

'But this he has not done . . . or has he?'

Now I had arrived at a most delicate pass. 'What troubles Cortes' soul, I believe, is that he does not know, nor do I, nor can we, for it is the woman who speaks for him, no one among us understands the language in which she speaks, and for all we know—'

'But if *she* tells this blasphemous lie, not Cortes, he is blameless! He need only forthrightly deny it!'

'His problem, Father, I think, is that he is not sure that he should, for by purging himself of that sin, he might be committing a greater one.'

'A greater one is hard to imagine!'

'Condemning thousands or even millions of souls to eternal damnation would be such a sin, would it not, Father Olmedo?'

As we conversed, our pace had slowed so that we had fallen behind the bulk of our company, and now Father Olmedo stopped, and bade me do likewise until the rest had passed.

'We seem to have fallen into grave matters, Alvaro de Sevilla,' he said after they had, and did not resume walking until we were bringing up the rear well out of earshot.

'Hernando Cortes may be a seeker after riches and glory, Father,' I said, 'but I do believe, and I believe that you believe too, that he has the soul of a true Christian whose highest duty here is to win souls away from Satan and damnation and to salvation through our Lord Jesus Christ.'

'I will grant him both,' Olmedo said somewhat owlishly, 'though perhaps I am less certain of the order of his priorities than you are.'

I shrugged in a comradely acknowledgement. 'Be that as it may, and no aspersion on your formidable persuasive powers, it seems plain that these people here cannot be brought to the Cross by persuasion alone, for they are as ignorant of our ways as we are of theirs, and it is like their papas trying to convert us to the worship of Huitzilopochtli.'

'But many of them have taken communion,' Father Olmedo protested rather weakly.

'Their gods are fed the bodies and the blood of men, Father, and as you might well imagine, they might be pleased at the thought of a God who offers up his own instead.'

'What are you trying to tell me?'

And now we had come down to it.

'I am certain that Cortes has concluded that before their souls can be brought to Christ, these Indians must be liberated from the yoke of Montezuma and Huitzilopochtli, and that this can only be accomplished by force of arms. And as anyone with the slightest knowledge of the military arts must realize, this cannot be done by five hundred Spaniards. And so, as Captain-General, he knows that he must raise the Totonacs against them.'

'And this might be accomplished were they to believe that he was their . . . awaited savior, Quetzalcoatl.'

'There you have it.'

Father Olmedo stopped dead in his tracks.

'And you would have me absolve him of any sin in so doing?'

I nodded.

We stood there silently for a long moment, regarding the tiny force of Christians marching away through the beauteous tropical paradise, a feast for the eyes and ears and nostrils, which, nevertheless, in that moment seemed haunted by the hidden demons and minions of Satan. At its head rode a lone man on horseback towards whatever he would confront in Cempoala.

'You are a good man and a good friend to him, Alvaro de Sevilla,' Father Olmedo said, 'but I do not see how I can do such a thing.'

'Could you not at least absolve him of the sin of not denying it?' I pleaded.

'And allow it to fall upon the woman?'

'She is willing. She has shouldered it already.'

'It is a hard thing you ask of me, Alvaro de Sevilla. Indeed you ask me to take upon my own soul the very decision you would lift from that of Cortes.'

'Is that not why you are a priest?' I said.

The wan smile of this priest of a Church which had burned countless numbers of my brethren and who would have burned me had he known who and what I was nevertheless touched my heart to the point where I would have been less than the Christian I was not, and even less the Jew that I was, if I did not have it in my own soul to risk all by attempting to grant him the absolution I sought for Hernando Cortes.

'I am not a learned man,' I lied, 'and the Jews are a fallen people. But I was once told a tale by a child of Abraham of a rabbi who was asked whether it was a sin to break the laws of their sabbath in order to save a life, be it that of a Jew or an unbeliever. And the rabbi replied that there was no greater virtue than to do so, and by so doing, take a sin upon one's own soul in order to save another.'

Father Olmedo seemed to look right through me, through all my artifices and pretensions, straight to the secrets of my soul.

'So be it,' he said. 'You are . . . a better man than you might think, Alvaro . . . de Sevilla.'

Our eyes locked and something seemed to pass between us.

But he said nothing more.

'This rabbi was a Jew, and an unbeliever, and no doubt would have denied it at the very stake, but I do believe that Jesus Christ spoke through him,' I told him. 'And so, I do believe, has He now spoken through you, Father Olmedo.'

And in that moment, I, who was no true Christian, nevertheless somehow did believe it.

12

WE FOLLOWED THE RIVER inland and upland during most of the rest of the day, passing by a few more deserted villages but skirting them without entering for fear of encountering further horrors.

When we paused for lunch, I observed Cortes deep in conversation with Father Olmedo, and before we resumed our march I was able to speak with Hernando briefly and confirm that he had indeed received the dispensation that I had secured for him, albeit with the caveat that he was never to go so far as to wear any of the items of finery of Quetzalcoatl, nor to call himself by that name.

Our spirits had been darkened by the sight of the remains of that cannibal feast, and as we continued to march through the paradisiacal country, the very beauty of it seemed to mock us, as if every stand of wild roses had been fertilized by blood, every parrot's squawk might be the shriek of a Satanic demon, every flowering tree hid its lurking serpent.

As the sun waned, our train was approached by a party of some dozen Totonacs, and Cortes' first reaction was to call a halt and order the crossbowmen and arquebusiers to load and cock their weapons. But when they reached us, they proved to be bearing heavy loads of flat breads, bean mash, dressed turkeys, and pulque for our pleasure, and words of welcome and greeting from Tlacochcalcat, the paramount cacique of Cempoala, and hence, in effect of the Totonacs, who had sent them to guide us directly to the city.

This pleasant surprise, a good dinner under a splendid sunset outlining the distant mountain range in gorgeously luminous golden orange, and a sweet sleep under a brilliant starscape, went a long way to erasing foul memories, and in the morning our march away from the river and directly to Cempoala became a high-spirited parade along a kind of highway through a well-tended and most fruitful farmland of orchards and fields of both food crops and a dazzling assortment of cultivated flowerbeds.

Both men and women turned out to greet and observe our spectacle, and better dressed than anything we had yet seen; the women wearing long white cotton gowns dyed in complex and brightly colored patterns, the men in cloaks of a similar style over their loincloths, and both wearing gold earrings, necklaces and nose rings. They were also heavily bedecked with wreaths of flowers, and carrying more, which they put around our necks as we passed, so that we proceeded in a cloud of floral perfumes, in a gaily good-natured parody of a Roman triumphal procession.

Cempoala was an impressive metropolis. The public edifices were of well-dressed stone or well-crafted brick whitened with stucco, the ordinary houses of adobe similarly whitened and thatched with fresh green palm fronds, and the main avenues were laid out in a regular grid centered on several plazas, while the smaller streets, though narrow and more chaotically arranged, were clean and orderly after their more modest fashion, and their districts not at all the foul-smelling warrens all too common in such environs in Europe.

How many inhabitants Cempoala boasted I know not, but judging by the number of people crowding the streets of our passage to watch the parade, there were certainly some tens of thousands, and whether this was their everyday custom or reserved for such gala occasions, all of them were awash in flowers, headily perfumed red roses dominating.

We were led through the city to the residence of the paramount cacique, a large single-storied white edifice embellished with colored frescos and made grander by being built upon a kind of truncated pyramidal platform like the lower third of one of their temples, its entrance approachable by a flight of stone stairs.

Tlacochcalcat honored us by descending these to greet us, no mean feat, if not on his part, for he was enormously fat and borne on a feather-bedecked and umbrella-shaded litter by half a dozen men who had quite a time carrying their burden down some dozen or more steeply pitched steps.

Cortes, to his credit, managed to watch this with a solemn mien, an impressive diplomatic feat in itself, though many of us, myself I must confess among them, were less successful in stifling our mirth.

Once safely delivered, however, Tlacochcalcat, through Marina, delivered a dignified enough greeting, which Cortes returned in kind without any mention of Quetzalcoatl in either Spanish or Nahuatl, or so Marina assured me later, and we were then escorted to suitably spacious, if not entirely ecclesiastically correct, quarters.

These were a series of apparently priestly apartments in low buildings surrounding a large courtyard on three sides, the fourth being ominously occupied by a towering and glowering temple. But no papas were in evidence, and the apartments themselves had been scrupulously cleaned and fumigated with incense. Here a veritable banquet was laid on, meats and fowl both roasted and served in a variety of piquant sauces which hopefully did not dress the flesh of humans, along with the usual bean mash, maize breads and pulque, as well as a judicious offering of the sweet and invigorating frothy brown chocolatl. Gifts of cotton cloth and gold jewelry were also presented, which, like the chocolatl, while satisfying, also served to whet a thirst for much more.

Despite this royal welcome, Cortes positioned the small cannon so as to cover the entrances to the courtyard and posted a guard for the night, and we passed the night wondering nervously at our good fortune, for these Totonacs, though they chafed under the yoke, were vassals of the great Montezuma, who had enjoined us at the coast to proceed no further.

Was Tlacochcalcat, despite his comical appearance, a heroic would-be rebel, or was all this a velvet trap but awaiting the word of Montezuma to be sprung?

As Montezuma was to explain to me later, it was a little of both and quite a bit of neither.

'It was I, of course, who ordered Teuhtlile to withdraw provisions from the Teules and avoid further contact with them when they refused to leave Totonaca, and he did obey, which lightened my heart, but Tlacochcalcat's invitation to Cempoala, if not quite against my orders, was certainly against what he must have known would be my wishes,' he told me so many great and terrible events later. 'And the tidings that Malinche had chosen the finery of Quetzalcoatl from what had been offered him, and worse still, then proceeded to don them, vexed me severely. Still more when I was shown *this*!'

And he produced a most peculiar painting of Christ on the Cross. It was recognizably a bearded Jesus, but the Crown of Thorns was replaced by one of quetzal feathers, the bleeding wound that should have been in His side was moved to where His heart would have been were it not a gaping hole, and the nose was a mere pair of reptilian nostril slits, the mouth lipless, and the browless eyes clearly those of a serpent.

'I do not quite understand,' I lied, but when he explained, it turned out to be the truth.

'This, I was told, was one of the idols of their god which they set up everywhere, and behold, it displayed the attributes of Quetzalcoatl! And what their papas proclaimed was that this was the Son of their paramount god, whose name they did not know or feared to pronounce, and their Virgin Goddess; a god himself, who had been offered up as a sacrifice, but who would return one day to end this world and bring a better next one. And that all who did not bow down to him then would be sacrificed to a terrible demon called Satan.

'If this was Quetzalcoatl, and he had truly returned, how could I oppose him, for not only would I surely fail, it would be a terrible wrong, for which I and all the Mexica would be sacrificed to Satan, nor would ours be an honorable flowery death, but punishment for disobeying the will of all of the gods, not only Huitzilopochtli, but the gods of the Totonacs and the Texcocans, the Tabascans and the Cholulans, and all the vassals of Mexico.'

'*All* of them?'

Montezuma's eyes grew furtive, as the eyes of this Emperor who ruled all he surveyed of his earthly realms so often did when he entered these celestial waters. 'Each of these nations may be favored by its own god, and we war against each other at their command to secure hearts and blood to feed them, but the gods do not war among themselves. Indeed . . .'

He paused. His eyes now seemed haunted. 'Nezahualcoyotl, the great King of Texcoco, was not great because he was a great leader in war, for in the end, he must be restored to his rule by us, so beginning the Triple Alliance led by the Mexica,' he told me, 'but rather because he was a great poet and . . . delver of the mysteries. And he proclaimed that the gods as we know them are but the children or the . . . masks of a greater and singular god whose name and aspect men may not know—'

'The Ain-Soph!' I exclaimed.

Montezuma regarded me with lidded incomprehension.

'Others have believed thusly,' I told him. 'But please do go on . . .'

'Not many others believed what Nezahualcoyotl declared nor understood it, nor do I truly understand, but I am not sure he was wrong, and if so . . . if so, to oppose the will of one god is to oppose the will of this greater one and so of all, is it not? Worse still if that god is Quetzalcoatl.'

'How so?'

Montezuma's mien became stranger still, he seemed consumed with some arcane combination of fear, envy, what might even have been shame. 'Quetzalcoatl is the god of the *Toltecs!*' he proclaimed, as if that explained everything.

'The Toltecs came before us,' he went on when he saw that it didn't, 'the fathers of us all, who created the arts of architecture and painting and sculpture and the writing of codexes, and passed on all the knowledge of their world to us when it ended, as all worlds must, a world that was greater and finer than this one. The Toltecs departed with their world, but gods do not die, and when Quetzalcoatl departed to the east with them, he left behind a promise, like that of Jesus the Christ, to return one day to bring back that greater and better world.'

'You are saying that Jesus and Quetzalcoatl may be one and the same?'

Montezuma shrugged. 'If Nezahualcoyotl was right, are not all gods one and the same, or perhaps . . . masks worn by the god who is the one and only?'

His discourse had become breathtaking, and I longed to speak to him of the Kabbalah and the Ain-Soph and the Sephiroths, but of course I dared not, for he was then also in the habit of conversing with Cortes, and the moment passed as he descended to more worldly matters.

'Yet would a god display such open greed for gold and conquest? And would a mere man possessed of both such greed and the knowledge I have just vouchsafed to you not use it to his own advantage? What must I do? I had to know before either laying my empire at the feet of the true Quetzalcoatl of the Toltecs or destroying an imposter. Of course, I knew I must do what Huitzilopochtli would have me do, but though I offered him two hundred hearts, and the blood from my own tongue and penis, he refused to either speak to my heart or provide me with any omen. And so . . .'

'And so?'

'And so I must use other means to persuade Huitzilopochtli to speak clearly, or if he still would not, at least provide an omen myself . . .'

And so Montezuma did, though on that first night in Cempoala, neither I nor Cortes nor any of us was aware of the mission he dispatched to seek it out, let alone of the alien theological depths behind it.

The next morning, Cortes was summoned to the residence of Tlacochcalcat, and, taking precautions, arrived not only with Marina and myself, but a guard of some fifty men. Tlacochcalcat, while not making the arduous descent of the stairs to greet us, sent down well-dressed and feathered nobles to garland Cortes with roses and usher the entire party up them and into a central courtyard where Cortes, thus reassured, was persuaded to leave his guards behind, and he, Marina and myself proceeded through a long hallway past many apartments, and into what in Europe might have been deemed a sort of throne room.

The walls were hung with bright featherwork tapestries depicting fabulous creatures and bizarre gods. The corpulent Tlacochcalcat reclined on a couch covered with the spotted pelt of something like a leopard, and while none such were supplied to us, the stone floor was well padded with petatl mats, and servants brought each of us a small silver cup, into which chocolatl was decanted from earthenware jugs as quickly as they were emptied, which was frequently during the entire proceedings.

Tlacochcalcat himself consumed the delicious and invigorating brown liquid almost continually, slurping down his cup of the frothy stuff in a gulp or two, after which it was speedily refilled with more. Through Marina, he introduced himself as the paramount cacique of all the Totonacs, boasting that his nation comprised some thirty towns and villages and could field some hundred thousand warriors, a daunting figure if it were to be entirely believed.

He then paused to invite Cortes to do likewise, and Cortes, in Spanish, warned Marina to take care to translate accurately this time and add no untoward embellishments.

'I am the Captain-General of an expedition dispatched by . . . a great ruler across the sea, who having been informed of . . . the situation prevailing here, and being of noble heart, has sent us to . . . provide succor and enlightenment to the suffering people thereof,' he began carefully. 'And while our numbers may seem small in comparison to your mighty armies, the Tabascans have learned that they are quite sufficient to overcome forces of a similar size, for we are possessed of . . . arts and power unknown to this land, and moreover, are . . . servants of . . . the One True God, whose will it is that we shall always prevail, and whose . . . powers pass beyond all human understanding.'

Tlacochcalcat digested this with another cup of chocolatl before speaking again. 'I have been informed of what transpired at Potonchan, and this is what has aroused my interest,' he said. 'But how are you to be addressed?'

This was a delicate pass, for while Cortes was under Father Olmedo's dictum not to call himself 'Quetzalcoatl', calling himself 'Hernando Cortes' would be to deny what was politic here not to deny, and he and Marina engaged in a rapid consultation in Spanish, as if this were a delicate problem in translation, as indeed it was.

'I should tell him we call you "Malinche", which means something like the "Captain" you are in Nahuatl,' she told Cortes.

What she did not tell him was that 'Marina' tended to become 'Malina' in that tongue, and that 'Malinche' could have the punning connotation of '*Malina's* Captain' in this context, for it was Malina who was the voice of Malinche, and it was both disrespectfully amusing and the cause of a kind of awe to the Nahuatl speakers that such a great leader did not deign to address them directly but spoke through an intermediary, albeit a mere woman, as might a god.

This Tlacochcalcat accepted with a somewhat bemused and consternated expression when she put it into Nahuatl for him. 'And is your god, then, simply called "God"?' he asked in a similar vein.

When this was translated to Cortes, he all but heaved a sigh of relief. 'Tell him that this is exactly so, for in truth there is no other.'

What Marina said in Nahuatl I do not know, but Tlacochcalcat regarded Cortes with unmistakable pity. 'How unfortunate,' he replied sympathetically. 'For we have gods who, properly fed, supply us with sunshine and rain, who cause the crops to grow, and the hunt to succeed, and the animals as well as ourselves to bring forth young, and surely this must be too much to ask of your poor single god.'

'Tell him that while his gods demand hideous human sacrifices and are demonic lies of Satan, ours is the One True God, who offered up His Only Son to save us,' Cortes demanded hotly of Marina when this was translated.

'You must not insult him with this!' Marina insisted.

'Well then tell him that we have been sent to bring knowledge of . . . this God to his people, and once they have understood it, they will come to . . . love him.'

Shaking her head ruefully, Marina complied this time, though no doubt glossed it more smoothly in Nahuatl, for Tlacochcalcat passed on to other matters.

'This succor your King offers to us interests me more than his offer of enlightenment,' he said, 'for we suffer greatly as the unhappy tributaries of the mighty and terrible Mexica, whom we must propitiate with heavy taxes in cotton and cacao and feathers and even gold, and worse, in hearts to feed Huitzilopochtli, which only makes him more rapacious and the Mexica stronger, lest the invincible armies of the great Montezuma sweep down upon us and exact a vengeance too terrible to be imagined.'

Cortes' ears pricked up at this. 'I assure you that we have been sent to relieve you of such outrages, and neither God nor my King would ever allow us to commit such atrocities,' he told Tlacochcalcat, 'and as for Montezuma's invincible armies, the Tabascans too believed their armies invincible until they so foolishly presumed to match arms with *us.*'

Tlacochcalcat seemed to consider this with great interest. 'We are not the only province subservient to the Mexica who suffer so, and even the Tlascalans, a nation of great warriors whose lands lie between us and the Mexica and who have never been conquered by them, are maintained in such a state by Montezuma's forbearance only so that he may war with them at his pleasure and Huitzilopochtli's need in order to secure a sure supply of warriors to meet the flowery death on his altars and so furnish him with noble warriors' hearts . . .'

He paused to regard Cortes skeptically. 'Your King would put an end to this?' he asked.

'If he would not, I would not be here,' replied Cortes.

'And what would he demand in return for so great a service?' Tlacochcalcat asked even more skeptically.

'Only that you accept him as your sovereign and swear allegiance as his vassals and make the One True Faith your own.'

'No tribute would be required?'

'A certain amount of gold and other goods to be agreed upon as is always customary in such arrangements across the sea, even as here,' Cortes assured him blithely.

'No hearts for the altar of your god?'

'No hearts for the altar of *our* god,' Cortes told him with heartfelt sincerity, 'for the Heart of Jesus Christ bleeds for *us*, and not the other way around.'

Tlacochcalcat's eyes widened at this, no doubt in astonishment and perhaps disbelief, but also, as it turned out, with a certain cautious interest, for while he did not straightaway abandon his forced allegiance to Montezuma and swear allegiance to the Spanish sovereign, he not only told Cortes that he would take all he had heard under careful consideration, but gave us friendly leave to proceed to Quiahuitzlan and establish a settlement there and provided us with some four hundred tamanes to carry our baggage.

And so the next day we made a swift passage through the rich and fruitful lands of the Totonacs to the cliffs above the harbor where the fleet had long since made anchor and where Quiahuitzlan was situated commanding it. We were welcomed much as we had been in Cempoala, being greeted before it by a party of nobles garlanding us with roses, but Cortes declined their offer of quarters, preferring to descend to the beach to quarter our main force with the landing party from the ships via a steep path quarried down the cliff face.

Having delivered the glad tidings of Tlacochcalcat's permission to site the municipality of Vera Cruz there, and after seeing to the unloading of the ships and the beginning of its construction the next morning, Cortes, Marina, myself and a small formal guard made the arduous ascent back up to the city a bit after noon.

We were escorted to the only plaza of this smaller town. There was a temple at one side and market stalls around the other three, offering maize, vegetables and fruits, cotton and agave cloth, turkeys and other such merchandise, all neatly and logically laid out in sections devoted to each. The central area had been cleared out to make room for a general civic convocation.

A semicircle of petatl mats had been put down on the bare earth before the temple steps upon which were seated some dozen or so caciques in their feathered finery, and more set out for us facing them. Our dozen guards, though, were constrained to seat themselves on the bare earth behind us.

The rest of the square was crowded with curious onlookers, men and women both, and even children; some as well dressed as the caciques, but more than not wearing only simple cotton shifts for the women and similar cloaks and loincloths for the men, indeed many of the men wearing loincloths alone.

The conference began with the usual formalities, the caciques being introduced by names which I have long since forgotten, and Cortes, via Marina, introduced in the judicious manner adopted at Cempoala. Cortes thanked them for their friendship and hospitality, assured them of our beneficent intent, and then began an exchange of questions and answers, of which, in terms of useful knowledge gained, we got much the better of the bargain.

The caciques of Quiahuitzlan learned that we were the envoys of a mighty monarch across the sea and servants of the One True God come to liberate them from servitude to the Mexica and the darkness of Satanic superstition, and that we had the military force with which to do so – no more than a reiteration of what they knew already.

But under the clever questioning of Cortes, greatly aided by Marina's wider and deeper knowledge of matters on this side of the ocean, we learned much of military and political value.

We learned that what the Mexica ruled and what we confronted was a complex empire of many peoples who more or less considered themselves separate subject nations, subdued and made vassals by Mexica military might, subject to onerous levies of goods and blood, kept loyal to Montezuma and the Mexica by fear alone, and certainly not by anything like love.

We learned that the heartland of the Mexica empire was Anahuac, the great Valley of Mexico, which lay across the lofty range of mountains to the southwest, and that the center of this valley was occupied by a large lake or series of lakes on whose shores were several cities subservient to the Mexica, and two cities, Tacuba and Texcoco, which were their unequal partners in something known as the Triple Alliance.

We also learned that the Empire of the Mexica was a comparatively recent construction in historical terms, only a century or two old perhaps, and that the Texcocans, their ally, while a secondary military power, were admired as a more cultivated and sophisticated people than the Mexica, a more direct and worthy heir of the venerated Toltecs.

It seemed to me that we had stumbled upon no simple barbarian empire, but a political situation as complex as that of Spain during the long decades of the Reconquest and then some, with all the rivalries of Europe itself, and with a history equally long and perpetually fluid.

From the expression with which Cortes took all this in, he was of like mind, but its eager avidity betrayed a judgement which I did not quite share – that the empire of Montezuma was restive, ripe for rebellion, and ready for easy conquest.

One item of information, however, gave even his ebullient spirit pause. The Mexica had not built their great capital, Tenochtitlan, on the shores of the lake. Instead, it was somehow built in or above the lake itself, connected to the mainland only by a few narrow and easily defended causeways, and therefore entirely impregnable.

All this was informative and fascinating, but there was a preliminary air about these proceedings, as if the caciques were passing the time with tale-telling while waiting for the real business of the meeting to begin, something with which I was all too familiar from the court of Boabdil.

At considerable length, this was proven true when Tlacochcalcat himself arrived amidst much commotion, preceded by a phalanx of warriors, and borne on his litter, accompanied by servants who perfumed his way with incense. The litter was set down before the caciques, and no sooner had this been accomplished than more servants began preparing chocolatl, with which he was well supplied throughout, nor did he ever deign to rise from it to speak.

And when he began to speak, it was the caciques he addressed, not Cortes, or so Marina told us, for this could not be discerned from his posture, since he made no attempt to turn to face them.

He began with a series of greetings and ceremonial niceties which Marina did not bother to translate, and then finally got down to the subject at hand.

'We have long suffered under the cruel and greedy levies of the Mexica, our goods going to enrich Montezuma, and the blood and hearts of our best young warriors feeding Huitzilopochtli, and now this . . . Malinche has appeared among us, with a tiny band of warriors which has nevertheless by magic defeated the great army that the Tabascans raised against him, offering us salvation from the Mexica if only we will swear our fealty to his . . . King across the sea and worship his god,' he began, at which Cortes' eyes lit up with anticipation and murmurings swept the semicircle of caciques.

'Malinche promises us that if we do so, the tribute required of us will be lighter, nor will it include the flesh and the blood of our warriors to feed his god to keep him powerful,' he went on, 'for, or so it is claimed, his god is already so all-powerful that he needs no such nourishment, and indeed offers up his own blood and flesh to his worshippers instead.'

On hearing this, the caciques gasped, and the intake of breath spread to the surrounding crowd, leaving in its wake a vast breathless silence.

'But the Totonacs have not submitted to the Mexica because we are cowards, but because, having fought them, we have learned all too well that we cannot stand against them, for their armies are greater than anything we can raise, and Tenochtitlan cannot be taken by anyone. And against this that we know, we have only the promise of . . . Malinche . . .'

Tlacochcalcat paused, and now, with great effort, he half-turned his enormous bulk so that he was facing his caciques as he spoke. 'And so now, the Totonacs face the most fateful decision we have ever been forced to make, and I do not believe myself wise enough to make it alone. Do we remain unwilling tributaries of the Mexica, or do we swear a new allegiance to Malinche and his King? If we remain as we are, we may be refusing a great good change in our fortunes. But if we choose Malinche, and his promises prove false, or his powers insufficient, the Totonacs will surely be destroyed utterly, for Montezuma's wrath would be greater than any fury this world has ever known, his vengeance terrible, and all of our hearts, down to the last of our children, will be fed to Huitzilopochtli.'

The caciques began shouting to each other in a cacophony that Marina was powerless to translate, while Tlacochcalcat turned his back on them once more, and slurped down another cup of chocolatl. In a minute or two, the word of what was being angrily debated spread to the crowd, and the din became enormous.

On and on it went, until at length Cortes rose from his petatl, whipped out his sword, and waved it furiously as high above his head as he could reach for all to see. When this failed to accomplish anything, he turned to his guards, three of whom were armed with arquebuses, and ordered them to fire a volley without shot in their barrels.

The thunderous roar and the billowing acrid smoke produced the desired silence.

What Cortes would have spoken into it no one shall ever know, for before he could, there was a great commotion at the eastern edge of the square, and the Totonacs hastily parted to make way for five men, whom, by appearances, they regarded as they might the advent of a conquering army, even though they were accompanied by but a few attendants armed only with fans to brush away insects and censers to perfume their passage.

These lordly creatures languidly minced their way through the parting crowd towards the caciques as if merely touching the ground with their sandals was an offense to their dignity. Their long lustrous black hair was tied up atop their heads and adorned with quetzal feathers, their cloaks were entirely feathered, and they wore golden jewelry in their ears, noses and lips, and heavy necklaces of gold set with slabs of blue-green turquoise. Their noses, held high in the air, were yet buried in enormous bouquets of roses encircled by smaller blue flowers, as if not even the cloud of incense in which they moved was sufficient to shield them from the stink of common humanity.

Only Tlacochcalcat maintained anything like a semblance of dignified tranquility, ordering up another cup of chocolatl with a negligent wave of his hand, and sipping at it slowly as they approached, passing directly in front of Cortes without appearing to even notice his existence, and their apparent leader began addressing him and his caciques in a Nahuatl dripping with arrogance even to those of us who did not understand its words.

A slow red blush rising to his cheeks betrayed Cortes' fury as he bent down to demand of Marina who these men were and what they were saying.

'These are . . . you would say . . . Montezuma's gatherers of tribute—'

'Tax collectors,' I interrupted. 'Who else could be so hated and feared!'

'—and they are telling these caciques how angry Montezuma is at the hospitality they have given you when he commanded you to be gone.'

'Are they?' Cortes growled, his hand twitching and clenching as it slid towards the hilt of his sword.

Tlacochcalcat's face now displayed a fearful and protesting outrage as he exchanged words with the chief tax collector.

'What now?' Cortes demanded of Marina.

'As punishment, Montezuma demands twenty more warriors to sacrifice to Huitzilopochtli.'

At this, Cortes' hand tightened around the hilt of his sword as if it had a will of its own, and perhaps it did, or at least a wisdom, as if it too understood what I immediately realized.

'Arrest the tax collectors!' I hissed at him. 'Nothing is more sure to win a man favor anywhere than that!'

'Indeed!' cried Cortes, drawing his sword, at which our guards leapt to their feet with theirs, and the arquebusiers, without need of an order, trained their weapons on the Mexica, who now were forced to acknowledge our existence.

'Tell Tlacochcalcat and his caciques that . . . Malinche and his King forbid all such Satanic sacrifices,' he commanded Marina, 'and therefore these evil men must be seized and held under arrest until the proper punishment for such an outrageous demand is decided.'

When this was translated, Tlacochcalcat blanched, his caciques shrank back in terror, and the tax collectors, their faces contorted more in fury than fear, began expressing it at the top of their lungs all at once.

'SILENCE!' roared Cortes in the loudest voice I had ever heard, so loud that even though it was in Spanish, no translation was needed to achieve, at least momentarily, the desired effect.

'We cannot do such a thing,' Tlacochcalcat said in a craven whine, which, though Marina did provide a translation, likewise needed none to make its import plain. 'Montezuma would slay us all!'

Cortes, motioning for Marina to attend him, now strode up to Tlacochcalcat's litter, straight past the tax collectors – and now it was *he* who imperiously deigned not to acknowledge *their* existence – leaned close to Tlacochcalcat and beckoned Marina to do likewise so that they could not hear.

When she later told me what had been said, I understood that in such matters, Hernando Cortes was subtler than I, if only because more pragmatically ruthless.

'Arrest these men in the name of the Totonacs, and I will protect you from Montezuma and liberate the Totonacs from his terrible rule, and you will be a hero to your people as long as the tale is told,' he told Tlacochcalcat. 'If you do not, I will be forced by the Will of God to slay them right here and now with the thunder and lightning you have just seen, and then it will be a war to the death between the Mexica and my army with neither of us having a care for the fate of the Totonacs.'

And then he clapped a comradely arm around the shoulders of Tlacochcalcat. 'Be brave, my good friend,' he cooed in an abrupt change of tone, 'and my all-powerful God will protect you as He protects me, for as surely as the sun rises in the east and sets in the west,

God sends the right, and marches into battle with the righteous.' And then he withdrew.

Tlacochcalcat sat there silent and immobile for a long moment. Then he motioned to a servant for a cup of chocolatl, which he slowly sipped until it was drained.

And then, even more slowly, and with an arduous and heroic effort, he raised his ponderous bulk to its feet and managed to stand shakily upright.

'Arrest these Mexica and bind them,' he declared, and sank back onto his litter with a great sigh of exhaustion.

13

FORCING TLACOCHCALCAT TO arrest Montezuma's tax collectors was a ruthless masterstroke, for with it Cortes made war between Montezuma's forces and the Totonacs seemingly inevitable and himself their only protector. Tlacochcalcat forthwith swore an oath of fealty to the far-off King of Spain, and caciques from their towns and villages swarmed in terror into Quiahuitzlan to ratify it and so shelter under the protection of 'Malinche'.

Tlacochcalcat and the assembled caciques were of the unanimous opinion that there remained only one chance, however improbable, of evading the wrath of Montezuma, namely to kill the captured tax collectors in secret, so that there would be no one to carry the tale of what had happened back to Tenochtitlan, and they might claim when inquiries came from there that they must have suffered a misfortune along the way of which the Totonacs were innocently ignorant.

But Cortes reminded them that since the tax collectors' servants had fled in the confusion and thousands of people had seen them arrested, such a ridiculous lie would have no chance to be believed, would only make Montezuma even more furious, and since these men were his nobles, they might at least at some point prove useful as hostages.

When this was pointed out, they quickly came to their senses, though if anything, their terrorized state became worse, which perhaps had been Cortes' intent, and which he used to stunning advantage.

'If you fear to hold these men lest Montezuma discover that you have them, I do not,' he told them. 'So I will guard them for you, and let Montezuma presume to attempt to take his vengeance on *me*, which would only be to his sorrow.'

The sighs of relief at this all but produced a wind that shook the fronds of the palm trees. But two nights later, Cortes had two of the prisoners secretly brought to him, and released them with a truly outrageous lie to carry to Montezuma. Nor was that the end of his breathtaking dissembling.

The next morning, the Totonacs were outraged and terrified at the news of this 'escape', and Cortes pretended to be even more furious. He straightaway ordered the 'incompetent' guards to be hauled off to imprisonment on one of the ships, where, of course, they were immediately released.

The three remaining prisoners were then chained together and likewise dragged off to a ship, where, Cortes assured Tlacochcalcat, they would be so secure that the Totonacs would never be constrained to set eyes on them again. This was a promise that Cortes did keep, after his own fashion, for he soon thereafter released *them* as well from a boat up the coast, without the Totonacs ever knowing what had happened.

And what, you ask, was the message sent back by these means to Montezuma? I fear, dear reader, you would scarcely believe it if I told you. Best you hear it in the words of Montezuma himself, recorded by me during his captivity:

'I was naturally furious, as surely any man would be. Though perhaps, I reasoned when my full reason returned, the Totonacs, hardly famed for excessive and foolhardy bravery, had probably been forced into their seizure of my tax collectors and rebellion against me by this . . . Teule who called himself by the title of "Malinche" who had, by guile and fear of his magical weapons, made them fear him more than me.

'Under the urging of my nephew, Cuatemoc, and the lord of Iztapalapa, Cuitlahuac, both younger and more hot-blooded than I, though at the time my own rage was great and needed no urging, I determined to assemble an army of at least a hundred thousand warriors not merely to punish them but to destroy the Teules, be they led by Quetzalcoatl himself or not, for surely none of this could be tolerated.

'But as preparations were begun, first two, then the other three, of the men they had captured arrived at Tenochtitlan with the most astonishing story. Malinche, they swore, had not only secretly procured their release, but assisted in their safe passage.

'But is it not true that the same Malinche had insisted that the Totonacs arrest them and forced them to swear allegiance to his King? I demanded of them in agitated confusion.

'They confirmed that this appeared to be so.

'How could both of these things be possible? I demanded.

'They were even more baffled by such a contradiction than I was. All they could do was repeat the message with which Malinche had dispatched them.

'This incomprehensible Teule *apologized* for their undignified and treacherous arrest by the Totonacs, which he himself had fomented, and expressed his good will towards me! As proof of which, and despite my lack of hospitality towards him, at great risk to himself, he had seen to it that my nobles were returned to me unharmed.

'When I demanded of them how any man could act and speak thusly, one of them ventured that perhaps no *man* could, but what man could truly comprehend the mind and will of Quetzalcoatl?

'What man indeed, if this were so?

'Was this the whole of the message? I asked.

'Malinche told us only one more thing to convey to you, I was told. That all would be explained, and much precious knowledge besides, to your great good benefit, when you received him at Tenochtitlan.

'What was I to make of this? How must I react to a man or a Teule or even Quetzalcoatl himself when he acted as my enemy and yet then proceeded not only to profess friendship and good will but to offer me proof of it by deed?

'Many of my nobles and warriors, Cuatemoc most forceful among them, declared that I must ignore this deceitful and contradictory ploy, whatever it was, and march on the Totonacs and the Teules, perhaps delaying a bit to assemble an even larger and more irresistible army.

'But when I consulted the papas, they were of the opinion that I should do nothing until Huitzilopochtli had spoken. Scores of them pierced themselves to draw blood for two days, but Huitzilopochtli remained silent. Thirty warriors were willingly sacrificed to him, and still Huitzilopochtli would not speak. Finally I myself ascended his temple, stood before him, and offered up the blood of my own tongue and penis.

'Then, at last, Huitzilopochtli granted me an omen. Upon disconsolately descending, I saw a rat pursued from above by an eagle. Frantically seeking sanctuary, it spied the mouth of a burrow that appeared to be of its own people. When it dashed inside, it was seized and devoured by a serpent.

'When I demanded a reading of this by the papas, I was reminded that Tenochtitlan had been founded in the lake where an eagle was seen seizing a serpent on a small rocky island, so surely both the eagle and the serpent spoke of the city, and the rat could only be an enemy thereof who had willingly entered its precincts to be destroyed. Perhaps, rather than march on my enemy, I should allow him to scurry into my stronghold, since that was what he professed to wish.

'*If* Malinche was a man and my enemy.

'But could not the serpent and the feathered eagle also be taken as attributes of Quetzalcoatl? And who then was the rodent?

'Huitzilopochtli had spoken, but only to sow more confusion.

'I offered him more of my blood but there was no further omen.

'And so I finally decided that perhaps *confusion* itself was the advice he had given.

'Both Huitzilopochtli and Malinche had sown confusion in my spirit.

'Until Huitzilopochtli, at least, spoke more clearly, should I not respond in kind?'

Thus Montezuma's confusion at Cortes' strange actions, and when I brought my own to him at the time, Hernando just told me: 'If you are mystified, Alvaro, then so will he surely be.'

And Cortes laughed. 'And surely confusion is the father of curiosity,' he said, and laughed again, and would say no more.

Cortes spent the next days scurrying back and forth between Vera Cruz and Cempoala. At his own municipality, he must see to the construction of fortifications, housing and a church, but the capital of the Totonacs was where the work of consolidating his rule over them needed to be conducted. He stationed the larger part of his army there, and in particular the cavalry and most of the cannon, in order to maintain an impression of power and force, for there was no need of them at Vera Cruz.

This proved to be a major benefit, as if God indeed was with him if you would thus believe, or if he was simply the luckiest of men if you would not. For while he was in Cempoala, a deputation from Montezuma arrived unexpectedly, or at least unexpected by anyone but Cortes, who, as he told me later, had hoped to produce just such an effect when he released the tax collectors with his incomprehensible profession of friendship.

This was the highest-ranking embassy from Tenochtitlan that Cortes had yet received, headed by one Motelchiuh, a major military tribune or uiznahuatl, and including two nephews of Montezuma himself, four venerable advisers, the usual train of tamanes and servants, as well as a troop of 'Eagle' and 'Jaguar' warriors from the military elite.

The Totonacs were quite frightened by this advent, scattering in terror as the minions of Montezuma marched imperiously through their capital to the residence of Tlacochcalcat, where the high officers and advisers ascended to Tlacochcalcat's 'throne room' for a private audience with the Totonac cacique and 'Malinche', accompanied, of course, by Marina.

I was not there at the time, but as Cortes told me with no little relish, it was quite a mystifying affair to Tlacochcalcat.

'Motelchiuh, who did the talking, frostily ignored him, while the others spent the whole time glaring at him contemptuously, nor did he get to speak, spending the whole time guzzling chocolatl and fidgeting, in fear to begin with, and at the end, in dumbfounded amazement.

'Motelchiuh effusively thanked me for rescuing his tax collectors from the treacherous Totonacs, and Tlacochcalcat, knowing nothing of this, gave me a look of amazement and outrage, though he dared not utter a word of it. To make matters worse for him and better for me, Motelchiuh, casting a sidelong threatening glance at Tlacochcalcat, then told me that this act of friendship was the only reason he had thus far spared the Totonacs from his vengeance.

'I was then told that Montezuma was surprised and angered at our seeming support of their rebellion, but in his magnanimity of spirit would at least conditionally operate under the assumption that this had been the result of treacherous advice on their part, to which we had been vulnerable, since it appeared that we were the bearded inheritors of the Toltecs who would one day return from the east, and therefore ignorant of what had come to pass during their long absence.

'To wit that a ruler directly descended from that same illustrious lineage, namely himself, had happily attained the rulership of their former lands and much more besides, which he had held in respectful stewardship against their return, and therefore, among brothers, as it were, the previous misunderstandings could surely be easily overcome and a suitable compact arrived at.

'Overjoyed at this, but hardly about to show it, I replied that no doubt this was so, and a resolution of any difficulties would surely be arrived at when I paid my respect to him at Tenochtitlan.

'To this Motelchiuh neither protested nor assented. Instead, he but nodded, and led us outside to the square as if this were his own palace, where a considerable crowd had summoned up the courage to view an astonishing spectacle.

'The Mexica tamanes had laid out a wide area of petatl mats upon which were displayed well-woven and embroidered cotton cloths, feathered cloaks, and no stingy amount of gold jewelry, utensils and statuettes. All those who were there, and no doubt all who heard the tale later, were quite dumbfounded and no little relieved when Motelchiuh, amidst a cloud of incense and much flowery ceremony, presented them to me as gifts of Montezuma to "he who now chooses to be known as Malinche".

'Among these gifts was a small gold statue which, by this time, I could readily recognize as an idol of Quetzalcoatl, and while I had been enjoined never to don any of his costume, this was not an item of his personal adornment, and so, under the circumstances, I saw no harm, and much good, in paying conspicuous attention to it while inspecting the presents, holding it aloft and fondling it with a special smile, the reaction to which you might well imagine.

'The ceremony concluded, and before returning the favor by treating the Mexica delegation to a fine display of military might, I told Tlacochcalcat that neither of us would be well served should the matter of the released prisoners ever be broadcast abroad, to which he readily enough agreed, amazed at how I had pacified the wrathful Montezuma without recourse to anything more than words, no little gratified, and, I do believe, in that moment, more than half convinced that I must therefore truly be Quetzalcoatl.

'As for the Mexica, while I cannot say that they were exactly pleased by the ensuing cavalry parade, salute to them with arquebuses, displays of swordsmanship, and climactic cannonade in their honor, I warrant they bore a report suitable to my purpose back to the great Montezuma.'

After the Mexica had departed, Tlacochcalcat, perhaps as a test of Cortes' true identity and the mysterious powers of his word, prevailed upon him to go to a nearby city, and, as the new overlord of Totonaca, settle some obscure dispute with its cacique over tribute. This Cortes readily agreed to do. The dispute proved to be a minor affair, easily enough resolved by him by splitting the amount down the middle, and Cortes returned to Cempoala to a celebration of his new achievement as a peacemaker and new role as effective Chief Justice of the Totonacs.

As a reward, however, Tlacochcalcat presented him with eight comely maidens as a gift to his womanless troops, and this produced a serious contretemps in which the matter of who was to 'wed' them proved to be the least of it.

Under the prodding of our priests, Cortes told Tlacochcalcat that his men could have no such congress with unbaptized women. This did not greatly vex Tlacochcalcat, his caciques, or the general population, but Cortes then made the mistake of pressing the matter further, declaring that the Totonacs, having forsworn their political allegiance to Montezuma in favor of his King, must now do likewise in the religious realm by casting down their idols in favor of Christ and the Cross.

Worse still, the women had been presented to Cortes in a ceremony in the square before the main temple, before most of his troops in the city and a goodly number of its inhabitants, including a number of papas, so this demand was made openly in public.

Poor Tlacochcalcat was thus put in an extremely awkward position.

If he resisted the demand, he would face the ire of the Spanish troops, but if he did not, he would face the wrath of his papas and his own people.

'Our gods have served us well enough, since by the prosperous and fruitful condition of our lands, it is obvious that they have not failed to deliver the rains, made the sun to shine, ripened the crops in the fields, and given fair value for the tribute in hearts and blood that we have delivered to them . . .' he began.

At this, Cortes, Father Olmedo and Father Diaz scowled, and the Spaniards before the temple shouted out imprecations, and seeing this Tlacochcalcat sought to escape through equivocation. 'But it is also evident that he who Malinche simply calls "God" has well served us in easing the wrath of Montezuma against us, so it is well to pay him proper tribute too, whether it be to allow his Cross to be erected, or to be sprinkled with his sacred water, or to accept the generous gift of his blood and flesh to eat, or whatever other propitiation may be required to retain his favor.'

I stood next to Marina, who stood next to Cortes and our priests as this was delivered, and I could not help but grin in approval, for this was a speech worthy of the most skilled Talmudic hair-splitter and the most cunning Greek pragmatist. Marina could not help but do likewise in process of translation, and when our eyes met for a moment, it was clear that our appreciation was shared.

But not by the jeering Spaniards in the square, nor by Cortes, and certainly not by Father Olmedo and Father Diaz, the former who met it with a scowl, and the latter who burst into a purple rage.

'Your gods are but demons sent by Satan to drag you down into eternal torment in the fiery pits of Hell!' Father Diaz bellowed. 'They send neither the sun nor the rain nor the crops and certainly not the salvation of your immortal souls! There is but One True God who has created the Heavens and the Earth and all things under it! The God Who sent His only begotten Son to redeem us all! The God who has declared it a mortal sin to kill your fellow man and certainly to *eat* him! A mortal sin to worship any other god! A mortal sin to worship false idols! These must be forsaken and cast down from your temples and replaced by the Holy Cross!'

'I cannot translate such a thing!' Marina hissed in Cortes' ear in no little terror.

'I command you!' shouted Father Diaz.

'Do as he says!' ordered Cortes.

Marina turned to me imploringly, but before either of us could do or say anything, further speech was rendered irrelevant as a score or more Spaniards rushed towards the temple steps, egged on by shouts and screams of approval from their fellows. Seeing this, scores of Totonac warriors in the crowd pushed forward brandishing maquahuitls and lances, likewise encouraged by the outraged Totonacs who crowded towards the temple in their van howling most horribly in rage, and a bloody riot seemed certain to ensue.

Cortes drew his sword and backed up towards the temple steps and the litter of Tlacochcalcat, his left hand held before him to stay his own men at least for a moment. 'Not one step further without my command!'

And then he shouted over the din at the cacique: 'Stop your people at once, for if a single Spaniard is harmed, I shall slay you, your caciques and your papas, and abandon the Totonacs to the mercy of Montezuma!'

Tlacochcalcat needed no translation, and with surprising speed gained his feet, spread his arms, and boomed out a few words in Nahuatl.

The scene became a painting of a battle about to commence, contorted faces, straining limbs, upraised weapons, the writhing and the rushing, the very spewing spittle of rage, frozen for a brief eternal moment of time.

'What did Tlacochcalcat say?' I demanded of Marina as she dashed forward to translate the cacique's words.

'Let the gods defend themselves,' she told me. 'Let Quetzalcoatl preserve us from Montezuma!'

'Don't let the priests hear that in Spanish!'

'The God of . . . Malinche has proven that we cannot prevail against him,' Tlacochcalcat went on, 'nor can we prevail against Montezuma without his favor. And so we must give him his tribute, or he will sacrifice us to the wrath of Huitzilopochtli.'

Cortes and our priests, not to say the Spanish soldiers, were less than pleased at this niggardly conversion to their One True Faith when his words were translated, but the fiery Totonac rage began to subside into grumbling embers, and the more practical Father Olmedo spoke to Marina.

'Tell him that the . . . tribute required is the destruction of their idols and the erection of the Cross in their place.'

When this was relayed to the Totonacs by Tlacochcalcat the crisis was past. Grumble, weep and moan though the crowd did, tear at their own flesh and hair shrieking and howling though their papas did, two score or so Spaniards were allowed to ascend the temple unmolested. A few minutes later, idols of stone and idols of wood came tumbling and crashing down the steps. The former cracked and fractured, and the latter were hacked into flinders by Spanish swords, piled into a bonfire, and set ablaze.

The next afternoon an impressive spectacle was staged by Father Olmedo. The temple exterior and the shrine at its crown had been more or less washed clean of dried blood and the remaining stains covered over with white stucco. Half a dozen of the more pragmatic papas had been induced to trade their ragged and filthy black robes for the clean white ones of Catholic acolytes, though not to shave the filthy and blood-caked tresses from their pates, and handed candles. A new Cross had been nailed together, whitewashed, and garlanded with roses. A portrait of the Virgin was fetched and garlanded. A procession was formed up across the square with an aisle cleared through the center of the crowd of assembled Totonacs for its parade.

Father Olmedo and Father Diaz led it through the square to the temple, followed by Cortes himself bearing the heavy Cross in an almost Christlike manner, followed by a Spanish soldier and a Totonac cacique carrying the Virgin, and then the converted papas in a double line with their candles.

I stood near the temple steps at the fringe of the crowd observing the proceedings with Marina, choosing by unspoken agreement, or so it seemed, to stand aside from this ceremony that was alien to both of us.

Marina turned to me as if to acknowledge this as the Cross and the Virgin reached the steps of the Totonac temple.

'You are no more a true believer in this . . . One and Only God of the Spaniards than I am, are you, Alvaro de Sevilla?' she whispered.

In that moment, I longed to tell her the truth, to share with this woman of an alien land what I could not reveal to any of my 'compatriots', not even to Cortes, especially not to Cortes, and so relieve myself of the loneliness of my heart. Instead I cravenly opted for a half-truth.

'I do believe in a God who is One and Only,' I told her.

'You do not fool me, Alvaro. You do not worship this Christ on his Cross any more than I worship the man I make love with as Quetzalcoatl.'

'I . . . believe that there is one God whose true nature and countenance will for ever remain unknowable,' I continued to prevaricate. 'And it may be that Christ and Huitzilopochtli and Quetzalcoatl and all the rest are but different masks he dons to speak to different peoples.'

Cortes reached the foot of the stairs and began to carry his Cross up them to the newly sanctified altar at its pinnacle, followed by the Virgin borne by men of two different continents.

'Or masks we create for our own purposes,' Marina said knowingly, nodding towards Cortes, 'even as together we have feathered that serpent.'

At this I could not suppress a sardonic smile of acknowledgement.

'We are alone, each of us in our way, are we not?' said Marina. 'I have told you the story of my life and my true name. Won't you tell me yours, so we might share our secrets and share our aloneness and so ease it?'

I longed to do so but fear froze the tongue in my mouth.

'You are afraid that I will reveal your secrets in the night to Hernando . . .' said Marina.

At least I had the courage to nod in agreement.

And then I felt her take my hand.

'Then I will put my danger in your hands to guard you against it,' she told me.

'How?'

Marina, who had been Malinal, smiled at Alvaro de Sevilla, who had been Alvaro Escribiente de Granada, who in his heart was still Avram ibn Ezra or in truth Avram ben Ezra.

The Cross and the Virgin disappeared from sight within the shrine atop the temple.

'In the usual way,' she said. 'As a woman in the faithless secrecy of the night.'

14

I WAS TOO OLD A MAN to spend sweaty hours longing for the embrace that Marina had promised, too mature to delude myself that she found me more arousing than Cortes. On the contrary, I found myself avoiding her as much as possible. Not, I confess, because I had moral qualms over cuckolding a man who was already cuckolding his own wife, nor because I feared to display inadequacy when the moment came, but because I feared what might be the consequences of revealing my true self to her, the price she had set on such intimacy, putting my fate in the hands of a woman who would be proving her questionable loyalty to anyone but herself in the very act thereof.

And so while she stayed close to Cortes as he arranged preparations for our march to Tenochtitlan with the Totonac leaders in Cempoala – securing not only a thousand tamanes to carry our baggage and haul our cannon but some thirteen hundred warriors to serve as auxiliaries – and warming his bed at night, I busied myself during the day learning about what we might face on the way forward, which was precious little, and my nights fretting over how much I could reveal to Marina to keep my side of the bargain when the time came, which I feared could only be too much.

About all I did manage to learn, mostly from maps shown to me, was that there were two possible routes between Cempoala and the Valley of

Mexico, or rather two roads to the singular practical pass through a mighty range of mountains, several of them active volcanoes to judge by the drawings.

The southern route passed through a city and principality called Cholula, and by the gestures and scowls accompanying the pointing thereto, held in low and suspicious repute by the Totonacs. The more northerly route passed through Tlascala, which, by the drawings of many warriors covering a considerable territory and that of a city also called Tlascala, appeared to be held by a more numerous and warlike people, but who, to judge by the pantomime, were held in high repute by the Totonacs.

When I reported this to Cortes, his interest was piqued, but even more so his frustration at the paucity of what I had managed to learn without a translator, and so, as fate would have it, he commissioned Marina to remain behind with me in Cempoala while he arranged things at Vera Cruz for the expedition, ordering us to question Tlacochcalcat closely as to the political and military implications thereof.

He departed before noon, telling us he would return in a day or two to begin the march, and so we went straightaway to the residence of Tlacochcalcat, whom we questioned for long hours over a veritable ocean of chocolatl.

The more of it he drank, the more loquacious he became, and the more we drank, far more than I had yet consumed at a single sitting, the more incisive my questioning became and the greater my endurance, for chocolatl, unlike wine or pulque, far from fogging the mind and fatiguing the body, seemed to enhance the energy of the latter and cause the former to wax ever quicker and brighter.

The Cholulans, we learned, or at any rate were told, were a weak and unwarlike people, but great craftsmen of metals, weavers of cloth, potters and traders.

Tlascala was a much larger nation of fierce and accomplished warriors, reinforced moreover by the Otomis, a primitive tribe who excelled at nothing but battle and who served them as mercenaries.

'Why then,' I demanded, 'are we counseled to avoid pacific Cholula and attempt to pass instead through the lands of the fierce Tlascalans?'

The Cholulans, Tlacochcalcat explained, were loyal to the Mexica, for while they paid tribute, the favorable location of their capital made it the trading hub of the plateau east of the great mountains and their skill as traders enabled them to stay rich by taking full advantage of the situation, so that the last thing they would want to do was ally themselves against their most profitable market and military protector, Tenochtitlan. Moreover, according to Tlacochcalcat, being a nation of wily traders, they were by nature a cunning, deceitful and self-serving lot, and hence not at all to be trusted.

The Tlascalans, on the other hand, were a race of proud, noble and honorable warriors, who, in their mountainous redoubt, had long maintained a sort of independence from the rule of Tenochtitlan by endless flowery warfare against the Mexica, whom they therefore hated.

'*Flowery* warfare?' I chided Marina. 'Surely you have mistranslated.'

'Surely I have not,' she huffed indignantly. 'That is exactly what he said.' And she spoke to Tlacochcalcat in Nahuatl to extract an elucidation.

The Mexica, Tlacochcalcat then explained, could at any time have overwhelmed the Tlascalans, but they actually *preferred* continual warfare with them of this 'flowery' variety.

There were three categories of victims to be sacrificed to Huitzilopochtli, a gourmet of human hearts. The most easily obtained and therefore most numerous were the victims required as tribute from vassal states, but these were merely his basic bread. His most special treat, provided only on rare high ceremonial occasions, were handsome young Mexica warriors, honored as princes and demigods for a year, who then were fed a cactus called 'peyotl' or a mushroom known as 'teonanecatl', or both, under whose mystical influence they willingly and joyously ascended to the altar stone to offer themselves up to the 'flowery death'.

Such a delicacy was hard to provide, and the next-best banquet with which to please Huitzilopochtli's voracious palate was the hearts of noble warriors seized in brave and honorable battle, the most choice among them the Tlascalans, who, being devotees of Huitzilopochtli themselves under another name, were most likely to please him by accepting the flowery death as a transcendent honor even on the altar of their enemies.

The Tlascalans favored captured Mexica warriors with the same honor, though unfortunately for them in unequal numbers, an imbalance it would not displease them to redress, and so might be more hospitable to the passage of an army that might weaken their partners in this flowery warfare.

By the time this bizarre and amazing intelligence had been extracted, it was nearing sunset, my head was reeling with these revelations, and both of us were fairly vibrating with chocolatl like the strings of a lute, and so was my manly member, more so than at any time I could remember since I was a very young man.

Caution having been washed away by the frothy brown liquid, which, if not the true aphrodisiac fruitlessly sought by generations of mages, was the next-best or next-worst thing, and without any words of significance passing between us, we proceeded to the inevitable.

We repaired to the more modest apartment provided for me, for it would have been going too far and more dangerous to commit the act in the grander quarters normally shared by her and Cortes.

There was nothing romantic about it, or even truly passionate, aside from the sheer animal lust provoked by the chocolatl, the long delay between the promise and its fulfillment, and the dark piquancy of tasting forbidden fruit.

We did not kiss, we did not engage in any sort of tender preliminary embrace at all. Marina drew off her shift, revealing a slender but nubile young body, the like of which I had not seen for many years, and stood there regarding me expectantly but quite coolly.

My flesh, such as it was, had already been quite aroused and now was only more so, but I was reluctant to reveal its less appetizing state to such young beauty and hesitant to commit myself to the act. This not because I feared I would not be physically up to it, for a secret hidden from young bravos only to be happily revealed much later, is that men of mature years, once aroused and being in reasonably good health, have a greater staying power than they do, once the act is commenced. Rather it was a Rubicon I hesitated to cross, fearing not the passage itself, but what I would face on the other side.

Sensing this, Marina began removing my shirt and fumbling with my pantaloons, a more difficult disrobing than simply throwing off a shift, contriving to rub her nudity against me in the process, at the touch of which my reticence was dissolved, and finishing the stripping of my vestments together, we fell back onto the petatl mat in a rather clumsy embrace.

Gallantry forbids me to provoke your salacious interest with a lubriciously detailed description of what came next, dear reader, but it would seem relevant to inform you that it was Marina who immediately presumed to take the more active role, just as she had in proposing the assignation, and as she would in what she demanded afterward, forthrightly mounting me and riding me to a satisfying conclusion, at least to myself.

Afterward, there was somewhat more tenderness than the mood in which we had begun, or more properly a greater closeness, as we lay side by side barely touching, but I had scarcely caught my breath before she passed on to a demand that I now fulfill my side of the bargain.

'And so now it is time to tell me the true history of Alvaro de Sevilla.'

When I proved even more reluctant to strip away my masks than I had been to reveal my mere body's nakedness, she persisted with a peculiarly logical form of persuasiveness under the supposedly sensual circumstances, but one that proved effective.

'The deed is done, Alvaro,' she told me, 'and the secret which we now share and must keep from all others is far more dangerous to both of us than anything you will now tell me, and so you can surely tell me without fear, for our lives are now in each other's hands.'

'Which was your purpose to begin with . . .' I said dryly.

'You knew that then as now,' she pointed out, 'but what I did not know, though I suspected it, is that a man of your . . . knowledge and subtlety makes for an . . . interesting lover, not that I am not physically dissatisfied with the ability of Cortes, for we are—'

'Birds of a feather?' I suggested with a little laugh, and when she smiled wryly at that, it was enough to loosen my tongue, and once it had been, it all poured out in a torrent of passionately angry relief.

'So you too are a fallen . . . noble of a sort,' she said when I had given her the brief history.

'Of a sort . . .'

'And the empire in which you enjoyed such a position was also con-quered by these Spaniards, as the Empire of the Mexica will be if what we have begun is fulfilled,' she said. Then, more somberly, 'And the god of your people was cast down by them and they were forced to worship the god of the conqueror as ours are being cast down and so we too must.'

'It's a little more complicated than that, Marina. The Jews have but one God, who, like the Christians, they believe is the One and Only, and we had lost our land and wandered as a conquered people for more than a thousand years before our refuge in Granada was conquered and became a part of their Spain.'

'So these . . . Muslims before the coming of the Christians already forced you to worship their . . . Allah.'

'No,' I told her, 'they were more subtle than that. We were allowed to remain . . . infidels, for we were of great service to them—'

'As the two of us are to Cortes and his Spaniards! Though the God of the Cross seems far more demanding than Allah, almost as demand-ing as Huitzilopochtli!'

I laughed at this, but immediately afterward realized that it was a shrewd perception of the deep truth.

'You have no idea how true that is,' I told her, for while I had made brief mention of the Inquisition, I had not burdened her with the full horror of its methods. Now I did.

She was silent for long moments afterward before she spoke.

'These . . . Christians . . . who demand that we give up sacrificing hearts to our gods in the flowery death with the mercifully quick stroke of the obsidian knife *burn victims alive* in sacrifice to *theirs*?' she mut-tered in appalled outrage.

'They do,' I said. For in truth, while I had never quite thought of it that way, once hearing it voiced, what other way was there to think of it?

'And then their priests eat their arms and legs, leaving only the wine and the little flat cakes they pretend are the meat and blood of their God for the common folk?'

'No,' I reminded her, 'the Christians consider eating human flesh a hideous abomination.'

'Is it less an abomination to roast the life from the bodies of sacrifices and then waste the meat?'

We were both silent for quite a while after that.

'Why do you serve these . . . these . . . these *Spaniards* then, Alvaro . . . Avram?' Marina finally demanded.

It was a good question for which in that moment I had no quick answer.

'Why do you?' I said. 'Vengeance?'

'I was sold as a slave by my own mother and given by the Tabascans as a slave to the Spaniards, and a slave I would have always remained had I not made myself valuable to Hernando Cortes,' she reminded me. 'Is that not reason enough? But you . . .'

'But me?'

'I knew none of this before you told me,' she said, 'but *you* knew, and still—'

'Perhaps my reason is little different from yours,' I told her to cover my shame. 'If you had known then what you know now, would you have done differently?'

I felt her shoulder shrug against me.

'And knowing it now?'

Marina sighed. 'Better to be Doña Marina than be burned as Malinal at the stake . . .' she said softly.

'Birds of a feather,' I murmured in kind. 'And that is why we must go on . . .'

'Perhaps there is more to us than that, Avram . . .'

'How so? And you must never call me anything but Alvaro.'

'Tenochtitlan,' she said.

'Tenochtitlan?'

'When I was a girl, I heard tales of the city on the lake, the greatest city in all the world, a . . . magical city beyond all imagining, and the pictures I saw of it seemed like the painters' visions or dreams . . . And when I was a slave, I longed to see it before I died, and perhaps that is what kept me strong enough to stay alive and unbroken, for in visions and dreams, it called to my spirit, and now . . .'

'I knew nothing of Tenochtitlan when I set sail with Cortes from Cuba, but I had seen the fall of a greater civilization than that which conquered it, and when I fled there and heard the tale of an unknown New World beyond the waters, everything I then did was driven by my passion to see it for myself,' I told her.

And so told myself.

'I cared not for conquest, I cared not for gold, for in my heart, I remained a Jew, and through the centuries without a land, without an army, with nothing to sustain us in our endless wanderings as a vassal people everywhere but the knowledge we accumulated and wrote down to remember, all else was stripped away save the passion to know *more*, to know *everything*, were that possible. Or better, knowing that however far we voyaged upon the sea of knowledge, its final shore would never be reached, that there would always be a Tenochtitlan beyond the next horizon.'

Stunned, amazed, yet also raised above my survivor's cynicism by what I had told to this woman and by so doing discovered in my own heart, I fell silent and moved closer to her.

'And now we are on our way there,' said Marina.

'Whatever it takes. Whatever sins with which it may weigh down our souls.'

'Birds of a feather,' whispered Marina.

'With which we beautify the serpent we must ride there.'

And then, at last, we did embrace.

We did not spend the night together, nor would we ever, for the danger of discovery would be too great, and from this outset our relationship was never what anyone could call a romantic one, rather a friendship of co-conspirators, bound together by occasional carnal intercourse and the shared danger thereof.

The next day, a messenger arrived from Vera Cruz ordering me to return there with all possible haste, and when I inquired as to the reason for urgency, he shrugged and replied that all he knew was that a Spanish ship had arrived in the harbor and Cortes had need of my presence at once.

My curiosity was piqued to the point where I even steeled myself to proceed to Quiahuitzlan on horseback in order to slake it as soon as possible, the discomforts of which I care not to detail here, lest the memory thereof be fully awakened. When I arrived in Vera Cruz, I found there was indeed a new caravel in the harbor, and that Cortes was in something of a frenzy.

Upon entering the house that had been carpentered for him, I found Hernando behind a rude desk piled with a jug of chocolatl and a midden of papers and busily scribbling more.

'My friend Francisco de Salcedo has found us some three score men to add to our army,' he told me distractedly by way of greeting. 'Along with the tidings that my prophecy has been fulfilled, and King Charles is now indeed Holy Roman Emperor.'

'Then why are you so distressed by two such favorable advents?' I asked him in total confusion, for his mood was clearly not a happy one.

'He has also brought evil tidings,' Cortes told me. 'The treacherous Velazquez has secured from Castile a writ to . . .' He fumbled among the documents so as to read from the relevant one aloud. '. . . "seek, at his own cost, islands and mainland territory which up till now had not been discovered."'

He waved the document about as if it were a sword. 'This thing further gives him all the profits, minus the King's fifth, of the expedition that I have mortgaged my entire fortune to pay for, plus a twentieth of all derived from any colony established, and in perpetuity! And furthermore, Salcedo informed me that he received this license the very day I left Santiago de Cuba! In other words—'

'He would have had to apply for it about the time you were mortgaging your holdings to him in order to mount it—'

'The fat bastard deliberately swindled me twice over!' Cortes roared. He poured himself another cup of chocolatl, which, to judge from the brown stains on a goodly number of the papers, was far from his first of the day, and slurped it down.

'That's why I need your help, Alvaro,' he told me when he had. 'This mess is my attempt to write a letter to the King, and I need you to put it into the best possible form as quickly as possible.'

'Its intent?'

'To give a full and grand account of all that I have thus far accomplished here, emphasizing that with Tabasco, and now Totonaca, I, on my own initiative and with no help financial or otherwise from Diego Velazquez, have already brought under his sovereignty far more land and subjects than all his previous holdings in this New World combined. And that this is only the smallest beginning to what I will achieve, and that he would be much better served by empowering me to continue as his de facto viceroy and Captain-General here than to place his trust in some lazy, incompetent, cowardly tub of lard resting on his fat buttocks in Cuba who has never so much as laid eyes on these shores.'

'That should about cover it,' I said dryly, 'though I believe I can phrase it in somewhat more diplomatic language than that.'

'Then do so at once!' Cortes ordered irritably, shoveling the choco-latl-stained pile of papers in my general direction. As I gathered them together, I was struck by a further notion, albeit one that I doubted would greatly please him to hear. 'I do have an idea which I am sure will tip the balance . . .' I ventured nervously.

'Well?' Cortes demanded, refilling his cup.

'Deeds speak more loudly than words, and greed is a greater moti-vator of men than logical persuasion,' I began cautiously, 'and so—'

'Spit it out!'

'This letter would be much more persuasive accompanied by His Majesty's first installment of tribute, and the more of it the better, since what he would be expecting is only the royal fifth, and if you were to send say . . . half of what has been secured, the wealth of the lands you have already won for him would be greatly enhanced in his eyes . . .'

Knowing Cortes' greed for gold and his strained financial circum-stances, I broached this ploy with no little trepidation. Cortes did indeed bang his fist on the desk, but not in consternation.

'A stroke of genius, Alvaro!' he exclaimed. 'Half? By Jesus Christ and all twelve of His Apostles, I'll send him *all of it*!'

'*All of it?*'

'All of it,' Cortes said much more calmly. 'For surely that would be a treasure to put me so much higher in his favor than Velazquez that the letter must surely succeed, and the dangling promise for so much more would whet the greed of Croesus himself!'

'You would give up your entire share of what we already have?' I exclaimed in disbelief.

'Has not most of it been given to us by Montezuma?' Cortes told me craftily. 'And would he have given so much if that was not piddling compared to what the Empire of the Mexica must therefore have? And has he not given up this gold in an attempt to preserve his rule over that empire? And would I not be a fool and a cowardly miser like Diego Velazquez if I were unwilling to give it up for a royal license to replace his rule with my own?'

'Your grandeur and courage amaze me, Hernando,' I told him quite sincerely.

Cortes laughed. 'Sometimes it amazes me as well,' he said. 'But it is best to be amazed afterward, is it not? Besides, when Tenochtitlan is in my hands, the King's share of the much more will be reduced to the customary fifth, and my fifth will be restored. You must make it clear in the letter that what I am sending with it *is* but a fifth.'

'That would be an outright lie,' I pointed out gently.

'Then make it less than outright,' said Hernando Cortes.

'I suppose I could simpy enumerate the booty, call it the King's share, and leave it at that . . .'

'There you have it!' Cortes exclaimed with a grin and a clap of my shoulder, and downed his cup of chocolatl in a single self-satisfied gulp.

What I had not understood was that when Cortes said 'all of it', he meant not just his own share but that of the officers and men as well. I was too busy putting his series of less than coherent drafts into proper final form to attend the proceedings, but he called a meeting of his officers and persuaded them to go along by much the same appeal to greed that motivated the letter I was writing.

Namely that this was a modest investment that would be paid back at least a hundredfold, and his belief in such an outcome was proven by the fact that he, who had a mountain of debt and nothing more, had already pledged his own fifth. Since the Captain-General and all his officers had already agreed to do so, when the same argument was put to the ordinary soldiers, not a man would sully his honor or place himself in the jeopardy of isolation by refusing to relinquish his own presently piddling share. Cortes cleverly chose Puertocarrero, who had high connections at court, and Montejo, who had been a Velazquez loyalist, as the couriers to deliver the letter and the treasure to Spain.

Under the grimly watchful eyes of the entire populace of Vera Cruz, the great wheels of gold and silver were rolled out onto the beach before the dock against which the treasure ship was moored. Feathered cloaks were piled up. Cotton cloth. Golden statues. Heaps of jewelry. Gems, golden bells, and much, much more.

Then, in a procession more solemn and much more somber than any in a cathedral, the officers, and then the common soldiers, added their comparatively modest booty to what at the time must have been the greatest treasure ever seen in one place at one time by European eyes.

Though the process was almost as boring and tedious to watch as it must have been arduous to perform, most of those present remained during the hours it took to do the loading.

When the ship was finally loaded and riding low in the water, one could imagine its timbers fairly groaning, but the groaning on the beach when it was warped from the dock and unfurled its sails was all too audible, like mourners at a funeral lamenting the departure of their most beloved friend.

Unsurprisingly, dear reader, there were those who, upon reflection, felt that the donation of their gold to the greater cause had been extracted under a cunning form of duress and lamented its loss long after the treasure ship had disappeared beyond the horizon.

Certain men who still retained a loyalty to Velazquez, or at least their own mendacious self-interest, realized that if they acted quickly to seize one of the lighter and faster brigantines, they could reach Cuba in time for Velazquez to send out ships to intercept Montejo and Puertocarrero's vessel on the way to Spain. Cortes' letter to the King would never be delivered, Velazquez's license would remain in force, and the location of Vera Cruz would be known. Velazquez could dispatch a large force to seize control of the colony and the enterprise, and they would surely be rewarded with high positions in it.

Moreover, since the treasure ship and the accounting that accompanied it would fall into the hands of Velazquez before the King knew of its existence, the latter could easily be adjusted so that His Majesty would be none the wiser if a sizeable portion of the treasure were to disappear into the coffers of the governor of Cuba and his friends before the remainder was delivered.

The leaders of this enterprise, encouraged by Father Diaz, were Velazquez de Leon, Diego de Ordaz, the governor's ex-page Alonso

Escobar, the chronically discontent Juan Escudero, the required pilot, Diego Cermeño, and others.

Too many others for the necessary secrecy to be maintained, for conspiracies hatched in the dead of night by so many are all too likely to be betrayed by a single conspirator with second thoughts, or for that matter who never harbored a loyalty to the conspiracy in the first place.

In this case the betrayer of the betrayers was a minor conspirator, one Bernardino de Soria, who slunk into Cortes' dwelling as he and Marina were preparing for bed.

'The man claimed that he had been approached by Father Diaz, who made him swear an oath of secrecy before even being told what he was to hold in secret,' Cortes told me. 'Only then was he taken to a meeting of the plotters and learned who they were and what it concerned. Fearful for his own life if he did not, he pretended to join them, not only to safeguard himself, he assured me, but so as to obtain a full list of the traitors before betraying the affair to me.

'As to de Soria's true motivations, I found it hard to take them at face value from a man who first joined a conspiracy to betray me and then betrayed his fellow conspirators, reckoning that it was much more likely a sudden loss of courage or a calculation that it was not likely to succeed, which, though it served my own interests, I found dishonorable and repugnant.

'Nevertheless, I thanked him profusely for his courageous loyalty to me, and, while my immediate impulse was to round every last one of them up, the priest included, and slay them all with my own sword, I had the presence of mind to allow my temper to cool so as to take a more pragmatic course.'

This Cortes told me after the trial over which he presided, by way of explaining its 'merciful' results.

'Upon reflection, I realized that, our force being small as it was, I could not afford to waste manpower by executing them all, and so I opted for setting a few examples so as to cow the rest, and anyone else who might later harbor such ideas, into loyal submission,' he explained. 'Nor would it be politic to attempt to punish a priest when I might be overruled by appeal to the ecclesiastical authority of Father Olmedo.'

So Father Diaz was merely chastised privately, and at the swift conclusion of the trial the conspirators were imprisoned on the flagship to contemplate their sins, though brought forth to be 'lightly punished' and bear witness to the exemplary punishments of a handful of their number: one Gonzalo de Umbria, and the unfortunate Escudero and Cermeño, chosen as representatives of the ringleaders for the maximum sanction.

A double gallows was constructed in the main square of the little town and all of us presently in Vera Cruz rather than Cempoala were assembled to endure witness.

The first act of Cortes' cautionary theater piece was a multiple whipping. The miscreants were brought forth, stripped to the waist and made to kneel to expose their bare backs to, as memory serves, perhaps a hundred strokes. These were laid on with flails of knotted rope rather than actual whips, so that after the screaming and bleeding was done, they would recover their fitness for military duty.

Umbria was then made to stand upright and barefoot before Cortes, who chopped off the toes of his left foot with a small ax, eliciting a sharp shriek of pain, immediately put to shame by a greater and more prolonged howling and blubbering when the stumps were cauterized with the flat of a heated dagger.

The climactic act was the hanging.

The double gallows was a crude affair, a narrow board long enough for two men to stand on laid across two trestles little more than a man's height above the ground, with two nooses dangling ominously above it from uprights.

Escudero and Cermeño were shoved up onto the board by a ladder, their hands bound behind them, but their faces nakedly exposed to the audience, and the nooses fitted around their necks. The board was then pulled out from under them and down they plummeted.

But not fast enough or far enough to snap their necks. Instead they hung there for minutes that seemed an eternity, choking and gurgling through open mouths, their faces purpling, their limbs twitching and jerking, piss wetting the front of their pantaloons and spreading brown stains blossoming on the seats thereof for all the world to see, as they turned this way and that at the ends of their ropes before finally expiring.

★

To say that I was disgusted and appalled by this spectacle is merely to proclaim that I am human. Yet now, upon long reflection, I believe there was more to it than that, for after all, I had witnessed more terrible deaths at the battle of the plain of Ceutla, and many more of them, and had seen the fresh results of bloody human sacrifice and cannibalism.

But the former was war, and the latter a barbarous rite performed no doubt in a state of frenzied religious conviction, whereas Cortes had carried out his own act in cold blood, the sacrifice of human lives to equally cold pragmatic purpose. And was this not as good a definition of ruthlessness in its purest form as can be devised?

I still cannot decide whether Cortes harbored this within his breast from the outset, or whether the spirits of this land had entered into him and changed him, or whether the potential for such ruthlessness sleeps within us all waiting to be called forth by circumstance. Would I be capable of such a deed? Would the Quetzalcoatl of the noble Toltecs? Of a certainty, the Quetzalcoatl I had had a hand in crafting had done so.

Be that as it may, the sacrifice was successful. Never again did Hernando Cortes suffer such a rebellious conspiracy against him. But at the time Cortes enjoyed no such assurance. If anything, the failed conspiracy aroused his fear that another might at any time arise, and so he himself formulated a conspiracy of his own to make that impossible.

This he confided to no one save those necessary to carry it out: the pilots of the ships and enough of the crews to accomplish the deed. Nor did he broadcast his intent before it had already been done.

Nor was he present to witness it. He was in Cempoala, where most of the troops that were to march to Tenochtitlan had already been marshaled, along with the accompanying Totonac auxiliaries, and he did not even announce that the deed had been done, preferring to let rumors sweep the encampment to pave the way for a risky dramatic confrontation.

Sailors were flooding into Cempoala to take up arms as soldiers, their former occupation having been rendered obsolete by the final act required of them as seamen, and I heard it myself from one of them who had been constrained to take part:

'Our pilot gathered us together, and told us that nine of the ships, our own included, had become unseaworthy due to the rotting of hull timbers caused by lying too long at rest in these tropical waters and the holes bored into them by the marine worms infesting them.

'I knew enough of how things went in these steamy harbors to believe that such damage was native to them, but found it hard to believe that it had gone so far, though this was a bone of contention among us seamen.

'We were then ordered to perform a final duty that would sadden and outrage any sailor. The nine ships must be beached, deliberately shipwrecked! Our protests were answered by being told that the order came directly from the Captain-General himself, and when this failed to cool down our outraged dismay, we were told that the masts, yards and rigging, which were sound, along with the fittings and sails and what timbers proved usable when inspected, would be salvaged, and used, along with fresh lumber, to construct sound new vessels when the time came.

'And so I took part in the saddest sight I have ever seen in my life at sea. The ships were warped away from the docks, their sails were unfurled for the last time, we sailed them far enough away from the shore to catch a fair following wind. Then the yards were crowded with all the sail they would carry, and the fleet was turned to catch it, and, as if we were returning eagerly to home port after a hard voyage, we sailed towards the beach with all the speed we could muster.

'One by one, our ships ran hard aground upon the beach, to lie on their sides like broken and dying whales, and, when it was my vessel's turn, the shock of the impact and cracking and crashing of its death agony was the most terrible moment of my entire life.'

As these sailors' tales swept through the army in Cempoala, so too did angry and fearful embellishments. The crews had been forced to carry out the beachings at swordpoint. Several men who had refused to obey had been executed. Cortes had bribed the pilots from a secret store of gold.

No sailor claimed to have seen such swordpoint coercion of his fellows, nor any execution, and no seaman ever turned up missing, but knowing Cortes, I had little difficulty crediting that gold might have changed hands, though he was never to admit this to anyone.

In twos and threes, and finally in greater numbers, ad hoc deputations accosted Cortes at his quarters, as he made his rounds of the preparations, everywhere he went. Cortes put them off for a day, with a promise to address the matter to all on the morrow.

By the time the sun had reached its zenith the next day, most of the army had gathered before Cortes' quarters; an angry, surly mob, quarreling and shouting among themselves, with many swords already ominously free of their scabbards.

When Cortes finally emerged, the din was both terrible and incoherent. No one imprecation could be made out over the general furious tumult of outrage.

Cortes stood before his rebellious and outraged army with his arms folded across his chest, letting it go on as long as it would without any call for silence in which to speak. His eyes were as cold and unreadable as a reptile's and his visage as stony as a statue's, as if he had frozen his face into the mask of Quetzalcoatl.

Finally the shouted demands that he answer for his action were subdued by impatient expectation into the silence necessary for him to do so.

'The ships were rotten to the core and would have only served to carry those whose fighting spirit and faith were likewise rotted away by cowardice to a well-deserved death at the bottom of the sea,' he began, which was greeted by jeers and cries of outrage.

'And of what use would they have been to those of us eager to march inland to gain an empire for our King and riches for ourselves and souls for Christ and the Cross? Only those of craven spirit have reason to mourn their useless loss, for when the glorious time comes, we will build new ships from their wreckage, our only problem being to build enough stout ships to carry the treasure with which they will be groaningly laden without sinking to the bottom of the sea under their golden cargos.'

There was spontaneous laughter at this, nor was it drowned out by the scattering of catcalls.

'I remind you that those ships were bought with all I had in this world, and if anyone should mourn their necessary loss, it is I! I now stand before you pauperized, naked to fortune, and like you, determined to win it! The deed is done, there is no turning back, not for me, not for those true soldiers of the King and Cross among us!'

Once more, Hernando Cortes had won a victory with words alone, as ruthlessly calculated as the deed, and backed by lion-hearted bravery and iron-willed conviction that could only put to shame any man who wished to consider himself worthy of such leadership, for as the breaking of a thunderstorm clears the air of the sullen black clouds that birth it, so did his thunderous words freshen the atmosphere.

And then Cortes sealed it with a challenge.

'As for me, I will remain here while there is a single one of you to stand by my side. If there is any among you so craven as to shrink from our glorious enterprise, I say farewell, go home, for who among us would wish to force your company upon us! Spend your dotage regaling your grandchildren with the story of how you deserted your commander and comrades and stood heavily downcast on the Cuban docks as we sailed triumphantly into port laden with gold and honor!'

For the first time Cortes allowed a smile to crease his lips.

'There are still two sound ships,' he said. 'They are yours. Surely they are more than enough to carry what cowards there may be in this company of heroes back to Cuba.'

A great cheer rang out. There were cries of 'On to Mexico!' and 'Tenochtitlan!' and 'Saint James and the Cross!'

And of course in the end no one took him up on his sardonic offer.

Madness? Hubris? Leadership in its most pure and perfected form?

Call it what you will, no one was immune to the call to destiny of our Feathered Serpent.

Even I, who well knew what mendacious and ruthless cunning lurked behind the very mask I had had such a hand in crafting, found my spirit captured.

15

AND SO, WITH SOME four hundred Spanish infantry, a score or so arquebusiers and crossbowmen, seven cannon, about a dozen horses, thirteen hundred Totonac auxiliaries, and a thousand tamanes to transport the baggage, Hernando Cortes led his little army towards the mountains to conquer the Empire of the Mexica.

How this was to be accomplished he seemed to regard as a minor detail. 'God has given us good evidence that He is with us. We have founded a colony, we have secured the Totonacs as vassals and won them to Christ, and we are on our way to Tenochtitlan.'

'And what do you intend to do if and when we get there?'

'That depends on Montezuma,' Cortes told me. 'If he agrees to treat with me, I will persuade him to accept the One Truth Faith on behalf of his people, and swear vassalage to our Holy Roman Emperor, who, after all, is far away and out of sight, and so would present no obvious threat to his own standing.'

'And if he refuses us entry to Tenochtitlan in the first place?'

'Would his curiosity permit him to deny a face-to-face encounter with Quetzalcoatl?' Cortes said dryly. 'And if it does . . . Then we shall have to conquer Tenochtitlan by force of arms.'

'Simply storm a city in the middle of a lake approachable only by a few narrow causeways?'

'What Our Lord wills, Our Lord will provide His soldiers with the means to accomplish,' Cortes said blithely. 'And why would He not wish to see these heathens brought out of their slavery to Satan and into His One True Faith?'

Our army began the march in high spirits, enhanced by the delightful landscape through which it passed, the fruitful fields and balmy savanna westward of Cempoala, sprinkled with copses of palms, enlivened by the songs and squawkings of brilliantly colored birds, the air alive with butterflies and perfumed by wild roses and the heavier scents of waxy tropical flowers.

On the morning of the second day, the land began to slope upward towards crests of the great cordillera, but it was a mildly pitched approach and the day's ascent was not particularly arduous, and moreover the temperature cooled as we moved upward.

We reached the town of Xalapa just before dark, a town owing fealty to Cempoala, where we were hospitably received, spent a tranquil night, and the next morning were greeted by the most beauteous and spectacular sunrise it has ever been my pleasure to witness.

The sun arose, a deeply burnished golden orange, from the gleaming blue mirror of the distant sea, its light stepwise rolling towards us across the lush flower-strewn green of the tropical lowlands, and as it rose further, it flashed highlights off the snow-whitened peak of a distant mighty mountain we were told was called Orizaba. Behind us, pine forests bearded the ascending slopes of the mountain chain, rising and receding in the distance through white fogs that assumed glorious tints of azure and purple as the sunlight slowly and gently burned them away.

Before leaving Xalapa, Father Olmedo preached a sermon to those inhabitants who were abroad and curious, which might have fallen on largely uncomprehending ears, but Cortes followed with a speech declaring the town 'liberated' from the yoke of the Mexica and no longer to pay tribute thereto, and promising to hold it under his protection as long as they continued to give over human sacrifice and venerated the Cross and the Virgin.

This was taken with more enthusiasm, and as we had a journey of unknown length before us and this was a ceremony both Cortes and our priests wished to perform at whatever settlements we passed through, and as we were running out of paintings of the Virgin and Child, the Spaniards set up a Cross, presented as a gift rather than an obligation, a local artist was shown one of those paintings remaining, given a handful of trade beads as payment, and hired to produce his own version.

We then began a harder climb via a winding and treacherous road up the steeper shoulders of the mountains, beneath rugged slopes covered with pine forests, and through rocky defiles, which broadened from time to time into little verdant meadows, several with villages numbering only a few hundred inhabitants, cowed and terrified by the appearance of what to them was an enormous army.

At the first of these, Cortes delivered the same proclamation of liberation and its terms as he had at Xalapa before Father Olmedo preached, and this became the formula as we climbed upward. As at Xalapa, the Spaniards erected the Cross, but here there was no artist, and so a volunteer from among the Totonacs was pressed into service to produce a colored drawing of the Virgin and Child, a curious version to European eyes, with a deep brownish tinge to the skin tones, local clothing style, and haloes rendered as wreaths of unnaturally golden quetzal feathers, but acceptable enough to Indian tastes.

We passed through several more such alpine villages during the next four days, repeating this procedure in each, and as we did, it was evolved and perfected. In the end, the Spaniards gifted the Indians in each village with a Virgin and Child drawn by our Totonac artist, who with practice began to turn them out ever more rapidly, and who began to teach the locals to produce the portraits, however crudely, and rather than erect the Cross themselves, the Spaniards instructed the Indians in this simple piece of carpentry.

Thus, it was hoped, might Christianity spread among these tribes, as a new flower, once planted, might spread its seeds on the wind to find fertile soil, and germinate, and take root, to bear full fruit only later.

After four days of this, with the climate growing colder, wetter and more unpleasant as we climbed, the pine forests sparser, and the landscape more rocky and forbidding, we reached a much larger alpine meadow with a river running down it, high above the range we had thus far traversed, but at the foot of another range even higher. Here,

supported by the required extensive fields of maize, was Zautla, a settlement of some thousands which might fairly be deemed a city.

Its cacique, Olintecle, we were told by Mamexi, the commander of
our Totonac auxiliaries, paid tribute to Montezuma, but through the
intermediary of the Totonacs, so that when we were received in a cordial manner, it was ambiguous as to whether this was due to the feudal
hierarchy, or the direct orders of Tenochtitlan. And Olintecle seemed
bent on preserving that ambiguity.

We were all fed – modest fare consisting of maize bread, bean mash,
peppers, a few turkeys, some pulque, but no chocolatl – and housed in
decent dwellings for the night. But my dreams, and no doubt those of
others, were haunted by what we saw on the way to our quarters as we
passed through the main square. Dominating the square was the usual
temple. At its foot was a large wooden framework containing a great pile
of well-weathered human skulls, thousands of them, and the ground
around it was strewn with fresher human arm and leg bones, some with
scraps of flesh still clinging to them.

I dreamed that night of skulls: full-sized ones, tiny ones, skulls of
intermediary sizes, an abundance of snow-white skulls, piled high
everywhere, in small village squares, in the streets of some strange great
city, offered up as produce in a marketplace, played with as toys by children, munched on like sweets, a horrendously joyous festival of skulls,
and a procession parading through them behind a Cross upon which
was crucified a crudely carved Jesus with the face of a skull and haloed
by the feathers of Quetzalcoatl and a brightly painted idol of the Virgin
Mary with skin as dark as that of a black African.

On the morrow, Cortes, Father Olmedo, Marina and myself were
conducted to a meeting with Olintecle at his dwelling. This was built on
a model similar to that of Tlacochcalcat, but smaller, more spare, and
sitting on the ground rather than atop a grandiose stone pedestal.
Olintecle himself was a lanky man in middle age, whose sharp-boned
visage well justified the hoary term 'weathered'.

Cortes curtly chastised Olintecle for what he assumed were his ghastly
sacrifices to Huitzilopochtli. Olintecle just as brusquely informed him
that while Zautla had been constrained to place an idol of Huitzilopochtli
in its temple, this being a harsh land of intermittent heavy rains and

short growing seasons entirely dependent on the maize crop for its livelihood, the gods who mattered and whose favor must be sought and maintained with blood and hearts were the rain god Tlaloc and Xipe Totec, god of springtime renewal.

'You are a vassal of Montezuma?' Cortes asked in some confusion. 'Or are you not?'

'Who is not a vassal of the great Montezuma, one way or another?' Olintecle replied laconically. 'Even the Tlascalans, who forever war with Tenochtitlan, supply him with tribute after their fashion.'

'*I* am no vassal of Montezuma,' Cortes told him. 'Rather am I the servant of a far greater and more powerful King who has sent me here to liberate the people from servitude to him.'

'Ah yes, Quetzalcoatl, sent by some Toltec King across the sea whom no one has seen to reclaim his rightful domains from the Mexica usurpers,' Olintecle replied sardonically.

Cortes' visage froze, save for a clamping of his jaw, and a vein that throbbed in his temple, clearly angered, but just as clearly loath either to deny this outright or to affirm it in the presence of Father Olmedo.

'Swear allegiance to . . . my sovereign, give over your evil sacrifices and accept Jesus Christ as your savior, and you will be placed under His and my protection and freed from paying blood tribute to the Mexica for ever,' he finally said, sidestepping the dilemma.

'Will I now?' Olintecle said skeptically. 'What I have seen is some hundreds of your warriors, some ferocious beasts at your command, and perhaps a thousand Totonac warriors incapable of fighting off half their number in Tlascalans. Montezuma, for his part, commands some thirty great caciques as vassals, each of whom can field a hundred thousand warriors. Tenochtitlan sits on a lake approachable only by four long causeways whose many bridges can be easily enough raised to prevent the entrance of any army.'

He bared rotten teeth in a grimacing smile. 'You will pardon me, therefore, if I do not place the lives of my people in the hands of your promise, however generously intended. And even were I foolhardy enough to do so, they would never accept it.'

Cortes was at a loss to counter this pragmatic argument. Frowning, shrugging in frustration, Cortes nodded at Father Olmedo.

'Will you not at least give over your beastly human sacrifices, throw down your idols, and allow us to replace them with the Cross and the Virgin?' Father Olmedo asked rather wanly.

Olintecle shrugged. 'We are not the Tlascalans and you have enough warriors to force us to do whatever you like,' he said. 'So if you wish to install your idols alongside ours and Huitzilopochtli, I will not prevent you. Because, after all, I *cannot* prevent you.'

'And if we throw your idols down and smash them to pieces?' Cortes demanded hotly.

Olintecle stared at him unwaveringly for a long moment. 'They are emblems of Tlaloc and Xipe Totec, not the gods themselves, just as your Cross of wood and drawing of a woman and child are not your gods either, now are they, for you make more of them as you go, and even teach others to do so, and we know how to carve the emblems of our gods already,' he finally said, making his meaning all too plain.

'Will you not at least let Huitzilopochtli be destroyed and his place remain vacant?' Father Olmedo fairly whined.

'There is no great favor for Huitzilopochtli here, for he hardly favors us,' said Olintecle. 'But should the tribute collectors of Montezuma arrive to find his place vacant . . .' He grimaced and shrugged eloquently enough.

There was then a long moment of confrontational silence. Olintecle finally broke it. 'Perhaps I have not spoken plainly enough,' he said in a conciliatory tone. 'No one in Zautla will mourn if you should over-throw the rule of Montezuma, and no one truly venerates Huitzilopochtli. In return for hearts, Tlaloc brings the rain, and Xipe Totec allows the maize to come forth in the springtime, whereas Huitzilopochtli takes our tribute and gives us nothing. So should you somehow triumph over the Mexica, we will accept your god in his place, for, I am told, he requires no tribute. So I give you leave, because I must, to place your idols beside our own and that of the Mexica, and when the issue is decided, let those of the victor remain.'

If I found Olintecle's canny equivocation the only wise and responsible course to be taken by a prudent ruler under such circumstances, Cortes was in no mood to appreciate such cleverness, and was determined to move on to Tlascala as soon as the way was diplomatically prepared.

He sent forth four Totonac chieftains as envoys with a message to the Tlascalan cacique, Xicotencatl the Elder, a wise centenarian if Mamexi was to be believed, to the effect that we were on our way to ally ourselves with the great and noble warriors of Tlascala in order that together we might vanquish the evil forces of Montezuma, hoping to appeal to the martial nature of a nation of warriors who we had been assured were far from loath to battle the armies of Tenochtitlan even without such assistance.

When Olintecle learned of this, he cautioned us against crossing the border of Tlascala at all, for Xicotencatl the Elder fought off all trespassers, and his son, also called Xicotencatl, was a great and fierce general who delighted in any opportunity to give battle. Better to proceed through Cholula, a nation which prospered under vassalage to Montezuma, and was no more likely to resist us by force than Zautla.

Since this was a course against which he had already been cautioned, Cortes would have none of this advice, and after waiting four days for the return of the envoys, which was not forthcoming, he decided to proceed without it to Tlascala.

We followed the course of the river upstream towards Tlascala and the higher mountains beyond, passing through a long string of small villages along its banks, pausing in most of them only long enough to announce to the indifferent inhabitants that they were now liberated from the Mexica and vassals of King Charles and to plant the Cross and the Virgin, spending the night where sundown caught us.

As we neared the end of the valley, it began to narrow, and the land to rise into a series of rocky foothills, atop the broadest and highest of which was a town of some size, which Mamexi told us was called Iztaquimaxtitlan. It was well situated to command the route up the valley to the frontier of Tlascala, which was of course also the route downward, along which any Tlascalan army would have to proceed should the Tlascalans seek to invade the lands below paying tribute to Mexico.

But Mamexi told us that such an invasion had never happened, for the Tlascalans, having found themselves a mountain fortress of a country, were content to defend it, rather than seek to expand into the valley at the expense of the Mexica, who would surely send an expedition of overwhelming force to eject and punish them most severely if they tried.

Nevertheless, the Mexica maintained a garrison in Iztaquimaxtitlan to keep the Tlascalans reminded of their presence should such a foolish thought otherwise come into their heads, and serve to delay any such foray long enough for a larger force to arrive, for which purpose a stone-walled fortress had been constructed which the small garrison could hold against a larger Tlascalan force for at least a week.

This information gave Cortes some pause, but Mamexi pointed out that the last thing the Mexica would want to do would be to emerge from their fortification to confront his larger force in the open, and so they should present no problem. Besides which, Cortes was quick to realize, his cannon could if necessary make short work of a stone fort built to withstand nothing more than javelins and fire-arrows.

The envoys sent to Tlascala still not having returned, and the border of Tlascala being nearby, Cortes decided that the best course was to enter Iztaquimaxtitlan and tarry there a while to wait for them, but to proceed cautiously.

Cortes rode into the city accompanied only by half a dozen horsemen and Marina and was received by the cacique in a guardedly polite manner. He made no mention of his mission to liberate the downtrodden vassals of the Mexica or the One True Faith, saying instead that he was simply passing through these lands on his way to Tenochtitlan to visit the great Montezuma at his invitation.

The cacique swallowed this whole, or found it prudent to pretend to do so, or for all we could know, might be acting under the orders of Montezuma himself, who, we had begun to realize, was as much a master of confusing ambiguity as Cortes was of evasive prevarication, and we were welcomed into the city.

It was an elusively ominous welcome. We were given quarters in the apartments surrounding the temple square, kept well fed, and even presented with a few featherwork cloaks and minor gold trinkets. But always within sight, glowering above us from its craggy eminence, was the fortress of the Mexica garrison, where warriors continually paraded atop the walls to assure us of their attention.

Cortes countered by placing four of his cannon to cover the entrances to the square and positioning the others in the center, where those atop the fortress could clearly observe their barrels pointing up at them, staging cavalry drills to keep them entertained, ordering his men to wear their armor at all times, even while sleeping, and never to have their weapons more than a hand's reach away. He also refrained from any attempt to deliver a Requerimiento or to disturb whatever lurked atop the temple.

Thus we enjoyed several days of tense leisure, the tension growing ever more dominant as the envoys sent to Tlascala still did not arrive.

At length, at interminable length, Cortes decided that there was no recourse but to go to Tlascala without waiting any longer for them or the sought-after invitation. And so we left Iztaquimaxtitlan, left the alpine valley, and marched inward and upward.

Once we climbed out of the valley, the climate swiftly became harsher and the landscape more and more forbidding. Rocky and sparsely vegetated slopes became the cliffs on either side of cramped and winding defiles strewn with the debris of rock falls through which we were forced to proceed in narrow file with uneasy caution. Cold winds blew down these canyons, sometimes bearing dank mists, sometimes drenching showers. It was bad enough for Spaniards and difficult for the horses, but the Totonacs, unaccustomed to such climes and not at all dressed for them, suffered greatly.

It became easy enough to understand how the Tlascalans could hold this fortress of a landscape against the much more numerous Mexica indefinitely if the approaches to it were all like this.

But there was worse to come.

Rounding the bend of one of these rocky canyons, we were confronted with a wall across it entirely blocking the way forward.

It was perhaps ten feet tall and equally thick, if the square faces of the large stone blocks with which it was constructed proved to be those of cubes. There was a parapet atop it behind which defenders could shelter against arrows and javelins, but there were no defenders in evidence. There also seemed to be no entrance.

Cortes kept the Totonacs and the Spanish infantry lined up well back of this threatening fortification, dismounted, and walked cautiously toward it, accompanied by Alvarado, Sandoval, Olid, Mamexi, Marina and myself.

'What *is* this thing?' Cortes demanded of Mamexi.

'The frontier of Tlascala,' Mamexi told him, as if that were necessary.

We came up to the wall, and upon closer inspection, saw that there *was* an entrance, albeit a devilish one. In the center, the wall was in fact doubled for about forty paces, that is it became two overlapping semi-circular walls, from the exterior appearing almost like the foundation of a castle tower. Peering around the open edge of the outer wall, we saw that there was a passage no more than ten paces wide between them, leading no doubt to a similar opening in the inner wall at the other end, invisible from this vantage around the curve of the passage.

Meaning that the only way to pass through was perhaps five men or two horses abreast, utterly vulnerable all the while to devastating attack from above.

'Why have they built this wall only to leave it undefended?' Cortes asked Mamexi.

'This is not usual, they keep it well manned with Otomis as far as I have been told,' Mamexi said, regarding the wall with the perplexed eyes and wan smile of a man who had no good answer but was searching for one that might conceivably serve in its stead.

'You have sent out envoys seeking passage,' he finally ventured. 'Perhaps leaving the entrance to Tlascala unguarded is their way of invitation?'

'Invitation to *what*?' Cortes grumbled, peering intently at the wall as if his vision might pierce the stone, and certainly wishing it could. 'And how can I be sure from here that the other side *is* unguarded?'

We returned to the army lined up all the way around the bend of the canyon, and it took only a brief discussion among Cortes and his officers to decide on the only possible course of action. He positioned his little troop of cavalry double file at the head of the army with himself in the lead, and ordered them to keep their swords sheathed and their lances lashed to their saddles, hold their shields above their heads, and gallop through the passageway as quickly as possible. The rest of the army was to follow five abreast at a dead run.

I began the run with Marina near the rear of the Spanish formation and was sufficiently out of breath soon after it began to be passed by half of the following Totonacs, so I had to rely on Cortes to learn what did not and did happen.

'Though the gallop through that passage took only moments, they were among the most terrifying moments of my life, a terror that was surely shared by the men I led, so that when we emerged unscathed and unchallenged out the other side the relief was so complete as to be intoxicating, and many of us, myself included, burst into laughter at what we beheld.

'Which was nothing but a broad, flat, grassy plateau stretching out to some low hills to the northwest, with not a foe in sight! Such was the giddiness engendered by this sight that high spirits overcame caution, and I led our little party of a dozen horsemen trotting forth across the plain toward the hills to reconnoiter without waiting for the infantry to pass through behind us.

'We could not have advanced more than three or four miles at this pace when I spied a small party of Indians, perhaps a few score, in the far distance. Seeking to learn from them what might lie between us and the city of Tlascala rather than to give battle, I brought my troop up to a gallop.

'As soon as they spied us approaching, they turned and ran towards the hills, but we easily enough outpaced them, waving and shouting that we meant no harm, which, since none of us spoke their language and they in any case couldn't hear us, only spurred on their futile flight.

'When we closed the distance sufficiently to see that they were wearing quilted cotton armor and were armed with shields and those blade-fringed paddles called maquahuitls, they realized there was no outrunning our horses, and turned to face us.

'Accustomed as we were to the terror struck into Indian hearts at the sight of mounted cavalrymen, I was surprised but strangely pleased when, instead of displaying cowardice, they ran towards us, screaming, whistling, slashing the air with their weapons, and then slashing at us with them when we closed.

'They gave quite a good account of themselves, slicing at our greaved legs with their maquahuitls and at the bodies and legs of our horses, while we fended them off with thrusts of our lances, rearing our mounts to bring their hoofs down among them to keep them at bay.

'Smartly adapting to these tactics, they altered their own, the greater part of their number continuing to slash at us with their weapons, while a score or so bravely grabbed at the lances thrust down at them, seeking to pull us off our mounts.

'To no avail, for we switched over to our swords, and while cotton armor is effective at protecting from slashing attack such as the limits of their weapons accustomed them to, it is little protection from the pointed thrust of good Toledo steel, and though we were outnumbered and surrounded, it was as if reapers were encircled by stands of grain as we cut these brave warriors down.

'In the heat of battle, rearing my horse, piercing the breasts of screaming men, fending off maquahuitls with my shield, I did not realize that this engagement had been the opening move of a clever tactic, for I did not at first see the veritable horde of warriors, thousands of them, descending upon us while we were surrounded and thus hampered from rapid and easy escape.

'When I finally did, I dispatched a reluctant cavalryman to flee the impending battle to urge our infantry to rush into the fray with all haste, clearing a path for him with my own sword, and then the main force was upon us.

'It was a terrible battle, with the issue in perilous doubt. We formed ourselves into a tight formation with our lances outward in a protective circle of sharp points so as to neutralize their overwhelming numbers, but once more the foe grabbed at them, succeeding in dragging one of our number off his horse to suffer grievous wounds which later proved to be fatal, and we were forced to revert once more to swords.

'Seemingly indifferent to the danger, the Tlascalans crowded around us, those in the rear pressing forward into the smallest gap as we cut those in the front ranks down, even pushing through their comrades to engage us with their maquahuitls. Trapped as we were, our vantage atop our mounts gave us a good defensive edge, and I believe that had the battle continued thus for hours, only their great superiority in numbers, allowing them to pour in fresh warriors when we were finally exhausted, would have allowed them to bring us down.

'These Tlascalans, however, showed no fear of our horses, and great and clever warriors that they were, several of them realized that their exposed necks were within reach of their fearfully sharp maquahuitls and began slashing at them.

'The counter to this was to rear the horse upward away from the blow before it could be delivered and bring its hoofs down on the attacker, but one of our company was late in executing this maneuver, and a maquahuitl sliced through the underside of the poor animal's throat to such a depth that its head flopped over sideways as it fell, neighing piteously one last time, its neck fountaining gore.

'Encouraged by this success, two Tlascalans likewise attacked a horse together, joined by a third, and with equally deadly result. We were thus forced to give over our swords in favor of lances to fend them off our mounts, and once more the Tlascalans countered by grabbing at them. We then spontaneously developed the tactic of splitting our numbers, some of us protecting the horses with lances, others chopping off the hands that grabbed at them with swords.

'Thus the battle seemed stalemated, though if it had gone on indefinitely like this, in the end we would surely have been lost, thanks to my foolhardy mistake. But at length I heard a distant booming of cannon, and never was there music sweeter to my ears than that of this fusillade.

'Shot whistled high overhead and tore into the rear ranks of the Tlascalans out of my sight, but I could hear the cries of pain and terror, and so could the warriors immediately surrounding us. Another cannonade was fired, and another, and another, and the fighting around us became a panicked confusion as some of the Tlascalans continued to attack while more of them turned and fled.

'Seizing the opportunity, I shouted out a command to retreat in good order, and we cut our way back through the thinning ranks to face the welcoming sight of Spanish infantry, crossbowmen and arquebusiers at the front, the great number of Totonacs bringing up the rear, advancing towards us at a run.

'I turned to lead my advancing army in pursuit of the fleeing enemy, and we got close enough for the crossbows and arquebuses to give a good account of themselves. But the Tlascalans, even in their fear, proved to be proper soldiers, organized into good defensive formation with archers protecting their rear, as they retreated before us at a run.

'Realizing that they could make at least as much speed afoot as our infantry, that this was country they must well know whereas we did not, and having once been led into a trap, I contented myself with what had already been accomplished and gave up the chase.'

This Cortes dictated to me after we had camped for the night by a stream where the inhabitants of a small village had fled at our approach, for the events of the day had decided him to provide posterity with a clear and forthright account of his adventures, for the purpose of which I was to record events as freshly afterward as possible, and what I did not witness, he would relate to me as soon as leisure presented itself, to be put into better form later when the time for such rewriting came.

The peculiar event that intervened between the battle and our taking refuge for the night, I did witness, though I made no more sense of it at the time than did Cortes.

We were making our way across well-cultivated fields of maize and stands of maguey no more than three hours later when we spied four figures coming toward us from the direction of the city of Tlascala. When they reached us, they proved to be two of the missing Cempoalan envoys accompanied by two Tlascalans, who, by their featherwork cloaks and extravagant headdresses, seemed to be of high rank.

Through the translation of Marina, they offered profuse, indeed groveling, apologies for the attack on us, declaring that Xicotencatl the Elder, most senior of the ruling four caciques of Tlascala, had waxed furious when he had learned of it, all the more so because it had been the insubordinate act of his own son and namesake Xicotencatl, a great general, but possessed of a rash nature and love of battle that had overcome both prudence and hospitality as well as the orders of his own sovereign and father.

'Is this true?' Cortes demanded of the Cempoalans.

'So it would seem,' he was told, 'for the cacique Xicotencatl, though exceedingly old and frail and apparently blind, had flown into quite a robust rage.'

'And what of my other two envoys to him?'

'These he keeps by his side so that when you reach Tlascala they may regale you with the tale of the hospitality he has lavished upon them in recompense.'

Cortes made no sight of his skepticism to the Tlascalans, but I could read it on his face, and when we were encamped and he had finished dictating his tale of the battle, he inquired as to whether I placed any more credence in what the Tlascalans had professed than he did.

'Less, if anything,' I told him, 'for I have made some simple calculations. They arrived from their capital not much more than three hours after the attack in question. Three hours for the unexpected news of the battle to reach Tlascala, for Xicotencatl the cacique to dispatch envoys with his apologies for it, and for them to reach us with them. A feat which Hermes himself might just have managed to accomplish, but hardly mortal men afoot. He must have known in advance.'

16

DESPITE MAMEXI'S ASSURANCE that night attacks were unheard of in these lands, Cortes posted the usual sentries that night and kept a hundred men armed and awake for four hours at a time, for the Totonacs' intelligence as to the disposition of the Tlascalans now seemed a good deal less than reliable. Marina and I were also kept awake during the first watch interrogating the two Cempoalan envoys and the two Tlascalans they had returned with in hopes of acquiring better information as to the true political situation presently prevailing in Tlascala.

Tlascala, it seemed, was made up of four principalities, each ruled by its own cacique, the four assembled being collectively responsible for decisions affecting the state as a whole. While the four were formally co-equal, Xicotencatl the Elder, being the cacique of the principality containing the largest city, and having ruled it for so many decades, was, however, the senior in terms of effective influence.

So he could have acted independently, all the more so since his own son commanded the largest part of their army, and the Tlascalans admitted that the approach of the Spaniards had generated acrimonious debate among the four paramount caciques and their immediate subordinates.

Some believed that 'Malinche' might indeed be Quetzalcoatl and the bearded white men the prophesied return of the Toltecs and the enemies of the Mexica, in which case it would be best to greet them with hospitality and seek to make alliance. Others pointed out that the Teules were travelling in the company of the Totonacs, vassals of Montezuma, had been favored by him with lavish gifts, and had declared that they were on their way to visit Tenochtitlan by imperial invitation. Still others, quite perplexed, pointed out that they had desecrated temples and set up idols to previously unknown gods all along the way, hardly what either Quetzalcoatl or any ally of the worshippers of Huitzilopochtli would be likely to do.

Xicotencatl's view had prevailed, which was that since it was presently impossible to make an informed judgement, the Teules should therefore be allowed to proceed to Tlascala where their true nature and intent might be better discerned.

The Tlascalans swore that this was all they knew, and the Totonacs affirmed that it was true to the best of their knowledge, and that Xicotencatl had personally dispatched them with the invitation.

When we reported to Cortes, he mused that it might be prudent to apply the methods of the Inquisition to the Tlascalans to see if another story might emerge under torture. But when I pointed out that if it did not and Xicotencatl *was* at least tentatively well disposed towards us, this would only be likely to tip his opinion in a hostile direction, he thought better of it.

And so on the next morning we set forth in defensive formation as an army marching through possibly hostile territory.

Cortes led the cavalry in the van, riding three abreast, and instructed never to charge separately if attacked, hold their lances short rather than thrusting, and train their points at the faces of the foe, for surely the Tlascalans, like any men, would be most distracted from attacking by threat to their eyes. Close behind came the Spanish infantry marching in close ranks, with the crossbowmen and arquebusiers among the foremost so as to afford them clear fields of fire, enjoined to stagger their volleys so that some would always be firing while others were reloading. Behind the infantry came the cannon, drawn by Totonac tamanes, and bringing up the rear our Totonac warriors. Marina, myself, the priests and the two Tlascalans, the latter under guard, were positioned just behind the Spanish infantry.

We proceeded in this manner through the morning towards the hilly land beyond which lay the city of Tlascala until, soon after noon, we were met by the two remaining Totonac envoys dashing towards us across the plain. Cortes called a halt to await them, and when they reached us, they were in a state of exhaustion and terror.

Cortes summoned Marina to translate and myself to record the conversation, for such, he had decided, would be a useful general procedure for when the time came to send the next letter to the King and when his memoirs must be prepared to inform future generations of his exploits.

The envoys told us that, far from being lavishly feted, they had been held in captivity to be sacrificed, or at least so they had been told by the Tlascalans who had aided their escape.

'*Aided your escape?*' Cortes exclaimed. 'Why would any of them do that?'

'We only know what we were told—'

'Which was?' Cortes demanded.

'That they were the agents of a faction opposed to what Xicotencatl had persuaded the others to do . . .'

'*Which was?*' demanded Cortes, quite exasperated.

'To let the decision be made by your god and theirs on the field of battle—'

'To allow his son to test the Teules. If he was victorious, you could not be Quetzalcoatl, nor your army Toltecs, nor, whoever you might be, would you be useful allies against Montezuma. But if you prevailed against the army of Tlascala led by its greatest general, then you would make mighty allies, and the blame for arousing your ire and losing the war could be laid upon his hot-blooded, impetuous and rebellious offspring.'

Incredibly, Cortes not only broke into an approving grin, but actually laughed aloud.

'These Tlascalans would certainly make most valuable allies!' he exclaimed. 'So let us take up their worthy challenge and win them to our side as they themselves would have it!'

We had not gone forward for more than two hours before an

opportunity to do so presented itself. In the distance we spied a group of Tlascalans, perhaps a thousand of them, a band we and the Totonacs outnumbered. Out of politesse, and perhaps reluctant to give full credence to our most recent information, Cortes, rather than firing the cannon at them or charging, had us proceed toward them at a measured and unthreatening pace until he was within earshot.

He then summoned Marina to his side, and I, emboldened by curiosity, went forward with her. Cortes ordered her to tell the Tlascalans that we meant them no harm, but were merely passing through their country in friendship.

When this was greeted by a hail of stones, atlatl-launched javelins, arrows, jeers, whistles and hostile imprecations, Cortes ordered the charge. Marina and I hastily retreated to our previous position behind the Spanish infantry, huffing and struggling to maintain this relative safety as the whole army, Totonacs and all, surged forward, and so I glimpsed what ensued in confused fragments, and herein have relied on Cortes' later account to give mine coherence.

The Tlascalans held their ground and continued to rain missiles until the cavalry and the front rank of the infantry, with the crossbowmen and arquebusiers returning fire on the run, were almost upon them. Then they retreated in what Cortes approvingly described as excellent order.

Half of them fled across the plain towards the hills which were now nearby, but not so rapidly as to abandon a rearguard, who at first contrived to continue throwing stones and launching javelins and arrows while running backwards.

When the cavalry and the front of the infantry closed with them, they held their ground, giving a good account of themselves with spears and maquahuitls. But Cortes' new tactics proved successful, making it difficult for them to grab onto lances or attack the horses, and steel swordpoints rather than slicing sweeps were quite effective at penetrating cotton armor.

Still the Tlascalan rearguard refused to flee from what was becoming a fearful slaughter, giving ground only reluctantly, foot by foot, inch by bloody inch, and the rest of their force, seeing their heroic resistance, returned to the fray to reinforce them.

'But they seemed to have little notion of how to deploy more than their front ranks in any effective manner,' Cortes told me, 'those at the rear seeking to press through the ranks of their own comrades like small boys trying to get closer to a parade rather than even trying to outflank us, and at length we seemed to have slain enough to dishearten them, and they gave over trying to hold ground against us, rather seeking to escape towards the hills, though still in a more or less proper retreating order.'

Upon reaching the range of hills, the Totonacs did break and run, and this much I was able to see from where I was, as they fled into a sort of narrow valley with Cortes and the cavalry in hot pursuit, but the rest of our number had to first form up in narrower file in order to follow. What happened next, therefore, I did not see myself, and must rely on Cortes.

'We found ourselves pursuing them through a valley with a stream running through it that must have done considerable meandering, for the ground was strewn with rocky rubble, making for gingerly passage with the horses, and the whole rendering the cannon following far behind virtually useless. Had there been warriors atop the hills enclosing the defile, we would have been in desperate straits, and though none were in evidence, it was impossible to know what might lurk behind the crests. Seeing that they were fleeing towards a widening of the valley just around a final bend, with no confining heights visible beyond, I believed we would have them when we chased them out onto another open plain. Instead, when we emerged, we found ourselves confronting an enormous army.'

Later accounts have given figures for the size of this Tlascalan army ranging up to a hundred thousand, nor was Cortes himself immune from this tendency to hyperbolic quantification, but I being present and therefore knowing all too well the impossibility of performing such a head count in the heat of battle, shall refrain from doing so, and merely tell you, dear reader, that there were certainly some scores of thousands, and that they covered the plain before us.

The Tlascalan army did not immediately charge Cortes' enormously outnumbered cavalry contingent, nor was Cortes mad enough to advance towards it until the rest of his own army had caught up to him.

Rather, he told me, they held their ground, beating drums, whistling, jeering, brandishing their forest of weapons, as if to impress him with their grand martial display, or even, possessed of a certain chivalry, to allow him to fully deploy his own forces before testing them in fair battle.

And a grand display it was, for the Tlascalans wore headdresses of brightly colored plumes and waved shields likewise decorated with colorful feathers, and their bodies were painted with white and yellow stripes, and hundreds, if not thousands, of standards – cloth banners, featherwork on poles – were raised high above their army.

'Frightening though it was,' Cortes told me, 'there was a beauty to it that my soldier's soul could not help but admire.'

As for me, emerging from the valley to suddenly see the endless ranks of Tlascalans ranged across the plain from behind the Spanish infantry, such esthetic admiration was not exactly my first reaction.

Mamexi, close behind me, pointed at something in the distance, the largest and most proudly prominent of the Tlascalan standards, a veritable tower of feathers done up in the likeness of a heron perched on a rock, and shouted something in Nahuatl, the only word of which that I could understand was 'Xicotencatl'. This must be the ensign of the great Tlascalan general himself.

The Spanish infantry spread out into double ranks on either side of Cortes' little skirmish line of cavalry so as to afford clear lines of fire for the arquebusiers and crossbowmen, and seeing this the army of Xicotencatl charged forward in a single great mass.

The arquebusiers and crossbowmen fired continuous volleys as they had been instructed, but they could not have gotten off more than three or four before the Tlascalans closed the ground, and it was swords against maquahuitls, lances against spears, men against men, close enough to smell each other's blood and sweat, to spray each other with the spittle of their cries of rage and pain.

'Never have I seen such fierce and courageous warriors,' Cortes told me, 'pressing forward undaunted against lances, swords, horses, seeking forthrightly to overwhelm us with their numbers no matter the cost to themselves, which was terrible, for their cotton armor was little protection against pointed sword-thrusts, the obsidian blades of their maquahuitls shattered on contact with metal, and, moreover, they seemed more intent on inflicting bloody wounds than on cleanly slaying.'

Nor, I was told after the battle, did Xicotencatl seem to have any clear notion of how to take tactical advantage of his great advantage in numbers, or perhaps the Tlascalans had no good means of coordinating their forces.

'Were I him,' Cortes told me, 'I would certainly have charged along a wide front to flank our line on both sides in great depth with my superior forces, so as to surround and crush us as a fist might squeeze a peach.'

Instead the Tlascalans confined themselves to charging with a front no wider than that of the Spanish infantry, neutralizing their advantage in numbers by causing the bulk of their army to pile up far behind their fighting edge in an unruly mob where each man jostled his fellows in a futile attempt to reach the forefront.

Worse than futile as it turned out, for the Spanish infantry not only held, but, aided by the efforts of Cortes' cavalry and the arquebusiers and crossbowmen thinning the enemy ranks as quickly as their eager replacements pressed through over the bodies of the fallen, began to push the Tlascalans back.

At length there was enough room behind the fighting front to deploy the cannon and protect them as they fired blindly over it at the deep rear ranks of the Tlascalans.

The carnage wreaked by cannonade after cannonade among these tightly massed warriors was quite terrible, but more terrible still must have been the effect upon their spirits of the mighty continuous thunder, the reeking pall of gunsmoke, the sudden mangled deaths of their comrades all around them, a monstrous and continuous slaughter which could only have been the wrath of the god of the Teules called down upon them, since not a single human adversary was there to be seen.

Emboldened by this spectacle, the Totonacs did what the Tlascalans had failed to do, breaking into two wings so as to surge forward on either flank of the Spanish infantry, and fall upon the flanks of the attacking Tlascalans.

Now Cortes led a cavalry charge through the center of the Tlascalan attack, cutting their front in two, and Spanish infantry poured through the gap and spread out, so that the Tlascalans found themselves fragmented into several groups, each all but surrounded by Spaniards and Totonacs.

At the same time, the cannon continued to bombard the Tlascalan rear, so that those at the front were receiving fewer and fewer reinforcements as they were cut down, and their resistance crumbled.

Finally, Xicotencatl displayed the general's skill in defeat that had failed to gain him victory. His army turned tail so as to flee out of range of the cannon, but in a clever order, behind a rearguard courageously harrying what was now a trotting advance of the Spanish and Totonac forces with arrows and javelins launched by atlatls, so that the cannon could not be brought forward fast enough to further decimate their retreating comrades.

Cortes, seeing that the sun would soon go down, the damage done already terrible, and the victory won, gave up the pursuit, and we repaired to a rocky butte easily defended in case of night attack to dress wounds and celebrate the triumph.

The account we later concocted to send back to the King painted this battle as a most perilous one whose outcome hung on Spanish fighting spirit and valor, and later versions made it seem that the victory had been won only with the aid of divine intervention. But in cold unromantic truth, it was a one-sided slaughter, masked by the overwhelming preponderance of the Tlascalan forces.

For these Indians took battle as an endless number of individual combats, and so seemed to have little understanding of how to marshal and maneuver their forces to take tactical advantage of their superior numbers, and they had never faced cannon and shot before.

This battle, and the dissection of it by Cortes and his captains afterward, might have been but the beginning of my military education, but one did not have to be a well-schooled general to know that no other army of valiant innocents could have done much better than that of poor Xicotencatl.

But Xicotencatl was yet to be convinced that he had lost the war. The next day, Cortes released two captured Tlascalan chieftains with a message congratulating him on the valor of his troops in hopelessly confronting the most powerful force on earth, to wit an army rendered invincible by the infinite power of the One True God, and offering an honorable end to the hostilities, after which he would visit Tlascala with an offer of alliance which would be to their great advantage.

He whiled away the next two days waiting for a response by leading foraging parties into the countryside. On the third day, while Cortes was off on one of his foraging expeditions, the two Tlascalan messengers he had sent out did finally return, and in his absence they were given to Marina and myself for immediate questioning in the presence of the assembled captains remaining in the camp.

We were haughtily informed that they had had little problem in seeking out Xicotencatl, for he had assembled an even greater army only a few miles away, fifty thousand warriors at the least if they were to be believed, a combined army of all four principalities of Tlascala and the Otomis as well, assembled behind the standards of their own caciques as was customary, but united under the command of Xicotencatl by agreement of all.

The senior of them then delivered Xicotencatl's response to Cortes' message:

'The Teules are welcome to make their way to Tlascala for a great feast at which they will be honored by the flowery death upon the altar of Huitzilopochtli, and, moreover, after he has eaten their hearts, they will be further honored by having their flesh serve as the main item of the following banquet, not merely roasted, but elegantly prepared with an impressive variety of savory sauces. Should the Teules reject such a generous invitation, he and his army will pay them a courtesy visit on the morrow.'

You may well imagine the outrage and terror with which this was greeted so soon after what we had all assumed was a decisive victory, but when Cortes returned and was informed, he was positively buoyant.

'This is good tidings indeed,' he told the army after assembling it before him. 'For when we defeat the Tlascalans this time, as we surely will, we will have defeated their entire army, not merely that of Xicotencatl alone, after which the war will have been won, we will have proven the invincibility of Spanish arms fighting behind the Cross, and they will surely be eager to accept Christ as their Savior and King Charles as their sovereign, and we shall gain a mighty ally whose valor and worthiness has already been proven to us on the field of battle.'

With this piece of blustery bravado to match that of Xicotencatl and then some, our Feathered Serpent raised the fighting spirit of his troops, and, as always, preferring attack to defense, set out on the morrow with his entire army – save myself, Marina, the priests, what captives we held, the too severely wounded, and a small garrison force – to take the battle to the Tlascalans before they could take it to him.

Thus, being mercifully not present at this fray, I must rely entirely on Cortes for this account of the battle:

'Seeing as we were to advance across an open plain and having learned to avoid all confining terrain at some cost, I spread the infantry out along as wide a front as our numbers would permit, backed by our Totonac allies. Rather than lead with my small cavalry contingent, I positioned the horsemen along the infantry line by twos, like towers reinforcing a castle wall, each of them flanked by arquebusiers and crossbowmen. Rather than keeping the cannon well back, I spread them out immediately behind the horsemen.

'Xicotencatl, it seemed, had sought to benefit by his hard schooling as well, for when we spied his army in the distance, it too was spread along a wide front, wider than ours, though its enormous numbers formed up a huge square behind it.

'A splendid sight it was too! Like a formal garden, for it was mustered into four separate companies behind tall feathery standards flanked by banners, and each contingent of warriors was painted in its own colors, matching those of these ensigns. The white and black heron of the house of Xicotencatl was prominently in the center, close by a standard taller than any of the others, a great gilded eagle chased with silver and encrusted with emeralds that gleamed like cats' eyes in the sunlight, no doubt the sigil of united Tlascala itself.

'Upon sighting us, the Tlascalans held their ground, apparently awaiting our charge so as to form a crescent with their greater flanking forces and so embrace us in its deadly arms.

'I therefore did not order the charge, but held formation and advanced steadily towards them at a slow walk. As we approached, the

Tlascalans remained immobile, content to set up a provoking din with the beating of drums, shrill whistling, screams of outrage, and shouted imprecations which no doubt would have been highly insulting had we understood them.

'When we were within extreme range of their most powerful weapon, the obsidian-tipped javelins whose reach and force was enhanced by atlatls, they launched a great fusillade, most of them falling short, the others too spent to do real damage, obviously another attempted provocation.

'But instead of rising to the bait, I halted our advance, and ordered the horsemen to stand aside to provide a clear vantage for the cannon to fire, not at high trajectory upon the Tlascalan rear, but straight and level at their front at close range.

'The cannonballs tore into the Tlascalans, through their front rank and three or four ranks behind, slaying scores in a moment with each shot. Bloody gobbets of flesh showered down on those not slain, whole arms and heads were sent flying, and the cries of pain and fear were terrible.

'But to the credit of their bravery if not their prudence, the Tlascalans held their ground through several cannonades, launching javelins and equally futile arrows, even stepping forward over the abundant remains of their comrades to fill gaps in the line.

'And then they charged, the whole army rushing forward straight into the teeth of our cannonade. I had the cannon fire two more fusillades at ever-decreasing range, causing even greater carnage, then ordered the charge to meet them, leaving the cannon behind to continue the bombardment in relative safety, but firing in high arcs at their rear, concentrating their fire on the standard of each contingent in turn, in hope of slaying chieftains and sowing confusion.

'As we advanced, I adopted an ancient tactic of the Romans, forming my infantry into squares of four men each, so that they were sheltered on all sides behind shields, from behind which to deliver short thrusting strokes at the enemy. The Totonacs were ordered to attempt a flanking maneuver and then left to their own devices, while the arquebusiers and crossbowmen were pulled back behind the squares to dispatch any Tlascalans who penetrated. I repositioned the cavalry into a strong triangular unit and led it myself toward their center.

'After that, all I can report is the chaos of combat, the bite of obsidian blade on my thigh, the shattering of maquahuitl against my shield, the crash of hoofs on heads and bodies, the yielding of flesh to Toledo steel, the stink of horse dung and ruptured intestines, the war cries and the screams of pain, the crackling reports of arquebuses, and above it all like the battle drums of the gods, the sweet bass music of the continuous roar of the cannon.

'How long it lasted, or what ground it traversed, I cannot say, for I was no longer a general, but only one more soldier, enveloped in the small sanguinary world of sword and blood, moments of fear and moments of exultation, no larger than the sweep of my sword and the forest of foes surrounding me.

'At length, the music of the battle underwent a welcome change, Spanish voices crying out in triumph, Tlascalan voices diminishing in volume, and their attacks lessened, waned, and then were no more. Rearing my horse for a better view, I beheld the beautiful and glorious sign of a greatly diminished Tlascalan army fleeing in no little disorder across a corpse-strewn plain, and it was over.'

As we were to later learn, bombarding the contingents clustered around the battle standards had worked to telling effect, for one of the chieftains had ordered his warriors to retreat from this onslaught, precipitating a partial disintegration of the Tlascalan army and aiding greatly in the Spanish victory.

But the war was still not quite over. Mamexi had assured us that night attacks were unknown in this land, in part because there was some kind of superstitious injunction against them, in part because they were a violation of both the Tlascalan and the Mexica code of chivalrous military conduct. Which was probably why Xicotencatl the son tried one anyway as the most desperate last resort he could imagine. But since the Tlascalans were unaccustomed to mounting night attacks, even their greatest general made a botch of it, verging on farce.

Attempting it on a cloudless night illumined by a full moon was hardly a brilliant strategy when it came to the necessary stealth. Then too, the Tlascalan force sought to creep up on the butte upon which we were encamped under cover of a maize field, but the crop was yet not head-high, nor did the warriors deign to remove their feathered head-dresses, and one of the sentries that Cortes always posted spotted them while they were still moving through it.

Cortes roused his troops, mounted his cavalry, rolled the cannon to the edge of the incline, positioned the arquebusiers among them, and all waited silently until the Tlascalans had reached the foot of the butte.

He then shouted out the most blood-curdling battle-cry he could muster, the signal for everyone to do likewise, the cannon boomed out an ear-splitting if largely ineffective volley in the general direction of the Tlascalans, the arquebusiers, their weapons more suited to the steeply downward angle, did likewise to much more telling effect, and the cavalry came galloping down the hillside followed by the infantry and the Totonacs, all this as simultaneously as could be managed.

Not being accustomed to fighting at night to begin with, the shock of such a fearsome eruption of noise, acrid smoke, and demons seemingly possessed of the power to see through the darkness quite unmanned them, and they fled in ignominious disarray.

Two days later, a party of Tlascalans, a dozen or so warriors under white banners which Mamexi informed us were sigils of truce, arrived at our encampment, followed by some half a hundred tamanes bearing foodstuffs and some golden trinkets, with word from Xicotencatl that, if Cortes permitted, he would personally visit to sue for peace.

What followed was a shameful business by my lights. Cortes took it into his head that they were spies, or at any rate that it would be prudent to proceed under the assumption that they might be. He had several of these Tlascalan envoys put to the torture, under which they confessed to this violation of the politesse of truce. Whether this was true or not, I cannot tell you, dear reader, for this evil art had been well perfected by the minions of the Inquisition, under whose coercion almost anyone would tell the torturers whatever they wished to hear just to have their torments ceased.

Worse still, upon hearing what he wished or feared or expected to hear, Cortes had their hands cut off, and sent them back to Xicotencatl with a message that any further treachery would be punished with a good deal less mercy.

Perhaps Cortes committed this foul outrage *because* it was such a foul outrage, in order to convince the Tlascalan general, his father, and the generality of Tlascalans, that he was a harder man than any of them. Perhaps because his sojourn in these lands of human sacrifice and cannibalism had indeed made him so.

Or perhaps not. For as a Jew who had fled from an Inquisition which habitually extracted religious conversion and even admissions of Satanic congress under torture, I knew that two generations of Spaniards believed sincerely that what was spoken under such terminal duress must be the truth.

For if this was not so, was not the Inquisition and its methods a monstrous evil? And if it was, were they and the faith in the service of which such evil was practiced not servants of the very Devil they professed to abhor?

Several days later, Xicotencatl arrived under two great standards – the yellow, white and black heron banner of his own house, and the golden emerald-encrusted ensign of Tlascala itself. He was accompanied by several hundred warriors wearing the white and yellow, servants perfuming his way with incense, and tamanes bearing modest tribute of food, a few featherwork cloaks, and bolts of crude maguey-fiber cloth.

Cortes lined up his whole army to welcome Xicotencatl. Xicotencatl saluted him by touching his hand to the ground and then to his brow in the usual Indian manner, and Cortes replied with the ghost of a bow.

The Tlascalan general must have been the very late progeny of his supposedly centenarian sire, for he could not have reached his fortieth year. He was a muscular man, taller than most Tlascalans, with a sharply chiseled profile, an aquiline nose, and hard dark eyes that maintained their pride and dignity even under these circumstances. I could sense an instant respectful admiration pass between these two hopefully former foes, which was only enhanced when Marina translated the words Xicotencatl spoke.

'I believed you to be the enemy of Tlascala, even though you professed to come in peace, even though your declaration that you wished to ally yourself with us against the Mexica was believed by my father and our caciques, for you also arrived in the company of his vassals and declared you were on your way to visit Montezuma in Tenochtitlan at his invitation. I still do not understand how both these things can be possible at the same time.

'But you have bested me in fair battle, and it may be that you are indeed Quetzalcoatl come to bring back the wise rule of the Toltecs by means only you can understand. I fought you entirely on my own as a Tlascalan general and the responsibility for waging and losing this war is entirely mine, but now I speak to you under the eagle standard of all Tlascala to pledge our fealty to you . . .'

He doffed his feather cloak and spread his arms wide to expose his bare chest. 'And to seal our alliance, if you so accept, I willingly offer up my heart to the flowery death so that you may feed it to your mighty god and so assure him that my word is good and I speak the truth.'

There was a mass intake of breath at the nobility of this gesture, wrong-headed and blasphemous though it was to Spanish hearts, for this was the heart of a warrior speaking to warriors' hearts, and even I could not but love him for it.

'Though no heart could be greater than yours, it is yours to keep,' Cortes told him, 'for the One True God abhors such sacrifice, however well intended. I do believe that had you known me and I known you before we met on the field of battle, my words would have been believed as I now believe yours, and many brave men who died would still be counted among the living. So as the Christ commands us, let us forgive our ignorant sins against each other and seal the friendship between us in His Grace.'

How much of this Xicotencatl could truly comprehend was questionable, for his face showed considerable perplexity as Marina translated it, but the essence of it seemed to penetrate, for his visage softened, and though he could hardly have been familiar with the foreign custom when Cortes held out his hand, after hesitant consideration, he finally understood enough to take it.

17

WE ONLY TARRIED ON OUR hilltop for a few days, but to our amazement, it proved long enough for word of events in Tlascala to reach Montezuma, for him to dispatch an embassy to that far butte, and for it to reach us before we departed for the city of Tlascala. An impressive embassy paraded through the lands of his Tlascalan enemy to deliver his peculiar message, accompanied by the lavish gifts of gold, embroidered cotton finery and featherwork cloaks to which Cortes was by now accustomed, if not under such bizarre circumstances.

There were five richly dressed Mexica nobles, scores of servants sending up clouds of incense, hundreds of tamanes bearing the treasure, but only ten warriors, each bearing white banners of truce, which the Tlascalans were compelled by diplomatic custom to honor.

What Cortes was told was such a farrago as to be impossible to believe as the truth.

Cortes was not only congratulated for his victory over the Tlascalans, but thanked for being of such service to the great Montezuma, as token of which he was presented with such gold as to surely whet his appetite for more.

'The great Montezuma would like nothing more than to receive you in Tenochtitlan with the pomp and hospitality which you have so well earned by this proof of your friendship and thank you himself. Alas, his true friendship for you renders this impossible, for Tenochtitlan is an enormous city with a huge and often fractious population, there are those who might plot to raise the people against you, and so your safety cannot be guaranteed.'

'How could you have expected Cortes to believe such words coming from the absolute monarch of all the Mexica?' I asked Montezuma in utter befuddlement much later.

'I did not care,' Montezuma told me. 'For if he did, it would be proof that this was no Quetzalcoatl and these were no Toltecs, and I would send an army to crush him. And if he did not, it would entice him here, where I would learn the truth, and either accept the rule of Quetzalcoatl and the Toltecs, or trap a tribe of mere men who would usurp my rightful rule, as Huitzilopochtli would have it.'

'You *wanted* him to come to Tenochtitlan?'

'I wanted nothing but to know what the gods would have me do, and since I was granted no clear omen, I sought my own by seeking not to prevent what they would have Malinche do, but making it as difficult as possible.'

Cortes allowed two of the envoys to return to Tenochtitlan with an equally smarmy reply to the effect that the command of his sovereign forbade him to eschew a face-to-face meeting with his brother Emperor, no matter the danger to his own person, and the cautionary tale of how thoroughly the Teules had conquered Tlascala and won the Tlascalans' allegiance. The rest of the delegation he took with us to Tlascala in like manner so that they might witness our triumphal entry.

Thousands of its citizens and folk from the surrounding countryside turned out to watch our army parade into their capital city. But the manner in which the Tlascalans greeted us was strangely delightful and delightfully strange. Men and women turned out in their best embroidered and feathered finery, festooned themselves with wreaths of roses, hung them around the necks of Spaniards and even the horses. Amazingly enough, there were even scores of papas in their filthy robes and blood-matted tresses perfuming the air we breathed with the sweet smoke of their censers.

Our way had to be cleared by the city guard as we passed through the gates of the stone wall surrounding the city, so crowded were the streets, and the flat roof-terraces of the dwellings were lined with avidly cheering spectators, their façades hung with roses and honeysuckle, rough boughs of which were gaily tossed at our train.

It was as if the Tlascalans were greeting their own victorious warriors rather than an army of conquerors. Caesar himself could not have wished for more upon his triumphal entries to Rome after his conquests.

In this manner we made our way to the palace of Xicotencatl the Elder, a large, low, sprawling edifice, where the old man himself, supported by two retainers, toddled out to greet us. If he were not truly a hundred years old, he must have been approaching that count, for his skin was as wrinkled and leathered as ancient parchment, his features skeletal. In his beautiful featherwork cloak, earrings, labret, and necklace of emerald-embellished gold, richly embroidered tunic, and towering headdress of iridescent green quetzal plumes, he presented a spectacle both comic and pathetic: a corpse decked out in the vestments of an Emperor or a Pope.

When Cortes dismounted to receive his greeting, Xicotencatl ran shaky fingers gently over his face, for it seemed he was indeed blind. We were all then conducted into an enormous banquet hall hung with cloth and feathered tapestries and liberally strewn with roses, and seated on petatl mats.

After the usual formal exchange of greetings, Cortes rose to speak, first for the benefit of our notary Godoy, for he straightaway recited the formula of the Requerimiento, claiming all Tlascala as a vassal state of the Holy Roman Emperor, King Charles of Spain, though by now I was conversant enough with Nahuatl to know that in Marina's translation Charles became 'our sovereign', nor was that of which he was sovereign identified by name.

Xicotencatl declared, in a firm voice at variance with his frail appearance, that nothing could have pleased him more than this alliance that was now sealed between Tlascala and 'the nation of Malinche', which he likened to that of the so-called Triple Alliance of the Mexica with Texcoco and Tacuba which had established the Mexica rule that this new and mightier alliance would now soon overthrow.

Then the feast began as servants brought out scores of well-painted and glazed clay bowls filled with different elaborately prepared dishes, all of them morsels of meats and vegetables swimming in both subtle and fiery sauces. Pulque was served from jugs, and as much chocolatl as anyone desired, and my Nahuatl was sufficiently lubricated so that I could hold something of a conversation with Xicotencatl, with only occasional aid from Marina, who sat between him and Cortes, with myself opposite.

'How is it that you so open-heartedly greet your conquerors?' I managed to ask him after this fashion.

'I am a very old man,' he replied, 'and never in my lifetime have we been truly free of the Mexica, though never in my lifetime have they subdued us either. Texcoco, though a greater nation than the Mexica in everything save military power, is well served by its lesser role in its alliance with Tenochtitlan, and so may Tlascala be in such an alliance against them with you.'

He displayed a vulpine smile that was more gums than teeth. 'Especially since the ruler whom we have now accepted as our sovereign is much further away than Montezuma and conveniently out of sight.'

Cortes demanded a full translation of this from Marina, after which his interest was piqued, and he joined in the conversation, making it rather slower and more difficult, but no less interesting.

'Ask him to explain the nature and brief history of this alliance.'

'The Mexica now claim descent from the Toltecs, or at least their nobles do, but that is one of their more ridiculous fabrications, for in fact they wandered into Anahuac as a barbarous tribe from the great northern desert long after the Toltecs were gone, claiming to have come from the great nation of Aztlan at that time, conveniently unreachable across impassable wastes, which will give you a good notion of their character, and which is why the other tribes of what they now presume to style "the Valley of Mexico" slyly refer to them as "Aztecs", though not to their faces,' Xicotencatl told us contemptuously with a sly smirk.

'A, you say, *word*-play?' Marina said, when our expressions made plain that neither Cortes nor I had understood the jest.

'Pun,' I informed her.

'*Pun* . . . The *pun* is that "Aztec", which may be taken to mean someone from "Aztlan" if spoken quickly and not too clearly, can be taken to mean something like "barbarian from nowhere" if one is of a mind to take it thus.'

'Just so,' said Xicotencatl when this was translated into Nahuatl for him. 'They amounted to so little that they were driven out everywhere and the only place they could find to settle was the middle of a lake, later to claim that they adopted this desperate measure under command of a sign given by Huitzilopochtli, who at that time himself amounted to little more than the paramount god of the lowliest tribe in Anahuac.'

He paused to down a cup of chocolatl, and continued his version of Mexica history with even more scornful relish.

'Itzcoatl, a rude man but a great war leader, conquered some of the weaker peoples around the lakeshore from the safety of Tenochtitlan, but there would have been no Triple Alliance if not for the misfortune of Nezahualcoyotl, the great King of Texcoco, the true inheritors of the Toltecs if ever there were any. Nezahualcoyotl was a great poet, a deep delver of mysteries, and a wise ruler, but his prowess as a survivor of intrigues against him left much to be desired, and one of the plots against him cost him his kingdom. Itzcoatl took advantage of this and used the resulting divisions in Texcoco to restore him to power as something more than a vassal but less than an equal, and that was the beginning of the Triple Alliance, Tacuba not being much then or now.'

'How long ago was this?' I asked.

'My father was a boy at the time,' replied Xicotencatl. 'But the alliance would not have lasted without Tlacaelel, counselor not only to Itzcoatl, but to both the first and greater Montezuma who succeeded him, and Axayacatl, who succeeded *him* in turn, a man whom I was privileged to meet on several occasions when I was a boy.'

His blind eyes seemed to gaze off into some misty land of memory and for the first time he displayed a smile that was almost beatific. 'Tlacaelel!' he exclaimed. 'Now there was a great man! The only great man the Mexica have ever produced. Wise. Clever. Devious. Quite ruthless. No poet, but in his way a great artist of the word, and certainly when it came to using it to practical advantage.'

'How so?' asked Cortes.

'He revised the history of the Mexica into something more suitable for the overlords of an empire,' said Xicotencatl. 'It was he who declared that the Mexica were descended from the Toltecs, and thus gained them the awe in which they are now held by their vassals and the ridiculous pride in themselves which fills their barbarous hearts. And he did more. As Itzcoatl, under his guidance, made Nezahualcoyotl a King once more, so did Tlacaelel raise up Huitzilopochtli over Quetzalcoatl.'

'He did *what*?' I exclaimed.

'Quetzalcoatl was the god-king of the Toltecs, god of the life-giving sun, god of knowledge, god of wisdom, god of valor, or perhaps an ancient hero, or perhaps both, since with the Toltecs, men, it is said, were like gods, and gods walked among them. As for Huitzilopochtli, he arrived in Anahuac as the simple war god of a barbarian tribe. But Tlacaelel stole the powers of Quetzalcoatl for him.'

'How does one steal the powers of a god?' Cortes asked softly, as if wondering if there was some way he might do likewise, as if I and Marina had not helped him steal a certain portion thereof already.

The canny Xicotencatl, catching this in his voice even in Spanish, laughed.

'Only to give them to another god,' he said sardonically. 'Tlacaelel made changes in the rites of the Mexica. Huitzilopochtli became the god of both life and death, of the sun and of war. As the Sun, his tears of light brought life to the Earth, and to keep the cycle of growth and death and rebirth turning round, he must be fed with what those tears became in the world below the sky – blood, the Tears of the Sun, contained by the flesh which they nourished. As the god of Death, he must be fed Life to keep the circle complete, and as god of War, he must be fed the hearts of brave warriors, the spirits of their bodies willingly liberated in the flowery death to increase his power. Which in turn, Huitzilopochtli, thus satisfied, returns to the hearts of the next generation of warriors to make them brave and strong.'

Upon hearing this translated, Cortes could not refrain from crossing himself against the horror. Xicotencatl, who could not have understood the import of this sign, would have understood its meaning from the stricken look on Cortes' face had he not been blind. And he somehow seemed to sense it anyway, for he laughed grimly, and turned his unseeing eyes on Cortes in a most unsettling manner.

'An excellent belief for a warrior nation, don't you think?' he said. 'It has served the Mexica so well that, with a change of the war god's name, we have adopted it for ourselves.'

I left that banquet with my stomach bloated and my head spinning, nor did the thoughts that the tales Xicotencatl set revolving in my mind abate during the next days, as I was free to wander alone through Tlascala observing the life of the city and seeking to comprehend the inner lives of its inhabitants.

Cortes, always accompanied of necessity by Marina, spent most of this time seeking to persuade Xicotencatl the general, Xicotencatl the Elder, and the council to supply him with troops to reinforce his march on Mexico, denying that he intended to use them to storm Tenochtitlan, which they unanimously considered suicidal, while *they* sought to persuade *him* to remain in Tlascala to protect his new 'vassals' from the armies of Montezuma the next time they were attacked.

Cortes was elated with his great victory and eager to make good use of his new allies, but vexed with these negotiations with the said allies, who seemed primarily interested in making defensive use of *him*.

'But what use *would* you make of the Tlascalans if you get your way?' I asked him once. 'Attack Tenochtitlan? Besiege it?'

Cortes seemed to have no good answer, and that vexed him even more. 'That is a Rubicon I will worry about bridging when I get there,' he grumbled. 'Much the best course would be to subdue the Mexica by winning Montezuma to King and Cross.'

Leaving him to his own devices, or rather being left by him to my own, I continued my solitary exploration of Tlascala.

The city was laid out in the orderly pattern with which we had become familiar, though here the main market square was separate from that of the chief temple around which our quarters were ranged, and there was a Spartan cleanliness to the streets and an orderliness to the well-policed markets where magistrates were stationed to adjudicate commercial disputes and municipal guards to enforce their edicts.

Foodstuffs were in reasonable abundance, but the choice was not large; mainly maize, maize breads, beans, turkeys, peppers, and a few varieties of vegetables, with little fruit, no cacao, and no salt. My

Nahuatl by now was good enough for me to learn that Tlascala, in its mountain fastness far from the sea, with its cool climate, could not grow tropical fruits or cacao of its own, nor did it have a source of salt, and the Mexica made trade with the outside difficult if not impossible, so that the banquet we had enjoyed must have been supplied at great expense and no little danger by smugglers.

The inhabitants of the city, while displaying no hostility to the Spanish and little more to the Totonacs, seemed aloof and guarded, perhaps owing to a generally parsimonious nature engendered by the climate, the harsh rocky slopes surrounding their plateau, and the discipline required to earn their living; mountaineers rather than the more expansive tropical lowlanders to whom we were accustomed.

In addition to the main temple, there were many others, all with their hideous collections of skulls proudly displayed on the ceremonial racks, which, I learned, were honoured with the special name of 'tzompantli', and papas aplenty casting their evil eyes at passing white faces. As I wandered alone through the streets of this alien city, passing among its inhabitants like a ghost, it was truly brought home to me that we were not merely in a foreign land as Britain might be to a Spaniard, but in another world entire.

No doubt this mood was greatly enhanced by Xicotencatl's history lesson, which had revealed a complexity of intrigues that might put the Roman Empire to shame, but even more by his theological discourse. I had previously believed that the life of the spirit forms the life of a nation, but here it seemed that the beliefs of the peoples, the very identities and attributes of the gods, had more than once been changed for political ends.

Was this mere cynicism, or was it something else that hovered beyond my comprehension? For the Tlascalans, like the Totonacs and the Tabascans, seemed to sincerely credit the existence of their pantheon of gods and the vital functions they must be paid in blood and hearts to perform, even though their very natures and powers seemed to swirl mutably on the winds of state.

I had lived in nations professing two different religions while practicing a third, so one would have thought that my familiarity with their variety would have prepared me for those of this New World. But here

I had encountered not merely a difference in religious beliefs but an elusive difference in the nature of the relationship between men and their gods itself.

In this mood, I chanced to encounter Father Olmedo likewise wandering alone through one of the smaller marketplaces, his pensive mien, as it turned out, matching my own.

'You are obviously an educated man, Alvaro de Sevilla, you have the ear of Cortes, and once before you have persuaded me to take your good advice upon such matters.'

'Such matters?'

'This may seem strange coming from a priest to a layman,' Father Olmedo said uneasily, 'but I would have your advice on how I might succeed in truly bringing these heathen to Christ.'

How strange this really was, I of course could not betray out of fear for my own safety, but there was something affecting in the plaintive tone of this Christian priest seeking such counsel from a secret Jew.

'They allow us to tear down their idols and erect the Cross, but they are only bowing to superior force, surely we both know that,' he told me. 'They consent to be baptized, but it is only a sort of lark. They gather to mass, but for them it is merely entertainment. They partake of the wine and the wafer but only because the novelty of devouring the body and the blood of a god is a reversal of their own hideous sacrifices. They listen to my sermons, but I am not so naive or full of myself as to believe that I really touch their hearts . . .'

'Perhaps you cannot reach their hearts until you understand them?' I suggested.

'And you believe you do?'

I could only shrug and repeat what Xicotencatl had told us. By the time I had finished, we had left the market and were strolling at random down a narrow street towards another square.

'What awful blasphemy!' Father Olmedo exclaimed predictably.

'What else would you have expected to hear?'

'At least blasphemy of a lesser kind,' he muttered, frowning more as if he were struggling with a difficult concept to grasp than in outrage. 'These people . . . these people blaspheme even their own gods!'

'Perhaps not.'

'What then?'

Now it was my turn to wrestle with a concept my mind could barely contain. 'We believe in and worship a single God,' I told him truthfully, for in this at least, Christian, Jew and Muslim were in accord. 'They believe in a plethora of godlings, some in charge of rain, others of the ripening of the crops, sunshine, war. And while each tribe may have its paramount deity, each does not discredit the existence of that of the others, indeed may propitiate them, for even farmers must on occasion wage war, even warriors must cultivate maize, and all men must have sun and rain. Thus, depending upon changing fortunes and way of life, they must change the god they mainly propitiate that he might be persuaded to serve them.'

'What cynicism!' Father Olmedo exclaimed, but I found that my words were now coming faster than my thoughts, clarifying what had been elusive as they emerged from my lips, as if some sapient god were speaking through me.

'I think not,' I told him, 'for they do not *worship* their gods as we do ours. We seek to obey the Will of God and serve Him by living right-eously and according to His commandments, but *they* seek to persuade *their* gods to serve *them.*'

The look on Father Olmedo's face as he stopped dead in his tracks might have appeared on that of Saul thunderstruck by revelation on the road to Damascus.

'Before you can hope to convert them to the service of Christ, you must first persuade them how, if they do, Christ will serve them.'

'By saving their souls from eternal damnation in the fires of Hell of course!'

It was growing clearer and clearer in my mind. If Tlacaelel could rewrite the religion of the Mexica to suit his worldly purposes, why could not the Christian faith be rewritten a bit to serve ours? And who better to do it than a Jew?

'That is not their concern,' I said. 'Jesus Christ must give them what they require of *their* gods, not what we require of *ours.*'

We had reached the edge of the next square, this a modest one, devoted to a minor temple, which nevertheless was caked with dried blood, and had a ceremonial tzompantli of some scores of human skulls proudly displayed before it.

'What would you have me do?' Father Olmedo demanded, pointing angrily at this obscenity. 'Have them sacrifice human hearts to Jesus, and add the skulls of the victims to that pile?'

And then I had it entire.

'I do believe I know how to have them give up such loathsome practices,' I told him.

'You do?'

'This is not *worship* of their gods, this is payment for services that must continue to be provided . . .'

'The logic of the marketplace . . .' Father Olmedo muttered contemptuously.

'Exactly,' I told him. 'And so they will readily enough give it over if the nourishment that Jesus requires is less onerous tribute.'

'You would have me preach a blasphemous sermon?'

'Not at all. And since this is a warrior race, better it be delivered by Cortes, the victorious warrior of Christ, who, after all, derives his powers from Him, and what Jesus requires as food is something they value not at all. Something that He in truth eats already.'

Father Olmedo goggled at me.

'What else?' I told him. 'Sin.'

Having convinced Father Olmedo that the conversion of the Tlascalans must be accomplished by adapting the precepts of Christianity to their desires instead of the other way around, I was then commissioned to write the sermon which would accomplish this feat of theological prestidigitation, but while Tlacaelel had only to satisfy a singular master when performing his similar literary task, I was burdened with three.

Cortes was all for it when I explained it to him, for the victorious general of Christ rendered invincible by the One True God was something he believed he was already, and pragmatist that he was, he immediately saw how turning the Prince of Peace into a war god who could replace Huitzilopochtli in the hearts of Tlascalans would go a long way toward persuading them to follow wherever his favorite general chose to lead.

This was not how I had put it to Father Olmedo, who was hardly about to endorse the forthright transformation of Jesus Christ into

Mars, and the result was endless redrafting of the speech to square this circle and produce a text which could win the approval of both.

And then there was Marina, who was going to have to translate it into Nahuatl, so that each draft had to be gone over with her. The happy result was that we had an excellent excuse to spend much time alone together, not all of which was spent preparing the two texts. The unhappy result was that she had her own idea about how to accomplish the desired effect, and while I had to agree that it would work, I knew full well that it would never be countenanced by Father Olmedo.

'Why are you so . . .you say *dense*? Alvaro? Jesus is both God and man. Quetzalcoatl is both god and man. Cortes is Quetzalcoatl. Jesus died with the promise to return at this battle you call "Armageddon" to defeat the evil Satan and bring a new and better world. Quetzalcoatl left the same promise behind. So . . . the Second Coming of Quetzalcoatl is the Second Coming of Jesus and Montezuma is Satan.'

'And our Hernando is therefore Jesus Christ in battle armor?' I groaned.

'Yes! It is perfect!'

'We can't do it. Father Olmedo would never allow it.'

'You do not know that.'

'Oh yes I do!'

'You must at least ask him.'

'Oh no I mustn't!'

At this point in each version of this argument, Marina would turn seductive, would appeal to both the courage and desire of my manhood, arousing and satisfying the latter in the transparent hope of thus arousing the former to terminal folly.

In the afterglow of which, I would once more patiently explain that even suggesting such a thing to a Catholic priest was likely to get both of us burned at the stake for heresy, she would express her disbelief, and I would entertain her with pillow talk of the horrors of the Inquisition, which I could never convince her were not stories I was making up to cover my cowardice.

In the midst of this process of literary frustration mingled with amatory bliss, an embassy arrived from Tenochtitlan with a message contradicting Montezuma's last one which seemed to make bringing it to a rapid conclusion imperative.

Now Cortes was cordially invited to visit him in Tenochtitlan, entreated to eschew any alliance with the barbarous Tlascalans or further passage through their lands, and to proceed instead through Cholula, a city loyal to him where a friendly reception and safe passage could therefore be assured.

You can no doubt imagine, dear reader, the uproar this caused, for we were in Tlascala because the Totonacs had warned us against the treacherous Cholulans, and the Tlascalans, who scorned and detested them as willing collaborators with the Mexica, were even more adamant in their insistence that this was a trap.

'There is a large Mexica garrison only a few hours' march from Cholula,' Xicotencatl the general told Cortes.

'Would you betray the alliance you so recently made with us at the orders of Montezuma against whom you have promised to protect Tlascala?' Xicotencatl the Elder demanded reasonably but not without ire.

Cortes was caught in Montezuma's trap, for surely this must be a political snare set for him, if not so surely a military one. If he now rejected what Montezuma had finally deigned to grant, or declined to proceed by a route along which the Emperor had guaranteed his security, the insult would ensure that he would never receive another. But if he did as Montezuma bade at the cost of losing the Tlascalan alliance, he would be more or less at the mercy of the Mexica as he passed through the heart of their empire.

'I'm afraid, Alvaro, that my sermon to the Tlascalans is going to have to parse this conundrum as well,' Cortes told me.

'At least tell me what outcome you wish to produce,' I groaned.

'Obviously the only course is to proceed to Tenochtitlan through Cholula accompanied by a sizeable force of Tlascalans,' he told me.

'As simple as that?'

'Indeed,' said Cortes blithely.

The next day, envoys arrived from Cholula confirming the invitation and pressing Cortes to allow them to return with his acceptance. The

Tlascalans provided him with an excuse to prevaricate by huffily declaring that these were men of insultingly low rank, which was their opinion of all Cholulans, but which allowed Cortes to send them back with no more than a haughty demand for envoys more suitable to his own station.

Which also provided him with the excuse to tell me to get the speech written *now*, and 'Father Olmedo be damned!'

But Father Olmedo was more likely to damn *me* than himself if I produced what he would consider blasphemy, and it took three more sweaty days to accomplish the task, by which time another embassy from Cholula had arrived, this one a deputation of caciques dripping gold and feather finery and accompanied by tamanes bearing gifts of same, so that there could be no question of sending them back without a definitive answer.

And so a convocation was held in the main temple square where a Cross and an altar had already been set up. Xicotencatl the Elder, the other three principal caciques, and Xicotencatl the general, surrounded by nobles and officers, were positioned in the front ranks, the former reclining on a litter in practical deference to his age and infirmity, the rest standing. Flanking the Cross and altar were contingents of the Spanish army, and the rest of the square filled up behind them with townspeople and nervous-looking papas.

I myself, a good deal more nervous than any of these filthy wretches, positioned myself within the Spanish ranks, just in case the effect produced by what I had written was other than what was planned.

Father Olmedo said mass, after which Cortes took his place before the altar with Marina at his side, and began to read from the prepared text, which I had insisted was prudent he do under the circumstances, and also, to be truthful about it, because I was quite proud of what I had managed to write in the end.

Cortes delivered it in small segments, pausing after each for Marina's translation, but herein I shall reproduce it without pause in its entirety, to indulge you the better, dear reader, while admittedly indulging myself.

'The peoples of these lands have long believed that they were constrained to feed their gods the flesh and blood of men, none more so than the benighted Mexica who have warred endlessly with Tlascala to feed the flower of *your* warriors to the ravenous maw of Huitzilopochtli, thereby weakening you and strengthening themselves. So too have you believed it necessary to feed your war god with the hearts of *their* warriors to weaken them and strengthen yourselves.

'But I have been sent here by the One True God to put such sacrifices to an end and liberate you from the onerous yoke of Tenochtitlan, and I tell you in His Name, which no man dare pronounce, that these great and noble tasks are one and the same!

'In the long ago, there reigned in these lands the noble Toltecs, under the wise rule of him who was long venerated as both a god and a man, and Quetzalcoatl was his name. Then he departed from this world and left it to the forces of blood and darkness, but promising to return at the end of this evil age to bring back the light in a great battle against them, after which victory would come a new world greater than any ever before known.

'In the long ago, in lands across the sea, there reigned another empire of blood and darkness, and the One True God, seeing this, descended into it to become a being both a god and a man, and Jesus Christ was his name. And He who was both God and man allowed himself to be sacrificed upon the Cross to bring such evil to an end. For the One True God, Who is both omniscient and omnipotent, saw that if the battle to bring back the light and call forth the blessed new age was fought then and there, the rest of the world that He had made would remain in darkness.

'And so He allowed Himself to be slain as proof of His love for all His creation everywhere and for all time. And He too promised to return one day to slay the forces of darkness everywhere they ruled.

'But the One True God, the All-Powerful, the Merciful, needs not to be nourished by the blood and flesh of men, for He is all things unto Himself, as a token of which He gives his own ever-renewed body and blood to men as nourishment to their spirits. And so that all men will believe the glorious message with which He left the world and with which He returns to redeem it.

'I speak to you now in the language of a distant land and you hear my words in your own. The words are different and so too the names, but

I say to you that the name of the messenger matters not, for the message is the same over all the Earth.

'And the message is this:

'The One True God is not to be fed with the hearts and blood of men. The One True God is to be fed with the sins of your enemies. For by feeding Him the hatred in your hearts for the wrongs committed by them, you free yourselves from it, and such freedom is a mighty sword, as evidence of which I remind you that we who feed our God with the forgiveness of your sins have defeated you who have fed yours with hearts and blood. And by feeding Him the forgiveness of your enemies' sins against you, even those of the Mexica, you too will gain that power, and no one can stand against us, for it is the greatest pleasure of the One True God to eat such sins, and rid all men of them, and thereby transform them into His Grace and us all into the invincible soldiers of Christ behind whose shield we are destined to become the redeemers and rulers of the world.'

Then Cortes and a dozen of his soldiers went to the great rack of skulls before the temple steps and smashed the tzompantli with their swords so that the skulls tumbled in an avalanche that rumbled into the front ranks of the dumbstruck crowd.

Cortes raised his sword high, and knelt before the Cross.

'Onward to Mexico!' he roared. 'Onward for Christ and liberty!'

As they had been schooled, all the Spaniards dropped to their knees as one man.

One by one, then in groups, with gathering momentum, all the Tlascalans before that great temple to death and blood did likewise, until only the papas with their blood-caked hair and filthy robes were left standing there, bereft, abandoned, and quite alone.

Thus did a Christian sermon written by a Jew with a little help from the Koran transform the Prince of Peace into the Messiah of Armageddon bearing fire and the sword and the Gospel which in the hands of the Inquisition ruled the continent across the sea with a cruel iron hand into the war cry of liberty.

In the name of the Father and the Son and the Holy Spirit.

Inshallah.

Adonoi Elohenu.

Blessed and terrible be His Name.

18

T HUS WERE THE TLASCALANS converted into Holy Warriors of the Cross and an expedition of conquest into something like an Islamic jihad. Nor, I must confess, was I innocent of what I was doing, for I knew that this was how Mohammed, Prophet and general, had united the fractious tribes of Arabia into a force that had swept over half his known world during his lifetime.

But I had not anticipated the effect Cortes' speech would have on the Spaniards, who had found it convenient to believe that their cause was a holy one already. Righteous fervor was kindled, and Cortes was convinced more than ever by the words I had put in his mouth that even Montezuma could be subjugated by the Gospel according to me.

We would proceed to Tenochtitlan, crushing whatever benighted heathens presumed to oppose us, converting them afterward by the sweet reason of conquest and the natural human desire to enlist in a winning cause, and when we got there, Cortes would convert Montezuma by an alliance between religious logic and the threat of invincible force, thereby gaining his empire for Christ, King and himself as the conversion of Constantine had won the Roman Empire for the Cross.

Now the opportunity to proceed through Cholula seemed God-given. For Cholula was a city whose founding was lost in the mists of time; older than the Empire of the Mexica, older perhaps than even the coming of the Toltecs, and was to the heathens of all these lands what Jerusalem was to Jews and Christians alike, the fount and holy city of their faiths, and to win it for the Cross would be like unto the Crusaders retaking Jerusalem from Islam.

Now the Tlascalans, emboldened by the martial fervor sweeping their city, were all for marching on it with us with overwhelming force behind the promised shield of the Cross, and by the tens of thousands petitioned to accompany us.

But Cortes foresaw that the approach of a large army of their enemies would surely be taken by the Cholulans for the army of conquest the Tlascalans wished it to be, and the nearby Mexica garrison could hardly fail to become embroiled if there was an attempt to take the city by force. Cortes would then find himself drawn into what both he and Montezuma himself had thus far prudently avoided – direct battle between an army of Tenochtitlan and his own.

So Cortes allowed a force of no more than six thousand Tlascalans to march with us and the Totonacs, who were on friendly terms with the Cholulans, and so we set forth.

The march to Cholula was short and uneventful and our reception more or less as promised. The city sat on a high but most fruitful plain, well watered by both streams and irrigation canals, and though by marching into the evening hours and perhaps the edge of night we could have reached it in a single day, Cortes chose to make camp by one of these streams before the sun was down and proceed to the city the next morning. For an approach under cover of dusk by a far larger force than had been invited, including thousands of hostile Tlascalans, would be perceived as a threat rather than the acceptance of a cordial invitation.

How right he was!

The next morning several caciques and their retainers arrived to usher us into their city, and when they saw thousands of Tlascalan warriors glowering at them, they protested in fear and politely guarded outrage. After short and less than acrimonious negotiations, it was agreed that the Tlascalans would remain where they were while the Spaniards and Totonacs visited Cholula.

As at Tlascala, our parade into the city was well attended, but the crowds that lined the road to Cholula seemed more restrained, decked out in finery and flowers to be sure, garlanding Spaniards upon occasion, serenading us with drums and flutes in manner too orderly to seem wholehearted, and there was little cheering or gaiety. Then too the crowds were salted with an overabundance of papas, silently observing and waving censers in a manner suggestive of fumigation.

The innocent among us might have taken the mood as being merely one of cautious curiosity, but I, being of a more saturnine nature, sensed that this was a formal welcoming, carefully arranged.

The city itself was unlike any I had yet seen. The streets were so wide as to be fairly styled avenues and scrupulously clean, and they were laid out in a rectangular gridwork that Euclid might have admired.

There were temples everywhere, large ones, small ones, so that one was always in sight of several of them. In contrast to the pristine avenues, they were all encrusted with well-aged dried blood, and the stones of many of them were so weathered and softened by erosion than they must have been centuries old. More of the dwellings than not were also of stone, and even the fresh whitewash on the majority of them could not conceal their venerability.

The people in the streets were better-dressed than any I had yet seen, their mantles more finely and artfully embroidered, featherwork cloaks more extravagantly crafted, the jewelry most cleverly worked and in much greater abundance; the rich and cultivated citizenry of a great center of commerce and art. Yet among them were thousands of papas, who, in their bloodstained robes, with their filthy and tangled blood-stiffened tresses, would be taken as the lowliest of beggars in any city in Europe or Araby. But here, the manner in which they strutted through the throngs, and the deferential manner in which way was made for them, made it plain that in Cholula they were effectively princes of the city.

There were markets in profusion, offering every manner of goods, including an abundant supply of the elegant metalwork and pottery for which Cholula was known, but they seemed to have been set up in the available interstices of a far older city which had been erected of a piece for ceremonial purposes by some lost race, as if a series of Arabian souks had grown up at the feet of the Great Egyptian Pyramids.

An apt metaphor as it turned out as we approached the center of the city, for we saw that Cholula was dominated, in every sense of the word, by a truly immense pyramid, perhaps not nearly as tall as the greatest thrown up by those ancient Egyptians, but squatter and truncated into a huge flat platform at its top from whose heights glowered down a large stone idol, so that its base must have occupied nearly as much ground.

We were led to its foot, where a great crowd had gathered, not to witness some ceremony, it was obvious, but to observe our reaction, for to a man they stood there silently and expectantly facing not the temple but Cortes as he rode slowly past it. Marina ran up to him, said something, and Cortes halted and looked up at the idol, and then I saw why.

Its stones were even more rounded than any of the others in the city, and, caked with dried blood as they were, still the verdigris of even greater age was visible peering here and there from the dirty brown crust. Thousands of skulls were racked before it, many of them cracked and splintered. The idol atop it was roofed over by a kind of open-faced stone pavilion, but from the ground, its features could be vaguely discerned. The thing was crafted of some black stone. Its visage was that of a serpent. It was decorated with turquoise, gold and silver earrings, pendants and necklaces which had to be much newer than its obsidian flesh. It was crowned by a headdress of stone feathers freshly painted bright green. Its identity was unmistakable and its proclamation loud and clear.

This was Quetzalcoatl and the city was his, and had been since its deepest antiquity and perhaps beyond, as the Kaaba had been worshipped by wandering tribes long before there was an Islam or a Mecca.

Cortes gazed up at Quetzalcoatl uncertainly for a long moment, as well he might, presented as he was with this conundrum, for it was plain that a sign from him was what the Cholulans required. He dismounted and held a brief parley with Father Olmedo while the crowd held its collective breath.

Then a tall wooden Cross was brought forth and Cortes took it, facing the Spanish army, which then knelt down before it, facing both the Cross and the temple behind him. Cortes did not kneel, nor did he speak. He turned, and with a visible effort raised up the heavy Cross to Quetzalcoatl, a perfect gesture under the circumstances, I thought, for it could be taken as either a salute or a challenge.

The great throng remained silent as Cortes handed the Cross to a soldier, remounted, and rode on, and only then did the silence dissolve into a chaotic and collectively muttering babblement.

We were quartered, as usual, in apartments surrounding a secondary temple square on three sides, were welcomed with formal hospitality by a deputation of caciques in the usual manner, and well supplied with food and drink, including a generous amount of chocolatl.

But though the apartments had been well cleaned, the temple was still there with its crust of dried blood and its rack of skulls, and the atmosphere was therefore rather ominous. Cortes positioned the cannon to cover the entrances to the square, and posted a heavy guard.

The next few days passed tranquilly and uneventfully enough. We continued to be lavishly fed, and were free to wander the city unmolested. A Cross was erected in the center of the square, and an altar, and mass was said daily, but no Cholulans arrived to observe, which was odd, since Cholula was known as a nexus of pilgrimage for the devotees of the temples to a profusion of gods, and one would have thought that this ceremony to a new one who might or might not be the second coming of Quetzalcoatl would at least have drawn a throng of the curious.

The city seemed to be waiting for something. At length, a deputation of Mexica arrived, and paid a brief visit to our compound, but there was only a half-dozen of them, they were merely warriors, or at most captains, they bore no gifts, seemed to be using the paying of their respects primarily to observe our deployments, and soon took their leave to consult with the caciques of the city.

Here I fear, dear reader, my tale becomes a murky one, for the why of the massacre never became clear, not even when I later sought the truth of it from the captive Montezuma when he would have seemed to have no further self-interest in dissembling. I suspect that by that time he himself had forgotten what it was, for far from greeting my questions with stony silence, he presented a different version each time I inquired.

'I did not send those envoys into Cholula, they were sent by the commander of the nearby garrison in order to assess the situation, which was only prudent and natural.'

'I invited Malinche to pass through Cholula so that I might have a sign when he confronted the great and ancient temple of Quetzalcoatl.'

'My brother Cuitlahuac, representing many of my nobles and captains, demanded that we attack the Teules in the high mountain passes, and I pacified them by inviting the Teules to first go to Cholula, where, I told them, such an attack would be most advantageous, should I decide to mount it.'

'When I was told that Malinche had arrived at Cholula with an uninvited army of Tlascalans, I naturally saw this as hostile, and had to take the necessary precautions.'

'It was decided by the Cholulans alone, as witness that the Mexica garrison never came to the rescue of the city.'

And so forth. Even now I can only report the dreadful events as I witnessed them.

After the Mexica left Cholula, the atmosphere grew more and more ominous. There were no more visits by caciques to our compound. The food supply that had been offered to us daily was reduced to maize breads and bean mash and a parsimonious amount at that, and there was no more chocolatl.

Cortes' captains, chief among them Alvarado, Olid and Sandoval, counseled him to leave the city and rejoin our Tlascalan allies. But in somewhat larger groups than before, Spaniards and Totonacs wandered freely about Cholula, and while they were unmolested, the Totonacs, who were more familiar with such tactics, reported that they had seen barricaded streets, rooftops piled with stones, pits hidden under branches: signs that the Cholulans were preparing to impede a retreat from their city.

Then a messenger from the Tlascalans, disguised as a Totonac, arrived to inform Cortes that their scouts had seen a ceremony held well outside the city where some hundreds of men and children had been sacrificed; whether to Quetzalcoatl or Huitzilopochtli could not be discerned.

Finally an unclear event occurred which nevertheless seemed to clarify the situation. Marina and I, accompanied by six Spanish soldiers, three of whom were armed with arquebuses, for we no longer went abroad unguarded, were visiting a marketplace in search of additional provisions and what intelligence we might secure in the process when she was approached by an apparently ordinary woman doing likewise who asked to speak to her alone on 'a matter of interest only to women'.

Marina's interest was piqued, but I was adamantly opposed to it.

'Do not be foolish, Alvaro,' she insisted, nodding towards the woman, of an age approaching cronehood. 'I can easily enough take care of myself should she attempt any treachery.'

'Unless there are others lurking about, which would seem likely.'

'Then give me a sword,' she demanded, and made to snatch one from one of the guards, who pulled back.

A secure arrangement was finally agreed upon. We were led with our guards to quite a modest dwelling. The guards went inside to inspect the house, and when they reported that there was no one inside, Marina was allowed to enter alone with its mistress.

She remained inside for perhaps ten minutes, then emerged with her face carefully composed into a bland mask, behind which agitation was nevertheless visible. 'Have me escorted away from here as if I am a prisoner,' she whispered.

Agitated myself, I did as she bade.

'Well?' I demanded when we were sufficiently distant.

'First she asked if I was a prisoner of the Teules,' Marina told me, 'and seeing that she would tell me nothing if I denied it, I put up a show of anger at the Spaniards, and told her a tale of the cruelties they put me to. The woman then told me that this was not her house but one she had borrowed for the occasion, and that she was the wife of a cacique, seeking to save a fellow woman from the slaughter soon to befall the Teules. Find some means of escaping your captivity, and I will shelter you here so that you will later be able to return unharmed to your people, she told me.'

'And you believed that the wife of a cacique would really do such a thing?'

Marina regarded me as if I were a dimwit. 'Do you of all people take me for such a fool, Alvaro?' she said scornfully. 'Obviously this was a message from someone and I am expected to deliver it.'

'From whom? Her husband?'

Marina shrugged. 'She claimed that Montezuma had ordered the Teules to be attacked in the streets when they tried to depart from the city, aided by the Mexica garrison who would block the exits. Perhaps this is true. Perhaps the warning comes from a faction here that fears the consequences if the attack fails. Perhaps it is not true, and the Cholulans will act alone, but her husband or his faction seeks to blame whatever happens on Montezuma. Does it matter?'

When we informed Cortes, he straightaway called a meeting of his captains. Most of them were of a mind to leave the city at once, and without warning, opining that the element of surprise would be the best hope of escaping the trap. But Cortes demurred.

'I am all for surprise,' he declared. 'But rather than use it to escape this trap, I would use it to ensnare those who would spring it, and in the bargain teach the Cholulans, and Montezuma, and whoever else in these lands ever hears the tale, a lesson they will not soon forget in the fate of those who would seek to use treachery against an army of the Cross.'

Cortes returned the messenger to the Tlascalans with the order to make themselves ready to attack Cholula as soon as cannonfire was heard in the city. He then sent a message to the caciques of Cholula, informing them that he intended to leave their city for Tenochtitlan on the morrow. He requested that two thousand tamanes be assembled in our compound to transport our baggage, and that the caciques should accompany them, 'so that they might be repaid in full for the openhearted and generous hospitality which has been shown us'.

In the hours before dawn, arquebusiers and crossbowmen were stationed on the flat roofs of the buildings on three sides of the square, from which vantage to rain down a devastating crossfire. As the sun rose, infantry was positioned before each building in the orderly manner of guards of honor.

While the Spanish captains and soldiers went about setting this ambush with no little relish and vengeful anticipation of what was to come, though the Cholulans surely planned to do as much to us, I found my heart filled with guilt for my part, however small, in instigating this sanguinary affair, and I lurked back against the building at the far end of the square as far away as possible.

As the Cholulans approached, the cannon were rolled aside from the entrances to the square to allow them easy entry. Cortes mounted his horse, all the cavaliers did likewise, and he awaited their arrival at the far end of the square from the temple at the head of what appeared to be a formation of formal salutation.

Some half-dozen caciques entered the square by one of the entrances beside the temple and made their way slowly past the Cross in its center towards Cortes, followed by tamanes wearing only breechclouts, by the hundreds, by the thousands, so that it took quite a while for the square to fill with them, during which the caciques and Cortes regarded each other in still silence.

When the square was filled and tamanes had ceased to enter, one of the caciques spoke.

'Here are the bearers you have requested, Malinche, and I see that now that you have them, you are ready to depart.'

'We have one more task to perform first,' Cortes told him.

The caciques stared at him uncomprehendingly. Cortes smiled, the rictus of an Inquisitor about to light the pyre of an auto-da-fe.

'As you remember, I promised to repay you in kind for the hospitality which you have shown us,' he said smoothly. 'And now you shall have your just reward . . .'

He paused, and when he went on, it was in a voice of thunder. 'The just reward for your treachery! The repayment for your plan to murder us as we attempted to depart your city in peace! Did you really think you could hide your evil intent from the all-seeing eyes of the One True God? Did you really think you could butcher an army of the Cross as easily as you rip out the hearts of your countrymen?'

This true accusation was met with cries of terror, astonishment and lying denial; terror at what was to come, astonishment that Cortes or his god seemed to have seen into every dark nook and cranny, lying denial in a futile attempt to escape what could not be escaped.

'An evil lie of the Tlascalans!'

'It was Montezuma who ordered it!'

'The Mexica garrison would have punished us if we dared to disobey!'

'The Mexica will destroy you if you harm Cholula!'

That the caciques, in their fearful consternation, told such contradictory lies did nothing to aid them. 'It matters not who ordered this outrage!' Cortes roared. 'For the lesson in what retribution such treason will bring must be learned by all foolish enough to seek to commit its like again!'

He drew his sword to give the signal and it began.

The arquebusiers and crossbowmen atop the roofs aimed a withering crossfire into the densely packed tamanes, cutting them down by the screaming scores. There was another volley, and another, and another, so that hundreds lay dead or writhing in agony with their flesh torn open or bolts piercing their bleeding bodies before any of their remaining number could even summon up the forlorn wit to charge towards the buildings from which the carnage continued to rain down.

In any case, it was to no avail. From three sides of the square the infantry advanced, wielding swords of Toledo steel, against which the tamanes were utterly defenseless, even those scores among them who had hidden obsidian daggers in their breechclouts, and the Spaniards advanced in orderly and unhurried ranks, like lines of reapers bringing in a ripe crop of grain with their scythes.

Then Cortes led a cavalry charge through the center of the square which swiftly dispersed into a bloody chaos of individual horsemen cutting down all before them, and then, as the numbers of the living tamanes dwindled, chasing down pitiful remnants.

By this time, Cholulan forces outside the square were rushing towards the entrances at its four quarters, but Cortes, anticipating this, had the cannon aimed straight down the streets leading to them. The first volleys tore the narrow front ranks of the advancing Cholulans to pieces, and sent those who had escaped reeling back against the press of their fellows, only to be blown to bloody fragments by the second fusillades.

Their work in the square done, and the infantry dispatching those few Cholulans remaining alive, the cavalry formed up into four groups and charged through the entrances past the cannon. Though the horsemen were greatly outnumbered, the streets beyond were too narrow for more than a half dozen warriors to confront them at any one time, and in such circumstances they were invincible, cutting down the front rank with ease, then the one behind it, and the one behind that, until the Cholulans turned tail and fled with their tormentors harrying them back through the streets of the city in murderous pursuit.

That was all of the massacre I witnessed, for I had no desire to leave the safety of the square to appall myself with more. I remained there with Marina and a small detail of soldiers guarding the caciques, whom Cortes had ordered to be spared and taken prisoner. For at least an hour I listened to distant cries and screams and watched palls of smoke arise over every quarter of the city, learning later that the Tlascalans had entered the city to indulge themselves in an orgy of slaughter, arson, pillage and looting.

For all that time, Marina and I stood there without speaking, for what was there to say to each other about what our clever scheming had unwittingly wrought?

Before us was a great expanse of earth reddened with pools of blood and all but covered with the mangled and bloody bodies of the dead and the slowly dying. Beyond this ghastly midden towered the gore-encrusted pyramidal temple to some bloodthirsty god with its proud tzompantli rack of the skulls of his victims. And rising triumphantly in the midst of the battlefield as if to mock that sanguinary deity, or worse, much worse, to proclaim a dreadful brotherhood with it, was the pure white Cross.

Surely that said it all.

19

W E LINGERED IN CHOLULA for two weeks after the massacre, as Cortes, in much higher spirits than my own, put things back in order, or rather put things into the new order, which somewhere along the line had been christened 'New Spain'.

He recited the Requerimiento before a pliant new paramount cacique he installed, who straightaway forswore loyalty to Montezuma and swore fealty to King Charles on behalf of his nation and to 'Malinche' himself as his viceroy in New Spain. He removed the Tlascalans from the city, and soon enough, and with a surprising lack of rancor, caciques from the surrounding towns and villages arrived to ratify Spanish rule, and people began flocking in from the countryside to reinforce the diminished populace of the city.

When I expressed my surprise at how easily this had been accomplished in the aftermath of such an atrocity, Cortes told me that the 'necessary lesson' had been a great aid rather than a hindrance.

'It established that the wrath of Malinche, or Quetzalcoatl, or whatever they choose to call me, is much more to be feared than that of Montezuma, and the fact that the nearby Mexica garrison made no move to impede us established that Montezuma fears me far more than I fear him, which further erodes his authority.'

He waxed quite ebullient over what he had accomplished.

'Consider what would have happened if a Muslim army had done likewise in a Christian city while a Christian force sat on its hands nearby. Surely the rule of the Christian sovereign who let it happen would crumble. And that is what is happening here. In Tabasco, in Totonaca, in Tlascala, and now here in Cholula, it has already happened. New Spain already exists, it already covers a territory as large as most nations of Europe. We have already seized an empire from Tenochtitlan, and without even being opposed by a single Mexica soldier. I tell you, Alvaro, Montezuma's empire is rotten to the core. It is now clear that it was fractious and fragile before we even arrived on these shores, and we need only enter its capital to put an end to it. Indeed, if Montezuma is at all wise, he must realize that his only hope of retaining some shadow of his lofty position is to swear fealty to the Spanish Crown and serve as my viceroy as I serve under King Charles, an office I will magnanimously grant him if he is quick about it.'

I found this hard to credit until emissaries arrived from Montezuma accompanied by tamanes bearing extravagant gifts by way of apology for the outrageous treachery of his disloyal Cholulan vassals. Far from protesting the atrocity that Cortes had committed, Montezuma thanked him for relieving him of the necessity of sending in his own troops to punish their perfidy, the Mexican garrison being stationed in the area in the first place in order to keep the unruly Cholulans in their place!

Of course I could not swallow this whole and neither did Cortes, but after he had heard it and graciously granted his forgiveness, he laughed, and winked at me, as if to say 'I told you so.'

The only setback was that our Totonac allies insisted on returning home, for they feared the welcome that they might receive in Tenochtitlan, the savagery of the Tlascalans had frightened them, and the repute of the great mountains yet to be crossed for cold and mist and harshness of terrain cowed them as natives of a much more clement clime from continuing further, all the more so since they had no garments fit for such a passage.

And so, with a series of outlying vassal states secured behind us, an army of some several thousand Tlascalans and at least as many tamanes, we resumed our march to Tenochtitlan to complete the conquest of New Spain.

As we followed the road that led across a fertile and well-cultivated upland savanna but distantly overshadowed by the mighty cordillera and its snowcapped peaks shrouded in cloud, the shadows of what lay behind began to lift from my spirit, for it was an easy march, and a triumphal one. No one sought to impede us; far from it, the caciques of the villages we passed not only turned out to greet us, but readily enough acceded to their liberation from the yoke of Montezuma, swore their allegiance, and allowed the Cross to be planted.

It all seemed as Cortes had told me: we were a liberating army of Christian soldiers parading through a fair countryside towards final victory over a hated and bloodthirsty tyrant, expanding the borders of New Spain as we went and leaving in our wake a grateful peasantry won over to Christ and King.

I was almost able to persuade myself that the massacre we had put behind us was justified. For had not this lesser evil produced a greater good, the liberation of whole nations from far more sanguinary cannibalistic sacrifice, and in a pacific manner?

In this sophistic conversion, I was aided by Marina. 'Do not be foolish, Alvaro,' she told me when I expressed my qualms. 'Do not torment yourself. At Tenochtitlan, they feed ten times as many lives to Huitzilopochtli each year as Cortes fed to his Jesus Christ, and his sacrifice has proven much more effective. He is at war, and those whom he killed sought to kill us all on their altars, after all. Be happy, Alvaro, we are on our way to see great Tenochtitlan, as is both our hearts' desire.'

'But at what cost?'

'Whatever the cost, you may take it from one who has been a slave, better that your enemies pay it than you do!'

But after traversing the pleasant plain, we reached the foothill approaches to the daunting cordillera, the weather and the terrain grew ever harsher and our progress more labored as we climbed towards it, nor could the mood remain unaffected.

As we moved up through the densely wooded foothills, what had been a coolly refreshing climate began to turn cold. Gray mists hid the sun as often as not. Biting winds blew down from the canyons still high above us, canyons we must approach and traverse, rather than avoid.

As we began to climb through rugged ascending defiles, it grew colder still, and drizzle from what came to seem like a permanent gray deck of clouds began to slowly drench us, and fog rolled down through the passes. Higher yet, and the forests above them became pine, and then began to thin out, and the rains and the fogs became united in a single element, for now we had ascended into a cloud layer. The mighty snowcapped major peaks which previously had been intermittently visible were now permanently hidden from view as we crawled ever upward, while the air turned ever colder and the defiles steeper and rockier, and our world became an ominously gray-roofed tunnel clogged with dank and swirling mist.

If the Hell of the Christians was one of heat and fire, this was the cold, dark Hades of the pagan Greeks, and I at least, who was no Christian, began to take it as punishment for the terrible sin with which this grim journey had so blithely begun.

And then we reached the first evidence of the hand of man that we had encountered in what seemed like an eternity. But there was nothing comforting about it, only further diabolic torment.

The road – or rather rocky path – that we had been so laboriously following came to a fork. The righthand path was clear, but the lefthand path had been blocked with a barricade of large rocks and the trunks of trees whose greenness gave evidence that the barrier had been erected but recently to impede us.

Or to channel us.

Such was the mood that Cortes declared that we must not proceed as its builders had so obviously wished, but take the road they would not have us take. And so, like an army of Sisyphuses, albeit with less futile result, we were constrained to roll aside the stones and logs as a further chastisement.

Onward we climbed through the clouds, passing beyond the treeline, and the very soil became something darkly otherworldly; a pitch-black sandy loam laid down as lava and bolides by the great volcano Popocatepetl and ground down by the ages.

And then, miraculously, we were *above* the clouds and looking *down* on them, on a grimy grayish-white false landscape of slowly but visibly moving ethereal humped hills and misty valleys, as if we had ascended not merely to the sky but beyond it, to gaze down in discomfited wonder upon a grim parody of an angel-less and Godless Heaven.

But there were deities of a sort to be seen rising even above that. On our left hand rose the mighty snowcapped peak of Ixtaccihuatl, the 'white lady'. And even this mountain, dwarfing anything in Europe, was overshadowed by that which rose on the right: Popocatepetl, 'the mountain that smokes', a black peak that rose even higher, its summit freed of any snowcap by the fire of its volcanic eruptions, from which rose the plume of grayish-black smoke which gave it its name.

Truly we had left the world we had known behind us.

Here we paused, exhausted and dumbfounded, to rest and wonder. The Tlascalans, who had a dread of Popocatepetl both superstitious and quite practical, declared that it was a habitat of demons, and that no man had ever ascended it and returned alive. One of the Spanish soldiers, a mountaineer from the Pyrenees, piqued by the implied dare, declared his intention to climb to the summit of the volcano and nine of his comrades accepted the challenge, as well as a few fearful Tlascalans who were determined to prove that they were no lesser breed than Spaniards.

Climb the mountain they did, though not quite to the peak, and return they did also, with a daunting tale.

The ascent started easily enough along a steep but gentle slope of loam as black as the heart of Satan. But then the loam became deep dry black sand, and the climb a lead-footed slog through it. And further on, their breathing became labored, and they entered a strange but not entirely unpleasant dreamlike state in which their feet seemed disconnected from their bodies and they seemed to be floating upward with exaggerated slowness, as if walking through an ocean of viscous air.

Then, as they approached the summit, the sand gave way to rock, and the rim of the crater at the summit became visible, billowing black smoke, shooting out bright sparks and hot cinders, and exuding a choking Satanic stench of burning brimstone. All but overcome by the thinness of the air, the heat of the volcano and the showers of cinders, and perhaps fearing that they might encounter a portal into Hell itself if they peered over the crater rim, they turned back and returned to tell the tale without ever quite encountering Satan.

The next day we continued our passage through this unearthly infernal landscape, through a winding pass between the great mountains, which seemed like two forbidding sentinels guarding it. But that afternoon we rounded a bend and beheld a sight that took the breath away and transformed bleakness into soul-soaring wondrous delight in the blink of an eye.

As if we had been granted a sign from God, the curtain of cloud far below had been drawn aside, and we gazed upon Anahuac, the Valley of Mexico entire, glittering like an immense sapphire set in an even grander emerald.

The great valley was verdant with rich croplands and flourishing forests. In the center of it was an enormous lake. On its shores and inland rose more cities than the eye could count, and in the greater ones soared pyramids like unto those in ruins in Egypt, but gleaming white and entirely intact. A profusion of small boats hovered on the edge of visibility on the lake. Gardens floated magically on the waters.

There was nothing remotely like this constellation of cities anywhere in Europe. And if these cities were stars in a celestial constellation, great Tenochtitlan was a mighty sun, and I doubted that there was anything like it anywhere on Earth, or that Marco Polo could have felt anything like the wonder I did then when he first set eyes on the cities of Cathay.

Tenochtitlan was tremendous. Everything about it declared its grandeur. Its extent was immense. The avenues were so broad as to be dimly visible even at this distance as an enormous grid centered on a plaza larger than any I had ever seen or imagined. The city was huge enough, or so it seemed, that it might hold the entire populace of Castile.

But size was somehow the least of it. Tenochtitlan indeed sat in the lake connected to the shores only by four long straight causeways, like a great spider in the center of its web. The city shimmered in the haze the bright sun burned off the waters, so that it seemed to be not so much floating in the middle of the lake as hovering in the air above it as if by magic.

Who could have known? What extravagant tale could have prepared the soul for the reality? What eater of the lotus could have even imagined it?

I was enthralled, enchanted, overwhelmed with wonder. It was like falling in love. In some manner, I suppose I *did* fall in love. And I felt the hand of Marina, who stood beside me, covertly steal into my own for a moment, as if to affirm that this sight, this vision, was indeed all we had schemed and conspired to attain, that this was a moment shared between us as between none of those in our company of would-be conquerors.

Conquer *this*?

Yet when I glanced sideways at Cortes, what I saw on his lips was a feral grin, in his eyes was greedy determination. *Mad* determination. For my perception of who and what we were and where we were and what we had presumed to conquer had turned upside down.

We were not the army of a superior civilization across the sea confronting an empire of rude and uncouth barbarians. We were a troop of Greek adventurers washed up on its mythical shore presuming to storm Atlantis.

20

LESS THAN AN HOUR AFTER we were vouchsafed that magical sight of the Valley of Mexico, the clouds rolled in to conceal it once more, but nothing could remove it from the mind's eye, and the mood among us had quite changed, for now, rather than struggling towards the unknown, we were proceeding towards the foreglimpsed vision of the ultimate goal of the whole adventure.

There was trepidation among the Spanish troops over the presumptuousness of seeking to conquer such vastness with what now seemed like a pathetically tiny army, but Cortes was as eager as a virgin youth on his way to his first assignation, as greedily avid as Midas within sight of a golden hoard, and as bold as El Cid, and his spirit proved infectious.

'We have proceeded from victory to victory without a defeat even when we were but a few hundred against scores of thousands,' he reminded the fearful, 'and now we have thousands of allies marching with us. We have not only conquered the Tabascans, the Totonacs and the Tlascalans, but won their fealty and loyal support. We have done all this and slain thousands who would have slain us in Cholula with a Mexica garrison nearby, and no Mexica force has ever presumed to offer battle. Why should we fear the Mexica when they so obviously fear *us*? When Montezuma, rather than fall upon us with his armies, has sought to bribe us so lavishly to be gone, and that having failed, finally acceded to our demand to enter Tenochtitlan? I tell you the heathen empire of the Mexica is as ripe for conquest as that of the Moors in Spain so recently overcome by our fathers, and for the same reason – being in thrall to false gods, it is built on sand, whereas our foundation is the Rock called Peter upon which Jesus Christ built His Faith, and we are therefore the invincible soldiers of the Cross.'

This he did not preach to the Tlascalans, but there was no need, for their conquest had convinced them of it already as a rationale for their defeat which had saved their warriors' pride, besides which, the prospect of penetrating to the heartland of the Mexica for the first time in the long history of their warfare filled them with no little glee.

I retained my skepticism, but it did little to dampen my own glee, for I was about to achieve fulfillment of the dream that had propelled me on this adventure from the very first, back there an age and a world ago on that beach in Cuba. And what sort of sour spirit would I be if I could find no joy in the anticipation of that?

The descent into the Valley of Mexico validated Cortes' ebullient optimism. We came down from the cold and dank rocky wastes of the high cordillera into more clement forested slopes sheltering well-culti-vated alpine meadows and peasant villages whose inhabitants turned out to gawk at the spectacle. Whether out of fear or at the command of Montezuma to welcome our passage, or both, we were never impeded, and when we paused for rest, a meal, or the night, these modest folk feted us within their modest means with maize cakes, bean mash and pulque.

Furthermore, when their chieftains had shared a sufficient amount of the latter with us, they were emboldened to complain of the tribute in maize, beans, peppers and the like exacted from them by Tenochtitlan. And while this could be taken as the universal moan of peasants every-where against the cities whose populations their toil must maintain, the human tribute exacted for the altar of Huitzilopochtli was a far more unjust tax, peculiar to these lands and the source of much more pas-sionate consternation.

Seizing upon such opportunities, Cortes would recite the Requerimiento, announcing that they were now subjects of a far more benign sovereign who would make no such evil and outrageous demands. Father Olmedo would deliver a briefer and more pacific version of the sermon I had written, to the effect that human sacrifice was evil and the gods who demanded it somehow both non-existent and the minions of Satan, that Jesus Christ was a redeemer come to liberate them from the evils committed against them by Montezuma, and, far from devouring their flesh and blood, offered up his own as a bond between men and His Benevolent Father.

This would be greeted with cautious interest, and promises to honor the Cross that was erected, with the caveat that changes of worldly fealty and to which god obeisance must be paid were matters far too dangerous to be decided by such powerless folk as themselves, who must prudently await the outcome of the confrontation between Malinche and Montezuma, between Jesus and Huitzilopochtli, and then obey the will of the victor.

Prudence likewise dictated that Cortes could hardly demand more of them, and so we descended onto the rich and fertile floor of the Valley of Mexico unmolested, and with the good will and hope of the villages through which we passed, if not with their foolhardy commitment.

Likewise Montezuma opted for his customary prevarication. 'How would you have done otherwise?' he moaned to me later, over one of the endless cups of chocolatl he had taken to consuming almost continually during his incarceration.

'Despite all my efforts and the tributes I had lavished on them, an army of Teules or barbarians or perhaps Toltecs had penetrated to the heart of my empire and was marching on Tenochtitlan. But was it not in the end at my invitation? And did not Malinche profess friendship? Yet his Tlascalans had certainly not been invited and were no friends of the Mexica! But had he not conquered these enemies of mine? Might he not therefore be bringing these thousands of them to Tenochtitlan as my own warriors would after such a victory, to be offered up as a most worthy gift to Huitzilopochtli?'

The poor man became as agitated in the telling as he must have been fretting at this conundrum in his palace while caciques and chieftains and papas grew more and more agitated at his vacillation.

'I was overcome with demands and advice. Everyone freely offered their opinion save the gods. I offered hundreds of hearts to Huitzilopochtli, I gave my own blood until I became lightheaded and my penis throbbed with pain, for surely if he willed that the hearts of the Teules be fed to him, he would grant me an omen to tell me so. But there was only silence. I turned to Quetzalcoatl and likewise beseeched him, for if it were truly he approaching with an army of Toltecs to end this world and usher in the next one and I must not and could not escape my sad destiny, he would tell me, would he not?'

Montezuma sighed. 'But he did not. No god would speak. And so I could only turn to men for counsel. I summoned only two, my brother Cuitlahuac, lord of Iztapalapa, who I knew wished to fall upon the Teules and the Tlascalans before they could advance further, and Cacama, King of my Texcocan ally, who, though young, was, like most Texcocans, of a more cautious, less hot-blooded and more devious disposition.'

'A Socratic dialogue, as it were . . .'

Montezuma stared at me blankly.

'Yes,' he exclaimed when I gave him a brief explanation. 'Exactly. I wished to hear them contend with each other, that through such contention the gods might finally speak to me.'

For the sake of clarity, dear reader, I shall herein attempt to reproduce that dialog and the thoughts it engendered as conveyed to me by Montezuma, but since I was not even writing it down as he spoke, I cannot vouch for its accuracy. On the other hand, by way of apology, I might point out that Socrates himself wrote nothing down, and all we have of his dialogues is what was reproduced later from memory by Plato.

'The Teules demand you subordinate yourself to some King across the sea who may or may not exist, and are therefore our enemies,' Cuitlahuac told me. 'Even with their Tlascalans, they are few. Destroy them now.'

I had heard this before, but this time it granted me a new thought. 'This Jesus Christ, I have been informed, is sometimes known as the "King of Kings",' I said. 'What if this King to whom Malinche demands

I pay tribute and obeisance is not a man but a god? Then I dare not oppose his servant, but becoming his vassal would change nothing in this world and there would be no reason to resist.'

'If it *is* the god on the Cross and not a human King who demands your fealty, Montezuma, perhaps this *would* be the wise course,' said Cacama.

'How so?' demanded Cuitlahuac.

'When Nezahualcoyotl was restored to rule in Texcoco by Tenochtitlan, Texcoco became a kind of vassal nation of the Mexica within the Triple Alliance, under which we have prospered,' said Cacama. 'And if that King is not a man but an all-powerful god, accepting a similar status under him may not be to our disadvantage . . .'

Cuitlahuac would have none of this. 'The Teules are marching through the heart of our empire raising hope of rebellion among the discontented,' he pointed out.

'The weak many who must pay tribute to the powerful few are always discontented,' said Cacama, 'and so anything new may raise their hope of rebellion.'

'All the more reason to crush the Teules before matters grow worse,' said Cuitlahuac.

'But what if we fail?' I said.

'A few hundred Teules and a few thousand Tlascalans against the armies of Mexico!'

'Those few hundred Teules *defeated* scores of thousands of Tlascalans,' Cacama pointed out.

'*Tlascalans*,' Cuitlahuac said scornfully. 'They have never faced an army of Mexica.'

'The Tlascalans have often enough, and fare better against us than they have against the Teules,' said Cacama. 'The Teules would make much better allies than enemies.'

'Tell that to Malinche!' scoffed Cuitlahuac.

'But you have done that already, have you not, Montezuma?' said Cacama. 'And perhaps he is coming to Tenochtitlan to make just such a pact.'

'They are coming here to conquer us!' insisted Cuitlahuac.

'*A few hundred Teules and a few thousand Tlascalans against the armies of Mexico?'* Cacama said, mocking him with his own words. Cuitlahuac fell silent.

'Perhaps you are right, Cuitlahuac,' Cacama continued. 'Perhaps the Teules do fear the armies of Mexico as we fear them, for even as we have not sought battle with them, they have avoided all battle with us.'

'By marching into the Valley of Mexico with an army of Tlascalans?'

'By our Emperor's invitation to Tenochtitlan,' Cacama pointed out. And then it was that a god spoke to me through him.

'How so?' I asked Montezuma, for even long after the fact, I still could not follow his peculiar logic, and I fancy that neither Socrates nor Plato would have fared much better.

Montezuma downed another cup of chocolatl. 'I had forgotten the omen of the rat, the raptor and the serpent that Huitzilopochtli *had* granted me,' he said. 'Fleeing the bird of prey, the rat sought refuge in the burrow of the serpent, and so was devoured.'

I stared at him blankly. He stared back.

'You do not understand? Malinche was scampering directly into my burrow, into Tenochtitlan, into the one place where he might most easily be destroyed should it prove necessary. Why seek to prevent him? Only because his passage was serving to rally those chafing under my rule to rebelliousness behind his standard. And Cacama had given me the remedy for that.'

'He had?'

Even in his captivity, even though it had not saved him, Montezuma could not quite suppress a smile at the memory of his own cleverness.

'If Malinche and the Teules, rather than being seen marching through the Valley of Mexico as an invading army, were to be seen obediently led and escorted by a Mexica King and his entourage, the effect upon the discontented would be quite different,' Montezuma told me. 'I of course could not deign to descend to such a task, but the King of Texcoco . . .'

Of course neither Cortes nor I nor any of our company knew any of this as we debouched onto the valley floor and began making our way to the lakeshore.

We reached Amecameca, the first true town we had encountered west of the mountains, of modest size, but with even the ordinary dwellings built of stone and kept cleanly whitewashed with stucco, often painted in brilliant colors, the usual temple in its square, and a market-place not only bustling with a well-dressed populace, but offering an abundance of rich goods such as we had not seen elsewhere.

There were small dogs which the Mexica used for food, much cacao, turkeys, small hairy pigs, as well as the usual maize and beans and scores of varieties of peppers, as well as piles of previously unknown fruits. There was well-crafted pottery, implements of obsidian, cotton cloth both plain and embroidered, featherwork cloaks and tapestries, and great piles of assorted bright plumages. There was jewelry of turquoise and silver. And there was quite a bit of gold, in the form of necklaces, labrets, bracelets, and clever little statues of animals and deities, some of them, strangely enough, on wheels, though never had we or would we see this otherwise sophisticated civilization put larger wheels to any pragmatic purpose.

Here we were received with much the same hospitality as in the foothill villages, but the reception given Cortes' recitement of the Requerimiento was much more guarded, the cacique refusing to take it as anything more than a demand for tribute and handing over a respectable amount of gold to see us gone, to the point where Cortes prudently refrained from proceeding to religious matters.

We rested there for two days while Cortes and Marina questioned some of the chieftains, and we managed to put together a crude map of the Valley of Mexico or 'Anahuac'. The great central lake was not one lake but a system of several connected bodies of water. The central lake was Lake Texcoco, much the largest, with the city of Texcoco situated on its eastern shore. The northern lake was called Xaltocan, with the city of Xaltocan on an island in it. Lakes Chalco and Xochimilco were two much smaller bodies of water to the south. Tenochtitlan itself was sited off the western shore of Lake Texcoco, where that lake itself squeezed down into a comparatively narrow channel between the major body of Lake Texcoco and two smaller lobes thereof, and where the shortest of its four causeways joined it to the mainland near Tacuba.

Cities and towns were sited all around the shores of this lake system, connected to each other, to the rest of Anahuac and to the hinterlands of the empire by an elaborate system of roadways.

Cortes decided to avoid Texcoco and proceed west to the shore of Lake Chalco, around its southern bank, across a causeway separating it from Lake Xochimilco, and thence to the southern shore of Lake Texcoco itself, following it to the Tacuba causeway, the shortest available route to Tenochtitlan.

The road to Lake Chalco passed through fields of maize stretching as far as the eye could see, interspersed with extensive plantations of maguey cactus, some of which were in the process of being harvested by well-organized teams of laborers. This was agricultural country, and the road through it therefore unlikely to be a major highway. Nevertheless, there was considerable traffic; long strings of tamanes bearing maize and maguey to the cities of the lakeshore, and more proceeding in the opposite direction with empty panniers, accompanied by Mexica dressed in the manner of their nobles. These, however, Marina informed us, were either trading merchants or collectors of tribute on their way to the outlying provinces. Upon occasion, singular runners dashed by us in both directions; couriers of the extensive relay system that conveyed messages, documents and intelligence throughout the valley and the empire beyond at a speed unknown to our Old World.

This countryside seemed as densely cultivated and well ordered as any sustaining the great cities of Europe and then some, and this was confirmed by Spaniards hailing from such precincts, who declared that they had never seen its like at home.

The road reached the shore at Ajotzinco, a town of no great size, but a wonder nonetheless to European eyes, for there was nothing like it in Europe save Venice, which few of our number had ever seen, but which those who had declared it like unto the city of the Doges in miniature.

Part of it was built on the shore, but the greater part of the buildings had been erected offshore on pilings, and a network of canals, or more properly channels, served as its streets. As in Venice, these were thick with waterborne traffic: large pirogues and square-prowed barges carrying goods, small canoes carrying its inhabitants thither and yon, and all sizes of craft inbetween. There were docks serving as a fishing port, and others supporting craft that ranged farther conducting commerce and transport upon the lakes.

The caciques of this little aquatic metropolis greeted us with the unstinting but cautious hospitality to which we had become accustomed, but alas, given our numbers and the restricted space available on the waterborne wonderland, we were quartered ashore.

The next morning, as Cortes was marshaling his army on the road, a runner arrived, informing him that Cacama himself, King of Texcoco, the great ally of Tenochtitlan, and nephew of Montezuma, was on his way to greet him.

Realizing that it would be impolitic lèse-majesté not to await such an august personage, Cortes had us all linger there on the road for his arrival for two or three hours which seemed like a fretful eternity. But when Cacama finally did arrive, the breathtaking splendor of his advent proved a sight well worth the wait.

Although he appeared a vigorous man no older than thirty, he was carried up to Cortes reclining on a sort of imperial litter fit for a Pharaoh. Its elaborately carved wooden framework was embellished with so much gold plate and gems that it took six strong men to bear it. He was shaded from the sun by a canopy of brilliant green quetzal feathers supported by pillars that appeared to be of solid gold and encrusted with yet more gemstones.

On either side of him were four censer-bearers, so that he proceeded within a perpetual cloud of perfume. Before him were two standard-bearers holding aloft great golden eagles with emeralds for eyes, and beside them two retainers carrying instruments which curiously seemed to be brooms. Immediately behind him were two lines of extravagantly accoutered warriors, scores to a file, those on the left hand wearing eagle-headed helmets, those on the right the full pelts of something like a leopard, with the head crowning their own craniums. Behind them were perhaps a hundred or two tamanes.

Cacama wore a kind of tunic entirely covered with embroidery dotted with jewels, a sort of crown sprouting a crest of quetzal plumage, and so much gold jewelry in the form of necklaces, earrings, labret and pendants that they seemed to weigh as much as he did. Although he was a young man, his visage seemed to have the gravitas of someone much older.

Cortes had mounted to greet him, the better to awe him on the one hand, and show his respect by dismounting on the other, which he did as Cacama's litter halted about ten feet before him. Cacama did him one better. Retainers carpeted his way with petatl mats so that the soles of his sandals would not be defiled by contact with the earth. That not sufficing, the men with the brooms, and that proved to be exactly what they were, swept them clear of the dust of the road before he descended, strode in a mostly lordly manner up to Cortes, and touched the palm of his right hand to the pristine matting, then to his forehead, in the Mexica salutation of one high personage to another.

'I am Cacama, King of Texcoco, nephew of the great Montezuma, sent here at his bidding to welcome you to the heartland of his empire, and provide a fitting escort to convey you to Tenochtitlan with the highest honor,' he proclaimed. 'The great Montezuma regrets that he himself is not here in my stead, for he must await you in Tenochtitlan to prepare a more appropriate reception himself. I beg of you to forgive the simple modesty of this roadside display on his behalf and my own, but it was the best that could be arranged at such short notice.'

This was delivered with solemn dignity, but the gleam in the young man's clever bright eyes indicated that he knew quite well that whether Cortes liked it or not, this was a guard of honor he had been put in no position to refuse.

The consternated look in Cortes' eyes revealed that he understood this all too well, if not the why of it, but he otherwise maintained full diplomatic politesse, and after the formal niceties, off we went.

Cacama's litter led the way in its cloud of fragrant smoke behind the eagle standards of Mexico. Then came the 'Eagle Knights', elite troops of Tenochtitlan. Behind them was the Spanish army, led by Cortes and his cavalry, followed by our tamanes and those of the Texcocan King. Next were the Tlascalans, fretful and none too pleased with the honors, for bringing up the rear were the so-called 'Jaguar Knights', since that was the name of the large wild cat whose skins they wore, regarding their backsides with scornful disdain, completing the enclosure of the foreign armies, and making the symbolic import of the parade all too clear.

Surrounded by this escort of state, we paraded west along the coastal road around the southern shore of Lake Chalco, here and there shaded by cultivated fruit orchards, otherwise bordered on the inland side by endless fields of maize well irrigated by lake waters carried throughout them by a system of narrow canals.

This appeared to be a major highway, thronged as it was with tamanes bearing produce, the caravans of traders, and the occasional contingent of warriors, one of which guarded a long line of captives bound and strung together by a stout maguey-fiber rope.

Cacama's standard-bearers moved ten yards or so ahead of his litter, so as to keep the way clear, a necessary redeployment, since even the captives, destined I suspected for some bloody sacrificial altar, could not but slow their pace to gape and stare at the horses, the light-skinned men in gleaming steel vestments, the cannon being dragged by tamanes, the unprecedented advent of scowling and armed Tlascalans in the heart of the Valley of Mexico, all being escorted towards the capital by an elite guard of the Emperor's Eagle and Jaguar Knights and the King of Texcoco traveling in full state.

In this manner we reached the western end of Lake Chalco, where it narrowed down to meet a similar narrowing of the eastern end of Lake Xochimilco, though it appeared that the two lakes had once been connected, for a dike built of solid stone now divided them; a mighty work of men rather than nature, some five miles long and wide enough in most places for eight horsemen to ride abreast, the first such causeway we had encountered.

Cacama led the procession onto it and northward along its length, and we beheld hundreds of boats plying the waters on either side, some apparently those of fishermen, more of them than not carrying freight, still others small canoes transporting one or two men on errands unknown. Our passage raised quite a commotion among the boatmen as they crowded to both sides of the dike to stare in amazement, but their wonder was matched if not exceeded by our own.

Behind us, we could see, dwarfed by the distance, a veritable necklace of towns fringing the southern shores of the lakes. The waters themselves were dotted with towns built on islands, natural or artificial, their whitened buildings gleaming in the sun, so that the more distant of them took on the aspect of geese or swans riding the waves.

More wondrous still were the verdant islands of crops and flowers of every brilliant hue which could be seen *moving* upon the waves and currents of the lakes. These we later learned were the so-called chinampas, great rafts of soil held firmly together by the root systems of the plants which grew upon them to form true islands that truly floated, though at the time they seemed quite magical. And even knowing the art by which the hand of man had created a form of landscape that had never existed in the natural world, might not one deem it magical still?

There was a town in the middle of the dike, flanking it on both sides, built up on landfill and pilings, with docks and a channel through it and beneath the roadway, here a bridge of wood, by which means boats might make their way from one lake to the other. It was not large, but the buildings were of extravagant beauty; many painted blue to mirror the lake and the sky, some decorated with the varicolored shells of lake creatures, most of them festooned with flowering vines, the whole surrounded by fragrant and colorful floating gardens.

Here we paused for a noon repast provided by its inhabitants at the lordly behest of Cacama before moving on to reach the northern end of the dike, from which terminus we marched north across the peninsula between the two southern lakes and Lake Texcoco to the southern shore of that largest of the lakes at the city of Iztapalapa, where we halted to pass the night and enjoy the hospitality of its cacique, Cuitlahuac, brother of the great Montezuma himself.

Cuitlahuac had prepared quite a state reception in his palace. Its great hall was roofed in fragrant cedarwood, the walls were covered in featherwork tapestries, and when we arrived, it was already thronged with lords and dignitaries in their best fineries.

Cuitlahuac greeted Cortes with the proper formalities, which included an impressive amount of gold, and the banquet that was served left nothing to be desired, yet there was something strained about the whole affair.

Cuitlahuac was an older man than Cacama, his nature seemed more rough and blunt, and while he wore a similar quetzal-plume crown and cloak, the rest of his vestments were plainer, he wore much less jewelry, and carried a functional-looking maquahuitl. The manner with which he regarded Cortes, while never quite incorrect, seemed both frosty and measuring, certainly nothing like deferential, and what little conversation passed between them via Marina was entirely pro forma.

It seemed to me that Cuitlahuac was playing his role under sufferance by order of his brother, and would have been better pleased to apply his maquahuitl to Cortes' throat.

This was confirmed the next morning when it was Cacama, not Cuitlahuac, who escorted Cortes, his captains, Marina and myself on the tour of the gardens of Iztapalapa, for surely these were the pride of his city, and just as surely any ruler thereof would otherwise revel in escorting foreign dignitaries through such a marvel.

The gardens covered more land than any temple square we had seen. They were laid out in a pattern of square plots, each planted with the flora of a single quarter of the empire, as if to display its bounty and beauty in itemized entire. There were fruit trees of scores of varieties. There were cacti, some as tall as trees themselves, others displaying waxy blooms. There was cacao, and maguey, and maize, and perhaps a hundred different kinds of bushes upon which grew red and green peppers of many sizes and shapes. There were even plots of mushrooms and sparse saltmarsh grasses.

And there were flowers everywhere, cleverly planted so that each plot reproduced the very fragrance of the district it represented. The paths between them were trellised over with roses and honeysuckle. The gardens were watered by a network of tiled aqueducts and ditches, at the major intersections of which were ponds stocked with aquatic plants, fishes, and even frogs. A canal wide enough to pass boats bisected the gardens, and fed an enormous round stone basin sporting sculptured fountains that cooled and humidified the air.

But the finest feature of this gardens, the like of which was unknown in Europe, was the aviary, or rather aviaries, dozens of huge cages, housing a great collection of birds, some of which, if caged together, would no doubt be at each other's throats. There were raucous cages of red, blue, green and yellow parrots. There was a cage filled with iridescent green quetzals. There was a cage where brilliantly colored birds no larger than a man's thumb with long curved beaks hovered humming in the air like flies. There were cages of eagles and cages of hawks. There were cages where water birds were supplied with fish-stocked ponds. There were even cages of several varieties of large and hideous buzzards and vultures dining on rotting carcasses.

Surely this was an eighth wonder of the world, fit to put the Hanging Gardens of Babylon or even Eden itself to shame.

A strange venue therefore for what occurred at its margin as we left it wide-eyed with blissful wonder. Cuitlahuac had finally made an appearance, but at one of the garden entrances, and as Cacama was leading us out. Cortes and Marina were with Cacama, but I lagged behind, saw what seemed a less than genteel conversation taking place, but could not hear it, for it was over before I arrived.

Cuitlahuac and Cacama were already departing, and Cortes was in a foul mood. 'There has been a change in plans,' he told me sourly. 'By the order of Montezuma, or so his brother claims, we are not to proceed to Tenochtitlan by the short western causeway at Tacuba, but by the much longer southern one that begins near here and crosses half of Lake Texcoco.'

'Why should that vex you so?' I asked. 'As I remember, it is the most direct route, avoiding skirting many miles of lakeshore, and so will get us there all the more quickly.'

'That is what Cuitlahuac told me,' said Cortes. 'But it also avoids showing our flags and banners to a wide stretch of country, besides which it seems to reinforce the fact that we have proceeded as if we were captives or trophies, or perhaps even sacrifices on the way to the altar, ever since Cacama took us under escort at Ajotzinco—'

'Surely you don't think they're planning to—'

'Of a certainty, we have been cleverly isolated from the populace by the soft hand of this "guard of honor". Now we are to cross a long narrow causeway over a wide lake where we would be hard put to defend ourselves from waterborne attack, and to make the smell of it worse, Cuitlahuac is to rush on ahead of us to "prepare our welcome to great Tenochtitlan", whatever sort of welcome that may be.'

He frowned deeply. 'Were I Montezuma and determined to attack us, I would find our deployment in narrow file along that causeway with my warriors already to our front and rear the ideal place to do it.' He shrugged. 'But there is nothing for it. If I refuse, Cuitlahuac would take it as hostility, and an attack might just be launched right here, before I could even set eyes on Montezuma, let alone submit him to reason and my powers of persuasion.'

But Cortes' fears proved unfounded, and we proceeded along the Iztapalapa causeway unmolested, though the fear of attack was always with us, made all the more acute by the nature of the causeway itself.

The Iztapalapa causeway, crossing as it did the breadth of Lake Texcoco, a stone roadway wider than the causeway we had already crossed, was built on pilings and high enough above the waters for the lake traffic to freely pass under it. But the roadway was interrupted by easily raised wooden bridges, clearly designed to deny entry by any army to Tenochtitlan, or to trap one between the gaps.

There were towns along the causeway, built entirely on piles and surrounded by floating islands of croplands, so that the total population of this strange linear series of little Venices might have exceeded that of the Italian metropolis, if not that of Tenochtitlan, the immense grandeur of its temples and towers, and the extent of its precincts, gleaming brilliantly in the hazy distance.

About a mile from Tenochtitlan the causeway was blocked by a wall of stone twice the height of a man, anchored by parapeted towers, and with a shielded battlement atop its width. The only way forward was through a gateway in the center, open to our passage now, but equipped with two stout wooden doors which could quickly be closed.

This, we were proudly told by the leaders of the delegation who emerged through it to greet us, was the fortress of Xoloc, never breached, and quite impregnable. There were hundreds of these dignitaries, and every one of them must be formally introduced to Cortes, a process which took nearly two hours, while Cortes, gritting his teeth to maintain politesse, fretted and fumed. Having been privy to his fears, I knew he must be thinking that this ceremony must have been concocted to delay us while Cuitlahuac reached the city and prepared whatever he had gone ahead to prepare.

At last we passed through and proceeded to a drawbridge close by a gateway to Tenochtitlan itself, crowded with richly dressed onlookers. The city wall was high, but towering above it we beheld the peaks of three enormous pyramidal temples whitened to brilliance and with smoking fires burning at their crowning platforms, the greatest of which held not one stone reliquary but two.

The gateway was open and through it we could see a long straight stone-paved avenue wider than anything in Europe, which seemed to stretch all the way through the mighty city to dwindle from sight at the horizon. Likewise did the crowd that thronged it seem to extend backward to its very limits behind the procession approaching us.

First came three functionaries carrying tall golden wands. Behind them was what could only be the imperial palanquin of Montezuma himself. It appeared to be crafted entirely of solid gold, carved and bejeweled. This was carried forward not by tamanes but by six nobles as richly dressed as Cacama. Four more nobles shielded him from the sun with a separate canopy held aloft on gilded poles; an enormous umbrella of bright green quetzal feathers, fringed with silver pendants, and so dusted with multicolored gems as to give the appearance of the fan of some celestial peacock.

Montezuma was accoutered in a bejeweled and embroidered cotton robe secured around his neck by a huge gold brooch carved in the likeness of the sun. He wore no crown, but rather a headdress of quetzal plumes with a train depending down his back from it longer than he was tall. His earrings, labrets and necklaces were of gold. Even the very soles of his sandals were platforms of gold.

Cacama went forward to the right flank of the palanquin and Cuitlahuac emerged from the company behind to take his position to the left. Nobles spread out an imperial carpet of embroidered cotton tapestries, rather than mere petatls, for him to walk on. More nobles sprinkled the carpeting with rose petals for good measure.

Cacama took him by one arm, Cuitlahuac by the other, and together they supported him as he paraded, under the peacock canopy, toward Cortes, who had dismounted to greet him. Every last Mexica save his brother and his nephew bowed their heads, and many prostrated themselves on the ground.

Montezuma was a tall man for a Mexica, and wiry. His hair was the usual black, but he seemed rather lighter-skinned than most. He maintained a visage of lofty imperial composure verging on indifference.

Only the rapid blinking of his keen dark eyes as he studied Cortes betrayed anything less.

Cortes regarded the Emperor with an eagle-eyed gaze, and for a long moment the two men stood there measuring each other, perhaps both trying to decide who should speak first. It was Montezuma, as the host, who finally broke the silence, in a clear firm voice, which, however, seemed a bit higher-pitched than one might have expected.

'It pleases me to see that you have safely arrived to honor my invitation to visit my city,' he told Cortes through Marina. 'While circumstances may not allow your stay to be as long as we might both wish, I assure you that we will have ample opportunity to discuss matters of interest and importance, that you and your entourage shall enjoy the freedom of the city, and that every step will be taken to ensure your security and ease. You and your entourage will furthermore enjoy the privilege of being housed in the palace of my own father Axayacatl, left vacant in his honor ever since his death, of a size and luxury second only to my own. Welcome to Tenochtitlan.'

'I thank you for your freely given invitation and the munificence you have showered upon us along our long journey to this most happy moment of my life,' Cortes responded as we had prepared, 'and I assure you that you will be repaid many times over by the glad tidings and bounteous knowledge with which it shall be my pleasure to grace you and your subjects in return. In times to come, great Montezuma, this meeting of our two noble and mighty civilizations will be known as an event which changed history and enlightened the world.'

Cortes then produced a necklace of cut crystal strung on a silver chain, and made to drape it over Montezuma's neck. But as he did, any number of Mexica lords dashed angrily forward to restrain him from touching the imperial person, two of them seizing him by the arms.

But Montezuma waved them away with a negligent hand and an indulgent smile. 'You must be fatigued by your long journey,' he told Cortes. 'We will meet again when you are well rested and the omens are correct.'

He turned and walked slowly back to his litter, escorted by Cacama and Cuitlahuac, who helped him to mount. 'As a gesture of my true friendship,' he told Cortes, 'I entrust you to the care of my own brother

Cuitlahuac, who will escort you to the palace of our father and assure that your every need is met, and your safety and comfort are amply assured.'

With this, the great Montezuma departed, leaving behind a Cuitlahuac whose smile might be less than friendly but which for the first time seemed all too sincere.

21

C UITLAHUAC LED OUR procession onto the southern terminus of the broad stone-paved avenue that was the continuation of the Iztapalapa causeway, lined with residences constructed of a stone of a peculiarly reddish hue. These were single-storied, but large and well decorated with tiles and paintings, and the roofs of all of them were parapeted terraces, no few of them planted with flowers or even small palm trees, and all of them clogged with richly dressed onlookers.

Crowds of more simply dressed folk lined both sides of the avenue, held back from blocking our way by warriors who served as a municipal guard. Between our entry and our arrival at the Temple Square, we must have been gaped at by scores of thousands of people, while traversing merely one avenue through a quarter of the city.

But if the inhabitants of Tenochtitlan marveled at our horses, our steel armor, our cannon, our pallid faces, and the golden hair of such as Pedro Alvarado, we could not but marvel at the wonders of their city.

The avenue was so broad that from the beginning of our parade we could see that it led to a large plaza of central importance, and the buildings of the precincts through which it passed being low, the flat crowns of three great pyramids were likewise visible from afar towering over them.

The avenue intersected more than a score more modest streets lead-ing away into more modest residential districts and it crossed four interior canals over wooden bridges before it debouched into the great square that was the heart of Tenochtitlan, both religious and political, a veritable city within the city.

It was indeed square, and it was so enormous, dear reader, that I am at a loss to give you a European equivalent, for no such exists. The Forum and the Coliseum of Rome and the Parthenon of Athens would have been lost in it, I warrant, with perhaps room for Solomon's Temple besides.

Two massive pyramids dominated the far side, each with a single stonework cupola atop its truncated crown; one, as we were to learn, the temple of Xipe Totec, god of the springtime renewal, the other dedi-cated to Tezcatlipoca, god of night. These were set in spacious stone-paved courtyards fringed with the low apartment dwellings of the priests and other structures of less obvious nature that might have been secondary altars, and each boasted its impressive rack of sun-bleached human skulls.

The eastern side of the great square was dominated by a grander pyramid still. Here the stern steep stairways led up to a platform that might have done service as the courtyard of many a church in Christendom. And there were two temple cupolas crowning it, rather than one: the temples of Tlaloc the rain god and the sanguinary Huitzilopochtli standing together side by side. And as if to proclaim their paramount status, the collection of skulls gracing their shared pyramid was twice the size of those of Xipe Totec and Tezcatlipoca combined.

Ceremonial fires which never went out burned atop each pyramid, raising eternal smoke plumes into the sky. A low wall, not quite man-height, enclosed the pyramids, the apartments of the papas, and the extensive plazas and secondary altars at their feet, delineating a Sacred Precinct, another square occupying the greater part of the plaza. There no one was to be seen abroad save scores of papas, their bloody robes and filthy matted hair at bizarre variance with the grandeur over which they presided.

We were not permitted to defile the Sacred Precinct either, for our party was led past a vast single-story maze of interconnected buildings and courtyards that occupied the southeastern quarter of the Temple Square to a similar complex not that much smaller by its northeastern edge.

Both were constructed of reddish stone. Both were enclosed by gated and parapeted walls topped with walkways connected to a rooftop maze of terraces and gardens. Both were whitened in places with stucco to give their façades a pleasing red and white pattern. Both were embellished with stone statues, painted frescoes, and fretwork of gold and silver. Both seemed fit to be the palace of an Emperor.

Which is what they both were.

The former was the palace of Montezuma himself.

The latter had been the palace of his father, and was to be *our* palace, our fortress, our prison; before this tale is over, all three.

The palace of Axayacatl was a warren of huge communal chambers, spacious apartments, storerooms, and rooms that seemed to have no particular purpose, arrayed around open courtyards large and small, so that one moved from one to the other either directly through portals or across courts, for neither doors nor hallways were a feature of Mexica architecture.

As I have said, there was a parapeted wall around the palace complex with buttressing towers and a walkway from which other walkways connected it to the rooftop terraces, ideal for commanding the approaches to the palace with cannon and arquebuses. Cortes' first order of business was to have some of the cannon hauled up there and to station sentries and guards. Only after this was accomplished and more guards stationed at the ground level entrances to the palace, did he turn to assigning quarters.

Several of the interior courtyards were quite huge, with shade trees growing in their soil; large enough to accommodate among them our entire company of several thousand Tlascalans, who, cowed and awed by the grandeur of Tenochtitlan, and rendered fearful at finding themselves surrounded by such vast numbers of their traditional enemy, preferred being quartered under the open sky.

The rest of us were allowed to quarter ourselves in the generous selection of apartments. There were hundreds of them and they managed to be both luxurious and Spartan. The major ones were of great size and even the more ordinary ones had ceilings of fragrant woods and walls covered with brightly colored tapestries, but the only items of furniture were low wooden stools, a few simple low tables, and sleeping mats of cotton or maguey cloth stuffed with palm leaves or straw.

The palace fairly crawled with slaves, servants, cooks and the like, put at our disposal, and after the practical arrangements were made, the entire company of Spaniards was treated to a lavish banquet ordered up by Cuitlahuac, laid on in a kind of communal dining hall large enough to hold us all.

Swarms of servants plied us with scores of different dishes served in well-made pottery bowls. Some of these were comparatively simple roasted fowls and joints of meat whose ingredients were readily enough identified, but more than not were savory stews of bits of meat and vegetables enrobed in sauces, to be scooped up with maize cakes or poured onto bean mash to be eaten together with it in the same manner. The sauces were tasty and savory, but many were overly fiery, requiring much pulque to quench the flames, which in turn led to a post-prandial siesta more essential than most.

The siesta did not last long, for soon we were roused from our stupors by being told that Montezuma was in the process of arriving, a process that took some doing, for we were all scattered about the palace and word had to move from room to room.

By the time I had arrived in the banquet hall, the detritus had been cleared, most of the Spaniards had already arrived, and Montezuma's gold palanquin was being carried inside, escorted once more by Cacama and Cuitlahuac and a few other nobles who seemed to hold similar status.

Cortes had ordered servants to bring in stools for those of us who hadn't thought to bring one along from our rooms, myself included, nor had I had the wit to bring writing implements, so that when Cortes spied me and motioned for me to come forward to record the proceedings, these had to be fetched for me.

Cortes seated himself before Montezuma, who remained reclining on his litter. Marina sat down to his right, with myself to his left and slightly behind, and the Spaniards all took seats, but the Mexica nobles remained standing during the entire conversation, nor did anyone but Cortes and Montezuma speak throughout it all, save for Marina's necessary translation.

It swiftly became a verbal fencing match, or better, the exploratory opening moves of a game of diplomatic chess between two masters of the art.

'By what name do you choose to be called?' Montezuma inquired.

Cortes and Marina exchanged quick glances.

'I seem to have become known here by the name of Malinche,' he said, 'and by now I am comfortable with it.'

'You have no other in your own land?'

'I hope to make this land my own . . .'

At this Montezuma frowned, but seemed to let it glide by. 'And your King?'

'He is called Charles.'

'He has no other names?'

Cortes regarded Montezuma as if arduously attempting to discern where this was leading, and quite failing. 'Where I come from, Kings accumulate many names and titles . . .' he ventured.

Montezuma nodded. 'Among them . . . Jesus Christ?' he asked.

There was a collective gasp from the Spaniards. Cortes seemed frozen. 'Tread carefully, Hernando,' I presumed to whisper in his ear. 'Admit nothing, deny nothing, if you can.'

'Why do you ask that?' said Cortes.

'I am King of the Empire of the Mexica,' Montezuma told him, 'but you have asked me to swear fealty to your King across the sea. I am considering your proposition.'

'I do not understand,' was all that Cortes could manage.

'I have been informed that your Jesus Christ is known as the King of Kings,' Montezuma told him. 'I have also been told that he is both a man and a god. I would not become the vassal of a man. But there might be advantage and no dishonor in making alliance under a god who is King over many Kings.' He nodded in the direction of Cacama. 'Even as the Kings of Texcoco benefit from their alliance with Tenochtitlan under myself.'

Cortes seemed even more consternated than before. 'If you are asking me a question,' he said rather plaintively, 'I'm afraid I do not quite understand what it is.'

'It is simple,' Montezuma told him. 'Are Charles and Jesus Christ one and the same? Do you ask me to place myself and my empire under a god or a man?'

Answering such a question without either rejecting the political advantage of lying or committing the outright blasphemy of doing so was anything but a simple task. But Hernando was up to it.

'King Charles is also known as the Holy Roman Emperor, indeed King over many Kings,' Cortes told Montezuma truthfully. 'But he is vassal to the Holy Father the Pope in Rome who rules all who accept the One True Faith, who in turn derives his authority from Jesus Christ Himself, who indeed is both God and man. Thus, by swearing allegiance to my King the Holy Roman Emperor, you swear allegiance to the Pope through him, and through the Pope to Jesus Christ Himself, and therefore to God, rather than a mere man.'

Montezuma frowned with narrowed eyes, making a great effort to wrap his mind around this peculiar concept, but I saw that Father Olmedo was grinning at this politic squaring of the theological circle, and so was I.

'Even as I rule through Kings and caciques and Huitzilopochtli rules through me,' Montezuma finally muttered. 'I wonder if your Jesus Christ speaks more plainly than he does.'

'His Word is written down for all to read,' said Cortes.

'And what tribute does he require?'

'Only the tribute of what is in a good man's heart.'

'Then he does not value the tribute that you yourself value above all others . . . Malinche?' said Montezuma.

Now it was Cortes' turn to narrow his eyes in incomprehension.

'The tears of the sun,' said Montezuma 'Though they mean nothing to your god, perhaps *you* would like more?'

'The tears of the sun?'

'He means *gold*,' I heard Marina whisper into Cortes' ear.

Montezuma nodded towards Cacama, who clapped his hands and a train of tamanes began trooping into the banquet hall bearing enough gifts, and in particular jewelry and statues crafted of that so highly prized yellow metal, that none of us left it afterward crying for lack of his portion of the tears of the sun.

Which is not to say that the insatiable lust for such tribute was not aroused to dream of much more. Nor that Montezuma was not observant enough to see that this was so, and smile at what he saw with a certain guarded satisfaction.

After the sun was well down, Cortes had the cannon fire off a brave salute, as much to keep up the spirits of his own troops as to impress the inhabitants of Tenochtitlan with thunder and brimstone. For the Spaniards could not escape the realization that conquering the heart of his empire by force had been reduced to a fantasy by confrontation with the unexpectedly daunting reality, and the Tlascalans knew that their hearts could all be fed to Huitzilopochtli at Montezuma's pleasure.

How the others passed our first night in the city I do not know, but I slept but fitfully, and dawn found me prowling about the rooftop terraces, deserted at this hour except for the guard detail.

And Hernando Cortes.

I was strolling around the terrace surrounding the largest of the interior courtyards, where most of the Tlascalans were still slumbering, when I spied him close to the western edge of the palace roof, gazing out over the Temple Square and the Sacred Precinct within it. The terraces of the rooftops were interspersed with many gaps looking down into courtyards, so that there was no direct path from anywhere to anywhere up there, and it took several minutes for me to reach him, during which time he seemed not to move at all.

'We are a long way from Cuba, are we not, Hernando?' I said by way of greeting.

'A long way even from Vera Cruz,' Cortes muttered dreamily.

Behind us, the sun was peering over the peaks of the great cordillera separating us from our coastal settlement, but the waters of the lake still lay in shadowy darkness, as its first rays bathed the summits of the whitened pyramids in a golden glow spreading imperceptibly down their stepped inclines. Papas began to ascend them out of the darkness to tend to the temple fires and here and there cookfires winked into existence in the awakening city. A breeze blew in from the lake carrying the tropical odors of the floating island plantings and another smell drifted up to us from the great body of the city, compounded of frying maize and boiling beans and the bodies of hundreds of thousands of its people, and things beyond the ken of the European nose.

'Another world entire,' I said. 'Unlike anywhere else on Earth.'

'Unlike anything even in our most extravagant dreams, is it not Alvaro?'

I could only nod, and we stood there silently as the sun cleared the distant mountaintops, turning the lake into an enormous scintillating mirror ringed by its shoreside necklace of cities and villages strung together like white pearls, sliced into quadrants by the long straight causeways, and began to fully illumine the city before us, so much grander than any in Europe.

The whole city stretched out before us, endless streets of white buildings and green rooftops further than the eye could see, but nowhere a dwelling of men more lofty than our own or any that much lower, for here the vertical seemed a dimension reserved for the gods.

Far to the north, a distant pyramid towered high above the common ground, sending a black smoke plume skyward. Three enormous pyramids rose immediately before us doing likewise, utterly dwarfing the dwellings of the surrounding residential quarters, and even quite overshadowing the sprawling palace of Montezuma to our south with their overbearing height and bulk. The attendant papas climbing their stairs, the priests beginning to scurry about the Sacred Precinct, the people beginning to enter or cross the Temple Square, the foot traffic on the avenues and streets, all seemed like the comings and goings of tiny creatures as inconsequential to what dwelt in the city of the gods above them as those of ants beneath our feet.

Christians, Muslims, Jews, we might fight and slay each other over the name of the One True God, we each might deem our own culture superior, but together we believed that Europe or Araby held the crowning civilization of the world. Yet where else had men built a city to rival Tenochtitlan? Where was there a constellation of cities such as surrounded these lakes, fed by an empire that turned the valley in which they arose into the garden that sustained them?

'Who could have imagined that the jungled shore of an unknown savage continent concealed a civilization like this?' I said softly.

Cortes turned to regard me with a brotherly smile. '*We* did, did we not, Alvaro, back there in Cuba?'

'Or so at least we hoped.'

'Am I mad to have believed I could conquer this place with an army of a few hundred Spaniards and a few thousand Indians, Alvaro?' asked Cortes.

'I would say that depends on whether you believe it still,' I told him.

Cortes gazed back out over the city, wakening to ever more boisterous life. Canoes and pirogues plied its canals. More were becoming visible on the lake. There was a metropolitan buzz in the air.

'I do believe I do,' he said. 'And you do not?'

What was the population of Tenochtitlan? A hundred thousand? Two hundred thousand? How many Mexica dwelt in this great valley? A million?

'I don't see how,' I told him.

'We have seen that the empire of Montezuma is hollow and restive,' said Cortes. 'Tabasco, Totonaca, Tlascala, we have conquered wherever in it we've gone. Why not here?'

'We led ourselves astray by the ease with which outlying provinces were raised against their overlords,' I told him. 'But they were constrained to pay heavy tribute to the Mexica, and those who pay tribute always resent those who receive its benefits, just as the peasants of any countryside resent the cities they feed. But the Mexica have no more reason to resent such an arrangement than the citizens of Rome had to resent the plunder of the provinces that the Caesars brought back to them.'

'True,' said Cortes. 'Nevertheless, Rome fell.'

'Look at this city! It would take a full European army to stand up to what Montezuma could field from the population here alone.'

'But Rome was conquered by one man conquering one heart,' said Cortes.

I regarded him with silent befuddlement. The rising sun seemed to light a fire in the hard dark eyes of Hernando Cortes as he looked back at me with a grimace that was half determination and half something I could not quite fathom.

'Jesus Christ conquered the heart of Constantine and so was Rome conquered for the Cross,' he said.

Though I knew full well that Constantine had been the sort of scheming reptile the term 'Byzantine' had been invented to describe, and he had conquered the Church as much as it had captured him, seeing Cortes' current state of practical Christian fervor, I prudently forbore to enlighten him.

'Montezuma is not Constantine,' I pointed out instead. 'And you surely do not believe that you are—'

Cortes broke the solemn mood with a welcome sardonic laugh. 'Of course not!' he exclaimed. 'But in certain benighted environs, I *am* taken for Quetzalcoatl, am I not?'

He turned to regard the squares formed by the intersecting streets of the city once more, the mighty pyramids spewing smoke into the heavens, the monstrous racks of grinning skulls, the foul papas, the palace of Montezuma.

'We must think of it as a game of chess,' he told me. 'Behold the board! To win a war, you must overcome an army. But to win a game of chess, you need only checkmate the King. And this may be accomplished even by a lone knight. If he can make the right move.'

And upon descending from the rooftops, Cortes sent a messenger to request an audience with Montezuma in his own palace, for the purpose of converting the Emperor to the Christian faith, and thereby causing his fealty to the Cross to flow backwards from Christ, to the Pope, to the Holy Roman Emperor, and thence to himself.

'Is that all?' I scoffed.

'He has already expressed a willingness to swear allegiance to Christ, has he not?' Cortes insisted.

'Only by way of declaring that while he might consider a position in an alliance under a god who is King of Kings, he is not about to swear fealty to any mere man.'

'Bah, do not be so dour, Alvaro. Once his soul sees the true light as Saul did on the road to Damascus, the rest will follow easily enough.'

'As simple as that? You will convert him with the power of your words alone?'

'God converted Saul then, and if He so wills, it will be He who converts Montezuma now, and I will only be His instrument,' said Cortes.

'Such humility becomes you, Hernando,' I said dryly. But the irony was lost on Cortes.

'Indeed,' he said with humorless enthusiasm. 'For God may use any instrument to work any miracle that pleases Him, and why would He not be pleased to use me to win Montezuma and his great heathen empire for Christ and the Cross?'

To my surprise, Montezuma saw fit to send back a messenger granting Cortes' request, and off we went; Cortes, Marina, myself, Pedro de Alvarado, Juan Velazquez, Diego de Ordaz, Gonzalo de Sandoval, and a five-man guard led by Bernal Diaz, prudently or arrogantly leaving our priests behind.

But Montezuma, as he was to explain to me later, had something of more worldly practicality in mind than the salvation of his immortal soul. 'By then Malinche had declared that neither he nor his Emperor was more than a man, though Jesus Christ King of Kings was indeed a god, perhaps Quetzalcoatl himself by another name, for the gods have remade the world several times, and men speaking different tongues may know the same god by different names. And some say that Quetzalcoatl is also both a god and a man. So perhaps I *should* pay tribute to Malinche's King of Kings. Perhaps I would gain greatly thereby.'

'How so?'

'The Teules clearly valued the tears of the sun above all things, and in return for such tribute, might I not obtain things of greater value?'

'Greater value than gold?' Even I found this notion difficult to grasp.

'It is a metal of great beauty, it is easy to work, and it never tarnishes, but it is soft. Why the Teules hold it to be of greater value than the silver which is harder than obsidian and does not shatter, from which they make their metal armor and their terrible swords, I still do not understand. It would have certainly been to my advantage to exchange tribute in what they call "gold" for equal weight of weapons and armor made of this "steel". For with such weapons, and with the thundering "cannon", the armies of Mexico would have been invincible and could seize as much tears of the sun as might be needed to keep the King of Kings well pleased.'

Montezuma's palace was nearby, and built with a similar lack of plan to that of his late father, out of the same reddish stone, called 'tezontl', but within it seemed like a different world.

The many interior courtyards through which we passed on the way to the throne room were cooled by fountains and perfumed by the blooms of well-tended gardens. The rooms and apartments were similar in form and construction to those of the palace of Axayacatl, but the tapestries of embroidered cloth and featherwork were all but ubiquitous and worked in the likenesses of flowers, insects, animals and birds in amazingly fine and realistic detail. What wall space they did not cover was hung with the pelts of animals like lions or leopards or bears. Clouds of incense created a sultry dreamlike atmosphere.

But the greatest contrast was that while the palace of Axayacatl was that of the current Emperor's dead father pressed into service as a barracks, the palace of Montezuma was brilliantly alive. It swarmed not only with hundreds of servants, but with richly dressed courtiers, men and women alike, some bustling about on matters of importance at least to them, but at least as many idling, conversing, lolling about the courtyard gardens, quaffing the chocolatl that seemed to be available on demand; the atmosphere reminding me of nothing so much as the lost and lamented Arabic court of the palace of Boabdil.

The officers escorting us to our audience with the Emperor paused at the entrance to his reception hall to remove their sandals and don coarse maguey-fiber robes over their finery like penitents donning sackcloth. We were enjoined to do likewise, since for anyone other than direct blood relatives of the Emperor to approach him in this venue dressed otherwise was considered lèse-majesté.

Cortes was not about to submit himself or his entourage to such a gesture of submission, nor when the Mexica escort led us into the room with humbly downcast eyes did he or the rest of us refrain from walking proudly upright and looking straight ahead at the object of all this servile deference.

Montezuma's 'throne room', if I may so style it, though he sat on a simple stool, was spacious enough to seem rather empty occupied only by himself and half a dozen men likewise seated flanking him. Of these, I recognized Cacama and Cuitlahuac, the only two who, like the

Emperor, were dressed in fine robes and feathered cloaks and had sandal-shod feet; the rest, apparently not of royal blood, were obsequiously garbed like our escort.

The escort departed, stools were brought in for us, and the chess match began.

'I promised that your magnanimous generosity towards us would be just as generously rewarded, and now I have come to fulfill that vow,' Cortes began, surely an excellent opening with which to attract the favorable interest of even an Emperor.

'I ask no tribute of you, Malinche,' replied Montezuma. 'Of course if you wish to honor me with some trifling tokens of friendship, I would not insult you by refusing your gifts.'

'What I now offer you is no trifling token, Montezuma, but the greatest gift one man may offer to another . . .'

When Marina translated this, Cacama, Cuitlahuac and the other Mexica nobles came to visibly avid attention, but Montezuma at least feigned imperial indifference, and with the slightest wave of his hand merely silently bade Cortes continue.

'The gift I have come to give you,' said Cortes, 'is that of your own immortal soul.'

This, unsurprisingly, was not quite what the Mexica would have wished to hear, and the expressions of all of them save Montezuma drooped at once into sour frowns. Only the Emperor himself did not display disappointment or any other emotion.

'Since I possess it already, I do not see how you can give it to me, Malinche,' he pointed out not unreasonably.

'You possess it now, or you believe you do, but unless you give over your wicked practices and accept the gift of Salvation freely offered to all men by Our Lord Jesus Christ, your soul and those of your subjects will all belong to Satan, and you will suffer torment in the fires of Hell for all eternity.'

Cacama, and particularly Cuitlahuac, took obvious umbrage at this, but it did not seem to faze Montezuma, who smiled indulgently as he held up a negligent hand as if to indicate that there was no good reason for Cortes to go on since he had heard all this before. Which turned out to be more or less exactly the case.

'You need not trouble yourself to repeat the story of the god who became a man and died upon a Cross and who feeds men with his flesh and blood, Malinche,' the Emperor told him goodnaturedly. 'For you have told this tale many times, and nothing here escapes my attention. The god who is both the father of Jesus Christ and his own son created the first world, which was a lush garden, but a demon called Satan, who he had cast down into a pit called Hell, turned into a serpent, and took his vengeance by feeding men a forbidden fruit which gave them the wisdom of the gods. So the jealous god destroyed the first world, and created the second. Still men would not offer up the correct tribute, so he destroyed the second world by a flood. But worshippers of the demon came to rule the third world, so it was destroyed with plagues. Men were then given a fourth world, but yet again failed to pay proper tribute, and so the god, in desperation, became Jesus Christ to bring about the present fifth world with the sacrifice of his own body and blood. When he returns, there will be a sixth world, which will be a per-fect garden like unto the first.'

As you might well imagine, dear reader, the mouths of Cortes and the rest of the Spaniards gaped open by the time Marina had finished translating this brief synopsis of both testaments of the Bible. Not even Hernando Cortes could find a word to say.

'That is *your* tale of the five worlds, is it not, Malinche?' said Montezuma with an absolutely straight face.

Indeed it was. I myself could only marvel at its succinctness and admire Montezuma in a new light, for clearly this was no mere barbaric potentate, but a man not only of intellect, but perhaps possessed of a sense of irony, though given my imperfect command of Nahuatl and Marina's equally straight-faced translation, the latter was harder to judge. But that might have been Montezuma's intent.

Still Cortes could find no words.

'We too have knowledge of the four worlds before this one,' Montezuma told him. 'We too await the return of a god who was once a man to bring a sixth world which will be greater than the one we now know. You may call him Jesus Christ, we may call him Quetzalcoatl, but since we do not speak the same tongue, it is not surprising that we do not call him by the same name.'

'I would not have thought to have heard such blasphemy even in a mosque or a synagogue!' I heard Alvarado growl under his breath.

'Quiet!' Cortes hissed at him angrily.

'What you have recited does indeed resemble what is written in the Bible,' he finally managed to tell Montezuma diplomatically. 'And it may very well be that omnipotent God has in His infinite wisdom and mercy seen fit to reveal the history of the world to men here in your own language and in a manner you may more readily understand than my own poor rendering of Holy Scripture, for I am not a man of great learning and eloquence.'

'Nor am I,' Montezuma told him with what seemed to me a smarmy false modesty to match Cortes' own. Then, however, his expression became almost dreamy. 'But Nezahualcoyotl, a true man of knowledge and the greatest poet our tongue has ever known, expressed the notion that beyond the gods that make themselves known to men is a greater god who does not reveal himself, whose nature men can never know.'

And I was certain that I beheld a man who, though he might be engaged in some political chess game with Cortes, was fascinated by knowledge and philosophic speculation for its own sake.

'The One True God,' muttered Cortes.

Montezuma shook his head. 'Some say this was Nezahualcoyotl's meaning, some that the gods men know are simply his vassals. But Nezahualcoyotl further mused that it might be that the gods men know – Huitzilopochtli, Xipe Totec, Tlaloc, Quetzalcoatl, your Jesus Christ, and all the rest – are but masks worn from time to time by this singular hidden god, as Xipe Totec wears the skin of a man. Why this hidden god chooses to do this, we will also never know, and might not even understand were we told.'

Montezuma's vassals seemed vexed by this detour into theological discourse, and the Spaniards too were obviously impatient for Cortes to get on with the promised process of converting the Emperor to the One True Faith. Cortes himself frowned in consternation, and glanced towards me as if seeking counsel, for he was enough of an unquestioning Christian on the one hand and a sufficiently clever one on the other to realize that Montezuma had dragged him out into blasphemous waters beyond his theological depth.

I could offer him nothing better than a shrug, for though the Kabbalah hints at something akin to Nezahualcoyotl's vision as what it calls the Ain-Soph, what Montezuma was proposing was a novel theology to me as well.

Though not without its attractions. I would not have you believe, dear reader, that in that very moment, my eyes met those of the Emperor and we recognized each other as kindred spirits, but I do believe that this was the moment when my journey to the mountain refuge where I am writing this account truly began.

'And so,' said Montezuma, 'while I may pay tribute to my gods, and you and your King to yours, if Nezahualcoyotl was right, Huitzilopochtli, and Jesus Christ, and whatever gods there may be in lands yet unknown to us all, are all either vassals of the same hidden god whose nature and true desires none of us can ever know or merely masks he chooses to wear for the same unknowable purposes. And so . . .'

'And so . . . ?' Cortes muttered disconsolately.

'And so,' said Montezuma in quite another mode, 'there is little reason to trouble ourselves further with such matters, is there, Malinche? Since you have told me that your King is vassal to this Pope who is vassal to your King of Kings, who in turn is either a vassal or a mask of the hidden God of gods, then by swearing allegiance to him, I but reaffirm that I rule these lands as a fellow vassal of that King of Kings and God of gods. Is that not so, Malinche?'

And he favored Cortes with a warm fraternal smile.

'Well spoken,' was all that Cortes could manage, eyeing the emperor suspiciously.

'And so, Malinche, since you affirm this too, I do affirm that he is my sovereign, that I rule these lands in his name, even as he rules his lands in the name of Jesus Christ King of Kings, even as that god and all others rule the world in the name of the hidden God whose name will never be revealed,' said Montezuma. 'And so, there is nothing further to be decided now.'

He rose, having brought the audience to his desired end, and Cacama, Cuitlahuac and the other Mexica nobles sprang to their feet with what seemed like great satisfaction and relief.

'At our leisure, we may discuss the petty details of what tribute your King may require of me,' said Montezuma, beaming at Cortes, albeit in the manner of a cat who has cornered his mouse. 'And what new means, he in return, as my sovereign, may provide me to further secure my reign over the lands I now rule in his name and to extend our rule over more.'

22

AFTER AFFIRMING HIS allegiance to King Charles in this peculiarly disconcerting manner, Montezuma granted us the freedom of the city, and I set out to explore it. Cortes sternly enjoined his soldiery against committing outrages against public decency or seeking to take advantage of the honor of honorable females. But there were those of less punctilious honor to be found here as in any metropolis, and there was no shortage of pulque as well as an herb called tobacco whose fumes, when inhaled, proved to be mildly intoxicating.

I myself was no devotee of pulque, a drink which dulled my senses and sapped my energy, preferring the chocolatl which sharpened the former and enhanced the latter, though I did try the tobacco, which was loaded into a hollow reed through which the smoke was then breathed, but only once, for I found the lightheaded nausea it produced less than exhilarating.

I was told that the amatory skills of the local damsels of easy virtue were considerable, but I had no inclination to avail myself of their services, for Marina was often at liberty during the daylight hours, and while to be modestly frank or frankly modest about it, we passed much more of our time together exploring the city than each other, there was enough of the latter to keep me well satisfied.

Indeed, had I been condemned to perfect monkish celibacy I might barely have noticed the lack, for Tenochtitlan, no less for myself than for Marina, was the fulfillment of a soul-deep fantasy. And so during a magical four days we wandered through Tenochtitlan as wide-eyed explorers.

It was a city of both visual splendor and sophisticated municipal design beyond anything I knew or had heard tales of in Europe.

Venice might have its lagoon and grand canals, but Tenochtitlan was surrounded by water that gleamed and sparkled under a tropical blue sky, upon which drifted the magical chinampas, floating isles of flowers out of some sultan's hashish dreams. The waters of Lake Texcoco were brackish and therefore unsuitable for drinking or cooking, and so fresh water was brought to Tenochtitlan from a source on the mainland at Chapultepec, and such was the care with which the public amenities were planned, that it was brought in by two aqueducts rather than one, so that there would always be running water while one was being cleaned or repaired.

These main aqueducts fed an extensive network of secondary piping which not only served the practical purpose of keeping basins and catchpools throughout the city well filled with fresh water at all times and seasons, but likewise fed the many ornamental fountains which beautified it. The canal system was extensive and heavily used by the populace, completing the vision of a great white city arising from the water and floating upon it.

Amazingly, this mighty metropolis and much more besides had been built without benefit of either beasts of burden or the simplest use of the wheel. And while the former lack could be laid to the absence of suitable animals in these lands, as I had seen, the Mexica did produce small statues on wheels, so that why they never thought to attach larger wheels to wooden platforms and thereby construct at least rude carts, was a mystery to me then, and remains incomprehensible even now.

The city was kept cleaner than any I knew in Europe, the streets were well paved with either stones or a kind of cement, and its teeming populace was likewise unusually clean and sweet-smelling by the far less fastidious standards of European cities. There were no beggars or obvious cutpurses in evidence, and aside from the filthy-robed papas, the men and women, even those of modest means, wore clean togas or gowns of cotton or maguey fiber, often richly embroidered, the more affluent sporting cloaks of feathers or furs, and jewelry of silver and gold.

Once, when Marina was unavailable, I conversed in my less than perfected but by now serviceable Nahuatl with a telpochtlatoque, a schoolmaster of sorts in one of the telpochcallis, simple but universally available schools set up by the clan elders of the city's quarters for the sons of people of ordinary means. I learned that there were also universities of higher learning, called calmecacs, maintained by the priesthood for the scions of the nobility and the training of papas, not unlike those of Catholic Europe, though preserving a very different intellectual patrimony.

Whether in the company of Marina or practicing my Nahuatl on my own, Tenochtitlan was a paradise for a man of my scholarly inclinations, one which I could have spent several lifetimes delving; in short, as you might well imagine, dear reader, I was in my element.

But not Hernando Cortes.

Montezuma had sworn fealty to the Spanish throne and expressed his willingness to pay tribute in gold. Cortes was now effective viceroy of the King whom Montezuma recognized as his suzerain, and therefore ruled here, did he not? He *should* be pleased, should he not?

But of course, dear reader, unless you are hopelessly naive, you already realize that he was not.

'How am I any different from that lion he has caged up in that menagerie of his?' he growled at me for want of a more just target, indeed for want of any clear target.

This was on our fifth day in the city. We had just returned to the palace of Axayacatl from a tour of Montezuma's most impressive zoological gardens, where we had seen a large tawny golden-eyed cat padding in obsessively repetitive circles around its enclosure, and Cortes was pacing around one of the secondary courtyards of the palace of Axayacatl in very much the same manner, though *his* cage was far more spacious and luxurious and its bars much more subtle.

So subtle as to be not even quite visible.

Montezuma's palace lay within sight and his menagerie in turn lay within sight from its rooftop pavilions, so it took but the smallest flight of fancy to imagine the emperor gazing upon our quarters and regarding us as another of his exhibits of exotic fauna.

Indeed, in addition to a series of gigantic aviaries which put those of Iztapalapa to shame, the lizards and serpents, the wild cats of various sizes and colors, the rodents and deer and boar, Montezuma's menagerie *did* contain human specimens. There were dwarfs and giants. There were two girls joined at the head, and two boys joined at the buttocks. There was a woman with a thick pelt and a beard. There were several persons with peaked and pointed skulls and eyes vacant of all sapience. And much more which I need not raise your gorge and mine by describing.

Why not, then, a good number of 'Teules' or 'Spaniards' with their Tlascalan retainers, their exotic raiments and artifacts, nicely caged in the liberty of his capital and the palace of his father to complete Montezuma's collection?

'I am still not sure what has happened,' moaned Cortes. 'How does a man say "no" by saying "yes"?'

'Perhaps in the same manner that a woman says "yes" by saying "no"?' I suggested archly.

Cortes summoned up the spirit to laugh at this wan jest, which sufficed to somewhat lighten the darkness of his mood.

'Seriously, Alvaro, I am at a loss for what to do now. I have been granted what I demanded, but in name only, for in truth rather than conquerors, we are prisoners in this opulent trap.'

'Perhaps not,' I told him. 'We have been granted the liberty to return to Vera Cruz, or for that matter to Cuba or even Spain unimpeded and with all the considerable golden booty we have already collected.'

'Oh of a certainty! And it wouldn't surprise me if Montezuma would add quite a bit more just to see us gone!'

'Would that be so terrible?' I said, though in truth quitting Tenochtitlan and the civilization which was ruled from this city of marvels which I had just begun to explore for the rude environs of Vera Cruz, let alone the colonial crudeness of Cuba, was the last thing that I wanted.

'And then what?' demanded Cortes.

'And then we would all be rich, and together we would write your memoirs, and you would go down in history as a greater explorer than Columbus and the King would probably shower you with honors, and . . .'

Cortes' black look and disbelieving smirk were enough to silence my blather in midstream, for it told me that he knew full well that I placed no more credence in what I was telling him than he did.

'And Diego Velazquez will mount an expedition of thousands of soldiers and hundreds of horsemen and cannon to conquer what we could not, or the King will do it himself, and I will meet the final fate of Columbus too, which, you may remember, was not exactly a retirement to riches and honor and glory.'

'What then do you propose to do?'

Cortes ceased his pacing. 'I do not know,' he told me. But then a predatory look came into his eyes, and there seemed to be something behind it that frightened even Hernando himself. 'Or perhaps I do . . .' he muttered. 'But I am not yet desperate enough to contemplate it seriously now.'

And he would say no more.

As you might well imagine, dear reader, the Spaniards languishing in the tense boredom of their genteel confinement soon began to grow restive. The avidly martial likes of Pedro de Alvarado and his brotherly retinue longed for a final gloriously triumphant battle and began to call for one. Less suicidal gallants such as young Gonzalo de Sandoval fretted from inaction as well, but at least realized that such a victorious climax was hardly within our grasp. Former Velazquez loyalists like Diego Ordaz and Velazquez de Leon began to muse aloud that the best course might be to return while we could to Cuba, or at least to Vera Cruz, with the abundant booty already secured. The priests, and Father Diaz most strongly, began to campaign for an effort to convert these heathen.

Although Montezuma had given us the freedom of the city, Cortes had not tested how far it truly went by marching his forces through it en masse, but now he decided, for reasons of both morale and a showing of our standards to its inhabitants, that our entire company, minus the

Tlascalans, should visit the main market of Tenochtitlan at Tlatelolco, in the city's northern precinct.

'I have been told it is a great marvel,' he told me, 'and it will allow us to remind the inhabitants of the city that we are still here and in force by giving *them* something to marvel at.'

But even Cortes was not imprudent enough to attempt to parade his main force through the length of Tenochtitlan without warning, and so he sent messengers to the Emperor politely requesting his permission.

'Should he refuse to allow it, at the very least our true position will be nakedly clarified, and if he does not, my point will have been made.'

Montezuma went him one better. Not only was permission rapidly and readily granted, not only did he dispatch caciques to serve as guides, he sent word to Cortes that upon his return, he would do him the high honor of greeting him personally atop the city's center of worship, the great pyramid or 'teocalli' dedicated to Huitzilopochtli and Tlaloc which dominated the Sacred Precinct.

We set forth in much the same order as we had first entered the city, with our hosts leading the way on foot, followed by Cortes at the head of his cavalry, and the rest of us on foot, the main differences being that the cannon and the Tlascalans had been left behind, and his troops were displaying every flag, banner and standard they could muster.

The spectacle of our procession turned out great numbers of the curious, crowding the overlooking rooftops and lining both sides of the main avenue up which we proceeded, all the more so since Cortes had his drummers beating out a rhythm to accompany the clatter of horses' hoofs and trumpeters continuously proclaiming our advent from afar.

But when we reached the Tlatelolco market, our musicians fell silent, we were no longer a parade, and we became the curious rather than the object of curiosity. Indeed, so vast was the market that were it not for our horses and our fair skins and our strange clothing, a few hundred Spaniards might have gone unnoticed. By now, dear reader, you have probably grown weary of my declarations that this or that in Tenochtitlan went beyond anything of its like in Europe, but I crave your indulgence one more time, for the Tlatelolco market exceeded even those poor attempts at hyperbole.

That this market was far larger than anything in Europe was the least of it. More amazing still was its completeness, and, quite unlike a great Arabic souk, its orderliness. I warrant that there was nothing produced in the entire empire which paid tribute to Tenochtitlan and far beyond which could not be found in the Tlatelolco market, and all neatly arranged and displayed according to its kind in its own assigned sector.

There was a vast area devoted to foodstuffs, and there was order within it. More than a hundred varieties of peppers were displayed side by side. Beans were heaped up with beans, ears of maize with ears of maize, ground maize flour with flour. Here were fruits of the tropics, there fruits of more clement climes, with the respective vegetables elsewhere. Dressed meats had their own sectors, separate from the live turkeys, boar, water fowl and small dogs, each with their own stations. There was a separate fish market. Then there were the heaped-up spices, and the prepared maize cakes, the cacao beans, the jugs of pulque.

There was a gloriously fragrant section devoted to flowers, and another given over to the merchants of incenses and pungent gums and oils. There were cotton merchants and maguey cloth merchants, leather tanners, furriers, sandalmakers. There was a large section devoted to arms and cotton armor. There were goldsmiths and silversmiths and purveyors of gems and turquoise. There was pottery in several recognizable styles. Paintings and the materials for creating them. Tobacco and mushrooms and cacti and medicinal herbs. Piles of feathers and finished cloaks and tapestries made from them. Stools and tables and mats. Statues of stone and statues of wood.

The babbling cacophony of the throngs of buyers and sellers haggling in a foreign tongue was ear-splitting and yet exhilarating. Likewise the mingling and clashing odors of fruit and dung, flowers and fish, meat and leather, sweat and chocolatl, somehow combined in a perfume that intoxicated the senses and inspired visions. Here, within the compass of one enormous souk, was the food and drink, the art and the arms, the flora and the fauna, of a great civilization.

Here was Mexico entire.

Or so I thought as we strolled through the Tlatelolco market, but when we returned to the Temple Square, to the Sacred Precinct, to the great pyramid that ruled over it, to Cortes' rendezvous with Montezuma atop it, we were reminded that there was a deeper and darker heart to the empire that he ruled.

Our party was met at the foot of the temple to Huitzilopochtli and Tlaloc by two papas and four caciques. The former informed Cortes through Marina that the Emperor awaited himself and 'his retainers' at the top of the pyramid, and the latter, solicitously assuming that he must be fatigued from the day's exertions, declared that Montezuma had commissioned them to spare him the arduous climb by carrying him up to the top.

Cortes haughtily refused to be carried, a foolish mistake by my lights, for Marina, Father Olmedo, Alvarado, Sandoval, Bernal Diaz, Ordaz and myself were chosen for the honor of accompanying him, and I would certainly not have refused this courtesy.

Not only was the pyramid over a hundred feet tall, it was stepped in five stages, and for some perverse reason the ascending stairways were positioned so that one must trudge halfway around each landing to reach the next one, so that one must circle it three times in order to reach the platform at the top. Worse still, its faces were pitched at a steep forty-five-degree angle and so, of necessity, were the stairs. And if that wasn't enough, the steps themselves were unnaturally narrow, unnaturally high, and unnaturally close together, so that one was constrained to mince up them all the way like a dainty damsel.

I will spare you the aching legs, panting lungs, sweaty brow and thumping heart which were the price that I had to pay for the privilege, and mercifully pass you, dear reader, to the reward gained thereby. To wit the magnificent view from the top, which I would deem breathtaking had my breath not long since been taken away before I arrived there.

From this vantage the entire city was laid out below as if it were a master cartographer's most artful rendering, and one could encompass its glory entire: the broad avenues and the network of canals, the great northern marketplace, the hundreds of streets laid out in regular pattern, the secondary temples sending their plumes of smoke skyward, the swarms of inhabitants reduced to scurrying ants, the causeways linking the city to the mainland and the distant cities fringing the lakeshore, the glassy mirror of Lake Texcoco itself with its floating gardens and tiny boats, the mighty mountains enclosing the Valley of Mexico in the misty distance.

The sight was lovely indeed, but when we turned our attention to the plaza that crowned the pyramid upon which we now stood, it was another matter.

The platform atop the pyramid was quite large and paved with stone. At the side furthest away from where the final stairway had deposited us stood two more or less similar shrines. These were likewise of stone and in the form of small squat towers with open porticos facing in our direction, crowned with elaborately carved and painted woodwork. Before each of them was a stone altar upon which burned an eternal flame.

Montezuma awaited us midway between these two shrines, flanked by two papas who no doubt were the high priests of Huitzilopochtli and Tlaloc. In order to reach him, we had to pass by an imposing block of red-and-white marbled stone set up in the center of the platform. It was about as high as a man's waist, roughly round, with a diameter of about two man-lengths. As we neared it, we could see that there was a depression in it near its center, from which a channel had been chiseled to the far edge.

Passing by, we saw that the depression was half-filled with blood which flowed through the channel to ooze drippingly into a chalice of black stone set on the stone of the plaza to catch it.

We knew full well what sanguinary rites were held throughout the Empire of the Mexica. But to have ascended to this ultimate height above the gleaming white and magnificently civilized capital thereof only to be so intimately confronted with what lay beneath its grandeur and at the core of its soul made the horror suddenly vividly personal.

And for me, at least, that much more paradoxical.

How could the civilization that had built Tenochtitlan rip out human hearts on such a bloody altar?

How could the civilization that worshipped a Prince of Peace who commanded men to love their neighbors as themselves burn human beings at the stake in His name?

How could those who worshipped an Allah who was styled the Beneficent and the Merciful behead the infidels who would not bow down to Him?

How could the Jews, after suffering slavery in Egypt, sack Jericho and dispossess its rightful inhabitants in the name of the God who had freed them from the yoke?

Anger contorted the features of Alvarado; Sandoval, Diaz and Ordaz simply looked pale and stricken; Marina's face was calmly unreadable, and Father Olmedo crossed himself with eyes half shut. Cortes, who was now going to have to deal diplomatically with the Emperor without whose permission such atrocities could not be committed, seemed to be struggling to chew down his fury as he led us slowly towards Montezuma.

'Behold the sacred abode of the heart of Mexico, Malinche,' said Montezuma. 'For as Tenochtitlan is the heart of my empire, so is the twin teocalli of Huitzilopochtli and Tlaloc the heart of my people, for it is Tlaloc who brings the rain which waters the maize that allows us to live, and it is Huitzilopochtli who led us across the northern desert from Aztlan and gave us the strength to conquer all foes and so for our own heart to prevail. Without the favor of Tlaloc, we would surely perish, and without the favor of Huitzilopochtli, we would no longer rule.'

'I . . . thank you for extending this . . . high honor,' Cortes managed to reply through his clenched jaw and with a vein throbbing in his temple.

Montezuma then led our party on a brief walk around the edge of the temple platform so as to afford us a vision of his capital entire from on high like the proud proprietor thereof that he indeed was, though leaving it to the high priests to point out landmarks and provide commentary. This little tour quieted our gorges somewhat and cooled Cortes' ire, to the point where I heard him suggest to Father Olmedo that this might be the perfect place to erect a large Cross to dominate the city once these heathen were enlightened.

As for what sort of enlightenment Montezuma was seeking to provide to *us* by inviting Cortes to this bloody sacred venue, I could not fathom at the time, nor could Hernando or any other of our party, which was exceedingly regrettable, for if he had, he might have acted differently.

'My purpose, of course, was to seek an omen,' said Montezuma when I asked after it later. 'To confront Malinche with Huitzilopochtli and the god with him, for if they were pleased with each other, my alliance with his King of Kings would surely be propitious, and if not, it had best be rescinded.'

But neither Cortes nor I suspected any such thing at the time, and so the audience atop the temple did not go well at all.

After the display of his worldly role as Emperor of all we could see from horizon to horizon, Montezuma then assumed his role as sovereign of the invisible realm, and when we beheld what lay within the shrines, all of us no doubt wished it might have remained so.

We were ushered into the shrine of Huitzilopochtli, a large chamber dominated by the large idol of the war god at its rear. Seemingly of painted wood, this effigy had a more or less human head with the eyes, fanged lips and nasal slits of a serpent, and a human upper torso which devolved below into the coils of an enormous snake like a hideous parody of a mermaid. In his left hand he held a clutch of arrows and in his right a bow. His feet were the clawed talons of a great bird, probably an eagle. He wore a headdress of some green stone carved to emulate quetzal feathers. The lower body was completely covered in pearls and gemstones. Around his neck was a heavy chain composed of alternating hearts of gold and silver.

Upon the stuccoed walls the ghosts of full-colored paintings were dimly visible beneath an encrustation of what at first appeared to be dark reddish-brown rust, until the earthy pungent stink of ancient dried blood and fresher gore that could not be masked by the heavy incense smoke filling the chamber assailed the nostrils.

And before Huitzilopochtli, attended by three papas whose vestments and hair were likewise encrusted, was a black stone altar upon which lay three human hearts so slick with fresh red blood that they seemed to almost be beating.

Marina covered her nose and mouth with the back of her hand. Father Olmedo crossed himself, and frantically worked the beads of his rosary. Alvarado's face fairly purpled with rage. The other captains seemed to turn a greenish pale. I felt a bubble of nausea rising up my gullet, for the awful sight made the fetid stench all but overpowering.

Montezuma seemed to be studying Cortes intently as Cortes regarded Huitzilopochtli with fists that kept clenching and unclenching, a jaw set so sternly against outraged reaction that I feared his teeth might crack, an Adam's apple that, like mine, seemed to be suppressing a gag, and eyes within which disgust warred with fury.

No one said a word. No one moved. It was as if the immobile Huitzilopochtli exerted his power over us all, as if he and Cortes were engaged in a silent contest of wills which the implacable war god was winning.

And when Montezuma finally broke the silence, it was as if Huitzilopochtli spoke through him.

'Outside is the fresh heart of a Jaguar Warrior who willingly offered himself up to the flowery death,' he told Cortes in a most generous tone. 'There is no more welcome and propitious offering, Malinche, and it is yours to make if you choose to do so.'

When Marina translated this magnanimous proposal, it was all Cortes could do to refrain from drawing his sword and shouting his outrage, in lieu of which he turned on his heel and stormed out of the foul and putrid shrine into the fresh air and sunlight, immediately followed by the rest of us with no little relief, let me tell you, dear reader.

'How can you ask me to take part in such a vile Satanic rite?' Cortes demanded angrily of Montezuma when he had emerged behind us. 'I am a Christian, not some barbarous cannibal! You would have me commit a most foul and evil sin that would have my immortal soul cast down into the nethermost pit of Hell for all eternity!'

Alvarado's expression of outrage well mirrored that of Cortes, and the other captains likewise, if somewhat less floridly, but Father Olmedo quailed before this impolitic onslaught, and Marina, looking more fearful than I had ever seen her, remained silent.

'Translate my words!' Cortes ordered, rounding on her.

'I cannot do that—'

'I order you to—'

'She means it would not be wise,' interjected Father Olmedo.

'Now I am accused of stupidity for my faithfulness to the Cross?' roared Cortes.

Montezuma had been regarding this conversation in Spanish with growing consternation; now he barked something which his expression and even my imperfect Nahuatl told me was an imperial command to Marina to tell him what was being said.

'Not stupidity for your faithfulness to the Cross, Hernando,' I said quickly, screwing up my courage, 'but it is not exactly wisdom to so insult any monarch thus in his own capital, let alone his god atop his own temple, and certainly not one whose loyalty you would wish to win who could have us all slain if his ire were sufficiently aroused.'

To his credit, Cortes was able to cool himself to the point where he could recognize such pragmatic necessity. 'Tell him then that as a good Christian I cannot take part in such heathen blood rites, nor as an admirer of his own sagacity and wisdom can I comprehend how he can be so deluded as to put his faith in such false gods and evil spirits. Tell him further that as his good friend, I must warn him that these are snares of the Devil, and that if he does not repent of such sins, throw down these idols, and allow us to erect a Cross here to which he and his people may then cleave with confidence in their salvation, he, and they, will suffer what I would, should I take part in such evil rituals, namely an eternity spent in the torments and fire of Hell.'

This was a much prettier speech, but its import seemed unlikely to greatly please the ears of Montezuma, and Marina once more was reluctant to put it into Nahuatl. But this time Cortes would have none of it, and made her do so.

As she did, Montezuma's visage at first became unmistakably enraged, but by the time she had finished, and he was ready to reply, it was as if he had become one of his own stonily stolid idols.

'Our gods have served us well as long as we have served them properly,' he told Cortes. 'They have caused the rising sun to banish the night and brought the night to give rest to the day's exertions. They have given the rain and allowed the seeds of the spring planting to ripen into maize and preserved that bounty against the harvest. And Huitzilopochtli, greatest of them all, has granted us his special favor, leading us out of the wilderness to victory after victory and conquest after conquest until all you see from this height and much beyond is now under the rule of his favored warriors. Have I insulted your god as you have mine? Had I known you would do so, I would never have honored you with admission to his temple.'

Cortes stood there silent, unable, for once, to frame any reply. Nor did he have to. Montezuma then dismissed us all with a wave of his hand.

'Go now,' he ordered. 'Because of what you have done, because of my part in allowing you to commit this outrage, I must propitiate Huitzilopochtli myself lest his favor be withdrawn and his wrath fall upon us. And the task will be long and arduous.'

As the sun sank over the peaks of the western horizon, sending long lengthening shadows across the waters of the lake towards Tenochtitlan and silhouetting the temple of Tlaloc and Huitzilopochtli in a fiery aura, from the rooftop terraces of the palace of Axayacatl a long line of figures could be seen ascending its staircases in a steady unbroken file.

Smoke rose above the temple, reddened by the setting sun as the sky purpled toward black, and the distant cries of sharp pain continued until the full fall of night with a dreadful and relentless regularity, each followed some moments afterward by the sight of another corpse making its long heartless tumble downward.

None of us could abide the somber and terrible spectacle for long, but none of us could refrain from bearing witness, however brief, for none of us, and certainly not Cortes, could truly deny that these murders were on our knowing souls, at least in some measure, as much as they were upon the oblivious souls of their perpetrators.

23

THERE HAD BEEN LITTLE discord among Cortes' captains since our arrival in Tenochtitlan, but now an eruption of fear, outrage and horror made for a night of restive recrimination. Small groups met, argued, dissolved, soldiers and captains drifted from one to the other, Father Diaz exhorted to righteous action, Father Olmedo tried to calm the stormy waters. Sometime after midnight, Cortes summoned to his quarters a small selection of officers and the priests to try to put an end to it.

I too was summoned, not to write down what was all too likely to occur but no doubt because Hernando valued my counsel and knew that I maintained an indifferent distance from the bickerings and factionalism once more arising among his lieutenants and soldiery, so what follows is my re-creation from memory alone of what transpired.

Both priests were there, the iresome Father Diaz and the more prudent and practical Father Olmedo. Cortes' loyal partisans were represented by the two most respected thereof: Gonzalo de Sandoval, the closest thing to a true knight of the Cross among our company, a Galahad if you will, but of a modest nature which would have caused him to blush at such a comparison, and Cortes' favorite, Pedro de Alvarado, a man incapable of blushing at anything, but after Hernando, the strongest leader of men in the army.

Also attending were Diego de Ordaz and Velazquez de Leon, both former partisans of the governor of Cuba, won over by success, but now made once more restive by catastrophe and in the forefront of those demanding a retreat from Tenochtitlan while it still might be possible or else some strong punitive response to the atrocity Montezuma had forced us to witness.

'How can you still call yourselves soldiers of Christ after hiding behind these walls like cowards while hundreds of victims were slain in a hideous Satanic ritual?' Father Diaz demanded.

'For one thing, we are at least still alive to do so,' Cortes replied sourly.

'But do we have the right to still call ourselves soldiers of the Cross?' Sandoval asked sincerely and earnestly.

'What would you have done in my place, Gonzalo?' Cortes demanded rather mildly.

Sandoval had no answer to that.

'*I* would have marched through the gates and up the pyramid and put a stop to it!' Alvarado blustered.

'Oh would you?' said de Leon.

'And how?' demanded Ordaz. 'And with what result? Our own deaths on the altar?'

'He is right,' said Father Olmedo. 'I too found it appalling to watch such monstrous evil while doing nothing, but had we tried to prevent it, it would no doubt have only resulted in all of us joining the death march to the top of the pyramid.'

'Such martyrdom would have cleansed our souls of a lifetime of sin and sent us all directly to Heaven!' Father Diaz proclaimed with righteous fervor.

'A destination we would all like to attain,' said de Leon, 'but at as late a date as possible.'

This provoked wan laughter.

'Besides which, seeking after such martyrdom would be a selfish act in the eyes of God,' said Father Olmedo.

'How so?' demanded Father Diaz.

'Winning absolution with such martyrdom would mean not only the failure to conquer the worldly Empire of the Mexica but the abject failure to win its soul for Christ, and thus buying our salvation by deny-ing these benighted heathens theirs.'

'Just so,' said de Leon. 'Best we escape, assuming that we can, and return to the safety of Tlascala or even Vera Cruz and petition Diego Velazquez for reinforcements.'

On and on it went to no useful end, with Cortes mute during most of it, as if he knew all too well that he had made a dreadful mistake, but also that owning up to it, by draining confidence in his leadership, would only make his personal position and that of the collectivity he led that much worse, glancing sidewise at me from time to time apparently imploring me to intervene somehow.

But what could I say? Montezuma had laid a trap from which Cortes could not have escaped no matter what he did or did not do. There was little doubt that Montezuma would have contrived to take the same umbrage at Cortes' refusal to offer up a heart to Huitzilopochtli no matter how sweetly he had managed to pose it. For while the Emperor might truly fear the outrage of Huitzilopochtli, offering him the hearts of so many victims within our sight was probably as much a premedi-tated political act as a rite of propitiation.

Namely a demonstration of our impotence. It certainly made it impossible to maintain the delusion that Montezuma's oath of fealty to the Holy Roman Emperor or Jesus Christ as 'King of Kings' had any practical significance, for it was a stark demonstration that he still ruled here, that he was not about to forsake his war god for any Prince of Peace, and that the palace of Axayacatl could become our prison any time the Emperor chose to make it so.

But Cortes kept imploring me silently, and I finally gathered up the courage to speak. 'It seems to me, if I may be so bold, that instigating this contention was exactly the intent of Montezuma, and it therefore serves no purpose but his own,' I ventured. 'His deed is done, as is our response to it or our failure to mount one. Neither can be undone, therefore it would be best to give over any recriminations and turn to consideration of how our situation might best be retrieved.'

I had spoken but reluctantly, and had said nothing but the blandly obvious, but the glares with which my mild intervention was met made me wish I had held my silence. But it seemed I had served the purpose Cortes had assigned me.

'Well spoken!' he declared. 'For I did not summon you here to consider whether it would have been better to have fought and died and failed as noble Christian martyrs than sagaciously survived to triumph later as soldiers of the Cross, but to consider how the latter may be accomplished.'

'Well spoken yourself!' declared Alvarado.

'Noble words,' Ordaz said skeptically, 'but how *do* you propose to accomplish it?'

'I was hoping one of your number might have a suggestion,' said Cortes, but his eyes became guarded, and I could tell he was dissembling.

'Return to Vera Cruz and send for reinforcements,' declared de Leon.

'Or at least to Tlascala,' said Ordaz, 'where you were offered ten times the warriors we brought with us and you refused them.'

'You have no plan of your own?' exclaimed Sandoval, in a tone of surprised disappointment.

This appeared to be what Cortes had been waiting for all along.

'I do have a notion . . .' he said slowly. 'Though it is so audacious that I had hoped I would be presented with a better alternative . . . but since I have not—'

He cut himself short, shook his head. 'But no,' he said, 'I must sleep on it before even broaching it as a proposal . . .'

And with that, the conclave was concluded.

But early the next morning, so early that the sun had not fully risen, and no one else was up and about to see him do it, Cortes slunk into my quarters and roused me from slumber.

'I need your aid, Alvaro,' he told me as I rubbed sleep from my eyes, 'and in a manner in which you have aided me before. The truth is I dissembled last night. I had more than a notion. I had already decided what must be done.'

'Let me guess . . .' I muttered blearily. 'It is something that you deem it best should appear to originate elsewhere and perhaps be forced upon you, and you want me to plant the seed in some fertile ear.'

'There you have it!' said Cortes, far more brightly than the light of the hour.

'And what is this brilliant stratagem that must be forced upon you by your captains?'

Cortes' mien became a good deal more sober. 'No brilliant stratagem,' he told me, 'but the only alternative I can see to extract success from this dire situation. We must capture Montezuma and hold him prisoner.'

This brought me to full wakefulness as might a bucket of cold water suddenly poured over my head. 'Is that all?' were the only words I could find to utter.

'I believe I likened the situation before to a game of chess in which the capture of the King is decisive, regardless of the strength and positions of any other pieces on the board,' said Cortes.

'I believe that your idea at the time was to convert Montezuma to the Cross and thus win his fealty to the King as Holy Roman Emperor and thus rule through him,' I pointed out, beginning to think clearly. 'And now he *has* sworn fealty to the King or to the King of Kings, or some such thing, but it seems to have availed us nothing . . .'

Cortes nodded. 'To you, in confidence, I will confess that I not only seriously underestimated the extent and power of his empire, but also the sophisticated cunning of Montezuma,' he said. 'But he has had the wit to trap us within a palace within his capital in the middle of a lake, surrounded by a vast countryside and outnumbered by his forces by thousands to one, and all without a single armed confrontation.'

'Not bad for an ignorant heathen,' I said dryly. 'And now, it seems, he has performed his hideous mass human sacrifice before our eyes to rub our faces in it. But to what end?'

'Obviously to be quit of us without a battle,' said Cortes. 'As witness the fact that he has been showering us with gold since we landed on these shores in hopes of buying such an outcome. And then swearing a meaningless oath of fealty to the Spanish Crown. If it was his first choice to overcome our cannon and horses and steel swords with sheer numbers, he would have done so already. I do believe that if we demanded yet more tribute and decided to leave, he would let us retire across the mountains to Vera Cruz without opposition. I believe that he demonstrated his atrocious savagery and power over the lives of his subjects in order that we might be grateful for such an outcome and seize it.'

'Instead you would seize *him*.'

'Just so,' said Cortes. 'He has already made known his oath of fealty to the sovereign I represent, so once I hold him here, I can rule through him.'

'As long as his legitimacy in the eyes of the Mexica is maintained. Assuming he cooperates. Assuming you can capture him in the first place. And how do you propose to accomplish all that, Hernando?'

Cortes shrugged and favored me with a smile that was at once smarmy and ruefully sardonic. 'I was hoping that you might also aid me in working out these minor details, Alvaro,' he told me.

That very morning, before any solution to the said 'minor details' could present itself to either of our minds, a discovery occurred which increased the urgency of finding one.

The events of the previous day had made the setting up of a proper Christian altar to counter the Satanic pall they had cast over the spirits of our company seem urgent, and in the process of seeking out the best possible location, one of our carpenters, Alonso Yañez, had happened upon a wall which seemed to have been recently replastered and repainted, as if a portal had been blocked up and then less than perfectly concealed.

Yañez brought the matter to Juan Velazquez de Leon and Francisco de Lugo, who brought it to Cortes, and Cortes had him break through the wall in the presence of the three of them. There was indeed a secret chamber.

'It is filled with gold!' Cortes told me immediately afterward. 'Plates! Jewelry! Statues! Great mounds of nuggets! Casks of dust! And the room is as large as the largest of the apartments in this palace! As much gold as we have already sent back to His Majesty! Perhaps even more! Enough to make us all fabulously wealthy!'

'A shame we cannot have it,' I found myself blurting.

And then I had one of those chains of insights, one leading to the other with such rapidity that they seem to emerge from the nethermost regions of the mind of a single piece.

'If this treasure was so recently sealed away, Montezuma certainly did not mean for us to discover it, which is to say he certainly does not mean for us to have it,' I told him. 'And if he does not mean us to have it, and since we can hardly hide it in our baggage, he will not let us leave here with it in our possession.'

'Oh,' said Cortes, with the crestfallen expression of a small boy who has been shown a huge plate of his very favorite sweets, only to have it snatched away as he reached for it.

I laughed. 'Be of good cheer, Hernando!' I told him. 'It's perfect!'

'It is?' said Cortes, regarding me as if I had gone quite mad.

'Let everyone have a good long secret look at it to set them drooling,' I said. 'And then seal it away again. Their minds will surely become quite occupied with the desire to possess it. If someone else does not point out that Montezuma will not willingly let us depart with it, it will be easy enough for me to lead someone to such a logical conclusion. After which, the rest will either follow of their own accord, or be easily enough pointed in the obvious direction.'

'They will?' said Cortes, looking choicely perplexed. '*What* obvious direction?'

'That if we leave Tenochtitlan voluntarily, we must leave without this treasure.'

Now it was Hernando's turn to laugh as his eyes lit up with comprehension. 'So the only way we can have it is by Montezuma's permission, and the only way to achieve that—'

'—is by taking him prisoner.'

Once the news of the hidden treasure spread, most of the Spaniards wanted to take it and be gone, and it took a conversation with young Bernal Diaz, who had well served as such a conduit in the past, to set abroad the unfortunate realization that Montezuma was not about to let us do so. Once this had been wafted into the air, the truth of it, being all too painfully obvious, produced the desired effect. Or something more or less like it.

'The deputation arrived in my quarters in the middle of the night,' Cortes told me the next morning. 'Velazquez de Leon, Ordaz, Sandoval, Alvarado, and of course your young friend Bernal Diaz. The first three treated me to an interminable exposition of the precariousness of our position, that Montezuma could cut off our supplies any time he chose to, that if we had to fight our way out of Tenochtitlan, the situation would be all but hopeless, that the human sacrifices he had forced us to witness proved that his oath of fealty to the King was a sham, that we could never convert him to Christ, and so forth, as if I was a thick-witted ignoramus who had to be told all this.'

Cortes shook his head and grimaced. 'It was all I could do to contain my ire at such endless insult to my intelligence, but I managed it, hoping they would reach our desired conclusion on their own. But they did not. At length, I had to cozen them into it. What would you have me do? I finally asked them ingenuously. I could ask Montezuma's leave to depart, and I do believe he would allow it . . .'

Cortes laughed. 'Diaz and Alvarado were both so quick to point out that Montezuma would never let us leave with the treasure he had hidden from us that I do not remember which of them protested first, and when I sweetly suggested that we could always leave without it, you can imagine the consternation among them all!'

'And then they came out with the notion of taking Montezuma prisoner?'

Cortes shook his head ruefully. 'I had to lead them by their noses. What else can we do? I asked them. Stay here as guests of the Emperor until he grows weary of our presence and attacks? Can any of you come up with a reasonable strategy for taking this city? And so forth, bringing up all the possibilities I could think of save the one I wanted *them* to think of in a manner that exposed the rest as hopeless. It was Pedro de Alvarado who finally came out with it as if it was a stroke of brilliance. We must take Montezuma prisoner! he shouted. The rest of them instantly agreed, though Ordaz and Velazquez de Leon simply wanted to use the Emperor as a shield behind which to make off with the gold. It was Alvarado who pointed out that once we had Montezuma, we might very well have the city, if not the entire empire, and Sandoval and Bernal Diaz, being young and idealistic, swiftly came to his support.'

'And you, Hernando?' I asked.

'I congratulated Pedro on his sagacity and the three of them on their loyalty to King and Cross above gold, and inquired as to how they believed we could capture Montezuma, seeing that he dwelt in a palace surrounded by warriors and guards.'

'*And?*'

'And nothing,' said Cortes. 'Finally Sandoval suggested that the best course would be to entice him here to our quarters, where we could hold him easily enough and force him to do our bidding by threatening his life if he didn't.'

'To be accomplished *how*, Hernando?'

'One final detail that remains for us to work out, Alvaro,' Cortes told me with a smarmy little false smile.

As it turned out, destiny or God took care of this minor detail for us, if you are of a mind to view it thus, or Cortes seized upon what seemed at first telling to be a catastrophe and turned it to his own great advantage if you, like myself, dear reader, are more inclined to believe that such men make their own destiny out of whatever materials are made available to them.

The very next day, two Tlascalan messengers arrived with word that Juan de Escalante, whom Cortes had left in command at Vera Cruz, had been killed, along with six other Spaniards, a horse, and an indeterminate number of Totonacs, whose lives the Tlascalans held of little consequence.

I was not present at the interrogation of the Tlascalans, but Marina told me of what had transpired soon afterward, or at least as much of it as she comprehended.

'The Mexica still had a tax collector or an envoy named Qualpopoca in Nauhtla, some fifty miles or so from Vera Cruz in the lands of the Totonacs. Either he had not heard that Tlacochcalcat had sworn allegiance to Hernando and his King, or he did not care, or he sought to find favor with Montezuma, this was not clear, but he demanded the usual tribute for Tenochtitlan from some towns around Cempoala. The Totonacs told him that Malinche had forbidden it. Escalante threatened Qualpopoca, Qualpopoca threatened him, the Teules marched on Nauhtla, there was a battle, and seven Spaniards, a horse, and some Totonacs were killed.'

Marina told me this much in an indifferent manner, as if she were simply translating from the Nahuatl, which in a way she was, but then she frowned and shook her head, and became openly confused. 'Hernando's reaction to this I do not understand,' she told me. 'It was very strange.'

'How so?'

'At first, he was very upset and angry, but by the time it was all over, he was almost rubbing his hands together happily. You can explain this, Alvaro?'

'I'm afraid not, Marina,' I told her. 'It makes no more sense to me than it does to you.'

But it did to Cortes.

'This is what we have been waiting for,' he told me soon thereafter.

'It is? For an uprising against our garrison in Vera Cruz? For seven of our number to be slain, along with who knows how many Totonacs who are supposed to be under our protection?'

'Exactly,' said Cortes. 'For it was Montezuma's henchman who performed this outrage, was it not? And after he himself swore an oath of fealty to our King. It might therefore be construed as an act of treason.'

'Do you really believe Montezuma was behind this, Hernando?'

Cortes shrugged. 'Does it matter, Alvaro?' he asked. 'True or not, it will certainly be useful to confront him with such an accusation. Which he will no doubt deny. At which point, would it be unreasonable to demand that he himself bring the miscreant before us as a proof of his own innocence?'

'Here, rather than in his own palace?'

'We *are*, after all, the offended party, are we not?' Cortes said with a lupine smile. 'And that *would* be a courteous gesture.'

The next morning Cortes sent a messenger to courteously request an audience with Montezuma on 'a matter of mutual interest', and Montezuma just as courteously granted it.

Cortes chose two dozen soldiers to infiltrate Montezuma's palace in small groups – no difficult task, since the place was continually abuzz with the comings and goings and idle amusements of Mexica nobles and the occasional Spaniard, and so vast and labyrinthine that their seemingly random and gradual concentration in the vicinity of Montezuma's audience chamber would be unlikely to be noticed until the deployment was accomplished.

He then chose five officers to accompany him – Alvarado, Sandoval, Velazquez de Leon, Francisco de Lugo, and Alonso de Avila – and off he went. They were all accoutered in full armor, a style of formal dress to which the Mexica were so accustomed that no suspicion was likely to be raised by it and which would allow them to bear swords into the imperial presence without demur.

Marina went along to translate, but I was left behind to fret, and fret I did, not only for the extremely problematic success of what seemed like an audaciously mad enterprise, but for her safety. And for my own as well, for I was under no illusion that any of us in the palace of Axayacatl would likely survive a failed attempt to capture Montezuma.

Thus it was with as much surprised relief as wonder that I beheld the amazing spectacle proceeding across the Temple Square to our palace-turned-fortress some four hours later.

Leading the procession was the great Montezuma himself, reclining on his golden litter borne by four well-accoutered nobles, shaded from the sun by the umbrella of quetzal feathers, wearing his quetzal-plume headdress and an abundance of gold and jeweled finery, preceded by three functionaries bearing golden wands, perfumed by clouds of incense, followed by a train of nobles, servants, wives and concubines – the Emperor of the Mexica apparently arriving to assume his captivity in full state.

This much I could see from atop the wall where I had awaited just this advent, if without more than wan hope that it would arrive, and also that Cortes, Marina, Sandoval, Alvarado, Avila, Lugo and Velazquez de Leon marched directly behind the Emperor's litter, but no more, save that Montezuma seemed to be waving dismissively to the small crowd through which this imperial parade was constrained to pass.

But by the time I had rushed down to the main palace gate, Montezuma's palanquin was in the process of entering through it, and he passed by me close enough so that I could see his eyes blinking most rapidly, like those of a newly caged bird, and making a not entirely successful effort to avoid glancing anxiously this way and that, belying the impassive mask he had made of his face. For a moment his eyes met mine, and seemed to rest there for a brief instant, as if seeking succor, or silently asking some question I could not understand.

And then he was gone, and Cortes and Marina were passing before me; she acknowledging me with a strange little self-satisfied smirk, he seemingly triumphant.

As you might imagine, I was impatient to find out how this amazing and perilous coup had been accomplished, and not to keep you in more suspense than I endured, without further delay I shall convey to you the tale as I finally learned it from each of them separately.

Let Cortes speak first, dear reader:

'We were received quite graciously, indeed lavishly, for Montezuma not only served us chocolatl, not only presented each of us with gold trinkets, but actually offered me the hand of one of his daughters in marriage to seal our alliance, which, of course, vexed Marina. Worse still, when of necessity my tongue slipped and I couched my polite refusal in the revelation that Christians practice monogamy, and I already had a wife back in Cuba!'

Here I cannot resist interjecting what Marina told me of her true reaction to this revelation:

'Hernando seemed to believe I was angry when he told Montezuma that Christians were allowed only one wife and that he already had one elsewhere, when I was only amused, for you had told me of this wife he remembered only when it served his own purpose. As for this strange Christian practice, who should know better how little it matters to Hernando Cortes!'

To return to Cortes' account:

'We spoke of this and that of little consequence until I had judged that my men in the palace would be positioned outside the audience chamber, and then I asked Montezuma most politely to have his servants and retainers leave so that we might converse confidentially on that matter of mutual interest previously alluded to. When he then demanded that I should dismiss my own men, I replied that they were already privy to this matter, which it would not be at all in his interest to have made known to Mexica ears other than those of the Emperor himself, and I swore that when its nature was revealed he would immediately understand why these captains of mine must be present and be grateful for my insistence.

'As soon as my conditions had been met, I confronted Montezuma with the whole story of Qualpopoca's treason and the murder of the Spaniards and the horse in the most outraged tone of high dudgeon I could muster and accused him of ordering it. Montezuma replied in a tone of wounded innocence that not only had he issued no such order but that this was the first he had heard of what Qualpopoca had done, and if he had not acted on his own, it had certainly been at the instigation of one of the Emperor's enemies, for who else would wish to so poison the friendship between himself and me?'

Here it would perhaps be best to continue with Marina's version, for reasons which will become apparent:

'Montezuma had to be lying, because whether Qualpopoca had acted under his orders or not, no one in the world received tidings of such matters before the Emperor did, and so he must have already known what Hernando had told him.

'But Hernando told Montezuma he believed him, and that was why he wanted to speak to him about it in secret, so as not to make him look foolish in front of his servants, who would surely spread the story if he let them live after they heard it. Then he told him that friends and kinsmen of the dead Spaniards were in an angry and suspicious mood, which was why he needed the men he had brought with him to witness the conversation because it was believed that he had grown too friendly with the Emperor. And finally that the only way the murdered men's friends and kinsmen would believe that the Emperor was innocent was if Qualpopoca and his accomplices were brought to Tenochtitlan by order of Montezuma to be tried before them.

'Montezuma agreed to this, had me summon one of the nobles waiting outside, and told him to see to it that Qualpopoca and his men be brought at once to Tenochtitlan on the order of the Emperor.

'I think Montezuma ordered Qualpopoca to do what he did to test Hernando, because his surprise and anger did not sound very real in Nahuatl, and I am sure he did not believe that Hernando feared the anger of his own warriors. I believe that neither of them believed the other, that this was some kind of dance of lies and they were both enjoying it.'

And perhaps they were, though the Spanish audience, as Cortes explained to me, was not:

'I could see that my captains, and the irascible de Leon in particular, were growing impatient with this pavane, and Montezuma could not help but notice them glowering threateningly at him already, so as soon as we were alone with him again, I told him that to satisfy my own men, and indeed his own subjects, it would be best if we conducted the trial of Qualpopoca and his men jointly, to which, of course, he had every reason to agree. But when I declared that since the crime had been committed against us, Qualpopoca's confinement, trial and punishment should take place in the palace of Axayacatl, he grew suspicious.

'"We will speak of this when he is brought to Tenochtitlan, Malinche," Montezuma told me in a manner that seemed intended to dismissively conclude the audience. Upon hearing Marina's translation of this, my five captains served me well by muttering, glowering fiercely, and inching their hands towards the hilts of their swords.

'This allowed me to frown at them in fearful agitation, and approach closer to Montezuma, accompanied by Marina, as if to confide my disquiet in a brotherly manner.

'"I'm afraid we must settle this now," I said in Spanish, so softly that it appeared I did not wish my men to hear me, "for there is a great fury in my army at this murderous perfidy, and while I am quite convinced that you had no part it in, my soldiers do not believe this, and unless a gesture is made to convince them of your sincerity, I cannot answer for your safety or my own."

'I do believe that at this moment Montezuma had an inkling of what was coming, for his expression grew stony, his eyes grew cold, and his face turned as pale a hue as is possible for a man of his race to attain.

'"What are you suggesting, Malinche?" he said.

'"Were you to accompany us now to the palace of Axayacatl as our honored guest until Qualpopoca's judgement for the murder of their fellows is accomplished, I cannot see how any of my men could continue to doubt your innocence," I told Montezuma. "And if any should then do so in my presence, on my oath, I would have him severely punished."'

'"Become your prisoner!" Montezuma shouted, albeit shrilly, rather than with a properly leonine imperial roar. "How dare you suggest that I submit to such degradation in the very capital of the land that I rule!"'

Let Marina have the concluding words of the tale, for it was her words which sealed the accomplishment of the deed:

'Hernando told Montezuma that what he was suggesting was nothing like taking him prisoner, but a common practice among the kings of Europe. Kings there often visited fellow kings, bringing with them as many servants, retainers and nobles as they wished, and ruling their kingdoms from the court of their brother monarchs as honored guests.

'Montezuma would have none of it. "You are not a King," he told Hernando, "and even if I were to accept such a thing, my subjects surely would not."

'"But after all, the palace of Axayacatl is *your* palace not ours, and we are already your guests there," Hernando reminded him, "so you would be doing nothing more than moving from one of your own palaces to another."

'Still Montezuma would not agree.

'"If some happy day King Charles would wish to visit Tenochtitlan, would you not afford him the courtesy of allowing him to set up his court in premises you provided for him?" Hernando said. "And when he invites you to visit him in state in his own capital in the same manner, would you insult him by refusing his hospitality?"

'Montezuma regarded Hernando with eyes as cold as those of a dead fish in a marketplace.

'"I am his ambassador to your court," said Hernando. "His loyal servant. And therefore by refusing the hospitality I offer by his authority, would that not be exactly what you would be doing?"

'Montezuma remained silent.

'"Enough fancy words wasted on this barbarian!" Velazquez de Leon shouted, and not to the Emperor but to Hernando. "We have gone too far to retreat now! He either comes with us or we kill him! Tell him that, Cortes!"

'And he drew out his sword.

'Montezuma jumped to his feet, trembling; with rage or fear or both. The angry look Hernando gave de Leon I think was genuine, for he shouted at the man to put his weapon away. But de Leon did not, and Alvarado also drew his sword.

'And it was to me, not any of the Teules, that the Emperor spoke, demanding a translation to Nahuatl of what had been said. And I knew that doing that would be wrong, and so I told a lie which I hoped Montezuma would believe, for a Mexica warrior would feel the same way in the same circumstance.

'"The man who drew his sword first is a brother of one of the Teules who was killed by Qualpopoca, and so is in a mad and murderous rage. The one with the golden hair also lost a kinsman. Malinche tries to restrain them both, but I fear for your life and his if you do not come with us to the palace of Axayacatl, for these men are not convinced you had no part in the deaths of their kinsmen, and their honor demands satisfaction even if it would mean their own."

'And this Montezuma did believe.'

And so it was that the great Montezuma, trapped in a room in his own palace by six desperate armed men and with a score and more lurking in the halls outside, was in the end made captive not by Spanish valor and Toledo steel, but by the cunning prevarication of a woman placed in our Feathered Serpent's mouth.

24

I T WAS A STRANGE CAPTIVITY as we tensely awaited the arrival of Qualpopoca. Montezuma, the 'prisoner', installed himself, for the choice was his, in the largest suite of apartments in his 'prison'. Within hours of the Emperor's arrival they had been swept clean, their walls had been freshly whitewashed and draped with luxurious tapestries of embroidered cotton and featherwork, fresh petatl mats laid down, new furniture set out, the whole fumigated with copal incense, and an abundance of flowers brought in.

Nor was Montezuma unaccompanied by an appropriate imperial retinue: body servants, cooks, waiting maids, pages, messengers, and an impressive number of wives and concubines. One large room in his apartments was set up as his throne room or audience chamber, from which he was allowed to conduct the normal affairs of the empire, for Cortes wisely realized that holding him incommunicado would almost certainly provoke either a rescue attempt or a struggle for power among the nobles of Tenochtitlan or both.

So Montezuma was allowed to 'govern' his empire much as before by permission of Cortes, who stationed a guard of some dozen men a shift just outside the Emperor's quarters. This Cortes placed under the command of Velazquez de Leon, as a grim warning to Montezuma and a chastisement of de Leon, who was ordered to 'guard the Emperor's life as it were your own, for if he dies or escapes it will be'. Cortes also kept the garrison inside the palace of Axayacatl in a state of alert, ordering that all his men go armed and armored at all times, and posted heavy guard patrols outside.

But it might just as well be said that Montezuma 'allowed' himself to be held prisoner, for the prison was the palace of his own late father, and though it would almost certainly mean his death, his jailers could be easily enough overwhelmed by the forces at his command in the city surrounding the jail.

Who was the prisoner of whom? Which was the true pretense? That Montezuma was an honored royal guest who had merely chosen to rule from a different venue for a time, or that he was a hostage through whom Cortes ruled?

It seemed to me that it hinged on what was meant by 'rule' and by 'govern', and the fine distinction between them. Cortes held Montezuma's life in his hands, and so ruled him, and through him the Empire of the Mexica. But Montezuma still governed, for neither Cortes nor any other Spaniard had the knowledge of the economic, political and legal details needed to make the specific decisions required to supervise the empire. And only orders Cortes issued through Montezuma would be obeyed; if he attempted to govern in his own name or that of his sovereign, there would surely be rebellion.

Thus Montezuma still governed but did not rule, but Cortes ruled only as long as he allowed Montezuma to govern. It was not a stable condition, and I warrant that no one, down to the dimmest Spanish soldier or the lowest kitchen scullion of Montezuma's entourage, did not feel the strain of the unresolved tension.

Certainly Cortes himself was acutely aware that Montezuma might not be the only one caught in this clever trap. 'The truth of it is, I do not understand the man, Alvaro,' he confided to me. 'I would certainly not have surrendered so easily in his place.'

'What then *would* you have done, Hernando?'

'Drawn my sword and died fighting?' Cortes suggested with a consternated frown, as if trying it out and finding it wanting. 'Shouted for my guards with the same result?' He shrugged. 'The truth of it is that I do not know! But I have never been either a barbarian or an Emperor, and Montezuma is both. I have captured him, but what am I to do with him? He is my prisoner, but I have the uncanny feeling that even now he is wondering what *he* is to do with *me*! Even now, he has requested that I supply him with a Nahuatl-speaking interlocutor to inform him of our ways and history, and I suspect his true desire is to see into my alien mind as I would see into—'

Cortes stopped himself in midstream to suddenly regard me. I nodded my agreement. It was obvious. And it would obviously satisfy my fondest intellectual passion as well.

'Who else is there?' Cortes said. 'You are the only Spaniard who really speaks his tongue. And even if you weren't, I warrant you are the only one among us who could match wits with him in such a manner.'

'Excluding you, of course, Hernando, were you conversant with Nahuatl.'

Cortes merely narrowed his eyes and grunted.

And so began the seances with the Emperor Montezuma which many months later would lead me to this mountain refuge with the records I made thereof, and the paintings and codexes I saved from the fires, and my memories of the man and what understanding of his spirit I might have obtained from these sources, and now to the writing of this very account, and thence, perhaps, if one day you shall exist, to your perusal of it, dear reader.

Our first such meeting was held in Montezuma's audience chamber. In Europe, such a session might have been held over a luncheon table, but it was the imperial custom here for the monarch to dine alone behind a screen, so that no lower personage would observe him masticating. So we sat on stools facing each other, with supernumerary functionaries standing against the distant walls, and servants keeping us steadily supplied with chocolatl, a stiff and awkward situation for such conversation, at least by my lights.

I introduced myself by name, he graciously complimented me on my command of his language, however awkward it in truth was, and after these niceties Montezuma asked me to describe the land from which we came.

I began with a description of the geography of Europe, which inevitably passed to that of Asia and Africa, and thence to the global nature of the world entire, and as I delivered this exposition, Montezuma sat there silently, regarding me with a keener and keener interest, and at length with his dark eyes asparkle with something that seemed very much like pleasure.

'It is round, like a ball?' he finally said when I had more or less concluded. 'Your gods have told you this?'

'Men have discovered this for themselves,' I told him. 'You may discover it yourself by standing on the shore of Lake Texcoco and watching a canoe disappear as it moves towards the line of the horizon. First the body of the canoe disappears from view, then the men in it, finally their heads, and then it is seen no more . . .'

'Yes, yes, I have seen this!' Montezuma said excitedly.

'This is caused by the curve of the ball that is the Earth,' I told him.

Montezuma squinted at me, obviously having difficulty with the concept. He ordered a retainer to fetch a tomatl. He held the round red fruit close by his nose with a finger extended across the top, then slowly withdrew it behind the curve. It might have been deemed a comical sight, but there was nothing comical about the enlightenment that glowed in the man's eyes when he had completed his little experiment.

'You are a man of knowledge, Alvaro de Sevilla!' he exclaimed in delight.

'And you, I warrant, are another,' I told him sincerely, and with no little pleasure myself, for in that moment, I knew that I had encountered a kindred spirit.

And so it began.

In that first session, I played the teacher, and the great Montezuma the avid pupil, hungrily eager to learn everything I might teach him all at once. He was an adept pupil, and there is such a thing, dear reader: one who asks the right question at the proper time and does not drag the teacher off on irrelevant tangents.

From geography, we passed to the political organization of Spain, the simplified exposition of which I needed to convey carefully, confining myself to a description of the feudal system of hierarchies, not unlike that which obtained in Montezuma's own empire and so readily enough understood by him, omitting the sanguinary recent history of its Reconquest by the Catholics from the Muslims, and of the Inquisition.

By this time, two or three hours must have passed, though in a manner that had neither of us counting the time, which was measurable only by the fidgeting of the imperial functionaries standing silently against the distant walls, and the session ended.

The next day's session was conducted in the same venue and much the same manner, and concerned the creation of Creation, as it were. I gave Montezuma the version in Genesis, agreed upon by Christians, Jews and Moslems alike, and for the first time Montezuma favored me with a brief reversal of roles, in which he delivered a quite fascinating discourse on the Mexica version thereof, which involved the doings of many more gods than the One, and the concept that they had destroyed and rebuilt the world several times over.

But what opened new vistas in my mind was the grandeur of the Mexica concept of *time*, far vaster than our own. The notion that the world and all that dwelt upon its lands and within its seas and in the heavens above us had been created in six days and was no more than a few thousand years old seemed quite petty to the Emperor. For the Mexica had an exceedingly complex calendar, or rather two of them, and they interacted in a manner which produced long cycles, and cycles of cycles, so that the Mexica vision of time encompassed tens or hundreds of thousands of years, perhaps even millions.

With my mind reeling from the opening up of such a temporal vista, Montezuma then constrained me to provide him with a more coherent exposition of the Christian religion than he had heretofore received, referring to matters which were a good deal further from my intellectual heart and upon which I must carefully refrain from speaking my true feelings.

And so I confined myself to the official version as recorded by Matthew, Mark, Luke and John, left off with the Resurrection, and went from there directly to the Second Coming and the Final Judgement, passing over the millennial history of the Catholic Church, and finishing with as good an exposition of the sacraments as an unbeliever in them might muster.

All this being a sufficient mental banquet for any two intellectual gourmands to ruminate upon, the seance then concluded.

But not before Montezuma beckoned me closer and leaned forward to speak for my ears alone. 'I believe it might be useful to meet where there are no other ears but ours to hear, Alvaro de Sevilla,' he told me. 'For here I must speak as Emperor of the Mexica, and you must speak as the servant of Malinche, and I would converse with you as one man of knowledge with another, for in such a manner, we both might more easily find more of it to gain.'

And so it was arranged that our next session would take place alone in one of his private rooms, but before that could happen, Cortes impatiently demanded to know what I had thus far learned.

'I have thus far confined myself to gaining his confidence,' I told Hernando, 'for after all the man *is* an Emperor, and he *is* a captive, and one must therefore proceed somewhat gingerly.'

'Have you not yet learned why he so readily *agreed* to this captivity?'

'I do have a theory,' I told him. 'Perhaps it is a matter of learning as much of us and our ways as he can.'

'As simple as that?' said Cortes. 'The man submits to captivity in order to learn more about his jailers?'

'As you have pointed out, he may not exactly be our captive and we may not exactly be his jailers, and curiosity is no simple thing, Hernando. Some men seek knowledge for pragmatic purposes alone, some for the pleasure of its own sake, some few for both, and I suspect that Montezuma is one of these.'

'And for this an Emperor puts his life in peril?' scoffed Cortes. 'You are telling me you believe he is mad?'

'But his life was already in peril when Velazquez de Leon drew his sword, and so he succumbed to prolong it, and there is nothing mad in that.'

'Nothing honorable either,' muttered Cortes. 'A craven way for a sovereign to act!'

To this I could make no reply, for what I would have said was that by my lights, risking one's life and one's honor and even one's sovereignty in the passionate pursuit of knowledge was anything but cowardice. Or if it was, I must count myself among the most craven of cowards, for it was nothing else that had brought me to this very moment in this very place.

But Hernando Cortes was first of all a warrior with a warrior's heart, and this was a hierarchy of priorities I doubted he could comprehend, and so I held my tongue.

'Pray extract something more useful than that, Alvaro,' said Cortes. 'For this Qualpopoca and his treacherous cohorts will surely arrive any day now, and when they do, I must decide how to act.'

'No doubt as would a brave and honorable sovereign,' I could not quite refrain from replying in a dangerously sardonic tone.

But, perhaps fortunately, the irony was lost on Hernando Cortes. 'In order to finally establish just who is to be truly sovereign here!' he replied humorlessly and with grim determination. 'I have captured the body of Montezuma. What I need to know is how to conquer his spirit.'

Our next meeting being conducted alone in a modest room of the Emperor's apartment, and time and Cortes beginning to press upon me, I decided to ask Montezuma the very question whose answer Cortes had sent me to him to obtain. Montezuma responded, but what he told me was neither quite what I had expected nor what I was as yet equipped to understand.

'Had I called out for my guards, I would almost certainly have been slain before they could rescue me.'

'It was simply a matter of saving your own life?' Was Cortes then right? Had Montezuma acted out of cowardice and nothing more?

But as if reading my thoughts, Montezuma shook his head. 'My life is as much in the hands of Malinche now as it was then, is it not?' he said, fixing me with a knowing regard that revealed another complexity of what I was coming to understand was an exceedingly complex man.

'What then?' I asked in no little perplexity.

'Had I cried out and been slain, Malinche and his captains would surely have been slain after me, and then all within the palace of my father would surely have been slain by my successor, and then the Teules in Tlascala and Totonaca,' Montezuma told me in quite a matter-of-fact manner. 'And I would never have known whether I had done the right thing.'

'Whether destroying the Spaniards was worth the sacrifice of your own life?'

Montezuma gave me a disparaging look, as if I had said a foolish or contemptible thing.

'Whether ridding your empire of the invaders would have been worth the terrible loss of life?'

Montezuma regarded me in precisely the same manner.

'What then?' I demanded in utter befuddlement.

'Whether I had obeyed the will of the gods and destroyed Teules who had sought to overthrow them and so would have brought famine and disaster to the lands they had entrusted to my rule, and thereby acted correctly, or whether in my impatience I had wrongly acted to preserve this fifth world ruled by the Mexica under Huitzilopochtli and thereby prevented the destined creation of the sixth world brought in by the return of the Toltecs led by Quetzalcoatl.'

Having had prior knowledge of this Mexica theology, the information contained in his words carried no surprise, but as an answer to my original question, it was hardly enlightening.

'I am afraid I still do not understand why this caused you not to resist this . . . this . . .'

'Captivity?' Montezuma said plainly, sensing my distressed reluctance to speak it plain. 'Yes, of course I am a captive here in the palace of my own father, just as my captors are captive in my capital, and we are all captives of the will of the gods. And that is your answer, Alvaro de Sevilla. I allowed myself to be taken captive so that I would not be slain. I could not allow myself to be slain because my death at the hand of Malinche would have been a sign for my people to rise against him. But it would have been a sign to destroy the Teules given only by an Emperor, not an omen granted by any god. Surely the destinies of worlds should not be decided without one.'

I must remind you, dear reader, that while I have in the writing of this narrative given you the benefit of what deeper understanding of Montezuma I may have gained from subsequent conversations, at the time of this one, they had not yet happened, and this was the moment when I began to understand just how much the Emperor was in thrall to the wills of his gods as he perceived them. Or, failing to be granted an omen enabling him to perceive their will, how given he was to procrastination when forced to rely on his own.

'You decided to live to await an omen from your gods?' I said, scarcely crediting my understanding of what I had just heard.

'Of course,' said Montezuma. 'Such was my duty to Huitzilopochtli, my people, and Quetzalcoatl, if he had truly returned. To do otherwise would have been a cowardly and selfish act, would it not?'

I then made the mistake of reporting the gist of this conversation to Cortes. I call it a mistake because I can only deem what it led to a physical and moral horror, and therefore a sin which to this day lies heavy on my spirit. But Cortes deemed it exactly what he had been seeking.

'Montezuma is *that much* a slave to his omens from his non-existent gods?' he exclaimed in both glee and a certain disbelief.

'So it would seem.'

'It is difficult to believe that even a barbarian prince could be in the habit of ruling an empire in such a manner!'

'Unless, of course, his gods were in the habit of granting him his omens as required,' I replied, not quite certain whether I was being sardonic or not.

Cortes eyed me as if he wasn't either. 'If it's an omen he requires, an omen he shall have,' he said, but with a wolfish set to his jaw and hardly in a tone of voice bespeaking generosity. 'You have done well, Alvaro. With this knowledge, I shall break him like a wild stallion and tame him to be my steed.'

I shuddered at the sound of this without quite knowing why, but I forbore inquiry, knowing all too well that I would soon find out, and I soon did, for the very next day Qualpopoca and his entourage arrived in Tenochtitlan.

For a miscreant summoned to justice, Qualpopoca arrived in the court set up in Montezuma's audience chamber in quite an arrogant manner. He was a burly man in middle years with thick black hair, an eagle's beak of a nose, hard brown eyes, and thick lips set in a fierce grimace. Borne on a litter carried by six of his chieftains, he was accompanied by nine more of his accused accomplices as well as his young son. He wore a plain white cotton loincloth and cloak, but also gold earrings and labret and a headdress of quetzal feathers, and he carried a maquahuitl in the manner of a scepter.

Cortes had arranged things so that Montezuma met him seated upon a stool that served as a sort of throne, dressed in his full finery and flanked by high-ranking functionaries. Qualpopoca's entourage donned the required robe of coarse maguey cloth upon entering the imperial presence and made the mandatory gesture of obeisance. Qualpopoca himself did likewise, but there was nothing repentant in his manner.

Cortes, accompanied by Marina, myself, Alvarado, Sandoval, Velazquez de Leon, Ordaz and a few guards, stood well back towards the rear of the chamber to begin with, to allow Montezuma the useful illusion of presiding over the trial.

But this did not extend much beyond the ceremonial opening, in which Qualpopoca formally greeted his sovereign, and Montezuma coldly acknowledged the presence of his vassal, and then turned the proceedings over to Cortes – as a decidedly unjust combination of aggrieved party, prosecutor, and, as it turned out, adjudicating magistrate.

'You are a subject of Montezuma, Emperor of the Mexica?'

'And who else might anyone here serve?' Qualpopoca replied in a surly manner.

'You were his representative in Nauhtla?'

'And still am.'

'You attempted to take tribute from several towns in the vicinity of Cempoala?'

'As was my accustomed duty.'

'You were told that Tlacochcalcat, cacique of Cempoala, had sworn fealty to the King of Spain through myself?'

'What of it?'

'You were informed that I had forbidden the taking or forwarding of such tribute?'

'I was informed by a subject of Montezuma that he had committed treason,' Qualpopoca replied, casting a scornful glance at the Emperor, 'and demanded what was rightfully his in his name.'

'And when Tlacochcalcat refused your demand, and sought aid from the Spanish garrison at Vera Cruz, what happened then?'

'The Teules raised threats against me if I refused to desist, I replied that I was not in the habit of being threatened by barbarians, and that if they persisted in interfering with the performance of my duties as required by my rightful sovereign, I would be forced to . . . chastise them.'

'Chastise them?'

'War upon them, capture a respectable number of them, and offer up their hearts to Huitzilopochtli.'

'Which you did?'

'Before I could, the Teules came to Nauhtla and attacked me there.'

'And you killed seven of them, a number of Totonacs, and a horse?'

Qualpopoca addressed his answer to Montezuma in an apologetic manner. 'They had powerful weapons, they fought in a strange and cowardly manner, and so I was prevented from taking prisoners for the altar of Huitzilopochtli, and for this I beg pardon.'

'But for nothing else?' demanded Cortes.

Qualpopoca glared at him silently.

'Not for killing Juan de Escalante?'

'Who?'

'The commander of the Spanish garrison.'

Qualpopoca shrugged with a great display of diffidence. 'I take no notice of the names of barbarians.'

'You then admit to all these things?'

'I admit to doing my duty,' said Qualpopoca, deliberately looking away from Cortes and straight into the eyes of Montezuma.

Cortes then seemed to puff himself up like a fighting cock.

'You have admitted to treason to His Majesty King Charles of Spain and Emperor of the Holy Roman Empire, to whom Montezuma, Emperor of the Empire of the Mexica has sworn fealty, and also to the murder of seven of his Spanish subjects, a horse, and an uncounted number of Totonacs, likewise sworn vassals of the Spanish Crown,' he declaimed in a most arrogant and pontifical manner. 'You and your accomplices are therefore condemned to death at the stake for these most heinous crimes.'

At this, Qualpopoca finally displayed full outraged umbrage, shouting not at Cortes but at Montezuma, who sat there absorbing it as if his face were carved from stone. 'We are condemned to death for doing our duty as Mexica warriors as ordered by our Emperor. I will not plead for our lives from this Teule, but from my Emperor I plead for a flowery death upon the altar of Huitzilopochtli rather than a dishonorable death at the hands of this barbarous invader.'

There was a long, long moment of still silence, as Qualpopoca glared at Montezuma, and Montezuma looked beseechingly at Cortes, and Cortes regarded the Emperor with the cold reptilian eyes of the Feathered Serpent, which, in the eyes of Montezuma, and indeed in my own, in that dreadfully decisive and decisively dreadful moment, he had at last truly become.

Cortes shook his head almost imperceptibly.

Montezuma allowed his head to droop slightly as he lowered his gaze.

Qualpopoca turned his back in a gesture of his utter contempt.

Some of the smaller buildings in the Temple Square served as armories, and Cortes had these ransacked for kindling in the form of bows, arrows, javelins, maquahuitls and the like, which he had piled up before the main entrance of the palace of Axayacatl just outside the Sacred Precinct, but in full challenging sight of the great temple of Tlaloc and Huitzilopochtli.

Cortes turned out a hundred of his men in full armor, including all his arquebusiers and crossbowmen, and rolled out four of his cannon as well, but that was not the only reason there was no challenge from the crowd that began to gather to witness the proceedings.

Cortes had announced that Qualpopoca and his entourage were to be executed 'by order of Montezuma' for 'treason' and the 'murder' of the Spaniards. But since the Spaniards were the aggrieved party, the execution was to be carried out in their accustomed style, and it was a crowd of spectators who gathered rather than any angry mob, curious to see how such a rite was conducted.

Seasoned lumber was piled up into a huge but well-built pyre atop the kindling of armaments and seventeen green logs well planted atop it, for while such mass public burnings were not common Inquisition practice, let it not be said that Spaniards did not know how to prepare a proper auto-da-fe.

Let it also not be said that Alvaro de Sevilla, or Avram ibn Ezra if you prefer, and I myself then did, was not already racked with guilt for his part in the production of this hideous spectacle, for while it might be Hernando Cortes who had fashioned this 'omen' with which to 'break Montezuma like a wild stallion' and 'conquer his spirit', it was I who had supplied him with the knowledge he needed in order to craft it.

The Emperor was brought out onto the rooftop upon his imperial litter and set down just behind the parapet overlooking the great pyre, shaded by his brilliant green quetzal-feather parasol, flanked by retainers bearing his standards, bedecked with gold and jewels and his imperial headdress, perfumed by incense; for all the world the absolute monarch of all he surveyed sitting in state to preside over the carrying out of his own iron will.

As penitence, I chose to bear witness among my fellow perpetrators rather than from on high, and so I did not see what the Mexica crowd could also not see from their groundling vantage, and it was Montezuma who had to tell me soon thereafter, as a broken man fighting to hold back the tears in his eyes.

'Malinche and his woman, along with one of his warriors bearing what I took to be bracelets of the silver-colored metal they call steel linked together with a chain of the same metal, appeared in my private chamber as my attendants were finishing dressing me, and Malinche told me to dismiss them since he wished to add the final ornament to my finery himself.

'Thinking only that this gift of jewelry was a strange one, but curious about the new metal from which it was made, I granted his wish. But as soon as the four of us were alone, Malinche turned on me in a fury, and accused me of having given the orders that resulted in the death of his men and his animal. I was too outraged to even begin to protest before he declared that were I not the Emperor my punishment would be death. But since I was, and since he had come to love me as a brother, and since mercy was a great Christian virtue, I would get off with a mere token chastisement. And . . . and then . . .'

And then in the telling Montezuma did shed tears, did lose his manly dignity, as he had lost his imperial dignity in the moment being recalled, nor shall I further violate it by detailing his words or the manner in which he uttered them.

Suffice it that Cortes had his ankles fettered.

Suffice it to say that the great Montezuma upon his golden litter of state and beneath his umbrella of royal quetzal plumes was constrained to preside over the hideous rite which conquered his spirit already broken to harness and shackled by hidden chains.

Qualpopoca, his son and his fifteen lieutenants were brought out with their hands tied behind them and stripped of all but their loincloths and their dignity, for they walked upright with their eyes fixed straight ahead and their visages frozen in fierce and contemptuous warriors' grimaces, the only protest they deigned to make as they were led to the pyre and tied to the stakes.

A soldier lit a torch and handed it to Cortes. Cortes took a few steps forward towards the pyre, then halted, half-turned, looked up at Montezuma, and raised the torch in salute, or as if seeking formal permission, for when Montezuma remained still as an idol of his Huitzilopochtli, Cortes nodded as if he had received it, marched briskly up to the pyre, and set it ablaze.

Strange to say, I had never before witnessed an auto-da-fe. Or perhaps not so strange, for this had been a matter of deliberate avoidance, both of the horrible death itself, and the sight of braver folk whose faith mattered more to them than their lives suffering it in my stead.

The pyre, though larger than that for any auto-da-fe I had heard of erected by the Inquisition in Spain, was well built, and the kindling caught quickly. Within a minute or two, flames were licking at the feet of Qualpopoca and his men. They did not scream. Their faces were masks against what must already have been considerable pain, yet they would not even deign to struggle futilely against their bonds.

The onlooking Mexica crowded somewhat closer. I saw neither anger nor pity in their eyes. Only a sort of avid curiosity, perhaps at the spectacle of such a novel new form of sacrifice, or perhaps a curiosity to learn whether their fellow Mexica would meet it in as honorable a manner as that with which so many met their flowery deaths upon the altar of Huitzilopochtli, who himself might be looking down from his great temple on the growing conflagration and wondering the same thing.

The seasoned lumber caught and serpents of fire like living vines climbed the victims' legs towards their chests. Still they would not scream, though now they could be seen writhing in their agonies. The flames rose higher, engulfing them like a great ocean wave, the heat of it driving back the crowd.

Flesh began to blacken. The sweet and savory odor of roasting meat tantalized the senses obscenely and so tormented the mind. Hair caught fire, there was a faint sickening stench behind the cookfire aroma, and heads were haloed by brilliant orange feathers of flame.

And then, at last, the fire reached its full maturity, and even the green stakes crackled and fumed, and a curtain of flame was drawn across the final agonies.

Black smoke billowed up from the auto-da-fe of the Spanish Christians and their Prince of Peace. Lesser plumes of black smoke from the eternal flames at the apex of the temple where I had seen the pagan Mexica conduct no lesser sacrifice to their god of war likewise defiled the heavens.

Orange highlights flickered on the polished metal armor of the Spaniards and gleamed in their eyes. The Mexica crowd stood silently watching their countrymen bake to a well-crisped turn, and I had the terrible notion and the more terrible vision that many of their number were hoping for their own morsel of the expected post-sacrificial cannibal feast.

Never had I felt more a Jew in the tormented secrecy of my cowardly hidden heart.

Never had I been further from any place I could ever call home.

Never had I been more alone.

Did I feel the weight of his gaze upon me or was the wish father to the fancy?

I turned my face to look up at the figure upon his gilded throne beneath the feathered canopy of royal quetzal green.

Did our eyes meet?

It mattered not.

For there, in all this vast crowd of strangers who had been his people and mine, was the only kindred soul.

25

A ND SO WAS THE GREAT Montezuma reduced to the puppet of Hernando Cortes, and so did the Empire of the Mexica become a vassal state of the Spanish Crown baptized 'New Spain'.

Or so at least it seemed.

Within the audience chamber of Montezuma in the palace of Axayacatl, envoys from provincial governors came and went, disputes were adjudicated, tribute accounted for, nobles and caciques received, and all orders necessary for conducting the business of the state given by the Emperor. But Cortes controlled access to Montezuma, and while he allowed Montezuma free rein in matters that did not concern his own interests, when he wished to issue a command on matters that did, he made his will known to the Emperor, and Montezuma obediently issued it as his own.

Cortes now made the use of the swift and extensive Mexica system of couriers his own, and so communication between himself and his minions in Cempoala, Tlascala and Vera Cruz became rapid and regular, and since the messages that the runners carried were written in a language that only the Spanish could understand, security was assured. So too did he gain the use of as many tamanes as might be required to carry tribute or supplies.

Thus did Cortes dispatch Alonso de Grado to replace the slain Escalante, thus did he receive reports that de Grado's administration was slothful and incompetent, thus did he replace him with the trusted and equally scrupulously honest Sandoval. Thus too, when Cortes decided that two brigantines must be built to give him naval command of the lakes and free his forces in Tenochtitlan from their total reliance on the four causeways for any necessary exit or reinforcement, was he easily able to have the nails, sails, yards and fittings salvaged from the beaching of the fleet shipped across the mountains, and to secure the timbers from Montezuma's own royal forests.

The changes in Montezuma were invisible to the casual eye but extreme to closer and deeper observation. I have drawn a merciful veil over his own words describing his fettering, but I find that I cannot avoid his description of his release:

'No sooner had the Christian rite ended and I was returned to my apartments, than Malinche arrived, knelt down before me like any subject, and freed me from the shackles with his own hand! And . . . and he offered an abject apology for his act, declaring that he had only inflicted this minor punishment so as to satisfy the ire of his own men and thus prevent something much worse.'

'And you believed him?' I could not refrain from exclaiming in sour amazement.

Montezuma's reply was passingly strange, but stranger still was the tranquil manner in which he delivered it, like a Christian whose active life was over resolved to become a monk, like a Sufi mystic withdrawing from all but the contemplation of the will of Allah.

'It no longer matters what I believe, for the fifth world in which I ruled in the service of Huitzilopochtli ended and the sixth world was born when Malinche made his rite of sacrifice before both of us, the man watching powerlessly in chains, and the god remaining silent while the offering to the god of the new sixth world was made before his very temple.'

My gorge rose to hear this, for I knew full well how deeply I was responsible for what had happened, the extent to which I had feathered the serpent who had done it, and how much of what he had done had been planted by me in his cunning and ruthless mind. And being confronted with its effect not upon a nation or an empire but the soul of this singular man made the evil of it all the more poignant.

'You then believe that Malinche is Quetzalcoatl?' I said, preparing to reveal my own and Marina's part in the creation of this conquering fiction. But Montezuma's reply disarmed me.

'That too no longer matters,' he said. 'It may be that Malinche is Quetzalcoatl. It may be that the Teules are the descendants of the Toltecs. Or it may be that his Jesus Christ is Quetzalcoatl. Or it may be that the sixth world will be dominated by a god neither Malinche, myself, Jesus Christ nor Quetzalcoatl has ever known. Or that all of them are but masks worn for a time by a greater and hidden god whose name we can never know. How can we of the world that has ended know such things? What I do know, Alvaro de Sevilla, is that it was prophesied that bearded men with white skins would come from the east to destroy the fifth world and bring the sixth, and that has happened. It happened when Huitzilopochtli allowed it to happen.'

'You are content with this? You just accept it?' I demanded.

And the poor man shrugged and sighed wistfully. 'Does it matter whether I am content?' he said. 'How can I do other than accept it?' And he studied me with a shrewd but hopeless regard. 'You are a clever man. And I think you might also be wise. Can you tell me how I might reject what both your gods and mine have already decided, Alvaro de Sevilla?'

Not my God, I almost declared, but I held my bitter silence.

But if I nursed bitterness in my heart, Montezuma displayed none at all. He behaved as might a European monarch who had inherited his crown without inheriting any particular desire or ability to rule, and so was content to enjoy the prerogatives of kingship without the responsibilities. Perhaps, having been unwillingly shorn of the power of rule and therefore the responsibility, Montezuma had gained the freedom to simply enjoy being an exceedingly wealthy and exceedingly pampered man.

He continued to dine lavishly in his solitary manner. His consumption of chocolatl became almost continuous. He continued to enjoy the presence of his wives and concubines. He seemed to take genuine interest in the military exercises performed by the Spanish troops in the palace courtyards and in particular the equestrian figures. He would banter in an awkward manner with some of the captains. He would bestow what to him were little gifts of gold quite freely. He would even gamble with Cortes and his lieutenants.

When the boats were finished, he sailed upon them, always with delight, but always under guard, to the hunting preserves he maintained on the lake shores. Likewise did Cortes, after some convincing, allow Montezuma to pay his respects to his gods atop the nearby temple, though again, only under Spanish guard, and without offering human hearts.

In return, Montezuma allowed himself to be hectored by Father Olmedo on the subject of Christian doctrine and the Satanic falsehood of all other faiths, and not without the avid encouragement of Cortes, who knew full well that the conversion of a vassal monarch to the conqueror's religion would swiftly lead to the conversion of his subjects, and thus, hopefully, would seal for ever the conquest of their territories by the conquest of their collective soul.

But though Montezuma submitted to these sermons, he was swayed by none of it, habitually replying that while Jesus Christ might have triumphed over Huitzilopochtli and the next world might be his, the gods of the Mexica were still needed to bring the rain, and cause the sun to rise and set, and the crops to ripen in the fields. Besides which, even should he declare himself a Christian, his people would never accept the faith, and the result would surely be a rebellion, which, whether victorious or not, would result in more carnage and catastrophe than would be deemed desirable by the worthy priests of this God of Mercy and Prince of Peace.

Perhaps this was when Montezuma and I became, if not exactly friends, then intellectual companions, strange creatures to each other, but closer in our passions for the life of the mind than any other either of us could find in that place and time. And I warrant that just as the distance I found myself putting my heart from whatever true friendship I had previously had with Hernando Cortes drove me towards his company, so did his loss of what had been the most meaningful active life in the land drive his attention inward, and therefore towards mine.

It was at this time that he began to reveal to me his version of the events leading up to this captive afterlife and encouraged me to record them. For he had accepted that his former life as a mover and shaper of great events was over, and like most such men when they know they have finished their turn on the world's stage, he wished to leave some sort of explanatory and exculpatory memoir behind.

Then too, even as an absolute monarch, this omen-obsessed Emperor had been of a mystical bent, and shorn of his worldly power he became all the more so, not least because he was convinced that he had been a pawn of gods – his, Cortes', the Toltecs', perhaps a god unknown – in the greatest of all possible events, the death of one world and the birth of the next.

And the more I conversed with Montezuma on these matters, the more I became convinced that in some manner he must be right. For in the span of a lifetime, half of the globe had been discovered, Muslim rule on the European continent ended, the Jews become a fugitive race, the fractious kingdoms of the Iberian peninsula united in a kingdom called Spain, and now the rule of the Mexica over an empire greater than that kingdom had passed over to it. In both the Old World across the sea and here in this world new only to Europeans, worlds had indeed ended and begun.

Nor could it be denied that the dominion of whatever gods there be over these worlds had shifted. The God of Abraham had scarcely a refuge over which to raise His head; Allah was in retreat across the Mediterranean; Huitzilopochtli, Quetzalcoatl and the rest of the Mexica pantheon were on their way to join that of the ancient Greeks, and the God of the Cross was on His way to gain an entire new world.

The notion of Nezahualcoyotl and the Kabbalists that there not merely existed a greater god over these petty warring pantheons, but that the deities of all of them were but masks donned for a time by that Hidden God, that Ain-Soph, whose singular countenance would never be revealed because none such existed, was something I began to consider more and more comforting.

And thus did Montezuma and I drift inward and towards each other, towards greater and greater mutual confidence, I at length unburdening the secrecy of my true name and what beliefs I might still truly hold, he determining to tell his story as best as might be possible via my second-hand account herein to a posterity even more unimaginable to him then than it is to me now.

*

Beyond the walls of the palace of Axayacatl, things seemed to proceed with an eerie normality, for a people habituated to obeying the will of an absolute monarch for generations would seem to be at a loss to do otherwise, even if they knew that he was transmitting the orders of a conqueror. Nobles and men of war aside, most of the people of Tenochtitlan, like those of any city, naturally cared little about such changes in power in high places as long as those in the said high places left their own pursuits and interests undisturbed.

But the men of power, and the extensive priesthood, who *were* concerned with affairs of state, were another matter, and beneath the calm surface and across the tranquil waters of Lake Texcoco, a conspiracy was brewing.

This seemed to have been instigated by the King of Texcoco, the very Cacama who had counseled Montezuma to act cautiously and allow the Teules to enter Tenochtitlan as honored and captive guests, the very nephew of Montezuma who had been dispatched by his uncle to carry out the mission he himself had proposed.

Cacama, who now had the sagacity to admit his mistake, and the courage to seek to rectify it, was attempting to put together a coalition of lakeside princes to rescue his uncle if possible and oust the Teules from Mexico.

'The most worrisome thing about it,' Cortes told me in some agitation, when he summoned me to his quarters to counsel, 'is that he may have recruited Cuitlahuac, who is not only the lord of Iztapalapa, but is also the Emperor's *brother*, and whose legitimacy to succeed him might therefore be readily enough accepted if a coup were successful.'

Yes, I still counseled Cortes, and yes, I continued to serve as his scribe and literary collaborator, and yes, perhaps because I felt a ghost of my friendship for him, if no longer any comradeship. And I had learned that there was a fine distinction between them. Comradeship was an emotion of the will, the union of two persons in a common enterprise, but friendship required no such comradeship, being an emotion of the heart, which could be won by the worst of blackguards were he charming enough, not at all an unfitting description of Hernando Cortes.

Besides, I wished to live to continue to enrich my store of knowledge of this fascinating new world, and so I was equally concerned by the prospect of a bloody rebellion against us. But my desire was not to find a way to crush it, but to avoid its advent in the first place.

'How did you find this out, Hernando?' I first asked.

Cortes shrugged. 'In the usual manner,' he told me. 'Far too many mouths are involved for the tidings not to have reached ears paid to listen. The question is, what do I do about it? They do not seem to have yet marshaled any forces, and it is unclear as to whether it has gone beyond mere talk. It might be best to march on Texcoco now and crush Cacama before it can . . .'

I shuddered at this madly rash notion. 'You would attack the second greatest city in the Valley of Mexico with a few hundred Spaniards, leaving a puny garrison here? Marching in narrow file down a long causeway to get there?'

'We could use the brigantines to bring our troops across Lake Texcoco, we could use the Tlascalans,' Cortes muttered unconvincingly, in a manner that I began to realize meant he wanted me to talk him out of it, a task which I ardently and cravenly wished to accomplish.

'If you used Tlascalan troops against the second city of the Triple Alliance, most of Anahuac would rise against us in outrage, and Tenochtitlan certainly would, and all that you have thus far won would be lost, not to mention our own lives,' I told him hastily. 'Besides which, fortunately, you can't do it. The two boats could only transport a few hundred men fully laden, and you could never move the Tlascalans down any of the causeways.'

'There is that,' Cortes admitted with what seemed suspiciously like relief. 'What then?'

'I don't know,' I admitted myself. 'But let me speak with Montezuma before you do anything precipitous.'

'You would inform him of this plot to rescue him from my clutches?' Cortes exclaimed in astounded outrage.

'Why not? What harm can it do? You control all his communication with what lies outside the walls of this palace, and in the end, he still *is* in your clutches.'

★

And so I found myself once more a servant of the machinations of the serpent I had feathered, this time in the service of nothing grander than the saving of my own skin.

And in the process, perhaps that of Montezuma himself, who, however, seemed fatalistically disinterested in the whole affair when I informed him of it.

'What would Malinche have me do?' he asked with baffling mildness.

'He doesn't know.'

'What then would *you* advise me to do, Avram ibn Ezra?'

'I don't know either,' I replied in some agitation, 'and please do not develop the habit of calling me that!' I paused for thought, for I did not even know what *I* wanted him to do. 'Would Cacama obey your order to give up his plan?'

Montezuma seemed unsure. 'I do not know,' he said after pondering. 'But I think none but perhaps Cuitlahuac my brother would follow him on a futile attempt to rescue me without my own order to do so.'

'Futile? If he raised an army from all the cities of the lakesides and controlled the causeways to Tenochtitlan into the bargain?'

'He might capture Tenochtitlan and feed the hearts of Malinche and the Teules to Huitzilopochtli, but I would never live to see it, for Malinche would surely hold my life hostage against it, and feed it to his own god on the fire if he saw that his cause was lost.'

Would he? I was not sure he wouldn't and I certainly didn't want to find out.

'And Malinche would not allow me to order such an attack on Tenochtitlan in any event.'

That much, at least, was certain!

'Would you act to . . .' I hesitated, realizing that I had been about to appeal to his cowardice.

'Save our lives?' Montezuma said with a faint smile. 'No, I would not prevent Cacama from following the honorable path of the warrior to save my own life, and certainly not that of Malinche and his Teules, but . . .'

'But?'

The Emperor's eyes grew dreamy, they seemed to be regarding another world, while speaking into this one. 'Since the burning of

Qualpopoca and his followers, I had had no omen, nor sought one, for I believed Huitzilopochtli had left the dying world, or the Hidden God had donned his new mask. But three days ago, I sought one in the visions brought by the sacred mushroom teonanecatl, and the vision I dreamed was a terrible one.'

Now Montezuma's eyes became darkly alert, his visage hardened, yet his body trembled almost imperceptibly.

'I saw Tenochtitlan burning. I saw the sky above the Valley of Mexico choked with a gray and silvery mist that burned the eyes and rasped the throat. I saw the waters of the lakes turn to sand, and the causeways broken. I saw mountains of corpses, and no altar upon which their hearts had or could have been fed, for the temple of Huitzilopochtli and Tlaloc was cast down, and in its place in the Sacred Precinct was a monstrous squat building of ugly gray stone with many doorways and with two towers topped by the Cross of the Teules, and in them huge bells sounded a fearful din like the end of a world. I smelled noxious fumes. I saw, and I smelled, and I heard, and I felt in my bones, that nothing we had built would survive such a horrible death of the fifth world to succor the Mexica in the sixth. I saw a proud people humbled. The children and their children of those who had built Tenochtitlan and mastered the Valley of Mexico would survive only as slaves cursing the memory of my name.'

Montezuma glared at me, and in that moment he was both the broken man he had become, and the mighty Emperor he had been. '*That* . . . Alvaro de Sevilla,' he said, 'I would act to prevent.'

And so he eventually would, and with a treacherous betrayal to match any such act performed by the master thereof, Hernando Cortes. But first Cortes entered into a futile correspondence with Cacama via couriers; both of them, I warrant, knowing it would be futile.

Cortes accused Cacama of plotting against himself and the Emperor. Cacama sent back a message to the effect that as King of Texcoco he would not deign to answer the accusations of a foreigner abusing his position as his uncle's guest and would only treat with Montezuma himself. Cortes ignored this and sent back a message declaring that the King of Spain now being the sovereign of all of the Empire of the

Mexica and he being that sovereign's viceroy, Cacama must deal with him, or he would deal with Cacama in a less pacific manner.

Cacama declared that he 'recognized no such authority, knew nothing of the Spanish King, had no desire to see that ignorance relieved, and would engage in no further negotiation as King of Texcoco and therefore equal sovereign of the Triple Alliance other than with his equal ruler, Montezuma himself'.

At this point, Montezuma was induced to send his own message to his nephew more or less dictated by Cortes: a smarmy and hardly credible missive to the effect that he was simply a guest of the Spaniards who were his friends, and inviting Cacama to come to Tenochtitlan to resolve whatever differences with them he might have with the aid of the imperial mediation.

Cacama was not fool enough to believe that this was other than a transparent ruse to take him prisoner, and his reply was suitably scathing to such an insult to his intelligence:

'It is plain, my uncle, that such dishonorable and cowardly words could not be your own, but could only have been extracted from you under duress or torture by Malinche. I therefore assure you that when I next visit Tenochtitlan, it will not be to crawl before this Teule, but to rescue the city and the empire of the Triple Alliance, our gods, and your own person and honor, from him. Since you are unable to communicate freely with me, and I have no wish to communicate with Malinche, this correspondence is now over, and in the future I will let my maquahuitl speak for me.'

I was present in Montezuma's audience chamber, along with Marina, when this final communiqué was read out to Cortes. He turned on the Emperor in what appeared less than sincere fury.

'Your nephew has not only entirely ignored your authority as Emperor, has not only now openly threatened to take your capital by force, but has called you a liar into the bargain!' he roared. 'I demand to know what you are going to do about it!'

I do not know who was more stunned by Montezuma's quiet, calm, and quite unexpected answer; myself or Cortes.

'The Kings of Texcoco maintain a lakeside villa, and if you will allow me to communicate with my agents in the court of Texcoco, it will be easy enough to arrange for them to send word to Cacama that they wish to discuss joining his venture there, away from the many eyes and ears of the city. The main house is built on pilings over a dock, and so it will be easy enough for them to seize Cacama, put him in a waiting canoe, and row him across the lake to Tenochtitlan.'

Cortes' jaw dropped in amazement, even as his eyes gleamed with vulpine approval for a clever treachery he would have been proud to have conceived himself. I could see that he wanted to ask Montezuma why he was willing to do such a thing, but this was a question that would have been far too impolitic to ask, and so he held his tongue.

I, who knew of the vision of terminal destruction that must have motivated such dishonorable treachery, understood the desperate why of it, but was stunned by its ruthlessness, and reminded abruptly that my intellectual companion and fellow spiritual seeker had once had twenty thousand hearts ripped out merely to celebrate his own coronation, without the slightest moral qualm.

But I, who had played no small part in bringing Hernando Cortes to these shores to satisfy nothing more than my selfish passion for knowledge, and therefore in bringing Montezuma to this very desperate pass, felt in no position to deliver a moral lecture to a man acting unselfishly to preserve what he might of his own people's civilization at the cost of everything else.

And so I too held my tongue.

In short, it was done. Cacama was seized and brought as a prisoner to Tenochtitlan, to the palace of Axayacatl, to the audience chamber of his uncle, before the imperial throne. Cortes staged this before several dozen nobles and caciques, his assembled captains as well as Spanish guards in full armor, and Fathers Olmedo and Diaz. Marina was there to translate, I was there to record the proceeding in Spanish, as well as Mexica scribes to record it in paintings and pictographs, for Cortes wished to make it known far and wide so as to crush any more rebellious ambitions.

Montezuma was dressed in his full imperial finery and was seated somewhat ludicrously by my lights on his golden litter of state, even shaded by the great quetzal-feather umbrella, though the proceedings were being held indoors.

But Cacama was neither impressed nor cowed. When he was handed the required rough robe of maguey cloth with which to cover his own fine dress, he threw it to the floor. Nor would he touch his hand to the ground or avert his gaze from the imperial visage.

'As King of Texcoco, I declare the Triple Alliance ended until Tenochtitlan is cleansed of these Teules, proper respect for the gods shown once more, and a man of honor whose word can be trusted restored to the throne,' he fairly snarled. 'And as your nephew, uncle, I say you are no longer worthy to serve as Emperor of Mexico, having disgraced yourself with your cowardice and now your falsehoods and your treachery.'

Montezuma glared at him silently, struggling not to bow his head at this furious but truthful assault. Cacama then spoke in quite another tone.

'Or perhaps I misjudge you, uncle,' he crooned insinuatingly. 'Perhaps you have brought me to Tenochtitlan to prove to me that you still truly rule here. If so, you will now have these Teules seized, return to your own palace, and feed their hearts to Huitzilopochtli upon his altar. Do these things, and I shall repent of my harsh words, rally all of Texcoco to your side, and together our armies shall march against the Tlascalans, the Totonacs, and all who have betrayed us to the Teules, cleanse the land of them, and put things right.'

Once more, Montezuma could find nothing to say, but now his lower lip seemed to tremble under the weight of its golden labret, and his eyes blinked furiously. Cortes, who stood behind and to one side of Cacama, signed to one of his guards, who came forward with open shackles, then, grimacing, nodded at Montezuma to proceed with the climax of the spectacle he had planned.

'As Emperor of Mexico and ruler of the Triple Alliance, I declare that Cacama, King of Texcoco, by reason of his plot to rebel against me, is deposed, and is to be replaced by his brother, Cuicuitzca.'

The assembled nobles and caciques gasped, but did no more. And before the eloquent Cacama could even find the words to express his outrage, Cortes had him shackled and dragged off in chains.

Thus was Cacama's conspiracy thwarted and crushed, and thus was a puppet of Cortes' puppet installed as King of Texcoco, and thus was proud Texcoco reduced from an ally to a vassal state. For though Cuicuitzca was barely more than a boy, the Texcocans did not rise or even protest openly against his appointment by Montezuma.

But that was not enough for Hernando Cortes. He ordered Montezuma to order his minions to seize all who had joined in Cacama's conspiracy, who were then clapped into an improvised dungeon along with him. The conquest of Mexico would now seem to be effectively complete.

But *still* that was not enough for Hernando Cortes. The submission of the Emperor of Mexico to the King of Spain must be formalized in a recitation of the Requerimiento before a great conclave of his own vassals.

And, of course, as Cortes confided in me, when we were able to report to King Charles that this great new territory of New Spain had been thus formally, legally, and with proper pomp and ceremony, added to his dominions by none other than himself, certainly his appointment as Viceroy thereof would likewise be officially sealed.

Do you find, as I do, something curiously similar, in the obedience of Montezuma's subjects to his will even when they knew he was in thrall to Cortes, to Hernando Cortes' unquestioned submission to the King of Spain?

The nobles and caciques who witnessed the humiliation of Cacama and thereby the humiliation of Montezuma *could* have deemed him unfit to continue to rule, and fomented a rebellion against the Spaniards within Tenochtitlan that probably would have succeeded. And Cortes, even now as I write this and his conquest of Mexico is long since complete, has never to my knowledge entertained the slightest thought of declaring himself King thereof, when he could have easily done so without King Charles being in any practical position to stop him.

Why? you may well ask. Because the Emperor of Mexico and the King of Spain and Holy Roman Emperor held their thrones by divine right granted them by the will of the gods of their respective empires? Because even their wiliest and most ruthless and otherwise unprincipled subjects were thereby rendered incapable of even forming such thoughts in their minds?

If this is a mystery to you, dear reader, so it still remains to me, but such a blindness to the obvious has no doubt played a part in the history of many lands, not only New Spain, which otherwise might have been the Kingdom of Mexico under Hernando the First.

And the ceremony Cortes conducted in the assembly chamber of the palace of Axayacatl was utterly loyal to his sovereign and designed to formally seal *his* rule over the lands that Cortes had conquered and not his own. Even so it was the single greatest act of arrogance I had witnessed since we set foot on these shores.

This was the largest room in the palace of Axayacatl, but it was so filled with caciques and nobles from the far reaches of the Empire of the Mexica that there was little room for anyone else, so that the only Spaniards within were Cortes, his notary, Father Olmedo, Father Diaz, Pedro de Alvarado, the captain of 'Montezuma's guard' Velazquez de Leon, and myself, constrained to stand just inside the rear entrance.

Extravagant new featherwork tapestries hung on the walls depicting both the eagle standard of the Mexica and the lion of Spain, the latter curiously sporting blotchy spots. Likewise were the same standards, in solid gold and gilded brass, set up beside the two thrones at the far end of the chamber.

To the left sat Montezuma upon a stool of solid gold encrusted with green gemstones, wearing his accustomed headdress of quetzal feathers and a magnificent cloak of the same iridescent green plumage draped over his shoulders and flowing to the floor. He wore so many heavy gold and turquoise necklaces that his neck almost bowed under the weight, and the huge gold labret pulling down his lower lip was set with an emerald the size of a grape.

To his right sat Hernando Cortes, upon a grotesque simulation of a European royal throne constructed to his design by one of his carpenters; a huge high-backed wooden affair, all curves and curlicues and gilt paint, the back and seat cushions upholstered in red and yellow featherwork, so that the thing could hardly survive the day's affair intact. Cortes wore a gilded helmet and full armor polished to a mirror sheen, black velvet pantaloons and tunic, and a red velvet cloak fastened around his neck by a length of gold braid secured by a golden choker.

This being an audience with the Emperor, or so the assembled Mexica notables had been told, whatever finery they might have arrived in was now concealed beneath rough maguey-cloth robes, and, as

Cortes had ordered, it was Montezuma who spoke, a stilted speech written for him by Cortes with the aid of the notary and translated by Marina, for I had found the limit to how far I would go, and managed to beg off by the use of flattery, telling Cortes that this would become a legal document, and he had had some legal education whereas I had none.

'All here know that before us these lands were ruled by the great and noble Toltecs under the great and noble Quetzalcoatl, and so too do we all know that when they departed across the ocean in the direction of the sunrise, they left behind a promise to return in the form of bearded white men riding upon fierce animals who spoke a different tongue and so honored Quetzalcoatl under another name . . .'

There was considerable baffled muttering, for this was a deliberately confused amalgamation and transmogrification of at least two legends which they *did* know into a combined version they had never heard before. Could I have rewritten it into something more elegant? No doubt, but the perplexity among the Mexica and the stench in my own nostrils would have been much the same.

'The . . . glad tiding is that they have now returned to reclaim their rule and our loyalty, for Malinche, who sits beside me, and whose beard and white skin are there for all to see, is the representative sent by him who in our tongue was called Quetzalcoatl and in another Charles, and in the most sacred of languages Jesus Christ, to rule in his sacred name . . .'

I was too far away to see whether there were tears in Montezuma's eyes as he hesitated as if choking on the climactic foul morsel he was now constrained to regurgitate, but there were in mine to witness such a man reduced to this, and the catch in his voice as he began to utter the words told it all.

'And as you have all been and remain my loyal vassals, so do I now declare in your name . . . and my own . . . fealty to this . . . this King of Kings beyond the waters, and I . . . command you to pay him trib-ute . . . as your lord as . . . as . . . as he is now mine.'

No one spoke into the stunned silence that reigned when Montezuma had finished. Not a cry of protest, not a word of agreement. The Mexica who knew all too well the nature of Cortes' 'hospitality' to their

Emperor and the fate of the former King of Texcoco and his allies, and it must have been at least half of them, had only witnessed the ceremonial confirmation of what had long since become a fait accompli. The others were either credulous enough to swallow Montezuma's speech at face value or were so dazed as to be incapable of coherent thought on the matter, let alone speech.

Hernando Cortes then rose to conclude the ceremony by delivering the Requerimiento, first uttered beside a modest tree in the little provincial city of Potonchan, and now at last proclaimed in a palace before the now former monarch of an empire larger and richer than all Iberia and in a capital city grander than anything the Old World knew.

'In the name of Charles, King of Spain and Holy Roman Emperor, I, Hernando Cortes, his most loyal vassal and servant, do take possession of this city of Tenochtitlan, all lands ruled by it and from it by the Emperor Montezuma, who by this formality likewise becomes his loyal vassal, and any and all of its dependencies for the Crown of Castile. Long live New Spain!'

I have said that this ceremony was the greatest act of arrogance I had witnessed since we had set foot on these shores, but there was another ceremony to come that put it into the shade, for nothing so mortifies a race, as the Jew knows all too well, than the casting down and humiliation of its gods.

Sooner or later it was going to have to come to this, for while the True Faith of the Cross had been able to make great inroads as a religion of liberation among the tribes who chafed as vassals under the yoke of the Mexica and Tenochtitlan, despite all efforts, it had gained little interest among those who benefited by their own rule under their war god Huitzilopochtli.

And now that secular rule had passed to Spanish Christians, the time had come for the Cross to rise triumphant atop the great temple of Huitzilopochtli and Tlaloc which rose above the Sacred Precinct to dominate the Hell-bound souls of the inhabitants of Tenochtitlan.

'You can well imagine the reaction of Montezuma when I demanded that the Satanic idols atop the pyramid be replaced by the Virgin and the Cross!' Cortes told me. 'He knew better than to protest on spiritual or theological grounds, but he was clever enough to declare that this would surely be enough to provoke a spontaneous uprising among his people.'

'He didn't have to be very clever to tell you that,' I told him, certain that nothing good could come of such a profanation.

But Cortes laughed. 'I told him that if it was *not* done by his consent, the ire of *my* people would constrain me to accomplish it by force,' he told me. 'When he continued to protest, I offered him a compromise. Since there are two sanctuaries, we would cleanse and consecrate only one for our needs, and because I was a generous man, he could choose whether Tlaloc or Huitzilopochtli might remain.'

He laughed again, with sardonic heartiness. 'Our Montezuma proved a practical man. His war god having clearly failed him, after some thought, he chose to preserve the shrine to the god that brought the rain!'

'I tell you as friend, and if not as a friend, then as one of the lives you will surely put in danger, do not do this thing, Hernando,' I pleaded. 'You go too far. You court disaster.'

'And what do I court if I do not?' Cortes snapped back at me, angered at my attempt to hector him out of his exultant mood. 'Eternity in Hell!'

It was the last time that I ever offered Hernando Cortes advice that I knew he did not want to hear.

The ceremony took place in the late afternoon, just as the setting sun began to tint the western sky behind the pyramid with wisps of pale orange and lavender and cast its long somber shadow across the crowd gathered in the Temple Square beyond the bounds of the Sacred Precinct.

All the Spaniards were to take part, but I managed to feint a sprain of the ankle to avoid it, and observed from the roof of the palace, in a puerile attempt to distance my soul from both this alien rite to a Christian god in whom I could not believe and the worshippers of the sanguinary god it was meant to overthrow. But if the God of Abraham was looking down, and if I still believed in Him, or He in me, I could not delude myself that this absolved me of my part in bringing about all that had happened, all that was about to happen, and whatever might be to come.

I was startled when Marina came out onto the roof to join me. We had grown distant from each other as I grew distant from Cortes, as I withdrew from active complicity, or so at least I had told myself, in the continuing events in which she still played such a vital part.

'Why are you standing here with me, rather than at the side of Hernando Cortes in his ultimate hour of triumph?' I asked her bitterly.

'I am here to watch, rather than stand beside Hernando, who I would have told how stupid this is if I believed he would listen instead of condemning me as a heretic for trying. And you?'

'The same,' I told her. 'We may have schemed, perhaps unknowingly, to bring this very moment to pass, and so in some sense this rite is our creation, but it does not belong to us, nor we to it.'

Marina nodded. 'Nor will either of us really belong in the sixth world we are about to see being born,' she muttered.

I could only nod my silent agreement. I had been a secret stranger in the world that I had helped so thoughtlessly to bring to this land. This was the funeral of the fifth world into which Marina had been born, and while she might become a Doña Marina and a great Christian lady in the sixth world whose birth it heralded, she would also become a traitor in the eyes of those who would mourn the world that was passing, and so it could never truly be home to her divided heart.

We spoke no more. There was nothing more to say.

The entire Spanish army was lined up in narrow file behind Cortes and Father Olmedo and Father Diaz, the former bearing as large a whitened wooden Cross as he could carry, the latter a portrait of the Virgin. The soldiers wore full armor polished to a mirror sheen, but were bare-headed. Each man bore a candle and a red rose in lieu of a sword. Cortes himself was dressed like the others, save for a long red velvet cloak trimmed with gold-threaded piping.

Father Olmedo raised the Cross, stepped forward, and the procession began. Slowly the Christian soldiers marched through the conquered Mexica behind the Cross, slowly and deliberately did they enter the Sacred Precinct itself, and cross it, and then, triple file behind Cortes and the priests, the ascent of the pyramid began.

The temple, as I have said, was built in stages, with each stairway between stages halfway around the surrounding platform from the next, so that one had to climb round and round the pyramid to gain the apex, and the steps themselves were narrow and steeply pitched, so that one must also climb at an unnaturally deliberate pace.

Thus the procession wound slowly up the pyramid like a snake coiling round its petrified prey, with scales of burnished steel lit along its length by flickering orange candlelight, its head a pure white Cross tinted a deeply reddening orange by the last rays of the sun peering over the top of the temple, where the shrine of Huitzilopochtli had been cleansed and consecrated and an altar set up before it, and it remained only for his eternal flame that still burned there to be finally snuffed out.

The procession began to intone some hymn as the Cross attained the crown of the temple, whose words could not be made out at this distance, but whose solemn yet martially triumphant tone made its meaning all too plain to the Mexica below, who began to softly low and moan like corralled cattle.

At long last, the tail of the steel serpent slithered up over the lip of the temple platform, and there was a long silence broken by a great groan from below as the fiery light of Huitzilopochtli was put out, and its final plume of black smoke ascended past the smoldering disk of the setting sun behind his sanctuary to disappear upward into the purpling sky and then be gone.

The Cross was erected, and I could make out the tiny figures kneeling before it, and then they rose, and the resonant tones of the Te Deum sung by hundreds of deep male voices rolled down upon the Temple Square as a new fire was lit, a large one burning bright, so that the Cross Triumphant would be whitely visible from the surrounding precincts of the great city as the sun sank for the last time on the sanctuary of its war god and a holy night descended upon Tenochtitlan.

And as it did, I was granted one of Montezuma's omens, or rather a vision was inflicted upon me, for this was the baleful vision inflicted upon the Emperor by his sacred mushrooms, and whether it was the memory of his words painting it across my mind's eye and overlaying it upon my quotidian sight, or a true vision of the sort produced by such plants or fasting meditations or ardent prayer, I cannot say. I can only tell you what I saw.

The pristine white Cross atop the temple became two Crosses atop the shrines of Huitzilopochtli and Tlaloc. The Crosses turned to weathered stone. The shrines grew and grew to become the steepled bell towers of a glowering gray cathedral arising where the temple had been to dominate the far side of an immense stone square, empty save for the tiny figures of strangely dressed people, neither Mexica nor Spanish, yet somehow both, crawling over it disconsolately like starveling ants on a bonepile.

And under my breath I found myself muttering the Kaddish.

The Hebrew prayer for the dead.

26

THE GREEKS HAD A SINGLE word for the overweening pride that brings about self-earned disaster, and for those who so smugly prided themselves on being the conquerors of 'New Spain', that word was all too apt, to wit, hubris. The rule of Malinche and Spain over the Empire of the Mexica was now secure, and the Spaniards were lords of this particular corner of creation.

Or so it seemed.

Montezuma was now thoroughly broken to harness. And I have heard it said that once a wild stallion is so broken, he may be used to lead his former herd, which still blindly follows him as their sovereign, into an acceptance of subjugation.

As for the Cross, those vassal tribes previously constrained to feed him the hearts of the flower of their youth had little reason to mourn the passing of the sway of Huitzilopochtli, and every reason to welcome the much more powerful war god of the Spaniards as their liberator.

Then too the Spaniards' obsessive passion for gold above all other worldly goods had a pacifying effect itself. As I write this, I live among the simple peasantry of this land, and know their lives well, and it is obvious to me now, as it had only begun to dawn on me then, that the Spanish hunger for gold came as a kind of liberation for the ordinary folk of the countryside whose main hunger was, and still is, and no doubt always will be, for food and survival.

Under Montezuma, forced tribute flowed to the Valley of Mexico and Tenochtitlan from the provinces and the countryside in the form of varied foodstuffs to be sure, but human tribute in the form of soldiers for the Mexica armies and hearts for the altars drained the countryside of more than maize and beans.

The Spaniards too now demanded tribute, but their food requirements were hardly felt, they had forbidden human sacrifice, they placed little value on quetzal feathers, cloth finery and the like, for they regarded gold alone as true wealth. Give the Spaniards their gold, pay the requisite obeisance to their god, and they will more or less leave you alone. It is not hard to see why the yoke of Spain and Malinche was generally preferred as otherwise much lighter than that of Tenochtitlan.

I digress with this little treatise on the successful pacification because the aforementioned hubris did not allow Cortes, his priests, or any of his lieutenants, to see that little of it applied to the Mexica of Anahuac and none of it inside Tenochtitlan.

What was onerous tribute exacted by Tenochtitlan from the outlying provinces was a bounty of riches to the central power in the Valley of Mexico, and what might tax the Mexica peasants of the valley became wealth to the citizens of the capital. And while Christianity might be a religion of liberation to the suppliers of hearts to the altars of Huitzilopochtli and his compatriot deities, it found no favor with their abundant priesthood.

And so while Cortes saw to the collection of golden tribute, sent out expeditions to secure and drain the sources of gold, and he and his compatriots gambled and squabbled and occasionally fought over the ever more abundant booty, there were ominous stirrings beneath the placid surface of Tenochtitlan.

Indeed the placidity had become a sullen one as soon as the Cross had been raised above the paramount temple of the city. The crowd observing it had dispersed disconsolately, and in a few days the mood had settled like a brooding miasma upon the city. We still had the freedom of Tenochtitlan, we still frequented the gardens and marketplaces, but no one would choose to look a Spaniard in the eye could they avoid it.

No one would smile upon us. No one would engage us in any conversation. We were the conquerors. We must be obeyed. We must be served. But that was all. If we were not yet quite hated, we were certainly not loved.

Did I sense this at the time? Truth be told, I cannot tell you, dear reader, trying to recall such subtleties of the spirit so much time and so many terrible events later. But surely I knew that something had changed for the worse by the time I realized that Montezuma had been avoiding my company.

After the erecting of the Cross atop the pyramid, Montezuma took to spending more and more time closeted with the papas, a practice which Cortes mistakenly took as a harmless diversion until the day when he sought me out in a great state of angry agitation as I strolled in the morning sunlight atop the palace roof terraces.

'Did you know about this, Alvaro?' he demanded.

'Know about what?'

'What Montezuma has been plotting with those stinking pagan priests, or vice versa!'

'I have no idea what you're talking about, Hernando,' I told him. 'I haven't spoken with him in days.'

'The man . . . summoned me to his quarters as if he still ruled,' Cortes told me indignantly. 'He proceeded to tell me that his ridiculous pantheon of pagan demons had held some kind of conclave and informed the papas of their livid outrage. According to these lying sons of Satan, the gods informed them through omens and mushroom-induced visions that if the Teules were not forthwith sacrificed to appease them, or at the very least driven out, their wrath would fall upon the city and it would be destroyed.'

'You cannot say I did not warn you that displacing Huitzilopochtli with the Cross atop his temple would lead to no good,' I blurted. I did not need the black look that Cortes gave me to immediately realize my mistake, for no man is comforted by being forced to admit to himself that he has harmed his own cause by rejecting sage advice. 'What did you say to Montezuma then?' I asked quickly to cover my error.

'Before I could reply at all, he became cravenly wheedling. The only reason he was telling me this, he claimed, was because he was my friend and concerned for our welfare. He believed he could curb the demands that our hearts be fed to Huitzilopochtli, but only if we quit the city and returned across the waters from whence we came. If not, the whole Valley of Mexico would rise against us, there would be nothing he could do to prevent us from being overcome by an infuriated populace whose rage had been inflamed by the papas and sacrificed upon the rededicated altar of Huitzilopochtli, though even in such circumstances, as a friend, he would try to ensure that our flesh was well prepared and dined upon honorably by nobles rather than tossed to the beasts in his menagerie.'

Cortes' face reddened with the memory as he recited this, and by the time he was finished, veins stood out on his temples, and I wondered how Montezuma had escaped being cut to pieces by his sword in a rage then and there. If indeed he had.

'To which you replied . . . ?' I inquired in a fearful whisper.

'Had it not been for Marina urging caution and wisely refusing to translate the foul curses that were my first response, I probably would have replied with my sword. But by the time I had finished chastising her for her entirely sage disobedience, my blood had cooled to the point where I could contain my rage within sarcasm,' said Cortes, and as he did, so did the flush leave his face now.

'I told him with dripping sweetness that I supposed Marina did not entirely render in translation that I regretted very much being forced to leave in such precipitous circumstances, since I had no ships to carry my party back across the waters, and it would take many months to send for them and more for them to arrive,' Cortes continued.

'Why did you tell him a thing like that, Hernando?' I asked in utter perplexity.

Cortes actually managed a wan laugh. 'Because it is the truth, is it not?'

'*The truth!*' I exclaimed. 'You really intend to pack up and return to Cuba?'

'Of course not!' said Cortes, regarding me as if I had gone mad. 'But it *would* take months and months to either send for the needed ships and have them arrive or build them here ourselves, and in the meantime we would be in dire danger, I told Montezuma. And so, when we retreated to Vera Cruz, I would be forced, against my own tender feelings for him, to bring him along for the duration as a hostage.'

'You bought time, then?'

Cortes nodded. 'I bought more than time, for Montezuma grew fearful, and such a state seems to sharpen the man's cleverness rather than sap it. He offered to send as many workmen to the coast as might be required to build the ships under our direction as quickly as possible, and with such a practical assurance that we intended to be gone, he could then restrain the populace of the city and the valley from rising against us before the work was completed.'

'And when it is?'

Cortes shrugged. 'I shall order our shipwrights to see to it that such an event remains as far in the future as possible,' he said. 'And in the meantime . . .' He shrugged again.

'No man likes to be reminded of the sage advice he has ignored,' he grumbled, 'but I am not such a blockhead as to let my pride stand in the way of seeking more of it when I need it. So . . . what say you now, Alvaro?'

I could think of no clever stratagem to offer. Yet I had to offer something.

'I think Montezuma must have been more or less speaking the truth,' I said somewhat haltingly. 'We know that there has been no influx of warriors into the city, so if there *is* an uprising brewing, it would have to be a general rising of the populace fomented by the papas—'

'But nevertheless I had best position cannon to seal the causeway approaches in case someone like Cuitlahuac, who is still out there loose, might seek to bring troops into the city to take advantage of any such chaos,' Cortes interrupted. 'What else, Alvaro?' he demanded.

What else indeed?

'Perhaps we should now retreat to Vera Cruz, or at least as far as Tlascala?' I suggested. 'For in either Tlascala or Totonaca, we have reasonably powerful allies whose loyalty we can count on . . .'

Cortes shook his head, frowning. 'And how long would any of Montezuma's former vassal tribes remain loyal to us after the Mexica were seen to be ejecting us from their capital without even a fight and with our tails between our legs?'

'You could do as you threatened, and take him with us as an open hostage . . .'

Cortes shook his head even more vigorously. 'That was a bluff, and I do believe both of us knew it. If the papas *are* looking for an excuse to ignite a general rebellion, that would be handing them the ideal casus belli.'

'What then?'

Cortes shrugged yet again. 'You have told me often enough that Montezuma is a prevaricator who delays decisions as long as he can in hopes of finally being granted a heavenly omen,' he said. 'Well, it seems that now my only course is to do likewise and pray to Christ and the Virgin and Saint James for one of my own.'

I cannot vouch for the diligence of Cortes' prayers, but in the end an omen was indeed forthcoming, though I doubt it was sent by such holy Christian sources, for it was hardly what Cortes could have expected or desired.

True to his word, Montezuma sent an army of tree-cutters and workmen to the coast at Vera Cruz, and true to Cortes' orders, the Spanish shipwrights and carpenters proved the most meticulous of task-masters, rejecting half the logs as of inferior quality, and half the timbers arduously hewn with obsidian tools from the rest as improperly trimmed, piling up enough lumber by this tedious process to construct a veritable armada before a single ship even began to be constructed.

Cortes kept his army in Tenochtitlan on permanent alert status. The causeway entrances were covered by cannon at every hour, likewise the approaches to the palace of Axayacatl, and the soldiery was ordered never to be without weapons or armor, even when sleeping.

Once more true to his word, Montezuma prevented any popular rebellion, or rather the knowledge that Mexica workmen were arduously occupied under Spanish supervision in building the ships that would take them back across the sea was enough to maintain a tense and brooding municipal patience.

And then Cortes' 'omen' arrived.

It was Montezuma himself who delivered it.

'Never have I seen this dour man beaming so,' Cortes told me fresh from the interview. 'He showed me one of those marvelous colorfully painted reports of his. And upon it, quite clearly delineated, were what could only be Spanish ships approaching the coast under sail! There were eighteen of them. You see, Montezuma told me positively joyously, now there is no need to continue building your ships. You can leave at once, for your King has sent these ships of his own to bring you home.'

'Do you really think—'

'Do you really remember my requesting any such thing?' Cortes snapped sardonically. 'And then he gave me *this* one for my very own,' he said, and produced the colored drawing in question.

The ships were now clearly at anchor, though the artists had neglected to furl the sails. Horses as fierce-looking as lions, more than a score of them, paraded along the sandy strand, ridden by bearded white men in full armor. There were what I believed I could make out as crossbowmen and arquebusiers, also by the score and more. And men afoot. And cannon.

'Certainly well-armed reinforcements, it would seem. But from where? And sent by whom?'

Cortes replied with no more than a lidded stare. And then we uttered the obvious together:

'Diego Velazquez.'

Cannon fired blank charges! Likewise arquebusiers! Soldiers shouted and hugged each other and guzzled pulque and sang martial and obscene songs! It was joyous pandemonium in the palace of Axayacatl!

Cortes had informed his troops of the 'glorious news' with a happy face and allowed the drawing given to him by Montezuma to circulate among them, figuring that it was better to lift the morale of the ordinary soldiery than to further trammel their minds with his grim forebodings before they could be confirmed or, hopefully, laid to rest.

But after making a show of sharing their pleasure at this arrival of a formidable array of 'reinforcements', he summoned Diego de Ordaz and Velazquez de Leon to his quarters in quite another mood. Alvarado was there too, and Olid, but it was they Cortes wished to consult, being former intimates of the governor of Cuba, which was why I was there as well.

'These troops must have been sent by Velazquez,' Cortes began dourly. 'Where else could they have come from?'

'Why not from Spain?' suggested Alvarado. 'You *did* send Montejo back with much gold for the King and the promise of much more, so why would he not—'

'Hardly an army of royal proportions,' said Ordaz. 'More the niggardly style of Diego Velazquez.'

Cortes nodded. 'They must be Velazquez's forces.'

'What do you think, Alvaro?' Cortes demanded of me. 'You know the man well.'

I replied cautiously, not that I had anything incautious to offer. 'It is hard to imagine that if Diego Velazquez has learned of the treasure here, he would allow an attempt by anyone else short of the King himself to mount an expedition to seize it. If that is what this is.' I shrugged. 'The rest is pure conjecture.'

'Indeed,' said Cortes. 'The question for now is what do we do about it?'

'There is nothing we can do but obey if this army has been sent by the King, is there?' ventured Olid.

'And if it has been sent by Velazquez?' said Cortes.

'If you're asking whether we would fight at your side to retain all we have won here rather than turn it over to the governor of Cuba, relative or not, I declare I am with you!' declared Velazquez de Leon.

'And I as well!' said Diego de Ordaz.

And I realized that such had been the sole purpose of the whole exercise, for under the circumstances, it was the only practical purpose the meeting could have had.

'I thank you for your support,' said Cortes. 'Perhaps as his kinsman,' he told Velazquez de Leon, 'you would be the best envoy to see whether the governor of Cuba has sent this expedition or not, and to treat with whoever is leading them if he has.'

But before Velazquez de Leon could make his arrangements to depart, a Spanish soldier arrived bearing a letter from Gonzalo de Sandoval making the situation all too direly clear, so direly that Cortes straightaway closeted himself with me in his own quarters without first informing any of his lieutenants, handed me the thing, demanded that

I read it as quickly as possible, and sat there frowning, fidgeting, and all but chewing on his beard while I did.

The Spanish force had indeed been sent by the governor of Cuba, Diego Velazquez, nor were the troops 'reinforcements'. Montejo and Puertocarrero had arrived safely in Spain, but not before stopping off in Cuba for reasons unclear, and thereby allowing Velazquez to learn of the early successes of Cortes' expedition – chief among them, in Velazquez's eyes, the securing of abundant supplies of gold. Cortes' envoys had presented his huge tribute of same to the King, along with our petition to proceed under his direct authority. King Charles was most pleased to receive the former, but the latter somehow passed out of his attention owing to his preoccupation with other matters concerning his grander crown, and no decision had been made.

Velazquez then decided to take matters into his own greedy hands, and dispatched the current expedition under Panfilo de Narvaez, who had been his chief military officer in the conquest of Cuba. Worse, Narvaez's force, according to Sandoval, was even more formidable than Montezuma's drawings had indicated. It consisted of some nine hundred soldiers, eighty of whom were cavalrymen supplied with the requisite mounts, eighty arquebusiers, one hundred and fifty crossbowmen, and an unknown but formidable number of cannon.

To make matters still worse, Narvaez soon encountered one of the scouting parties Cortes had sent out in search of further sources of gold, whose leader innocently and boastfully informed him of all that Cortes had accomplished. Narvaez forthwith announced his intention to punish Cortes for his 'rebellion' against Velazquez and seize all he had conquered and gained for the governor of Cuba.

He then dispatched a delegation to Vera Cruz, which was how Sandoval had been rudely informed of these matters. And rudely was the word for it. Narvaez's delegation consisted of four soldiers and a notary, led by an arrogant priest named Guevara, who demanded that Sandoval submit to the authority of Narvaez and through him to the governor of Cuba. Sandoval just as forthrightly told him that were he not a priest, he would have him flogged, which, I surmised, was probably why Narvaez had dispatched a priest rather than an officer in the first place.

A shouting match ensued. Guevara demanded that the notary be allowed to read out some proclamation of authority. Sandoval demanded to know whether it came from the King. Guevara refused to tell him. Sandoval replied that unless it did, it was meaningless, and if the notary then attempted to read it aloud, he would be arrested or worse. Guevara apparently replied in language entirely inappropriate to a man of the cloth. Sandoval told him that he was under the command of Hernando Cortes until Cortes or the King told him otherwise, and therefore his business was with Cortes in Tenochtitlan.

Vexed with Guevara, Sandoval then kindly aided Narvaez's delegation in traveling to this appropriate venue by seizing them, trussing them like turkeys bound for market, and packing them off to Tenochtitlan on the backs of tamanes and under guard, and that was where Sandoval's letter ended.

Cortes and I stared at each other silently and blankly after I had finished reading the missive, both of us struggling to encompass this vast and vastly indigestible morsel. For my part, the most stunning aspect was the sudden intrusion of events and agents from a tired Old World that had had at most a wan memory's existence and good riddance. As for Cortes, having made himself the master of an empire, what ire and chagrin he must have felt at being reminded of a realm in which he was regarded as a rebellious vassal of the fat and greedy governor of a threadbare island colony!

'Well, Alvaro?' Cortes finally demanded.

'Well, Hernando?'

'Have you nothing to say?'

'Where is Narvaez's delegation now?' was the best I could manage to fracture our mutual stupefaction.

At this, Cortes managed a small smile. 'Still tied up under guard on the mainland.'

'Well then, the first step would be to bring them here and treat them in a far more liberal manner than has the valorous and loyal but excessively impetuous Sandoval.'

'Why, may I ask?' Cortes asked sourly.

'For one thing, to see what is in that proclamation,' I told him. 'From what Sandoval says, it almost certainly cannot be from the King—' I caught myself short, for I felt my wits unfreezing.

'What is it, Alvaro?'

'Since we know it is not from the King, you can pretend that you don't, and tell this Guevara that if it is, as a loyal subject of the Crown, you will obey it to the letter. But if it is not . . .'

'Which it won't be . . .'

'If it is not,' I heard myself saying as I fell once more into the unwanted role of Cortes' scheming vizier, 'you must loosen his tongue and learn more of the true nature and situation of Narvaez's forces.'

'Torture a priest!' Cortes exclaimed with such righteous but visibly speculative indignation that it was all that I could do to keep from bursting out in laughter.

'Hardly,' I told him. 'You cannot match Narvaez in the number of men, horses or armaments, but there is one weapon mightier than any other in which your supply reigns crushingly superior.'

Cortes peered at me in owlish consternation for a moment before he comprehended and his countenance became brighter than it had been at any time since he showed me Sandoval's letter.

I nodded.

'Gold!' said the conqueror of New Spain.

Cortes had dispatched not only officers with orders for the release of Narvaez's delegation, but six horses to carry them into the city in a state appropriate to their assumed diplomatic station, and greeted them in a dining hall in a luxuriously appointed apartment provided for their comfort, with the walls draped with rich featherwork tapestries, the air perfumed with incense and bouquets of roses, and a repast of some score of succulent and well-sauced dishes already laid out for their pleasure, as well as an abundance of chocolatl and pulque.

Cortes wore black Spanish velvet, a steel breastplate and a Toledo sword, but also a heavy golden pendant in the Mexica manner, and several pounds of gold chains, though eschewing labret, earrings or nose plug. I too was decked out in a display of golden finery, the whole being designed to show that he had so much gold to bestow that even his lowly scribe went around wearing as much as a European prince.

The notary and the four soldiers went to greedy and famished work on the lavish banquet, but Father Guevara, a swarthy, wiry and sharp-featured man, looking a good deal the worse for wear, arrived in an understandably irascible mood, which, according to Sandoval, seemed to be his characteristic humor.

'You will pay for this outrage, Hernando Cortes!' he roared by way of greeting.

'Indeed I will,' Cortes replied in the most friendly manner. He clapped his hands, and, as had been arranged, six Mexica servants entered bearing baskets the size of helmets and deposited one before each of the guests.

'I must apologize for the rudeness of my commander at Vera Cruz, and also for the presently modest nature of what I am now offering in recompense, for I had little time to prepare more suitable tokens of atonement, which will be provided later,' he purred as the notary and the soldiers pawed excitedly through their baskets, which were filled with assorted items of gold jewelry and little statues.

Father Guevara's countenance did not soften until he looked down into his, the central feature of which was a heavy gold crucifix attached to a rosary crafted of rounded nuggets of gold inlaid with emeralds, at which point his jaw dropped and his eyes bugged out in a most unecclesiastical manner.

'Perhaps there has indeed been merely an unfortunate misunderstanding,' he owned somewhat grudgingly.

'Of a certainty,' said Cortes, 'but before we discuss such matters, you must refresh yourselves.'

To this, Guevara and his companions readily agreed, indeed his companions were already at it, and as they seemed to prefer the pulque to the chocolatl and many of the dishes offered up were piquantly spiced, it took a liberal amount of it to wash them down, and so, as the banquet proceeded, tongues became loosened and lubricated.

The four soldiers, it thus emerged, and by extension many of their comrades, were not particularly enamored of the leadership of Panfilo de Narvaez, an intemperate and arrogant man, and no great military leader according to them. Moreover, they had been recruited with funds from the less than generous Velazquez and vague promises of shares in the sort of abundant booty which Cortes had just bestowed upon them, each basket of which was of more value than the paltry wages paid to the whole expedition.

It further emerged that they had been recruited with the promise that the worst they would be constrained to combat would be savages armed with spears and bows, and only recently had Narvaez revealed his intention to use them against fellow Spaniards and Christians if legal means were insufficient to persuade Cortes to submit to the authority of the governor of Cuba.

In short, Narvaez's army might fight for the Crown itself out of patriotism, but were otherwise disgruntled mercenaries with no particular loyalty to Diego Velazquez.

'Well, let us have a look at this proclamation which so exacerbated young Sandoval,' Cortes finally said when this was all digested, if the meal certainly was not. Guevara handed over the papers, and Cortes appeared to read them carefully and diligently. When he was finished, he put on an expression of great surprise, and even went so far in the mime as to scratch the top of his head in a theatrical gesture of perplexity.

'I don't understand,' he said. 'This is no license from the King. This is no more than a plea for my obedience from the governor of Cuba on no higher authority than his own assumption!'

Father Guevara, who by this point was quite bloated with food, and if not quite drunk, feeling no ire or pain, shrugged in a friendly manner. 'I am merely the messenger,' he said. 'Perhaps Narvaez kept his license from the King to himself, fearing that your Sandoval would do just what he did, or even destroy it.'

'Perhaps,' agreed Cortes, 'for if I was in possession of the only copy of such a document, I would certainly not let it out of my hands.' Which, of course, was the truth. 'And if Narvaez can indeed produce such a document, I would of course immediately submit to his authority.' Which, I was fairly certain, was a lie, albeit one that Cortes knew could never be found out.

'I'll tell you what, Father, might you be willing to carry *my* message to Narvaez, once you are well rested, along with suitable tokens of my esteem for him and his troops to prove my sincerity?'

'However I arrived here,' said Father Guevara, 'that is more or less what I was commissioned to do.'

'Excellent!' declared Cortes, turning to me. 'Scribe, note this down and prepare a suitably worded version to be carried to Panfilo de Narvaez over my signature: my dear Señor Narvaez, noble brother in arms, and so forth, and so on, I beg of you not to betray any differences that may have arisen by misunderstanding between us to the natives of these lands, lest, seeing us divided, it may come into their heads to rise against whichever Spanish authority may in the end prevail, to our mutual detriment. And indeed there is plenty here for both of us, and I am more than willing to share the fruits of my conquest and subjugation with you, either as my loyal chief captain, or as your obedient servant, should you produce a commission from the King requiring me to do so. Your friendly brother in arms, fellow soldier of Christ, loyal vassal of the King, and so on and so forth, Hernando Cortes.'

And I dutifully scribbled it all down, even though the full text of the letter had been drafted and carefully rewritten hours ago.

27

Not content with returning his own envoy to Narvaez laden with the letter we had drafted and an impressive amount of gold, Guevara hardly had time to cross the mountains when Cortes decided to dispatch Father Olmedo as his own envoy.

'Of what use is that?' I asked, when he required me to produce another letter couched as a report on all that he had accomplished here addressed to 'our fellow Christians, Spaniards, and brothers in arms', rather than specifically to Panfilo de Narvaez.

'The gold I sent back with Guevara and his party is under their control, and if I may be pardoned for questioning the generosity of their natures, I strongly suspect they may be tempted to retain it. With Father Olmedo, I shall send back a much larger supply in the form of small trinkets, with instructions to distribute them far and wide, along with the tales of how much there is and how liberal I am with it, and how much more the troops of Narvaez would therefore gain by a cooperative attitude towards the effective viceroy of Mexico, rather than risking their lives for the sake of the greed of Narvaez and Diego Velazquez.'

'You seriously believe that Narvaez will allow such subversion?' I scoffed.

'Father Olmedo will read the document to the assembled troops without revealing its contents beforehand,' Cortes told me.

'Narvaez will certainly not allow it.'

'Oh, and how will he stop it? Arrest a *priest* sent as my envoy? After Olmedo has distributed his tokens of my largesse far and wide in advance?' Cortes laughed. 'And even if he does, it will hardly gain him the favor of the recipients thereof or solidify his command over them, now will it?'

And so it was done. Two weeks and several days later, Father Olmedo returned to Tenochtitlan. Narvaez, unable to arrest a priest who had made himself and Cortes so popular with his troops by the distribution of gold and the promise of more, had expelled him with a demand that Cortes come to heel or be overcome by his superior force and hanged as a traitor.

This Cortes dismissed as the rantings of a checkmated blowhard, but the report from Sandoval he received only days later was quite another matter. Narvaez had moved his encampment to the outskirts of Cempoala, and himself and his immediate entourage into luxurious quarters within the city, where he had proclaimed to Tlacochcalcat that he had been sent to seize Cortes as a traitor to his King and a usurper of their own rightful sovereign Montezuma, whom he intended to rescue from his captivity. He also seemed to have put abroad a rumor that he and Montezuma were already in communication.

Sandoval reckoned that this latter was a falsehood, but falsehood or not, Narvaez had stirred up a hornets' nest among the Totonacs with the revelation that the Spaniards, far from being either the Second Coming of the Toltecs or 'Teules' united under their One True God, were as prone to factional warfare among their own tribes as were the inhabitants of their own world.

And Tlacochcalcat, being pragmatically and cautiously devoted to the interests of his own people over those of any other – be they Spanish or Mexica or Tlascalan – oath of fealty to Malinche notwithstanding, was hosting Narvaez, sitting on the fence, and waiting to see where advantage might eventually lie.

What to do now?

Cortes brooded and fumed for days, seeking no one's counsel but allowing his lieutenants to hear Father Olmedo's tales of his time among the troops of Narvaez, and to read Sandoval's report, thereby enabling the tidings to diffuse among his own troops in an indirect and natural manner.

My familiarity with Cortes' mode of cozening his troops into believing they were forcing the decision he wanted to make upon him led me to believe that this was more of the same. Or perhaps not, and Cortes might for once have been genuinely indecisive and genuinely wished to benefit from the unforced opinions of the generality.

There were few alternatives, and, so it seemed, no promising ones.

Cortes and his army could accept the authority of Narvaez and lose all they had gained, but anyone bruiting this about would brand himself a coward. Yet coward or not, who would want to put his life in the hands of a mediocre commander when the Mexica were growing ever more restive?

There seemed nothing for it but a clash of Spanish arms against Spanish arms.

Cortes could draw all his forces into Tenochtitlan, and dare Narvaez to march through a factionating countryside to besiege a perfect fortress where his superiority in numbers might be neutralized by the defenders' tactical advantage.

Or he could march against Narvaez with all he had, hoping for the support of the Tlascalans and Totonacs to augment his outnumbered forces.

Both military strategies seemed desperate courses of action at best.

Narvaez would have great difficulty marching through Totonaca and Tlascala with a promise to restore the rule of Montezuma from which Cortes had liberated them, but if he reached Anahuac, the Mexica would rally to his cause for that very reason, and a siege of Tenochtitlan would ignite the uprising that the papas were fomenting within the city.

But attacking an army that outnumbered Cortes' by more than two to one and with overwhelming superiority in cavalry and cannon would mean relying on the loyalty of indigene caciques like Tlacochcalcat and Xicotencatl the Elder, who might see their own best interests in watching the Spaniards battle it out and either rallying to the victor or finishing off his remnant forces themselves if they were sufficiently weakened. It would also mean abandoning Tenochtitlan to the control of Montezuma, or worse still to the papas if the Emperor was dragged along as a hostage.

I had no inkling of what Cortes was about to decide or what he was going to say to rally his troops to it when he assembled them in the largest courtyard within the palace of Axayacatl to hear it, for this was one speech I had no part in crafting. Yet a mighty speech it was, I must admit.

Cortes mounted his horse to address them, the better to be seen, and perhaps to enhance his authority.

'Brothers in arms, soldiers of the Cross, gallant conquerors of New Spain, together we face both the greatest danger and the greatest opportunity put before us by destiny and Almighty God since first we set foot on these shores. The danger we know all too well, and need not dwell on it, for we face a demand for craven surrender by the commander of an army of *Spaniards* armed with Toledo steel and many cannon, and with infantry and cavalry and crossbowmen and arquebusiers who greatly outnumber us. And so I say to you all, if there are those among you daunted by these seemingly hopeless odds against us, go now, make your peace if you can with Panfilo de Narvaez, and none will call you cowards, for to remain under my command and essay what I propose requires a company entirely composed of heroes.'

That the most anyone did to entertain this offer was to steal a sidelong glance at a few men stealing sidelong glances at them was hardly surprising.

'But now let us consider the great gift which God in His Mercy and Wisdom has offered up to us,' Cortes went on. 'We have conquered an empire to our honor and His and to our great enrichment, but now we are threatened with rebellion against our meager numbers. And so God, seeing our plight, has sent us His boon, and what more could we ask in our hour of need – nine hundred and more Spanish soldiers, with horses and cannon and abundant supplies, and all we need do to secure them is win our Christian brothers away from the miserly avarice of Diego Velazquez and his lackey Panfilo de Narvaez and to our own noble cause of New Spain, King Charles, and the Cross! And if this is not what God intended, then why would He have sent them to us?'

And I styled *myself* an accomplished sophist! But if Cortes was a more accomplished sophist than I, he was also an accomplished orator, which I was not, and knew better than to give his audience time to think.

'And if God did not intend us to prevail and so save the souls of millions of these benighted heathens, would He have allowed us to accumulate so much gold that we may use the smallest part of it to win over to our cause our fellow Christian soldiers from the evil and niggardly and treasonous and thieving intent of Panfilo de Narvaez and Diego Velazquez?'

At this there began to be murmurs of approval, for that Mammon had allied with God in their behalf was the perfect marriage of spiritual and practical encouragement, and these greedy troops found it entirely credible that those of Narvaez would rather fight for gold and the Cross than for penury and the governor of Cuba.

'And so,' said Cortes, 'I will leave the bulk of our forces here to keep Tenochtitlan and our treasure secure under the valorous Pedro Alvarado. I myself will lead but seventy volunteers to the camp of Narvaez, to win his men for our cause by appeal to reason, honor and avarice if God so wills it, or by force of arms and miracle if that is what the Lord should require. And who among you would doubt that God would march with us against Narvaez's mere thousand, when He has so stalwartly stood by our side against the heathen hordes in their tens and hundreds of thousands? I say to you that to suppose that He would quail and abandon us now would be to accuse the Lord Our God of cowardice in the face of His own enemies! Who among you would do that? Who among you would fail to place your lives and the fortunes you have won and your honor in the hands of the God Who has given them unto you? Who among you is not a Christian soldier?'

There was a moment of dumbfounded silence while the troops struggled to swallow down this huge overripe morsel, and then confused mutterings, and finally a ragged cheer began to build. For what martial Christian soul could in the end fail to be stirred by such an extravagant appeal? And if one did, he could hardly wish his faintheartedness to be seen by his assembled comrades.

*

And so Cortes departed to work his martial miracle, leaving the bulk of his little army behind under the command of Pedro de Alvarado. Marina went with him as translator, but I stayed behind, for Cortes planned to move as fast as possible and the presence of such as myself would only be a hindrance.

In retrospect, I was to chide myself often for stifling my instinct to attempt to persuade Cortes not to leave the hotblooded and headstrong Alvarado in charge of the garrison in Tenochtitlan.

Alvarado was the sort of cavalier that soldiers are prone to love, admire, and wish to be led by. He was a great horseman and swordsman, brimming with physical energy, fearlessly brave, a good tactician and a hearty companion, and these were the qualities which had raised him high in Cortes' own esteem, and which made him an excellent chief lieutenant when held on a tight enough leash.

But given an independent command, his equally extravagant flaws were, at least to me, all too apparent. His very martial skills made him arrogant. The ease with which he charmed all under his command prevented him from developing the necessary skills of more complex leadership, perhaps because he was not particularly clever. Pedro de Alvarado was the quintessential soldier's soldier, the perfect battlefield commander, but not the sort of man to be made a commanding general with no authority, military or civil, present above him.

Still less under the conditions now prevailing in Tenochtitlan. The atmosphere had been tense and ominous even before the advent of Narvaez, the fiery stew of rebellion stirred by the papas and whoever might be their clandestine allies kept from boiling over only by the false promise of Cortes to Montezuma to leave once the departure fleet was ready. But now that a Spanish fleet large enough to evacuate the forces of Malinche had arrived, not to effect this withdrawal but to disgorge even more Spaniards who declared themselves the enemies of Malinche, the result was a viper's nest of chaos, hopes, fears and confusions.

According to what paltry intelligence penetrated the walls of the palace of Axayacatl, the papas were using the departure of Malinche and the third part of the Spanish garrison to work up the courage of the general populace to a storming of our redoubt. The revelation of the factionalism within the forces of the distant King of Spain had destroyed any remaining belief either that Malinche was Quetzalcoatl or that these pale-skinned, gold-hungry and fractious foreign tribesmen could possibly be the descendants of the noble Toltecs. There were rumors that Montezuma had already made an alliance with Narvaez, and that an uprising would be the sign for him to march on Tenochtitlan to assure its liberation. There were rumors that Malinche had not departed to give honorable battle to Narvaez, but rather to proceed to Tlascala and bring back a huge army of Tlascalans.

To make matters worse, Alvarado was almost entirely dependent on Montezuma for intelligence as to what prevailed outside the walls of what had effectively become the Spanish fortress. If he held the Emperor incommunicado, he would be effectively blind. Therefore, so as long as Montezuma seemed sufficiently forthcoming to make the bargain seem worthwhile, papas, and even the occasional noble, were allowed to come and go, despite what mischief they might be carrying back from the captive ruler into the city.

I was no more a favorite of Pedro de Alvarado than he of me, but I was the most proficient in Nahuatl of anyone remaining in the palace of Axayacatl, and as much an intimate of Montezuma as anyone among our company could be, so at first he had demanded that I be present at what meetings he might allow between the papas or nobles and the Emperor.

Montezuma bridled at this, and Alvarado bridled in return at the Emperor's insubordination. Montezuma pointed out quite reasonably that if a Spanish spy was present, his interlocutors would not be about to speak freely, and therefore the presence of one would obviate the very reason for his presence.

At length, a compromise was negotiated. Montezuma would be allowed to conduct his seances without my presence, but I would interview him afterward and report back to Alvarado. This was hardly the ideal situation, but as even Pedro Alvarado had the wit to acknowledge, it was better than nothing.

And so Montezuma reported to me on the rumors his papas reported to him, and I filtered them back to Alvarado. It was an exceedingly unpleasant situation for both of us. As a friend or companion or even passing acquaintance, I would have chosen Montezuma over

Alvarado without a second thought, but Tenochtitlan was on the edge of rebellion, I was among those whose hearts would be fed to Huitzilopochtli if it occurred and succeeded, and so my loyalties were divided. The Emperor knew that I knew that he could hardly be delivering fully truthful reports and not issuing orders, but that was the fiction we both needed to preserve.

At length, I essayed an attempt to break through the façade of this charade.

'Tell me one thing true, at least,' I pleaded. 'Do you wish to see a rising in Tenochtitlan or not? I swear by all that is holy and any number of foul oaths that are not, if your answer is the former, it shall go no further.'

Montezuma studied me for a long moment. His slenderness had turned gaunt of late. He seemed to have put on years in a matter of weeks. There was a weakness in his gaze, and yet behind it, the strength one occasionally sees in the eyes of a man with a terminal illness who has achieved his acceptance of the inevitable.

'Like any ruler of a proud people, what I wish is for my empire to survive in its full glory and for its capital to stand both undestroyed and unconquered,' he finally told me. He sighed most deeply, and reached for the ever-present cup of chocolatl. 'But my empire has been seized from me, and I am a prisoner in my conquered capital, and in the last omen which has been inflicted upon me, I have seen Tenochtitlan become a city foreign to the Mexica and its inhabitants reduced to a fallen people. And yet . . .'

'And yet?'

'And yet, since the coming of the other Spaniards, I have considered that this vision told me nothing of what is to befall the Mexica outside Tenochtitlan. Might it be that the city must be sacrificed that the empire might live? And if so, does that mean the people should rise up? Or does it mean that Tenochtitlan might be given over to this Narvaez or Malinche in return for the life of the empire?'

Yes, to the very end, this strange man still sought after omens and visions to follow. And in their absence, sought to create them.

'The papas have reminded me that they must soon hold the greatest and most joyful of our ceremonies, the Perfuming of Huitzilopochtli, which has always been held before his temple in the Sacred Precinct,' Montezuma told me after a conclave with his priests a few days later. 'And so I will have my omen, and it will be for all to see, and it will be given not by Huitzilopochtli but by Pedro de Alvarado. For if he should forbid, prevent or hinder this rite, no Emperor will be able, even were he willing, to prevent a rising in outrage.'

'A foul heathen ritual before our very eyes and at the foot of the temple where we have raised the Cross against such Satanic worship!' Alvarado exclaimed in outrage when I reported this to him. 'Out of the question!'

'I'm afraid it *is* the question,' I told him, 'for unless you answer in the affirmative, the answer will surely be the very one we fear.'

'And how do I know if I permit this blasphemy, with the square right before our palace filled with reveling savages, no doubt inflaming themselves with pulque and incited by filthy bloodthirsty priests, that the feeding of our hearts to their demon will not be the planned climax of the ceremony, and will not serve as the signal for an uprising?'

'You don't,' I was forced to admit.

'Or even the ideal deployment from which to launch it . . .' Alvarado muttered under his breath. And his eyes became narrowed and lidded. Perhaps I should have guessed the dark thought seeping into his brain behind them. But alas, I did not.

'But what other choice is there?' I said in my innocence. 'You could, indeed you should, take defensive measures . . .'

'Indeed . . .' Alvarado said to himself thoughtfully. 'I could grant conditional permission, could I not? No human sacrifices. And Montezuma must be kept within the walls of the palace. And . . . most important of all, ceremonial or not, no one taking part can be permitted to bear arms . . .'

At this point, I could see that some sort of hidden strategy was being contemplated, but I could not imagine what. How could I? I ask you, dear reader.

The days leading up to the Perfuming of Huitzilopochtli were fraught with tension within the palace of Axayacatl, and intrigues as well, and the Tlascalans, who knew the nature of this festival, spread a lurid and fearful description of the rite.

According to them, human sacrifice was the very centerpiece thereof. The 'Perfuming of Huitzilopochtli' was an annual rite of renewal. A handsome young warrior, chosen the very day after the previous such rite, became a living effigy of Tezcatlipoca, an ambiguous deity who might have been the war god of a previous paramount tribe, and was honored and feted for a year in the lap of luxury. On the day of the ritual, he was fed a powerful dose of the sacred mushroom teonanecatl in order to prepare him to participate willingly, indeed ecstatically, in what was to come. At the climax of the ritual he would ascend the great pyramid, there to have his living heart cut out and offered up to Huitzilopochtli in the 'flowery death', so that the passage of the powers of Tezcatlipoca to Huitzilopochtli would thereby be renewed for another year.

Thus, without this sacrifice, and lesser but more numerous ancillary human sacrifices, the ritual would fail. Thus any promise to hold the rite without human sacrifice must be a lie. Thus the flowery death would occur, to what those holding it must know would be the ire of the Spaniards, and thus it would be the signal for a general uprising to begin.

There were rumors and signs and omens. The usual deliveries of food by the Mexica to the palace stopped and Alvarado had to dispatch parties of soldiers to the markets to fetch them. When the Mexica began erecting elaborate canopies of cloth and featherwork around the court-yard before the great temple, Alvarado himself went to inspect the premises and discovered tall stakes being pounded into the ground and assortments of pots, knives and other cooking implements, and was informed by the Tlascalans that these were no doubt preparations for the sacrifice of the Spaniards and the preparation of their flesh for a celebratory feast.

Here matters become murkier, for the truth was contained within the skull of Pedro de Alvarado, and considering the disaster his action pre-cipitated, what he later told Cortes could not have been other than an attempt at self-serving exculpation.

Did he truly believe that the Mexica were plotting a massacre of the Spaniards and the Tlascalans or did he use the rumors thereof sweep-ing through the palace of Axayacatl to rally his troops to a preplanned massacre of *them*?

Not having been privy to the plans of Alvarado, let alone his thoughts, nor to those of the Mexica, I shall of necessity confine myself to reporting what I witnessed and nothing more.

On the day the festival began an effigy of Huitzilopochtli was carried into the Sacred Precinct before the temple by four Jaguar Warriors and four Eagle Warriors in all their furred and feathered finery, though innocent of weapons. This monstrosity was twice the size of a man, made of dough mixed with the fresh blood of human victims and allowed to dry, or so the Tlascalans claimed, and an inspection by several Spaniards close enough to the thing to smell it seemed to confirm this. It wore huge turquoise and gold earrings in the form of serpents, a gold snout, a tunic embroidered in the likeness of human skeletons and skulls, and a ghastly cloak of what appeared to be freshly severed human heads, and it held a sheaf of arrows in one hand and a shield in the other. One could hardly expect this demon to be satisfied with tribute of incense and flowers.

The first three days of the festival were celebrated in other parts of the city, and none of us within the palace of Axayacatl cared to venture out to witness them for fear of being dragooned into playing a most unwelcome part, and so I cannot describe them save what they aroused in the fearful mind's eye.

For the Tlascalans insisted that abundant human sacrifices played a part and that the evening feasting featured the flesh thereof, and that well-spiced Spaniard would be a most prized delicacy. By day, from the palace rooftops, we could see distant colorful processions winding and dancing through the streets, elaborately decorated barges on the lake, and hear the insistent and interminable pounding and clack of distant drums, the thin nasal echoes of flutes, punctuated all too often by what no one could explain as other than hideously human screams of pain.

At night, it was even worse, for though little could be seen but scattered fires in the darkened precincts of the city and shadowy figures skulking about in the wan starlight, the darkness, and the continuing drumming and fluting, caused the disquieted imagination to transform Tenochtitlan in the mind's eye and ear into an ominous urban jungle infested with lurking cannibals and demons working themselves up into a frenzy.

I will pass over the nightmares engendered when fitful sleep was possible and proceed directly to the final day of the 'Perfuming of Huitzilopochtli' and what I was constrained to witness directly with my waking eyes and ears.

By noon the Temple Square was filled with onlookers, for only warriors and nobles were permitted into the Sacred Precinct to take active part. The Sacred Precinct itself then began to fill with nobles and warriors dancing to the music of drums and flutes, and they were elaborately and beautifully dressed, sporting headdresses of quetzal feathers or bright red plumage, cloaks of fur and feathers, earrings, labrets and nose-plugs of gold and turquoise, pendants and chains of gold, jade and seashells. Their faces and bodies were painted in extravagant colors and patterns, and they wore little gold bells on their ankles that tinkled as they danced in a manner most pleasant to the ears.

By the time the Sacred Precinct was filled, there must have been a thousand dancers crowded into it, accompanied by dozens of drummers and flutists, and at least from my vantage just beyond the wall enclosing it, I can testify that I saw no weapons among them, and in other circumstances this ritual might have been taken for and enjoyed as a gay fete.

I can also testify that Pedro de Alvarado, along with three score or so soldiers, pretended to be doing just that, entering the Sacred Precinct smiling and shuffling their feet to the music, and spreading out through the periphery of the reveling throng. I can also testify that, as was their normal habit, they were armored and armed. There were three entrances to the Sacred Precinct, and Spanish soldiers lounged at each of them, as if to enjoy a better perspective of the whole.

The dance was presided over by some sort of major domo who stood by the idol of Huitzilopochtli, marking time with a ceremonial staff. As the dancing went on, the dancers worked themselves up into an ecstatic frenzy, gyrating their buttocks and pelvises most obscenely, waving their arms, rolling their heads with upturned eyes, the whole yet so ritualized that, magically, none seemed to jostle another.

And then—

And then a horn sounded somewhere, and a handsome youth dressed in the finery of Tezcatlipoca was borne into the Sacred Precinct on a gilded litter bedecked with feathers and flowers, accompanied by an entourage of papas and flutists, and though way was made for him, the dancing and drumming redoubled in frenzy.

And then—

'Kill them!' roared Alvarado, and he rushed up to the leader of the dance, and with a single stroke of his sword, sliced off his head, releasing a fountain of gore and pandemonium. At this signal, the Spanish soldiers spread out around the throng and waded in swinging their swords, and for several long moments the Mexica didn't seem to understand what was happening, as the Spaniards appeared to be joining in their dance with a frenzy to match their own, albeit a killing frenzy that turned it into a dance of death.

But as the screaming began and the blood flew and men fell, the dance dissolved into a chaos of killing and outraged terror. From where I stood, or rather from where I backed away in shock and horror, it became a maelstrom of screams of pain, flashing swords, thrashing limbs, battle cries, flying spatters of blood, falling bodies and feet tripping over them, the most hideous and awful and piteous sight I had yet seen or imagined. And, in bitter irony, the litter of him who was supposedly being saved from sacrifice to the god of war was overturned, and he was slain by Spanish swords and trampling feet. Those who attempted to flee were cut to pieces by the soldiers barring the entrances, and their dying bodies kicked back into the melee.

It was no more a battle than the actions of knackers doing their bloody work in a corral of cattle, for despite Alvarado's later claims to the contrary, the victims were unarmed, the resistance all but non-existent, and the speed with which a few score armed Spaniards produced a tightly packed midden of a thousand bloodily hacked and decapitated Mexica corpses was limited only by the efficiency of their sword strokes, which, I warrant, the most experienced of butchers might admire.

The surrounding crowd in the Temple Square milled about in panicked confusion, some fleeing, some braver Mexica seeking to press forward into the forbidden Sacred Precinct, the rest trapped between these two conflicting surges. And after what could not have been a quarter of an hour of butchery, Alvarado's men, wild-eyed and covered with blood, and worked up into a terrible killing rage, turned their sanguinary attention on them.

Though Alvarado was later to claim that warriors and ordinary Mexica in the crowd had ransacked outbuildings in the Temple Square to seize weapons which had been secreted there in preparation for his general uprising, I saw no evidence of this as I retreated towards the safety of the palace of Axayacatl as fast as I could run. What I did see was Spanish soldiers pouring out of the Sacred Precinct, screaming and howling and wielding their swords against a crowd so tightly packed that flight was as impossible as resistance.

And then I was inside the palace walls, dashing across the main courtyard, inside the nearest building, and up a ladder to the rooftops, from which vantage I beheld not only the slaughter in the Temple Square but mobs of Mexica careening towards it down the streets beyond, brandishing spears, impromptu clubs, maquahuitls. Men were climbing up the lower steps of the temple seeking to escape; higher up, priests were screaming something, and atop the pyramid, drummers beat out a warlike rhythm, picked up by unseen drums in the city beyond.

Cannon fired within the palace, but these were charges of powder only, meant as warnings, for the Spaniards in the Temple Square were inextricably mingled with their victims, so that artillery could not be brought into play.

After two or three such ragged volleys, Alvarado, his helmet askew, his yellow hair reddened with the blood of a head wound, leapt up atop the low wall surrounding the Sacred Precinct, from which vantage he could see the mobs of armed and unarmed men advancing through the nearby precincts of the city towards the fray.

From my own more distant vantage, and above the screams and shouts, I could not hear what he shouted, but clearly it was the order to retreat behind the walls of the palace of Axayacatl, for his soldiers began to hack their bloody way through the populace in a purposeful direction, like machete-wielding woodsmen breaking path through the undergrowth of a jungle of living human flesh.

When all were inside, the gate was closed, arquebusiers and crossbowmen climbed to the rooftops, and began firing down into the vast mob of Mexica now surrounding what had become our besieged fortress, fruitlessly seeking to climb the walls, hurling stones, javelins, spears, howling and shrieking in furious outrage. Upon the lake, the two brigantines were burning. The city throbbed with drumming. The cannon in the courtyard roared back, blindly firing shot after shot into the midst of the besieging crowd.

A pitiless jihad had begun.

28

I F YOU HAVE EVER OBSERVED a horde of ants swarming around a sweet piece of fruit they have discovered, you will have some notion of the melee of Mexica swarming around the palace of Axayacatl in the same sort of frenzy, for we were under attack by the populace of a city as avid for vengeance and our hearts as such insects for their sugary morsel.

Townspeople roiled at the foot of the walls, undeterred by the arquebusiers and crossbowmen firing down from the roofs into their midst, fruitlessly hurling whatever came to hand up at the defenders. A mob of them violated the sanctity of their own Sacred Precinct by scrambling and shambling up the pyramid to tear down the Cross that had been erected atop the temple and fling it down the steps into the cheering and triumphantly gesticulating crowd below, scores of whom began the arduous task of picking up the doughy idol of Huitzilopochtli and restoring him to his rightful place of honor in his shrine at the pinnacle.

The cannon on the walls began firing into the rear ranks of the mob, but even the smoke and noise and carnage wreaked by the shot failed to deter the citizenry of Tenochtitlan from their wild attempts to scale the walls with makeshift ladders, wooden planks, poles set against them. But it was as impossible for the Mexica to scale the walls as it was for the Spaniards to drive them off, for no sooner did the top of a ladder or a pole gain the parapet, than Spanish soldiers flipped it and its climbers back down into the mob.

It did not go on like this for long, for the drumming throughout the city had begun by the time the gates of the palace compound had been closed behind us, and it soon gathered more organized Mexica forces in the form of warriors from all the districts of Tenochtitlan, armed with javelins, bows, maquahuitls, and the heavy spears launched by atlatls. Among them were some dozen Jaguar and Eagle warriors who had donned their regalia in order to assert their leadership.

The situation now became much more dire, and my view of it much more problematical, for the Mexica warriors below kept far enough back from the walls to assume a shallow enough angle to launch a continuous, if uncoordinated, barrage of arrows, javelins and heavy spears at the top of the walls, causing all of us there, myself emphatically included, to dive for cover behind the parapet on our bellies, from which ignominious vantage return fire continued much more blindly, and my own observation became rather occluded.

The battle raged on like this, fearsome but inconclusive, for an hour or two perhaps; I cannot be sure, dear reader, for I learned that a minute of such mortally desperate straits can seem like an hour, and an hour can contract to an infinite moment of fear.

Then the noise suddenly diminished and then died away into a low guttural muttering silence, and the rain of missiles attenuated and then ceased, and I tentatively rose to my feet to see what had happened, albeit no further than a crouch which would allow me to drop back down again at the slightest provocation.

The Emperor Montezuma had come out onto the roof and advanced to the parapet facing the temple. He wore little of his jewelry but he did wear the great green quetzal-plume headdress, so that he had been immediately recognizable even to the farthest reaches of the furious mob below.

What the crowd could not see from below was the shackles on Montezuma's feet and Pedro de Alvarado kneeling behind him with a dagger at his back.

A little later on – and yes, there was a later on, else I could not be writing this – Montezuma told me how things had come to such a pass in a tone of outrage softened into melancholy by terminal despair:

'As soon as he was back inside the palace of my father, Pedro de Alvarado burst into my apartments with his sword drawn, in a terrible rage, and with his face streaming blood from a scalp wound, so that his visage was that of a true Teule. He was accompanied by a soldier whose Nahuatl was as the grunting of a swine compared to your own, Alvaro, but good enough to make Alvarado's equally swinish meaning plain.

'"See what you and your treacherous people have done to me!" he shouted.

'"What *we* have done to *you!*" I told him, equally outraged, but even more fearful, so that even in my fury I tried to keep my voice under calmer control. "If you had not begun this slaughter, my people would not have done this. You have ruined yourself and me also."

'At this, Pedro de Alvarado's pale face turned red with anger and his lips moved without being able to form words, for even such a fool could not deny to himself the truth of this, and then, cursing most foully, he ran out again.

'Later, he returned with the blood now drying on his face, and a colder anger. Cacama and most of the other Mexica prisoners had been executed by his men. He first said that this had been an act of enraged vengeance, but then he swore it had been done as an example of what would happen to me if I now disobeyed him and my brother Cuitlahuac would join them as well if I did. I was then shackled at the ankles, and, as you saw, forced to order my people to stop the fighting with a dagger at my back.'

This the poor man then did, with his face ashen, and his lower lip trembling.

'Hear, O Mexica!' he managed to shout in a voice loud and firm enough to momentarily quell the tumult. 'The battle is a noble one, but it must be abandoned!'

At this, there were roars of disdain and disapproval, and a few stray stones and arrows were launched in his general direction. Montezuma shook his head, seemed to try to retreat, but Alvarado prodded him back with the point of his dagger, and when he spoke again, his voice might have been almost as loud, but his speech was tentative and halting as he searched for words that would make his subjects obey without at last entirely destroying his imperial authority to do that very thing.

'We cannot . . . we cannot . . . defeat the Spaniards . . . within the fortress they have made of the palace of my father . . . for . . . for they have the weapons of thunder that will only slaughter more of our number . . . and . . . and they will slay your Emperor and lay waste to the city . . . and . . . and . . .'

The cries of outrage became jeers and they became louder, and more missiles were launched towards the pathetic figure atop the parapet, though strangely enough, even those thrown from an easy distance seemed deliberately hurled to fall short as mere gestures of protest, as if the Mexica could not quite form the concept of disobeying their absolute ruler, even when they knew his words were put in his mouth by his captors, let alone seek to slay him.

'We . . . we must . . . at least pause . . . to gather up our dead and perform the proper ceremonies to placate their spirits . . . or . . . or their ghosts will chastise us for failing to soothe them with the proper rituals and sacrifices . . .'

The jeers and cries of outrage hardly diminished, though the rain of protesting missiles began to falter. Alvarado scowled and pricked him once more with his dagger.

And then Montezuma performed the most singular act of both cowardice and bravery that I have ever witnessed. Prodded by the threat to his life of the dagger at his back, the Emperor scrambled clumsily up onto the parapet and advanced to its very edge. The mob gasped and moaned as they clearly beheld his shackles, and then fell into stunned silence.

'If this battle continues, I shall leap to my death in your midst, and offer up my Emperor's heart to Huitzilopochtli in sacrifice! But this will be no honorable flowery death, for you by your disobedience shall have murdered your own Emperor, and if the Spaniards do not destroy Tenochtitlan, Huitzilopochtli in his terrible vengeance surely will!'

And thus was the fighting suspended. And thus was a battle transformed into a siege. For who among the Mexica could have then conceived of now disobeying he who had been their absolute monarch, whose person was sacred and whose will must be obeyed?

Even, for the moment, when they beheld him in chains.

This was the moment when Montezuma's authority was finally and irrevocably destroyed and the Mexica rendered leaderless, for they likewise had never conceived of a means to replace a living Emperor. But this too was the moment when the authority of the Spaniards to rule through him was therefore likewise destroyed.

No one now ruled in Mexico.

Save the war god Huitzilopochtli now restored to the bloody pinnacle of his temple.

Inside the palace of Axayacatl, the mood in the next days was angry, contentious, frustrated, and above all fearful. We could do nothing but wait and hope and pray to God for a miracle, or to Hernando Cortes for something all too similar – a defeat of the forces of Panfilo de Narvaez against seemingly impossible odds, followed by the conversion of his troops to our cause, and an heroic ride by a heavily reinforced Spanish army to our rescue.

We had few means to discern what was transpiring in the hostile city around us.

The Mexica stripped the corpses in the square of their clothing, piled them up in an enormous heap upon a pyre at the foot of the temple, and there they sat for four days, picked at by carrion birds and rats, swarmed over by great clouds of flies, and wafting a terrible rotting stench in our direction.

Thousands of warriors patrolled the area surrounding our fortress, shouting imprecations, offering us recipes for the preparation of our own flesh, and firing occasional volleys of spears and arrows over the parapets, to which Alvarado ordered that no response be made, in order to conserve our ammunition for the day when the assault must come or impending starvation forced us to sally forth.

By day, we could see squads of papas coming and going up and down the pyramid and resuming full control of the Sacred Precinct, while the re-ignited eternal flame of Huitzilopochtli atop it sent its plume of black smoke skyward, mirrored by scores of similar pillars of smoke arising throughout the far-flung quarters of the city. Drums boomed dolefully. The sounds of thousands of lamenting voices arose like the howlings of distant wolfpacks.

By night, it was worse. The drumming continued. The lamentations seemed louder. The darkness of the city was punctuated by numerous smoldering orange bonfires, transforming it into the landscape of Hell in the fearful mind's eye, aided in no little measure by the demonic pantomime put on by firelight outside the walls for our ghoulish entertainment.

Human heads, whitened, hideously painted, and yellowly bewigged with straw to emulate Spaniards, danced atop poles. Headless bodies, likewise done up as Spaniards, writhed and groaned. Monsters with the faces of jaguars, serpents, eagles, and things that hopefully never were, pranced and capered.

On the fourth day, the papas staged an elaborately horrible ceremony. We were forced to helplessly watch as some hundreds of men, their faces whitened and bearded with straw, were led to the altar atop the temple. When this mass ascension had been completed, the pile of rotten corpses was set ablaze, sending a huge greasy black pall of smoke hovering heavily over the Temple Square, and replacing the rotten stink of decaying flesh with the far worse tantalizing aroma of roasting meat.

And then the shrieks of pain began. One after another, at regular intervals no more than a minute or two apart. And one after another, following the same rhythm, bodies with bright red blood still gushing from gaping holes in their chests came tumbling down the temple steps. When they reached the bottom, they were dragged away to an impromptu butchery, where their arms and legs were hacked off with obsidian axes and neatly piled up.

By the time this mass sacrifice of pantomime Spaniards had been completed, Huitzilopochtli's temple was emblazoned from behind by the bloody light of early sunset, the pyre had burned down to a great heap of redly glowing charcoal embers, and the air was laden with an overpowering aroma of well-crisped meat fit to set any cannibal's appetite to salivating. And upon this well-made barbecue, hundreds of Mexica roasted the arms and legs of their victims and proceeded to dine upon them, chewing heartily with exaggerated smacking of their lips, gnawing the last morsels of flesh from the bones, then tossing them on piles which rose like little models of the great pyramid behind them.

I will not dwell on that night's nightmares, nor linger long on the next two days' debates, as those terrified into demanding that we now sally forth and die quickly and cleanly with honor contended with those too fearful to contemplate such a doomed final battle.

Suffice it to say that the will to attack was lacking, and perhaps too all hope had not entirely been lost. For we had had no word of the outcome of Cortes' confrontation with Narvaez. And even if Narvaez had prevailed, as seemed all too likely, surely he would then march on Tenochtitlan with his greater force to claim the prize he had come to secure for himself and Diego Velazquez, and therefore, however inadvertently, march to our rescue.

Such was the dream that restrained our courage and sustained our last dying hopes, a dream so desperate and hopes so wan that when word swept the palace that a lookout had spied morning sunlight flashing on metal on the Tacuba causeway, no one dared believe it as we rushed as a man to the rooftops to peer westward.

At first, all we could see was flashes of light from the morning sun on the western causeway. But a minute or two's observation then told us that they were moving up it towards us, and we held our breath. Soon we could discern that there was a very long train of figures stretched out along the length of the causeway, and the murmuring started.

Then we saw that the flashes were bobbing up and down in the manner of armored men riding horses, and the cheering began. Yes, there were armored horsemen! And there seemed to be perhaps as many as a hundred of them! And behind them marched soldiers in gleaming armor! Scores! No, hundreds! A thousand! And behind *them*, thousands of warriors in the colors and feathers of Tlascala.

A great cry of joy and deliverance went up. The rescuing army cleared the causeway and advanced into the city towards us with score upon score of arquebusiers firing volley after volley of blank charges, so that it proceeded towards us with a continuous salute of gunfire and amidst an incense of acrid smoke, scattering whatever Mexica were abroad before them in terror. Never, I warrant, was such music so thrilling to the ear or such perfume so sweet to the nostrils.

Before the martial parade could reach the Temple Square, it had quite emptied out, but so too had our cheering died away into tense anticipation, for surely this mighty relieving army must be under the command of Panfilo de Narvaez, and who was to say what the man who had condemned us as a force of brigands and traitors would make of the remnants of the army of his fallen enemy?

And then—

And then we beheld the head of the parade entering the Temple Square, and a roaring cheer went up such as must have shaken the hearts of all Tenochtitlan as it raised up ours, and tears came into the eyes of grizzled and desperate soldiers, nor could I fail to cry with them.

For there, at the head of the Spanish army, with his standard flying beside him, upon a prancing stallion, visage grim and stern, but eyes gleaming as brightly as his well-polished helm and armor, rode the Captain-General of New Spain, Hernando Cortes.

'How in the name of everything holy, and any number of things that are not, did you do it, Hernando?' were the first words I spoke to Cortes upon his return.

'In the name of the Father, the Son, and the Holy Spirit, as well as Saint James, the Virgin, and Lucifer himself, how could I have been so stupid as to leave Pedro de Alvarado in command here?' were the first words he spoke to me. 'And what am I to do now?'

This was late that night as I was about to retire, and after a long day of triumphal celebration during which he was constrained to smile and backslap and play the confident conquering hero, followed by what had apparently been a dressing-down of Alvarado, and a full briefing on the still perilous situation. Cortes had appeared in my quarters looking haggard, furious, and more openly desperate than I had ever seen him.

He was also lugging two clay cups and a formidable jug of pulque, and by the way he poured a cupful for himself, bolted it down, bade me do likewise, and repeated the process before continuing the conversation, I had the impression that he intended us to drain it. This was quite alarming, for Hernando Cortes was no drunkard, and I had never seen him resort to fortifying his spirit thusly.

'I tell you, Alvaro, that the fool has turned conquest into catastrophe, and my victory over Narvaez into ashes, and any advice from the one man here I can admit this to would be desperately welcome,' he admitted when this had been accomplished.

'About the only advice I can give you, bleak though it is,' I told him, 'is quit Tenochtitlan, or at least try to, as quickly as possible, preferably tonight. At least the reinforcements will give us a fighting chance to escape.'

'Escape!' Cortes fairly roared. 'I seek advice as to how to pacify Tenochtitlan, not escape it! I now command over a thousand Spaniards, nearly a hundred cavalry, and thousands of Tlascalans. Surely that is enough to put down this petty disorganized rebellion!'

'Surely not,' I told him gloomily. 'I don't know what Alvarado has told you, but I fear he has gilded the black lily to escape your wrath.'

'I assure you that my wrath was not escaped!' Cortes snarled.

'Your *full* wrath, then. For I doubt even the brave Alvarado was foolhardy enough to tell you the worst of it.'

'Tell me, then,' Cortes muttered disconsolately.

I fortified myself with another cup of pulque and I did. And as I did, Cortes' visage turned red with fury and pale with despair alternately. 'So you see,' I concluded, 'Montezuma's authority is now so completely eroded that you can accomplish nothing by putting words in his mouth, the Mexica nobility has been decimated, they have no effective leader, and what you are faced with is the entire enraged populace of a city of some hundreds of thousands howling for Spanish hearts for their altars and Spanish flesh for their cannibalistic feasts.'

'I will not surrender all I have won and slink out of Tenochtitlan with my tail between my legs like a whipped dog in the night!' Cortes insisted.

'But Tenochtitlan is *not* all you have won, Hernando,' I told him, beginning to formulate a strategy to persuade him to do just that, for to be frank, dear reader, saving my own life was my chief, if not only, goal at the time.

'Is it not?' said Cortes.

'Tell me now how you managed to make your way to Cempoala, overcome Narvaez's superior force, win over his troops, and return here with them.'

'I hardly think this is the moment for vain boasting!'

'I have a more pragmatic reason, I assure you,' I told him.

'Tell me what it is, then.'

'Tell me at least of your journey to the scene of your triumph, and I will.'

Cortes sighed, shrugged, poured himself more pulque, and sipped at it as he did.

'We crossed the Iztapalapa causeway, traversed the valley, and crossed the mountains without incident, for the Mexica and the Texcocans seemed to be keeping their distance. It was much the same as we reached Cholula, which was still in Spanish hands – our own, not those of Narvaez. There I was greatly buoyed to find that one of the exploratory expeditions I had sent out before the advent of Narvaez had arrived. Thus reinforced, we proceeded to Tlascala, again without incident, where Xicotencatl the Elder received us cordially enough. When I requested his aid, he even dispatched six hundred warriors to march with us.'

Cortes frowned. 'Though as we left Tlascala and entered the territory of the Totonacs, they began to desert in dribs and drabs, and, no longer trusting in their usefulness or loyalty, I dismissed the rest of them.' He peered at me owlishly. 'Why am I telling you this now, Alvaro? Of what relevance is all this to our present dilemma?'

'Quite a bit, I am beginning to be heartened to believe,' I told him.

'You are?' said Cortes, and a faint glimmer began to kindle in his eyes.

I nodded. 'Do continue.'

Cortes shrugged, cocked his head at me in somewhat irate impatience, but he did.

'As we approached Cempoala, I was met by Sandoval with some

sixty men, including a number of deserters from Narvaez's army, which was indeed heartening,' Cortes recalled, and as he did, the memory seemed to likewise hearten him, and he began to lose himself a bit in the enthusiasm of the telling of his tale of military triumph.

'Sandoval was also full of useful and far from disheartening intelligence, having been in contact with Tlacochcalcat and others in Cempoala. Narvaez's army was ensconced in the city, and Narvaez and his chief lieutenants in the lap of luxury therein. His soldiers had less love for him than for the gold Olmedo had distributed among them and were not at all eager for battle with fellow Spaniards.'

'And the fat cacique himself?'

Cortes grimaced. 'Everyone's host and no one's ally or enemy as long as he could avoid it.'

'Excellent!'

'*Excellent?*'

I nodded, and now Cortes, warmed to the happy task of telling the sort of boastful tale of victory dear to any general's heart, needed no further prodding to continue.

'Some fifteen miles or so from Cempoala, we were met by an embassy from Narvaez, led once more by Guevara. He relayed Narvaez's usual demand for me to surrender to his authority, but now there was no talk of arrest or treason, rather a magnanimous offer to transport me and my men, along with what treasure we had thus far accumulated, to whatever destination we might choose. And then it was that I began to formulate my battle plan, for in truth, before then, I had had none.'

Now Cortes grinned wolfishly, and quite forgot his current predicament and his impatient curiosity at my reason for this interrogation, and became quite happily and enthusiastically lost in his tale of glory, living it once more in the memory thereof.

'This display of faintheartedness on the part of Narvaez encouraged me to believe that he had no stomach for battle, or he believed that his men didn't, or both. Moreover their sprawling deployment within a city seemed slovenly defensive tactics. And so I decided on a decapitation attack, a stealthy infiltration of Cempoala at night, aimed at the capture or killing of Narvaez and his lieutenants as they lay sleeping in their quarters, hopefully after a heavy meal washed down with a liberal amount of pulque.'

Now Cortes actually summoned up the spirit to laugh. 'And so I sent Guevara back with a conciliatory missive of my own,' he told me. 'I proposed that we parley at some neutral site in two days' time. If he produced a royal commission, I would submit to his authority and accept his generous offer. If not, perhaps we might come to some mutually advantageous agreement, for as he must surely know by now, there was more than enough gold to be had here to make us both richer than Croesus and certainly richer than the governor of Cuba.'

'You lied, I presume?'

Cortes gave me a look that said, *Does the tongue of a serpent fork at its tip?*

'As soon as Guevara's embassy was out of sight, I made for Cempoala, for I intended to attack that very night. I disposed of fewer than three hundred men to Narvaez's thousand and more, but his cavalry was outside the city guarding the obvious approach roads, and from what I had heard, his forces within were not on alert, and my little . . . falsehood should make them all the less so.

'We approached the city at dusk, not by road, but by the most arduous route, which required the fording of a river a mile or two from the city, and as I had hoped, the slovenly fool had left it unguarded. I broke our forces into three parts. Sandoval, with sixty men, was charged with making straight for Narvaez's lair and capturing or killing him and his lieutenants as the situation warranted. The bulk of the remaining force was to cover Sandoval's thrust and mount a diversionary attack on the artillery, which could hardly be brought in to play against them within the cramped confines of a city. I myself took only twenty men, to act as opportunity presented.

'We forded the river without being spotted, and likewise entered the city. Narvaez had had the effrontery to quarter himself in the shrine atop the main temple pyramid, guarded by arquebusiers and crossbowmen. There were two secondary temples in the area garrisoned by infantry, and he had stupidly stationed his cannon in the square between them, defended by horsemen, where they were indeed secure from a frontal attack on the city, but in the present circumstances, worse than useless.

'As we approached the temple square down an avenue leading into it, the alarm was finally sounded. Narvaez's cavalrymen mounted, his artillerymen staggered to their cannon, and managed to fire a ragged volley in our general direction, but since we were running down the avenue and pressed close to the walls of the buildings, it was entirely ineffective, and before they could reload, for whatever good it might have done them, we were upon them.

'It was thus easy enough for my main force to overcome the cannoneers in a twinkling and gain possession of their cannon, while my own force and some of the others dealt handily enough with the horsemen, who were hopelessly outnumbered.

'Sandoval, meanwhile, led his men straight for the temple, and scrambled up the steps under a hail of crossbow bolts and arquebus balls, but what with the darkness, and the steep downward angle, and the confusion of the marksmen, this did little damage and was little hindrance.

'According to Sandoval, however, when they reached the top it was another matter. To his credit, Narvaez himself led his men out of the shrine onto the platform, and in the fierce hand-to-hand fighting he was wounded several times, but continued to fight until his left eye was pierced by a sword or spear, and he fell screaming that he had been slain. This, alas, proved to be not quite the case, and his men retreated into the shrine, dragging Narvaez with them, from which cover they proved most difficult to dislodge.

'One of Sandoval's men finally set fire to the thatched roof, and that drove them out, and they were moreover constrained to flee the flames and smoke a few at a time, so that the first few were slain, and Narvaez was captured, and that was the end of their resistance.

'Meanwhile, having seized the cannon, and seeing that Narvaez and his men atop the main temple had either been killed or captured, I turned my attention to the infantry atop the two secondary pyramids.

'Seeking to save their lives for my own future uses, I brought the cannon to bear on them and shouted out the tidings of the situation, followed at once by a magnanimous offer of friendship, enlistment in my victorious army, and liberal sharing in the bounteous golden fruits of my conquests, past, present and future.

'When this was not immediately answered, I had the cannon fire a single volley at each of the pyramids, taking care that the balls impacted well below the pinnacle platforms where they huddled. This provided sufficient enlightenment for reason, cowardice and cupidity to prevail, and they surrendered.'

By this time, Cortes' eyes were fairly glowing, he was waving his arms, and he gulped down a cup of celebratory pulque to calm himself. 'A brilliant victory if I do say so myself!' he crowed. 'And all the more so because only half a dozen of my men were slain and not much more than twice as many of the former enemy, so that the rest were most grateful for their lives and my promised munificence, and the cavalry afield then readily joined this united Spanish army which today rode to the rescue of this hideous catastrophe in Tenochtitlan.'

Now, having concluded his stirring tale, Cortes frowned at me in impatient consternation. 'Now that you know it all,' he demanded, 'perhaps you will—'

'But I do not know it all, Hernando! What of the march from Cempoala to here?'

'What of it?' demanded Cortes. 'Aside from the expected privations of the mountain crossing, it was strangely uneventful, and there is little to tell of it.'

'Then tell me the little, tell me of the uneventfulness, for I do believe it may be the key to everything.'

'Nothing is the key to everything?'

'I hope so,' I told him, pouring us both more pulque. 'Humor me for one more small tale and one more large cup, and then I shall be entirely forthcoming.'

Cortes drank, and shrugged, and then went on in a flat tone of voice entirely at variance with his previously martial animation.

'We dressed our wounds at Cempoala, were well provisioned by Tlacochcalcat, ever one to follow in whatever direction the victor's wind blew. We proceeded to Tlascala, where we were received as victorious allies, and garnered some two thousand warriors eager to have at the Mexica with such a greatly reinforced Spanish army. We crossed the mountain passes into Anahuac and marched unmolested to Tacuba, and there you have it.'

'*Unmolested?*' I said sharply. 'And how were you welcomed?'

Now Cortes frowned. 'Strangely. That no one would challenge or harry such a force was only natural, but we were hardly welcomed either. When I demanded provisions, they were supplied, neither grudgingly nor with any show of hospitality or celebration. Otherwise, we were carefully avoided. Except, that is, for the advice of the Tacubans, who saw fit to warn us that Tenochtitlan had descended into murderous madness, and if we valued our lives, we would proceed no further.'

He put down his cup and placed his hands on his hips in an expectant gesture. 'Well, now?' he demanded quite crossly.

Now I had been provided with the ammunition that I hoped would suffice to win him, against all his brave martial inclinations, to the only possible course I could see.

'Now I know enough to venture to speak my mind,' I told him, 'though I fear your enthusiasm for my advice will be muted. I pray you at least hear me out before you express your ire.'

'Speak your mind at last, Alvaro,' Cortes told me. 'I am not so dense as to refuse to listen to advice other than the fawning and apologias and bluster I have been subject to today, else why would I be here demanding it?'

And so I did.

'I pray you to heed your head and myself now, rather than your otherwise admirable lion's heart. The tale you have told me confirms what we both already knew. Before the advent of Narvaez, you had already broken the fear with which the hated Mexica ruled their subject tribes, whose loyalty had never been based on anything else, save the self-interest of their allies in the Triple Alliance, the Texcocans and the Tacubans. But once you arrested Cacama and installed your puppet there, the Texcocans could no longer fancy themselves anything but vassals of the Mexica, and through Montezuma of you and Spain. And now, the Tacubans, having seen this, likewise no longer harbor any illusions that the Triple Alliance still exists, or any loyalty to Tenochtitlan.'

'So?' said Cortes, eyeing me intently.

'So the Empire of the Mexica had become New Spain before

Narvaez arrived, and your lighter hand was much preferred to Montezuma's. No one could have believed that Narvaez intended to restore the rule of Tenochtitlan by "rescuing" him from you rather than replacing you as his puppeteer. Therefore none of the tribes here had the slightest self-interest in the outcome of your conflict with Narvaez. Which is why they stayed clear of your march to Vera Cruz, and why Tlacochcalcat played host to Narvaez until you had defeated him, and then became your loyal vassal once more. Likewise, when you marched back to Tenochtitlan with your enlarged army, none of the tribes between sought to impede you, neither did they wish to do anything that might paint themselves as your allies.'

'All this is true,' muttered Cortes, 'but all of it is obvious.'

'Nevertheless, Hernando, you seem to have avoided the obvious conclusion.'

'*Which is?*'

'Which is that just as none of them had the slightest self-interest in the outcome of the war between you and Narvaez, none of them save the Tlascalans have much self-interest in the outcome of this war between us and the Mexica of Tenochtitlan. Oh, no doubt some might prefer to be subjects of the distant King Charles and Malinche, but not enough to fight for the privilege, and others might prefer the rule of brother Indians to that of European Teules, but certainly not enough to fight your greatly reinforced army in the service of restoring an imperial rule which would resume feeding the hearts of the flower of their youth to Huitzilopochtli!'

'Mmmm . . .' muttered Cortes, at last grown thoughtful. 'But where does all this lead, Alvaro?'

'For the love of God, New Spain, the Cross, the King, and our own hides, *out of here*!' I declared with all the force I could muster. 'Tonight! While the shock of your new army's arrival just might make it possible! We are trapped in a fortress inside a city in the middle of a lake with the only links to the mainland being four long narrow causeways, outnumbered by hundreds of thousands of Mexica—'

'I hardly need you to remind me of this!' Cortes snapped sourly.

'But imagine the reverse!' I told him. 'If your army were on the mainland lakeshore, none would dare confront you or wish to, and the remaining enemy *would be trapped in Tenochtitlan themselves*! It would be child's play to hold the landward entrances to the causeways. Hundreds of thousands would be sealed in the city without means of resupply. How could such a siege fail? It could only end in the final surrender of the Mexica or their death by thirst or starvation.'

'By Saint James and the Cross, you are right!' Cortes exclaimed. But then he frowned, and moaned, and shook his head. 'I only wish I could do it,' he muttered disconsolately.

'It will be difficult, but I have faith that you can,' I lied, or at least exaggerated, in desperation. 'The Mexica are cowed for the moment by your army's arrival, they are presently uncoordinated and leaderless. If the cavalry led the way to the Tacuba causeway, and if Montezuma was seen to be our hostage, and if it was done under the cover of night, and—'

'That is not the problem,' declared Cortes.

'Then what in the name of Heaven is?' I demanded.

'The army I have so recently overcome and incorporated into my own was promised conquest and riches, I have led them here to rescue my own men from what they conceive of as primitive savages and to retake the Mexica capital,' Cortes said. 'Do you really imagine they will then loyally obey the order of their new commander to immediately turn tail and flee Tenochtitlan through what will no doubt be a hail of arrows, stones and spears, without so much as putting up a fight to retain the glittering prize they presently believe they have captured?'

My stomach sank. My heart skipped a beat. 'But it is that or we all die,' were the only words I could find to utter.

'I fear you may be entirely right,' Cortes told me grimly. 'But you are no general. Those who have already experienced the horrors the Mexica have inflicted here might just be willing to follow your advice. But those of our old comrades fresh from a glorious victory against seemingly impossible odds are presently in no mood to accept such cowardice, and as for Narvaez's former troops, now the greatest part of the forces needed to accomplish such a fighting retreat, never. Never . . .'

And then a cold gleam came into the eyes of Hernando Cortes, such that I half-expected a forked tongue to emerge from his expressionless lips at any moment, the whole a sight almost as terrifying as our predicament.

'Perhaps not . . . never . . .' said Cortes. 'But not before they have quite convinced themselves that it is indeed that or die and be eaten.'

'And how do you propose to accomplish that?'

Was it a trick of the mind's eye or the soul's deeper vision?

'That is not my task,' said Cortes. 'That is the task of the Mexica.'

For a moment I saw his face transformed into the quetzal-feather-crowned serpent's mask of Quetzalcoatl.

'And from what you have seen,' he said, 'they are quite accomplished at it.'

29

I NOW KNEW THAT CORTES' plan was to attempt to escape the city, since the plan was my own, but how he was going to convince his army that escape was the only possible alternative was another matter. All he would tell me was 'there can be such a thing as strategic failure,' a dishonorable and cynical strategy he proceeded to implement to my growing comprehension, horror, and self-disgust for inadvertently calling it into being.

He ordered Montezuma to open the Tlatelolco market, presently closed by its overseer, his cousin Cuatemoc, to the Spaniards. When Montezuma told him that he must send a high-ranking emissary into the chaotic city to accomplish this, if it could be accomplished at all, and suggested his own brother, Cuitlahuac, presently and conveniently held prisoner in our fortress, Cortes acceded, which seemed self-defeating, for the cacique of Iztapalapa had long made no secret of his hostility to the Spaniards.

Cortes deflected the protests at this bizarre choice of envoys by declaring that Cuitlahuac would hardly be likely to do anything to endanger his brother's life, and as the brother of the still formally sitting Emperor, would be the man with the most authority to convince Cuatemoc that the order came directly from him, and therefore the one most likely to succeed in accomplishing this admittedly problematic mission.

Unsurprisingly, Cuitlahuac never returned or sent back word, nor was the market opened to us.

The same day Cuitlahuac set out, Cortes also dispatched a messenger to Vera Cruz, ostensibly to inform Sandoval of his safe arrival at Tenochtitlan, but, I suspected after he returned bloody and beaten within twenty minutes, only so that he could fail, barely escaping with his life and the dire tidings that the shortest avenue to a causeway, the one to Tacuba, was blocked by irate and armed Mexica.

Cortes then sent out a force of some three hundred soldiers, among them a few arquebusiers and many crossbowmen, under the command of Diego de Ordaz and Juan Gonzalez Ponce de Leon, to clear the avenue and teach the Mexica a stern martial lesson.

A lesson was indeed taught, but it was not the Mexica who learned it. Half an hour later, the Spaniards came fleeing back at a dead run, with a howling horde of Mexica warriors and townspeople after them, hurling stones, throwing spears and firing arrows. As Ordaz reported the moment he was inside the fortress, the flat rooftops of the buildings flanking the avenue had swarmed with Mexica who rained down stones and heavy rocks which had been piled up there for the purpose.

Half a dozen of this sally were killed, and by the time the last of them were inside and the gates shut fast behind them, the pursuing Mexica had surrounded the palace of Axayacatl and began a massive if disorganized assault on its walls.

There were thousands of them, enough to fill most of the Temple Square in front of the palace. The stones thrown over the walls and against them, and the volleys of arrows and javelins, did little more than keep the defenders hunkered down behind the parapets, with the aim of the crossbowmen and arquebusiers thus hindered from any hope of driving the attackers away from the walls. The cannon could only fire on high arcs, the balls falling in the rear of the mob, slaying many potential reinforcements, but just as ineffective at clearing the Mexica away from the foot of the walls.

Then the Mexica brought up logs and torches and obsidian axes.

Most of the logs were piled against a section of the wall and set ablaze. Teams of Mexica took to hammering against the wall through the flames with the longest and stoutest of them, soon to be joined by hundreds more madly hacking away with axes, knives, stones, even fists and nails, and the situation became most dire.

The fire weakened the adobe holding the stone blocks of the wall together, and slowly but inexorably, the Mexica rammed a breach through it. First a single block fell inward, then another, and a third, and then the Mexica were within the breach, ripping, hammering, and tugging it larger.

Many swordsmen were wounded holding them back until Cortes could bring up arquebusiers and crossbowmen. These were then positioned in four solid ranks before the opening, so that at any given moment one rank was firing while the others were reloading, and the way inside was blocked by a continuous and massive fusillade of shot and bolts fired directly into Mexica flesh at point-blank range.

The carnage was terrible. Wave after wave of the attackers went down, and those waiting behind trod upon their bodies to be dealt with likewise, until the breach was so clogged with the dead and the dying that they must drag their fallen comrades aside in order to face their own certain deaths.

It lasted until sundown, when there were too many dead to be cleared away in order to continue, and more added every moment, so that the breach was closed from top to bottom with a barricade of corpses several ranks deep, and the Mexica, perhaps also overcome by their habitual distaste for night fighting, at last gave it up and retreated.

Cortes' full army was now thoroughly battle-blooded. Some eighty men, including a score of those who had been brought to these shores by Narvaez, were wounded, though not all that many severely, and even Cortes himself had an arrow wound to display.

As the wounded were cared for, and the breach in the wall frantically mended, and the beating of hundreds of drums and the shouts of war-cries and howled curses from tens of thousands of the enemy investing the buildings surrounding our redoubt peopled the night with unseen demons, none could doubt that they were no longer in a battle for gold and conquest. Each man must now know that the stake was his own life.

Though the Mexica never again attempted to break through the walls, the fighting went on for days, and fell into a regular pattern. Cortes himself had small breaches knocked through the walls through which the cannon could fire, keeping the Mexica at bay. Outside the walls, the Mexica swarmed in the Temple Square in their tens of thousands, the inchoate mob shouting and screaming but more or less keeping their distance, while every hour or so organized formations of warriors, clearly under some manner of coherent command to judge by the Jaguar and Eagle warriors to be seen scattered among them, launched purposeful if futile assaults.

Several hundred archers would be stationed at the rear, and before them a somewhat smaller number of warriors armed with heavy spears and the atlatl spear-throwers with which to increase their force and range. The front ranks consisted of warriors armed with maquahuitls, many of them carrying crude scaling ladders.

At a shouted command, the whole mass would dash forward, with the archers and spear-throwers launching fusillades on the run in an attempt to force the arquebusiers and crossbowmen atop the walls to hunker down behind the parapets. This was usually successful, but the cannon always took a fearful toll of the charge before the front lines reached the wall. Those who survived to attain the wall, where the cannon could no longer hit them, flung their ladders against it, and attempted to climb to the parapet. Mostly, the Spaniards atop the wall were able to throw down the ladders before any Mexica warriors could reach them, and when they did, it was Toledo steel versus obsidian maquahuitl blades, to the latter's great disadvantage.

When the attempt to scale the wall failed, and it always did, the Mexica, at another shouted command, would pull back, brandish their maquahuitls and shields, and shout imprecations in Nahuatl, which, though the words could not be understood by their enemy, were clearly accusations of cowardice and challenges to come out and fight fairly and nobly like true warriors.

The Spaniards would reply with arquebuses, crossbows and cannon, the Mexica would retreat back out of range of all but the latter, regroup, rearm, and resume the futile carnage somewhat later. Though the cost to them in lives was huge, it bought a continual decline in our store of shot and powder.

Realizing that once this was exhausted we would lose our most vital advantage and be overwhelmed sooner or later, a situation not at all lost on his grumbling troops, Cortes organized several attempts to pass to the attack and seize the initiative, supposedly to shore up their waning morale.

The Mexica were unaccustomed to fighting in the hours of darkness, perhaps believing that the night was peopled with demons, perhaps because their mode of battle was between massed and lavishly accoutered armies coming together honorably on a well-chosen open field under full light of day, and, I suspect, probably both.

Cortes sought to take advantage of this by sending forth attacks an hour or so before sunrise. Under cover of darkness, he would open the main gate, roll out cannon, and position them in a line well in front of the palace. Several cannonades would be fired to clear the Temple Square of any Mexica brave enough to congregate there during the night, and then a contingent of cavalry would ride out, followed by infantry. The size and composition of these assault forces varied, but the results, alas, were always more or less the same.

The Spaniards would attempt to capture buildings in the streets around the palace and the Temple Square, most often along the avenue leading to the Tacuba causeway, for by now, I warrant, Cortes already had in mind clearing this shortest of the escape routes, and if nothing else, these sallies served the purpose of performing fighting reconnaissance thereof.

The cavalry rode down the street, clearing away any Mexica who emerged blearily from the houses to oppose the foray, while the infantry stormed into the houses, slaying anyone inside, and attaining the rooftops. There they would quickly throw whatever stones and rocks were piled up there down into the street, and if they had time, make a half-hearted attempt to set fire to the stone or adobe building.

They had to work fast, for as soon as the sun was up, Mexica warriors in great force would pour down the avenue and cross-streets, and they would be forced to retreat behind a shield of cavalry, taking many wounds, and some few fatalities from stones and arrows and atlatl-launched spears in the process.

Where was I during these days of battle, need you ask, dear reader? Up on the battlements with sword or arquebus? Sallying forth with the brave soldiers? Supplying Cortes with more of the sage advice that had led him to send his own men into futile battle for no other reason than to convince them of its futility?

Hardly. Call me a coward, call me wise, call me the only one among us who realized that risking his life would only be in the cause of failure, but say also that I survived to tell the tale of this shameful and pointless carnage. I stayed in the central courtyard or within the palace apartments, as far away from the fray as possible, pathetically salving my smarting conscience by tending to the wounded, passing ammunition to the cannon, and staying as far away from Cortes as possible.

There being no need of translation between Spanish and Nahuatl of this martial discourse, Marina might spend what hours of sleep or dalliance might be cadged during the fearful nights with him, but otherwise also steered clear of Cortes, who, still following his perfidious secret strategy, nevertheless seemed to take demonic pleasure in the clash of arms itself, like all too many of his officers.

We could therefore have passed what idle waking hours we had in each other's company, but on those few occasions when our paths crossed and our eyes met, what I saw in hers, aside from the universal fear, was a cold and hardening determination to cleave to her Malinche and her identity as 'Doña Marina', despite her part in bringing such death and destruction to what in some small corner of her heart she must surely still regard as her people. Was there contempt in those eyes for a man who had loyalty to no one and nothing, or did my own eyes betray my deeper and darker guilt if not its source?

Nor did I converse with Montezuma, for never during this time was I summoned. Indeed, I surmised that the fallen and broken Emperor might be the only man in the palace who shared my numbness of spirit, trapped in the terrible battle, but unwilling to be of it.

By now, the majority of the Spanish troops were all in favor of escaping from Tenochtitlan, if only they knew how, and Cortes would seem to have achieved his secret objective, for the petitions to do so were becoming ever more frequent and rebellious. But by now, things had gotten out of hand to the point where success in fighting our way out had become a dubious proposition, and became more so day by day.

Cortes took to protesting against the popular demands to take the very action whose acceptance he had schemed to foment, but I do suspect that this time, aflame with the heat of battle, his declarations of his determination to fight on in the city until the rebellion was crushed were becoming madly and dangerously sincere, else the attempt to retreat would have been essayed long since.

I suspect that Cortes at this point was genuinely of two minds, for out of the dialectic between somehow winning the unwinnable battle and giving escape the maximum chance emerged an 'invention' of his designed to achieve either.

This he dubbed the 'manta', after the medieval siege towers called 'mantelets', a war machine dating back at least to Roman times, but adapted to the present circumstances. This was a much smaller two-tier version enclosed and roofed over by planking nailed to a light framework, and sheltering some score or so arquebusiers who could fire through loopholes in the cladding. It was set on rude axles and wheels appropriated from gun carriages, and would be pulled by a team of Tlascalans harnessed like dray horses, for there were many more of them than the real thing, and much more expendable.

Two of the things were built, but before they could be tried out, events intervened which changed everything.

The daily Mexica assaults seemed to have been rather impromptu affairs organized and directed by Eagle and Jaguar warriors, but the Mexica as a whole had seemed leaderless. But the morning after the construction of the mantas had been completed, a much more coordinated series of attacks was launched against all four sides of the palace at once, and these seemed to be commanded by some dozen or so grandees stationed well in the rear and well guarded by scores of warriors in the pelts and feathers of the Jaguar and Eagle.

Standards were erected beside them and a large embroidered cotton canopy over them. They wore lavishly embellished cloaks and feathered headdresses. Faces could not be made out at this distance, but one of them had presumed to don a headdress with a tail as long as a cloak made of the brilliantly iridescent quetzal feathers, like unto the imperial accouterment of state of the Mexica emperors.

This apparition both alarmed Cortes and presented an opportunity that brought him to his previously devious senses. The plan had been to bring Montezuma along as a hostage, or at least the conversation during which it had been hatched had led me to believe so. But now it seemed that the Mexica had either a new Emperor, or a pretender to the throne, or at the very least an overall war leader. It therefore occurred to Cortes that confronting whoever it was with Montezuma himself might accomplish one or more of several possible objectives.

First it would prove to all of Tenochtitlan that Montezuma was still alive. At the very least, this might split the loyalties of the Mexica and raise dissension in their camp. Better still, upon seeing this the man appropriating the imperial finery might submit to the rightful Emperor's authority. In which case, Montezuma might then be able to successfully order a truce, under cover of which we could retreat from the city. Or, I suppose, in the most extravagant of impossible fantasies, effect a Mexica surrender.

In the years since, there have been many different versions of what really happened, most of them, I warrant, self-serving versions put forth by both Spanish and Mexica chroniclers for their own purposes, and I was in the courtyard when it happened and so was not there to witness it, so I will give you Montezuma's own version, related to me on his deathbed some three days afterward, when he, at least, had no further self-interest to serve and knew it.

'Malinche demanded to know who these men were and who their paramount cacique who had donned the imperial mantle might be. I truthfully told him that they must be the highest leaders of my people he had not yet slain, but had no idea who he who wore the imperial quetzal feathers might be, though both of us must have surmised that if he lived, it must be my brother Cuitlahuac.

'Cortes then demanded that I go to the top of the walls and try to speak to him, order him to lay down arms and honor my oath of allegiance to the Spanish Crown, or failing that, at least allow the Teules to depart Tenochtitlan unmolested.

'I refused at first, telling Malinche that he had brought this disaster on himself and on me, I had no further desire to either serve him or live, and in any case, the only order from me that would be obeyed would be one to fight to the death of the last warrior.

'At this, Malinche flew into a fury. "If you do not do as I say, I swear by Saint James and the Cross that I will likewise fight on to the last Spaniard, and rather than fight to retreat, we will fight to kill as many of the inhabitants of the city as we can before that last Spaniard is slain, sparing not even women and children. We will set fire to all that will burn, tear down what will not stone by stone, poison the wells, and do to Tenochtitlan what Rome did to Carthage, so that no one will live there for a thousand years, and the names of those who did will be forgotten."'

This Montezuma told me as he lay dying of his wounds, his eyes rheumy and half-closed, his lips trembling and drooling spittle, and his breath shallow and labored, but then what remained of his spirit's will summoned up the last of his strength, and he spoke to me like a man who was indeed an Emperor, and, I dare to fancy, to the closest thing he had to a friend in his fallen days of captivity.

'I had thought I had nothing left in this world to fear, for everything I feared had already come to pass, Avram ibn Ezra,' he told me, 'and please allow me to utter your true name this one last time, for we both know I will not live to reveal it to another. I wish to do this because Malinche's terrible threats aroused in me the vision I have related to you and no other, Avram ibn Ezra, so that at least one man will understand why I submitted one last time to the will of Malinche. For I saw once more the temple of Huitzilopochtli thrown down and replaced by the monstrous gray stone building with the two Cross-topped towers, and I heard the deep and somber ringing of their awful demon's bells, and I beheld my fallen people skulking about the precincts of a city that was no longer Tenochtitlan, no longer theirs, even as I will soon not be its Emperor, even as they will not have one. And I knew that I had one last duty to perform. I must at least for once, at the end of my reign, at the end of my life, defy whatever god had sent me this omen, and try to prevent it.'

My eyes filled with tears when he said this, for he had not only related this vision to me, I had seen it myself, and I knew that it could not ever have been prevented. If we all died now in Tenochtitlan, it could not be prevented. If Montezuma had sent his armies and slain us at Vera Cruz, or Cholula, or as we emerged from the mountain passes, it could not have been prevented. If I and Marina had never been born to feather the serpent, it could not have been prevented. If Hernando Cortes had never left Cuba, it could never have been prevented. Even if Columbus had never set sail, it could not have been prevented, for Europe had the ships, and sooner or later someone would have discovered this New World.

And *that* was what made the fulfillment of Montezuma's omen inevitable. That was when the Empire of the Mexica became fated to be transformed into New Spain or the same thing under some other European name and flag. For this New World held treasure and unbounded virgin land unknown in the tired old one, and Europe had the greed to covet and the means to seize it. If it took a hundred thousand men and forty thousand horses and ten thousand cannon and a fleet of two thousand galleons, they would come. It was about as likely that these lands would remain unconquered by Europe as that a horde of famished bears would leave a forest of hives dripping with honey unmolested so as to avoid transgressing the territory of the bees who were its rightful owners.

I wept for Montezuma. I wept for the final ironic tragedy of this man who led his people to disaster by so loyally seeking to summon up and follow the omens expressing the will of his gods, only to die ignominiously in failure and dishonor the one time he bravely defied them in their service.

I spoke no more with the great Montezuma, who died on the morrow. I will let the account of how his death came about be his, the last words he ever spoke to his friend and betrayer, Avram ibn Ezra:

'And so I was taken to the top of the wall by a party of Teules who held their shields above and before me so that I could see nothing, only hear the drums and war cries of battle, the roar of the Teules' large thunder weapons and the crackling of the smaller ones, and the stones and arrows raining down on my metal fortress and prison.

'When I had thus been blindly escorted to the lip of the parapet, I heard a great shout, a murmuring as of the waves of the storm-whipped waters of the lake crashing upon the shore, and then a moment of silence.

'The shields before me were removed, but not the ones overhead, and I saw that my great gold eagle standard had been brought out to stand proudly beside me for the last time. And I beheld for the last time my people, stilled for the last time by the sight, and for the last time in their tens of thousands gazing up at me.

'Two men had come forward close enough for me to recognize and for us to hear the last words we would speak to each other.

'One was Cuatemoc. The other was my own brother Cuitlahuac, wearing the finery and quetzal-feather cloak of the Emperor of the Mexica.

'It was like beholding my ghost while I yet lived. It *was* beholding my own ghost, for I knew that this was the final omen of my life, and whatever words I now spoke would be futile. As I knew that my life had been futile.

'Nevertheless I tried to speak them.

'"Obey your Emperor! Lay down your weapons and allow the Teules to leave—"

'At this, a great roar of anger sounded, and stones were hurled in my direction, narrowly fended off by the shields of the Teules. But Cuitlahuac, out of loyalty or brotherly mercy, or so I foolishly thought, spread his arms to quell my subjects' ire, or at least have them cease throwing stones and allow him to speak.

'I will die wishing he had not, for the words he spoke struck harder than any stone and deeper than any arrow.

'"How dare the cowardly traitor Montezuma call to us with his womanlike soul to spare the Teules to whom he has betrayed us! Whore of Malinche! Traitor! Fool! Coward! You have betrayed our gods and our people and our honor! You are our Emperor while you yet live, but you are not fit to rule us. And so you must be removed and punished as what you are! A coward and a traitor!"

'And my brother turned his back and walked away. And as he did, a great thunder of fury sounded, and a torrent of stones and rocks fell upon the parapet where I stood, like a thunderstorm breaking.

'The Teules raised their shields to protect me and I heard the missiles of my just punishment battering and clattering against them. With all my body's strength, with all that remained of my honor, I pushed through the wall of shields to accept them in place of the flowery death I did not deserve and would never be granted.

'I was struck. And struck again. In the chest. On the shoulder. And then on my brow.

'Then there was only the welcome darkness of death.

'But then, Avram ibn Ezra, I awoke here.

'My spirit had died, but my heart had been rejected by Huitzilopochtli, and my body, alas, yet lived.'

30

WHILE MONTEZUMA LINGERED on for four days, and Cortes, realizing even before his death that his usefulness as a hostage was now at an end and our only hope of escaping the city was by main force alone, determined to clear the route to the Tacuba causeway before committing his entire force to the project. The force he assembled consisted of the mantas drawn by Tlascalans, who likewise lugged four cannon, followed by several score arquebusiers and a like amount of crossbowmen, followed by two hundred infantrymen led by Cortes himself on horseback with a score of cavalry. Needless to say, I was not among them, and so herein must rely on what Cortes related to me upon his ill-tempered return:

'Choosing to attack on the hour before dawn when the square before the palace would be clear of the daytime masses of warriors, we sallied forth behind the mantas and made straight for the avenue leading to the Tacuba causeway. The mantas laid down a fearful fire and cloaked themselves in gunsmoke. The few hundred Mexica who had lingered between the palace and the entrance to the avenue fled in terror as before fire-belching dragons, which, for all I know, they did believe they were confronting.

'We reached the avenue unimpeded, but the Mexica, now apparently better commanded by Cuitlahuac and having experienced all too many of our previous thrusts in this direction, had filled it with warriors, many of them archers, some several score armed with the spear-throwing atlatls, the rest with maquahuitls and spears, and the roofs of the buildings that had not been demolished were manned by stone-throwers.

'As soon as I saw this, I ordered the crossbowmen and arquebusiers within the mantas to commence and maintain a steady fire, and the sight of these horrific monsters advancing abreast towards them quite terrified the enemy, to the point where they did not even retain the wit to attack the Tlascalans drawing them, which certainly would have impeded our advance or even stalled it.

'I had brought the cannon to reduce the buildings along our path to the causeway to rubble, so that when I later brought our entire force down its length, it would not be under a rain of stones and rocks from the rooftops. We made good if sluggish progress, with the mantas driving the enemy before us, and cannon crumbling the buildings behind us, effectively slowed only by the lumbering pace with which the Tlascalans were able to draw them.

'Until, that is, we reached the first of the several canals between us and the entrance to the causeway.'

Now Cortes' visage darkened, and his tone became ireful and frustrated.

'Whether before the battle began, or during our unfortunately leisurely advance, I know not, but most of the Mexica had retreated to the other bank of the canal when we reached it, and had either demolished the bridge over it or withdrawn it behind them. And there they were, strung out for some score yards along the quay, where we could not get at them, archers and spear-throwers a dozen ranks deep, with endless reinforcement of the same behind them, and what had begun as an easy advance and demolition according to plan became a disorderly and fumble-footed disaster.

'The Mexica archers and spear-throwers now had angles from which to bombard the arquebusiers, crossbowmen and cavalry behind the mantas, and while their deployment allowed the crossbowmen, arquebusiers and cannon to fire around the mantas into them and give better than they got, we began to take casualties ourselves, and, being so greatly outnumbered, even if we killed ten of them to our one, we could therefore not win the contest of fusillades.

'Worse still, my infantry and cavalry, now blocked by both the mantas and the canal, could not advance against them, and thus were rendered useless. No doubt heartened by his successful reversal of the tactical advantage, whoever was in command on the other side of the canal recovered the wit to rain down arrows and spears on the exposed Tlascalans, to fearful effect. Brave as they were, the Tlascalans nobly held their ground, but as the mantas could now not advance further, their sacrifice was useless, and I withdrew them behind the mantas.

'The Mexica then began to concentrate the fire of the atlatls against the immobile mantas themselves, and as the atlatls effectively doubled the length of the throwers' arms, they were able to launch very heavy spears with more than human force, and at this range they began to splinter the wooden cladding.

'I must admit that at this point I was quite at a loss for an effective tactic, but the Mexica soon concentrated my battlefield wit by beginning to shoot fire arrows at the mantas.

'Desperation then dictated that I withdraw them out of range before they were destroyed, and upon realizing the necessity of pulling back the mantas before attempting any further advance, I realized also that I might be able to fill the canal with rubble from the buildings that had been destroyed behind us, and thus cross over with infantry, crossbowmen, arquebusiers and infantry at the very least, and perhaps even with cavalry.'

Cortes frowned, and struck the palm of his left hand with the fist of his right. 'Oh yes, a brilliant strategy!' he exclaimed in angry self-chastisement. 'But implementing it was a nightmare! I evacuated the mantas and ordered a party of the Tlascalans to drag them out of harm's way to the rear of the formation, which would also give the cannon, the crossbowmen and the arquebusiers a clear field of fire behind which the infantry and the cavalry might advance once the canal was filled, and at the same time sent more Tlascalans back to fetch the required fill.

'It was a great piece of stupidity! The Tlascalans had to drag the mantas back through the cavalry, the cannon, the arquebusiers, the crossbowmen and the infantry the length of an avenue between the narrow confines of buildings. To make matters worse, this had not been long under way when more Tlascalans came crashing through the melee in the other direction carrying fragments of masonry.'

Cortes moaned. 'Tlascalans bearing rubble barged into Spaniards seeking to allow the mantas to pass through them and advance around them, and Tlascalans pulling them collided with their fellow tribesmen, causing them to drop stones on the feet of various contingents, amidst curses, near fistfights, and a continuous hail of Mexica spears and arrows.

'Suffice it to say that when the Tlascalans finally managed to gain the canal bank with their rubble and began tossing it into the water, the Mexica on the other side began concentrating their fire on them to fearful effect, and our covering fire was simply insufficient to defend them.'

Cortes sighed and shook his head. 'And so I had no choice but to call the retreat from this ignominious failure. And the ignominy, Alvaro, is by no means the worst of it, for *this* is what we must face if we seek to fight our way out of Tenochtitlan! This multiplied by four! For that, if I have counted correctly, is how many canals cross the avenue to the Tacuba causeway, and that route is the shortest!'

'Surely you have not given up on escaping!' I exclaimed fearfully. 'What alternative is there?'

'I have not the slightest idea at the moment,' Cortes told me sourly. 'Perhaps I should seek out an omen like Montezuma, for all the good that it has done him.'

During the night after this fiasco, the mantas were repaired, and Cortes determined to use them as the forward element in an attempt to seize the temple of Xipe Totec and hold it hostage to effect a truce that would allow us to quit the city, this being a more modest nearby pyramid, and thus more easily stormed than that of Huitzilopochtli.

There was a garrison atop it, but the platform was likewise of modest size, and therefore it could not be a large one. At dawn the next morning, under an unusually fierce bombardment of the warriors before the palace, Cortes set forth with no more than three score men, infantry reinforced with arquebusiers and crossbowmen, all huddled behind the cover of the mantas. Having learned from his previous mistake, their Tlascalan haulers were now likewise protected behind them, a much smaller contingent constrained to perform the therefore more arduous but less dangerous task of pushing rather than pulling them forward. The crossbowmen and arquebusiers served as a rearguard enclosing the small formation, so that it lumbered through the masses of Mexica warriors surrounding it like a small mobile fortress.

This I observed from the safety of the palace wall, and an amazing sight it was. The Mexica swarmed around the mantas as they crept inexorably towards the low temple like an army of ants seeking to impede a carnivorous beetle on the way to their nest, firing fire arrows into the wooden planking, and spears, attacking it with axes and stones, while the arquebusiers and crossbowmen within and without mowed them down like a cow chewing and ambling its way through a field of grass.

By the time the mantas had reached the pyramid, their planking was splintered and smoldering, and I feared that whatever the outcome of what came next, Cortes and his men had lost all hope of escaping afterward.

Whether this trammeled their minds at the time, I know not, but it did not sap their mad courage, for the Spaniards emerged from within and behind the mantas and began scrambling up the pyramid. Warriors descended to meet them, and from my vantage, what I could behold was little more than what appeared to be a battle on the slopes of a great anthill between attacking insects and defenders that went on for perhaps half an hour, as the Spaniards slowly drove the Mexica upward, while bodies rolled down the stairs in horrifying profusion.

At last the Spanish ants gained the top in triumph, and now it was idols rolling down the steps to crash in pieces amidst the Mexica surrounding the pyramid, followed by their priests.

But strangely, the Mexica below did not rush up the pyramid in overwhelming numbers to avenge this outrage. They did not move. They fell silent. And then, moving through their ranks towards the pyramid, I saw the reason why.

Under a green quetzal-feather parasol, a litter borne by four Jaguar and four Eagle warriors was moving through them. The litter appeared to be either of gold or gilded. Before it a warrior carried the gold eagle standard of Mexico and before him two retainers carried the gold wands of state. I could not discern the face of the figure reclining upon it, but he wore the imperial quetzal-feather cloak and headdress of the Emperor of the Mexica.

I did not need Cortes to tell me later that it must be Cuitlahuac.

But being far too distant to hear anything, I must rely on his account to tell you what they said to each other when Cuitlahuac dismounted and Cortes came out to the lip of the platform so that the two of them could shout up and down at each other. This he told me as we walked together through the halls of the palace an hour so past noon towards the main courtyard, where he had assembled all his grumbling, blood-ied, angry, and by now quite terrified troops.

'I not speaking Nahuatl and he not speaking Spanish and Marina not being among us, and it being conducted as a series of shouts in my good Spanish and the primitive Spanish of some Indian who had learned enough of the tongue to more or less serve as a translator, it was a short and brusque conversation. And mendacious on both sides as well, I must admit.

'I pointed to the mantas, now in a state of smoldering dilapidation which I hoped Cuitlahuac would not discern, and declared that if he persisted in his rebellion I would construct a whole flotilla of the things, and reduce the entire city to rubble.

'Cuitlahuac countered with an offer to stop the war as soon as the last Spaniard had left the entire country. Otherwise, the Mexica would fight until the last Spaniard was killed or captured and the latter sacrificed to Huitzilopochtli and their flesh prepared as a savory stew with sufficient peppers and spices to mask the foulness of the meat.

'Seizing what seemed an opportunity, I ignored the threat and the insult and demanded to know how either of us could trust the other to keep such a bargain. Cuitlahuac declared that he would accept an oath sworn upon my gods and if I agreed to this solemn ceremony of honor, he would allow us to depart afterward via the Tacuba causeway.

'This was obviously a lie to entrap us, for the Mexica had only to allow us to pass over two or three of the canals, raise the bridges on the ones before us, send warriors down the side streets to remove the ones behind us, and our whole army would be trapped in a long thin line on the avenue with hope of neither advance nor retreat, and easily enough destroyed or starved.

'But I quickly saw that this falsehood might be turned against him with another, which, at the very least, might allow us to retreat back into the palace without the aid of the mantas, which were now useless, and might allow us the best possible chance to escape the city.

'And so I thanked him for his magnanimous offer and promised to give it serious consideration if he would allow me to return to the palace of Axayacatl to consult with my priests, without whose consent, of course, no such oath could be given, and give him my reply on the morrow.

'I held my breath while Cuitlahuac pondered this. I could not read his face at this distance, but I could easily enough imagine what was going on in the mind behind it by summoning up what my own thoughts would be if it were mine.

'I could slay Malinche and a few score of his men right now, but that would leave the main Spanish force still inside the palace, where they might still be capable of constructing many more of the terrible war-machines, and, moreover, they would probably then be commanded by the ferocious Pedro de Alvarado, who had already committed a most terrible slaughter. Would it not be better to allow Malinche his life for the moment, thereby allowing him to lead his entire army into my trap?

'At length, Cuitlahuac replied that he would suspend hostilities until the sun reached its zenith tomorrow, at which time, if I had not sworn my oath beneath a Cross taken to the top of the temple of Huitzilopochtli, it would be war to the death.

'Thus was my life and those of the brave men with me spared by the courtly pavane of his lies and mine, and thus may we likewise dance our way out of the trap we find ourselves in tonight.'

This set me back on my heels, and stopped me in my tracks. '*Tonight?*' I exclaimed. 'But you told Cuitlahuac you would give him your answer tomorrow!'

Cortes halted to regard me with the even-lipped smile and cold eyes of a fey serpent. 'I lied,' he said with an indifferent shrug.

'This does not at all trouble your honor?'

'I lied to a fellow liar,' said Cortes. 'Where is the dishonor in that? Indeed, by preventing Cuitlahuac from turning his words into a lie, may I not be said to have saved his honor? And thus does he not owe me a favor which I intend to collect tonight?'

I did not know whether to laugh at this one or choke on it and so I did neither.

'Be of good cheer, Alvaro,' Cortes told me perhaps only half sardonically, 'your plan is about to be carried out, is it not?' He nodded towards the entrance to the courtyard, where we could hear the loud murmuring and contention as we approached it. 'When I tell my troops what I have just told you, and relay your advice to me with my own mouth as if it emerged full-blown from my own brow, they will surely be enthusiastically willing to follow.'

'*My* advice?'

'Was it not you who told me that once we were back on the mainland, it would be Tenochtitlan trapped in the middle of a lake behind causeways that we can blockade, and thus the advantage will then be ours? Thus will not their terror be relieved and their wounded pride balmed by conducting a strategic fighting retreat that will turn the tables, rather than a flight in ignominious dishonor?'

And Cortes made to leave me and stride out of these shadowy corridors of our reptilian machinations and out into the bright sunlight as a lion-hearted general.

But before he could, Velazquez de Leon, captain of the guard set over the Emperor's deathbed, came running down them towards us. 'Montezuma is dead!' he shouted.

Cortes and I stared at each other for a long silent moment, not in shock, for this had been expected for days, but in deep and contorted contemplation.

From a Spanish perspective, Montezuma had been an enemy. From a Mexica perspective, he had been a weakling who had died as a traitor to his own people. From both perspectives, and I warrant from his own, his rule had been a failure. During his reign he had dragooned hundreds of thousands to bloody sacrifice atop the altar to his war god. Had he not been a monster?

And yet . . .

And yet there seemed to be genuine sorrow in Cortes' eyes, or perhaps respect. But this was almost immediately transformed into uncouth glee. 'Saint James and Our Lord have indeed answered my prayers with a true omen,' he cried.

Omen? Prayers?

Was this not bitter irony?

For Montezuma had been a more truly spiritual man than either of us. I had forsaken the God of my people in the service of my own survival, and Cortes' faith in his, while sincere in its own peculiar fashion, was equally sincere in the conviction that by serving his own self-interest, he served that of his God. But Montezuma had throughout sincerely sought to seek out the occluded will of his gods and carry it out, even when it ill-served his own interest, and even that of his people.

The great Montezuma, like myself, had sought to apprehend the unknowable visage of the Ain-Soph, of Nezahualcoyotl's Hidden God, behind the dance of masks. In this lay his greatness.

As a ruler he had been a monster and a disaster and an enemy.

But in this he had been my brother.

This was why, unbeknowst to myself until the moment of his passage, I had loved him.

Had Cortes somehow in his own way loved him too, or was this merely another cynical stratagem? Or, in the at once simple and labyrinthine soul of this beguiling liar and villain, was there somehow no contradiction?

For what Cortes did was both cunning and noble. He had the corpse of Montezuma dressed in his full imperial finery and laid out on his golden imperial litter. As we watched together from the wall, the gate to the palace of his father was opened and he was borne through it on the shoulders of six Spanish soldiers in gleamingly polished armor, each of their helmets adorned with a single quetzal feather.

As the Mexica surrounding the palace advanced gingerly and uncertainly towards it, a score of arquebusiers, likewise accoutered, emerged to stand behind the imperial bier. The Mexica halted.

The arquebusiers pointed their weapons skyward and fired a farewell salute towards the heavens.

I knew that this ceremony would well serve Cortes' self-interest by hopefully distracting the Mexica, whose priests were now advancing to retrieve the body, with rites of their own, while we made for the causeway tonight.

Nevertheless, it was a noble gesture that brought tears to my eyes, and when we turned to each other, I saw that Cortes was likewise on the verge of a martial species of weeping.

And I understood why men would loyally follow this lion-hearted and treacherous serpent of a man into the jaws of death or the depths of his unprincipled and ruthless machinations.

I hated this man for the evil that he had done. I hated him for what the faith he followed with fire and the sword had done to my own people. I hated him for how he had made me his perfidious collaborator, or worse still, himself my own. There were so many reasons for me to hate Hernando Cortes.

But most of all I hated him because there were moments like this, when no matter how I tried, I found it impossible not to love the bastard.

31

I T WAS DECIDED TO LEAVE at midnight, when the fewest Mexica would be abroad, and, if all went well, we would be able to gain the entrance to the Tacuba causeway and traverse it before the sun was up. The omens seemed good. The way to the avenue leading out of the Temple Square was empty, and to judge by the mournful, slow and somber drumming in the distance, the Mexica seemed to be occupied with funeral rites for Montezuma. A light rain was descending from an overcast sky that assured a dark and starless night.

A stout portable bridge had been constructed with which to cross whatever gaps in the roadway over the city canals or along the causeway might have been created by the Mexica to block or trap us, and the horses' hoofs had been padded with cloth and leather to muffle the sounds of their passage.

Two hundred foot soldiers led the way, commanded by Sandoval on horseback, and reinforced by a score of cavalry. The rest of the infantry, commanded by Alvarado and Velazquez de Leon, formed the rear-guard. In between was everything and everyone else, myself included – the cannon, the Tlascalans, the priests, Marina, the portable bridge carried by some forty men, and the baggage, including horses heavily laden with all the treasure that had been accumulated. Cortes himself, mounted, led from the center, directly commanding a troop of a hundred infantry and some half-dozen cavalry, to maintain close order and serve as a mobile relieving force to act where and when and if needed.

While everyone else save the Tlascalans, the priests and Marina was preoccupied with retaining the gold come what may, I was obsessed with safeguarding what to me had become the greater treasure – the transcriptions of Cortes' accounts and my own commentary to be sure, but most vitally the transcriptions of the words of Montezuma, and as many of the Mexica drawings as I could snatch up. For this knowledge had been vouchsafed to no other, and if I lost it, it would be for ever lost to the posterity which even then was becoming my obsession. These documents I secured in a leather pouch which I stuck in my belt and beneath my tunic, and I went so far as to secure a sword with which to defend them, praying, of course, that I would never have occasion to use it.

The omens continued propitious as we traversed the empty square and made our way down the avenue leading to the Tacuba causeway. No one was abroad as we passed through the precinct whose streetside buildings had been reduced to rubble. When we reached the first canal, whose bridge had been removed, the portable bridge was brought up, the entire army crossed without incident, it was taken up again, and we proceeded onward with heartening ease.

None of the bridges over the remaining canals passing beneath the road leading out of Tenochtitlan had been removed, the portable bridge need not be used, not a Mexica had been sighted, and to me at least, it was beginning to seem all *too* easy.

Many accounts have been given of what occurred that awful night, provided directly or at a remove by the hundreds of survivors, all of whom were more concerned with fighting for their lives and saving the gold than with future accuracy, and so they are all riddled with contradictions. I was in the middle of the Spanish army, and so experienced it only in confused and terrified bits and snatches. So I must attempt to relate what I can as a melange of my fragmentary experience and what I was able to piece together afterward.

Our vanguard reached the entrance to the causeway and proceeded along it to the first gap, where a bridge had been removed. The portable bridge was brought up and slammed down across it, and the leading infantry crossed it, followed by the middle ranks, myself, and apparently Cortes and his squadron.

All I can directly report of what happened next is a great noise of shouts and screams to the rear, followed quickly by drumbeats throughout the city behind us. Some say a woman collecting water from the lake sounded the first alarm, some say a lookout, some say a priest or priests atop the great pyramid. Of a certainty, it was given, and the Mexica, whether by happenstance or by cunning plan, were roused against us at the worst possible time, when we were strung out along the narrow causeway.

It was pandemonium. The vanguard apparently dashed on to a second gap in the causeway well before the whole army could cross the first, perhaps with Cortes' command backed up behind them. A huge rushing sound as of great waves moving across the darkened waters of the lake surged towards us from both sides. Arrows began to rain down, and stones.

And then we saw them.

Cuitlahuac had indeed laid a trap for us, albeit of a sort that was entirely unexpected.

Hundreds, if not thousands, of canoes filled with warriors were closing on the causeway from both sides, firing arrows, hurling stones, howling their impending triumph.

I can only dimly recollect the succeeding minutes. I cannot even remember how long it lasted. And relatively secure in the midst of the pack, I saw it only in terrified fragments. What seems to have happened is that the Mexica canoes reached the causeway and thousands of warriors in them, armed with maquahuitls, scrambled onto it, or at least attempted to gain it, along two fronts perhaps half a mile wide, and it was swords, and stones, and arrows, and cries of death and agony.

What most accounts agree on is that scores of Spaniards were quickly slain and many more Mexica, but the causeway was held, while Sandoval, or perhaps it was Cortes, sent back for the portable bridge, even as the rear of the army, likewise under ferocious attack, was still crossing the first gap. Still the causeway was held at the cost of terrible losses. I myself saw men go down, saw horses speared, sliced, dragged, neighing piteously, into the water, cannon overturned, cries, screams, and I even found myself slashing away at a warrior who had broken through before he was decapitated by a better soldier's sword, spattering me with blood.

At length, the whole army, or what was left of it, crossed the first gap, what was left of the bridging crew heroically brought the portable bridge up through the carnage, and made it fast across the second gap in the causeway.

What seemed to have happened as we desperately clambered across it, was that the vanguard dashed onward towards Tacuba, followed by all who had gained the opposite side, fighting every inch of the way and taking great losses, only to find themselves confronting yet another gap.

Again, accounts of what then happened vary, and, having already crossed over the portable bridge and put it well behind me, I was not there to bear direct witness.

All agree that Cortes ordered the portable bridge to be brought forward again. Some say the order was given to do so before the rear of the army had crossed over it. Others deny this as a cowardly order that Cortes would never have issued. But all agree that in practical terms it did not matter.

The portable bridge had been wedged so tightly into the gap by the passage of scores of cannon, cavalry and heavily laden horses that it could not be budged. The way forward was blocked, and no doubt the Mexica would now have blocked any retreat back into the city.

The whole army, surrounded along its entire length on both sides by lakeborne warriors, was trapped on the causeway.

Again, I was not there to see what happened next, but I was there to see the results, and they saved my life, and those of hundreds of others.

What I witnessed directly was long minutes of terrible battle around me as we were forced to hold our ground on the causeway. Wave after wave of Mexica assaulted the infantry guarding the banks, cutting down dozens of them, being thrown back bleeding or dead into the waters. A dozen or so broke through at any given moment, and yes, even I was constrained to do battle, taking cuts on both arms, and managing in my fugue of terror to bring down several.

At length, though, we found ourselves advancing once more, as if by a miracle, and when it was my turn to cross over the gap, I saw how it had been bridged. The water was relatively shallow here, and the gap was filled with the corpses of dead Mexica, dead Spaniards, dead and dying horses, the wreckage of canoes and gun carriages, the whole reddened by an ever-widening pool of blood. On this bridge of gore and wreckage did we cross over, feet slipping on blood and sinking most horribly into flesh.

The vanguard, with Cortes now leading it, pressed onward towards Tacuba. Some say the water beneath the final gap was shallow enough to ford, and they reached the safety of the shore before they gallantly turned back to the rescue of their hard-pressed comrades. Others claimed that they had turned back upon reaching that last gap in the causeway. Either way, Cortes realized the plight of the rest of us, and turned back to fill the gap with corpses and debris so that the cannon, the heavily laden baggage train, the rest of the infantry, and the Tlascalans, could cross.

The truth of it I do not know, for I crossed the final gap in the middle of the army, and by the time it was my turn to cross it, I had already seen Cortes and Sandoval and what had been the vanguard dashing further backwards to the rescue of Alvarado's and De Leon's sorely pressed rearguard.

The rest of the battle, at least for me, was a long forward dash through a dark tunnel of death and screams and blood and chaos. There was nothing forward to impede our flight to the shore now, for the Mexica could not keep enough men on the narrow causeway before us to avoid being swept away by cavalry charges or arquebusiers. But the attacks along the full length of our advance continued, and within it, attempts to halt the cannon long enough to bring them into play not only proved ineffective, but created chaos within our train.

At length, I heard a great cheering break out before me, a cheer which continued unabated until I joined in it, for at last I beheld the most welcome sight I had ever seen – a lakeshore village like a beacon at the end of the nightmarish tunnel.

By the time I had staggered breathlessly ashore, and turned to gaze on what lay behind me, the first purplish gray light of dawn somberly revealed a grim and terrible spectacle.

Perhaps half the army was still fighting its way along the causeway to the shore, albeit through diminishing attacks by the Mexica. For its entire length, corpses by the thousand, Mexica, Spaniards, horses, floated in two long and slowly widening sheens of blood, blackened and glistening in the light of the mocking sunrise. Canoes by the hundred drifted, empty and overturned. More canoes paddled through the gore back to the dark silhouette of their city, while others moved among the lakeborne wreckage, gathering up booty as tiny figures could be seen on the abandoned section of the causeway stripping armor and arms from the bodies of the abundant fallen Spaniards.

At last, the living last of our decimated army attained the shore. All the cannon were arranged in a line on the strand and bombarded the few scores of canoes making a desultory attempt to follow until they too gave it over and turned back to their island city.

The battle was over.

Later, when such things were counted, it was said that five hundred Spaniards had died. The wounded were never counted, for it was far easier to number the few of us that were unbloodied. No one bothered to count the thousands of dead victors.

How long I stood there silently gazing out over this terrible waterborne midden I do not know, but it must have been quite a while, for by the time Cortes came up beside me to do likewise, the sun had risen high enough to turn the spreading pool of blood into a sanguinary mirror of its golden fire, and scintillate on the surface of his cold eyes. Was that a grim smile or simply a more seemly death mask's rictus betrayed by a trick of the light?

'Congratulations, Alvaro,' he said in a voice devoid of irony or indeed of any discernible emotion. 'We have escaped from Tenochtitlan. Your plan has succeeded.'

Never in my life had I suffered such a loathsome compliment.

May I die before I hear its like again.

32

THE BLOODIED, WOUNDED, exhausted remnants of the Spanish army, amounting to little more than half of those who began the retreat from Tenochtitlan, were in a foul, disconsolate and defeated mood. The overwhelming desire was to make for Vera Cruz, where the fleet that had brought Narvaez was waiting to bring them safely back to Cuba with what treasure was not now at the bottom of the lake, which was still enough to buy them comfortable retirement as overlords of modest plantations.

But not Hernando Cortes. By noon the next morning, he had assembled his troops not far from the beach to listen to a post-mortem dissertation they were in no humor to hear. The half a thousand or so Spaniards clustered within earshot were greatly outnumbered by the thousands of Tlascalans he had gathered to surround them for some reason I could not fathom, for only the nearest of them would be able to hear his words, and only a dozen or so, if that, would have been dimly able to understand them if they could.

'My plan has succeeded,' were the first words he presumed to utter, and mine was not the only jaw to drop open.

'We have been delivered from the trap of Tenochtitlan by God and our own courage and force of arms,' he went on, 'and now we are ready to take the offensive, avenge our dead, and complete our conquest of Mexico.'

There were gasps of amazement and cries of outrage. There stood this poor decimated army, or at least those among them not too wounded to do so, with half their former comrades dead, a third of the gold gone, having escaped only barely themselves, and Cortes was blathering on about 'completing' a conquest that had quite fallen apart.

Only I understood that Cortes, for once, was telling a truth that seemed to be a lie rather than the reverse, for it was I, no soldier, who had given him the plan that I knew would succeed, if only to persuade him to flee Tenochtitlan in the service of nothing more than saving my own life. Now I was forced to stand there fidgeting, fuming and cursing myself as he reiterated it to his disgruntled forces in the service of persuading *them* to continue to fight this immoral war.

'What the Mexica now hold is no more than Tenochtitlan,' Cortes declared blithely, 'for their vassal tribes were loyal to them only out of the fear of their power, which we have long since broken, and surely none of those tribes forced to pay tribute to them in treasure and lives will fight at their side to overthrow the benign rule of King Charles and the Cross in order to resume the evil yoke of Tenochtitlan and once more feed the hearts of their youth to its demon-god rather than partake of the body and the blood of our Lord Jesus Christ and so gain the salvation of their souls in heavenly bliss everlasting!'

While there were no cheers at this true and truly outrageous declaration, it did bring silence, which, under the circumstances, surely must be counted as an impressive feat of oratory. As for myself, I do believe that this twisting of my own words was a feat of oratory which finally forced me to confront what should have been the obvious fact that this war *was* entirely immoral.

'What the Mexica have in Tenochtitlan is an army a hundred times the size of what we have here!' someone shouted out to general cries of agreement. 'We will be fortunate to escape this valley to Vera Cruz with our lives!'

'What we have that the Mexica do not have and will never have again is *allies*!' Cortes roared back. And he waved his right arm in the direction of the thousands of curious and befuddled Tlascalans surrounding the Spaniards.

'The fierce and noble warriors of Tlascala who fought them to a standstill for generations before we arrived! And who have not only sworn their allegiance to our King and the Cross but proven their hatred of the Mexica and their loyalty to us by standing beside us in battle! And while we, were we craven cowards, might board ship and slink ignobly back from whence we came to leave them to the vengeance of the Mexica, *they* have no recourse but to stand their ground and defend their homeland! *They* have fought bravely beside *us*! Who among us would be willing to have the tale told that *we* deserted *them* in their hour of need? Who among you would wish it said that while Spaniards turned tail and fled, leaving these lands to fall once more into Satanic darkness, Tlascalans stood alone as true soldiers of the Christ and the Cross that we deserted?'

It would be hyperbole to claim that I actually gagged on this invocation of faith and honor in the immoral cause of further slaughter and conquest, but I would have vomited out the anguished guilt for my part in bringing about all that had thus far occurred, and what I knew was to come, if that would have enabled me to rid myself of it.

Where was the moral cause in this war?

The Spaniards fought it for gold and land, the true word for both being *loot*, when the verdigris of King and Cross was cleaned off the noble monuments, and even the souls they professed to save they declared *won* for Christ, as if they were more of the same.

The Mexica fought to repel voracious invaders as so many peoples had down through the ages, and if there was no just cause in that, then the rising of the Maccabees against the Greeks, and the Gauls against the Romans, and the resistance of Charles Martel to the Moors at Tours, likewise had no moral justification. But if they succeeded, they would surely turn their attention to the resubjugation of the vassal tribes this war had for the moment freed, and would restore the reign of Huitzilopochtli and human sacrifice.

The Tlascalans?

Cortes opened his arms as if to embrace them. 'Let us stand up and cheer our noble brothers in Christ!' he exhorted the Spaniards.

'Together we will make our way to the safety of their capital, and once we have, there will be no safety for the Mexica, for we shall return with an invincible army of Spaniards and Tlascalans fighting side by side such as will sweep all before us and make the very foundations of Tenochtitlan tremble and the evil temples to their Satanic gods crumble! Tlascala! Tlascala! God send the right! Saint James and Tlascala! Onward to Tlascala!'

'Tlascala! Tlascala! Saint James and Tlascala!'

One by one, and then in a great chorus, the Spaniards began shouting it, until even all those not too gravely wounded to do so were on their feet waving their swords and shouting.

The Tlascalans might have been ignorant of what Cortes had said, but they knew enough to recognize the name of their nation shouted out in tribute from the throats of brothers in arms, Christ and the Cross or not, and they likewise roared their response and waved their weapons in a mad martial spirit.

The Tlascalans would surely fight to prevent their conquest by the Mexica as they always had, and perhaps, led by such as Cortes, and with cannon and horses, and firearms to reinforce them, would indeed be emboldened to fight to finally conquer their ancestral enemies. But their endless wars with the Mexica had been some barbaric form of sport in which neither side truly sought to definitively defeat the other. For if they did, who would there be to contest on the bloody gaming field of battle?

The Tlascalans did not fight to live. The Tlascalans lived to fight. That was what made them the Tlascalans.

There was no just cause here, mine emphatically included. Why had I come here but to seek after the form of loot peculiar to the greed of my own acquisitive spirit, to accumulate ever more knowledge, to see beyond whatever might be my present horizon, to engorge the treasury of my soul with insights and wisdoms snatched from those of the mages of unknown civilizations?

True, I might justify my quest by declaring that this form of looting harmed no one, but how can I justify the crimes I committed in the service of aiding Hernando Cortes in destroying the very civilization I came to marvel at that I might fulfill my own selfish desires?

I cannot, dear reader. I will not try. I can only pray, that if you can find pity in your heart as you read this account, you will accept my telling of it as some meager form of expiation.

I have little will to recount the events of our long march to Tlascala, until we reached the vicinity of Otumba and Teotihuacan, where Cortes fought the one significant battle at the former, and I received a revelation at the latter of far greater import to me than any famous victory. The rest was days of privation and skirmishes with war parties of Mexica sent forth by Cuitlahuac to harry us from the Valley of Mexico, and nothing more.

Cortes took a route west of the lakes and northward around them well away from the shores, in order to reconnoiter this previously un-visited territory and because it was more sparsely populated than the southern and eastern parts of the Valley of Mexico, and by smaller tribes who had already been less tightly held by Tenochtitlan before we had arrived therein. Yes, even as the retreat began, he was already plot-ting the strategy for his triumphant return, which was to conquer or win over the lands surrounding the lakes, isolate the Mexica within the island city, and complete the conquest by besieging it.

Cuitlahuac seemed to have taken our circuitous route, avoiding Texcoco, the second city of what had been the Triple Alliance, as a sign that the starveling remnant of a defeated Spanish army was slink-ing towards the mountains with no more in mind than escaping to safety beyond them. Apparently understanding that he would gain no significant support from the cities and towns along our line of march, he contented himself with merely harrying us onward out of the valley.

'Exactly what I would be doing were I him,' Cortes told me. 'He must believe we are already finished. Why expend forces to complete a task that is already done? Better to conserve and rebuild them, and wait until we are gone, after which it will be easy enough to fall upon the former vassal tribes that the craven Spaniards have left unprotected behind them, and inflict upon them such punishment that they will never think to rise against Tenochtitlan again.'

Yes, I did not find it possible to avoid conversation with Cortes, for since the strategy he had followed since we began our death march out of Tenochtitlan had been at my inspiration, if he had fallen from my favor, I had certainly not fallen from his. And since he was the Captain-General, and I still his scribe, I could hardly avoid congress with him, and what with his skill in drawing me out, and my habitually loose tongue, it seemed that I could hardly open my mouth without giving him advice, however inadvertently.

For the most conspicuous example, at one point he was reflecting on Cuitlahuac's unexpected naval attack on our retreat along the causeway. 'If only *I* had a navy to sweep those canoes from the lake, the siege would be perfected . . .' he muttered.

'Too bad you can't drag Narvaez's fleet over the mountains,' I replied sardonically.

Instead of grimacing, he gave me a sudden look of intense interest.

'Surely you're not thinking of—'

'Of course not. But if we built a fleet of ships closer to the lakes . . .'

'*Build* a fleet?' I exclaimed, goggling at him in no little amazement, for he actually seemed serious.

'You forget that in the service of seeing us gone, Montezuma was already having a fleet built for us.'

'But at Vera Cruz! And you took great pains to ensure that the work was never completed. There's nothing there but timber and planking and raw lumber! Besides which—'

'A lot easier to move inland than completed vessels!' Cortes enthused in full flower. 'And there's the cannon and rigging and sails we salvaged from our own beached ships . . .'

Yes, dear reader, it would seem that I was the inadvertent father, or at least godfather, of what would become the 'navy' without which the climactic battle for Tenochtitlan might have had another outcome. Try as I might, there seemed no way I could avoid further contributions to events that would redound only to my sorrow.

On the other hand, my usefulness to Cortes, and the favor in which it maintained me, allowed me to secure a boon which proved a source of considerable, if darkly shadowed, enlightenment.

This occurred at about the same time as Cortes' famous victory at Otumba. Into the bargain it allowed me also to escape witnessing that carnage, and now allows me to tell you of the gloomy wonder of Teotihuacan.

We had rounded the shore of the northernmost lake, Xaltocan, and had turned eastward, proceeding across a broad dry plain towards the mountains and the northern pass through them to Tlascala. Their peaks were already visible on the horizon to the north and to the east, but to the south I spied what first appeared to be a range of low hills jutting up out of the flat terrain. But upon considered perusal from afar, I realized that this could be no natural formation, for though they were covered with brush and vines, the tallest of them had an unmistakably pyramidal crown, and seeing this, I realized that others likewise appeared to be great overgrown buildings.

A lost city!

My heart began to beat faster and the blood rushing to my head and the avid curiosity to my spirit roused me from my disconsolate humor.

I questioned the first Tlascalan I could, and I received the single word 'Teotihuacan' in a tone of voice that indicated that, had he been a Christian, he would have crossed himself. Further rapid inquiries yielded much the same response and little more information. Yes, there were the ruins of a city out there. It was a great city. It was an old city. How old? Older than memory. Older than legend. Who had built it? No one knew. Perhaps the gods. Which gods? Gods whose very names had been forgotten. It had been deserted since before the time of the Toltecs. Even they had avoided it. I had the impression that it was believed to be haunted, though no one dared say it in so many words.

Need I tell you that I had to see it?

I most certainly told Cortes. The ruins are not far, I told him, and they lie across a flat plain, whereas you will be climbing into the mountains. I can go there, tarry but a few hours at most, and regain the main party while it is climbing.

'Too dangerous,' was his first response.

'No one lives there. Teotihuacan is not only entirely deserted, it is shunned by all.'

'I cannot let you go alone.'

'I have served you well, Hernando, humor me at least in this small thing.'

And so it went, but not for long, for Cortes shrugged, and assigned me a guard of half a dozen Tlascalans, who, though clearly unenthusiastic, were shamed into it by appeals to their manhood.

To my surprise and his, as well as his dismay, Marina insisted on joining my little expedition. Cortes, of course, adamantly refused. Marina rejoined that Christ would protect her, besides which, there was not a human within sight, and therefore there would be no danger. Cortes began to relent. Marina whispered things in his ear which seemed of a sexual nature, and this was enough to reluctantly convince him.

'Why were you so determined?' I asked her as we set forth.

'I have heard of Teotihuacan,' she told me. 'As I heard tales of great Tenochtitlan as a girl, and so as a girl I likewise always dreamed of living to see it.'

'But *why?*'

'Tenochtitlan, so the tales of it were told, is the greatest thing built by the hands of men, and I have seen it, and it was so,' she told me. 'Teotihuacan, so the tales said, is greater. And so . . .'

'And so . . . ?'

And her eyes became soft and dreamy, and for a moment the girl that had been seemed to emerge from behind the hard and haughty mask of 'Doña Marina'.

'And so,' she said, in that girl's voice, 'if this is true, must it not have been built by gods? And if *that* is so, would I not betray the dreams of my girlhood . . . as . . . as I have betrayed the gods of my own land if they exist, if, being so close, I did not see it also?'

As my visit to this millennial ruin occurred at about the same time as the battle, it is my arbitrary choice to allow Cortes to relate his tale of found glory before passing on to mine of glory lost and forgotten. Though given the state of mind in which I now write this in my mountain retreat, and the brooding cloud which hung over me from the escape from Tenochtitlan until what will be the conclusion of this tale, perhaps there is nothing arbitrary about it.

So let me relate Cortes' battle tale as he told it to me when I rejoined him afterward and be done with it.

★

'As we ascended the mountains, we approached a low hill guarding an upland meadow, which, according to the Tlascalans, was the only feasible route to the high pass through the peaks, and atop it was a town called Otumba. When we reached Otumba, it was deserted, and by what had been left behind, it seemed to have been evacuated but recently and in haste.

'When we passed through it and I gazed down into the meadow beyond, I beheld a vast Mexica army deployed upon the meadow and blocking the way forward. Ten thousand warriors at the very least awaited us in a solid mass, and at more or less regular intervals amidst this otherwise amorphous formation were tall featherwork standards indicating the positions of sector commanders.

'This sight quite daunted our heavily outnumbered and fatigued party, but it was clear that Cuitlahuac had previously husbanded his forces to constrain us to engage this great army on this well-chosen battlefield, for here lay our only way forward to the safety of Tlascala.

'I pointed this out to our gallant little band, which did little to hearten them. And so I reminded them that we had faced much the same situation at Ceutla, the difference here being in our favor, to wit that here we were reinforced by several thousand Tlascalans who were fiercely motivated to fight their way homeward.

'I left the cannon on the hilltop, an excellent position from which to bombard the rear of the Mexica army, positioned the cavalry in the van in a broad wedge formation, and instructed my cavaliers to use their lances, held short, as thrusting weapons. The infantry I stationed behind the cavalry wedge, with orders to thrust at faces with their swords, and all I reminded to make bringing down the leaders, who so kindly proclaimed their positions with standards, their priority. The Tlascalans I placed on either flank to fight freely as they would in their own accustomed manner.

'The bombardment was begun and I led the charge down the hill towards the center of the Mexica army. The Mexica held their ground under the cannonade, indeed there was nothing else they could do, for their army was solidly blocked by their own deployment within the confines of a small valley that they virtually filled, so that no lateral movement was possible.

'As we approached within range, we were greeted by a hail of stones, arrows and javelins, but these had little time to do damage, for the cavalry advanced at a measured but brisk trot, slowed only to the pace of the infantry dashing forward at a dead run behind us, and so the ground was quickly closed, rendering useless everything but spears and lances, swords and maquahuitls.

'Lances before us, our cavalry wedge slammed into the center of the Mexica army like a great plow, mowing down the front rank, and the one after that, and the third, and the fourth, before the charge began to stall.

'By this time, we had penetrated deep into the enemy army, and so were massively outflanked, but protected to some extent by our wedge formation, as I led us ever deeper, though at a much slower pace. The rear ranks of the infantry clustered within the wide arms of the cavalry wedge turned about to close the formation with a wall of Toledo steel, creating something like a Roman turtle, though an overlarge one, dedicated to pressing the attack forward like one huge knight encased in armor through a horde of dragooned peasant infantry. What the Tlascalans did, left to their own devices, I could not see, but I learned later that they simply attacked the Mexica on our flanks from the sides, taking heavy casualties all the while, but inflicting even greater damage.

'The battle wore on like this for about two hours; hand to hand, sword to maquahuitl, lance to spear, shield to shield. In this respect it was much like the battle of Ceutla, for our formation allowed the Mexica to confront it only with a number of warriors equal to that of our own front ranks at any one time, their great advantage in numbers served only to allow them to replace their fallen, while our superior weapons and disciplined tactics allowed us to bring down their fresh warriors as soon as they surged forward over the corpses of their comrades.

'But each man in our little army must fight for his life at every moment, while the very inability of the Mexica to bring more than a small portion of their force to bear at any one time meant that we were continuously confronting fresh unbloodied and unwounded warriors.

'We, though, were cut and bleeding to a man. I myself had a bleeding scalp wound which impaired my vision, and a worse one on my left hand, and fighting heroically for our lives though we were, the wounds, the loss of blood, the endless sword-thrusts, the heat of the sun, were fatiguing us to exhaustion, and I must confess that even I was losing heart, for my own waning strength told me that if the battle continued like this we would surely be overcome, if not by the inexhaustible supply of fresh Mexica warriors, then by our own sheer inability to wield our weapons.

'But then, at this very nadir of despair, God granted me a vision of salvation. By now we had penetrated deep into the midst of the Mexica army, and less than a hundred yards before me, I beheld a splendid sight.

'Rising higher above the fray than any other was a magnificent standard, a great pennant of quetzal feathers flying from a golden pole topped with a gold eagle. Beside it, surrounded by some dozen Eagle Warriors and shouting orders, was a man I excitedly first took to be Cuitlahuac himself, for he wore an abundance of gold jewelry, a headdress of iridescent green quetzal feathers, and a cloak of the same imperial plumage.

'A more careful glance at his face told me that it was not the new Emperor, but if it was not, it could only be the commander of the entire Mexica army.

'My wounds were forgotten. My fear was washed away. I raised my sword as I backed my horse away from the front and reared it to make myself better seen as I shouted:

'"Follow me! Victory is at hand!"

'Without looking back, I spurred my exhausted mount to one last mighty effort, and the gallant steed served me well by trampling through the Mexica before me as I threw down my lance, drew my sword, and used it and my shield, not to kill, but to slash and hammer my way towards my objective, heedless of whatever new wounds I took in the process.

'As I closed on the commander and his Eagle standard, I heard the pounding of horses' hoofs on either side of me, and out of the corners of my eyes I saw Sandoval, Alvarado, Olid and several others, cutting their way forward with me.

'This most welcome sight propelled me onward with even greater vigor, which in turn seemed to reinvigorate them, and we surged forward like demon soldiers of the Cross. Nothing could stop us. My battle companions engaged the commander's guards in a fury, while I galloped up to him, and with a single stroke of my sword sliced through his neck so that his head hung by a thread of gristle and bone on his shoulder.

'I grabbed it by the hair and with all the strength I could muster, yanked it free of his falling body, and raised it aloft as a barbaric battle trophy. With my other hand, I seized his standard, worked my hand down to the bottom of the pole, and held it even higher above the fray, rearing my horse, and shouting and screaming I know not what.

'Every Mexica in sight of me commenced crying and moaning in dismay and terror and fleeing from this awful vision, or omen if you like, of their defeat, and the panic spread among them in ever-widening circles.

'The great Mexica army quite fell apart, and fled the battlefield in all directions, harried by the Tlascalans, who, not content with mere victory, summoned up the savage glee to harry and butcher as many as they could of their vanquished ancestral enemies.

'Thus the glorious victory of the battle of Otumba, and no matter what may come, I shall never know a greater, for it was snatched from the jaws of despairing and exhausted defeat by a boon granted by God and my own sword, as it was meant to be, as the Knights of the Cross in songs and legend won the day for their noble cause in chivalrous single battle!'

While Cortes was winning his glorious, if not by my lights exactly chivalrous victory, Marina and I were contemplating the inglorious victory of vegetation and time over the works of man at Teotihuacan, likewise far from chivalrous and not at all glorious, having erased not only all the efforts of whoever or whatever had built this city, but even the memory of their name in song and legend.

Teotihuacan had not been nearly as large as Tenochtitlan, but the scale of its buildings and its single courtyard was enormous, as if it had indeed been the abode of a pantheon of vanished gods, and never inhabited by a teeming population of mere men.

The city was entirely overgrown by vegetation. The vast rectangular courtyard was a field of waist-high dry grass browning in the hot sun. On its long sides, it was enclosed by continuous stone galleries higher than a man's head, these heavily bearded by lichen, creepers, and starveling stunted cacti growing out of cracks in the blocks. The tops of the galleries became the lips of vast stone esplanades strewn with low crumbling ruins, likewise overgrown, so that they appeared to meld into the flat landscape, their limits discernible only where the cacti and lichens and creepers eking out an existence in the cracks in the stones gave way to grass growing in the dry and sandy earth.

There was a modest pyramid built atop one of the esplanades at the end of the great courtyard where we entered, its massive dark gray stone blocks peering blindly and bleakly out through the conquering overgrowth.

The courtyard led up to a single enormous pyramid at the far end, clearly the focal point of the entire construction, which must have been designed to enhance its grandeur. I have never seen the great Egyptian Pyramids, so I cannot tell you whether they dwarf it, or the reverse, but this one was squatter than the temple of Huitzilopochtli in Tenochtitlan and therefore more massive, somber and overbearing, quite intact and seemingly unconquered under its cloak of vegetation, as if time were running backwards and rather than slowly being subsumed by the natural realm, it was still shouldering its implacable way up through it.

Our Tlascalan escort feared to approach it, but of course Marina and I were inexorably drawn to it, and we stalked and stomped slowly through the high grass to the base of the pyramid, saying nothing until we had reached it.

'Sic transit gloria mundi,' I muttered as I gazed up along the overgrowth-covered steep stairway that formed the face of the pyramid, clear to the apex, invisible somewhere skyward from this perspective.

Marina, not having any Latin, looked at me questioningly.

'Thus passes all the glory of the world,' I told her. 'Not Spanish but the language of a mighty empire called Rome, of which there is likewise nothing left but its stones.'

'And its words,' Marina sagely corrected. 'And its name. But these have not been left behind to be remembered by whoever built *this*. "Teotihuacan" means only "City of the Gods", and in Nahuatl, not in whatever tongue might have been spoken by those who built it. If they spoke a human language at all . . .'

'You don't seriously believe that this was not built by men?'

Marina shrugged. 'Who is to say? There must have been a time when there were no men. And so *some* gods must have created them. Who knows how long ago that was? Who knows when Teotihuacan was built? All that is known is that it *was* built, and that the only memory that has passed down is the name it was given by the Toltecs, or whoever came before *them*, so that all we know is that whoever named it Teotihuacan believed it was indeed built by gods.'

'Shall we climb it?' I found myself blurting.

'*Climb it!*' exclaimed Marina. 'A woman and an old . . . a man well past his prime?'

'A woman and an old man past his prime have not only gotten this far, but may have played all too great a part in bringing down a mighty empire, so that a thousand years from now, there may be nothing more left of the glory that was Tenochtitlan than this,' I told her.

'Sac tronsit glorious . . .'

'Sic transit gloria mundi.'

'*Sic transit gloria mundi*,' Marina repeated perfectly the second time, frowning upward at the great ruin. 'Perhaps you are right, Alvaro. I have not said this before, or even wished to think it, but together we have done a thing, whether terrible or not, that is surely great. All we both wanted was to see and marvel at great Tenochtitlan. We loved something we had never seen very much to have done what we did to reach it. And perhaps that love will end in *destroying* the very thing we loved.'

'Who knows but that two people very much like us might have stood here thinking the same thoughts about Teotihuacan a thousand years ago,' I muttered.

'Or viewed what they had done from up there . . .'

And wept, I thought, but ventured not to say.

And so we climbed.

The slope was steep, the steps set too close together, and too narrow, as if the stairway had been built for a race of small-footed, long-legged dwarves, and they were thickly overgrown, so that the climb was long and arduous, as seemed only right, for to me at least this was a pilgrimage of expiation, and it would have been more fitting to have made it on Yom Kippur, the Jewish Day of Atonement.

But the vines, and the small plants growing through the cracks, rather than hindering us, aided us with handholds, and there was something meet about this too, as if the forces of nature, more primeval even than any gods who might have built the pyramid, wished us to complete this penitential task.

At length we reached the apex, scratched, sweating and panting. Below, the great ruin spread before us, seeming to be subsiding with the slowness of biblical aeons into the sere and deserted landscape of the high valley. From this elevated vantage, the whole plain was seen to be surrounded by mountains, and from horizon to horizon there was nothing to be seen of man or any of his works, and I realized for the first time that there could have been no human reason for building a city here. If Teotihuacan had not been built by gods, it surely could only have been built by humans seeking to commune with them.

Neither of us spoke for long moments as we caught our breath. Then Marina pointed silently to the northeast. I squinted, and there, at the very limit of my vision, I could barely spy out the only thing moving in all the world, a vague broken gray line crawling slowly up a distant mountain slope like one of the creepers growing up this very monument to the empty vastness – Cortes' army making its way to what would be his glorious victory.

I did not know at the time that there *would* be a battle at Otumba that would allow him to march into Tlascala in glorious triumph, but even if I had, it would not have changed what I felt atop the pyramid at lost Teotihuacan, for neither did the memory thereof fade when we climbed down from that vision to rejoin him in his glory.

For I stood upon a ruin that seemed older than anything I had seen in the marvelous Valley of Mexico and great Tenochtitlan. Older than anything in Europe. Older perhaps even than the Pyramids at Giza. And yet defeated and humbled by the vines and the lichen.

And I understood that as the Mexica traced their antiquity back to the Toltecs and the Toltecs must have traced theirs back to whoever had built Teotihuacan, so its builders too must have risen from their own antiquity; back, and back, to the first scattered tribes in those distant mountains who first set stone on stone, who first set grunt to grunt to form words, who first stood on a peak and sought to see what lay behind the starry black vault of a night sky.

This was not a New World. This was a world old beyond imagining.

That army crawling up the mountain and all that it might accomplish were but motes of dust that would vanish in the blink of its millennial eye. This was how the people of this land thought of themselves in time, I saw in that moment. Five worlds come and gone, and they within it. And now the breaking of the fifth and the coming of the sixth.

And yet I still could not believe that Teotihuacan had been built not by men but by gods. Or if by gods, it did not matter, for those gods had been as men; gone, with their words, and their tongue, and their very names forgotten, conquered by the slow, inexorable and insensate armies of time.

This was the moment when I do believe my journey to the millennial mountain village where I write this now began. For this was the moment when I realized that the highest knowledge that I sought was written not in that which passes but in that which is eternal.

And in the worlds of men, that which approaches closest to eternity is not that which is writ large in great monuments of stone and mighty empires, but that which is writ small in the villages and the very field furrows of tiny plots of land, in the souls of people of the land from which all the works of men must arise, and where what makes them what they are is conserved when they are crumbled into dust and forgotten.

'Sic transit gloria mundi,' I intoned, this time as a kind of prayer.

Marina stood there beside me watching the serpent we had feathered marching his army on to his great destiny. Like aphids crawling up the stem of some insignificant plant.

'I was a slave, so how could I love those who enslaved me? How could they be *my* people when they so betrayed me, when even my own mother betrayed me? I hated them all, and so why not betray them, Alvaro? All I had to sustain me was a dream to see great Tenochtitlan, the greatest wonder of the world. Only now do I know that if I hated its people, I loved our world. And now all that is left to me is to be Doña Marina. A great lady of New Spain. Who betrayed the only thing she loved so that she might live to see it. And by so doing, destroyed the glory of the world.'

For one last time, I embraced her, not as a sometime lover, but as a longtime brother in treachery and the passion from which it arose, a passion no less greedy and selfish in the end than that of the Spaniards for gold.

And yet . . .

'No Marina,' I told her. 'Thus passes all worldly glory. But not the glory of the world.'

33

CORTES ARRIVED IN TLASCALA as a conquering hero determined
to use the advantage to mold a true Tlascalan army, and after my
vision at Teotihuacan I was determined to have as little further to do
with his war of conquest as possible. He was welcomed along the route
to the capital as the commander of a victorious Spanish-Tlascalan army
which had humbled the Tlascalans' ancestral enemy, and he and his
captains were sumptuously quartered in the palace of Maxixca, one of
the four Tlascalan paramount caciques, and the one most openly favorable to his cause.

But while the Spaniards were nursing their wounds, Cuitlahuac dispatched an embassy to Tlascala under truce, and the caciques called a
meeting of their general assembly to hear their message from which all
Spaniards were barred. I was able to learn the gist of it from Xicotencatl
the Elder afterward, for he wished Cortes to learn of what had occurred
and his part in it in a politic indirect manner, and despite my vow to
maintain my distance from such machinations, I could not but transmit
it.

Cuitlahuac had proposed an unprecedented alliance between the
Mexica and the Tlascalans against the Spaniards, declaring that
despite their long history of mutual hostility, they had fought their

endless wars in a proper flowery fashion, they worshiped the same gods, spoke the same language, and thus were, if not quite brothers, at least cousins.

The Spaniards, the missive went on, scorned those same gods, desecrated their temples, and imposed a false god whose enforced worship suited their evil purpose to subdue all the inhabitants of what they forthrightly presumed to call 'New Spain' and force them all to bow down to a distant sovereign who might or might not exist. Therefore, if the Tlascalans did not take advantage of the current weakness of the nest of scorpions in their midst, seize them and mollify the infuriated gods by sacrificing them on their own altars, disaster would surely befall the Mexica and the Tlascalans alike. For if the Tlascalans made common cause with the treacherous Spaniards, once the Mexica were conquered, they would certainly then turn on their erstwhile allies, and if the Mexica succeeded against them both, the victorious armies of Tenochtitlan would then crush Tlascala.

'My headstrong son was all for accepting this offer of alliance,' Xicotencatl told me, 'but when I asked what would happen between Tenochtitlan and Tlascala in the matter of tribute and sacrifices for *their* altars once such a war against the Teules was successfully concluded, I was told by the Mexica ambassador that he had been given no instructions by the Emperor as to his reply to this unexpected question. Which, of course, was answer enough. Cuitlahuac had not even prepared a proper lie, a fault of which Malinche could never be accused.'

Xicotencatl expressed his unwillingness to make alliance with the Mexica in what he told me were moderate and cautious terms, but he was supported by Maxixca with a lavishly fawning speech praising the virtues of the Spaniards.

'This was the last thing I needed, for he agreed with me in a manner that had even me choking on it, and gave my hot-blooded son the opportunity to deliver an even more intemperate speech denouncing them. Nor would he obey when I ordered his silence. My son Xicotencatl may be a mighty warrior and a clever general, but the boy has the political intelligence of a jaguar, for his disobedience, while it truly angered me, outraged the assembly even more, and decided the cause against him. I pretended a greater rage than I felt, and had him thrown out of the conclave by force, shouting and screaming in a red rage, and that settled the issue.'

When I reported this to Cortes, he decided that the alliance between New Spain and Tlascala must be sealed in the blood of mutual victories as soon as possible.

Fortunately for him, he had in the meantime been provided with an outrage that could be turned into a casus belli. Upon departing for Tenochtitlan after defeating Narvaez, he had left a certain amount of the gold he had dispatched with Father Olmedo at Tlascala for safekeeping by wounded soldiers likewise left there, who were commissioned to take it to Tenochtitlan when they had recovered sufficiently. They had set out to do so at about the time we were escaping from the city, but they had been ambushed in Tepeaca on the way and massacred by the Tepeacans, who had helped themselves to the treasure.

The Tepeacans were a small and primitive tribe, vassals of the Tlascalans, and thus Cortes was provided not only with a perfect casus belli but an equally perfect prey. He whipped up the convalescent Spaniards into a gold-hungry fighting spirit, and declared to the Tlascalans that since they were the allies of the Spaniards and the Tepeacans were their vassals, they had committed treason against both and must be punished, which, given their meager forces, would amount to no more than a one-sided martial adventure.

Cortes being Cortes, he pretended innocence of the events in the assembly of which I had informed him, and, showering lavish praise upon the young Xicotencatl, offered him command of a Tlascalan force of several thousand warriors, declaring that he was the natural war leader of Tlascala, and there was no man on earth he would rather have fighting at his side.

Whether or not Xicotencatl swallowed this flattery whole, he certainly must have been relieved to have been offered such an opportunity to redeem himself from his unseemly public fit and his demeaning public disgrace at the hands of his father, and so he gratefully accepted.

Off they went to sharpen their military edge and practice their coordinated tactics at the expense of the Tepeacans. If I sound cynical about this, so be it, for it was a cynical operation, and I wanted no part of it.

Cortes found no need for my part in it either, and I was left to my own devices back in Tlascala, a situation that was allowed by unstated and undiscussed agreement to become habitual.

Cortes and the Tlascalans soundly defeated the unfortunate Tepeacans, to the point that he was confident enough in having sub-dued them to establish his headquarters in their capital, which was much closer to the porous frontier with Mexico than Tlascala, and therefore better suited to his current purpose, which was to pacify all the lands to the east of the mountain passes into the Valley of Mexico, a task that took some time, but which was not arduous after the example made of the Tepeacans. The towns and cities were won over by quick skirmishes or none at all with what in these precincts was an over-whelmingly powerful army, or straightaway sought protection from the Mexica under the arms of 'New Spain'.

Having thus established his sway over this eastern empire and secured his rear, Cortes was then emboldened to reduce the Mexica frontier garrisons so as to establish control over the passes through which he might invade the Valley of Mexico, or at least those on the eastern slopes of the great cordillera.

These generally consisted of fortified positions atop foothill cliffs or bluffs overlooking and thus commanding either cities, where there was one, or valleys leading to the pathways up into the mountains.

Where there was no city of significance below, these garrisons were not large, and mostly fled westward into the mountains at the approach of so large an army, numbering several hundred Spaniards and by now perhaps as many as twenty thousand well-schooled but still ferocious Tlascalans. If they did not flee without a fight, they were soon either sent packing by cannonade, or, upon descending to desperate attack, annihilated by superior forces.

What happened at a place and a city called Quauhquechollan ended all further attempts by these isolated Mexica border forces to hold the eastern approaches to the mountains. Here several thousand Mexica held a ridge flanked by two high-banked rivers and several thousand more occupied the city in the valley below.

Cortes was met by a party of caciques as his army approached the city, who complained of the hardships inflicted upon them by the

Mexica garrison within and sued for his relief. Seeing that the garrison on the ridge was in an all-but-impregnable position, he agreed, telling them that if they would organize a general uprising in the city to coincide with his approach, he would march on the city rather than the fortified ridge.

And so it was done. As Cortes neared the outskirts of the city with his large army of Spaniards and Tlascalans, the inhabitants rose up against the Mexica garrison within, forcing them back into the main temple square and atop its temple with much mutual carnage, while the Spaniards and Tlascalans entered the city unopposed.

What ensued was a bloodbath and a fearsome festival of fire. Knowing Cortes, I warrant that he allowed the Tlascalans to freely engage in an orgy of pillage, rape, plunder, slaughter, and perhaps impromptu cannibalism, so as to draw the other Mexica garrison down off the ridge to the rescue of their comrades.

Stupidly gallant, they descended to the valley and dashed down it in their several thousands to the rescue. By this time, the garrison within the city had been reduced to the point where the unfettered ireful bloodlust of its inhabitants was quite able to deal with the survivors, and Cortes withdrew all of his forces, save those that could not be dissuaded from continuing their rapine, to confront the Mexica on the open plain.

Where, of course, facing cannon, cavalry, arquebuses, crossbows, hundreds of Spanish infantry armed and armored with steel, and a much larger force of gleefully and triumphantly bloodthirsty Tlascalans, the Mexica were at an impossible disadvantage. For a time they fought bravely on and were slaughtered, but at length fled backward, cruelly harried all the way by the Tlascalans, up onto the ridge, and westward through the mountain pass.

Thus did Cortes more or less complete his preparations for the invasion of the Valley of Mexico. I say more or less, for the more of it was the events occurring behind him as he secured the eastern regions of what was fated to become New Spain.

Indeed, the region between the eastern slopes of the great cordillera and the sea had more or less become New Spain already. While Cortes was completing his pacification activities, the timbers, planks, cannon and riggings were brought up from Verà Cruz by a small army of tamanes, and his shipwright Martin Lopez put them to work building a fleet of thirteen brigantines.

As if transporting the pieces of a fleet of warships to Tlascala and then transporting them inland through the high mountain passes to Lake Texcoco were not a daunting enough task, Lopez decided that they must first be assembled right where they were, several of them launched on a nearby river to test the design for seaworthiness, and then all of them taken apart again and reassembled on the distant lakeside.

This seemed lunacy to me, and I suspect that Lopez, no lordly chief naval architect before, upon finding himself in command of a limitless supply of workers, enjoyed the task for its own sake, so that he wished to preside over it twice. On the other hand, I am no shipwright myself, and perhaps this was the prudent procedure, though I seriously doubt it.

I was sufficiently impressed by this great project to linger long enough in Tlascala to be on hand for the launching, spending many hours in the meantime watching Lopez and his minions beavering away, to the point that I just might now be able to supervise the construction of a brigantine myself if pressed to do so.

The rest of the time I passed with short excursions into the nearby Tlascalan countryside, sometimes accompanying small troops of soldiers on their errands, occasionally in the company of Father Olmedo, and as often as not alone, for the country was so thoroughly pacified and its inhabitants so leery of affronting their Spanish overlords that there was no real danger.

Tlascala was well along to becoming a province of New Spain in small ways as well as large, and observing this process was the main reason for my wanderings at the time. Why this was so, I cannot say simply even now. Perhaps my vision at Teotihuacan had implanted a passion in me to become intimate at ground level with this world that was passing before it was entirely gone. Perhaps as well they were a series of pilgrimages for the penitential task of expiating my guilt for the part I had played in this crime without a name.

And, nameless though it may be, it *was* a crime, as surely as what the Romans did to Carthage, or the Catholic Spaniards to what had been Al Andaluz, or what the Jews did to the former owners of Jericho, if more subtle.

Every town of any significant size had its rude adobe church, where Indians, many of them wearing crudely carved wooden Crosses, received the sacraments from travelling priests. Some of these priests were Spaniards, many of them were ordained Tlascalans, schooled in rudimentary Latin and more practical Spanish, a language that was slowly spreading among the populace by this means.

So too were Spanish modes of dress, in bits and pieces, and quite bizarrely. Crosses were sometimes worn as earrings or labrets, rosaries served as belts for cotton skirts, otherwise naked farmers tilled their fields in comically tailored maguey-fiber pantaloons or even Spanish castoffs of threadbare velvet.

Even the modes of tillage were beginning to change. Instead of planting their maize in individual holes with pointed sticks, some farmers were plowing furrows with crude plows of sharpened wooden planking, some of them cunningly fringed with obsidian blades like maquahuitls. I even saw a few bladed with pieces of broken steel swords.

The half-fearful deference bestowed by any peasantry on passing nobles of their own people was now transferred to anyone with white skin wearing European clothing, myself included. It was all too easy to elicit any conversation I wished to engage in, but difficult to improve my Nahuatl thereby, for anyone with even a smattering of Spanish words insisted on speaking a pathetic broken version of the master tongue of the Conquistadores.

Cortes had conquered the leadership and its armies for New Spain and New Spain was conquering the very lives of the ordinary people. But was this not a boon, were we not bringing civilization to benighted savages?

By my lights, it was not. We were not raising higher the not-inconsiderable civilization they had already built for themselves. We were bringing them *our own* civilization. And if in terms of science and knowledge and agriculture ours might be a so-called 'higher' civilization, the version we were imposing on them, or in truth that our very presence was causing them to impose on themselves, was a hand-me-down threadbare one.

That is the crime for which I have no name. Having conquered their lands, now we were conquering their spirit.

At last the brigantines were finished, and whatever my distaste for what the civilization that had built them with dragooned Indian labor was doing elsewhere, I had to admit that they were an amazing example of the prowess thereof.

Lopez, true to his beaverlike nature, had dammed a drying river to form a giant pond behind it. Three of the thirteen ships were dragged to its shores on rollers. All but the slightly longer 'flagship', as it was grandly styled, were about forty feet in length and double-masted. Only the flagship bore sails for this test of the hull design, though I was told that all would be similarly rigged; a single large square sail on the foremast for speed, and triangular fore and aft sails on the mainmast for ease of control and tacking. The cannon were not fitted, since the brigantines would be taken apart again to be transported.

Lopez had the three ships lined up side by side to be launched at once by his entire army of navvies. They shoved and grunted and sweated until at length the ships began to move forward on their rollers. The prows kissed the waters. The tamanes pushed until the ships were half off their rollers, and then, with a mighty effort, the front halves were on the water, then one more massive shove, and they were *in* it.

An enormous cheering rang out from all watching, which must have been the entire city, for who would miss witnessing such a spectacle, myself included.

The vanguard of the navy of New Spain was afloat and bobbing gently in the waters.

Not content with this, Lopez then boarded the flagship with a few mariners of some experience, and took a triumphant promenade around the pond several times, albeit rather clumsily in such confinement, to the utter awe and delight of the Tlascalans.

Having witnessed this great event, I had no desire to linger in Tlascala to see these proud ships taken to pieces. And so, on the next morning,

I set forth for Vera Cruz, in the company of six sailors of like mind returning to what they told me had become a true Spanish seaport.

This was not the first time I had heard such boasting, and I had not been there since we first departed for the then unknown Tenochtitlan, which no doubt was the reason for my curiosity.

What had been an arduous and dangerous journey up from Vera Cruz was now only fatiguing in the opposite direction, for the towns along the way were garrisoned, the inhabitants had been pacified and half-Christianized, and the route carried a certain amount of commerce – gold and various other items of loot going to the seaport, ammunition, arms, European clothing and the like being transported inland, for there was now some seaborne traffic between Vera Cruz and the islands, and even Spain.

But Vera Cruz, at least to me, proved to be a horror. There were ships in the harbor to be sure, and not only Narvaez's captured fleet, and wooden quays at which to dock them. The town had indeed grown. There was a proper church and courthouse on a square that was even half-heartedly gardened. There were painted wooden houses set back off real streets fanning out from it in more or less the Spanish style.

There were also several raucous waterfront taverns and a bordello staffed by the sourest collection of tarts imaginable – Totonac women, bejeweled in ears, nostrils and lips, in the local fashion, but stuffed into ill-fitting and filthy Spanish dresses cut down to the nipples in the bodice, their unacceptably dark faces whitened with chalk powder or some such stuff and smeared with rouge and kohl in a most hideously inexpert manner.

The air of this coastal environ had always been steamy and far from deserted by flies and mosquitoes, but now the rotting detritus of this ill-kept town of our higher civilization and the urine and occasional puddles of vomit anointing the bare earth around the taverns perfumed the air with a foul stench and provided a bountiful banquet for the insects.

A true Spanish seaport town indeed, albeit of the sort reduced to servicing petty smugglers and unsuccessful pirates. And if the town's inhabitants did not quite include pirates, nor exactly smugglers, the newcomers partook of some of the less than fastidiously honest aspects of both.

Diego Velazquez, informed of the Spanish settlement at Vera Cruz but not of the defeat of Narvaez and the defection of his army, had dispatched two ships laden with supplies, ammunition, arms and a few reinforcements for his general's force. These were straightaway appropriated by Cortes' own alcaldes, and upon hearing the tales of the riches to be had inland, the men enlisted in his army soon thereafter.

The governor of Jamaica, not to be outdone, had dispatched three troop ships to implant his own colony up the coast, but when they were greeted mostly roughly by the inhabitants, they put to sea again, lost one of their ships in a storm, and limped into Vera Cruz, where they were likewise recruited as reinforcements for the army of New Spain.

A ship from the Canary Islands heavily laden with arms and ammunition for sale had touched land in Cuba, and, upon encountering both Velazquez's stingy style of bargaining and tales of the riches to be had in the service of Hernando Cortes, made for Vera Cruz. Upon arriving it easily enough sold its military supplies to the alcaldes for a goodly amount of gold, and its crew also enlisted in Cortes' enterprise in search of more.

The tales of all these welcome newcomers were commonplace in the taverns, but with them, on one ship or another, another immigrant had washed up on this shore; one so unwelcome that news of its arrival was mentioned only in fearful and reluctant whispers, and its name hardly spoken aloud, though in the end this new ally of Cortes' was to prove more potent than all the others combined.

The small pox.

This plague was so called, some said, because of the nature of its pustules and buboes, others said to differentiate it from the true venereal pox, though there was nothing small about it, for unlike the pox, it required no sexual contact to spread, and was far more widely and immediately fatal.

I first became aware that something was amiss when I began to notice a number of Indians and a few Spaniards whose faces were pocked with fields of scars so that they seemed to have taken scattershot to the head yet had somehow survived. Upon buying sufficient wine to loosen most reluctant tongues, I learned that what they had survived was not the blasts of arquebuses, but smallpox, as the local familiarity with the plague had caused it to be called here. Further such inebriated inquiries informed me that a third of those who contracted smallpox died most horribly within a week or two, and that there was a mass grave a good distance from the town, where the ashes of the victims were buried after their corpses were thoroughly burned.

Smallpox, I learned from more sailors' tales, had apparently arrived in the Indies from our higher European civilization, and had already decimated the Carib populations of several islands, even to the point of near-extinction on some, for the Indians were much more susceptible to this invader than the Spaniards who had brought it. There were even a few ghoulishly devout sailors who professed to believe that it had been dispatched by God to aid in their conquest, for smallpox apparently swept through a populace in a matter of weeks, or months at the most, and then mysteriously disappeared, leaving much land vacant, and surely there must be the hand of Divine Providence in this.

Just as an injured man has difficulty refraining from picking at the scab over his healing wound against his own better judgement, I was similarly moved to see the effects of this loathsome disease in full flower before quitting what I now knew was a pestilential environ in more than metaphor.

By invoking my station as Cortes' scribe, supposedly commissioned to give him a full report on conditions at Vera Cruz, I was reluctantly escorted to a makeshift shack, once again well away from the town, where the poor wretches afflicted with smallpox were left to either recover or die as God saw fit. My escorts would not go inside, and so I entered this dark and shadowy hell-hole alone.

The light might be dim, but it was enough to show me more than I wanted to see, then or ever. Eight victims lay on straw matting in various stages of the disease. All but one were Indians. The stench of stale urine, feces and gangrenous human flesh was terrible, for no one was about to touch either the victims of the disease or the dung- and piss-saturated straw upon which they languished in agony.

Some of the victims displayed nothing more than an angry red rash. Some were quite covered in yellowish-white-pointed pimples. On others, the pimples had ripened into sacs bursting with pus, which were commencing to leak. The worst were covered with deep leaking lesions and sodden scabs.

As for my own sense of charity and pity, the best I could manage was to dash outside to vomit before my swiftly rising gorge overcame all control.

I quit Vera Cruz the next day, determined never to return and never to subject myself to such a sight again. The first vow I kept, but the second proved entirely futile, for by the time I arrived back in Tlascala the smallpox had preceded me, and the sight of its victims could not be avoided.

Cortes and his triumphant army of Spaniards and Tlascalans had likewise arrived in Tlascala to complete the preparations for the march on Anahuac and Tenochtitlan, and departure was imminent. The brigantines had been dismantled and were ready to be transported. His rear was secured. Supplies and reinforcements were arriving from Vera Cruz, and he sent out ships to fetch back more. He had assembled an army of tens of thousands of Tlascalan auxiliaries.

All that remained was to stage a grand parade.

Smallpox had struck down Maxixca, friend and ally of Cortes and New Spain, but the pall this might have cast on this proceeding was lifted soon before it began by the glad tiding that their Lord had sent the plague to Tenochtitlan before His army of Christian Soldiers. Among the many He had struck down was the Emperor Cuitlahuac himself. He had been replaced with Cuatemoc, the stripling nephew of Montezuma, about whom little was known save that his modest previous position had been no more than guardian of the Tlatelolco market.

God send the right!

As for me, I found no support in my heart for the cause of New Spain, though yes, I had determined to follow its trajectory to its bitter end, so as to complete the very task I am engaged in now; to wit, to tell the only version of what was surely going to be a famous and oft-told tale unhindered by passion for either side's cause. For while I had come to detest the burgeoning reach of New Spain, I could hardly wish to witness the bloody triumph of the vanishing Empire of Mexico either.

The parade rode and marched through the main square of the city before the temple which now served as a sort of reviewing stand for all the caciques and nobles of Tlascala. The other side of the square was thronged with reveling citizenry.

First came the squadrons of Spanish cavalry led by the Captain-General himself. Then the cannon drawn by Tlascalan tamanes. Behind marched rank after rank of Spanish infantry. These were greeted by continuous shouts, whistles, fluting, drumming, and the tossing of garlands of flowers.

Then the Tlascalans in their tens of thousands paraded past, splendidly attired in their own martial style; befeathered, bejeweled, bearing maquahuitls, bows, lances, atlatls, gaily decorated shields. They had been schooled to march, or rather strut, in regular battalions in the Spanish fashion, each behind the featherwork standard of its commander.

The salute from the crowd that greeted their own army was even louder and more tumultuous, and not only because it was a far larger force composed of their own warriors. For they had never seen their men parade in such a manner before; a manner, after all, designed to set the heart pounding with martial ardor, dismay any watching enemies, and lift the spirits of the populace it represented, a form of military theater given much attention and drilling in Europe, but of course worse than useless on any field of battle.

The mighty warriors of Tlascala had at least for the moment been molded into a fair simulation of a European army. No longer were they a barbarian horde defending their homeland and seeking sacrifices for Tlascalan altars. They had become an auxiliary army of New Spain.

The Jews, being by inclination and experience a sardonic race, generally grant their God a sense of humor, albeit a dark one to suit the taste of His worshipers, but the Christians accept what they are pleased to consider Divine Intervention without recourse to laughter at even the most bitter Divine Jest. Nor are the Tlascalans, let alone their bloodthirsty gods, gifted or cursed with this ironic perspective.

I, therefore, being the only son of Abraham to witness this glorious spectacle, was no doubt the only one present who appreciated the irony.

The Tlascalans cheered the Spanish army. The Tlascalans cheered their own warriors marching to battle in its service. Cortes saluted the Tlascalan paramount caciques as he rode past the temple. Both sides cheered and saluted each other as allies.

But no one cheered or saluted the mighty ally who had already reached the heart of the enemy capital and slain its sovereign. Not even I could spare a comradely salute for the invisible army of the smallpox.

34

MY FIRST CROSSING OF the great mountains had been a perilous and arduous journey toward an unseen legend, the second a flight from seeming disaster, but now I was in the train of a mighty army returning to finish the conquest of the Empire of Mexico according to a plan of my own inspiration which I doubted could fail, but which I now detested as the commission of an atrocious crime.

My only hope was that Cuatemoc, the new Emperor, might realize the hopelessness of his position and surrender Tenochtitlan without a struggle that would see this great wonder of his world destroyed, or that failing, that Cortes would have the patience to content himself with winning the city by siege alone, however long it might take.

The omens, as Montezuma would have had it, were not clear. Save for trees freshly felled across the path to slow the army's way forward and a few distant scouting parties, we traversed the high passes unopposed, a sign, perhaps, that Cuatemoc was husbanding his forces, depleted at Otumba and subsequent battles and by smallpox as well, for a final stand within the city in the lake.

But when we reached the other side of the passes and gazed down upon the Valley of Mexico, its cities and towns gilded by the afternoon sun, we saw, despite the bright daylight, signal fires burning on the heights of the foothills surrounding the valley and on high points within it, as if Cuatemoc was summoning all the inhabitants thereof to rise against us.

If so, it seemed that, even as I had predicted, the call to arms had gone unheeded. Cortes' plan was to march to Texcoco, close by the shores of the lake, where the brigantines could most easily be launched once they arrived, and use it as his base of operations. But Texcoco was the second city of Anahuac and the staunchest ally of Tenochtitlan, if indeed Cuatemoc had an ally remaining, and surely if he would fight for any of the lakeside cities he would make a stand before it.

So Cortes ordered the army into battle formation even as we descended to the plain. But as we marched westward to the shore, the only Mexica warriors to be seen were parties of a modest size clustered around their beacon fires atop distant high points, doing no more than observing our passage.

I see that I am using, or misusing, the collective pronouns 'we' and 'us', for there seems to be nothing else for it. While my spirit had detached itself from any loyalty to the cause of the forces of New Spain, my body was constrained to share the fate of the collectivity to live or to die. I was among them, if you will, but not with them, as Homer, if he had been there, might have marched with a cold eye amidst the army of Agamemnon against his admired Troy.

We, then, encountered no Mexica resistance until we reached a little river flowing through a narrow ravine. The bridge across it had been hastily half-demolished, and on the other side was a force of some several thousand Mexica warriors, who shouted and howled, and held their ground, shooting arrows, throwing stones and launching javelins. But a cannonade, a few fusillades of crossbow bolts and arquebus balls and the daunting sight of our much greater force caused them to retreat, albeit in good order, after a short while, and they were well gone before the bridge had been repaired and we crossed.

By this time the sun was going down, and Cortes decided to make camp beyond Texcoco and proceed to the city in the morning. That evening, he summoned me to his tent, and I had no recourse but to attend him.

'I like it not,' he told me as I arrived, on his feet and pacing in small fretful circles outside the tent.

'Why not? All would seem to be proceeding according to plan.'

'*Whose* plan, Alvaro, yours or this Cuatemoc's?' he growled, hunkering down on the bare earth and motioning for me to do likewise. 'He seems much more clever than Cuitlahuac. He takes care to observe our movements, but he offers no resistance. He clearly signals *something* to the entire valley, but *what?*'

I tried to reply with no more than a shrug, but Cortes would not have it. 'Come, Alvaro, one comrade to another, what do you think is in the man's mind?'

Once more, against my will, I found myself drawn into Cortes' service, or perhaps more truthfully seduced into playing my part in this fascinating game of deadly chess. For it is said that chess is the King of games, and so what game can be more seductive to an intellectual warrior than the game of war, upon which it is based?

'He is doing what I suppose I would do were I him,' I ventured. 'Realizing he will find no support from the former vassals of the lakeshores, he is reconnoitering our movements in some force, while withdrawing his armies into Tenochtitlan. Since siegecraft seems foreign to warfare here, he assumes you will be constrained to attack him in his stronghold, where, since a naval assault must be likewise beyond his comprehension, he believes he can hold the causeways against you.'

Of course I was trying to lead him into a tactic that might serve my only remaining cause, which was to preserve Tenochtitlan from destruction, but Cortes greeted this with a shake of the head and a frown. Nevertheless I pressed on.

'Therefore allow him to do so, pulling as many mouths as he may into the city, the worse to withstand a siege. You need only hold the causeways on the landward ends, no difficult task. Perhaps he plans to bring in supplies by canoe, but he cannot be reckoning with the apparition of a fleet of Spanish warships on his lake. You need only be patient, and sooner or later he must surrender the city without a fight. The worst possible result of a patient siege is that he holds on until everyone within dies of hunger or thirst, in which case you will still have the golden prize of a great intact city, if not its inhabitants.'

Cortes grunted, and shook his head more strongly. 'What if Cuatemoc's plan is to make his stand at Texcoco?' he demanded. 'If

Cuatemoc has withdrawn his main forces there and his most powerful ally will fight with them for their own city, there is no question of a siege, we will have to fight our way into a large city and pacify it, in which case victory may be possible, but hardly assured.'

'But you forget that you deposed Cacama and the Texcocans accepted your puppet King, Cuitcuitzca.'

'Who may or may not still rule. The latest intelligence is that he was being contested by one Coanco, about whom I know nothing. Who is to say who rules in Texcoco now? Who is to say therefore on which side they may come down?'

To make subsequent events less mystifying to you, dear reader, than they were to us at the time, we learned in the aftermath that Coanco, Cuitcuitzca's own brother, had deposed and exiled him as a traitor for his collaboration with the Spaniards, and had made a tacit alliance with Cuatemoc, who, as titular head of the Triple Alliance, had confirmed him in return as King of Texcoco.

But none of this was known when a delegation from Texcoco arrived in our encampment early the next morning before the final march on the city could begin, not only under a standard of truce, but bearing a modest amount of tribute in gold and a message from Coanco imploring Cortes to spare the territories of Texcoco, inviting him to accept the hospitality of the city, and even volunteering to swear allegiance to the Spanish Crown.

This was glad tidings, albeit of a sort that seemed too good to be swallowed whole, particularly when Cortes was enjoined to camp just outside the city the next night to give time for a proper reception to be prepared.

It seemed to Cortes that this would indeed give time to stage a proper reception, whose welcoming nature, however, would be taken for granted only by the most credulous naïf. And so he sent the envoys back to the city with his agreement to make camp, but as soon as they were beyond his sight, and therefore he out of theirs, he marched to Texcoco in battle formation more than half-expecting to fight.

We were greeted outside the walls of the city before noon not by an opposing army but by the very same delegation of nobles, who made no mention of their previous injunction, and instead welcomed the entire army, tens of thousands of Tlascalans included, into the city, with garlands of flowers and clouds of fragrant incense. The only thing that gave me pause was that Coanco, who after all had pledged to swear fealty to the Spanish Crown, was not there himself to greet its representative.

Texcoco was not as large a city as Tenochtitlan but it was of similar style, though the buildings were if anything more artfully decorated and more graceful of design, and the abundance of gardens was even greater; even the most modest of houses seemed all but roofed over with fragrant blooms.

We were led from the gate in the walls up a splendid avenue lined with what appeared to be the residences of nobles and rich merchants to a plaza not dissimilar to the Temple Precinct in Tenochtitlan and thence to a palace compound larger even than that of Axayacatl, which, we were told, was to house the entire Spanish army, with the Tlascalans permitted to camp outside. It was not a long distance from the gate to the palace compound, but long enough to be disquieting, for the avenue crossed a number of similar avenues on the way, as well as more modest streets, and there was no one abroad. Save for the clatter of horses' hoofs, the rumble of cannon carriage wheels on stone, and the patter of marching feet and sandals, Texcoco was as quiet as, well, a tomb.

The situation grew even more ominous as soon as we were ensconced in the palace compound, for the delegation which had greeted us departed, and not a Texcocan was to be seen within the walls or in the plaza outside it. Cortes decided to dispatch a few men to climb to the summit of the nearby pyramid to reconnoiter, and I, desirous of viewing this second-greatest metropolis in Anahuac from on high, decided to accompany them.

The climb was less arduous than the ascent of the great pyramid of Teotihuacan, for there was no hindering overgrowth, and the steps seemed designed for normal human ease, and less arduous too than the climb to the top of the temple of Huitzilopochtli in Tenochtitlan, for they went straight up the face of a smaller construct, but the view from the top was equally commanding.

What we beheld, however, was utterly dismaying.

The sight of the city itself from on high was as grand as that of Tenochtitlan, and even more beautiful, with its abundance of well-tended gardens and more lavishly colored buildings, a metropolis built more for providing a life of graceful ease for its inhabitants than bloody worship. But thousands upon thousands of Texcocans, women and children among them, as well as tamanes bearing baskets of food and jugs of liquid sustenance and even household goods, were streaming northeast out of the city across the plain. Worse still, a great and greatly disorganized fleet of very heavily laden canoes was paddling frantically across the lake towards Tenochtitlan.

Texcoco was being evacuated and the process was well advanced. Perhaps the Texcocans were of two minds, those fleeing inland hoping to save it thereby from a battle that would destroy its loveliness, but those making their way over the waters bent on reinforcing Tenochtitlan in making its final stand.

One thing, though, was certain: had we heeded the entreaties of Coanco's emissaries and delayed through another night, we would have entered an intact city as deserted as Teotihuacan.

Cortes immediately sent troops to fan out through the city, prevent those still within it from leaving, and seize whatever caciques and nobles remained. A few of these were rounded up, and from their number Cortes chose one Ixlilxochitl as his latest puppet King.

While this was going on, the Tlascalans committed a certain amount of rapine and plunder within the nearly deserted city, which went on for a few days afterward, but once Cortes brought them to heel and order was restored, many of the inhabitants who had fled inland, seeing their city but lightly damaged, returned, and delegations from the surrounding Texcocan territories streamed in to swear allegiance to their new King and seek protection under the wing of New Spain.

The city itself had been built about a mile from the lakeshore rather than directly upon it, but Nezahualcoyotl had built a garden estate on the shore with a canal connecting it to Texcoco, so a project was begun to widen and deepen it sufficiently to accommodate the brigantines when they were transported across the mountains and reassembled.

Cortes had now secured an ideal base, pacified the eastern side of the valley, and moreover had secured the landward entrance to the western causeway linking the lakeshore to Tenochtitlan. He now turned his attention to sealing a second of the four, the southern causeway which began at Iztapalapa.

Leaving a strong garrison in Texcoco under Sandoval, he took a force of some two hundred Spanish infantry, a score of cavalry and several thousand Tlascalans south along the eastern shore of Lake Texcoco and then westward along its southern shore towards Iztapalapa. Following my determination to record what significant events I could for this account, I went with them.

But nothing transpired of significance until we were within a few miles of the city. There, on the open coastal plain approaching it, Cuatemoc, perhaps by now beginning to understand the rudiments of what Cortes was about, had stationed an army of some two or three thousand warriors in a forlorn attempt to deny us control of the approach to the Iztapalapa causeway, which is to say to retain its use for himself.

Or so it seemed.

The Mexica force was entirely inadequate to such a defensive task, and although they put up a valiant show of resistance, they were soon routed and forced to fall back into the city. Given that Cuatemoc must surely have been apprised of the strength of the Spanish and Tlascalan forces, this should have aroused suspicion, but alas, at the time it did not, and neither did the passing sight of a score or so canoe-borne laborers out on the lake apparently repairing the dike separating the smaller brackish western lobe of Lake Texcoco from the larger eastern section of the lake.

Since Iztapalapa was situated on an isthmus between them and more of it than not was built out on pilings on the western side, and the western lobe was somewhat higher than the eastern, keeping this dike in good repair was a vital task, even in the face of a possible impending invasion, and in our haste to pursue the fleeing Mexica into the city before they could take up good defensive positions, no one paid the laborers much attention.

The Mexica warriors dispersed into the city in a disorderly manner, and while the Spaniards maintained discipline, the Tlascalans poured in after them in a vengeful and gleefully murderous horde. The majority of the inhabitants had apparently already fled toward Tenochtitlan along the causeway and by boat, in terror, or so it seemed, at the approach of the army of New Spain.

The result was slaughter, looting and destruction that went on well beyond the fall of night. The Tlascalans hunted down the Mexica warriors street by street, and likewise broke into the houses, vacant or not, helping themselves to the contents, killing what men, children and women had been left behind, raping the latter, and, in the sanguinary process, setting everything afire that would burn.

Since Iztapalapa was largely built on pilings, weight was an important factor, and the buildings over the water were built of wood and adobe, and moreover boasted rooftop gardens whose vines were often draped down the sides. As a matter of habit or fashion, much of the rest of the city was likewise constructed, so that hundreds, or more probably thousands, of buildings were set ablaze.

The fires conveniently illumined the city for the benefit of the Tlascalans, who descended into a rampage of murder, arson, looting, rape, and I warrant cannibalism. It was an incarnadine scene of fire and blood, cries of pain and howls of fury, acrid smoke and roasting flesh, that would have been perfectly acceptable to Satan as a choice precinct of Hell.

It also saved most of our lives.

Nothing could have stayed the Tlascalans until their own raging fire of the spirit had burned down to embers, and Cortes and the Spaniards were not so foolish as to even try, for it was all we could do to keep clear of the madness ourselves. We were broken up into several separate parties in the confusion, some in the main square, some in the abandoned palace, others elsewhere, and I found myself, along with perhaps two score others, huddling in the famous and beauteous gardens to which we had been escorted by none other than Cuitlahuac on our previous visit to the city, an island, at least for the moment, of Arcadian calm amidst the chaos without.

But the sounds and smells and fires of the melee were all around us, the soldiers had their weapons pointed outward to form a defensive picket against any Tlascalans, who, stumbling on this tranquil and darkened environ, might be so crazed as to mistake us for prey in the ghoulish fiery twilight, and our fearful ears were fitfully pricked up to detect the sounds of any such approach.

In such a situation, sleep was the furthest thing from our minds.

That is what foiled Cuatemoc's ruthless and desperate stratagem and saved our lives.

The sound we heard was not that of running feet but a great rushing rumble as of a great storm-whipped wave washing up on a nearby beach. But there was no beach nearby, and the sound did not break upon sand and vanish, rather it continued on and on like a wide river gushing through rocky rapids. There was a canal in the garden feeding waters of the lake into the ponds and fountains, and the water in it began to rise. It filled the ponds and fountains to overflowing, and then likewise its own banks, and in minutes the entire garden was ankle-deep in flood water, and still rising.

Who realized what was happening first in the confusion I do not know, in memory it was myself, but I warrant every Spaniard in the city must have escaped with the same memory, for we all broke and fled at once, each man for himself.

The workers at the dike had not been repairing it. They had been breaking it to flood the city with the waters of the western lobe of the lake and drown us within it.

Ankle-deep, shin-deep, knee-deep, I found myself running inland through the burning city, or rather slogging with agonizing slowness through the rising tide, as one does in a nightmare of futile flight from monstrous or demonic pursuers.

Still the waters rose, and I found myself swimming for my life through fitfully firelit darkness towards a shore whose distance and direction could only be discerned by the absence of flames beyond it.

I had never counted myself a strong swimmer, indeed not much of a swimmer at all, but necessity kept me afloat, and at length I felt my feet scrape bottom, and, staggering, panting, coughing, spitting out brackish water, I half staggered and half crawled up onto the refuge of the lakeshore.

Scores of Spaniards had already arrived, drenched and shivering in the night breeze, and we stood there in silent dismay and wonder looking back toward whence we had come. Yes, in wonder as well as despair, for it was a terrible yet evilly marvelous sight.

More scores of Spaniards were swimming and stumbling towards us, and thousands of Tlascalans. The corpses of hundreds more Tlascalans floated and bobbed on the flood. Beyond, the fires still burning atop the half-drowned buildings silhouetted the city in dancing flame against the starry night sky, mirrored by a second and upside-down Iztapalapa shimmering in orange and black on the water.

Ironically, had it not been for the rapine of the Tlascalans, we would have been asleep and drowned, and the very noise and horror of their terrible orgy of slaughter and destruction, rather than any cleverness or strategy on the part of Cortes, had foiled Cuatemoc's plan.

More ironic and terrible still, while my soul could not but mourn and sorrow at the destruction of fair and lovely Iztapalapa, may all the gods of this land and all others forgive me, the vista of a city perishing in both fire and water, mirrored on the lake, haloed by an unnatural sunrise that was in truth its sunset, was an image of beauty that surpassed that of its living avenues and verdant gardens to my immoral eye.

Nor was the irony diminished when Cortes returned with his army to Texcoco. Cuatemoc had evacuated those inhabitants of Texcoco still loyal to Tenochtitlan to reinforce it, not to save the city, but that was what he had accomplished; a Texcoco still standing and in the hands of his enemies. Taken together, the capture of Texcoco and the destruction of Iztapalapa had served the same purpose, that of Hernando Cortes.

For together they had made the situation starkly clear to all the cities and towns and villages in the Valley of Mexico. Cuatemoc would destroy any city but his own to slay the army of New Spain, but he would not defend them. And, having left but minor residual forces on the shores, he could not defend them against Malinche even if he would.

My plan had succeeded. The inevitability I had predicted had come to pass.

Tenochtitlan might still stand but the Empire of the Mexica had fallen.

Long live New Spain.

Delegations flocked in from everywhere to swear their fealty. Seeing the impending end of the rule of their erstwhile dire overlords fast approaching, many of the tribes sought to play their vengeful part in their final defeat and gain favor in the eyes of their new master in the bloody bargain.

Cortes welcomed them. Spanish adventurers from the Indies likewise flocked to his golden standard. Cortes welcomed them too. All was in readiness for the climactic siege of Tenochtitlan or a terrible battle for the city.

All save the fleet of brigantines to close the trap. Cortes sent Sandoval with a strong force to escort the disassembled brigantines to Texcoco, and to await their readiness before beginning the final assault, for what parties Cuatemoc sent out in canoes to seek supplies on the shore had been easily repulsed. Tenochtitlan was bulging with refugees from Texcoco and being ravaged by the smallpox, and time was on the side of Hernando Cortes.

But conditions on the western side of the lakes were uncertain, so Cortes decided to pass the time by leading a powerful expedition around them, northward around Lake Xaltocan and down the other side at least as far as Tacuba.

Before he was to depart, I sought to play a part in his war of conquest for the very last time, or rather to bring it to a less deplorable conclusion. 'Allow Cuatemoc to surrender Tenochtitlan intact,' I implored him.

'Allow it? Why would I seek to prevent it? Should he seek to surrender, I would gladly accept. But I have received no such entreaty.'

'Perhaps he believes it would be futile. You have given him no cause to believe otherwise.'

'I did not start this war!' Cortes declared angrily and quite outrageously.

'*You did not start this war?*' I shouted at him in a fury, quite losing control of myself. 'Montezuma arrived unbidden on the Spanish shore with his armies and demanded that Iberia bow down to Tenochtitlan and worship Huitzilopochtli or be conquered by force?'

In the next moment, I cringed at what I expected would be the reply of this conquering Captain-General to the presumptuous anger of his lowly scribe. But I was mistaken, for his visage softened and his eyes grew tender, and he favored me with the smile of the man who had been my friend, back there in Cuba, where it had all begun.

'You love that city, do you not, Alvaro?' he said. 'You love it more than you love any and all of its inhabitants. You love it more than you love the King or the Cross. You love it more than you love me. More, I do believe, than you love yourself.'

I could only nod, for in that moment, and for a long while before, there had been precious little love for myself in my heart.

'God save me,' said Cortes, 'but so do I.' His face hardened. 'But that will not prevent me from tearing it down stone by stone to complete the task I have been chosen to complete by that very same God. I fancy that there is some poet in me, and a whiff of the philosopher as well, but above all I am a Soldier of the Cross and a general of Spain, and I will not place anything above my sacred duty to both.'

And I saw that he spoke from the heart. He truly believed this. This was what Hernando Cortes really was. A monster and a cavalier. A hero and a villain. I hated him for it and I loved him for it. He was somehow both a better and worse man than I. Perhaps that is the necessary nature of 'great men'. Not being one of their company, I would not know.

'What would you have me do, Alvaro?' he said.

'Send a message to Cuatemoc offering generous terms of surrender.'

'In return for all you have done in aid of my cause, and out of friendship, this I will do,' said Hernando. 'If he surrenders the city, I shall not only leave it untouched, but he shall be allowed to continue to rule it as my vassal, even as I rule New Spain as a vassal of my own King.'

'You know full well he will never accept.'

Cortes shrugged. 'This much and no more, I do for you, Alvaro,' he said. 'The choice is his, not mine.'

And then he favored me with the crooked smile of the Feathered Serpent I had crafted him to be, or rather the one that had lurked within him all along waiting to be born. 'And I do it for myself, as well,' he said. 'For now the sins that I may be forced to commit if he refuses will be on Cuatemoc's soul, not mine.'

The message was sent.

Cortes departed on his expedition without waiting for a reply.

I remained behind in the admittedly futile hope that it would arrive before his return.

It did not.

There never was one.

By that silence was the doom of Tenochtitlan sealed.

35

M Y TALE NEARS ITS END, as did the Empire of the Mexica as Cortes made his tour around the lakes to Tacuba, though the greatest horror of the entire conquest was yet to come, a tragedy which I see that I am in the process of steeling myself to reluctantly describe.

I would say that my tale is reaching its *bitter* end, for bitter was my heart in the moment which will conclude this narrative, but as I write this it is years later, years of reflective contemplation among the people of this simple village, and while the bitterness lingers on, they have at length taught me anew the lesson I learned atop that pyramid at Teotihuacan. Greece fell, and so did Rome, and Al Andaluz. But the peoples thereof, in their towns and villages and farmsteads, remained, and remembered some of what had been, and their lives went on.

To say that the people of villages such as my own carry forward the torch of what had been the Empire of the Mexica would be a bathetic fallacy, for what now lies below in the lands the Mexica once ruled is indeed New Spain, ruled by Spaniards, filled with their churches, well along towards speaking their language, its captured wealth flowing towards Iberia, the imperial pride of the Mexica long subdued, even the spirit of rebellion fading away into servility.

From the vantage of its Spanish rulers and those of its natives who must seek their favor and toil for their benefit, this is a vanquished land. But from this isolated refuge which time has both preserved and forgotten, I can see, or perhaps merely hope, that the day will come when New Spain too will be no more; slowly and stealthily absorbed by the far vaster populace under its political and religious rule as it has now absorbed what was.

And then there will arise here something that is a melange of both, as the former Iberian principalities have melded with the peninsula's former Arabic kingdoms to become the still-young nation now calling itself Spain.

Even now it is beginning to have a name that is overwhelming that given it by the conquerors. The natives of the land are using it in Nahuatl, and it is seeping into the vocabulary of the Spaniards as well. This new name is spreading out from the great valley thereof which once owned it for the Mexica, who have begun to lose even that, being once more contemptuously called 'Aztecs' by their former vassals; a name, I remind you, which more or less means 'wanderers from the wastes' in Nahuatl.

Its peoples have begun to call *all* the lands of 'New Spain' 'Mexico' now. The name is even seeping into Spanish.

The Empire of the Mexica is no more. The Mexica are no more. Neither are the Tlascalans or the Totonacs or the Texcocans. The tribes are disappearing. And someday so will the ruling tribe that calls itself the Spaniards. The time will come when all they have conquered will call these lands by the new name which has reached even to these isolated heights. And then both the descendants of the Mexica who once ruled and the Spaniards who rule now will be *Mexicans* together, and New Spain, if not its imperial rule, will be gone.

But I see that I am not only getting beyond the end of my tale, but seeking to escape from it into more hopeful musing upon events that may or may not occur long after its author has departed from this world. I must screw up my courage and complete the task upon which I have embarked, no matter how tragically this true history must end.

Cortes' expedition around the lakes to Tacuba fought a few battles and skirmishes, but these were of little consequence, I was not there to witness any of it, and by the time he returned to Texcoco I had no stomach for any more boastful tales of military valor in the service of an already triumphant cause I had come to despise, so I will spare you them, dear reader, hoping that by now I have persuaded you to be of like mind.

The launching of the assembled brigantines, however, was both a decisive event and a magnificent spectacle; the entire population of Texcoco turned out to see it, and so did I.

The thirteen brigantines were rolled close to the canal side by side with wide spaces between. Then began the delicate and arduous task of shifting them all onto second sets of rollers at right angles to the first, so that when it was finally completed, they were lined up bow to stern to bow at the very lip of the bank, which had been dug in a short gentle slope to the water and moistened into slick mud.

Then all the tamanes and many volunteers from among the Texcocans and Tlascalans and Spaniards alike pushed them sliding down the mud-lubricated embankment more or less at the same time to the sound of mighty splashes and subsequent more modest ones as the waves stirred up buffeted back and forth in the narrow confines of the canal, while the unrigged ships heeled over at what seemed to me a perilous angle before the ballast in their hulls righted them of their own accord.

The crews then boarded, and though the brigantines were to be towed to the lake by tamanes on either bank of the canal, the triangular mainsails at least were raised, though tightly reefed, to make the naval parade all the grander.

One after the other, the brigantines were towed down the canal and into the lake, and one by one, as they attained their freedom, the mainsails were unreefed, the foresails unfurled, and they sailed out onto the lake in a line, like great ducklings triumphantly leaving the maternal nest for the last time.

The fleet sailed a modest distance from the shore, turned in the general direction of Tenochtitlan, and fired a great cannonade towards it, an even greater cheer went up, and a gay celebration that was to last into the night began.

Thus, might it be said, did the preparations end, and the battle for Tenochtitlan begin.

It was to end far less gloriously and there would be nothing gay about it.

Cortes divided his army into three more or less independent forces, each given a specific set of objectives, each numbering some score or so cavalry, a like number of arquebusiers and crossbowmen, a few cannon, about a hundred or so Spanish infantry, and several thousand Tlascalans and assorted other Indian allies.

One, under Alvarado, was commissioned to seize and hold the Tacuba causeway, the second, under Olid, was to do likewise at Coyoacan, while Sandoval's task was to secure the Iztapalapa causeway. The fourth, at Tepeyac, was to be left open, at least initially, to afford Cuatemoc's forces an opportunity to flee the city in vulnerable narrow file, allowing him in effect the dignity to surrender without humiliating formalities if he so chose.

The Captain-General transformed himself into an admiral and commanded the fleet. I, upon reflection, chose to accompany him on the flagship, for several reasons.

Personal safety was among them, for after surviving a voyage across the unpredictably stormy Atlantic and a true storm on the way here from Cuba, I had little fear of the placid waters of the lakes, whereas, had I inflicted myself upon Alvarado, Olid or Sandoval, who, shall we say, made little effort to enlist me, I would be in the thick of what fighting there might be.

Also, if I was to attempt to record as best I might the events of these disconnected campaigns, it seemed to me that the best vantage from which to do so would be at the side of the lakeborne commander of the whole operation.

But finally, I was encouraged that Cortes' plan seemed to be the one closest to my own heart, namely to seal off Tenochtitlan and subject it to a patient siege, rather than storm it, and this was certainly the only personal deployment whereby I might do what I could to persuade him to maintain it to the end.

Perforce, I could only learn of the exploits of the dispersed armies post facto, and even Cortes' intelligence during the campaign was habitually late and fragmentary, and so I am forced to relay it to you, dear reader, in a similarly terse, confused and fragmentary manner, though for clarity's sake I shall endeavor to integrate what I learned long after it occurred in a timely moment within the train of this narrative.

Olid and Alvarado set forth to secure the Coyoacan and Tacuba causeways at the same time. Their combined armies reached and occupied Tacuba without meeting resistance, and, according to plan, made a short march to the hill of Chapultepec, where there was a spring that was the main supply of fresh water to Tenochtitlan, and demolished the aqueduct carrying it to the city.

Olid then went on to seize the bridgehead to the causeway at Coyoacan. In both places, the Mexica had dug ditches across the causeways. The Spaniards would drive them off, and fill them in, the Mexica would return, usually under cover of night, to break through the causeways again, only to be driven off by the Spaniards, who filled them in once more.

This digging and filling in continued interminably and under fire by canoe-borne Mexica and by Spanish crossbowmen and arquebusiers, but there was little hand-to-hand, for the Spaniards sought not to imperil themselves by attempting to advance far up the causeways, nor did the foraying Mexica seek to drive them off.

Futile and desultory though these skirmishes might be, they were harbingers of far more desperate battles to come.

Nine days later, Sandoval's forces set out on the shorter march to Iztapalapa, arriving rapidly, and easily driving off a small Mexica force that had garrisoned the ruins, or at least those still not flooded, and the trap was all but completed.

I was not there to witness its setting, but I was when Cortes received the reports thereof two days after Sandoval had completed his task, and the Spanish fleet, accompanied by perhaps a thousand Texcocan canoes, sailed forth to close it with the naval blockade.

The plan had been to sail some few miles from the shore down the length of Lake Texcoco, to intimidate both any Mexica forces on the land and what canoe-borne enemy might be abroad on the lake by a grand showing of the flag, or rather of the sails, but this was delayed when we passed within easy sight of a small rocky island, where a Mexica garrison was spied sending up signals with a smoky fire.

Cortes decided to clear the lake of this outpost, which he supposed was keeping Tenochtitlan apprised of the movements of his fleet. He sailed the flotilla close to it, but far enough to be out of range of the futile arrows launched against it, and debarked for it with small boats holding about a hundred and fifty soldiers.

This was a battle, or rather little more than a skirmish, which I observed from afar on the flagship. It did not take long to accomplish the task, but while the battle was still under way, a fleet, or rather a disorganized horde, of Mexica canoes, several hundred of them, weighed down with warriors, came paddling furiously and laboriously across the lake towards us from the direction of Tenochtitlan.

By the time Cortes and his shore party had regained the brigantines, they were close upon us, but halted well out of arquebus range, and therefore with our ships out of range of their arrows and javelins, as if uncertain whether to attack. Cortes was likewise unwilling or unable to begin the first naval battle these waters had ever seen, for the wind, a light breeze to begin with, had entirely died, and while the brigantines were equipped with oars for such exigencies, rowing such heavy vessels against a multitude of light and far more maneuverable canoes would have put our fleet at a significant disadvantage, especially if the Mexica thought to employ fire arrows.

It was a bizarre several minutes as the two disparate fleets sat there regarding each other and shouting imprecations, a mighty European flotilla bristling with arquebuses and cannon, and the puny but more numerous canoes filled with Indians armed only with bows and javelins and wearing little more than loincloths, the navies of two different worlds confronting each other on the water for the first time, each at a loss as to what to do next.

One god or another finally decided to end the standoff by sending a breeze, which freshened into a wind that filled the sails of the fleet of New Spain. Cortes deployed his ships in a line facing the Mexica, piled on all the sail the yards would hold, and bore down upon them at frightening speed.

The bows of the brigantines rammed into the tightly packed canoes and plowed through them as if they were so much driftwood; splinter-ing, swamping, overturning scores of them with every yard they advanced, while the cannon and arquebuses laid down withering fire in all directions from within their midst.

The terrified Mexica put up no resistance at all; those who could turned and began paddling back in a total panic towards whence they came, while the fleeter brigantines pursued them through an ever-widening slick of wrecked canoes, debris and corpses, harrying them all the way back to the island shore of Tenochtitlan.

If hundreds of canoes had sallied forth, mere scores survived to dis-perse within the canal system of the city, where further pursuit was impossible, and Cortes, in modest emulation of Columbus, had made himself Admiral of the Inland Sea.

Emboldened by this total rout, Cortes, instead of making for the city of Iztapalapa, brought the fleet south around Tenochtitlan, turned west to the Iztalapala causeway, and anchored off the fortress of Xoloc, which guarded the entrance from the causeway to the city itself.

When, fearing all too well that I already knew the answer, I inquired as to what he was doing, he replied with a wild and triumphant gleam in his eyes that he was abandoning my unmartial and over-cautious plan for a better one of his own conceived of on the spot.

'A general must seize opportunity,' he told me excitedly.

And so he did.

Holding off the Mexica garrison with a naval bombardment, he landed troops on the causeway before the fortress under insignificant opposition. Rather than further reduce the fortress of Xoloc to rubble with cannon, coveting it for his own purposes, he stormed it from the causeway, a somewhat more perilous, but not very difficult task, occu-pied it, and declared that it, not the city of Iztapalapa, would be his 'forward headquarters' for the 'final assault'.

'*What* final assault?' I demanded plaintively. 'Tenochtitlan is now under an unbreakable siege by land and by sea. All we need do is rest at our ease and wait for it to fall into our hands.'

'Don't be a fool, Alvaro,' Cortes told me dismissively. 'We now control the entire Iztapalapa causeway as well as the entrance to

Tenochtitlan, so that we may enter the city and bring up as much reinforcement and supplies as what resistance we meet within may require. It would be unmanly and un-Christian to disdain a gift that God has deigned to place in my waiting hands. We shall have the city within days, not weeks!'

Three of the four causeways now being sealed, Cortes, in his inflamed state, gave over his knightly plan to offer Cuatemoc an honorable tacit surrender by allowing the defeated Emperor to flee the city via the northern causeway to Tepeyac and into his waiting arms. On the excuse that Mexica had been seen bringing supplies into the city along it, true or not, and such niceties had never mattered to Cortes, he dispatched Sandoval to close this last possible avenue of escape.

While he was bringing up more men and supplies from Iztapalapa and waiting for word that Sandoval had accomplished this task, the Mexica, seeing that they were about to be entirely trapped, with the enemy forces occupying the very fortress at their city gates built to keep such as them out, made continuous, desperate and foredoomed efforts to dislodge the army of New Spain from the fortress of Xoloc.

Night and day they attacked from canoes, sallying forth from the canals of the city to within arrow and stone range, launching quick fusillades, and retreating before the brigantines could come within arquebus and crossbow range, for they quickly learned that they were not about to fire cannonballs when they were close to the fortress for fear of striking the Spaniards in and before it.

Such was the complete futility on the eastern side of the causeway where the army of New Spain before the city was protected by the brigantines. On the western side, where it was not, the Mexica were able to paddle down the length of the causeway and attack along a broad front, spreading out the arquebusiers, crossbowmen and cannon upon it, so that, being willing to take heavy losses in the process, they were able to gain the causeway any number of times and had to be driven back in ferocious battles of swords against maquahuitls, inflicting losses in the process of taking many more.

Cortes was irksomely constrained to break a temporary breach in the causeway wide enough to sail two brigantines through to the western side to deal with them, after which the attacks began to die away.

About the time they had, word arrived that Sandoval now commanded the landward entrance to the Tepeyac causeway and all was ready for the supposedly overwhelming assault on Tenochtitlan itself to begin.

On a brilliantly sunny morning, a mass was said, and Cortes prepared his forces to enter the city. The infantry was placed in the van before the gates to the fortress of Xoloc, with Cortes unable to do other but lead the triumphant entry afoot. Behind was the cavalry, and then the cannon, and then the Tlascalans, all stretched out along the causeway as if preparing for the victory parade he seemed to expect it would be.

I stood well back between the cavalry and the cannon, for my only desire was to bear witness to the end, whatever it might be, and I sought earnestly to live long enough to do so.

The gates to the fortress of Xoloc were opened and Cortes led the march through them. Mere yards up the causeway, the bridge connecting the fortress to the city itself had, unsurprisingly, been removed. Far back as I was, I could only detect this by the fact that the advance had been halted.

But even from this vantage I could see that the Mexica had built a wall of stones on the other side of the gap and were bombarding the front ranks of our army with javelins and stones and arrows from the cover thereof, while the Spaniards answered with arquebuses and crossbows.

I expected Cortes to bring up the cannon to reduce this fortification, but instead our Admiral of the Inland Sea brought up a brigantine on each side of the causeway to smash it to pieces with a terrible crossfire that slammed cannonade after cannonade into the wall from the rear as well as the front and the sides.

Thus the Mexica, no longer at all sheltered by stone, took scores of casualties within minutes, and were quickly driven off before their fortification could even be demolished. Without waiting for orders, soldiers aboard the ships dove madly into the water, swam across it, and scrambled up the quay to either side of the crumbling wall.

No doubt seeing the advance into the city commence in such unseemly chaos, and not to be denied his rightful place leading it,

Cortes, I learned later, swam across the gap in the causeway, followed by much of the infantry.

This I did not see, for, along with the cavalry and the cannon, who did so out of necessity rather than prudence, I lingered behind until the gap had been filled with rubble and I could stumble across.

Two more canals must be crossed before the splendid avenue beyond the city wall could take us to the Temple Precinct, whose capture I hoped would bring about sufficient dismay to cause Cuatemoc to surrender. Unsurprisingly, the bridges had been removed and the far sides of the gaps likewise fortified and defended, and the way forward had to be negotiated in like manner.

Having traversed this path in the opposite direction, I was counting the pauses at the gaps. Call me mad, if you like, or favor me with bravery, which often enough, after all, amounts to the same thing; but, having brought Hernando Cortes from Cuba to this very pass, I had to enter Tenochtitlan at my Feathered Serpent's side.

And so, when I knew that only one canal remained to be crossed, I shouldered and elbowed my way to the fore, dove into the water with the soldiers doing likewise, and paddled and puffed, panting, to scramble up the other side.

Cortes had advanced several score yards up the great avenue to allow the forefront of his army to form up behind him and stood there gazing up it at the distant entrance to the plaza which was the bright fighting heart and dark mystic soul of Tenochtitlan, with his hands on his hips as might have Joshua surveying Jericho and about to trumpet it down.

When I reached him, the two of us stood there silently together contemplating the sight.

The avenue was a long straight canyon between two palisades of gleaming white buildings stretching away to the vanishing point of the entrance to the Temple Precinct, topped by beautiful gardens, brightly painted, here untouched by the ruinous demolitions inflicted upon its nether end when last we had been here, the pinnacle of the great pyramid of Huitzilopochtli peering above them beyond.

I would imagine that Cortes beheld the triumphal route of a Caesar returning with his conquering army to Rome. But I beheld no such impending glory. There were no crowds of citizens lining the parade route to garland the troops with flowers and the conqueror with laurels. The avenue was as empty of humanity as the great plaza at Teotihuacan.

What I beheld was another city inhabited by ghosts.

Not the ghosts of what had been, but the ghosts of what I feared was about to come.

Cortes strode up the avenue and I walked silently one step behind him until the hundreds of infantry had assembled on its pavement to his rear. The gap had now been filled with rubble, and the cavalry and all behind it had halted on the causeway, likewise waiting for the order to advance.

Cortes turned, drew his sword, raised it above his head, and finally spoke in a voice of thunder.

'Forward for Saint James and the Cross! Let nothing stand that would aid those who would oppose us! No retreat! No quarter!'

And then he swept his sword, right, left, up and down the avenue, and the horror that I had feared was begun.

'Demolish all that might be used as a fortress against us!' commanded the Captain-General of New Spain. 'Tear all this heathenish handiwork down to the ground!'

36

CORTES HAD BOASTED THAT his change of strategy from siege to attack would capture Tenochtitlan within a few days, and in the next hour or so, he seemed to have been right. Once his army had been assembled behind him, or rather the Spanish contingent thereof, for the Tlascalans took a long time crossing over the rubble dam in the canal and he was too impatient and too confident of quick victory to wait, he began the advance up the avenue towards the great plaza. The plan was to take the palace of Axayacatl, then quickly assault the former palace of Montezuma, where he assumed that the new Emperor must be residing, and with any luck, or, as he put it, by the Grace of God, 'win the game of chess by capturing the king within his lair'.

All went well as we proceeded up the avenue, indeed the Mexica did not even seek to impede our swift progress, but when we reached the point at which the avenue debouched into the plaza, we saw the reason why. Cuatemoc had withdrawn his warriors into this heart of the city to make a stand, and the entire plaza was filled with them.

Cortes halted the advance and brought up cannon, while I remained well back, so that I only saw the ensuing battle from the temporary safety of afar. I heard several reports and saw the smoke as the cannon fired into the warriors in the square, but nothing more until several minutes later, when the infantry at the fore began dashing into the plaza.

What I later learned was that the cannonade had driven the Mexica back into the Sacred Precinct surrounding the temple of Huitzilopochtli, and the Spanish infantry had charged into the square after them in hot pursuit. From my vantage, I could only hear battle cries and shouts in the distance, but hearing them dwindle, I assumed that the Spanish were driving the Mexica back, and so I ventured as far as the entrance to the plaza to see what it appeared was going to be the climactic victory for myself.

What I saw, however, was nothing of the kind.

The Sacred Precinct around the great pyramid was surrounded by a man-high wall with only three entrances, and there were a number of smaller buildings within it. Mexica warriors by the hundreds crouched behind the cover of these structures raining arrows, javelins and stones on the Spaniards, who were trying to fight their way into the Sacred Precinct through the narrow entrances, swords against maquahuitls.

Once more, Cuatemoc had proven a doughty and clever commander in desperate defensive constraints. The Sacred Precinct was fairly clogged with Mexica warriors, likewise the environs of the wall around it with Spaniards, but the two forces could only come to lethal blows at the entrances.

What followed was something like an hour of senseless stalemated slaughter. The obsidian blades of the maquahuitls were no match for Toledo steel and the Spaniards were well protected by armor, so that ten Mexica were slain for each Spaniard slain or forced to retire by wounds, but the Mexica within the Sacred Precinct were able to throw fresh warriors continuously at the Spaniards attempting to fight their way inside.

It was clear at once to me, if not to Cortes, that if he persisted in this attack every last attacking Spaniard would be slain, albeit at the cost of hundreds of Mexica lives.

At length, at pitiless length, Cortes ordered the retreat.

The Spanish infantry at first fell back towards the avenue in good order and at a measured pace, so that the cavalry, cannon, and by this time the Tlascalans, backed up along its length to the city gate, could make room to accommodate them.

Needless to say, I was eager to flee myself, but before I could retire into the supposed safety of the middle ranks, I saw the Mexica come streaming out of the Sacred Precincts after the retreating Spanish infantry in a great triumphantly howling tide, forcing them into a fighting retreat, which degenerated into a desperate dash for the entrance to the avenue.

I did not directly witness what happened next, except to see the cavalry advance towards the entrance to the square to form a defensive screen while infantrymen streamed through the horses in the other direction.

What I learned later was that the cavalry, quite able to block the avenue, gallantly held their ground until the last of the infantry reached shelter behind them, and then fought a slow deliberate retreat so as to inflict as many casualties as possible on the Mexica pressing forward against them.

It was a ghastly mistake.

Our retreat would have been slow enough, with the route back down the avenue clogged with troops, but the gallantry of the cavalry inspired scores of infantrymen to return to the fray to join them, the confusion making it slower still.

And Cuatemoc used the time gained to good advantage. Seizing the moment, or perhaps even having planned the strategy in advance, he dispersed most of the warriors in the square through side streets, so as to flank the avenue on both sides for almost all of its length, and gain the rooftops of what buildings remained along it from behind.

Thus we were forced to retreat all the way back to the edge of the city under a most awful and continuous hail of heavy and lighter stones. Not a man, I warrant, reached the fortress of Xoloc unharmed and unbloodied. Few might have been slain, but we were all wounded, the unlucky with broken bones and cracked craniums from the heavy jagged rocks, the fortunate, myself among them, escaping with no more than a multitude of cuts and bruises from the smaller missiles.

Sandoval and Alvarado, it turned out, had also battled their way up their respective causeways from Tacuba and Tepeyac, reaching the outskirts of Tenochtitlan before being driven back by Mexica attacking their front ranks afoot in the city and along the causeways by canoe, for they had no brigantines with which to defend them.

One would have thought that such a fiasco would cause Cortes to revert to the previous sage plan and content himself with laying siege. I certainly did. But when I began to broach this to him, he silenced me with a look as frosty as the summits of the Pyrenees in winter from eyes as hard as Toledo steel.

'You counsel me to patience, Alvaro?' he fairly snarled. 'I'll show you patience. I will patiently reduce this damnable city to rubble or Cuatemoc to surrender, whichever comes first!'

He dispatched three brigantines each to Sandoval and Alvarado to give them command of the waters around their causeways. He had Tlascalans thoroughly fill in all the breaches in his own with rubble all the way to the avenue leading to the Temple Precinct under cover of his brigantines and the cannon at the fortress of Xoloc.

He then made a second attack similar to the first which I did not have the heart or the stomach to observe. Once again, the Mexica had cleared gaps where canals crossed the avenue, which were bridged with the abundant rubble. This time, however, the army proceeded more slowly, taking care to add to the rubble by demolishing every building along the avenue as it went. Once more, he reached the Temple Square. Once more, it was filled with Mexica warriors, but now there were even more of them, and they were deployed hundreds of ranks deep blocking the entrance, and Cortes was forced to retreat.

This time however, with all the buildings along the route of the retreat destroyed, and the cavalry easily holding back the Mexica pursuit in the narrow confines of the avenue, it gave Cortes food for ultimately effective but hideous thought.

'It may be a plodding strategy, but a safe and sure one,' he told me. 'Advance into the city from all three sides by day along avenues as far as we have already leveled the buildings, and proceed only a bit further down them or along other streets, destroying the buildings as we go, then retire safely down them for the night, to repeat the process the next day, until, precinct by precinct, we have reduced the city to wastelands which we command.'

I dared not even express my horror, for it was all too clear that Cortes had now passed far beyond any sane or merciful advice.

But before this terrible relentless grinding down of Tenochtitlan into ruins as a millstone grinds grain, there was a worse atrocity to be committed, for this one was the destruction of beauty to no military purpose, rather, as Cortes proclaimed, to break its people's heart.

My own heart broke with theirs as I watched from atop the fortress of Xoloc.

Cortes had half a dozen of his brigantines rowed with no little difficulty into the canal closest to the Palace of Axayacatl, which was wide enough for them to navigate in this manner, to within easy cannon range.

Then they began their bombardment. Dozens of cannonballs crashed into the walls of the palace compound with each terrible volley. Within a quarter of an hour, the walls facing this assault crumbled, and the shot began to fall inside. Interior quarters were demolished, and fountains, and gardens with their trees, and still the brigantines continued their bombardment. After another ten minutes or so, something caught fire, and then the Palace of Axayacatl was burning. Still the bombardment continued, the cannoneers shooting their balls madly into the rising flames.

Rising and falling embers were carried by the breeze to fall upon the nearby great menagerie, and soon there were fires within its precincts as well. Under orders or not, cannonballs were sent into it too, and the flames grew, and even from this distance, my ears were assaulted by the piteous screams and cries and howls of the creatures trapped within.

And then—

And then one of the great wooden aviaries caught fire. And another and another and another. They went up like dried kindling, the cages reduced to ash in moments, releasing clouds of birds to rise into the blue skies above billowing balls of flame.

Birds whose feathers were burning. Birds with wings of fire rising up like great flocks of Phoenixes.

But these Phoenixes did not rise triumphant above the flames of their destruction. They careened upward madly no more than a hundred feet or so to fall, screaming, squawking, cawing, in awful agony, into the waters of the lake.

Atrocities committed against outlying cities of an enemy's empire may daunt him into fear or caution, but when they are committed within his very capital, they serve only to incite careless rage, as Cortes should have known, and all the more so when his situation is terminally desperate to begin with.

The destruction of the Palace of Axayacatl and the menagerie neither brought about Cuatemoc's surrender, nor diminished the will of his warriors to fight on. The grinding down of the city continued, day by day, street by street; the Spaniards advancing during the daylight hours, filling in the gaps broken across the canals with rubble and leveling the buildings as far as their progress allowed, the Mexica clearing them out at night. The process pushed the daily forays by the forces of Cortes, Alvarado and Sandoval ever deeper into the city.

At times I wandered through the ruins well behind Cortes' advance, seeing nothing but the wrecked buildings, the rotting corpses left behind, and occasional wretched and starveling women and children failing to scavenge sustenance like isolated ants futilely crawling over a bone-pile long since picked clean.

At its glorious height Tenochtitlan had boasted a population of some hundreds of thousands. For weeks now, the city had been cut off from all outside food supply, and the only water to be had was from wells within, now running dry. Then too, the city had been ravaged by the smallpox, and each day hundreds, if not thousands, of its defenders were slain.

Surely the population by now must have been halved, and of a certainty, half its precincts had been destroyed. I myself had lost all hope that great Tenochtitlan might by some miracle be saved, but the Mexica fought on, hopelessly or not, and now I feared that they were determined to fight on until the last building was razed and the last man had died.

How long this might take, I feared to contemplate. For while there had been a class of warriors among the Mexica which might have been deemed a regular standing army, every adult male was given some perfunctory martial training. There still must be at least a hundred thousand Mexica men remaining in the city, all of whom were now under arms and fighting, if only with rocks and stones, so that even if the Spaniards slew a thousand a day, it would take months to bring this madness to its bitter end. Only starvation and thirst were likely to bring a quicker but even more terrible end.

Still, I could not but admire the gallantry of the Mexica, even while I longed for them to surrender and put an end to this pointless slaughter before they were all dead, along with their women and children, and no stone was left standing upon another.

I knew that theirs was no chivalric gallantry, but rather born of utter forlorn desperation and the sheer inability to contemplate surrendering the city to the monsters bent on razing it, the gallantry of a bear defending its cubs from a pack of hounds because there was simply nothing else for it. They were fighting on to preserve the very identity of their souls at the cost of the bodies that contained them, a far more honorable cause than that of the Spaniards fighting for gold and the conquest of a land and a people that had never belonged to them.

The Mexica had their victories, which is to say the Spanish had their disasters. Several brigantines were destroyed. Several score Spaniards were slain and others taken prisoner, no doubt to be sacrificed and then eaten. But at length, the end seemed near.

At least half of the city had been demolished. Mexica resistance was slackening. Cortes advanced to the Temple Precinct to find it undefended. Alvarado had moved his headquarters into the city from Tacuba. Sandoval was in the northern precincts of the city and closing on the great marketplace of Tlatelolco, where Cuatemoc had concentrated the last of his forces.

Cortes now was ready for the final push to the end. He would go forward from the south, Sandoval from the north, reinforced by a sally by Alvarado from the east, and when the three armies converged on the Tlatelolco marketplace, it would be over at last.

But not quite.

There was one near-disaster to come for the Spaniards, followed by a final atrocity committed by the Mexica. I was fortunate not to be present at the former, and so was spared from all too possible participation in the latter, which I *was* constrained to witness, a horror that has revisited me in nightmare all too often, and no doubt will pursue me therein until the end of my days.

Cortes and a force of some hundreds of Spaniards and many more Tlascalans behind them had penetrated deep into the southern precincts of the Tlatelolco quarter towards the marketplace, across several canals, where, as usual, the Mexicans had broken the bridges, and he expected the gaps to be filled in with rubble behind his advance as usual. Further along, he encountered yet another such obstacle, and on the other side, a force of Mexica which commenced to bombard his front ranks with arrows, javelins and stones.

He ordered his infantry to pull back out of range, and for cannon, arquebusiers and crossbowmen to be brought forward to dislodge them. But before this double maneuver could be accomplished within the confines of the narrow street, there was a commotion to the rear.

Dashing back to see what was about, he discovered to his dismay and fury that the deepest and widest canal behind was now an open gap, either because the Mexica had removed the rubble bridge, or because his orders had somehow not been followed, or because the procedure had become so habitual that he had not bothered to issue them.

In any case, he had no time for recriminations, for the canal itself was clogged with Mexica canoes, more Mexica warriors were streaming down side streets towards the flanks of his forces, and, as he learned only later, a similar tactic was now being applied at the forward canal.

A desperate battle to escape the trap ensued. The cannon, arquebusiers and crossbowmen could not be brought into play, the cavalry was useless, and the quarters were too close for the Mexica to use stones or arrows, though their javelins, at such close range, took their toll.

But it was mostly swords against maquahuitls as the Spaniards dove into the water, or leapt directly into the canoes filled with warriors, to cut, swim and stagger to join the Tlascalans in safety on the other side. The Spaniards fought for their very lives, rather than to slay the enemy, and the Mexica seemed to be fighting to wound and capture prisoners more than to kill, for what dreadful purpose I shall soon reluctantly describe.

The fighting was desperately fierce, the carnage terrible, and Cortes himself barely escaped with his life, saved only by a gallant soldier, Cristobal de Olea, who sacrificed his own life in the process, never knowing that he had thereby escaped from the worst.

At some length, the arquebusiers and crossbowmen arrived, along with reinforcements from the front ranks, and drove off the Mexica, or rather, as subsequent events would seem to have indicated, they withdrew of their own accord, their grisly mission accomplished.

Some twenty Spaniards were slain.

They were the fortunate ones.

The fifty or so who were taken captive were not so lucky.

Whether as a final act of defiance, or an attempt to emulate Cortes with his own dismaying atrocity, or a last entreaty to the war god who had deserted him, Cuatemoc enacted a spectacle which reminded me that the Mexica, civilized as they might be in terms of art, poetry, and the erection of the greatest and most beautiful city that I had ever seen, were also a bloody-minded conquering race of pitiless overlords, with a Satanic darkness in their souls to match that of the Inquisition itself, or Genghis Khan, who had delighted, like them, in piling up mountains of skulls.

Even as Cortes' army was fleeing in disarray back towards the Temple Square, the forces of Alvarado and Sandoval were making headway. As they advanced, they were confronted not by great hordes of Mexica warriors, but by small parties of them, who dashed forward to fling only some dozen missiles before retreating in haste.

These were not rocks or stones but the severed heads of Spanish soldiers.

Invitations to the spectacle as it would turn out.

As the sun began to go down, word from lookouts on the masts of some brigantines reached the Temple Square that a great throng of Mexica seemed to be assembling in the Tlatelolco marketplace before a secondary temple dedicated to Huitzilopochtli.

And there were Spaniards among them.

Some impulse caused me to make the arduous ascent of the Great Temple to the same god in the Sacred Precinct. Were I a sincere Christian, I might say that I ascended to view what we all knew was to come from the final Station of the Cross; my own mournful Calvary, and that of Tenochtitlan itself. Be that as it may, no true Christian made this pilgrimage with me. I was alone at the pinnacle platform. Even the effigy of Huitzilopochtli was gone. Nor was Tlaloc there to weep tears of rain.

In all directions, I surveyed the crumbled ruins of what had been great Tenochtitlan. And if the gods shed no tears, at least I was there to do so, and I recited Kaddish, the Jewish prayer meant to be said over human dead, but appropriate to me now to honor the death of mere mortar and stones. May the God of Abraham forgive me for this, if not for my part in making it so.

I could see the brigantines moving close to the shore to bear witness. And the top of the fortress of Xoloc crammed with tiny figures.

And then it began.

A somber drumming. Papas ascended to the platform of the distant pyramid. And then, one by one, the Spanish captives, stripped naked, were dragged to the top of the pyramid. It took some time, for there were at least two score of them, and they struggled valiantly and vainly every one of the many steps of this final dreadful station of their own lives' way.

When they were all assembled before the black altar stone, their bare heads were adorned, if that is the word, with quetzal feathers, and fans of some sort were put in their hands, I suspect tied in place.

And then, prodded by maquahuitls, they were constrained actually to *dance* in front of the shrine of Huitzilopochtli, before their deaths at the pleasure of what to them in these final moments must have seemed Satan himself.

Then, one by one, they were stretched out upon the altar. I could see the arm of the priest raised again and again, but not the obsidian blade which tore out their hearts, nor the still gushing organ held high in tribute to Huitzilopochtli before, one by one, their ruined bodies were thrown tumbling down the stairs into what would be the subsequent cannibal feast.

They received no last communion save this, in which the Body and the Blood were their own. They were not even allowed to cross themselves for one last time, and who is to say whether any of them managed to even utter one last prayer.

And so there, atop the temple to the war god of the Mexica, a secret Jew said it as best as he was able; for these Christians, for these far from innocent Soldiers of the Cross, for the city and the world that they had destroyed, and, in the spirit of the greatest and deepest truth that their faith contained, for their murderers as well, driven to this act by the very worst crime ever committed in the blasphemed name of their beloved Prince of Peace.

I sank to my knees, may my own God forgive me.

Once more, I said Kaddish.

And followed with a fragment of another Hebrew prayer.

'Hear, Oh Israel, the Lord Our God, the Lord is One.'

And the same from the Koran: 'There is no God but Allah.'

Let Nezahualcoyotl be right.

Inshallah.

Let it be so.

Still the battle of Tenochtitlan was not over, and while Mexica resistance dwindled away in force from casualties inflicted by the Spaniards and starvation, it intensified in ferocity, and likewise the savagery of the Spaniards, for in the face of the atrocities committed by both sides, no quarter was given, either by the Mexica or by the Spaniards, let alone by the Tlascalans, whom Cortes in his ire gave free rein.

And so it went on for days that stretched into weeks, as starving refugees fled the ruins, as the destruction spread, as the remaining Mexica warriors were slowly driven back into a final refuge in the Tlatelolco quarter by short bloody battles and skirmishes so ferocious that the Mexica took to sacrificing what Spanish prisoners they were able to take directly on the field of battle and the Spaniards took to the destruction of even militarily useless structures for its own vengeful sake.

I shall spare myself and you, dear reader, by not describing this endless and pointless carnage and destruction that went on long after the outcome had become inevitable, for I have no stomach for it, and I would hope that you too possess sufficient humanity to now have had a surfeit of such tales.

Suffice it to say that the forces of Cortes, Sandoval and Alvarado occupied the last refuge of the Mexica in the Tlatelolco marketplace, were driven out, returned, and finally occupied it for good, with the remains of Cuatemoc's forces reduced to making their last stand in the ruins of the nearby streets, making only occasional forays to the galleries surrounding the marketplace.

Since the Mexica of New Spain, like the Jews of Lost Israel, like the Muslims of what is now Spain, are a conquered people, it seems appropriate to bury what has died according to the custom of the latter two, and hope that it will find favor with Nezahualcoyotl's Hidden God.

Let me therefore conclude this narrative with two ceremonies and a final vision which in my memory, and I would hope in yours, will serve as the final Kaddish over the death of the Empire of the Mexica and great Tenochtitlan, and allow me to draw the burial shroud over the corpse. For both Jews and Muslims, unlike Christians, long mourn the spirit of that which has died, but inter the body which housed it as soon after it is cold as they may.

Throughout this prolonged final moment of a war that should have long since ended, Cortes sent entreaties to Cuatemoc inviting his surrender, and there were endless rumors that he was about to submit, or that the remaining nobles would remove him and perform this final act of mercy themselves, all of which came to naught.

Finally, when the forces of Alvarado had advanced deep into the last Mexica redoubt, Cuatemoc made a final plea to Huitzilopochtli via an attempted act of magic. I was not there to witness it, but I heard the tale often enough from those who were.

According to the code of flowery warfare, the conclusion of such a war arrived when one side brought to the field of battle a so-called 'quetzal-owl warrior'. A great warrior was fitted with a framework of wood or reeds entirely covered with the green feathers of the quetzal and the gray plumage of the owl so that nothing showed but an outsized gold beak jutting out from between where the bird's eyes would have been. This effigy was then dressed in the full finery of Huitzilopochtli, armed, and sent forth into battle.

If Huitzilopochtli chose to inhabit the quetzal-owl warrior, which is to say if he led his side triumphantly through the ensuing combat, it was proof that the god had chosen his victor, and the enemy withdrew or surrendered. If he was slain, the god had made the reverse choice, and his minions accepted defeat at his unseen hand.

As Alvarado's troops sallied forth to close with what in these final days was a large force of Mexica warriors, that is, no more than a thousand, such a quetzal-owl warrior suddenly emerged from their ranks to the fore, or, if you believe the more extravagant versions of the tale, appeared out of nowhere in a cloud of incense, already charging at the Spaniards.

The Mexica, who the moment before had been waging a determined slow retreat, surged forward to a man against arquebuses, crossbows, cavalry and Toledo steel, madly heedless of personal consequences, fighting like demons, dying like a cloud of moths flying into a flame.

Nor were they fighting to take back ground or to kill. They sacrificed their own lives to secure Spanish captives to offer up directly and without ceremony to Huitzilopochtli, dragging them only far back enough from the front to allow papas to slice out their hearts with obsidian blades before the horrified eyes of their comrades and throw them as garlands of roses might be tossed in the direction of their quetzal-owl warrior.

This apparition fought on and on in the center of the fray with lance and maquahuitl in a frenzy that for a time did indeed seem more than human, possessed by the god, or enhanced by the ingestion of sacramental peyote or mushrooms, which to the Mexica mind, and no doubt his own, might have amounted to the same thing.

But finally Huitzilopochtli's last champion was brought down by the crush of superior forces, red blood seeping through his imperial feathers, the framework of his costume splintered and smashed by Toledo steel and Spanish feet, the featherwork trampled and torn, flesh and feathers and finery reduced to a pulped and terrible wreckage all too appropriate to mark and seal the final fall of his ruined city.

The Mexica broke off battle and fled in dismay and terror.

The war was over.

There was nothing left but the final ceremony of surrender.

This, however, was not immediately forthcoming. Delegations came and went. Negotiations went on to no effect. Cuatemoc, it seemed, would not even surrender to the will of the god who had so manifestly abandoned his cause.

Finally a delegation of Mexica came before Cortes to forlornly announce that Cuatemoc would surrender to him in the Tlatelolco marketplace on the morrow. Cortes, with his captains, assembled a force of several hundred Spaniards and thousands of Tlascalans there to witness the formalizing of his conquest. Of course, I was there to witness this ultimate event, as was everyone else of our company who could crowd into the marketplace.

Nothing happened.

We stood there expectantly for four hours and neither Cuatemoc nor any delegation made an appearance.

Cortes, thoroughly enraged, decided to put an end to the war without any such formality. He brought dozens of cannon, scores of arquebusiers and crossbowmen, the majority of his infantry and several thousand Tlascalans into the Tlatelolco marketplace for the final assault on the Mexica, who now were confined to a small quarter between the marketplace and the northern shore, and sailed all his brigantines close to it to bombard them from the lake.

When all was in readiness, the signal was given, and the irresistible ground forces advanced northward through the marketplace and into the last Mexica refuge while an enormous cannonade began devastating it from the rear.

It was as if two faces of a wine press were being brought together squeezing a torrent of Mexica – warriors, old men, women and children – streaming out the sides, where the Tlascalans fell upon them, slaughtering and harrying them in all directions back into the ruins of the city.

Still Cuatemoc would not give himself over to the Spaniards, deeming flight less dishonorable than surrender, or perhaps seeking to fight on after the fall of Tenochtitlan with what he could muster in the countryside. He fled to the shore, boarded a canoe, and was captured by a brigantine, only when the nobles accompanying him surrendered their Emperor under threat of cannonade.

Thus was the last Emperor of the Mexica spared the surrender of his own person.

But not that of his city or his empire or his spirit.

Cortes must have his ceremony.

Strangely enough, after all that had happened, it was conducted with honor and mercy.

The imprisoned Emperor was brought into the Tlatelolco market-place before a great assembly of all the Spanish captains, those Mexica nobles remaining in the city, formations of Spanish soldiers, and those remaining inhabitants willing to bear witness.

He was allowed or constrained to wear his full imperial finery: the gold, the jewels, the long headdress and cloak of quetzal feathers. And he was honored by being allowed or constrained to speak first.

'I have done all in my power to defend my empire and my people and my gods, but they have deserted me, and I have failed, for in the end your God proved more powerful, and as it was foretold, the fifth world over which I have ruled has come to its end, and the sixth world over which you now rule has begun. Therefore, I beg you, Malinche, grant me the honor of the flowery death denied me by my god, and let me have it by the will of your own at the hands of the worthy warrior who has defeated me.'

It was a noble speech and a cunning one, for by it the man still avoided giving his surrender.

True to his divided nature, Hernando Cortes responded with a mercy that was cruelty and a cruelty that was mercy.

'I can but respect and honor you for the valor with which you have defended your subjects and your city. My only regret is that peace had not been made before so many died and so much was destroyed. Forgiveness of one's enemies is the command of Our Lord Jesus Christ. And so now let there be peace between us. I will not slay you. Instead I will allow you to rule over all the lands you have once held as Emperor as my vassal, as I rule over you as the vassal of my own King.'

True also to his nature, Cortes lied.

Four years later he hanged Cuatemoc.

And so I have reached the end of my tale, dear reader. And so also did I then reach the end of my journey in the company of Hernando Cortes and begin my solitary journey to the telling thereof, accompanied only by the vision which perhaps in the end has been what has compelled me to write it.

When this last ceremony was over, I left the Tlatelolco marketplace without speaking with anyone, for there was nothing left which I could bear to say or wished to hear. I made my way through the endless ruins, through the rotting corpses and the small bands of desperately scavenging Mexica, to stand one last time in the Temple Precinct.

The plaza was deserted, save for the carrion birds and flies picking the last scraps of flesh from the corpses reduced to bleaching skeletons. The Palace of Axayacatl was a burnt-out ruin. The great temple pyramid still stood, but my mind's eye covered it with vines creeping up its sanguinary steps like featherless serpents, and vegetation sprouting between its stones bringing it to time's ruin.

In that moment it seemed to become the pyramid at Teotihuacan, and if this was a last vision sent by Huitzilopochtli to mark his final passage, then so be it.

And then the vision changed, and I saw the last omen that this terrible god had inflicted upon his most loyal and tormented servant, the great Montezuma. His temple was gone and in its place there arose from the stones of the plaza the great glowering gray cathedral I knew in the moment thereof that his own God would constrain Cortes to erect there.

Or perhaps I dare hope that both these visions were sent neither by the Mexica god of war and bloody human sacrifice nor by the God of New Spain and the Cross and the no less evil fiery sacrifices of the Inquisition, and yet by both and the God of Abraham as well.

For the Mexica had built beauty and glory under the aegis of their evil god. And the God of the Inquisition was both the God of Redemption and the Father of a Prince of Peace. And the God of Abraham was a God whose mask displayed just such a dark and sardonic sense of Holy Humor.

I offered up a silent prayer to all three of them.

I prayed that Nezahualcoyotl was right. That all of them were but masks worn for a time by the Hidden God whose name can never be known, who has no face to be seen, whose reasons for the masquerade can never be fathomed, from whose Being all descends; building and destruction, beauty and horror, the Good and the Evil.

The Ain-Soph, the One and the Only.

And then an eagle appeared out of the cerulean sky. It circled once, twice, thrice, about the twin towers of the cathedral. And then it swooped down to land on the ruined plaza, perching upon the skull of a bleached white skeleton.

In its right talon was a serpent. In its left was a Cross of gold.

We gazed at each other for a long moment.

Then the eagle arose.

As it did, the Cross and the serpent fell from its claws, to disappear when they touched the stones.

And then the vision passed and I was alone once more in the ruins.

Do not ask me what it meant. I do not know.

All I know is that I somehow know that my prayer was answered.

Albeit not in whatever manner I thought I had intended.

It was not sent to enlighten me.

It was sent to command me to a mission.

Namely the writing of this very narrative which is now concluded, for I believed then, and I still believe now, that the Hidden God willed me to write it, both to bear true witness to what was, and to bring something I will never know into the Light of His Being.

Perhaps you, dear reader, may be brought thereby to forgive what I have done, as I cannot.

May you live within that Light.

Inshallah.

Let it be so.